DEXTER: AN OMNIBUS
Darkly Dreaming Dexter
Dearly Devoted Dexter
Dexter in the Dark

Jeff Lindsay

Dexter: An Omnibus

This omnibus edition first published in Great Britain in 2008 by Orion Books,
an imprint of the Orion Publishing Group Ltd
Orion House, 5 Upper St Martin's Lane
London WC2H 9EA

An Hachette Livre UK Company

9 10 8

Darkly Dreaming Dexter © Jeffry Freundlich 2004
Dearly Devoted Dexter © Jeffry Freundlich 2006
Dexter in the Dark © Jeffry Freundlich 2007

The moral right of Jeffry Freundlich to be identified as the author of this work
has been asserted in accordance with the Copyright, Designs and Patents Act of 1988.

A CIP catalogue record for this book is available from the British Library

ISBN (Trade Paperback) 978 1 4091 0065 2

Printed in Great Britain by Clays Ltd, St Ives plc

The Orion Publishing Group's policy is to use papers that are natural, renewable and
recyclable products and made from wood grown in sustainable forests. The logging
and manufacturing processes are expected to conform to the environmental
regulations of the country of origin.

www.orionbooks.co.uk

Contents

Darkly Dreaming Dexter   1

Dearly Devoted Dexter   169

Dexter in the Dark   351

Darkly Dreaming Dexter

For Hilary
who is everything to me

Acknowledgements

This book would not have been possible without the generous technical and spiritual help of Einstein and the Deacon. They represent what is best about Miami cops, and they taught me some of what it means to do this very tough job in a tougher place.

I would also like to thank a number of people who made some very helpful suggestions, especially my wife, the Barclays, Julio S., Dr. and Mrs. A. L. Freundlich, Pookie, Bear, and Tinky.

I am deeply indebted to Jason Kaufman for his wisdom and insight in shaping the book.

Thanks also to Doris, the Lady of the Last Laugh.

And very special thanks to Nick Ellison, who is everything an agent is supposed to be but almost never is.

1

Moon. Glorious moon. Full, fat, reddish moon, the night as light as day, the moonlight flooding down across the land and bringing joy, joy, joy. Bringing too the full-throated call of the tropical night, the soft and wild voice of the wind roaring through the hairs on your arm, the hollow wail of starlight, the teeth-grinding bellow of the moon-light off the water.

All calling to the Need. Oh, the symphonic shriek of the thousand hiding voices, the cry of the Need inside, *the entity*, the silent watcher, the cold quiet thing, the one that laughs, the Moondancer. The me that was not-me, the thing that mocked and laughed and came calling with its hunger. With the Need. And the Need was very strong now, very careful cold coiled creeping crackly cocked and ready, very strong, very much ready now – and still it waited and watched, and it made me wait and watch.

I had been waiting and watching the priest for five weeks now. The Need had been prickling and teasing and prodding at me to find one, find the next, find this priest. For three weeks I had known he was it, he was next, we belonged to the Dark Passenger, he and I together. And that three weeks I had spent fighting the pressure, the growing *Need*, rising in me like a great wave that roars up and over the beach and does not recede, only swells more with every tick of the bright night's clock.

But it was careful time, too, time spent making sure. Not making sure of the priest, no, I was long sure of him. Time spent to be certain that it could be done right, made neat, all the corners folded, all squared away. I could not be caught, not now. I had worked too hard, too long, to make this work for me, to protect my happy little life.

And I was having too much fun to stop now.

And so I was always careful. Always tidy. Always prepared ahead of time so it would be *right*. And when it was right, take extra time to be sure. It was the Harry way, God bless him, that farsighted perfect policeman, my foster father. Always be sure, be careful, be exact, he had said, and for a week now I had been sure that everything was just as Harry-right as it could be. And when I left work this night, I knew this was it. This night was the Night. This night felt different. This night it would happen, *had* to happen.

Just as it had happened before. Just as it would happen again, and again.

And tonight it would happen to the priest.

His name was Father Donovan. He taught music to the children at St. Anthony's Orphanage in Homestead, Florida. The children loved him. And of course he loved the children, oh very much indeed. He had devoted a whole life to them. Learned Creole and Spanish. Learned their music, too. All for the kids. Everything he did, it was all for the kids.

Everything.

I watched him this night as I had watched for so many nights now. Watched as he paused in the orphanage doorway to talk to a young black girl who had followed him out. She was small, no more than eight years old and small for that. He sat on the steps and talked to her for five minutes. She sat, too, and bounced up and down. They laughed. She leaned against him. He touched her hair. A nun came out and stood in the doorway, looking down at them for a moment before she spoke. Then she smiled and held out a hand. The girl bumped her head against the priest. Father Donovan hugged her, stood, and kissed the girl good night. The nun laughed and said something to Father Donovan. He said something back.

And then he started toward his car. Finally: I coiled myself to strike and—

Not yet. A janitorial service minivan stood fifteen feet from the door. As Father Donovan passed it, the side door slid open. A man leaned out, puffing on a cigarette, and greeted the priest, who leaned against the van and talked to the man.

Luck. Luck again. Always luck on these Nights. I had not seen the man, not guessed he was there. But he would have seen me. If not for Luck.

I took a deep breath. Let it out slow and steady, icy cold. It was only one small thing. I had not missed any others. I had done it all right, all the same, all the way it had to be done. It would be *right*.

Now.

Father Donovan walked toward his car again. He turned once and called something. The janitor waved from the doorway to the orphanage, then stubbed out his cigarette and disappeared inside the building. Gone.

Luck. Luck again.

Father Donovan fumbled for his keys, opened his car door, got into his car. I heard the key go in. Heard the engine turn over. And then—

NOW.

I sat up in his backseat and slipped the noose around his neck. One quick, slippery, pretty twist and the coil of fifty-pound-test fishing line settled tight. He made a small ratchet of panic and that was it.

'You are mine now,' I told him, and he froze as neat and perfect as if he had practiced, almost like he heard the other voice, the laughing watcher inside me.

'Do exactly as I say,' I said.

He rasped half a breath and glanced into his rearview mirror. My face was there, waiting for him, wrapped in the white silk mask that showed only my eyes.

'Do you understand?' I said. The silk of the mask flowed across my lips as I spoke.

Father Donovan said nothing. Stared at my eyes. I pulled on the noose.

'Do you understand?' I repeated, a little softer.

This time he nodded. He fluttered a hand at the noose, not sure what would happen if he tried to loosen it. His face was turning purple.

I loosened the noose for him. 'Be good,' I said, 'and you will live longer.'

He took a deep breath. I could hear the air rip at his throat. He coughed and breathed again. But he sat still and did not try to escape.

This was very good.

We drove. Father Donovan followed my directions, no tricks, no hesitations. We drove south through Florida City and took the Card Sound Road. I could tell that road made him nervous, but he did not object. He did not try to speak to me. He kept both hands on the wheel, pale and knotted tight, so the knuckles stood up. That was very good, too.

We drove south for another five minutes with no sound but the song of the tires and the wind and the great moon above making its mighty music in my veins, and the careful watcher laughing quietly in the rush of the night's hard pulse.

'Turn here,' I said at last.

The priest's eyes flew to mine in the mirror. The panic was trying to claw out of his eyes, down his face, into his mouth to speak, but—

'Turn!' I said, and he turned. Slumped like he had been expecting this all along, waiting for it forever, and he turned.

The small dirt road was barely visible. You almost had to know it was there. But I knew. I had been there before. The road ran for two and a half miles, twisting three times, through the saw grass, through the trees, alongside a small canal, deep into the swamp and into a clearing.

Fifty years ago somebody had built a house. Most of it was still there. It was large for what it was. Three rooms, half a roof still left, the place completely abandoned now for many years.

Except the old vegetable garden out in the side yard. There were signs that somebody had been digging there fairly recently.

'Stop the car,' I said as the headlights picked up the crumbling house.

Father Donovan lurched to obey. Fear had sealed him into his body now, his limbs and thoughts all rigid.

'Turn off the motor,' I told him, and he did.

It was suddenly very quiet.

Some small something chittered in a tree. The wind rattled the grass. And then more quiet, silence so deep it almost drowned out the roar of the night music that pounded away in my secret self.

'Get out,' I said.

Father Donovan did not move. His eyes were on the vegetable garden.

Seven small mounds of earth were visible there. The heaped soil looked very dark in the moonlight. It must have looked even darker to Father Donovan. And still he did not move.

I yanked hard on the noose, harder than he thought he could live through, harder than he knew could happen to him. His back arched against the seat and the veins stood out on his forehead and he thought he was about to die.

But he was not. Not yet. Not for quite some time, in fact.

I kicked the car door open and pulled him out after me, just to let him feel my strength. He flopped to the sandy roadbed and twisted like an injured snake. The Dark Passenger laughed and loved it and I played the part. I put one boot on Father Donovan's chest and held the noose tight.

'You have to listen and do as I say,' I told him. 'You *have* to.' I bent and gently loosened the noose. 'You should know that. It's important,' I said.

And he heard me. His eyes, pounding with blood and pain and leaking tears onto his face, his eyes met mine in a rush of understanding and all the things that had to happen were there for him to see now. And he saw. And he knew how important it was for him to be just *right*. He began to know.

'Get up now,' I said.

Slowly, very slowly, with his eyes always on mine, Father Donovan got up. We stood just like that for a long time, our eyes together, becoming one person with one need, and then he trembled. He raised one hand halfway to his face and dropped it again.

'In the house,' I said, so very softly. In the house where everything was ready.

Father Donovan dropped his eyes. He raised them to me but could not look anymore. He turned toward the house but stopped as he saw again the dark dirt mounds of the garden. And he wanted to look at me, but he could not, not after seeing again those black moonlit heaps of earth.

He started for the house and I held his leash. He went obediently, head down, a good and docile victim. Up the five battered steps, across the narrow porch to the front door, pushed shut. Father Donovan stopped. He did not look up. He did not look at me.

'Through the door,' I said in my soft command voice.

Father Donovan trembled.

'Go through the door now,' I said again.

But he could not.

I leaned past him and pushed the door open. I shoved the priest in with my foot. He stumbled, righted himself, and stood just inside, eyes squeezed tight shut.

I closed the door. I had left a battery lamp standing on the floor beside the door and I turned it on.

'Look,' I whispered.

Father Donovan slowly, carefully, opened one eye.

He froze.

Time stopped for Father Donovan.

'No,' he said.

'Yes,' I said.

'Oh, no,' he said.

'Oh, yes,' I said.

He screamed, 'NOOOO!'

I yanked on the noose. His scream was cut off and he fell to his knees. He made a wet croaky whimpering sound and covered his face. 'Yes,' I said. 'It's a terrible mess, isn't it?'

He used his whole face to close his eyes. He could not look, not now, not like this. I did not blame him, not really, it *was* a terrible mess. It had bothered me just to know it was there since I had set it up for him. But he had to see it. He had to. Not just for me. Not just for the Dark Passenger. For *him*. He had to see. And he was not looking.

'Open your eyes, Father Donovan,' I said.

'Please,' he said in a terrible little whimper. It got on my nerves very badly, shouldn't have, icy-clean control, but it got to me, whining in the face of that mess on the floor, and I kicked his legs out from under him. I hauled hard on the noose and grabbed the back of his neck with my right hand, then slammed his face into the filthy warped floorboards. There was a little blood and that made me madder.

'Open them,' I said. 'Open your eyes. Open them NOW. *Look*.' I grabbed his hair and pulled his head back. 'Do as you're told,' I said. 'Look. Or I will cut your eyelids right off your face.'

I was very convincing. And so he did it. He did as he was told. He looked.

I had worked hard to make it right, but you have to use what you've got to work with. I could not have done it at all if they had not been there long enough for everything to dry up, but they were so very dirty. I had managed to clean off most of the dirt, but some of the bodies had been in the garden a very long time and you couldn't tell where the dirt began and the body stopped. You never could tell, really, when you stop to think about it. So dirty—

There were seven of them, seven small bodies, seven extra-dirty orphan children laid out on rubber shower sheets, which are neater and don't leak. Seven straight lines pointing straight across the room.

Pointing right at Father Donovan. So he knew.

He was about to join them.

'Hail Mary, full of grace—' he started. I jerked hard on the noose.

'None of that, Father. Not now. Now is for real truth.'

'Please,' he choked.

'Yes, beg me. That's good. Much better.' I yanked again. 'Do you think that's it, Father? Seven bodies? Did they beg?' He had nothing to say. 'Do you think that's all of them, Father? Just seven? Did I get them all?'

'Oh, God,' he rasped out, with a pain that was good to hear.

'And what about the other towns, Father? What about Fayetteville? Would you like to talk about Fayetteville?' He just choked out a sob, no words. 'And what about East Orange? Was that three? Or did I miss one there? It's so hard to be sure. Was it four in East Orange, Father?'

Father Donovan tried to scream. There was not enough left of his throat for it to be a very good scream, but it had real feeling behind it, which made up for the poor technique. Then he fell forward onto his face and I let him snivel for a while before I pulled him up and onto his feet. He was not steady, and not in control. His bladder had let loose and there was drool on his chin.

'Please,' he said. 'I couldn't help myself. I just couldn't help myself. Please, you have to understand—'

'I do understand, Father,' I said, and there was something in my voice, the Dark Passenger's voice now, and the sound of it froze him. He lifted his head slowly to face me and what he saw in my eyes made him very still. 'I understand perfectly,' I told him, moving very close to his face. The sweat on his cheeks turned to ice. 'You see,' I said, 'I can't help myself, either.'

We were very close now, almost touching, and the dirtiness of him was suddenly too much. I jerked up on the noose and kicked his feet out from under him again. Father Donovan sprawled on the floor.

'But *children*?' I said. 'I could never do this to children.' I put my hard clean boot on the back of his head and slammed his face down. 'Not like you, Father. Never kids. I have to find people like you.'

'What are you?' Father Donovan whispered.

'The beginning,' I said. 'And the end. Meet your Unmaker, Father.' I had the needle ready and it went into his neck like it was supposed to, slight resistance from the rigid muscles, but none from the priest. I pushed the plunger and the syringe emptied, filling Father Donovan with quick, clean calm. Moments, only moments, and his head began to float, and he rolled his face to me.

Did he truly see me now? Did he see the double rubber gloves, the careful coveralls, the slick silk mask? Did he really see me? Or did that only happen in the other room, the Dark Passenger's room, the Clean Room? Painted white two nights past and swept, scrubbed, sprayed, cleaned as clean as can be. And in the middle of the room, its windows sealed with thick white rubberized sheets, under the lights in the middle of the room, did he finally see me there in the table I had made, the boxes of white garbage bags, the bottles of chemicals, and the small row of saws and knives? Did he see me at last?

Or did he see those seven untidy lumps, and who knows how many more?

Did he see himself at last, unable to scream, turning into that kind of mess in the garden?

He would not, of course. His imagination did not allow him to see himself as the same species. And in a way, he was right. He would never turn into the kind of mess he had made of the children. I would never do that, could never allow that. I am not like Father Donovan, not that kind of monster.

I am a very neat monster.

Neatness takes time, of course, but it's worth it. Worth it to make the Dark Passenger happy, keep him quiet for another long while. Worth it just to do it right and tidy. Remove one more heap of mess from the world. A few more neatly wrapped bags of garbage and my one small corner of the world is a neater, happier place. A better place.

I had about eight hours before I had to be gone. I would need them all to do it right.

I secured the priest to the table with duct tape and cut away his clothes. I did the preliminary work quickly; shaving, scrubbing, cutting away the things that stuck out untidily. As always I felt the wonderful long slow build to release begin its pounding throughout my entire body. It would flutter through me while I worked, rising and taking me with it, until the very end, the Need and the priest swimming away together on a fading tide.

And just before I started the serious work Father Donovan opened his eyes and looked at me. There was no fear now; that happens sometimes. He looked straight up at me and his mouth moved.

'What?' I said. I moved my head a little closer. 'I can't hear you.'

I heard him breathe, a slow and peaceful breath, and then he said it again before his eyes closed.

'You're welcome,' I said, and I went to work.

2

By four-thirty in the morning the priest was all cleaned up. I felt a lot better.
I always did, after. Killing makes me feel good. It works the knots out of dar-
ling Dexter's dark schemata. It's a sweet release, a necessary letting go of all the
little hydraulic valves inside. I enjoy my work; sorry if that bothers you. Oh,
very sorry, really. But there it is. And it's not just any killing, of course. It has
to be done the right way, at the right time, with the right partner – very complicated, but very necessary.

And always somewhat draining. So I was tired, but the tension of the last
week was gone, the cold voice of the Dark Passenger was quiet, and I could be
me again. Quirky, funny, happy-go-lucky, dead-inside Dexter. No longer Dexter with the knife, Dexter the Avenger. Not until next time.

I put all the bodies back in the garden with one new neighbor and tidied
the little falling-down house as much as I could. I packed my things into the
priest's car and drove south to the small side canal where I had left my boat,
a seventeen-foot Whaler with a shallow draft and a big engine. I pushed the
priest's car into the canal behind my boat and climbed on board. I watched
the car settle and disappear. Then I cranked up my outboard and eased out
of the canal, heading north across the bay. The sun was just coming up and
bouncing off the brightwork. I put on my very best happy face; just another
early-morning fisherman heading home. Red snapper, anyone?

By six-thirty I was home in my Coconut Grove apartment. I took the slide
from my pocket, a simple, clean glass strip – with a careful single drop of the
priest's blood preserved in the center. Nice and clean, dry now, ready to slip
under my microscope when I wanted to remember. I put the slide with the
others, thirty-six neat and careful very dry drops of blood.

I took an extra-long shower, letting the hot hot water wash away the last
of the tension and ease the knots in my muscles, scrubbing off the small final
traces of clinging smell from the priest and the garden of the little house in
the swamp.

Children. I should have killed him twice.

Whatever made me the way I am left me hollow, empty inside, unable to
feel. It doesn't seem like a big deal. I'm quite sure most people fake an awful

lot of everyday human contact. I just fake all of it. I fake it very well, and the feelings are never there. But I like kids. I could never have them, since the idea of sex is no idea at all. Imagine doing those things – How can you? Where's your sense of dignity? But kids – kids are special. Father Donovan deserved to die. The Code of Harry was satisfied, along with the Dark Passenger.

By seven-fifteen I felt clean again. I had coffee, cereal, and headed in for work.

The building where I work is a large modern thing, white with lots of glass, near the airport. My lab is on the second floor, in the back. I have a small office attached to the lab. It is not much of an office, but it's mine, a cubicle off the main blood lab. All mine, nobody else allowed in, nobody to share with, to mess up my area. A desk with a chair, another chair for a visitor, if he's not too big. Computer, shelf, filing cabinet. Telephone. Answering machine.

Answering machine with a blinking light as I came in. A message for me is not a daily thing. For some reason, there are very few people in the world who can think of things to say to a blood spatter pattern analyst during working hours. One of the few people who does have things to say to me is Deborah Morgan, my foster sister. A cop, just like her father.

The message was from her.

I punched the button and heard tinny *Tejano* music, then Deborah's voice. 'Dexter, please, as soon as you get in. I'm at a crime scene out on Tamiami Trail, at the Cacique Motel.' There was a pause. I heard her put a hand over the mouthpiece of the telephone and say something to somebody. Then there was a blast of Mexican music again and she was back on. 'Can you get out here right away? Please, Dex?'

She hung up.

I don't have a family. I mean, as far as I know. Somewhere out there must be people who carry similar genetic material, I'm sure. I pity them. But I've never met them. I haven't tried, and they haven't tried to find me. I was adopted, raised by Harry and Doris Morgan, Deborah's parents. And considering what I am, they did a wonderful job of raising me, don't you think?

Both dead now. And so Deb is the only person in the world who gives a rusty possum fart whether I live or die. For some reason that I can't fathom, she actually prefers me to be alive. I think that's nice, and if I could have feelings at all I would have them for Deb.

So I went. I drove out of the Metro-Dade parking lot and got onto the nearby Turnpike, which took me south to the section of Tamiami Trail that is home to the Cacique Motel and several hundred of its brothers and sisters. In its own way, it is paradise. Particularly if you are a cockroach. Rows of buildings that manage to glitter and molder at the same time. Bright neon over ancient, squalid, sponge-rotted structures. If you don't go at night, you won't go. Because to see these places by daylight is to see the bottom line of our flimsy contract with life.

Every major city has a section like this one. If a piebald dwarf with advanced leprosy wants to have sex with a kangaroo and a teenage choir, he'll find his way here and get a room. When he's done, he might take the whole gang next door for a cup of Cuban coffee and a *medianoche* sandwich. Nobody would care, as long as he tipped.

Deborah had been spending way too much time out here lately. Her opinion, not mine. It seemed like a good place to go if you were a cop and you wanted to increase your statistical chance of catching somebody doing something awful.

Deborah didn't see it that way. Maybe because she was working vice. A good-looking young woman working vice on the Tamiami Trail usually ends up as bait on a sting, standing outside almost naked to catch men who wanted to pay for sex. Deborah hated that. Couldn't get worked up about prostitution, except as a sociological issue. Didn't think bagging johns was real crime fighting. And, known only to me, she hated anything that overemphasized her femininity and her lush figure. She wanted to be a cop; it was not her fault she looked more like a centerfold.

And as I pulled into the parking lot that linked the Cacique and its neighbor, Tito's Café Cubano, I could see that she was currently emphasizing the hell out of her figure. She was dressed in a neon-pink tube top, spandex shorts, black fishnet stockings, and spike heels. Straight from the costume shop for Hollywood Hookers in 3-D.

A few years back somebody in the Vice Bureau got the word that the pimps were laughing at them on the streets. It seems the vice cops, mostly male, were picking the outfits for the women operatives who worked in the sting operations. Their choice of clothing was showing an awful lot about their preferences in kinkiness, but it did not look much like hooker wear. So everybody on the street could tell when the new girl was carrying a badge and gun in her clutch purse.

As a result of this tip, the vice cops began to insist that the girls who went undercover pick their own outfits for the job. After all, girls know more about what looks right, don't they?

Maybe most of them do. Deborah doesn't. She's never felt comfortable in anything but blues. You should have seen what she wanted to wear to her prom. And now – I had never seen a beautiful woman dressed in such a revealing costume who looked less sexually appealing than Deb did.

But she did stand out. She was working crowd control, her badge pinned to the tube top. She was more visible than the half mile of yellow crime-scene tape that was already strung up, more than the three patrol cars angled in with their lights flashing. The pink tube top flashed a little brighter.

She was off to one side of the parking lot, keeping a growing crowd back from the lab techs who appeared to be going through the Dumpster belonging to the coffee shop. I was glad I hadn't been assigned to that. The stink of it came all the way across the lot and in my car window – a dark stench of Latin coffee grounds mixed with old fruit and rancid pork.

The cop at the entrance to the parking lot was a guy I knew. He waved me in and I found a spot.

'Deb,' I said as I strolled over. 'Nice outfit. Really shows your figure to full advantage.'

'Fuck off,' she said, and she blushed. Really something to see in a full-grown cop.

'They found another hooker,' she said. 'At least, they think it's a hooker. Hard to tell from what's left.'

'That's the third in the last five months,' I said.

'Fifth,' she told me. 'There were two more up in Broward.' She shook her head. 'These assholes keep saying that officially there's no connection.'

'It would make for an awful lot of paperwork,' I said helpfully.

Deb showed me her teeth. 'How about some basic fucking police work?' she snarled. 'A moron could see these kills are connected.' And she gave a little shudder.

I stared at her, amazed. She was a cop, daughter of a cop. Things didn't bother her. When she'd been a rookie cop and the older guys played tricks on Deborah – showing her the hacked-up bodies that turn up in Miami every day – to get her to blow her lunch, she hadn't blinked. She'd seen it all. Been there, done that, bought the T-shirt.

But this one made her shudder.

Interesting.

'This one is special, is that it?' I asked her.

'This one is on my beat, with the hookers.' She pointed a finger at me. 'And THAT means I've got a shot to get in on it, get noticed, and pull a transfer into Homicide Bureau.'

I gave her my happy smile. 'Ambition, Deborah?'

'Goddamned right,' she said. 'I want out of vice, and I want out of this sex suit. I want into Homicide, Dexter, and this could be my ticket. With one small break—' She paused. And then she said something absolutely amazing. 'Please help me, Dex,' she said. 'I really hate this.'

'Please, Deborah? You're saying *please* to me? Do you know how nervous that makes me?'

'Cut the crap, Dex.'

'But Deborah, really—'

'Cut it, I said. Will you help me or not?'

When she put it that way, with that strange rare 'please' dangling in the air, what else could I say but, 'Of course I will, Deb. You know that.'

And she eyed me hard, taking back her please. 'I *don't* know it, Dex. I don't know anything with you.'

'Of course I'll help, Deb,' I repeated, trying to sound hurt. And doing a really good imitation of injured dignity, I headed for the Dumpster with the rest of the lab rats.

Camilla Figg was crawling through the garbage, dusting for fingerprints. She was a stocky woman of thirty-five with short hair who had never seemed to respond to my breezy, charming pleasantries. But as she saw me, she came up onto her knees, blushed, and watched me go by without speaking. She always seemed to stare at me and then blush.

Sitting on an overturned plastic milk carton on the far end of the Dumpster, poking through a handful of waste matter, was Vince Masuoka. He was half Japanese and liked to joke that he got the short half. He called it a joke, anyway.

There was something just slightly off in Vince's bright, Asian smile. Like he had learned to smile from a picture book. Even when he made the required dirty put-down jokes with the cops, nobody got mad at him. Nobody laughed, either, but that didn't stop him. He kept making all the correct ritual gestures, but he always seemed to be faking. That's why I liked him, I think. Another guy pretending to be human, just like me.

'Well, Dexter,' Vince said without looking up. 'What brings you here?'

'I came to see how real experts operate in a totally professional atmosphere,' I said. 'Have you seen any?'

'Ha-ha,' he said. It was supposed to be a laugh, but it was even phonier than his smile. 'You must think you're in Boston.' He found something and held it up to the light, squinting. 'Seriously, why are you here?'

'Why wouldn't I be here, Vince?' I said, pretending to sound indignant. 'It's a crime scene, isn't it?'

'You do blood spatter,' he said, throwing away whatever he'd been staring at and searching for an-other one.

'I knew that.'

He looked at me with his biggest fake smile. 'There's no blood here, Dex.'

I felt light-headed. 'What does that mean?'

'There's no blood in or on or near, Dex. No blood at all. Weirdest thing you ever saw,' he said.

No blood at all. I could hear that phrase repeat itself in my head, louder each time. No sticky, hot, messy, awful blood. No splatter. No stain. NO BLOOD AT ALL.

Why hadn't I thought of that?

It felt like a missing piece to something I didn't know was incomplete.

I don't pretend to understand what it is about Dexter and blood. Just thinking of it sets my teeth on edge – and yet I have, after all, made it my career, my study, and part of my real work. Clearly some very deep things are going on, but I find it a little hard to stay interested. I am what I am, and isn't it a lovely night to dissect a child killer?

But this—

'Are you all right, Dexter?' Vince asked.

'I am fantastic,' I said. 'How does he do it?'

'That depends.'

I looked at Vince. He was staring at a handful of coffee grounds, carefully pushing them around with one rubber-gloved finger. 'Depends on what, Vince?'

'On who *he* is and what *it* he's doing,' he said. 'Ha-ha.'

I shook my head. 'Sometimes you work too hard at being inscrutable,' I said. 'How does the killer get rid of the blood?'

'Hard to say right now,' he said. 'We haven't found any of it. And the body is not in real good shape, so it's going to be hard to find much.'

That didn't sound nearly as interesting. I like to leave a neat body. No fuss, no mess, no dripping blood. If the killer was just another dog tearing at a bone, this was all nothing to me.

I breathed a little easier. 'Where's the body?' I asked Vince.

He jerked his head at a spot twenty feet away. 'Over there,' he said. 'With LaGuerta.'

'Oh, my,' I said. 'Is LaGuerta handling this?'

He gave me his fake smile again. 'Lucky killer.'

I looked. A small knot of people stood around a cluster of tidy trash bags. 'I don't see it,' I said.

'Right there. The trash bags. Each one is a body part. He cut the victim into pieces and then wrapped up each one like it was a Christmas present. Did you ever see anything like that before?'

Of course I had.

That's how I do it.

3

There is something strange and disarming about looking at a homicide scene in the bright daylight of the Miami sun. It makes the most grotesque killings look antiseptic, staged. Like you're in a new and daring section of Disney World. Dahmer Land. Come ride the refrigerator. Please hurl your lunch in the designated containers only.

Not that the sight of mutilated bodies anywhere has ever bothered *me*, oh no, far from it. I do resent the messy ones a little when they are careless with their body fluids – nasty stuff. Other than that, it seems no worse than looking at spare ribs at the grocery store. But rookies and visitors to crime scenes tend to throw up – and for some reason, they throw up much less here than they do up North. The sun just takes the sting out. It cleans things up, makes them neater. Maybe that's why I love Miami. It's such a *neat* town.

And it was already a beautiful, hot Miami day. Anyone who had worn a suit coat was now looking for a place to hang it. Alas, there was no such place in the grubby little parking lot. There were only five or six cars and the Dumpster. It was shoved over in a corner, next to the café, backed up against a pink stucco wall topped with barbed wire. The back door to the café was there. A sullen young woman moved in and out, doing a brisk business in *café cubano* and *pasteles* with the cops and the technicians on the scene. The handful of assorted cops in suits who hang out at homicide scenes, either to be noticed, to apply pressure, or to make sure they know what's going on, now had one more thing to juggle. Coffee, a pastry, a suit coat.

The crime-lab gang didn't wear suits. Rayon bowling shirts with two pockets was more their speed. I was wearing one myself. It repeated a pattern of voodoo drummers and palm trees against a lime green background. Stylish, but practical.

I headed for the closest rayon shirt in the knot of people around the body. It belonged to Angel Batista-no-relation, as he usually introduced himself. Hi, I'm Angel Batista, no relation. He worked in the medical examiner's office. At the moment he was squatting beside one of the garbage bags and peering inside it.

I joined him. I was anxious to see inside the bag myself. Anything that got a reaction from Deborah was worth a peek.

'Angel,' I said, coming up on his side. 'What do we have?'

'What you mean *we*, white boy?' he said. 'We got no blood with this one. You're out of a job.'

'I heard.' I crouched down beside him. 'Was it done here, or just dumped?'

He shook his head. 'Hard to say. They empty the Dumpster twice a week – this has been here for maybe two days.'

I looked around the parking lot, then over at the moldy façade of the Cacique. 'What about the motel?'

Angel shrugged. 'They're still checking, but I don't think they'll find anything. The other times, he just used a handy Dumpster. Huh,' he said suddenly.

'What?'

He used a pencil to peel back the plastic bag. 'Look at that cut.'

The end of a disjointed leg stuck out, looking pale and exceptionally dead in the glare of the sun. This piece ended in the ankle, foot neatly lopped off. A small tattoo of a butterfly remained, one wing cut away with the foot.

I whistled. It was almost surgical. This guy did very nice work – as good as I could do. 'Very clean,' I said. And it was, even beyond the neatness of the cutting. I had never seen such clean, dry, *neat*-looking dead flesh. Wonderful.

'Me cago en diez on nice and clean,' he said. 'It's not finished.'

I looked past him, staring a little deeper into the bag. Nothing moving in there. 'It looks pretty final to me, Angel.'

'Lookit,' he said. He flipped open one of the other bags. 'This leg, he cuts it in four pieces. Almost like with a ruler or something, huh? And so *this* one,' and he pointed back to the first ankle that I had admired so deeply, 'this one he cuts in two pieces only? How's come, huh?'

'I'm sure I don't know,' I said. 'Perhaps Detective LaGuerta will figure it out.'

Angel looked at me for a moment and we both struggled to keep a straight face. 'Perhaps she will,' he said, and he turned back to his work. 'Why don't you go ask her?'

'Hasta luego, Angel,' I said.

'Almost certainly,' he answered, head down over the plastic bag.

There was a rumor going around a few years back that Detective Migdia LaGuerta got into the Homicide Bureau by sleeping with somebody. To look at her once you might buy into that. She has all the necessary parts in the right places to be physically attractive in a sullen, aristocratic way. A true artist with her makeup and very well dressed, Bloomingdale's chic. But the rumor can't be true. To begin with, although she seems outwardly very feminine, I've never met a woman who was more masculine inside. She was hard, ambitious in the most self-serving way, and her only weakness seemed to be for model-handsome men a few years younger than she was. So I'm quite sure she didn't get into Homicide using sex. She got into Homicide because she's Cuban, plays politics, and knows how to kiss ass. That combination is far better than sex in Miami.

LaGuerta is very very good at kissing ass, a world-class ass kisser. She kissed ass all the way up to the lofty rank of homicide investigator. Unfortunately, it's a job where her skills at posterior smooching were never called for, and she was a terrible detective.

It happens; incompetence is rewarded more often than not. I have to work with her anyway. So I have used my considerable charm to make her like me. Easier than you might think. Anybody can be charming if they don't mind faking it, saying all the stupid, obvious, nauseating things that a conscience keeps most people from saying. Happily, I don't have a conscience. I say them.

As I approached the little group clustered near the café, LaGuerta was interviewing somebody in rapid-fire Spanish. I speak Spanish; I even understand a little Cuban. But I could only get one word in ten from LaGuerta. The Cuban dialect is the despair of the Spanish-speaking world. The whole purpose of Cuban Spanish seems to be to race against an invisible stopwatch and get out as much as possible in three-second bursts without using any consonants.

The trick to following it is to know what the person is going to say before they say it. That tends to contribute to the clannishness non-Cubans sometimes complain about.

The man LaGuerta was grilling was short and broad, dark, with Indio features, and was clearly intimidated by the dialect, the tone, and the badge. He tried not to look at her as he spoke, which seemed to make her speak even faster.

'No, no hay nadie afuera,' he said softly, slowly, looking away. 'Todos estan en café.' *Nobody was outside, they were all in the café.*

'Donde estabas?' she demanded. *Where were you?*

The man looked at the bags of body parts and quickly looked away. 'Cocina.' *The kitchen.* 'Entonces yo saco la basura.' *Then I took out the garbage.*

LaGuerta went on; pushing at him verbally, asking the wrong questions in a tone of voice that bullied and demeaned him until he slowly forgot the horror of finding the body parts in the Dumpster, and turned sullen and uncooperative instead.

A true master's touch. Take the key witness and turn him against you. If you can screw up the case in the first few vital hours, it saves time and paperwork later.

She finished with a few threats and sent the man away. 'Indio,' she spat, as he lumbered out of earshot.

'It takes all kinds, Detective,' I said. 'Even campesinos.' She looked up and ran her eyes over me, slowly, while I stood and wondered why. Had she forgotten what I looked like? But she finished with a big smile. She really did like me, the idiot.

'Hola, Dexter. What brings you here?'

'I heard you were here and couldn't stay away. Please, Detective, when will you marry me?'

She giggled. The other officers within earshot exchanged a glance and then looked away. 'I don't buy a shoe until I try it on,' LaGuerta said. 'No matter how good the shoe looks.' And while I was sure that was true, it didn't actually explain to me why she stared at me with her tongue between her teeth as she said it. 'Now go away, you distracting me. I have serious work here.'

'I can see that,' I said. 'Have you caught the killer yet?'

She snorted. 'You sound like a reporter. Those assholes will be all over me in another hour.'

'What will you tell them?'

She looked at the bags of body parts and frowned. Not because the sight bothered her. She was seeing her career, trying to phrase her statement to the press.

'It is only a matter of time before the killer makes a mistake and we catch him—'

'Meaning,' I said, 'that so far he hasn't made any mistakes, you don't have any clues, and you have to wait for him to kill again before you can do anything?'

She looked at me hard. 'I forget. Why do I like you?'

I just shrugged. I didn't have a clue – but then, apparently she didn't either.

'What we got is nada y nada. That Guatemalan,' she made a face at the retreating Indio, 'he found the body when he came out with the garbage from the restaurant. He didn't recognize these garbage bags and he opened one up to see if maybe there was something good. And it was the head.'

'Peekaboo,' I said softly.

'Hah?'

'Nothing.'

She looked around, frowning, perhaps hoping a clue would leap out and she could shoot it.

'So that's it. Nobody saw anything, heard anything. Nothing. I have to wait for your fellow nerds to finish up before I know anything.'

'Detective,' said a voice behind us. Captain Matthews strolled up in a cloud of Aramis aftershave, meaning that the reporters would be here very shortly.

'Hello, Captain,' LaGuerta said.

'I've asked Officer Morgan to maintain a peripheral involvement in this case,' he said. LaGuerta flinched. 'In her capacity as an undercover operative she has resources in the prostitution community that could assist us in expediting the solution.' The man talked with a thesaurus. Too many years of writing reports.

'Captain, I'm not sure that's necessary,' LaGuerta said.

He winked and put a hand on her shoulder. People management is a skill. 'Relax, Detective. She's not going to interfere with your command prerogatives. She'll just check in with you if she has something to report. Witnesses, that sort of thing. Her father was a damn good cop. All right?' His eyes glazed and re-focused on something on the other end of the parking lot. I looked. The Channel 7 News van was rolling in. 'Excuse me,' Matthews said. He straightened his tie, put on a serious expression, and strolled over toward the van.

'Puta,' LaGuerta said under her breath.

I didn't know if she meant that as a general observation, or was talking about Deb, but I thought it was a good time to slip away, too, before LaGuerta remembered that Officer Puta was my sister.

As I rejoined Deb, Matthews was shaking hands with Jerry Gonzalez from Channel 7. Jerry was the Miami area's leading champion of if-it-bleeds-it-leads journalism. My kind of guy. He was going to be disappointed this time.

I felt a slight quiver pass over my skin. *No blood at all.*

'Dexter,' Deborah said, still trying to sound like a cop, but I could tell she was excited. 'I talked to Captain Matthews. He's going to let me in on this.'

'I heard,' I said. 'Be careful.'

She blinked at me. 'What are you talking about?'

'LaGuerta,' I said.

Deborah snorted. 'Her,' she said.

'Yeah. Her. She doesn't like you, and she doesn't want you on her turf.'

'Tough. She got her orders from the captain.'

'Uh-huh. And she's already spent five minutes figuring out how to get around them. So watch your back, Debs.'

She just shrugged. 'What did you find out?' she asked.

I shook my head. 'Nothing yet. LaGuerta's already nowhere. But Vince said—' I stopped. Even talking about it seemed too private.

'Vince said what?'

'A small thing, Deb. A detail. Who knows what it means?'

'Nobody will ever know if you don't say it, Dexter.'

'There . . . seems to be no blood left with the body. No blood at all.'

Deborah was quiet for a minute, thinking. Not a reverent pause, not like me. Just thinking. 'Okay,' she said at last. 'I give up. What does it mean?'

'Too soon to tell,' I said.

'But you think it means something.'

It meant a strange light-headedness. It meant an itch to find out more about this killer. It meant an appreciative chuckle from the Dark Passenger, who should have been quiet so soon after the priest. But that was all rather tough to explain to Deborah, wasn't it? So I just said, 'It might, Deb. Who really knows?'

She looked at me hard for half a moment, then shrugged. 'All right,' she said. 'Anything else?'

'Oh, a great deal,' I said. 'Very nice blade work. The cuts are close to surgical. Unless they find something in the hotel, which no one expects, the body was killed somewhere else and dumped here.'

'Where?'

'Very good question. Half of police work is asking the right questions.'

'The other half is answering,' she told me.

'Well then. Nobody knows where yet, Deb. And I certainly don't have all the forensic data—'

'But you're starting to get a feel for this one,' she said.

I looked at her. She looked back. I had developed hunches before. I had a small reputation for it. My hunches were often quite good. And why shouldn't they be? I often know how the killers are thinking. I think the same way. Of course I was not always right. Sometimes I was very wide of the mark. It wouldn't look good if I was always right. And I didn't want the cops to catch *every* serial killer out there. Then what would I do for a hobby? But this one – Which way should I go with this so very interesting escapade?

'Tell me, Dexter,' Deborah urged. 'Have you got any guesses about this?'

'Possibly,' I said. 'It's a little early yet.'

'Well, Morgan,' said LaGuerta from behind us. We both turned. 'I see you're dressed for real police work.'

Something about LaGuerta's tone was like a slap on the face. Deborah stiffened. 'Detective,' she said. 'Did you find anything?' She said it in a tone that already knew the answer.

A cheap shot. But it missed. LaGuerta waved a hand airily. 'They are only *putas*,' she said, looking hard at Deb's cleavage, so very prominent in her hooker suit. 'Just hookers. The important thing here is to keep the press from getting hysterical.' She shook her head slowly, as if in disbelief, and looked up. 'Considering what you can do with gravity, that should be easy.' And she winked at me and strolled off, over toward the perimeter, where Captain Matthews was talking with great dignity to Jerry Gonzalez from Channel 7.

'Bitch,' Deborah said.

'I'm sorry, Debs. Would you prefer me to say, *We'll show her*? Or should I go with *I told you so*?'

She glared at me. 'Goddamn it, Dexter,' she said. 'I really want to be the one to find this guy.'

And as I thought about that *no blood at all*—

So did I. I really wanted to find him, too.

4

I took my boat out that night after work, to get away from Deb's questions and to sort through what I was feeling. Feeling. Me, feeling. What a concept.

I nosed my Whaler slowly out the canal, thinking nothing, a perfect Zen state, moving at idle speed past the large houses, all separated from each other by high hedges and chain-link fences. I threw an automatic big wave and bright smile to all the neighbors out in their yards that grew neatly up to the canal's seawall. Kids playing on the manicured grass. Mom and Dad barbecuing, or lounging, or polishing the barbed wire, hawkeyes on the kids. I waved to everybody. Some of them even waved back. They knew me, had seen me go by before, always cheerful, a big hello for everybody. *He was such a nice man. Very friendly. I can't believe he did those horrible things . . .*

I opened up the throttle when I cleared the canal, heading out the channel and then southeast, toward Cape Florida. The wind in my face and the taste of the salt spray helped clear my head, made me feel clean and a little fresher. I found it a great deal easier to think. Part of it was the calm and peace of the water. And another part was that in the best tradition of Miami watercraft, most of the other boaters seemed to be trying to kill me. I found that very relaxing. I was right at home. This is my country; these are my people.

All day long at work I'd gotten little forensic updates. Around lunchtime the story broke national. The lid was coming off the hooker murders after the 'grisly discovery' at the Cacique Motel. Channel 7 had done a masterful job of presenting all the hysterical horror of body parts in a Dumpster without actually saying anything about them. As Detective LaGuerta had shrewdly observed, these were only hookers; but once public pressure started to rise from the media, they might as well be senator's daughters. And so the department began to gear up for a long spell of defensive maneuvering, knowing exactly what kind of heartrending twaddle would be coming from the brave and fearless foot soldiers of the fifth estate.

Deb had stayed at the scene until the captain began to worry about authorizing too much overtime, and then she'd been sent home. She started calling me at two in the afternoon to hear what I'd discovered, which was very little. They'd found no traces of anything at the motel. There were so many tire tracks in the parking lot that none were distinct. No prints or traces in the Dumpster, on the bags, or on the body parts. Everything USDA inspection clean.

The one big clue of the day was the left leg. As Angel had noticed, the right leg had been sectioned into several neat pieces, cut at the hip, knee, and ankle. But the left leg was not. It was a mere two sections, neatly wrapped. Aha, said Detective LaGuerta, lady genius. Somebody had interrupted the killer, surprised him, startled him so he did not finish the cut. He panicked when he was seen. And she directed all her effort at finding that witness.

There was one small problem with LaGuerta's theory of interruption. A tiny little thing, perhaps splitting hairs, but – the entire body had still been meticulously cleaned and wrapped, presumably after it had been cut up. And then it had been transported carefully to the Dumpster, apparently with enough time and focus for the killer to make no mistakes and leave no traces. Either nobody pointed this out to LaGuerta or – wonder of wonders! – could it be that nobody else had noticed? Possible; so much of police work is routine, fitting details into patterns. And if the pattern was brand new, the investigation could seem like three blind men examining an elephant with a microscope.

But since I was neither blind nor hampered by routine, it had seemed far more likely to me that the killer was simply unsatisfied. Plenty of time to work, but – this was the fifth murder in the same pattern. Was it getting boring, simply chopping up the body? Was Our Boy searching for something else, something different? Some new direction, an untried twist?

I could almost feel his frustration. To have come so far, all the way to the end, sectioning the leftovers for gift wrapping. And then the sudden realization: *This isn't it. Something is just not right.* Coitus interruptus.

It wasn't fulfilling him this way anymore. He needed a different approach. He was trying to express something, and hadn't found his vocabulary yet. And in my personal opinion – I mean, if it was *me* – this would make him very frustrated. And very likely to look further for the answer.

Soon.

But let LaGuerta look for a witness. There would be none. This was a cold, careful monster, and absolutely fascinating to me. And what should I do about that fascination? I was not sure, so I had retreated to my boat to think.

A Donzi cut across my bow at seventy miles per hour, only inches away. I waved happily and returned to the present. I was approaching Stiltsville, the mostly abandoned collection of old stilt homes in the water near Cape Florida. I nosed into a big circle, going nowhere, and let my thoughts move back into that same slow arc.

What would I do? I needed to decide now, before I got too helpful for Deborah. I could help her solve this, absolutely, no one better. Nobody else was even moving in the right direction. But did I want to help? Did I want this

killer arrested? Or did I want to find him and stop him myself? Beyond this
– oh, nagging little thought – did I even want him to stop?

What would I do?

To my right I could just see Elliott Key in the last light of the day. And as
always, I remembered my camping trip there with Harry Morgan. My foster
father. The Good Cop.

You're different, Dexter.

Yes, Harry, I certainly am.

But you can learn to control that difference and use it constructively.

All right, Harry. If you think I should. How?

And he told me.

There is no starry sky anywhere like the starry sky in South Florida when you
are fourteen and camping out with Dad. Even if he's only your foster dad.
And even if the sight of all those stars merely fills you with a kind of satisfaction, emotion being out of the question. You don't feel it. That's part of the
reason you're here.

The fire has died down and the stars are exceedingly bright and foster dear
old dad has been quiet for some time, taking small sips on the old-fashioned
hip flask he has pulled from the outside flap of his pack. And he's not very
good at this, not like so many other cops, not really a drinker. But it's empty
now, and it's time for him to say his piece if he's ever going to say it.

'You're different, Dexter,' he says.

I look away from the brightness of the stars. Around the small and sandy
clearing the last glow of the fire is making shadows. Some of them trickle
across Harry's face. He looks strange to me, like I've never seen him before.
Determined, unhappy, a little dazed. 'What do you mean, Dad?'

He won't look at me. 'The Billups say Buddy has disappeared,' he says.

'Noisy little creep. He was barking all night. Mom couldn't sleep.'

Mom needed her sleep, of course. Dying of cancer requires plenty of rest,
and she wasn't getting it with that awful little dog across the street yapping at
every leaf that blew down the sidewalk.

'I found the grave,' Harry says. 'There were a lot of bones in there, Dexter.
Not just Buddy's.'

There's very little to say here. I carefully pull at a handful of pine needles
and wait for Harry.

'How long have you been doing this?'

I search Harry's face, then look out across the clearing to the beach. Our
boat is there, moving gently with the surge of the water. The lights of Miami
are off to the right, a soft white glow. I can't figure out where Harry is going,
what he wants to hear. But he is my straight-arrow foster dad; the truth is
usually a good idea with Harry. He always knows, or he finds out.

'A year and a half,' I say.

Harry nods. 'Why did you start?'

A very good question, and certainly beyond me at fourteen. 'It just – I kind of . . . had to,' I tell him. Even then, so young but so smooth.

'Do you hear a voice?' he wants to know. 'Something or somebody telling you what to do, and you had to do it?'

'Uh,' I say with fourteen-year-old eloquence, 'not exactly.'

'Tell me,' Harry says.

Oh for a moon, a good fat moon, something bigger to look at. I clutch another fistful of pine needles. My face is hot, as if Dad has asked me to talk about sex dreams. Which, in a way— 'It, uh . . . I kind of, you know, *feel* something,' I say. 'Inside. Watching me. Maybe, um. Laughing? But not really a voice, just—' An eloquent teenaged shrug. But it seems to make sense to Harry.

'And this *something*. It makes you kill things.'

High overhead a slow fat jet crawls by. 'Not, um, doesn't *make* me,' I say. 'Just – makes it seem like a good idea?'

'Have you ever wanted to kill something else? Something bigger than a dog?'

I try to answer but there is something in my throat. I clear it. 'Yes,' I say.

'A person?'

'Nobody in particular, Dad. Just—' I shrug again.

'Why didn't you?'

'It's – I thought you wouldn't like it. You and Mom.'

'That's all that stopped you?'

'I, uh – I didn't want you, um, mad at me. Uh . . . you know. Disappointed.'

I steal a glance at Harry. He is looking at me, not blinking. 'Is that why we took this trip, Dad? To talk about this?'

'Yes,' Harry says. 'We need to get you squared away.'

Squared away, oh yes, a completely Harry idea of how life is lived, with hospital corners and polished shoes. And even then I knew; needing to kill something every now and then would pretty much sooner or later get in the way of being squared away.

'How?' I say, and he looks at me long and hard, and then he nods when he sees that I am with him step for step.

'Good boy,' he says. 'Now.' And in spite of saying now, it is a very long time before he speaks again. I watch the lights on a boat as it goes past, maybe two hundred yards out from our little beach. Over the sound of their motor a radio is blasting Cuban music. 'Now,' Harry says again, and I look at him. But he is looking away, across the dying fire, off into the future over there somewhere. 'It's like this,' he says. I listen carefully. This is what Harry says when he is giving you a higher-order truth. When he showed me how to throw a curve ball, and how to throw a left hook. *It's like this*, he would say, and it always was, just like that.

'I'm getting old, Dexter.' He waited for me to object, but I didn't, and he nodded. 'I think people understand things different when they get older,' he says. 'It's not a question of getting soft, or seeing things in the gray areas instead of black and white. I really believe I'm just understanding things different. Better.' He looks at me, Harry's look, Tough Love with blue eyes.

'Okay,' I say.

'Ten years ago I would have wanted you in an institution somewhere,' he says, and I blink. That almost hurts, except I've thought of it myself. 'Now,' he says, 'I think I know better. I know what you are, and I know you're a good kid.'

'No,' I say, and it comes out very soft and weak, but Harry hears.

'Yes,' he says firmly. 'You're a good kid, Dex, I know that. I *know* it,' almost to himself now, for effect maybe, and then his eyes lock onto mine. 'Otherwise, you wouldn't care what I thought, or what Mom thought. You'd just do it. You can't help it, I know that. Because—' He stops and just looks at me for a moment. It's very uncomfortable for me. 'What do you remember from before?' he asked. 'You know. Before we took you in.'

That still hurts, but I really don't know why. I was only three. 'Nothing.'

'Good,' he says. 'Nobody should remember that.' And as long as he lives that will be the most he ever says about it. 'But even though you don't remember, Dex, it did things to you. Those things make you what you are. I've talked to some people about this.' And strangest of strange, he gives me a very small, almost shy, Harry smile. 'I've been expecting this. What happened to you when you were a little kid has shaped you. I've tried to straighten that out, but—' He shrugs. 'It was too strong, too much. It got into you too early and it's going to stay there. It's going to make you want to kill. And you can't help that. You can't change that. But,' he says, and he looks away again, to see what I can't tell. 'But you can channel it. Control it. Choose—' his words come so carefully now, more careful than I've ever heard him talk '—choose what . . . or *who* . . . you kill . . .' And he gave me a smile unlike any I had ever seen before, a smile as bleak and dry as the ashes of our dying fire. 'There are plenty of people who deserve it, Dex . . .'

And with those few little words he gave a shape to my whole life, my everything, my who and what I am. The wonderful, all-seeing, all-knowing man. Harry. My dad.

If only I was capable of love, how I would have loved Harry.

So long ago now. Harry long dead. But his lessons had lived on. Not because of any warm and gooey emotional feelings I had. Because Harry was right. I'd proved that over and over. Harry knew, and Harry taught me well.

Be careful, Harry said. And he taught me to be careful as only a cop could teach a killer.

To choose carefully among those who deserved it. To make absolutely sure.

Then tidy up. Leave no traces. And always avoid emotional involvement; it can lead to mistakes.

Being careful went beyond the actual killing, of course. Being careful meant building a careful life, too. Compartmentalize. Socialize. Imitate life.

All of which I had done, so very carefully. I was a near perfect hologram. Above suspicion, beyond reproach, and beneath contempt. A neat and polite monster, the boy next door. Even Deborah was at least half fooled, half the time. Of course, she believed what she wanted to believe, too.

Right now she believed I could help her solve these murders, jump-start her career and catapult her out of her Hollywood sex suit and into a tailored business suit. And she was right, of course. I could help her. But I didn't really want to, because I enjoyed watching this other killer work and felt some kind of aesthetic connection, or—

Emotional involvement.

Well. There it was. I was in clear violation of the Code of Harry.

I nosed the boat back toward my canal. It was full dark now, but I steered by a radio tower a few degrees to the left of my home water.

So be it. Harry had always been right, he was right now. *Don't get emotionally involved,* Harry had said. So I wouldn't.

I would help Deb.

5

The next morning it was raining and the traffic was crazy, like it always is in Miami when it rains. Some drivers slowed down on the slick roads. That made others furious, and they leaned on their horns, screamed out their windows, and accelerated out onto the shoulder, fishtailing wildly past the slowpokes and waving their fists.

At the LeJeune on-ramp, a huge dairy truck had roared onto the shoulder and hit a van full of kids from a Catholic school. The dairy truck flipped over. And now five young girls in plaid wool skirts were sitting in a huge puddle of milk with dazed looks on their faces. Traffic nearly stopped for an hour. One kid was airlifted to Jackson Hospital. The others sat in the milk in their uniforms and watched the grown-ups scream at each other.

I inched along placidly, listening to the radio. Apparently the police were hot on the trail of the Tamiami Butcher. There were no specifics available, but Captain Matthews got a lovely sound bite. He made it seem like he would personally make the arrest as soon as he finished his coffee.

I finally got off onto surface roads and went only a little faster. I stopped at a doughnut shop not too far from the airport. I bought an apple fritter and a cruller, but the apple fritter was gone almost before I got back into the car. I have a very high metabolism. It comes with living the good life.

The rain had stopped by the time I got to work. The sun shone and steam rose from the pavement as I walked into the lobby, flashed my credentials, and went upstairs.

Deb was already waiting for me.

She did not look happy this morning. Of course, she does not look happy very often any more. She's a cop, after all, and most of them can't manage the trick at all. Too much time on duty trying not to look human. It leaves their faces stuck.

'Deb,' I said. I put the crisp white pastry bag on my desk.

'Where were you last night?' she said. Very sour, as I'd expected. Soon those frown lines would turn permanent, ruining a wonderful face: deep blue eyes, alive with intelligence, and small upturned nose with just a dash of freckles, framed by black hair. Beautiful features, at the moment spattered with about seven pounds of cheap makeup.

I looked at her with fondness. She was clearly coming from work, dressed today in a lacy bra, bright pink spandex shorts, and gold high heels. 'Never mind me,' I said. 'Where were *you*?'

She flushed. She hated to wear anything but clean, pressed blues. 'I tried to call you,' she said.

'Sorry,' I said.

'Yeah. Sure.'

I sat down in my chair and didn't speak. Deb likes to unload on me. That's what family is for. 'Why were you so anxious to talk to me?'

'They're shutting me out,' she said. She opened my doughnut bag and looked inside.

'What did you expect?' I said. 'You know how LaGuerta feels about you.'

She pulled the cruller out of the bag and savaged it.

'I expect,' she said, mouth full, 'to be in on this. Like the captain said.'

'You don't have any seniority,' I said. 'Or any political smarts.'

She crumpled the bag and threw it at my head. She missed. 'Goddamn it, Dexter,' she said. 'You know damned well I deserve to be in Homicide. Instead of—' She snapped her bra strap and waved a hand at her skimpy costume. 'This bullshit.'

I nodded. 'Although on you it looks good,' I said.

She made an awful face: rage and disgust competing for space. 'I hate this,' she said. 'I can't do this much longer or I swear, I'll go nuts.'

'It's a little soon for me to have the whole thing figured out, Deb.'

'Shit,' she said. Whatever else you could say about police work, it was ruining Deborah's vocabulary. She gave me a cold, hard cop-look, the first I'd ever had from her. It was Harry's look, the same eyes, same feeling of looking right through you to the truth. 'Don't bullshit me, Dex,' she said. 'All you have to do half the time is see the body, and you know who did it. I never asked you how you do that, but if you have any hunches on this one, I want 'em.' She kicked out savagely and put a small dent in my metal desk. 'Goddamn it, I want out of this stupid outfit.'

'And we'd all love to see that, Morgan,' came a deep and phony voice from behind her in the doorway. I looked up. Vince Masuoka was smiling in at us.

'You wouldn't know what to do, Vince,' Deb told him.

He smiled bigger, that bright, fake, textbook smile. 'Why don't we try it and find out?'

'In your dreams, Vince,' Debbie said, slumping into a pout that I hadn't seen since she was twelve.

Vince nodded at the crumpled white bag on my desk. 'It *was* your turn, goody. What'd you bring me? Where is it?'

'Sorry, Vince,' I said. 'Debbie ate your cruller.'

'I wish,' he said, with his sharp, imitation leer. 'Then I could eat her jelly roll. You owe me a big doughnut, Dex,' he said.

'The only big one you'll ever have,' Deborah said.

'It's not the size of the doughnut, it's the skill of the baker,' Vince told her.

'Please,' I said. 'You two are going to sprain a frontal lobe. It's too early to be this clever.'

'Ah-ha,' Vince said, with his terrible fake laugh. 'Ah-ha ha-ha. See you later.' He winked. 'Don't forget my doughnut.' And he wandered away to his microscope down the hall.

'So what have you figured out?' Deb asked me.

Deb believed that every now and then I got hunches. She had reason to believe. Usually my inspired guesses had to do with the brutal whackos who liked to hack up some poor slob every few weeks just for the hell of it. Several times Deborah had seen me put a quick and clean finger on something that nobody else knew was there. She had never said anything, but my sister is a damned good cop, and so she has suspected me of something for quite a while. She doesn't know what, but she knows there is something wrong there and it bothers the hell out of her every now and then, because she does, after all, love me. The last living thing on the earth that does love me. This is not self-pity but the coldest, clearest self-knowledge. I am unlovable. Following Harry's plan, I have tried to involve myself in other people, in relationships, and even – in my sillier moments – in love. But it doesn't work. Something in me is broken or missing, and sooner or later the other person catches me Acting, or one of Those Nights comes along.

I can't even keep pets. Animals hate me. I bought a dog once; it barked and howled – at *me* – in a nonstop no-mind fury for two days before I had to get rid of it. I tried a turtle. I touched it once and it wouldn't come out of its shell again, and after a few days of that it died. Rather than see me or have me touch it again, it died.

Nothing else loves me, or ever will. Not even – especially – me. I know what I am and that is not a thing to love. I am alone in the world, all alone, but for Deborah. Except, of course, for the Thing inside, who does not come out to play too often. And does not actually play with me but must have somebody else.

So as much as I can, I care about her, dear Deborah. It is probably not love, but I would rather she were happy.

And she sat there, dear Deborah, looking unhappy. My family. Staring at me and not knowing what to say, but coming closer to saying it than ever before.

'Well,' I said, 'actually—'

'I *knew* it! You *DO* have something!'

'Don't interrupt my trance, Deborah. I'm in touch with the spirit realm.'

'Spit it out,' she said.

'It's the interrupted cut, Deb. The left leg.'

'What about it?'

'LaGuerta thinks the killer was discovered. Got nervous, didn't finish.'

Deborah nodded. 'She had me asking hookers last night if they saw any-thing. Somebody must have.'

'Oh, not you, too,' I said. '*Think*, Deborah. If he was interrupted – too scared to finish—'

'The wrapping,' she blurted. 'He still spent a lot of time wrapping the body, cleaning up.' She looked surprised. 'Shit. *After* he was interrupted?'

I clapped my hands and beamed at her. 'Bravo, Miss Marple.'

'Then it doesn't make sense.'

'Au contraire. If there is plenty of time, but the ritual is not completed properly – and remember, Deb, the ritual is nearly everything – what's the implication?'

'Why can't you just tell me, for God's sake?' she snapped.

'What fun would that be?'

She blew out a hard breath. 'Goddamn it. All right, Dex. If he wasn't inter-rupted, but he didn't finish – Shit. The wrapping-up part was more impor-tant than the cutting?'

I took pity on her. 'No, Deb. Think. This is the fifth one, exactly like all the others. Four left legs cut perfectly. And now number five—' I shrugged, raised an eyebrow at her.

'Aw, shit, Dexter. How should I know? Maybe he only needed four left legs. Maybe . . . I don't know, I swear to God. What?'

I smiled and shook my head. To me it was so clear. 'The thrill is gone, Deb. Something just isn't right. It isn't working. Some essential bit of the magic that makes it perfect, isn't there.'

'I was supposed to figure that out?'

'Somebody should, don't you think? And so he just sort of dribbles to a stop, looking for inspiration and finding none.'

She frowned. 'So he's done. He won't do this again?'

I laughed. 'Oh my God, no, Deb. Just the opposite. If you were a priest, and you truly believed in God but couldn't find the right way to worship him, what would you do?'

'Keep trying,' she said, 'until I got it right.' She stared hard. 'Jesus. That's what you think? He's going to do it again soon?'

'It's just a hunch,' I said modestly. 'I could be wrong.' But I was sure I was not wrong.

'We should be setting up a way to catch him when he does,' she said. 'Not looking for a nonexistent witness.' She stood and headed out the door. 'I'll call later. Bye!' And she was gone.

I poked at the white paper bag. There was nothing left inside. Just like me: a clean, crisp outside and nothing at all on the inside.

I folded the bag and placed it in the trash can beside my desk. There was work to do this morning, real official police lab work. I had a long report to type up, accompanying pictures to sort, evidence to file. It was routine stuff, a double homicide that would probably never go to trial, but I like to make sure that whatever I touch is well organized.

Besides, this one had been interesting. The blood spatter had been very difficult to read; between the arterial spurting, the multiple victims – obviously moving around – and the cast-off pattern from what had to be a chain saw, it had been almost impossible to find an impact site. In order to cover the whole room, I'd had to use two bottles of Luminol, which reveals even the faintest of blood spots and is shockingly expensive at $12 a bottle.

I'd actually had to lay out strings to help me figure the primary spatter angles, a technique ancient enough to seem like alchemy. The splat patterns were startling, vivid; there were bright, wild, feral splatters across the walls, furniture, television, towels, bedspreads, curtains – an amazing wild horror of flying blood. Even in Miami you would think someone would have heard something. Two people being hacked up alive with a chain saw, in an elegant and expensive hotel room, and the neighbors simply turned up their TVs.

You may say that dear diligent Dexter gets carried away in his job, but I like to be thorough, and I like to know where all the blood is hiding. The professional reasons for this are obvious, but not quite as important to me as the personal ones. Perhaps someday a psychiatrist retained by the state penal system will help me discover exactly why.

In any case, the body chunks were very cold by the time we got to the scene, and we would probably never find the guy in the size 7 ½ handmade Italian loafer. Right-handed and overweight, with a terrific backhand.

But I had persevered and done a very neat piece of work. I don't do my job to catch the bad guys. Why would I want to do that? No, I do my job to make order out of chaos. To force the nasty blood stains to behave properly, and then go away. Others may use my work to catch criminals; that's fine by me, but it doesn't matter.

If I am ever careless enough to be caught, they will say I am a sociopathic monster, a sick and twisted demon who is not even human, and they will probably send me to die in Old Sparky with a smug self-righteous glow. If they ever catch Size 7 ½, they will say he is a bad man who went wrong because of social forces he was too unfortunate to resist, and he will go to jail for ten years before they turn him loose with enough money for a suit and a new chainsaw.

Every day at work I understand Harry a little better.

6

Friday night. Date night in Miami. and believe it or not, Date Night for Dexter. Oddly enough, I had found somebody. What, what? Deeply dead Dexter dating debutante doxies? Sex among the Undead? Has my need to imitate life gone all the way to faking orgasms?

Breathe easy. Sex never entered into it. After years of dreadful fumbling and embarrassment trying to look normal, I had finally hooked up with the perfect date.

Rita was almost as badly damaged as I am. Married too young, she had fought to make it work for ten years and two kids. Her charming life mate had a few small problems. First alcohol, then heroin, believe it or not, and finally crack. He beat her, the brute. Broke furniture, screamed, and threw things and made threats. Then raped her. Infected her with some dreadful crack-house diseases. All this on a regular basis, and Rita endured, worked, fought him through rehab twice. Then he went after the kids one night and Rita finally put her foot down.

Her face had healed by now, of course. And broken arms and ribs are routine for Miami physicians. Rita was quite presentable, just what the monster ordered.

The divorce was final, the brute was locked up, and then? Ah, the mysteries of the human mind. Somehow, somewhy, dear Rita had decided to date again. She was quite sure it was the Right Thing to do – but as a result of her frequent battery at the hands of the Man She Loved, she was completely uninterested in sex. Just, maybe, some masculine company for a while.

She had searched for just the right guy: sensitive, gentle, and willing to wait. Quite a long search, of course. She was looking for some imaginary man who cared more about having someone to talk to and see movies with than someone to have sex with, because she was Just Not Ready for That.

Did I say imaginary? Well, yes. Human men are not like that. Most women know this by the time they've had two kids and their first divorce. Poor Rita had married too young and too badly to learn this valuable lesson. And as a by-product of recovering from her awful marriage, instead of realizing that all men are beasts, she had come up with this lovely romantic picture of a

35

perfect gentleman who would wait indefinitely for her to open slowly, like a little flower.

Well. Really. Perhaps such a man existed in Victorian England – when there was a knocking shop on every corner where he could blow off steam between flowery protestations of frictionless love. But not, to my knowledge, in twenty-first-century Miami.

And yet – I could imitate all those things perfectly. And I actually wanted to. I had no interest in a sexual relationship. I wanted a disguise; Rita was exactly what I was looking for.

She was, as I say, very presentable. Petite and pert and spunky, a slim athletic figure, short blond hair, and blue eyes. She was a fitness fanatic, spending all her off-hours running and biking and so on. In fact, sweating was one of our favorite activities. We had cycled through the Everglades, done 5K runs, and even pumped iron together.

And best of all were her two children. Astor was eight and Cody was five and they were much too quiet. They would be, of course. Children whose parents frequently attempt to kill each other with the furniture tend to be slightly withdrawn. Any child brought up in a horror zone is. But they can be brought out of it eventually – look at me. I had endured nameless and unknown horrors as a child, and yet here I was: a useful citizen, a pillar of the community.

Perhaps that was part of my strange liking for Astor and Cody. Because I did like them, and that made no sense to me. I know what I am and I understand many things about myself. But one of the few character traits that genuinely mystifies me is my attitude toward children.

I like them.

They are important to me. They matter.

I don't understand it, really. I genuinely wouldn't care if every human in the universe were suddenly to expire, with the possible exception of myself and maybe Deborah. Other people are less important to me than lawn furniture. I do not, as the shrinks put it so eloquently, have any sense of the reality of others. And I am not burdened with this realization.

But kids – kids are different.

I had been 'dating' Rita for nearly a year and a half, and in that time I had slowly and deliberately won over Astor and Cody. I was okay. I wouldn't hurt them. I remembered their birthdays, report-card days, holidays. I could come into their house and would do no harm. I could be trusted.

Ironic, really. But true.

Me, the only man they could really trust. Rita thought it was part of my long slow courtship of her. Show her that the kids liked me and who knows? But in fact, they mattered to me more than she did. Maybe it was already too late, but I didn't want to see them grow up to be like me.

This Friday night Astor answered the door. She was wearing a large T-shirt that said RUG RATS and hung below her knees. Her red hair was pulled back in two pigtails and she had no expression at all on her small still face.

'Hello Dexter,' she said in her too-quiet way. For her, two words were a long conversation.

'Good evening, beautiful young lady,' I said in my best Lord Mountbatten voice. 'May I observe that you are looking very lovely this evening?'

'Okay,' she said, holding the door open. 'He's here,' she said over her shoulder to the darkness around the couch.

I stepped past her. Cody was standing behind her, just inside, like he was backing her up, just in case. 'Cody,' I said. I handed him a roll of Necco Wafers. He took them without taking his eyes off me and simply let his hand drop to his side without looking at the candy. He wouldn't open them until I was gone, and then he would split them with his sister.

'Dexter?' Rita called from the next room.

'In here,' I said. 'Can't you teach these children to behave?'

'No,' said Cody softly.

A joke. I stared at him. What next? Would he sing someday? Tap dance in the streets? Address the Democratic National Convention?

Rita rustled in, fastening a hoop earring. She was rather provocative, considering. She wore a practically weightless light blue silk dress that fell to mid-thigh, and of course her very best New Balance cross-training shoes. I'd never before met, or even heard of, a woman who actually wore comfortable shoes on dates. The enchanting creature.

'Hey, handsome,' Rita said. 'Let me talk to the sitter and we're out of here.' She went into the kitchen, where I heard her going over instructions with the teenage neighbor who did her babysitting. Bedtimes. Homework. TV dos and don'ts. Cell phone number. Emergency number. What to do in case of accidental poisoning or decapitation.

Cody and Astor still stared at me.

'Are you going to a movie?' Astor asked me.

I nodded. 'If we can find one that doesn't make us throw up.'

'Yuk,' she said. She made a very small sour face and I felt a tiny glow of accomplishment.

'Do you throw up at the movies?' Cody asked.

'Cody,' Astor said.

'Do you?' he insisted.

'No,' I said. 'But I usually want to.'

'Let's go,' said Rita, sailing in and bending to give each kid a peck on the cheek. 'Listen to Alice. Bedtime at nine.'

'Will you come back?' Cody asked.

'Cody! Of course I'll be back,' Rita said.

'I meant Dexter,' Cody said.

'You'll be asleep,' I said. 'But I'll wave at you, okay?'

'I won't be asleep,' he said grimly.

'Then I'll stop in and play cards with you,' I said.

'Really?'

'Absolutely. High-stakes poker. Winner gets to keep the horses.'

'Dexter!' Rita said, smiling anyway. 'You'll be asleep, Cody. Now good night, kids. Be good.' And she took my arm and lead me out the door. 'Honestly,' she murmured. 'You've got those two eating out of your hand.'

The movie was nothing special. I didn't really want to throw up, but I'd forgotten most of it by the time we stopped at a small place in South Beach for a late-night drink. Rita's idea. In spite of living in Miami for most of her life, she still thought South Beach was glamorous. Perhaps it was all the Rollerblades. Or maybe she thought that anyplace so full of people with bad manners *had* to be glamorous.

In any case, we waited twenty minutes for a small table and then sat and waited another twenty for service. I didn't mind. I enjoyed watching good-looking idiots looking at each other. A great spectator sport.

We strolled along Ocean Boulevard afterward, making pointless conversation – an art at which I excel. It was a lovely night. One corner was chewed off the full moon of a few nights ago, when I had entertained Father Donovan.

And as we drove back to Rita's South Miami house after our standard evening out, we passed an intersection in one of Coconut Grove's less wholesome areas. A winking red light caught my eye and I glanced down the side street. Crime scene: the yellow tape was already up, and several cruisers were nosed into a hurried splay.

It's him again, I thought, and even before I knew what I meant by that I was swinging the car down the street to the crime scene.

'Where are we going?' Rita asked, quite reasonably.

'Ah,' I said. 'I'd like to check here and see if they need me.'

'Don't you have a beeper?'

I gave her my best Friday-night smile. 'They don't always *know* they need me,' I said.

I might have stopped anyway, to show off Rita. The whole point of wearing a disguise was to be seen wearing her. But in truth, the small irresistible voice yammering in my ear would have made me stop no matter what. *It's him again.* And I had to see what he was up to. I left Rita in the car and hurried over.

He was up to no good again, the rascal. There was the same stack of neatly wrapped body parts. Angel-no-relation bent over it in almost the same position he'd been in when I left him at the last scene.

'*Hijo de puta,*' he said when I approached him.

'Not me, I trust,' I said.

'The rest of us are complaining that we have to work on Friday night,' Angel said. 'You show up with a date. And there is *still* nothing for you here.'

'Same guy, same pattern?'

'Same,' he said. He flipped the plastic away with his pen. 'Bone dry, again,' he said. 'No blood at all.'

The words made me feel slightly light-headed. I leaned in for a look. Once again the body parts were amazingly clean and dry. They had a near blue tinge to them and seemed preserved in their small perfect moment of time. Wonderful.

'A small difference in the cuts this time,' Angel said. 'In four places.' He pointed. 'Very rough here, almost emotional. Then here, not so much. Here and here, in between. Huh?'

'Very nice,' I said.

'And then lookit this,' he said. He nudged aside the bloodless chunk on top with a pencil. Underneath another piece gleamed white. The flesh had been flayed off very carefully, lengthwise, to reveal a clean bone.

'Why he would do like that?' Angel asked softly.

I breathed. 'He's experimenting,' I said. 'Trying to find the right way.' And I stared at the neat, dry section until I became aware that Angel had been looking at me for a very long moment.

'Like a kid playing with his food,' is how I described it to Rita when I returned to the car.

'My God,' Rita said. 'That's horrible.'

'I think the correct word is *heinous*,' I said.

'How can you joke about it, Dexter?'

I gave her a reassuring smile. 'You kind of get used to it in my line of work,' I said. 'We all make jokes to hide our pain.'

'Well, good lord, I hope they catch this maniac soon.'

I thought of the neatly stacked body parts, the variety of the cuts, the wonderful total lack of blood. 'Not too soon,' I said.

'What did you say?' she asked.

'I said, I don't think it will be too soon. The killer is extremely clever, and the detective in charge of the case is more interested in playing politics than in solving murders.'

She looked at me to see if I was kidding. Then she sat quietly for a while as we drove south on U.S. 1. She didn't speak until South Miami. 'I can never get used to seeing . . . I don't know. The underside? The way things really are? The way you see it,' she finally said.

She took me by surprise. I had been using the silence to think about the nicely stacked body parts we had just left. My mind had been hungrily circling the clean dry chopped-up limbs like an eagle looking for a chunk of meat to rip out. Rita's observation was so unexpected I couldn't even stutter for a minute. 'What do you mean?' I managed to say at last.

She frowned. 'I – I'm not sure. Just— We all assume that . . . *things* . . . really are a certain way. The way they're supposed to be? And then they never are, they're always more . . . I don't know. Darker? More human. Like this. I'm thinking, of course the detective wants to catch the killer, isn't that what detectives do? And it never occurred to me before that there could be anything at all political about murder.'

'Practically everything,' I said. I turned onto her street and slowed down in front of her neat and unremarkable house.

'But you,' she said. She didn't seem to notice where we were or what I had said. 'That's where you start. Most people would never really think it through that far.'

'I'm not all that deep, Rita,' I said. I nudged the car into park.

'It's like, everything really is two ways, the way we all pretend it is and the way it really is. And you already know that and it's like a game for you.'

I had no idea what she was trying to say. In truth, I had given up trying to figure it out and, as she spoke, I'd let my mind wander back to the newest murder; the cleanness of the flesh, the improvisational quality of the cuts, the complete dry spotless immaculate lack of blood—

'Dexter—' Rita said. She put a hand on my arm.

I kissed her.

I don't know which one of us was more surprised. It really wasn't something I had thought about doing ahead of time. And it certainly wasn't her perfume. But I mashed my lips against hers and held them there for a long moment.

She pushed away.

'No,' she said. 'I – No, Dexter.'

'All right,' I said, still shocked at what I had done.

'I don't think I want to – I'm not *ready* for— Damn it, Dexter,' she said. She unclipped her seat belt, opened the car door, and ran into her house.

Oh, dear, I thought. *What on earth have I done now?*

And I knew I should be wondering about that, and perhaps feeling disappointed that I had just destroyed my disguise after a year and a half of hard maintenance.

But all I could think about was that neat stack of body parts.

No blood.

None at all.

7

This body is stretched out just the way I like it. *The arms and legs are secure and the mouth is stopped with duct tape so there will be no noise and no spill into my work area. And my hand feels so steady with the knife that I am quite sure this will be a good one, very satisfying—*

Except it's not a knife, it's some kind of—

Except it's not my hand. Even though my hand is moving with this hand, it's not mine that holds the blade. And the room really is sort of small, it's so narrow, which makes sense because it's – what?

And now here I am floating above this perfect tight work space and its tantalizing body and for the first time I feel the cold blowing around me and even through me somehow. And if I could only feel my teeth I am quite sure they would chatter. And my hand in perfect unison with that other hand goes up and arches back for a perfect cut—

And of course I wake up in my apartment. Standing somehow by the front door, completely naked. Sleepwalking I could understand, but sleep stripping? Really. I stumble back to my little trundle bed. The covers are in a heap on the floor. The air conditioner has kicked the temperature down close to sixty. It had seemed like a good idea at the time, last night, feeling a little estranged from it all after what had happened with Rita. Preposterous, if it had really happened. Dexter, the love bandit, stealing kisses. And so I had taken a long hot shower when I got home and shoved the thermostat all the way down as I climbed into bed. I don't pretend to understand why, but in my darker moments I find cold cleansing. Not refreshing so much as necessary.

And cold it was. Far too cold now, for coffee and the start of the day amid the last tattered pieces of the dream.

As a rule I don't remember my dreams, and don't attach any importance to them if I do. So it was ridiculous that this one was staying with me.

—floating above this perfect tight work space – my hand in perfect unison with that other hand goes up and arches back for a perfect cut—

I've read the books. Perhaps because I'll never be one, humans are interesting to me. So I know all the symbolism: Floating is a form of flying, meaning sex. And the knife—

Ja, Herr Doktor. The knife ist eine mother, ja?

Snap out of it, Dexter.

Just a stupid, meaningless dream.

The telephone rang and I almost jumped out of my skin.

'How about breakfast at Wolfie's?' said Deborah. 'My treat.'

'It's Saturday morning,' I said. 'We'll never get in.'

'I'll get there first and get a table,' she said. 'Meet you there.'

Wolfie's Deli on Miami Beach was a Miami tradition. And because the Morgans are a Miami family, we had been eating there all our lives on those special deli occasions. Why Deborah thought today might be one of those occasions was beyond me, but I was sure she would enlighten me in time. So I took a shower, dressed in my casual Saturday best, and drove out to the Beach. Traffic was light over the new improved MacArthur Causeway, and soon I was politely elbowing my way through the teeming throngs at Wolfie's.

True to her word, Deborah had corralled a corner table. She was chatting with an ancient waitress, a woman even I recognized. 'Rose, my love,' I said, bending to kiss her wrinkled cheek. She turned her permanent scowl on me. 'My wild Irish Rose.'

'Dexter,' she rasped, with her thick middle-European accent. 'Knock off with the kiss, like some faigelah.'

'Faigelah. Is that Irish for fiancé?' I asked her, and slid into my chair.

'Feh,' she said, trudging off to the kitchen and shaking her head at me.

'I think she likes me,' I told Deborah.

'Somebody should,' said Deb. 'How was your date last night?'

'A lot of fun,' I said. 'You should try it sometime.'

'Feh,' said Deborah.

'You can't spend all your nights standing on Tamiami Trail in your underwear, Deb. You need a life.'

'I need a transfer,' she snarled at me. 'To Homicide Bureau. Then we'll see about a life.'

'I understand,' I said. 'It would certainly sound better for the kids to say Mommie's in homicide.'

'Dexter, for Christ's sake,' she said.

'It's a natural thought, Deborah. Nephews and nieces. More little Morgans. Why not?'

She blew out a long breath. 'I thought Mom was dead,' she said.

'I'm channeling her,' I said. 'Through the cherry Danish.'

'Well, change the channel. What do you know about cell crystallization?'

I blinked. 'Wow,' I said. 'You just blew away all the competition in the Subject Changing Tournament.'

'I'm serious,' she said.

'Then I really am floored, Deb. What do you mean, cell crystallization?'

'From cold,' she said. 'Cells that have crystallized from cold.'

Light flooded my brain. 'Of course,' I said, 'beautiful,' and somewhere deep inside small bells began to ring. *Cold . . . Clean, pure cold and the cool knife almost sizzling as it slices into the warm flesh. Antiseptic clean coldness, the blood slowed and helpless, so absolutely right and totally necessary; cold.* 'Why didn't I—' I started to say. I shut up when I saw Deborah's face.

'What,' Deb demanded. 'What of course?'

I shook my head. 'First tell me why you want to know.'

She looked at me for a long hard moment and blew out another breath. 'I think you know,' she said at last. 'There's been another murder.'

'I know,' I said. 'I passed it last night.'

'I heard you didn't actually pass it.'

I shrugged. Metro Dade is such a small family.

'So what did that "of course" mean?'

'Nothing,' I said, mildly irritated at last. 'The flesh of the body just looked a little different. If it was subjected to cold—' I held out my hands. 'That's all, okay? How cold?'

'Like meat-packing cold,' she said. 'Why would he do that?'

Because it's beautiful, I thought. 'It would slow the flow of blood,' I said.

She studied me. 'Is that important?'

I took a long and perhaps slightly shaky breath. Not only could I never explain it, she would lock me up if I tried. 'It's vital,' I said. For some reason I felt embarrassed.

'Why vital?'

'It, ah – I don't know. I think he has a thing about blood, Deb. Just a feeling I got from – I don't know, no evidence, you know.'

She was giving me that look again. I tried to think of something to say, but I couldn't. Glib, silver-tongued Dexter, with a dry mouth and nothing to say.

'Shit,' she said at last. 'That's it? Cold slows the blood, and that's vital? Come on. What the hell good is that, Dexter?'

'I don't do "good" before coffee, Deborah,' I said with a heroic effort at recovery. 'Just accurate.'

'Shit,' she said again. Rose brought our coffee. Deborah sipped. 'Last night I got an invite to the seventy-two-hour briefing,' she said.

I clapped my hands. 'Wonderful. You've arrived. What do you need me for?' Metro Dade has a policy of pulling the homicide team together approximately seventy-two hours after a murder. The investigating officer and her team talk it over with the Medical Examiner and, sometimes, someone from the prosecutor's office. It keeps everyone on the same heading. If Deborah had been invited, she was on the case.

She scowled. 'I'm not good at politics, Dexter. I can feel LaGuerta pushing me out, but I can't do anything about it.'

'Is she still looking for her mystery witness?'

Deborah nodded.

'Really. Even after the new kill last night?'

'She says that proves it. Because the new cuts were all complete.'

'But they were all *different*,' I protested.

She shrugged.

'And you suggested—?'

Deb looked away. 'I told her I thought it was a waste of time to look for a witness when it was obvious that the killer wasn't interrupted, just unsatisfied.'

'Ouch,' I said. 'You really *don't* know anything about politics.'

'Well, goddamn it, Dex,' she said. Two old ladies at the next table glared at her. She didn't notice. 'What you said made sense. It *is* obvious, and she's ignoring me. And even worse.'

'What could be worse than being ignored?' I said.

She blushed. 'I caught a couple of the uniforms snickering at me afterward. There's a joke going around, and I'm it.' She bit her lip and looked away. 'Einstein,' she said.

'I'm afraid I don't get it.'

'If my tits were brains, I'd be Einstein,' she said bitterly. I cleared my throat instead of laughing. 'That's what she's spreading about me,' Deb went on. 'That kind of crappy little tag sticks to you, and then they don't promote you because they think nobody will respect you with a nickname like that. God-*damn* it, Dex,' she said again, 'she's ruining my career.'

I felt a little surge of protective warmth. 'She's an idiot.'

'Should I tell her that, Dex? Would that be political?'

Our food arrived. Rose slammed the plates down in front of us as though she had been condemned by a corrupt judge to serve breakfast to baby killers. I gave her a gigantic smile and she trudged away, muttering to herself.

I took a bite and turned my thoughts to Deborah's problem. I had to try to think of it that way, Deborah's problem. Not 'those fascinating murders.' Not 'that amazingly attractive MO,' or 'the thing so similar to what I would love to do someday.' I had to stay uninvolved, but this was pulling at me so very hard. Even last night's dream, with its cold air. Pure coincidence, of course, but unsettling anyway.

This killer had touched the heart of what my killing was about. In the way he worked, of course, and not in his selection of victims. He had to be stopped, certainly, no question. Those poor hookers.

Still . . . The need for cold . . . So very interesting to explore sometime. Find a nice dark, narrow place . . .

Narrow? Where had that come from?

My dream, naturally. But that was just saying that my unconscious wanted me to think about it, wasn't it? And narrow felt right somehow. Cold and narrow—

'Refrigerated truck,' I said.

I opened my eyes. Deborah struggled mightily with a mouthful of eggs before she could speak. 'What?'

'Oh, just a guess. Not a real insight, I'm afraid. But wouldn't it make sense?'

'Wouldn't what make sense?' she asked.

I looked down at my plate and frowned, trying to picture how this would work. 'He wants a cold environment. To slow the blood flow, and because it's, uh – cleaner.'

'If you say so.'

'I do say so. And it has to be a narrow space—'

'Why? Where the hell did that come from, narrow?'

I chose not to hear that question. 'So a refrigerated truck would fit those conditions, and it's mobile, which makes it much easier to dump the garbage afterward.'

Deborah took a bite of bagel and thought for a moment while she chewed. 'So,' she said at last, and swallowed. 'The killer might have access to one of these trucks? Or own one?'

'Mmm, maybe. Except the kill last night was the first that showed signs of cold.'

Deborah frowned. 'So he went out and bought a truck?'

'Probably not. This is still experimental. It was probably an impulse to try cold.'

She nodded. 'And we would never get lucky enough that he drives one for a living or something, right?'

I gave her my happy shark smile. 'Ah, Deb. How quick you are this morning. No, I'm afraid our friend is much too smart to connect himself that way.'

Deborah sipped her coffee, put the cup down, and leaned back. 'So we're looking for a stolen refrigerator truck,' she said at last.

'I'm afraid so,' I said. 'But how many of those can there be in the last forty-eight hours?'

'In Miami?' She snorted. 'Somebody steals one, word gets out that it's worth stealing, and suddenly every goddamn two-bit original gangsta, marielito, crackhead, and junior wise guy has to steal one, just to keep up.'

'Let's hope word isn't out yet,' I said.

Deborah swallowed the last of her bagel. 'I'll check,' she said. And then she reached across the table and squeezed my hand. 'I really appreciate this,' she said. She gave me a couple of seconds of a shy, hesitant smile. 'But I worry about how you come up with this stuff, Dex. I just . . .' She looked down at the table and squeezed my hand again.

I squeezed back. 'Leave the worrying to me,' I said. 'You just find that truck.'

8

In theory, Metro's seventy-two-hour meeting gives everyone enough time to get somewhere with a case, but is soon enough that the leads are still warm. And so Monday morning, in a conference room on the second floor, the crack crime-fighting team led by the indomitable Detective LaGuerta assembled once again for the seventy-two-hour. I assembled with them. I got some looks, and a few good-hearted remarks from the cops who knew me. Just simple, cheerful wit, like, 'Hey, blood boy, where's your squeegee?' Salt of the earth, these people, and soon my Deborah would be one of them. I felt proud and humble to be in the same room.

Unfortunately, these feelings were not shared by all present. 'The fuck you doing here?' grunted Sergeant Doakes. He was a very large black man with an injured air of permanent hostility. He had a cold ferocity to him that would certainly come in handy for somebody with my hobby. It was a shame we couldn't be friends. But for some reason he hated all lab techs, and for some additional reason that had always meant especially Dexter. He also held the Metro Dade record for the bench press. So he rated my political smile.

'I just dropped in to listen, Sergeant,' I told him.

'Got no fucking call to be here,' he said. 'The fuck outta here.'

'He can stay, Sergeant,' LaGuerta said.

Doakes scowled at her. 'The fuck for?'

'I don't want to make anybody unhappy,' I said, edging for the door without any real conviction.

'It's perfectly all right,' LaGuerta said with an actual smile for me. She turned to Doakes. 'He can stay,' she repeated.

'Gimme the fucking creeps,' Doakes grumbled. I began to appreciate the man's finer qualities. Of course I gave him the fucking creeps. The only real question was why he was the only one in a room filled with cops who had the insight to get the fucking creeps from my presence.

'Let's get started,' LaGuerta said, cracking her whip gently, leaving no room for doubt that she was in charge. Doakes slouched back in his chair with a last scowl at me.

The first part of the meeting was a matter of routine; reports, political maneuvers, all the little things that make us human. Those of us who are human, anyway. LaGuerta briefed the information officers on what they could and could not release to the press. Things they could release included a new glossy photo of LaGuerta she'd made up for the occasion. It was serious and yet glamorous; intense but refined. You could almost see her making lieutenant in that picture. If only Deborah had that kind of PR smarts.

It took most of an hour before we got around to the actual murders. But finally LaGuerta asked for reports on the progress in finding her mystery witness. Nobody had anything to report. I tried hard to look surprised.

LaGuerta gave the group a frown of command. 'Come on, people,' she said. 'Somebody needs to find something here.' But nobody did, and there was a pause while the group studied their fingernails, the floor, the acoustic tiles in the ceiling.

Deborah cleared her throat. 'I, uh,' she said and cleared her throat again. 'I had a, um, an idea. A different idea. About trying something in a slightly different direction.' She said it like it was in quotation marks, and indeed it was. All my careful coaching couldn't make her sound natural when she said it, but she had at least stuck to my carefully worded politically correct phrasing.

LaGuerta raised an artificially perfect eyebrow. 'An idea? Really?' She made a face to show how surprised and delighted she was. 'Please, by all means, share it with us, Officer Ein – I mean, Officer Morgan.'

Doakes snickered. A delightful man.

Deborah flushed, but slogged on. 'The, um, cell crystallization. On the last victim. I'd like to check and see if any refrigerated trucks have been reported stolen in the last week or so.'

Silence. Utter, dumb silence. The silence of the cows. They didn't get it, the brickheads, and Deborah was not making them see it. She let the silence grow, a silence LaGuerta milked with a pretty frown, a puzzled glance around the room to see if anybody else was following this, then a polite look at Deborah.

'Refrigerated . . . trucks?' LaGuerta said.

Deborah looked completely flustered, the poor child. This was not a girl who enjoyed public speaking. 'That's right,' she said.

LaGuerta let it hang, enjoying it. 'Mm-hmm,' she said.

Deborah's face darkened; not a good sign. I cleared my throat, and when that didn't do any good I coughed, loud enough to remind her to stay cool. She looked at me. So did LaGuerta. 'Sorry,' I said. 'I think I'm getting a cold.'

Could anyone really ask for a better brother?

'The, um, *cold*,' Deborah blurted, lunging at my lifeline. 'A refrigerated vehicle could probably cause that kind of tissue damage. And it's mobile, so he'd be harder to catch. And getting rid of the body would be a lot easier. So, uh, if one was stolen, I mean a truck . . . a refrigerated . . . that might give us a lead.'

Well, that was most of it, and she did get it out there. One or two

47

thoughtful frowns blossomed around the room. I could almost hear gears turning.

But LaGuerta just nodded. 'That's a very . . . *interesting* thought, Officer,' she said. She put just the smallest emphasis on the word *officer*, to remind us all that this was a democracy where anybody could speak up, but really . . . 'But I still believe that our best bet is to find the witness. We know he's out there.' She smiled, a politically shy smile. 'Or *she*,' she said, to show that she could be sharp. 'But somebody saw something. We know that from the *evidence*. So let's concentrate on that, and leave grasping at straws for the guys in Broward, okay?' She paused, waiting for a little chuckle to run around the room. 'But Officer Morgan, I would appreciate your continued help talking to the hookers. They know you down there.'

My God, she was good. She had deflected anyone from possibly thinking about Deb's idea, put Deb in her place, and brought the team back together behind her with the joke about our rivalry with Broward County. All in a few simple words. I felt like applauding.

Except, of course, that I was on poor Deborah's team, and she had just been flattened. Her mouth opened for a moment, then closed, and I watched her jaw muscles knot as she carefully pushed her face back into Cop Neutral. In its own way, a fine performance, but truly, not even in the same league as LaGuerta's.

The rest of the meeting was uneventful. There was really nothing to talk about beyond what had been said. So very shortly after LaGuerta's masterful putdown, the meeting broke up and we were in the hall again.

'Damn her,' Deborah muttered under her breath. 'Damn, damn, *damn* her!'

'Absolutely,' I agreed.

She glared at me. 'Thanks, bro. Some help you were.'

I raised my eyebrows at her. 'But we agreed I would stay out of it. So you would get the credit.'

She snarled. 'Some credit. She made me look like an idiot.'

'With absolute respect, sister dear, you met her halfway.'

Deborah looked at me, looked away, threw up her hands with disgust. 'What was I supposed to say? I'm not even on the team. I'm just there because the captain said they had to let me in.'

'And he didn't say they had to listen to you,' I said.

'And they don't. And they won't,' Deborah said bitterly. 'Instead of getting me into homicide, this is going to kill my career. I'll die a meter maid, Dexter.'

'There is a way out, Deb,' I said, and the look she turned on me now was only about one-third hope.

'What,' she said.

I smiled at her, my most comforting, challenging, I'm-not-really-a-shark smile. 'Find the truck,' I said.

*

It was three days before I heard from my dear foster sister again, a longish period for her to go without talking to me. She came into my office just after lunch on Thursday, looking sour. 'I found it,' she said, and I didn't know what she meant.

'Found what, Deb?' I asked. 'The Fountain of Grumpiness?'

'The truck,' she said. 'The refrigerated truck.'

'But that's great news,' I said. 'Why do you look like you're searching for somebody to slap?'

'Because I am,' she said, and flung four or five stapled pages onto my desk. 'Look at this.'

I picked it up and glanced at the top page. 'Oh,' I said. 'How many altogether?'

'Twenty-three,' she said. 'In the last month, twenty-three refrigerator trucks have been reported stolen. The guys over on traffic say most of 'em turn up in canals, torched for the insurance money. Nobody pushes too hard to find them. So nobody's been pushing on these, and nobody's going to.'

'Welcome to Miami,' I said.

Deborah sighed and took the list back from me, slouching into my extra chair like she'd just lost all her bones. 'There's no way I can check them all, not by myself. It would take months. Goddamn it, Dex,' she said. 'Now what do we do?'

I shook my head. 'I'm sorry, Deb,' I said. 'But now we have to wait.'

'That's it? Just wait?'

'That's it,' I said.

And it was. For two more weeks, that was it. We waited.

And then . . .

9

I woke up covered with sweat, not sure where I was, and absolutely certain that another murder was about to happen. Somewhere not so far away he was searching for his next victim, sliding through the city like a shark around the reef. I was so certain I could almost hear the purr of the duct tape. He was out there, feeding his Dark Passenger, and it was talking to mine. And in my sleep I had been riding with him, a phantom remora in his great slow circles.

I sat up in my own little bed and peeled away the twisted sheets. The bedside clock said it was 3:14. Four hours since I'd gone to bed, and I felt like I'd been slogging through the jungle the entire time with a piano on my back. I was sweaty, stiff, and stupid, unable to form any thoughts at all beyond the certainty that it was happening out there without me.

Sleep was gone for the night, no question. I turned on the light. My hands were clammy and trembling. I wiped them on the sheet, but that didn't help. The sheets were just as wet. I stumbled into the bathroom to wash my hands. I held them under the running water. The tap let out a stream that was warm, room temperature, and for a moment I was washing my hands in blood and the water turned red; just for a second, in the half-light of the bathroom, the sink ran bloodred.

I closed my eyes.

The world shifted.

I had meant to get rid of this trick of light and my half-sleeping brain. Close the eyes, open them, the illusion would be over and it would be simple clean water in my sink. Instead, it was like closing my eyes had opened a second set of eyes into another world.

I was back in my dream, floating like a knife blade above the lights of Biscayne Boulevard, flying cold and sharp and homing in on my target and—

I opened my eyes again. The water was just water.

But what was I?

I shook my head violently. Steady, old boy; no Dexter off the deep end, please. I took a long breath and peeked at myself. In the mirror I looked the way I was supposed to look. Carefully composed features. Calm and mocking blue eyes, a perfect imitation of human life. Except that my hair stuck up like Stan Laurel's, there was no sign of whatever it was that had just zipped through my half-sleeping brain and rattled me out of my slumber.

I carefully closed my eyes again.

Darkness.

Plain, simple, darkness. No flying, no blood, no city lights. Just good old Dexter with his eyes closed in front of the mirror.

I opened them again. Hello, dear boy, so good to have you back. But where on earth have you been?

That, of course, was the question. I have spent most of my life untroubled by dreams and, for that matter, hallucinations. No visions of the Apocalypse for me; no troubling Jungian icons burbling up from my subconscious, no mysterious recurring images drifting through the history of my unconsciousness. Nothing ever goes bump in Dexter's night. When I go to sleep, all of me sleeps.

So what had just happened? Why were these pictures appearing to me?

I splashed water on my face and pushed my hair down. That did not, of course, answer the question, but it made me feel a little better. How bad could things be if my hair was neat?

In truth, I did not know. Things could be plenty bad. I might be losing all, or many, of my marbles. What if I had been slipping into insanity a piece at a time for years, and this new killer had simply triggered the final headlong fall into complete craziness? How could I hope to measure the relative sanity of somebody like me?

The images had looked and felt so real. But they couldn't be; I had been right here in my bed. Yet I had almost been able to smell the tang of salt water, exhaust, and cheap perfume floating over Biscayne Boulevard. Completely real – and wasn't that one of the signs of insanity, that the delusions were indistinguishable from reality? I had no answers, and no way to find any. Talking to a shrink was out of the question, of course; I would frighten the poor thing to death, and he might feel honor bound to have me locked away somewhere. Certainly I could not argue with the wisdom of that idea. But if I was losing my hold on sanity as I had built it, it was all my problem, and the first part of the problem was that there was no way to know for sure.

Although, come to think of it, there was one way.

Ten minutes later I was driving past Dinner Key. I drove slowly, since I didn't actually know what I was looking for. This part of the city slept, as much as it ever did. A few people still swirled across the Miami landscape: tourists who'd had too much Cuban coffee and couldn't sleep. People from Iowa looking for a gas station. Foreigners looking for South Beach. And the predators, of course – thugs, robbers, crackheads; vampires, ghouls, and assorted monsters like me. But in this area, at this time, very few of them altogether. This was Miami deserted, as deserted as it got, a place made lonely by the ghost of the daytime crowd. It was a city that had whittled itself down to a mere hunting ground, without the gaudy disguises of sunlight and bright T-shirts.

And so I hunted. The other night eyes tracked me and dismissed me as I passed without slowing. I drove north, over the old drawbridge, through downtown Miami, still not sure what I was looking for and still not seeing it – and yet, for some uncomfortable reason, absolutely sure that I would find it, that I was going in the right direction, that *it* was waiting for me ahead.

Just beyond the Omni the nightlife picked up. More activity, more things to see. Whooping on the sidewalks, tinny music coming and going through the car windows. The night girls came out, flocks of them on the street corners, giggling with each other, or staring stupidly at the passing cars. And the cars slowed to stare back, gawking at the costumes and what they left uncovered. Two blocks ahead of me a new Corniche stopped and a pack of the girls flew out of the shadows, off the sidewalk, and into the street, surrounding the car immediately. Traffic stumbled to a half stop, horns blattered. Most of the drivers sat for a minute, content to watch, but an impatient truck pulled around the knot of cars and into the oncoming lane.

A refrigerator truck.

This was nothing, I said to myself. Nighttime yogurt delivery; pork link sausages for breakfast, freshness guaranteed. A load of grouper headed north or to the airport. Refrigerated trucks moved through Miami around the clock, even now, even in the night hours— This it was and nothing more.

But I put my foot down on the gas pedal anyway. I moved up, in and out of traffic. I got within three cars of the Corniche and its besieged driver. Traffic stopped. I looked ahead at the truck. It was running straight up Biscayne, moving into a series of traffic lights. I would lose him if I got too far behind. And I suddenly wanted very badly not to lose him.

I waited for a gap in traffic and quickly nosed out into the oncoming lane. I was around the Corniche and then speeding up, closing on the truck. Trying not to move too fast, not to be conspicuous, but slowly closing the space between us. He was three traffic lights ahead, then two.

Then his light turned red and before I could gloat and catch up, mine did, too. I stopped. I realized with some surprise that I was chewing on my lip. I was tense; me, Dexter the Ice Cube. I was feeling human anxiety, desperation, actual emotional distress. I wanted to catch up to this truck and see for myself, oh how I wanted to put my hand on the truck, open the door to the cabin, look inside—

And then what? Arrest him single-handed? Take him by the hand to dear Detective LaGuerta? See what I caught? Can I keep him? It was just as likely that he would keep me. He was in full hunting mode, and I was merely tagging along behind like an unwanted little brother. And why was I tagging along? Did I just want to prove to myself that it was him, *the* him, that he was out here prowling and I was not crazy? And if I was not crazy – how had I known? What was going on in my brain? Perhaps crazy would be a happier solution after all.

An old man shuffled in front of my car, crossing the street with incredibly slow and painful steps. For a moment I watched him, marveling at what life must be like when you moved that slow, and then I glanced ahead at the refrigerator truck.

His light had turned green. Mine had not.

The truck accelerated quickly, moving north at the upper end of the speed limit, taillights growing smaller as I watched, waiting for my light to change.

Which it refused to do. And so grinding my teeth – steady, Dex! – I ran the light, narrowly missing the old man. He didn't look up or break step.

The speed limit on this stretch of Biscayne Boulevard was thirty-five. In Miami that means if you go under fifty they will run you off the road. I pushed up to sixty-five, moving through the sparse traffic, desperate now to close the distance. The lights of the truck winked out as he went around a curve – or had he turned? I moved up to seventy-five and roared past the turn for the 79th Street Causeway, around the bend by the Publix Market, and into the straightaway, searching frantically for the truck.

And saw it. There – ahead of me—

Moving *toward* me.

The bastard had doubled back. Did he feel me on his tail? Smell my exhaust drifting up on him? No matter – it was him, the same truck, no question, and as I raced past him he turned out onto the causeway.

I squealed into a mall parking lot and slowed, turning the car and accelerating back out onto Biscayne Boulevard, southbound now. Less than a block and I turned onto the causeway, too. Far, far in front, nearly to the first bridge, I saw the small red lights, winking, mocking me. My foot crashed down on the gas pedal and I charged ahead.

He was on the up-slope of the bridge now, picking up speed, keeping the distance steady between us. Which meant he must know, must realize somebody was following. I pushed my car a little harder; I got closer, little by little, a few lengths closer.

And then he was gone, over the hump at the top of the bridge and down the far side, heading much too fast into North Bay Village. It was a heavily patrolled area. If he went too fast he would be seen and pulled over. And then—

I was up the bridge and onto the hump now and below me—

Nothing.

Empty road.

I slowed, looking in all directions from the vantage point at the top of the bridge. A car moved toward me – not the truck, just a Mercury Marquis with one smashed fender. I started down the far side of the bridge.

At the bottom of the bridge North Bay Village split off the causeway into two residential areas. Behind a gas station on the left a row of condos and apartments made a slow circle. To the right were houses; small but expensive. Nothing moved on either side. There were no lights showing, no sign of anything, neither traffic nor life.

Slowly I moved through the village. Empty. He was gone. On an island with only one through street, he had lost me. But how?

I circled back, pulled off onto the shoulder of the road and closed my eyes. I don't know why; perhaps I hoped I might *see* something again. But I didn't. Just darkness, and little bright lights dancing on the inside of my eyelids. I was tired. I felt stupid. Yes, me; ditzy Dexter, trying to be Boy Wonder, using my great psychic powers to track down the evil genius. Pursuing him in my supercharged crime-fighting vehicle. And in all likelihood he was simply a stoked-up delivery boy playing macho head games with the only other driver on the road that night. A Miami thing that happened every day to every driver in our fair city. Chase me, you can't catch me. Then the uplifted finger, the waved gun, ho-hum and back to work.

Just a refrigerated truck, nothing more, now speeding away across Miami Beach with the heavy metal station ripping from the radio speaker. And not my killer, not some mysterious bond pulling me out of bed and across the city in the dead of night. Because that was just too silly for words, and far too silly for level-headed empty-hearted Dexter.

I let my head drop onto the steering wheel. How wonderful to have such an authentic *human* experience. Now I knew what it was like to feel like a total idiot. I could hear the bell on the drawbridge in the near distance, clanging its warning that the bridge was about to go up. Ding ding ding. The alarm bell on my expired intellect. I yawned. Time to go home, go back to bed.

Behind me an engine started. I glanced back.

From behind the gas station at the foot of the bridge he came out fast in a tight circle. He passed me fishtailing and still accelerating and through the blur of motion in the driver's window a shape spun at me, wild and hard. I ducked. Something thumped into the side of my car, leaving behind it the sound of an expensive dent. I waited for a moment, just to be safe. Then I raised my head and looked. The truck was speeding away, crashing the wooden barrier at the drawbridge and powering through, leaping across the bridge as it started to raise up, and making it easily to the other side as the bridge keeper leaned out and yelled. Then the truck was gone, down the far side of the bridge and back into Miami, far away on the other side of the widening gap as the bridge went up. Gone, hopelessly gone, gone as if he had never been. And I would never know if it had been my killer or just another normal Miami jerk.

I got out of my car to look at the dent. It was a big one. I looked around to see what he had thrown.

It had rolled ten or fifteen feet away and wobbled out into the middle of the street. Even from this distance there was no mistaking it, but just to make sure I was absolutely without any doubt, the headlights from an oncoming car lit it up. The car swerved and smashed into a hedge and over the sound of its now-constant horn I could hear the driver screaming. I walked over to the thing to be sure.

Yes indeed. That's what it was.

A woman's head.

I bent to look. It was a very clean cut, very nice work. There was almost no blood around the lip of the wound.

'Thank God,' I said, and I realized I was smiling – and why not?

Wasn't it nice? I wasn't crazy after all.

10

At a little after 8 AM Laguerta came over to where I was sitting on the trunk of my car. She leaned her tailored haunch onto the car and slid over until our thighs were touching. I waited for her to say something, but she didn't seem to have any words for the occasion. Neither did I. So I sat there for several minutes looking back at the bridge, feeling the heat of her leg against mine and wondering where my shy friend had gone with his truck. But I was yanked out of my quiet daydream by a pressure on my thigh.

I looked down at my pants leg. LaGuerta was kneading my thigh as if it were a lump of dough. I looked up at her face. She looked back.

'They found the body,' she said. 'You know. The rest of it that goes with the head.'

I stood up. 'Where?'

She looked at me the way a cop looks at somebody who finds corpseless heads in the street. But she answered. 'Office Depot Center,' she said.

'Where the Panthers play?' I asked, and a little icy-fingered jolt ran through me. 'On the ice?'

LaGuerta nodded, still watching me. 'The hockey team,' she said. 'Is that the Panthers?'

'I think that's what they're called,' I said. I couldn't help myself.

She pursed her lips. 'They found it stuffed into the goalie's net.'

'Visitor's or home?' I asked.

She blinked. 'Does that make a difference?'

I shook my head. 'Just a joke, Detective.'

'Because I don't know how to tell the difference. I should get somebody there who knows about hockey,' she said, her eyes finally drifting away from me and across the crowd, searching for somebody carrying a puck. 'I'm glad you can make a joke about it,' she added. 'What's a—' she frowned, trying to remember, '—a sambolie?'

'A what?'

She shrugged. 'Some kind of machine. They use it on the ice?'

'A Zamboni?'

'Whatever. The guy who drives it, he takes it out on the ice to get ready for practice this morning. A couple of the players, they like to get there early? And they like the ice fresh, so this guy, the—' she hesitated slightly '—the sambolie driver? He comes in early on practice days. And so he drives this thing out onto the ice? And he sees these packages stacked up. Down there in the goalie's net? So he gets down and he takes a look.' She shrugged again. 'Doakes is over there now. He says they can't get the guy to calm down enough to say any more than that.'

'I know a little about hockey,' I said.

She looked at me again with somewhat heavy eyes. 'So much I don't know about you, Dexter. You play hockey?'

'No, I never played,' I said modestly. 'I went to a few games.' She didn't say anything and I had to bite my lip to keep from blathering on. In truth, Rita had season tickets for the Florida Panthers, and I had found to my very great surprise that I liked hockey. It was not merely the frantic, cheerfully homicidal mayhem I enjoyed. There was something about sitting in the huge, cool hall that I found relaxing, and I would happily have gone there even to watch golf. In truth, I would have said anything to make LaGuerta take me to the rink. I wanted to go to the arena very badly. I wanted to see this body stacked in the net on the ice more than anything else I could think of, wanted to undo the neat wrapping and see the clean dry flesh. I wanted to see it so much that I felt like a cartoon of a dog on point, wanted to be there with it so much that I felt self-righteous and possessive about the body.

'All right,' LaGuerta finally said, when I was about to vibrate out of my skin. And she showed a small, strange smile that was part official and part – what? Something else altogether, something human, unfortunately, putting it beyond my understanding. 'Give us a chance to talk.'

'I'd like that very much,' I said, absolutely oozing charm. LaGuerta didn't respond. Maybe she didn't hear me, not that it mattered. She was totally beyond any sense of sarcasm where her self-image was concerned. It was possible to hit her with the most horrible flattery in the world and she would accept it as her due. I didn't really enjoy flattering her. There's no fun where there's no challenge. But I didn't know what else to say. What did she imagine we would talk about? She had already grilled me mercilessly when she first arrived on the scene.

We had stood beside my poor dented car and watched the sun come up. She had looked out across the causeway and asked me seven times if I had seen the driver of the truck, each time with a slightly different inflection, frowning in between questions. She'd asked me five times if I was sure it had been a refrigerated truck – I'm sure that was subtlety on her part. She wanted to ask about that one a lot more, but held back to avoid being obvious. She even forgot herself once and asked in Spanish. I told her I was *seguro*, and she had looked at me and touched my arm, but she did not ask again.

And three times she had looked up the incline of the bridge, shaken her head, and spat 'Puta!' under her breath. Clearly, that was a reference to Officer Puta, my dear sister Deborah. In the face of an actual refrigerator truck as predicted by Deborah, a certain amount of spin control was going to be necessary, and I could tell by the way LaGuerta nibbled at her lower lip that she was hard at work on the problem. I was quite sure she would come up with something uncomfortable for Deb – it was what she did best – but for the time being I was hoping for a modest rise in my sister's stock. Not with LaGuerta, of course, but one could hope that others might notice that her brilliant bit of attempted detective work had panned out.

Oddly enough, LaGuerta did not ask me what I had been doing driving around at that hour. Of course, I'm not a detective, but it did seem like a rather obvious question. Perhaps it would be unkind to say that the oversight was typical of her, but there it is. She just didn't ask.

And yet there was more for us to talk about, apparently. So I followed her to her car, a big two-year-old light blue Chevrolet that she drove on duty. After hours she had a little BMW that nobody was supposed to know about.

'Get in,' she said. And I climbed into the neat blue front seat.

LaGuerta drove fast, in and out of traffic, and in a very few minutes we were over the causeway to the Miami side again, across Biscayne and a half mile or so to I-95. She drove onto the freeway and wove north through traffic at speeds that seemed a little much even for Miami. But we got to 595 and turned west. She looked at me sideways, out of the corner of her eye, three times before she finally spoke. 'That's a nice shirt,' she said.

I glanced down at my nice shirt. I had thrown it on to chase out of my apartment and saw it now for the first time, a polyester bowling shirt with bright red dragons on it. I had worn it all day at work and it was a trifle ripe, but yes, more or less clean looking. Somewhat nice, of course, but still—

Was LaGuerta making small talk so I would relax enough to make some damaging admission? Did she suspect that I knew more than I was saying and think she could get me to drop my guard and say it?

'You always wear such nice clothes, Dexter,' she said. She looked over at me with a huge, goofy smile, unaware that she was about to ram her car into a tanker truck. She looked back in time and turned the wheel with one finger and we slid around the tanker and west on I-595.

I thought about the nice clothes that I always wore. Well of course I did. I took pride in being the best-dressed monster in Dade County. Yes, certainly, he chopped up that nice Mr. Duarte, but he was so well dressed! Proper clothing for all occasions – by the way, what did one wear to attend an early-morning decapitation? A day-old bowling shirt and slacks, naturally. I was *à la mode*. But aside from this morning's hasty costume, I really was careful. It was one of Harry's lessons: stay neat, dress nicely, avoid attention.

But why should a politically minded homicide detective either notice or care? It was not as if—

Or was it? A nasty little idea began to grow. Something in the strange smile that flicked across her face and then away gave me the answer. It was ridiculous, but what else could it be? LaGuerta was not looking for a way to put me off my guard and ask more penetrating questions about what I had seen. And she did not truly give a winged fart about my hockey expertise.

LaGuerta was being social.

She *liked* me.

Here I was still trying to recover from the horrible shock of my bizarre, lurching, slobbering attack on Rita – and now this? LaGuerta *liked* me? Had terrorists dumped something in the Miami water supply? Was I exuding some kind of strange pheromone? Had every woman in Miami suddenly realized how hopeless real men are, and I had become attractive by default? What, in all very seriousness, the hell was going on?

Of course I could be wrong. I lunged at the thought like a barracuda at a shiny silver spoon. After all, what colossal egotism to think that a polished, sophisticated, career-track woman like LaGuerta might show any kind of interest in me. Wasn't it more likely that, that –

That what? As unfortunate as it was, it did make a kind of sense. We were in the same line of work and therefore, conventional cop wisdom said, more likely to understand and forgive each other. Our relationship could survive her cop hours and stressful lifestyle. And although I take no credit for it, I am presentable enough; I clean up good, as we natives like to say. And I had put myself out to be charming to her for several years now. It had been purely political schmoozing, but she did not have to know that. I was *good* at being charming, one of my very few vanities. I had studied hard and practiced long, and when I applied myself no one could tell I was faking it. I was really very good at sprinkling seeds of charm. Perhaps it was natural that the seeds would eventually sprout.

But sprout into this? What now? Was she going to propose a quiet dinner some evening? Or a few hours of sweaty bliss at the Cacique Motel?

Happily, we arrived at the arena just before panic took me over completely. LaGuerta circled the building once, looking for the correct entrance. It wasn't too hard to find. A cluster of police cars stood scattered outside one row of double doors. She nosed her big car in among them. I jumped out of the car quickly, before she could put her hand on my knee. She got out and looked at me for a moment. Her mouth twitched.

'I'll take a look,' I said. I did not quite run into the arena. I was fleeing LaGuerta, yes – but I was also very anxious to get inside; to see what my playful friend had done, to be near his work, to inhale the wonder, to learn.

The inside echoed with the organized bedlam typical of any murder scene – and yet it seemed to me that there was a special electricity in the air, a slightly hushed feeling of excitement and tension that you wouldn't find at any ordinary murder, a sense that this one was different somehow, that new and wonderful things might happen because we were out here on the cutting edge. But maybe that was just me. A clot of people stood around the nearby net. Several of them wore Broward uniforms; they had their arms folded and watched as Captain Matthews argued about jurisdiction with a man in a tailored suit. As I got closer I saw Angel-no-relation in an unusual position, standing above a balding man who was on one knee poking at a stack of carefully wrapped packages.

I stopped at the railing to look through the glass. There it was, only ten feet away. It looked so perfect in the cold purity of the newly Zambonied hockey rink. Any jeweler will tell you that finding the right setting is vitally important, and this— It was stunning. Absolutely perfect. I felt just a little dizzy, uncertain of whether the railing would hold my weight, as if I might simply pass straight down through the hard wood like a mist.

Even from the railing I could tell. He had taken the time, he had done it right, in spite of what must have seemed like a very close call on the causeway only minutes before. Or had he known somehow that I meant him no harm?

And since I brought it up anyway, did I, in fact, mean him no harm? Did I truly mean to track him to his lair and come up on point all aquiver for advancing Deborah's career? Of course that was what I thought I was doing – but would I be strong enough to carry through with it if things kept getting so interesting? Here we were at the hockey rink where I had whiled away many pleasant and contemplative hours; wasn't this even more proof that this artist – excuse me, I mean 'killer' of course – was moving on a track parallel to mine? Just look at the lovely work he had done here.

And the head – that was the key. Surely it was too important as a piece of what he was doing simply to leave it behind. Had he thrown it to frighten me, send me into paroxysms of terror, horror, and dread? Or had he known somehow that I felt the same way he did? Could he, too, feel the connection between us, and he just wanted to be playful? Was he teasing me? He had to have some important reason for leaving me such a trophy. I was experiencing powerful, dizzying sensations – how could he be feeling nothing?

LaGuerta came up beside me. 'You're in such a hurry,' she said, a slight edge of complaint in her voice. 'Are you afraid she'll get away?' She nodded at the stacked body parts.

I knew that somewhere inside me was a clever answer, something that would make her smile, charm her a little more, smooth over my awkward run from her clutches. But standing there at the rail, looking down at the body on the ice, in the goalie's net – in the presence of greatness, one might say – no wit came out. I did manage not to yell at her to shut up, but it was a very near thing.

'I had to see,' I said truthfully, and then recovered enough to add, 'It's the home team's net.'

She slapped my arm playfully. 'You're awful,' she said. Luckily Sergeant

Doakes came over to us and the detective didn't have time for a kittenish gig-gle, which would have been more than I could take. As always, Doakes seemed more interested in finding a way to get a good grip on my ribs and pull me open than anything else, and he gave me such a warm and penetrating look of welcome that I faded quickly away and left him to LaGuerta. He stared after me, watching me with an expression that said I had to be guilty of some-thing and he would very much like to examine my entrails to find out what. I'm sure he would have been happier someplace where the police were per-mitted to break the occasional tibia or femur. I circled away from him, mov-ing slowly around the rink to the nearest place where I could get in. I had just found it when something came at me on my blind side and hit me, rather hard, in the ribs.

I straightened up to face my assailant with a certain bruise and a strained smile. 'Hello, dear sister,' I said. 'So nice to see a friendly face.'

'Bastard!' she hissed at me.

'Quite probably,' I said. 'But why bring it up now?'

'Because, you miserable son of a bitch, you had a lead and you didn't call me!'

'A lead?' I almost stuttered. 'What makes you think—'

'Cut the crap, Dexter,' Deborah snarled. 'You weren't driving around at four AM looking for hookers. You knew where he was, goddamn it.'

Light dawned. I had been so wrapped up in my own problems, starting with the dream – and the fact that it had obviously been something more than that – and continuing on through my nightmarish encounter with LaGuerta, that it did not occur to me that I had wronged Deborah. I had not shared. Of course she would be angry. 'Not a lead, Deb,' I said, trying to soothe her feelings a bit. 'Nothing solid like that. Just – a feeling. A thought, that's all. It was really nothing—'

She shoved again. 'Except that it was *something*,' she snarled. 'You found him.'

'Actually, I'm not sure,' I said. 'I think he found me.'

'Quit being clever,' she said, and I spread my hands to show how impossi-ble that would be. 'You promised, goddamn you.'

I did not remember making any kind of promise that might cover calling her in the middle of the night and telling her my dreams, but this didn't seem like a very politic thing to say, so I didn't. 'I'm sorry, Deb,' I said instead. 'I really didn't think it would pan out. It was just a . . . a hunch, really.' I was certainly not going to attempt any explanation of the parapsychology involved, even with Deb. Or perhaps especially not with her. But another thought hit me. I lowered my voice. 'Maybe you could help me a little. What am I supposed to tell them if *they* ever decide to ask what I was doing driv-ing around down there at four AM?'

'Has LaGuerta interviewed you yet?'

'Exhaustively,' I said, fighting down a shudder.

Deb made a disgusted face. 'And she didn't ask.' It was not a question.

'I'm sure the detective has a great deal on her mind,' I said. I did not add that apparently some of it was me. 'But sooner or later, somebody will ask.' I looked over to where she was Directing the Operation. 'Probably Sergeant Doakes,' I said with real dread.

She nodded. 'He's a decent cop. If he could just lose some attitude.'

'Attitude may be all he is,' I said. 'But he doesn't like me for some reason. He'll ask anything if he thinks it will make me squirm.'

'So tell him the truth,' Deborah said deadpan. 'But first, tell it to me.' And she poked me again in the same spot.

'Please, Deb,' I said. 'You know how easily I bruise.'

'I don't know,' she said. 'But I feel like finding out.'

'It won't happen again,' I promised. 'It was just one of those 3 AM inspirations, Deborah. What would you have said if I had called you about it, and then it turned out to be nothing?'

'But it didn't. It turned out to be something,' she said with another push.

'I really didn't think it would. And I would have felt stupid dragging you in on it.'

'Imagine how I would have felt if he had killed you,' she said.

It took me by surprise. I couldn't even begin to imagine how she would have felt. Regret? Disappointment? Anger? That sort of thing is way beyond me, I'm afraid. So I just repeated, 'I'm sorry, Deb.' And then, because I am the kind of cheerful Pollyanna who always finds the bright side, I added, 'But at least the refrigerated truck was there.'

She blinked at me. 'The truck was where?' she said.

'Oh, Deb,' I said. 'They didn't tell you?'

She hit me even harder in the same place. 'Goddamn it, Dexter,' she hissed. 'What about the truck?'

'It was there, Deb,' I said, somewhat embarrassed by her nakedly emotional reaction – and also, of course, by the fact that a good-looking woman was beating the crap out of me. 'He was driving a refrigerated truck. When he threw the head.'

She grabbed my arms and stared at me. 'The fuck you say,' she finally said.

'The fuck I do.'

'Jesus—!' she said, staring off into space and no doubt seeing her promotion floating there somewhere above my head. And she was probably going to go on but at that moment Angel-no-relation lifted his voice over the echoing din of the arena. 'Detective?' he called, looking over at LaGuerta. It was a strange, unconscious sound, the half-strangled cry of a man who never makes loud noises in public, and something about it brought instant quiet to the room. The tone was part shock and part triumph – I found something important but oh-my-God. All eyes turned to Angel and he nodded down at the crouching bald man who was slowly, carefully, removing something from the top package.

The man finally pulled the thing out, fumbled, and dropped it, and it skittered across the ice. He reached for it and slipped, sliding after the brightly gleaming thing from the package until they both came to rest against the boards. Hand shaking, Angel grabbed for it, got it and held it up for all of us to see. The sudden quiet in the building was awe inspiring, breathtaking, beautiful, like the overwhelming crash of applause at the unveiling of any work of genius.

It was the rearview mirror from the truck.

11

The great blanket of stunned silence lasted for only a moment. Then the buzz of talk in the arena took on a new note as people strained to see, to explain, to speculate.

A mirror. What the hell did it mean?

Good question. In spite of feeling so very moved by the thing, I didn't have any immediate theories about what it meant. Sometimes great art is like that. It affects you and you can't say why. Was it deep symbolism? A cryptic message? A wrenching plea for help and understanding? Impossible to say, and to me, not the most important thing at first. I just wanted to breathe it in. Let others worry about how it had gotten there. After all, maybe it had just fallen off and he had decided to throw it away in the nearest handy garbage bag.

Not possible, of course not. And now I couldn't help thinking about it. The mirror was there for some very important reason. These were not garbage bags to him. As he had now proved so elegantly with this hockey-rink setting, presentation was an important part of what he was doing. He would not be casual in any detail. And because of that, I began to think about what the mirror might mean. I had to believe that, as improvised as it might be, putting it in with the body parts was exceedingly deliberate. And I had the further feeling, burbling up from somewhere behind my lungs, that this was a very careful, very private message.

To me?

If not me, then whom? The rest of the act was speaking to the world at large: See what I am. See what we all are. See what I am doing about it. A truck's mirror wasn't part of the statement. Segmenting the body, draining the blood – this was necessary and elegant. But the mirror – and especially if it turned out to be from the truck that I had chased – that was different. Elegant, yes; but what did it say about the way things really are? Nothing. It was added on for some other purpose, and that purpose had to be a new and different kind of statement. I could feel the electricity of the thought surging through me. If it was from that truck, it could only be meant for me.

But what did it mean?

'What the hell is that about?' Deb said beside me. 'A mirror. Why?'

'I don't know,' I said, still feeling its power throb through me. 'But I will bet you dinner at Joe's Stone Crabs that it came from the refrigerator truck.'

'No bet,' she said. 'But at least it settles one important question.'

I looked at her, startled. Could she really have made some intuitive jump that I had missed? 'What question, sis?'

She nodded at the cluster of management-level cops still squabbling at the edges of the rink. 'Jurisdiction. This one is ours. Come on.'

On the surface, Detective LaGuerta was not impressed with this new piece of evidence. Perhaps she was hiding a deep and abiding concern for the symbolism of the mirror and all it implied under a carefully crafted façade of indifference. Either that or she really was dumb as a box of rocks. She was still standing with Doakes. To his credit, he looked troubled, but maybe his face had simply gotten tired from its perpetual mean glare and he was trying something new.

'Morgan,' LaGuerta said to Deb, 'I didn't recognize you with clothes on.'

'I guess it's possible to miss a lot of obvious things, Detective,' Deb said before I could stop her.

'It is,' LaGuerta said. 'That's why some of us never make detective.' It was a complete and effortless victory, and LaGuerta didn't even wait to see the shot go home. She turned away from Deb and spoke to Doakes. 'Find out who has keys to the arena. Who could get in here whenever they wanted.'

'Uh-huh,' said Doakes. 'Check all the locks, see if somebody busted in?'

'No,' LaGuerta told him with a pretty little frown. 'We got our ice connection now.' She glanced at Deborah. 'That refrigerated truck is just to confuse us.' Back to Doakes. 'The tissue damage had to come from the ice, from here. So the killer is connected to the ice in this place.' She looked one last time at Deborah. 'Not the truck.'

'Uh-huh,' said Doakes. He didn't sound convinced, but he wasn't in charge.

LaGuerta looked over at me. 'I think you can go home, Dexter,' she said. 'I know where you live when I need you.' At least she didn't wink.

Deborah walked me to the big double doors of the arena. 'If this keeps up, I'll be a crossing guard in a year,' she grumbled at me.

'Nonsense, Deb,' I said. 'Two months, max.'

'Thanks.'

'Well really. You can't challenge her *openly* like that. Didn't you see how Sergeant Doakes did it? Have some subtlety, for God's sake.'

'Subtlety.' She stopped dead in her tracks and grabbed me. 'Listen, Dexter,' she said. 'This isn't some kind of game here.'

'But it is, Deb. A political game. And you're not playing it properly.'

'I'm not playing anything,' she snarled. 'There are human lives at stake. There's a butcher running loose, and he's going to stay loose as long as that half-wit LaGuerta is running things.'

I fought down a surge of hope. 'That may be so—'

'It *is* so,' Deb insisted.

'—but Deborah, you can't change that by getting yourself exiled to Coconut Grove traffic duty.'

'No,' she said. 'But I can change it by finding the killer.'

Well there it was. Some people just have no idea how the world works. She was otherwise a very smart person, truly she was. She had simply inherited all of Harry's earthy directness, his straightforward way of dealing with things, without latching on to any of his accompanying wisdom. With Harry, bluntness had been a way to cut through the fecal matter. With Deborah, it was a way of pretending there wasn't any.

I got a ride back to my car with one of the patrol units outside the arena. I drove home, imagining I had kept the head, wrapped it carefully in tissue paper, and placed it in the backseat to take home with me. Terrible and silly, I know. For the first time I understood those sad men, usually Shriners, who fondle women's shoes or carry around dirty underwear. An awful feeling that made me want a shower almost as much as I wanted to stroke the head.

But I didn't have it. Nothing for it but to go home. I drove slowly, a few miles per hour under the speed limit. In Miami that's like wearing a KICK ME sign on your back. No one actually kicked me, of course. They would have had to slow down for that. But I was honked at seven times, flipped off eight, and five cars simply roared around me, either onto the sidewalk or through oncoming traffic.

But today even the energetic high spirits of the other drivers couldn't cheer me. I was dead tired and bemused and I needed to think, away from the echoing din of the arena and the bonehead blather of LaGuerta. Driving slowly gave me time to wonder, to work through the meaning of all that had happened. And I found that one silly phrase kept ringing in my head, bouncing off the rocks and crannies of my exhausted brain. It took on a life of its own. The more I heard it in my thoughts, the more sense it made. And beyond sense, it became a kind of seductive mantra. It became the key to thinking about the killer, the head rolling into the street, the rearview mirror tucked away amid the wonderfully dry body parts.

If it had been me—

As in, 'If it had been me, what would I be saying with the mirror?' and 'If it had been me, what would I have done with the truck?'

Of course it had not been me, and that kind of envy is very bad for the soul, but since I was not aware of having one it didn't matter. If it *had* been me, the truck would be run into a ditch somewhere not too far from the arena. And then I would get far away from there fast – in a stashed car? A stolen one? It would depend. If it had been me, would I have planned on leaving the body at the arena all along, or had that come up as a response to the chase on the causeway?

Except that made no sense. He could not have counted on anyone chasing him out to North Bay Village – could he? But then why did he have the head ready to throw? And then why take the rest to the arena? It seemed like an odd choice. Yes, there was a great deal of ice there, and the coldness was all to the good. But the vast clattery space was really not appropriate for my kind of intimate moment – if it had been me. There was a terrible, wide-open desolation that was not at all conducive to real creativity. Fun to visit, but not a real artist's studio. A dumping ground, and not a work space. It just didn't have the proper feeling to it.

If it had been me, that is.

So the arena was a bold stroke into unexplored territory. It would give the police fits, and it would most definitely lead them in the wrong direction. If they ever figured out that there was a direction to be led in, which seemed increasingly unlikely.

And to top it off with the mirror – if I was right about the reasons for selecting the arena, then the addition of the mirror would of course support that. It would be a comment on what had just happened, connected to leaving the head. It would be a statement that would bring together all the other threads, wrap them up as neatly as the stacked body parts, an elegant underlining to a major work. Now what would the statement be, if it was me?

I see you.

Well. Of course that was it, in spite of being somewhat obvious. I see you. I know you're behind me, and I am watching you. But I am far ahead of you, too, controlling your course and setting your speed and watching you follow me. I see you. I know who you are and where you are, and all you know about me is that I am watching. I see you.

That felt right. Why didn't it make me feel better?

Further, how much of this should I tell poor dear Deborah? This was becoming so intensely personal that it was a struggle to remember that there was a public side to it, a side that was important to my sister and her career. I could not begin to tell her – or anyone – that I thought the killer was trying to tell me something, if I had the wit to hear and reply. But the rest – was there something I needed to tell her, and did I actually want to?

It was too much. I needed sleep before I could sort all this out.

I did not quite whimper as I crawled into my bed, but it was a very near thing. I allowed sleep to roll over me quickly, just letting go into the darkness. And I got nearly two and a half full hours of sleep before the telephone rang.

'It's me,' said the voice on the other end.

'Of course it is,' I said. 'Deborah, wasn't it?' And of course it was.

'I found the refrigerated truck.'

'Well, congratulations, Deb. That's very good news.'

There was a rather long silence on the other end.

'Deb?' I said finally. 'That is good news, isn't it?'

'No,' she said.

'Oh.' I felt the need for sleep thumping my head like carpet beaters on a prayer rug, but I tried to concentrate. 'Um, Deb – what did you . . . what happened?'

'I made the match,' she said. 'Made absolutely certain. Pictures and part numbers and everything. So I told LaGuerta like a good scout.'

'And she didn't believe you?' I asked incredulously.

'She probably did.'

I tried to blink, but my eyes wanted to stick shut so I gave it up. 'I'm sorry, Deb, one of us isn't making much sense. Is it me?'

'I tried to explain it to her,' Deborah said in a very small, very tired voice that gave me a terrible feeling of sinking under the waves without a bailing bucket. 'I gave her the whole thing. I was even polite.'

'That's very good,' I said. 'What did she say?'

'Nothing,' Deb said.

'Nothing at all?'

'Nothing at all,' Deb repeated. 'Except she just says thanks, in a kind of way like you'd say it to the valet parking attendant. And she gives me this funny little smile and turns away.'

'Well, but Deb,' I said, 'you can't really expect her to—'

'And then I found out why she smiled like that,' Deb said. 'Like I'm some kind of unwashed half-wit and she's finally figured out where to lock me up.'

'Oh, no,' I said. 'You mean you're off the case?'

'We're all off the case, Dexter,' Deb said, her voice as tired as I felt. 'LaGuerta's made an arrest.'

There was far too much silence on the line all of a sudden and I couldn't think at all, but at least I was wide awake. 'What?' I said.

'LaGuerta has arrested somebody. Some guy who works at the arena. She has him in custody and she's sure he's the killer.'

'That's not possible,' I said, although I knew it was possible, the brain-dead bitch. LaGuerta, not Deb.

'I know that, Dexter. But don't try to tell LaGuerta. She's sure she got the right guy.'

'How sure?' I asked. My head was spinning and I felt a little bit like throwing up. I couldn't really say why.

Deb snorted. 'She has a press conference in one hour,' she said. 'For her, that's positive.'

The pounding in my head got too loud to hear what Deb might have said next. LaGuerta had made an arrest? Who? Who could she possibly have tagged for it? Could she truly ignore all the clues, the smell and feel and taste of these kills, and arrest somebody? Because nobody who could do what this killer had done – was doing! – could possibly allow a pimple like LaGuerta to catch him. Never. I would bet my life on it.

'No, Deborah,' I said. 'No. Not possible. She's got the wrong guy.'

Deborah laughed, a tired, dirty-up-to-here cop's laugh. 'Yeah,' she said. 'I know it. You know it. But she doesn't know it. And you want to know something funny? Neither does he.'

That made no sense at all. 'What are you saying, Deb? Who doesn't know?'

She repeated that awful little laugh. 'The guy she arrested. I guess he must be almost as confused as LaGuerta, Dex. Because he confessed.'

'What?'

'He confessed, Dexter. The bastard confessed.'

12

His name was Daryll Earl McHale and he was what we liked to call a two-time loser. Twelve of his last twenty years had been spent as a guest of the State of Florida. Dear Sergeant Doakes had managed to dig his name out of the arena's personnel files. In a computer cross-check for employees with a record of violence or felony convictions, McHale's name had popped up twice.

Daryll Earl was a drunk and a wife beater. Apparently he occasionally knocked over filling stations, too, just for the entertainment value. He could be relied on to hold down a minimum wage job for a month or two. But then some fine Friday night he'd throw back a few six-packs and start to believe he was the Wrath of God. So he'd drive around until he found a gas station that just pissed him off. He'd charge in waving a weapon, take the money, and drive away. Then he'd use his massive $80 or $90 haul to buy a few more six-packs until he felt so good he just had to beat up on somebody. Daryll Earl was not a large man: five six and scrawny. So to play it safe, the somebody he beat on usually turned out to be his wife.

Things being what they were, he'd actually gotten away with it a couple of times. But one night he went a little too far with his wife and put her into traction for a month. She pressed charges, and since Daryll Earl already had a record, he'd done some serious time.

He still drank, but he'd apparently been frightened enough at Raiford to straighten out just a bit. He'd gotten a job as a janitor at the arena and actually held on to it. As far as we could tell, he hadn't beaten up his wife for ages.

And more, Our Boy had even had a few moments of fame when the Panthers made their run at the Stanley Cup. Part of his job had been to run out and clean up when the fans threw objects on the ice. That Stanley Cup year, this had been a major job, since every time the Panthers scored the fans threw three or four thousand plastic rats onto the rink. Daryll Earl had to schlep out and pick them all up, boring work, no doubt. And so encouraged by a few snorts of very cheap vodka one night, he'd picked up one of the plastic rats and done a little 'Rat Dance.' The crowd ate it up and yelled for more. They began to call for it when Daryll Earl skidded out onto the ice. Daryll Earl did the dance for the rest of the season.

Plastic rats were forbidden nowadays. Even if they had been required by federal statute, nobody would have been throwing them. The Panthers hadn't scored a goal since the days when Miami had an honest mayor, sometime in the last century. But McHale still showed up at the games hoping for one last on-camera two-step.

At the press conference LaGuerta played that part beautifully. She made it sound like the memory of his small fame had driven Daryll Earl over the edge into murder. And of course with his drunkenness and his record of violence toward women, he was the perfect suspect for this series of stupid and brutal murders. But Miami's hookers could rest easy; the killing was over. Driven by the overwhelming pressure of an intense and merciless investigation, Daryll Earl had confessed. Case closed. Back to work, girls.

The press ate it up. You couldn't really blame them, I suppose. LaGuerta did a masterful job of presenting just enough fact colored with high-gloss wishful thinking that nearly anyone would have been convinced. And of course you don't actually have to take an IQ test to become a reporter. Even so, I always hope for just the smallest glimmer. And I'm always disappointed. Perhaps I saw too many black-and-white movies as a child. I still thought the cynical, world-weary drunk from the large metropolitan daily was supposed to ask an awkward question and force the investigators to carefully reexamine the evidence.

But sadly, life does not always imitate art. And at LaGuerta's press conference, the part of Spencer Tracy was played by a series of male and female models with perfect hair and tropical-weight suits. Their penetrating questions amounted to, 'How did it feel to find the head?' and 'Can we have some pictures?'

One lone reporter, Nick Something from the local NBC TV affiliate, asked LaGuerta if she was sure McHale was the killer. But when she said that the overwhelming preponderance of evidence indicated that this was the case and anyway the confession was conclusive, he let it go. Either he was satisfied or the words were too big.

And so there it was. Case closed, justice done. The mighty machinery of Metro Miami's awesome crime-fighting apparatus had once again triumphed over the dark forces besieging Our Fair City. It was a lovely show. LaGuerta handed out some very sinister-looking mug shots of Daryll Earl stapled to those new glossy shots of herself investigating a $250-an-hour high-fashion photographer on South Beach.

It made a wonderfully ironic package; the appearance of danger and the lethal reality, so very different. Because however coarse and brutal Daryll Earl looked, the real threat to society was LaGuerta. She had called off the hounds, closed down the hue and cry, sent people back to bed in a burning building.

Was I the only one who could see that Daryll Earl McHale could not possibly be the killer? That there was a style and wit here that a brickhead like McHale couldn't even understand?

I had never been more alone than I was in my admiration for the real killer's work. The very body parts seemed to sing to me, a rhapsody of bloodless wonder that lightened my heart and filled my veins with an intoxicating sense of awe. But it was certainly not going to interfere with my zeal in capturing the real killer, a cold and wanton executioner of the innocent who absolutely must be brought to justice. Right, Dexter? Right? Hello?

I sat in my apartment, rubbing my sleep-crusted eyes and thinking about the show I had just watched. It had been as near perfect as a press conference could be without free food and nudity. LaGuerta had clearly pulled every string she had ever gotten a hand on in order to make it the biggest, splashiest press conference possible, and it had been. And for perhaps the first time in her Gucci-licking career, LaGuerta really and truly believed she had the right man. She had to believe it. It was kind of sad, really. She thought she had done everything right this time. She wasn't just making political moves; in her mind she was cashing in on a clean and well-lit piece of work. She'd solved the crime, done it her way, caught the bad guy, stopped the killing. Well-earned applause all around for a job well done. And what a lovely surprise she would get when the next body turned up.

Because I knew with no room for doubt that the killer was still out there. He was probably watching the press conference on Channel 7, the channel of choice for people with an eye for carnage. At the moment he would be laughing too hard to hold a blade, but that would pass. And when it did his sense of humor would no doubt prompt him to comment on the situation.

For some reason the thought did not overwhelm me with fear and loathing and a grim determination to stop this madman before it was too late. Instead I felt a little surge of anticipation. I knew it was very wrong, and perhaps that made it feel even better. Oh, I wanted this killer stopped, brought to justice, yes, certainly – but did it have to be soon?

There was also a small trade-off to make. If I was going to do my little part to stop the real killer, then I should at least make something positive happen at the same time. And as I thought it, my telephone rang.

'Yes, I saw it,' I said into the receiver.

'Jesus,' said Deborah on the other end. 'I think I'm going to be sick.'

'Well, I won't mop your fevered brow, sis. There's work to be done.'

'Jesus,' she repeated. Then, 'What work?'

'Tell me,' I asked her. 'Are you in ill odor, sis?'

'I'm tired, Dexter. And I'm more pissed off than I've ever been in my life. What's that in English?'

'I'm asking if you are in what Dad would have called the doghouse. Is your name mud in the department? Has your professional reputation been muddied, damaged, sullied, colored, rendered questionable?'

'Between LaGuerta's backstabbing and the Einstein thing? My professional reputation is shit,' she said with more sourness than I would have thought possible in someone so young.

'Good. It's important that you don't have anything to lose.'

She snorted. 'Glad I could help. 'Cause I'm there, Dexter. If I sink any lower in the department, I'll be making coffee for community relations. Where is this going, Dex?'

I closed my eyes and leaned all the way back in my chair. 'You are going to go on record – with the captain and the department itself – as believing that Daryll Earl is the wrong man and that another murder is going to take place. You will present a couple of compelling reasons culled from your investigation, and you will be the laughingstock of Miami Metro for a little while.'

'I already am,' she said. 'No big deal. But is there some reason for this?'

I shook my head. It was sometimes hard for me to believe she could be so naïve. 'Sister dearest,' I said, 'you don't truly believe Daryll Earl is guilty, do you?'

She didn't answer. I could hear her breathing and it occurred to me that she must be tired, too, every bit as tired as I was, but without the jolt of energy I got from being certain I was right. 'Deb?'

'The guy confessed, Dexter,' she said at last, and I heard the utter fatigue in her voice. 'I don't – I've been wrong before, even when— I mean, but he *confessed*. Doesn't that, that . . . Shit. Maybe we should just let it go, Dex.'

'Oh ye of little faith,' I said. 'She's got the wrong guy, Deborah. And you are now going to rewrite the politics.'

'Sure I am.'

'Daryll Earl McHale is not it,' I said. 'There's absolutely no doubt about it.'

'Even if you're right, so what?' she said.

Now it was my turn to blink and wonder. 'Excuse me?'

'Well, look, if I'm this killer, why don't I realize I'm off the hook now? With this other guy arrested, the heat's off, you know. Why don't I just stop? Or even take off for someplace else and start over?'

'Impossible,' I said. 'You don't understand how this guy thinks.'

'Yeah, I know,' she said. 'How come you do?'

I chose to ignore that. 'He's going to stay right here and he's going to kill again. He has to show us all what he thinks of us.'

'Which is what?'

'It's not good,' I admitted. 'We've done something stupid by arresting an obvious twinky like Daryll Earl. That's funny.'

'Ha, ha,' Deb said with no amusement.

'But we've also insulted him. We've given this lowbrow brain-dead redneck all the credit for his work, which is like telling Jackson Pollock your six-year-old could have painted that.'

'Jackson Pollock? The *painter*? Dexter, this guy's a butcher.'

'In his own way, Deborah, he is an artist. And he thinks of himself that way.'

'For Christ's sake. That's the stupidest—'

'Trust me, Deb.'

'Sure, I trust you. Why shouldn't I trust you? So we have an angrily amused artist who's not going anywhere, right?'

'Right,' I said. 'He has to do it again, and it has to be under our noses, and it probably has to be a little bigger.'

'You mean he's going to kill a fat hooker this time?'

'Bigger in scale, Deborah. Larger in concept. Splashier.'

'Oh. Splashier. Sure. Like with a mulcher.'

'The stakes have gone up, Debs. We've pushed him and insulted him a little and the next kill will reflect that.'

'Uh-huh,' she said. 'And how would that work?'

'I don't really know,' I admitted.

'But you're sure.'

'That's right,' I said.

'Swell,' she said. 'Now I know what to watch for.'

13

I knew when I walked in my front door after work on Monday that something was wrong. Someone had been in my apartment.

The door was not broken, the windows were not jimmied, and I couldn't see any signs of vandalism, but I knew. Call it sixth sense or whatever you like. Someone had been here. Maybe I was smelling pheromones the intruder had left in my air molecules. Or perhaps my La-Z-Boy recliner's aura had been disturbed. It didn't matter how I knew: I knew. Somebody had been in my apartment while I had been at work.

That might seem like no big deal. This was Miami, after all. People come home every day to find their TVs gone, their jewelry and electronics all taken away; their space violated, their possessions rifled, and their dog pregnant. But this was different. Even as I did a quick search through the apartment, I knew I would find nothing missing.

And I was right. Nothing was missing.

But something had been added.

It took me a few minutes to find it. I suppose some work-induced reflex made me check the obvious things first. When an intruder has paid a visit, in the natural course of events your things are gone: toys, valuables, private relics, the last few chocolate chip cookies. So I checked.

But all my things were unmolested. The computer, the sound system, the TV and VCR – all right where I had left them. Even my small collection of precious glass slides was tucked away on the bookcase, each with its single drop of dried blood in place. Everything was exactly as I had left it.

I checked the private areas next, just to be sure: bedroom, bathroom, medicine cabinet. There were all fine, too, all apparently undisturbed, and yet there was a feeling suspended in the air over every object that it had been examined, touched, and replaced – with such perfect care that even the dust motes were in their proper positions.

I went back into the living room, sank into my chair, and looked around, suddenly unsure. I had been absolutely positive that someone had been here, but why? And who did I imagine was so interested in little old me that they would come in and leave my modest home exactly as it had been? Because nothing was missing, nothing disturbed. The pile of newspapers in the recycle box might be leaning slightly to the left – but was that my imagination? Couldn't it have been a breeze from the air conditioner? Nothing was really different, nothing changed or missing; nothing.

And why would anyone break into my apartment at all? There was nothing special about it – I'd made sure of that. It was part of building my Harry Profile. Blend in. Act normal, even boring. Don't do anything or own anything that might cause comment. So had I done. I had no real valuables other than a stereo and a computer. There were other, far more attractive targets in the immediate neighborhood.

And in any case, why would somebody break in and then take nothing, do nothing, leave no sign? I leaned back and closed my eyes; almost certainly I was imagining the whole thing. This was surely just jangled nerves. A symptom of sleep deprivation and worrying too much about Deborah's critically injured career. Just one more small sign that Poor Old Dexter was drifting off into Deep Water. Making that last painless transition from sociopath to psychopath. It is not necessarily crazy in Miami to assume that you are surrounded by anonymous enemies – but to act like it is socially unacceptable. They would have to put me away at last.

And yet the feeling was so strong. I tried to shake it off: just a whim, a twitch of the nerves, a passing indigestion. I stood up, stretched, took a deep breath, and tried to think pretty thoughts. None came. I shook my head and went into the kitchen for a drink of water and there it was.

There it was.

I stood in front of the refrigerator and looked, I don't know how long, just staring stupidly.

Attached to the refrigerator, hair pinned to the door with one of my small tropical-fruit magnets, was a Barbie doll's head. I did not remember leaving it there. I did not remember ever owning one. It seemed like the kind of thing I would remember.

I reached to touch the little plastic head. It swung gently, thumping against the freezer door with a small *thack* sound. It turned in a tiny quarter circle until Barbie looked up at me with alert, Collie-dog interest. I looked back.

Without really knowing what I was doing or why, I opened the freezer door. Inside, lying carefully on top of the ice basket, was Barbie's body. The legs and arms had been pulled off, and the body had been pulled apart at the waist. The pieces were stacked neatly, wrapped, and tied with a pink ribbon. And stuck into one tiny Barbie hand was a small accessory, a Barbie vanity mirror.

After a long moment I closed the freezer door. I wanted to lie down and press my cheek against the cool linoleum. Instead I reached out with my little finger and flipped Barbie's head. It went *thack thack* against the door. I flipped it again. *Thack thack*. Whee. I had a new hobby.

I left the doll where it was and went back to my chair, sinking deep into the cushions and closing my eyes. I knew I should be feeling upset, angry, afraid, violated, filled with paranoid hostility and righteous rage. I didn't. Instead I felt – what? More than a little light-headed. Anxious, perhaps – or was it exhilaration?

There was of course no possible doubt about who had been in my apartment. Unless I could swallow the idea that some stranger, for unknown reasons, had randomly chosen my apartment as the ideal spot to display his decapitated Barbie doll.

No. I had been visited by my favorite artist. How he had found me was not important. It would have been easy enough to jot down my license number on the causeway that night. He'd had plenty of time to watch me from his hiding place behind the filling station. And then anyone with computer literacy could find my address. And having found it, it would be easy enough to slip in, take a careful look around, and leave a message.

And here was the message: the head hung separately, the body parts stacked on my ice tray, and that damned mirror again. Combined with the total lack of interest in everything else in the apartment, it all added up to only one thing.

But what?

What was he saying?

He could have left anything or nothing. He could have jammed a bloody butcher knife through a cow's heart and into my linoleum. I was grateful he hadn't – what a mess – but why Barbie? Aside from the obvious fact that the doll reflected the body of his last kill, why tell me about it? And was this more sinister than some other, gooier message – or less? Was it, 'I'm watching and I'll get you'?

Or was he saying, 'Hi! Wanna play?'

And I did. Of course I did.

But what about the mirror? To include it this time gave it meaning far beyond the truck and the chase on the causeway. Now it had to mean much more. All I could come up with was, 'Look at yourself.' And what sense did that make? Why should I look at myself? I am not vain enough to enjoy that – at least, I am not vain about my physical appearance. And why would I even want to look at myself, when what I really wanted was to see the killer? So there had to be some other meaning to the mirror that I was not getting.

But even here I could not be sure. It was possible that there was no real meaning at all. I did not want to believe that of so elegant an artist, but it was possible. And the message could very well be a private, deranged, and sinister one. There was absolutely no way to know. And so, there was also no way to know what I should do about it. If indeed I should do anything.

I made the human choice. Funny when you think about it; me, making a human choice. Harry would have been proud. Humanly, I decided to do nothing. Wait and see. I would not report what had happened. After all, what was there to report? Nothing was missing. There was nothing at all to say officially except: 'Ah, Captain Matthews, I thought you should know that someone apparently broke into my apartment and left a Barbie doll in my freezer.'

That had a very good ring to it. I was sure that would go over well with the department. Perhaps Sergeant Doakes would investigate personally and finally be allowed to indulge some hidden talents for unfettered interrogation. And perhaps they would simply fling me on the Mentally Unable to Perform list, along with poor Deb, since officially the case was closing and even when open had nothing to do with Barbie dolls.

No, there was really nothing to tell, not in any way that I could explain. So at the risk of another savage elbowing, I would not even tell Deborah. For reasons I could not begin to explain, even to myself, this was personal. And by keeping it personal, there was a greater chance that I could get closer to my visitor. In order to bring him to justice, of course. Naturally.

With the decision made I felt much lighter. Almost giddy, in fact. I had no idea what might come of it, but I was ready to go with whatever came. The feeling stayed with me through the night, and even through the next day at work, as I prepared a lab report, comforted Deb, and stole a doughnut from Vince Masuoka. It stayed with me during my drive home through the happily homicidal evening traffic. I was in a state of Zen readiness, prepared for any surprise.

Or so I thought.

I had just returned to my apartment, leaned back in my chair, and relaxed, when the phone rang. I let it ring. I wanted to breathe for a few minutes, and I could think of nothing that couldn't wait. Besides, I had paid almost $50 for an answering machine. Let it earn its keep.

Two rings. I closed my eyes. Breathed in. Relax, old boy. Three rings. Breathe out. The answering machine clicked and my wonderfully urbane message began to play.

'Hello, I'm not in right now, but I'll get back to you right away if you'll please leave a message, after the beep. Thank you.'

What fabulous vocal tone. What acid wit! A truly great message altogether. It sounded nearly human. I was very proud. I breathed in again, listening to the melodic BEEEEP! that followed.

'Hi, it's me.'

A female voice. Not Deborah. I felt one eyelid twitch in irritation. Why do so many people start their messages with 'It's me'? Of course it is you. We all know that. But who the hell ARE you? In my case the choices were rather limited. I knew it wasn't Deborah. It didn't sound like LaGuerta, although anything was possible. So that left—

Rita?

'Um, I'm sorry, I—' A long breath sighing out. 'Listen, Dexter, I'm sorry. I thought you would call me and then when you didn't I just—' Another long breath out. 'Anyway. I need to talk. Because I realized . . . I mean – oh hell. Could you, um, call me? If – you know.'

I didn't know. Not at all. I wasn't even sure who it was. Could that really be Rita?

Another long sigh. 'I'm sorry if—' And a very long pause. Two full breaths. In deeply, out. In deeply, then blown out abruptly. 'Please call me, Dexter. Just—' A long pause. Another sigh. Then she hung up.

Many times in my life I have felt like I was missing something, some essential piece of the puzzle that everybody else carried around with them without thinking about it. I don't usually mind, since most of those times it turns out to be an astonishingly stupid piece of humania like understanding the infield fly rule or not going all the way on the first date.

But at other times I feel like I am missing out on a great reservoir of warm wisdom, the lore of some sense I don't possess that humans feel so deeply they don't need to talk about it and can't even put it into words.

This was one of those times.

I knew I was supposed to understand that Rita was actually saying something very specific, that her pauses and stutters added up to a great and marvelous thing that a human male would intuitively grasp. But I had not a single clue as to what it might be, nor how to figure it out. Should I count the breaths? Time the pauses and convert the numbers to Bible verses to arrive at the secret code? What was she trying to tell me? And why, for that matter, was she trying to tell me anything at all?

As I understood things, when I had kissed Rita on that strange and stupid impulse, I had crossed a line we had both agreed to keep uncrossed. With that thing done there was no undoing it, no going back. In its own way the kiss had been an act of murder. At any rate, it was comforting to think so. I had killed our careful relationship by driving my tongue through its heart and pushing it off a cliff. Boom, a dead thing. I hadn't even thought about Rita since. She was gone, shoved out of my life by an incomprehensible whim.

And now she was calling me and recording her breathing for my amusement.

Why? Did she want to chastise me? Call me names, rub my nose in my folly, force me to understand the immensity of my offense?

The whole thing began to irritate me beyond measure. I paced around my apartment. Why should I have to think about Rita at all? I had more important concerns at the moment. Rita was merely my beard, a silly kid's costume I wore on weekends to hide the fact that I was the kind of person who did the things that this other interesting fellow was now doing and I wasn't.

Was this jealousy? Of course I wasn't doing those things. I had just recently finished for the time being. I certainly wouldn't do it again anytime soon. Too risky. I hadn't prepared anything.

And yet—

I walked back into the kitchen and flicked the Barbie head. *Thack. Thack thack.* I seemed to be feeling something here. Playfulness? Deep and abiding concern? Professional jealousy? I couldn't say, and Barbie wasn't talking.

It was just too much. The obviously fake confession, the violation of my inner sanctum, and now Rita? A man can take only so much. Even a phony man like me. I began to feel unsettled, dizzy, confused, hyper-active and lethargic at the same time. I walked to the window and looked out. It was dark now and far away over the water a light rose up in the sky and at the sight of it a small and evil voice rose up to meet it from somewhere deep inside.

Moon.

A whisper in my ear. Not even a sound; just the slight sense of someone speaking your name, almost heard, somewhere nearby. Very near, perhaps getting closer. No words at all, just a dry rustle of not-voice, a tone off-tone, a thought on a breath. My face felt hot and I could suddenly hear myself breathing. The voice came again, a soft sound dropped on the outer edge of my ear. I turned, even though I knew no one was there and it was not my ear but my dear friend inside, kicked into consciousness by who knows what and the moon.

Such a fat happy chatterbox moon. Oh how much it had to say. And as much as I tried to tell it that the time was wrong, that this was much too soon, there were other things to do now, important things – the moon had words for all of it and more. And so even though I stood there for a quarter of an hour and argued, there was never really any question.

I grew desperate, fighting it with all the tricks I had, and when that failed I did something that shocked me to my very core. I called Rita.

'Oh, Dexter,' she said. 'I just – I was afraid. Thank you for calling. I just—'

'I know,' I said, although of course I did not know.

'Could we – I don't know what you – Can I see you later and just – I would really like to talk to you.'

'Of course,' I told her, and as we agreed to meet later at her place, I wondered what she might possibly have in mind. Violence? Tears of recrimination? Full-throated name-calling? I was on foreign turf here – I could be walking into anything.

And after I hung up, the whole thing distracted me wonderfully for almost half an hour before the soft interior voice came sliding back into my brain with its quiet insistence that tonight really ought to be special.

I felt myself pulled back to the window and there it was again, the huge happy face in the sky, the chuckling moon. I pulled the curtain and turned away, circled my apartment from room to room, touching things, telling myself I was checking once more for whatever might be missing, knowing nothing was missing, and knowing why, too. And each time around the apartment I circled closer and closer to the small desk in the living room where I kept my computer, knowing what I wanted to do and not wanting to do it, until finally, after three-quarters of an hour, the pull was too strong. I was too dizzy to stand and thought I would just slump into the chair since it was close at hand, and since I was there anyway I turned on the computer, and once it was on . . .

But it's not done, I thought, *I'm not ready*.

And of course, that didn't matter. Whether I was ready or not made no difference at all. *It* was ready.

14

I was almost certain he was the one, but only almost, and I had never been only almost certain before. I felt weak, intoxicated, half sick with a combination of excitement and uncertainty and complete wrongness – but of course, the Dark Passenger was driving from the backseat now and how I felt was not terribly important anymore because he felt strong and cold and eager and ready. And I could feel him swelling inside me, surging up out of the Dexter-dark corners of my lizard brain, a rising and swelling that could only end one way and that being the case it rather had to be with this one.

I had found him several months ago, but after a little bit of observation I'd decided that the priest was a sure thing and this one could wait a little longer until I was positive.

How wrong I had been. I now found he couldn't wait at all.

He lived on a small street in Coconut Grove. A few blocks to one side of his crummy little house the neighborhood was low-income black housing, barbecue joints, and crumbling churches. Half a mile in the other direction the millionaires lived in over-grown modern houses and built coral walls to keep out people like him. But Jamie Jaworski was right in between, in a house he shared with a million palmetto bugs and the ugliest dog I had ever seen.

It was still a house he shouldn't have been able to afford. Jaworski was a part-time janitor at Ponce de Leon Junior High, and as far as I could tell that was his only source of income. He worked three days a week, which might be just enough to live on but not much more. Of course, I was not interested in his finances. I was very interested in the fact that there had been a small but significant increase in runaway children from Ponce since Jaworski had begun to work there. All of them twelve- to thirteen-year-old light-haired girls.

Light-haired. That was important. For some reason it was the kind of detail that police often seem to overlook but always jumped out at someone like me. Perhaps it didn't seem politically correct; dark-haired girls, and dark-skinned girls, should have an equal opportunity to be kidnapped, sexually abused, and then cut up in front of a camera, don't you think?

Jaworski, too, often seemed to be the missing kid's last witness. The police had talked to him, held him overnight, questioned him, and had not been able to make anything stick to him. Of course, they have to meet certain petty legal requirements. Torture, for example, was frowned on lately, for the most part. And without some very forceful persuasion, Jamie Jaworski was never going to open up about his hobby. I know I wouldn't.

But I knew he was doing it. He was helping those girls disappear into very quick and final movie careers. I was almost positive. I had not found any body parts and hadn't seen him do it, but everything fit. And on the Internet I did manage to locate some particularly inventive pictures of three of the missing girls. They did not look very happy in those pictures, although some of the things they were doing were supposed to bring joy, I have been told.

I could not positively connect Jaworski with the pictures. But the mailbox address was South Miami, a few minutes from the school. And he was living above his means. And in any case I was being reminded with increasing force from the dark backseat that I was out of time, that this was not a case where certainty was terribly important.

But the ugly dog worried me. Dogs were always a problem. They don't like me and they quite often disapprove of what I do to their masters, especially since I don't share the good pieces. I had to find a way around the dog to Jaworski. Perhaps he would come out. If not, I had to find a way in.

I drove past Jaworski's house three times but nothing occurred to me. I needed some luck and I needed it before the Dark Passenger made me do something hasty. And just as my dear friend began to whisper imprudent suggestions, I got my small piece of luck. Jaworski came out of his house and climbed into his battered red Toyota pickup as I drove past. I slowed down as much as I could, and in a moment he backed out and yanked his little truck toward Douglas Road. I turned around and followed.

I had no idea how I was going to do this. I was not prepared. I had no safe room, no clean coveralls, nothing but a roll of duct tape and a filet knife under my seat. I had to be unseen, unnoticed, and perfect, and I had no idea how. I hated to improvise, but I was not being offered a choice.

Once again I was lucky. Traffic was very light as Jaworski drove south to Old Cutler Road, and after a mile or so he turned left toward the water. Another huge new development was going up to improve life for all of us by turning trees and animals into cement and old people from New Jersey. Jaworski drove slowly through the construction, past half a golf course with the flags in place but no grass on it, until he came almost to the water. The skeleton of a large, half-finished block of condos blotted out the moon. I dropped far back, turned out my headlights, and then inched close enough to see what my boy was up to.

Jaworski had pulled in beside the block of condos-to-be and parked. He got out and stood between his little truck and a huge pile of sand. For a moment he just looked around and I pulled onto the shoulder and turned off the engine. Jaworski stared at the condos and then down the road toward the water. He seemed satisfied and went into the building. I was quite certain that he was looking for a guard. I was, too. I hoped he had done his homework. Most often in these huge uberdevelopments one guard rides around from site to site in a golf cart. It saves money, and anyway, this is Miami. A certain amount of the overhead on any project is for material that is expected to disappear quietly. It looked to me like Jaworski planned to help the builder meet his quota.

I got out of my car and slipped my filet knife and duct tape into a cheap tote bag I'd brought along. I had already stuffed some rubberized gardening gloves and a few pictures inside it, nothing much. Just trifles I'd downloaded from the Internet. I shrugged the bag onto my shoulder and moved quietly through the night until I came to his grungy little truck. The bed was as empty as the cab. Heaps of Burger King cups and wrappers, empty Camel packs on the floor. Nothing that wasn't small and dirty, like Jaworski himself.

I looked up. Above the rim of the half-condo I could just see the glow of the moon. A night wind blew across my face, bringing with it all the enchanting odors of our tropical paradise: diesel oil, decaying vegetation, and cement. I inhaled it deeply and turned my thoughts back to Jaworski.

He was somewhere inside the shell of the building. I didn't know how long I had, and a certain small voice was urging me to hurry. I left the truck and went into the building. As I stepped through the door I heard him. Or rather, I heard a strange whirring, rattling sound that had to be him, or—

I paused. The sound came from off to one side and I whisper-footed over to it. A pipe ran up the wall, an electrical conduit. I placed a hand on the pipe and felt it vibrate, as if something inside was moving.

A small light went on in my brain. Jaworski was pulling out the wire. Copper was very expensive, and there was a thriving black market for copper in any form. It was one more small way to supplement a meager janitorial salary, helping to cover the long, poverty-strewn stretches between young runaways. He could make several hundred dollars for one load of copper.

Now that I knew what he was up to, a vague outline of an idea began to take root in my brain. From the sound, he was above me somewhere. I could easily track him, shadow him until the time was right, and then pounce. But I was practically naked here, completely exposed and unready. I was used to doing these things a certain way. To step outside my own careful boundaries made me extremely uncomfortable.

A small shudder crawled up my spine. Why was I doing this?

The quick answer, of course, was that I wasn't doing it at all. My dear friend in the dark backseat was doing it. I was just along because I had the driver's license. But we had reached an understanding, he and I. We had achieved a careful, balanced existence, a way to live together, through our Harry solution. And now he was rampaging outside Harry's careful, beautiful chalk lines.

Why? Anger? Was the invasion of my home really such an outrage that it woke him to strike out in revenge?

He didn't *feel* angry to me – as always he seemed cool, quietly amused, eager for his prey. And I didn't feel angry either. I felt – half drunk, high as a kite, teetering on the knife edge of euphoria, wobbling through a series of inner ripples that felt curiously like I have always thought emotions must feel. And the giddiness of it had driven me to this dangerous, unclean, unplanned place, to do something on the spur of the moment that always before I had planned carefully. And even knowing all this, I badly wanted to do it. *Had* to do it.

Very well then. But I didn't have to do it undressed. I looked around. A large pile of Sheetrock squatted at the far end of the room, bound with shrink-wrap. A moment's work and I had cut myself an apron and a strange transparent mask from the shrink-wrap; nose, mouth, and eyes sliced away so I could breathe, talk, and see. I pulled it tight, feeling it mash my features into something unrecognizable. I twisted the ends behind my head and tied a clumsy knot in the plastic. Perfect anonymity. It might seem silly, but I was used to hunting with a mask. And aside from a neurotic compulsion to make everything *right*, it was simply one less thing to think about. It made me relax a little, so it was a good idea. I took the gloves from the tote bag and slipped them on. I was ready now.

I found Jaworski on the third floor. A pile of electrical wire pooled at his feet. I stood in the shadows of the stairwell and watched as he pulled out wire. I ducked back into the stairwell and opened my tote bag. Using my duct tape, I hung up the pictures I had brought along. Sweet little photos of the runaway girls, in a variety of endearing and very explicit poses. I taped them to the concrete walls where Jaworski would see them as he stepped through the door onto the stairs.

I looked back in at Jaworski. He pulled out another twenty yards of wire. It stuck on something and would pull no more. Jaworski yanked twice, then pulled a pair of heavy cutters from his back pocket and snipped the wire. He picked up the wire lying at his feet and wound it into a tight coil on his forearm. Then he walked toward the stairs – toward me.

I shrank back into the stairwell and waited.

Jaworski wasn't trying to be quiet. He was not expecting any interruption – and he certainly wasn't expecting me. I listened to his footsteps and the small rattle of the wire coil dragging behind him. Closer—

He came through the door and a step past without seeing me. And then he saw the pictures.

'Whooof,' he said, as though he had been hit hard in the stomach. He stared, slack-jawed, unable to move, and then I was behind him with my knife at his throat.

'Don't move and don't make a sound,' we said.

'Hey, lookit—' he said.

I turned my wrist slightly and pushed the knife point into his skin under the chin. He hissed as a distressing, awful little spurt of blood squirted out. So unnecessary. Why can't people ever listen?

'I said, don't make a sound,' we told him, and now he was quiet.

And then the only sound was the ratcheting of the duct tape, Jaworski's breathing, and the quiet chuckle from the Dark Passenger. I taped over his mouth, twisted a length of the janitor's precious copper wire around his wrists, and dragged him over to another stack of shrink-wrapped Sheetrock. In just a few moments I had him trussed up and secured to the makeshift table.

'Let's talk,' we said in the Dark Passenger's gentle, cold voice.

He didn't know if he was allowed to speak, and the duct tape would have made it difficult in any case, so he stayed silent.

'Let's talk about runaways,' we said, ripping the duct tape from his mouth.

'Yaaaooww – Whu – whataya mean?' he said. But he was not very convincing.

'I think you know what I mean,' we told him.

'Nuh-no,' he said.

'Yuh-yes,' we said.

Probably one word too clever. My timing was off, the whole evening was off. But he got brave. He looked up at me in my shiny face. 'What are you, a cop or something?' he asked.

'No,' we said, and sliced off his left ear. It was closest. The knife was sharp and for a moment he couldn't believe it was happening to him, permanent and forever no left ear. So I dropped the ear on his chest to let him believe. His eyes got huge and he filled his lungs to scream, but I stuffed a wad of plastic wrap in his mouth just before he did.

'None of that,' we said. 'Worse things can happen.' And they would, oh definitely, but he didn't need to know that yet.

'The runaways?' we asked gently, coldly, and waited for just a moment, watching his eyes, to make sure he wouldn't scream, then removed the gag.

'Jesus,' he said hoarsely. 'My ear—'

'You have another, just as good,' we said. 'Tell us about the girls in those pictures.'

'Us? What do you mean, us? Jesus, that hurts,' he whimpered.

Some people just don't get it. I put the plastic stuff back in his mouth and went to work.

I almost got carried away; easy to do, under the circumstances. My heart was racing like mad and I had to fight hard to keep my hand from shaking. But I went to work, exploring, looking for something that was always just beyond my fingertips. Exciting – and terribly frustrating. The pressure was rising inside me, climbing up into my ears and screaming for release – but release came. Just the growing pressure, and the sense that something wonderful was just beyond my senses, waiting for me to find it and dive in. But I did not find it, and none of my old standards gave me any joy at all. What to do? In my confusion I opened up a vein and a horrible puddle of blood formed on the plastic wrap alongside the janitor. I stopped for a moment, looking for an answer, finding nothing. I looked away, out the shell of the window. I stared, forgetting to breathe.

The moon was visible over the water. For some reason I could not explain that seemed so right, so *necessary*, that for a moment I just looked out across the water, watching it shimmer, so very perfect. I swayed and bumped against my makeshift table and came back to myself. But the moon . . . or was it the water?

So close . . . I was so close to something I could almost smell – but what? A shiver ran through me – and that was right, too, so right it set off a whole chain of shivers until my teeth chattered. But why? What did it mean? Something was there, something *important*, an overwhelming purity and clarity riding the moon and the water just beyond the tip of my filet knife, and I couldn't catch it.

I looked back at the janitor. He made me so angry, the way he was lying there, covered with improvised marks and unnecessary blood. But it was hard to stay angry, with the beautiful Florida moon pounding at me, the tropical breeze blowing, the wonderful night sounds of flexing duct tape and panic breathing. I almost had to laugh. Some people choose to die for some very unusual things, but this horrid little bug, dying for copper wire. And the look on his face: so hurt and confused and desperate. It would have been funny if I hadn't felt so frustrated.

And he really did deserve a better effort from me; after all, it wasn't his fault I was off my usual form. He wasn't even vile enough to be at the top of my TO DO list. He was just a repulsive little slug who killed children for money and kicks, and only four or five of them as far as I knew. I almost felt sorry for him. He truly wasn't ready for the major leagues.

Ah, well. Back to work. I stepped back to Jaworski's side. He was not thrashing as much now, but he was still far too lively for my usual methods. Of course I did not have all my highly professional toys tonight and the going must have been a little rough for Jaworski. But like a real trouper, he had not complained. I felt a surge of affection and slowed down my slapdash approach, spending some quality time on his hands. He responded with real enthusiasm and I drifted away, lost in happy research.

Eventually it was his muffled screams and wild thrashing that called me back to myself. And I remembered I had not even made sure of his guilt. I waited for him to calm down, then removed the plastic from his mouth.

'The runaways?' we asked.

'Oh Jesus. Oh God. Oh Jesus,' he said weakly.

'I don't think so,' we said. 'I think we may have left them behind.'

'Please,' he said. 'Oh, please . . .'

'Tell me about the runaways,' we said.

'Okay,' he breathed.

'You took those girls.'

'Yes. . . .'

'How many?'

He just breathed for a moment. His eyes were closed and I thought I might have lost him a little early. He finally opened his eyes and looked at me. 'Five,' he said at last. 'Five little beauties. I'm not sorry.'

'Of course you're not,' we said. I placed a hand on his arm. It was a beautiful moment. 'And now, I'm not sorry either.'

I stuffed the plastic into his mouth and went back to work. But I had really only just started to recapture my rhythm when I heard the guard arrive downstairs.

15

It was the static of his radio that gave him away. I was deeply involved in something I'd never tried before when I heard it. I was working on the torso with the knife point and could feel the first real tinglings of response down my spine and through my legs and I didn't want to stop. But a radio— This was worse news than a mere guard arriving. If he called for backup or to have the road blocked, it was just possible that I might find a few of the things I had been doing a little difficult to explain.

I looked down at Jaworski. He was nearly done now, and yet I was not happy with how things had gone. Far too much mess, and I had not really found what I was looking for. There had been a few moments where I felt on the brink of some wonderful thing, some amazing revelation to do with – what? the water flowing by outside the window? – but it had not happened, whatever it had been. Now I was left with an unfinished, unclean, untidy, unsatisfying child rapist, and a security guard on his way to join us.

I hate to rush the conclusion. It's such an important moment, and a real relief for both of us, the Dark Passenger and I. But what choice did I have? For a long moment – far too long, really, and I'm quite ashamed – I thought about killing the guard and going on. It would be easy, and I could continue to explore with a fresh start—

But no. Of course not. It wouldn't do. The guard was innocent, as innocent as anyone can be and still live in Miami. He'd probably done nothing worse than shoot at other drivers on the Palmetto Expressway a few times. Practically snow-white. No, I had to make a hasty retreat, and that was all there was to it. And if I had to leave the janitor not quite finished and me not quite satisfied – well, better luck next time.

I stared down at the grubby little insect and felt myself fill with loathing. The thing was drooling snot and blood all together, the ugly wet slop burbling across his face. A trickle of awful red came from his mouth. In a quick fit of pique, I slashed across Jaworski's throat. I immediately regretted my rashness. A fountain of horrible blood came out and the sight made it all seem even more regrettable, a messy mistake. Feeling unclean and unsatisfied, I sprinted for the stairwell. A cold and petulant grumbling from my Dark Passenger followed me.

I turned out onto the second floor and slid sideways over to a glassless window. Below me I could see the guard's golf cart parked, pointing in the direction of Old Cutler – meaning, I hoped, that he had come from the other direction and had not seen my car. Standing beside the cart, a fat olive-skinned young man with black hair and a wispy black mustache was looking up at the building – luckily, looking at the other end at the moment.

What had he heard? Was he merely on his regular route? I had to hope so. If he had actually heard something – If he stood outside and called for help, I was probably going to be caught. And as clever and glib-tongued as I was, I did not think I was good enough to talk my way out of this.

The young guard touched a thumb to his mustache and stroked it as if to encourage fuller growth. He frowned, swept his gaze along the front of the building. I ducked back. When I peeked out again a moment later I could just see the top of his head. He was coming in.

I waited until I heard his feet in the stairwell. Then I was out the window, halfway between the first and second floors, hanging by my fingertips from the coarse cement of the windowsill, then dropping. I hit badly, one ankle twisting on a rock, one knuckle skinned. But in my very best rapid limp I hurried into the shadows and scurried for my car.

My heart was pounding when I finally slid into the driver's seat. I looked back and saw no sign of the guard. I started the engine and, with the lights still off, I drove as quickly and quietly as I could out onto Old Cutler Road, heading toward South Miami and taking the long way home along Dixie Highway. My pulse still pounded in my ears. What a stupid risk to take. I had never before done anything so impulsive, never before done anything at all without careful planning. That was the Harry Way: be careful, be safe, be prepared. The Dark Scouts.

And instead, this. I could have been caught. I could have been seen. Stupid, stupid – if I had not heard the young security guard in time I might have had to kill him. Kill an innocent man with violence; I was quite sure Harry would disapprove. And it was so messy and unpleasant, too.

Of course I was still not safe – the guard might easily have written down my license number if he had passed my car in his little golf cart. I had taken brainless, terrible risks, gone against all my careful procedures, gambled my entire carefully built life – and for what? A thrill kill? Shame on me. And deep in the shaded corner of my mind the echo came, *Oh yes, shame,* and the familiar chuckle.

I took a deep breath and looked at my hand on the steering wheel. But it *had* been thrilling, hadn't it? It had been wildly exciting, full of life and new sensations and profound frustration. It had been something entirely new and interesting. And the odd sensation that it was all going somewhere, an important place that was new and yet familiar – I would really have to explore that a little better next time.

Not that there was going to be a next time, of course. I would certainly never again do anything so foolish and impulsive. Never. But to have done it once – kind of fun.

Never mind. I would go home and take an exceptionally long shower, and by the time I was done—

Time. It came into my mind unwanted and unasked. I had agreed to meet with Rita at – right about now, according to my dashboard clock. And for what dark purpose? I couldn't know what went on in the human female mind. Why did I even have to think about 'for what' at a time like this, when all my nerve endings were standing up and yodeling with frustration? I did not care what Rita wanted to yell at me about. It would not really bother me, whatever sharp observations she had to make on my character defects, but it was irritating to be forced to spend time listening when I had other, far more important things to think about. Most particularly, I wanted to wonder what I should have done that I had not done with dear departed Jaworski. Up to the cruelly interrupted and unfinished climax so many new things had happened that needed my very best mental efforts; I needed to reflect, to consider, and to understand where it had all been leading me. And how did it relate to that other artist out there, shadowing me and challenging me with his work?

With all this to think about, why did I need Rita right now?

But of course I would go. And of course, it would actually serve some humble purpose if I should need an alibi for my adventure with the little janitor. 'Why, Detective, how could you possibly think that I—? Besides, I was having a fight with my girlfriend at the time. Ah – ex-girlfriend, actually.' Because there was absolutely no doubt in my mind that Rita merely wanted to – what was the word we were all using lately? Vent? Yes, Rita wanted me to come over so she could vent on me. I had certain major character flaws that she needed to point out with an accompanying burst of emotion, and my presence was necessary.

Since this was the case, I took an extra minute to clean up. I circled back toward Coconut Grove and parked on the far side of the bridge over the waterway. A good deep channel ran underneath. I rolled a couple of large coral rocks out of the trees at the edge of the waterway, stuffed them into my tote bag, which was loaded with the plastic, gloves, and knife, and flung the thing into the center of the channel.

I stopped once more, at a small, dark park almost to Rita's house, and washed off carefully. I had to be neat and presentable; getting yelled at by a furious woman should be treated as a semiformal occasion.

But imagine my surprise when I rang her doorbell a few minutes later. She did not fling wide the door and begin to hurl furniture and abuse at me. In fact, she opened the door very slowly and carefully, half hiding behind it, as if badly frightened of what might be waiting for her on the other side. And considering that it was me waiting, this showed rare common sense.

'Dexter?' she said, softly, shyly, sounding like she wasn't sure whether she wanted me to answer yes or no. 'I . . . didn't think you were coming.'

'And yet here I am,' I said helpfully.

She didn't answer for a much longer time than seemed right. Finally, she nudged the door slightly more open and said, 'Would you . . . come in? Please?'

And if her uncertain, limping tone of voice, unlike any I had ever heard her use before, was a surprise, imagine how astonished I was by her costume. I believe the thing was called a peignoir; or possibly it was a negligee, since it certainly was negligible as far as the amount of fabric used in its construction was concerned. Whatever the correct name, she was certainly wearing it. And as bizarre as the idea was, I believe the costume was aimed at me.

'Please?' she repeated.

It was all a little much. I mean, really, what was I supposed to do here? I was bubbling over with unsatisfied experimentation on the janitor; there were still unhappy murmurings filtering through from the backseat. And a quick check of the situation at large revealed that I was being whipsawed between dear Deb and the dark artist, and now I was expected to do some sort of human thing here, like – well, what, after all? She surely couldn't want – I mean, wasn't she MAD at me? What was going on here? And why was it going on with me?

'I sent the kids next door,' Rita said. She bumped the door with her hip.

I went in.

I can think of a great many ways to describe what happened next, but none of them seem adequate. She went to the couch. I followed. She sat down. So did I. She looked uncomfortable and squeezed her left hand with her right. She seemed to be waiting for something, and since I was not quite sure what, I found myself thinking about my unfinished work with Jaworski. If only I'd had a little more time! The things I might have done!

And as I thought of some of those things, I became aware that Rita had quietly started to cry. I stared at her for a moment, trying to suppress the images of a flayed and bloodless janitor. For the life of me I could not understand why she was crying, but since I had practiced long and hard at imitating human beings, I knew that I was supposed to comfort her. I leaned toward her and put an arm across her shoulder. 'Rita,' I said. 'There, there.' Not really a line worthy of me, but it was well-thought-of by many experts. And it was effective. Rita lunged forward and leaned her face into my chest. I tightened my arm around her, which brought my hand back into view. Less than an hour ago that same hand had been holding a filet knife over the little janitor. The thought made me dizzy.

And really, I don't know how it happened, but it did. One moment I was patting her and saying, 'There, there,' and staring at the cords in my hand, feeling the sense memory pulse through the fingers, the surge of power and brightness as the knife explored Jaworski's abdomen. And the next moment—

I believe Rita looked up at me. I am also reasonably certain that I looked back. And yet somehow it was not Rita I saw but a neat stack of cool and bloodless limbs. And it was not Rita's hands I felt on my belt buckle, but the rising unsatisfied chorus from the Dark Passenger. And some little time later—

Well. It's still somewhat unthinkable. I mean, right there on the couch.

How on earth did *that* happen?

By the time I climbed into my little bed I was thoroughly whipped. I don't ordinarily require a great deal of sleep, but I felt as though tonight I might need a nice solid thirty-six hours. The ups and downs of the evening, the strain of so much new experience – it had all been draining. More draining for Jaworski, of course, the nasty wet little thing, but I had used all my adrenaline for the month in this one impetuous evening. I could not even begin to think what any of it meant, from the strange impulse to fly out into the night so madly and rashly, all the way through to the unthinkable things that had happened with Rita. I had left her asleep and apparently much happier. But poor dark deranged Dexter was without a clue once again, and when my head hit the pillow I fell asleep almost instantly.

And there I was out over the city like a boneless bird, flowing and swift and the cold air moved around me and drew me on, pulled me down to where the moonlight rippled on the water and I slash into the tight cold killing room where the little janitor looks up at me and laughs, spread-eagled under the knife and laughing, and the effort of it contorts his face, changes it, and now he is not Jaworski anymore but a woman and the man holding the knife looks up to where I float above the whirling red viscera and as the face comes up I can hear Harry outside the door and I turn just before I can see who it is on the table but—

I woke up. The pain in my head would split a cantaloupe. I felt like I had hardly closed my eyes, but the bedside clock said it was 5:14.

Another dream. Another long-distance call on my phantom party line. No wonder I had steadfastly refused to have dreams for most of my life. So stupid; such pointless, obvious symbols. Totally uncontrollable anxiety soup, hateful, blatant nonsense.

And now I couldn't get back to sleep, thinking of the infantile images. If I had to dream, why couldn't it be more like me, interesting and different?

I sat up and rubbed my throbbing temples. Terrible, tedious unconsciousness dripped away like a draining sinus and I sat on the edge of the bed in bleary befuddlement. What was happening to me? And why couldn't it happen to someone else?

This dream had felt different and I wasn't sure what that difference was or what it meant. The last time I had been absolutely certain that another murder was about to happen, and even knew where. But this time—

I sighed and padded into the kitchen for a drink of water. Barbie's head went *thack thack* as I opened the refrigerator. I stood and watched, sipping a large glass of cold water. The bright blue eyes stared back at me, unblinking.

Why had I had a dream? Was it just the strain of last evening's adventures playing back from my battered subconscious? I had never felt strain before; actually, it had always been a *release* of strain. Of course, I had never come so close to disaster before, either. But why dream about it? Some of the images were too painfully obvious: Jaworski and Harry and the unseen face of the man with the knife. Really now. Why bother me with stuff from freshman psychology?

Why bother me with a dream at all? I didn't need it. I needed rest – and instead, here I was in the kitchen playing with a Barbie doll. I flipped the head again: *thack thack*. For that matter, what was Barbie all about? And how was I going to figure this out in time to rescue Deborah's career? How could I get around LaGuerta when the poor thing was so taken with me? And by all that was holy, if anything actually was, why had Rita needed to do THAT to me?

It seemed suddenly like a twisted soap opera, and it was far too much. I found some aspirin and leaned against the kitchen counter as I ate three of them. I didn't much care for the taste. I had never liked medicine of any kind, except in a utilitarian way.

Especially since Harry had died.

16

Harry did not die quickly and he did not die easily. He took his own terrible long time, the first and last selfish thing he had ever done in his life. Harry died for a year and a half, in little stages, slipping for a few weeks, fighting back to almost full strength again, keeping us all dizzy with trying to guess. Would he go now, this time, or had he beaten it altogether? We never knew, but because it was Harry it seemed foolish for us to give up. Harry would do what was right, no matter how hard, but what did that mean in dying? Was it right to fight and hang on and make the rest of us suffer through an endless death, when death was coming no matter what Harry did? Or was it right to slip away gracefully and without fuss?

At nineteen, I certainly didn't know the answer, although I already knew more about death than most of the other pimple-ridden puddingheads in my sophomore class at the University of Miami.

And one fine autumn afternoon after a chemistry class, as I walked across the campus toward the student union, Deborah appeared beside me. 'Deborah,' I called to her, sounding very collegiate, I thought, 'come have a Coke.' Harry had told me to hang out at the union and have Cokes. He'd said it would help me pass for human, and learn how other humans behaved. And of course, he was right. In spite of the damage to my teeth, I was learning a great deal about the unpleasant species.

Deborah, at seventeen, already far too serious, shook her head. 'It's Dad,' she said. And very shortly we were driving across town to the hospice where they had taken Harry. Hospice was not good news. That meant the doctors were saying that Harry was ready to die, and suggesting that he cooperate.

Harry did not look good when we got there. He looked so green and still against the sheets that I thought we were too late. He was spindly and gaunt from his long fight, looking for all the world as though something inside him was eating its way out. The respirator beside him hissed, a Darth Vader sound from a living grave. Harry was alive, strictly speaking. 'Dad,' Deborah said, taking his hand. 'I brought Dexter.'

Harry opened his eyes and his head rolled toward us, almost as if some invisible hand had pushed it from the far side of the pillow. But they were not Harry's eyes. They were murky blue pits, dull and empty, uninhabited. Harry's body might be alive, but he was not home.

'It isn't good,' the nurse told us. 'We're just trying to make him comfortable now.' And she busied herself with a large hypodermic needle from a tray, filling it and holding it up to squirt out the air bubble.

'Wait . . .' It was so faint I thought at first it might be the respirator. I looked around the room and my eyes finally fell on what was left of Harry. Behind the dull emptiness of his eyes a small spark was shining. 'Wait . . . ,' he said again, nodding toward the nurse.

She either didn't hear him or had decided to ignore him. She stepped to his side and gently lifted his stick arm. She began to swab it with a cotton ball.

'No . . . ,' Harry gasped gently, almost inaudibly.

I looked at Deborah. She seemed to be standing at attention in a perfect posture of formal uncertainty. I looked back at Harry. His eyes locked onto mine.

'No . . . ,' he said, and there was something very close to horror in his eyes now. 'No . . . shot . . .'

I stepped forward and put a restraining hand on the nurse, just before she plunged the needle into Harry's vein. 'Wait,' I said. She looked up at me, and for the tiniest fraction of a second there was something in her eyes. I almost fell backward in surprise. It was a cold rage, an inhuman, lizard-brain sense of I-Want, a belief that the world was her very own game preserve. Just that one flash, but I was sure. She wanted to ram the needle into my eye for interrupting her. She wanted to shove it into my chest and twist until my ribs popped and my heart burst through into her hands and she could squeeze, twist, rip my life out of me. This was a monster, a hunter, a killer. This was a predator, a soulless and evil thing.

Just like me.

But her granola smile returned very quickly. 'What is it, honey?' she said, ever so sweetly, so perfectly Last Nurse.

My tongue felt much too large for my mouth and it seemed like it took me several minutes to answer, but I finally managed to say, 'He doesn't want the shot.'

She smiled again, a beautiful thing that sat on her face like the blessing of an all-wise god. 'Your dad is very sick,' she said. 'He's in a lot of pain.' She held the needle up and a melodramatic shaft of light from the window hit it. The needle sparkled like her very own Holy Grail. 'He needs a shot,' she said.

'He doesn't want it,' I said.

'He's in pain,' she said.

Harry said something I could not hear. My eyes were locked on the nurse, and hers on mine, two monsters standing over the same meat. Without looking away from her I leaned down next to him.

'I – WANT . . . pain . . . ,' Harry said.

It jerked my gaze down to him. Behind the emerging skeleton, nestled snugly under the crew cut that seemed suddenly too big for his head, Harry had returned and was fighting his way up through the fog. He nodded at me, reached very slowly for my hand and squeezed.

I looked back at Last Nurse. 'He wants the pain,' I told her, and somewhere in her small frown, the petulant shake of her head, I heard the roar of a savage beast watching its prey scuttle down a hole.

'I'll have to tell the doctor,' she said.

'All right,' I told her. 'We'll wait here.'

I watched her sail out into the hallway like some large and deadly bird. I felt a pressure on my hand. Harry watched me watching Last Nurse.

'You . . . can tell . . . ,' Harry said.

'About the nurse?' I asked him. He closed his eyes and nodded lightly, just once. 'Yes,' I said. 'I can tell.'

'Like . . . you . . . ,' Harry said.

'What?' Deborah demanded. 'What are you talking about? Daddy, are you all right? What does that mean, like you?'

'She likes me,' I said. 'He thinks the nurse may have a crush on me, Deb,' I told her, and turned back to Harry.

'Oh, right,' Deborah muttered, but I was already concentrating on Harry.

'What has she done?' I asked him.

He tried to shake his head and managed only a slight wobble. He winced. It was clear to me that the pain was coming back, just liked he'd wanted. 'Too much,' he said. 'She . . . gives too much—' he gasped now, and closed his eyes.

I must have been rather stupid that day, because I didn't get what he meant right away. 'Too much what?' I said.

Harry opened one pain-bleared eye. 'Morphine,' he whispered.

I felt like a great shaft of light had hit me. 'Overdose,' I said. 'She kills by overdose. And in a place like this, where it's actually almost her job, nobody would question it – why, that's—'

Harry squeezed my hand again and I stopped babbling. 'Don't let her,' he said in a hoarse voice with surprising strength. 'Don't let her – dope me again.'

'Please,' Deborah said in a voice that hung on the ragged edge, 'what are you guys talking about?' I looked at Harry, but Harry closed his eyes as a sudden stab of pain tore at him.

'He thinks, um . . . ,' I started and then trailed off. Deborah had no idea what I was, of course, and Harry had told me quite firmly to keep her in the dark. So how I could tell her about this without revealing anything was something of a problem. 'He thinks the nurse is giving him too much morphine,' I finally said. 'On purpose.'

'That's crazy,' Deb said. 'She's a nurse.'

Harry looked at her but didn't say anything. And to be truthful, I couldn't think of anything to say to Deb's incredible naïveté either.

97

'What should I do?' I asked Harry.

Harry looked at me for a very long time. At first I thought his mind might have wandered away with the pain, but as I looked back at him I saw that Harry was very much present. His jaw was set so hard that I thought the bones might snap through his tender pale skin and his eyes were as clear and sharp as I had ever seen them, as much as when he had first given me his Harry solution to getting me squared away. 'Stop her,' he said at last.

A very large thrill ran through me. Stop her? Was it possible? Could he mean – *stop* her? Until now Harry had helped me control my Dark Passenger, feeding him stray pets, hunting deer; one glorious time I had gone with him to catch a feral monkey that had been terrorizing a South Miami neighborhood. It had been so close, so almost human – but still not right, of course. And we had gone through all the theoretical steps of stalking, disposing of evidence, and so on. Harry knew that someday It would happen and he wanted me to be ready to do It right. He had always held me back from actually Doing It. But now – stop her? Could he mean it?

'I'll go talk to the doctor,' Deborah said. 'He'll tell her to adjust your medicine.'

I opened my mouth to speak, but Harry squeezed my hand and nodded once, painfully. 'Go,' he said, and Deborah looked at him for a moment before she turned away and went to find the doctor. When she was gone the room filled with a wild silence. I could think of nothing but what Harry had said: 'Stop her.' And I couldn't think of any other way to interpret it, except that he was finally turning me loose, giving me permission to do the Real Thing at last. But I didn't dare ask him if that's what he had said for fear he would tell me he meant something else. And so I just stood there for the longest time, staring out the small window into a garden outside, where a splatter of red flowers surrounded a fountain. Time passed. My mouth got dry. 'Dexter—' Harry said at last.

I didn't answer. Nothing I could think of seemed adequate. 'It's like this,' Harry said, slowly and painfully, and my eyes jerked down to his. He gave me a strained half smile when he saw that I was with him at last. 'I'll be gone soon,' Harry said. 'I can't stop you from . . . being who you are.'

'Being *what* I am, Dad,' I said.

He waved it away with a feeble, brittle hand. 'Sooner or later . . . you will – *need* – to do it to a person,' he said, and I felt my blood sing at the thought. 'Somebody who . . . *needs* it . . .'

'Like the nurse,' I said with a thick tongue.

'Yes,' he says, closing his eyes for a long moment, and when he went on his voice had grown hazy with the pain. 'She needs it, Dexter. That's—' He took a ragged breath. I could hear his tongue clacking as if his mouth was overdry. 'She's deliberately – overdosing patients . . . killing them . . . killing them . . . on purpose . . . She's a killer, Dexter . . . A killer . . .'

I cleared my throat. I felt a little clumsy and light-headed, but after all this was a very important moment in a young man's life. 'Do you want—' I said and stopped as my voice broke. 'Is it all right if I . . . stop her, Dad?'

'Yes,' said Harry. 'Stop her.'

For some reason I felt like I had to be absolutely certain. 'You mean, you know. Like I've been doing? With, you know, the monkey?'

Harry's eyes were closed and he was clearly floating away on a rising tide of pain. He took a soft and uneven breath. 'Stop . . . the nurse,' he said. 'Like . . . the monkey . . .' His head arched back slightly, and he began to breathe faster but still very roughly.

Well.

There it was.

'Stop the nurse like the monkey.' It had a certain wild ring to it. But in my madly buzzing brain, everything was music. Harry was turning me loose. I had permission. We had talked about one day doing this, but he had held me back. Until now.

Now.

'We talked . . . about this,' Harry said, eyes still closed. 'You know what to do . . .'

'I talked to the doctor,' Deborah said, hurrying into the room. 'He'll come down and adjust the meds on the chart.'

'Good,' I said, feeling something rise up in me, from the base of my spine and out over the top of my head, an electric surge that jolted through me and covered me like a dark hood. 'I'll go talk to the nurse.'

Deborah looked startled, perhaps at my tone. 'Dexter—' she said.

I paused, fighting to control the savage glee I felt towering up inside me. 'I don't want any misunderstanding,' I said. My voice sounded strange even to me. I pushed past Deborah before she could register my expression.

And in the hallway of that hospice, threading my way between stacks of clean, crisp, white linen, I felt the Dark Passenger become the new driver for the first time. Dexter became understated, almost invisible, the light-colored stripes on a sharp and transparent tiger. I blended in, almost impossible to see, but I was there and I was stalking, circling in the wind to find my prey. In that tremendous flash of freedom, on my way to do the Thing for the first time, sanctioned by almighty Harry, I receded, faded back into the scenery of my own dark self, while the other me crouched and growled. I would do It at last, do what I had been created to do.

And I did.

17

And I had. So long ago, yet the memory still pulsed in me. Of course, I still had that first dry drop of blood on its slide. It was my first, and I could call up that memory any time by taking out my little slide and looking at it. I did, every so often. It had been a very special day for Dexter. Last Nurse had been First Playmate, and she had opened up so many wonderful doors for me. I had learned so much, found out so many new things.

But why was I remembering Last Nurse now? Why did this whole series of events seem to be whipping me back through time? I could not afford a fond remembrance of my first pair of long pants. I needed to explode into action, make large decisions, and begin important deeds. Instead of strolling sappily down memory lane, wallowing in sweet memories of my first blood slide.

Which, now that I thought of it, I had not collected from Jaworski. It was the kind of tiny, absurdly unimportant detail that turned strong men of action into fidgeting, whimpering neurotics. I *needed* that slide. Jaworski's death was useless without it. The whole idiotic episode was now worse than a stupid and impulsive foolishness; it was incomplete. I had no slide.

I shook my head, trying spastically to rattle two gray cells into the same synapse. I half wanted to take my boat for an early-morning spin. Perhaps the salt air would clear the stupidity from my skull. Or I could head south to Turkey Point and hope that the radiation might mutate me back into a rational creature. But instead, I made coffee. No slide, indeed. It cheapened the whole experience. Without the slide, I might as well have stayed home. Or almost, at any rate. There had been other rewards. I smiled fondly, recalling the mix of moonlight and muffled screams. Oh, what a madcap little monster I had been. An episode unlike any of my others. It was good to break out of dull routine from time to time. And there was Rita, of course, but I had no idea what to think about that, so I didn't. Instead I thought of the cool breeze flowing across the squirming little man who had liked to hurt children. It had almost been a happy time. But of course, in ten years the memory would fade, and without that slide I could not bring it back. I needed my souvenir. Well, we would see.

While the coffee brewed, I checked for the news-paper, more out of hope than expectation. It was rare for the paper to arrive before six-thirty, and on

Sundays it often came after eight. It was another clear example of the disinte-
gration of society that had so worried Harry. Really, now: If you can't get me
my newspaper on time, how can you expect me to refrain from killing people?

No paper; no matter. Press coverage of my adventures had never been terribly interesting to me. And Harry had warned me about the idiocy of keeping any kind of scrapbook. He didn't need to; I rarely even glanced at the
reviews of my performances. This time was a little different, of course, since
I had been so impetuous and was mildly worried that I had not covered my
tracks properly. I was just a bit curious to see what might be said about my
accidental party. So I sat with my coffee for about forty-five minutes until I
heard the paper thump against the door. I brought it in and flipped it open.

Whatever else one can say about journalists – and there is a very great deal,
almost an encyclopedia – they are very rarely troubled by memory. The same
paper that had so recently trumpeted COPS CORRAL KILLER now screamed
ICE MAN'S STORY MELTS! It was a long and lovely piece, very dramati-
cally written, detailing the discovery of a badly abused body at a construction site just off Old Cutler Road. 'A Metro Miami police spokesperson' –
meaning Detective LaGuerta, I was sure – said that it was much too soon to
say anything with certainty, but this was probably a copycat killing. The paper
had drawn its own conclusions – another thing they are seldom shy about –
and was now wondering aloud if the distinguished gentleman in captivity,
Mr. Daryll Earl McHale, was actually, in fact, the killer. Or was the killer still
at large, as evidenced by this latest outrage upon public morality? Because, the
paper carefully pointed out, how could we believe that two such killers could
possibly be on the loose at the same time? It was very neatly reasoned, and it
occurred to me that if they had spent as much energy and mental power trying to solve the murders, the whole thing would be over by now.

But it was all very interesting reading, of course. And it certainly made me
speculate. Good heavens, was it really possible that this mad animal was still
running loose? Was anyone safe?

The telephone rang. I glanced at my wall clock; it was 6:45. It could only
be Deborah.

'I'm reading it now,' I said into the phone.

'You said bigger,' Deborah told me. 'Splashier.'

'And this isn't?' I asked with great innocence.

'It's not even a hooker,' she said. 'Some part-time janitor from Ponce Junior
High, chopped up at a construction site on Old Cutler. What the hell, Dexter?'

'You did know I'm not perfect, didn't you, Deborah?'

'It doesn't even fit the pattern – where's the cold you said would be there?
What happened to the small space?'

'It's Miami, Deb, people will steal anything.'

'It's not even a copycat,' she said. 'It isn't anything like the others. Even

LaGuerta got that right. She's already said so in print. Damn it all, Dexter. My butt is way out in the wind here, and this is just some random slasher, or a drug thing.'

'It hardly seems fair to blame me for all that.'

'Goddamn it, Dex,' she said, and hung up.

The early-morning TV shows spent a full ninety seconds on the shocking discovery of the shattered body. Channel 7 had the best adjectives. But nobody knew any more than the paper. They radiated outrage and a grim sense of disaster that even carried over into the weather forecast, but I'm sure a large part of it was caused by the lack of pictures.

Another beautiful Miami day. Mutilated corpses with a chance of afternoon showers. I got dressed and went to work.

I admit I had a minor ulterior motive in heading for the office so early, and I beefed it up by stopping for pastries. I bought two crullers, an apple fritter, and a cinnamon roll the size of my spare tire. I ate the fritter and one cruller as I cheerfully threaded through the lethal traffic. I don't know how I get away with eating so many doughnuts. I don't gain weight or get pimples, and although that may seem unfair, I can't find it in my heart to complain. I came out reasonably well in the genetic crapshoot: high metabolism, good size and strength, all of which helped me in my hobby. And I have been told that I am not awful to look at, which I believe is meant to be a compliment.

I also didn't need a great deal of sleep, which was nice this morning. I had hoped to arrive early enough to beat Vince Masuoka to work, and it seemed that I had. His office was dark when I got there, clutching my white paper bag for camouflage – but my visit had nothing whatever to do with doughnuts. I scanned his work area quickly, looking for the telltale evidence box labeled JAWORSKI and yesterday's date.

I found it and quickly lifted out a few tissue samples. There might be enough. I pulled on a pair of latex gloves and in a moment had pressed the samples to my clean glass slide. I do realize how stupid it was to take yet another risk, but I had to have my slide.

I had just tucked it away in a ziplock baggie when I heard him come in behind me. I quickly put things back in place and whirled to face the door, as Vince came through and saw me.

'My God,' I said. 'You move so silently. So you *have* had ninja training.'

'I have two older brothers,' Vince said. 'It's the same thing.'

I held up the white paper bag and bowed. 'Master, I bring a gift.'

He looked at the bag curiously. 'May Buddha bless you, grasshopper. What is it?'

I tossed him the bag. It hit him in the chest and slid to the floor. 'So much for ninja training,' I said.

'My finely tuned body needs coffee to function,' Vince told me, bending to retrieve the bag. 'What's in here? That hurt.' He reached into the bag, frowning. 'It better not be body parts.' He pulled out the huge cinnamon roll and eyed it. 'Ay, caramba. My village will not starve this year. We are very grateful, grasshopper.' He bowed, holding up the pastry. 'A debt repaid is a blessing on us all, my child.'

'In that case,' I said, 'do you have the case file on the one they found last night off Old Cutler?'

Vince took a big bite of cinnamon roll. His lips gleamed with frosting as he slowly chewed. 'Mmmpp,' he said, and swallowed. 'Are we feeling left out?'

'If we means Deborah, yes we are,' I said. 'I told her I'd take a look at the file for her.'

'Wulf,' he said, mouth full of pastry, 'merf pluddy uh bud is nime.'

'Forgive me, master,' I said. 'Your language is strange to me.'

He chewed and swallowed. 'I said, at least there's plenty of blood this time. But you're still a wallflower. Bradley got the call for this one.'

'Can I see the file?'

He took a bite. 'Ee waf awife—'

'Very true, I'm sure. And in English?'

Vince swallowed. 'I said, he was still alive when his leg came off.'

'Human beings are so resilient, aren't they?'

Vince stuck the whole pastry in his mouth and picked up the file, holding it out to me and taking a large bite of the roll at the same time. I grabbed the folder.

'I've got to go,' I said. 'Before you try to talk again.'

He pulled the roll from his mouth. 'Too late,' he said.

I walked slowly back to my little cubbyhole, glancing at the contents of the folder. Gervasio César Martez had discovered the body. His statement was on top of the folder. He was a security guard, employed by Sago Security Systems. He had worked for them for fourteen months and had no criminal record. Martez had found the body at approximately 10:17 PM and immediately made a quick search of the area before calling police. He wanted to catch the *pendejo* who had done this thing because no one should do such things and they had done it when he, Gervasio, was on the job. That was like they had done it to him, you know? So he would catch the monster himself. But this had not been possible. There was no sign of the perpetrator, not anywhere, and so he had called the police.

The poor man had taken it personally. I shared his outrage. Such brutality should not be allowed. Of course, I was also very grateful that his sense of honor had given me time to get away. And here I had always thought morality was useless.

I turned the corner into my dark little room and walked right into Detective LaGuerta. 'Hah,' she said. 'You don't see so good.' But she didn't move.

'I'm not a morning person,' I told her. 'My biorhythms are all off until noon.'

She looked up at me from an inch away. 'They look okay to me,' she said.

I slid around her to my desk. 'Can I make some small contribution to the full majesty of the law this morning?' I asked her.

She stared at me. 'You have a message,' she said. 'On your machine.'

I looked over at my answering machine. Sure enough, the light was blinking. The woman really was a detective.

'It's some girl,' LaGuerta said. 'She sounds kind of sleepy and happy. You got a girlfriend, Dexter?' There was a strange hint of challenge in her voice.

'You know how it is,' I said. 'Women today are so forward, and when you are as handsome as I am they absolutely fling themselves at your head.' Perhaps an unfortunate choice of words; as I said it I couldn't help thinking of the woman's head flung at me not so long ago.

'Watch out,' LaGuerta said. 'Sooner or later one of them will stick.' I had no idea what she thought that meant, but it was a very unsettling image.

'I'm sure you're right,' I said. 'Until then, carpe diem.'

'What?'

'It's Latin,' I said. 'It means, complain in daylight.'

'What have you got about this thing last night?' she said suddenly.

I held up the case file. 'I was just looking at it,' I said.

'It's not the same,' she said, frowning. 'No matter what those asshole reporters say. McHale is guilty. He confessed. This one is not the same.'

'I guess it seems like too much of a coincidence,' I said. 'Two brutal killers at the same time.'

LaGuerta shrugged. 'It's Miami, what do they think? Here is where these guys come on vacation. There's lots of bad guys out there. I can't catch them all.'

To be truthful, she couldn't catch any of them unless they hurled themselves off a building and into the front seat of her car, but this didn't seem like a good time to bring that up. LaGuerta stepped closer to me and flicked the folder with a dark red fingernail. 'I need you to find something here, Dexter. To show it's not the same.'

A light dawned. She was getting unpleasant pressure, probably from Captain Matthews, a man who believed what he read in the papers as long as they spelled his name right. And she needed some ammunition to fight back. 'Of course it's not the same,' I said. 'But why come to me?'

She stared at me for a moment through half-closed eyes, a curious effect. I think I had seen the same stare in some of the movies Rita had dragged me to see, but why on earth Detective LaGuerta had turned the look on me I couldn't say. 'I let you in the seventy-two-hour briefing,' she said. 'Even though Doakes wants you dead, I let you stay.'

'Thank you very much.'

'Because you have a feeling for these things sometimes. The serial ones. That's what they all say. Dexter has a feeling sometimes.'

'Oh, really,' I said, 'just a lucky guess once or twice.'

'And I need somebody in the lab who can find something.'

'Then why not ask Vince?'

'He's not so cute,' she said. 'You find something.'

She was still uncomfortably close, so close I could smell her shampoo. 'I'll find something,' I said.

She nodded at the answering machine. 'You gonna call her back? You don't have time for chasing pussy.'

She still hadn't backed up, and it took me a moment to realize she was talking about the message on my machine. I gave her my very best political smile. 'I think it's chasing me, Detective.'

'Hah. You got that right.' She gave me a long look, then turned and walked away.

I don't know why, but I watched her go. I really couldn't think of anything else to do. Just before she passed out of sight around the corner, she smoothed her skirt across her hips and turned to look at me. Then she was gone, off into the vague mysteries of Homicidal Politics.

And me? Poor dear dazed Dexter? What else could I do? I sank into my office chair and pushed the play button on my answering machine. 'Hi, Dexter. It's me.' Of course it was. And as odd as it was, the slow, slightly raspy voice sounded like 'me' was Rita. 'Mm . . . I was thinking about last night. Call me, mister.' As LaGuerta had observed, she sounded kind of tired and happy. Apparently I had a real girlfriend now.

Where would the madness end?

18

For a few moments I just sat and thought about life's cruel ironies. After so many years of solitary self-reliance, I was suddenly pursued from all directions by hungry women. Deb, Rita, LaGuerta – they were all apparently unable to exist without me. Yet the one person I wanted to spend some quality time with was being coy, leaving Barbie dolls in my freezer. Was any of this fair?

I put my hand in my pocket and felt the small glass slide, snug and secure in its ziplock. For a moment it made me feel a little better. At least I was doing something. And life's only obligation, after all, was to be interesting, which it certainly was at the moment. 'Interesting' did not begin to describe it. I would trade a year off my life to find out more about this elusive will-o'-the-wisp who was teasing me so mercilessly with such elegant work. In fact, I had come far too close to trading more than a year with my little Jaworski interlude.

Yes, things were certainly interesting. And were they really saying in the department that I had a feeling for serial homicide? That was very troubling. It meant my careful disguise might be close to unraveling. I had been too good too many times. It could become a problem. But what could I do? Be stupid for a while? I wasn't sure I knew how, even after so many years of careful observation.

Ah, well. I opened the case file on Jaworski, the poor man. After an hour of study, I came to a couple of conclusions. First, and most important, I was going to get away with it, in spite of the unforgivable sloppy impulsiveness of the thing. And second – there might be a way for Deb to cash in on this. If she could prove this was the work of our original artist while LaGuerta committed herself to the copycat theory, Deb could suddenly turn from somebody they didn't trust to get their coffee into flavor of the month. Of course, it was not actually the work of the same guy, but that seemed like a very picky objection at this point. And since I knew without any possibility of doubt that there were going to be more bodies found very soon, it wasn't worth worrying about.

And naturally, at the same time, I had to provide the annoying Detective LaGuerta with enough rope to hang herself. Which might also, it occurred to me, come in handy on a more personal level. Pushed into a corner and made to look like an idiot, LaGuerta would naturally try to pin the blame on the nitwit lab tech who had given her the erroneous conclusion – dull dim Dexter. And my reputation would suffer a much-needed relapse into mediocrity. Of course, it would not jeopardize my job, since I was supposed to analyze blood spatter, not provide profiling services. That being the case, it would help to make LaGuerta look like the nitwit she was, and raise Deborah's stock even more.

Lovely when things work out so neatly. I called Deborah.

At half-past one the next day I met Deb at a small restaurant a few blocks north of the airport. It was tucked into a little strip mall, between an auto parts store and a gun shop. It was a place we both knew well, not too far from Miami-Dade Headquarters, and they made the best Cuban sandwiches in the world right there. Perhaps that seems like a small thing, but I assure you there are times when only a *medianoche* will do, and at such times Café Relampago was the only place to get one. The Morgans had been going there since 1974.

And I did feel that some small light touch was in order – if not an actual celebration, then at least an acknowledgment that things were looking up ever so slightly. Perhaps I was merely feeling chipper because I had let off a little steam with my dear friend Jaworski, but in any case I did feel unaccountably good. I even ordered a *batido de mamé*, a uniquely flavored Cuban milk shake that tastes something like a combination of watermelon, peach, and mango.

Deb, of course, was unable to share my irrational mood. She looked like she had been studying the facial expressions of large fish, dour and droopy in the extreme.

'Please, Deborah,' I begged her, 'if you don't stop, your face will be stuck like that. People will take you for a grouper.'

'They're sure not going to take me for a cop,' she said. 'Because I won't be one anymore.'

'Nonsense,' I said. 'Didn't I promise?'

'Yeah. You also promised that this was going to work. But you didn't say anything about the looks I'd get from Captain Matthews.'

'Oh, Deb,' I said. 'He *looked* at you? I'm so sorry.'

'Fuck you, Dexter. You weren't there, and it's not your life going down the tubes.'

'I told you it was going to be rough for a while, Debs.'

'Well at least you were right about that. According to Matthews, I am this close to being suspended.'

'But he did give you permission to use your free time to look into this a little more?'

She snorted. 'He said, "I can't stop you, Morgan. But I am very disappointed. And I wonder what your father would have said." '

'And did you say, "My father never would have closed the case with the wrong guy in jail"?'

She looked surprised. 'No,' she said. 'But I was thinking it. How did you know?'

'But you didn't actually *say* it, did you, Deborah?'

'No,' she said.

I pushed her glass toward her. 'Have some *mamé*, sis. Things are looking up.'

She looked at me. 'You sure you're not just yanking my chain?'

'Never, Deb. How could I?'

'With the greatest of ease.'

'Really, sis. You need to trust me.'

She held my eye for a moment and then looked down. She still hadn't touched her shake, which was a shame. They were very good. 'I trust you. But I swear to God I don't know why.' She looked up at me, a strange expression flitting back and forth across her face. 'And sometimes I really don't think I should, Dexter.'

I gave her my very best reassuring big-brother smile. 'Within the next two or three days something new will turn up. I promise.'

'You can't know that,' she said.

'I know I can't, Deb. But I do know. I really do.'

'So why do you sound so happy about it?'

I wanted to say it was because the idea made me happy. Because the thought of seeing more of the bloodless wonder made me happier than anything else I could think of. But of course, that was not a sentiment Deb could really share with me, so I kept it to myself. 'Naturally, I'm just happy for you.'

She snorted. 'That's right, I forgot,' she said. But at least she took a sip of her shake.

'Listen,' I said, 'either LaGuerta is right—'

'Which means I'm dead and fucked.'

'Or LaGuerta is *wrong*, and you are alive and virginal. With me so far, sis?'

'Mmm,' she said, remarkably grumpy considering how patient I was being.

'If you were a betting gal, would you bet on LaGuerta being right? About anything?'

'Maybe about fashion,' she said. 'She dresses really nice.'

The sandwiches came. The waiter dropped them sourly in the middle of the table without a word and whirled away behind the counter. Still, they were very good sandwiches. I don't know what made them better than all the other *medianoches* in town, but they were; bread crisp on the outside and soft on the inside, just the right balance of pork and pickle, cheese melted perfectly – pure bliss. I took a big bite. Deborah played with the straw in her shake.

I swallowed. 'Debs, if my deadly logic can't cheer you up, and one of Relampago's sandwiches can't cheer you up, then it's too late. You're already dead.'

She looked at me with her grouper face and took a bite of her sandwich. 'It's very good,' she said without expression. 'See me cheer up?'

The poor thing was not convinced, which was a terrible blow to my ego. But after all, I had fed her on a traditional Morgan family delight. And I had brought her wonderful news, even if she didn't recognize it as such. If all this had not actually made her smile – well, really. I couldn't be expected to do everything.

One other small thing I could do, though, was to feed LaGuerta, too – something not quite as palatable as one of Relampago's sandwiches, though delicious in its own way. And so that afternoon I called on the good detective in her office, a lovely little cubby in the corner of a large room containing half a dozen other little cubbies. Hers, of course, was the most elegant, with several very tasteful photographs of herself with celebrities hanging from the fabric of the partitions. I recognized Gloria Estefan, Madonna, and Jorge Mas Canosa. On the desk, on the far side of a jade-green blotter with a leather frame, stood an elegant green onyx pen holder with a quartz clock in the center.

LaGuerta was on the telephone speaking rapid-fire Spanish when I came in. She glanced up at me without seeing me and looked away. But after a moment, her eyes came back to me. This time she looked me over thoroughly, frowned, and said, 'Okay-okay. 'Ta luo,' which was Cuban for *hasta luego*. She hung up and continued to look at me.

'What have you got for me?' she said finally.

'Glad tidings,' I told her.

'If that means good news, I could use some.'

I hooked a folding chair with my foot and dragged it into her cubby. 'There is no possible doubt,' I said, sitting in the folding chair, 'that you have the right guy in jail. The murder on Old Cutler was committed by a different hand.'

She just looked at me for a moment. I wondered if it took her that long to process the data and respond. 'You can back that up?' she asked me at last. 'For sure?'

Of course I could back it up for sure, but I wasn't going to, no matter how good confession might be for the soul. Instead, I dropped the folder onto her desk. 'The facts speak for themselves,' I said. 'There's absolutely no question about it.' And of course there wasn't any question at all, as only I knew very well. 'Look—' I told her, and pulled out a page of carefully selected comparisons I had typed out. 'First, this victim is male. All the others were female. This victim was found off Old Cutler. All of McHale's victims were off Tami-ami Trail. This victim was found relatively intact, and in the spot where he was killed. McHale's victims were completely chopped up, and they were moved to a different location for disposal.'

I went on, and she listened carefully. The list was a good one. It had taken me several hours to come up with the most obvious, ludicrous, transparently foolish comparisons, and I must say I did a very good job. And LaGuerta did her part wonderfully, too. She bought the whole thing. Of course, she was hearing what she wanted to hear.

'To sum up,' I said, 'this new murder has the fingerprint of a revenge killing, probably drug related. The guy in jail did the other murders and they are absolutely, positively, 100 percent finished and over forever. Never happen again. Case closed.' I dropped the folder on her desk and held out my list.

She took the paper from me and looked at it for a long moment. She frowned. Her eyes moved up and down the page a few times. One corner of her lower lip twitched. Then she placed it carefully on her desk under a heavy jade-green stapler.

'Okay,' she said, straightening the stapler so it was perfectly aligned with the edge of her blotter. 'Okay. Pretty good. This should help.' She looked at me again with her frown of concentration still stitched in place, and then suddenly smiled. 'Okay. Thank you, Dexter.'

It was such an unexpected and genuine smile that if I only had a soul I'm sure I would have felt quite guilty.

She stood, still smiling, and before I could retreat she had flung her arms around my neck to give me a hug. 'I really do appreciate it,' she said. 'You make me feel – VERY grateful.' And she rubbed her body against mine in a way that could only be called suggestive. Surely there could be no question of – I mean, here she was, a defender of public morality, and yet right here in public – and even in the privacy of a bank vault I would have been truly uninterested in being rubbed by her body. Not to mention the fact that I had just handed her a rope with the hope that she would use it to hang herself, which hardly seemed like the sort of thing one would celebrate by— Well really, had the whole world gone mad? What is it with humans? Is this all any of them ever thinks about?

Feeling something very close to panic, I tried to disentangle myself. 'Please, Detective—'

'Call me Migdia,' she said, clinging and rubbing harder. She reached a hand down to the front of my pants and I jumped. On the plus side, my action dislodged the amorous detective. On the negative side, she spun sideways, hit the desk with her hip, and tripped over her chair, landing sprawled out on the floor.

'I, ah – I really have to get back to work,' I stammered. 'There's an important, ah—' However, I couldn't think of anything more important than running for my life, so I backed out of the cubicle, leaving her looking after me.

It didn't seem to be a particularly friendly look.

19

I woke up standing at the sink with the water running. I had a moment of total panic, a sense of complete disorientation, my heart racing while my crusty eyelids fluttered in an attempt to catch up. The place was wrong. The sink didn't look right. I wasn't even sure who I was – in my dream I had been standing in front of my sink with the water running, but it had not been this sink. I had been scrubbing my hands, working the soap hard, cleansing my skin of every microscopic fleck of horrible red blood, washing it away with water so hot it left my skin pink and new and antiseptic. And the hot of the water bit harder after the cool of the room I had just left behind me; the play-room, the killing room, the room of dry and careful cutting.

I turned off the water and stood for a moment, swaying against the cold sink. It had all been far too real, too little like any kind of dream I knew about. And I remembered so clearly the room. I could see it just by closing my eyes.

I am standing above the woman, watching her flex and bulge against the tape that holds her, seeing the living terror grow in her dull eyes, seeing it blossom into hopelessness, and I feel the great surge of wonder rise up in me and flow down my arm to the knife. And as I lift the knife to begin—

But this is not the beginning. Because under the table there is another one, already dry and neatly wrapped. And in the far corner there is one more, wait-ing her turn with a hopeless black dread unlike anything I have ever seen before even though it is somehow familiar and necessary, this release of all other possi-bility so complete it washes me with a clean and pure energy more intoxicating than—

Three.

There are three of them this time.

I opened my eyes. It was me in the mirror. Hello, Dexter. Had a dream, old chap? Interesting, wasn't it? Three of them, hey? But just a dream. Nothing more. I smiled at me, trying out the face muscles, completely unconvinced. And as rapturous as it had been, I was awake now and left with nothing more than a hangover and wet hands.

What should have been a pleasant interlude in my subconscious had me shaking, uncertain. I was filled with dread at the thought that my mind had skipped town and left me behind to pay the rent. I thought of the three care-fully trussed playmates and wanted to go back to them and continue. I thought of Harry and knew I couldn't. I was whipsawed between a memory and a dream, and I couldn't tell which was more compelling.

This was just no fun anymore. I wanted my brain back.

I dried my hands and went to bed again, but there was no sleep left in this night for dear decimated Dexter. I simply lay on my back and watched the dark pools flowing across the ceiling until the telephone rang at a quarter to six.

'You were right,' Deb said when I picked up.

'It's a wonderful feeling,' I said with a great effort at being my usual bright self. 'Right about what?'

'All of it,' Deb told me. 'I'm at a crime scene on Tamiami Trail. And guess what?'

'I was right?'

'It's him, Dexter. It has to be. And it's a whole hell of a lot splashier, too.'

'Splashier how, Deb?' I asked, thinking *three bodies*, hoping she wouldn't say it and thrilled by the certainty that she would.

'There appear to be multiple victims,' she said.

A jolt went through me, from my stomach straight up, as if I had swal-lowed a live battery. But I made a huge effort to rally with something typically clever. 'This is wonderful, Deb. You're talking just like a homicide report.'

'Yeah, well. I'm starting to feel like I might write one someday. I'm just glad it won't be this one. It's too weird. LaGuerta doesn't know what to think.'

'Or even how. What's weird about it, Deb?'

'I gotta go,' she said abruptly. 'Get out here, Dexter. You have to see this.'

By the time I got there the crowd was three deep around the barrier, and most of them were reporters. It is always hard work to push through a crowd of reporters with the scent of blood in their nostrils. You might not think so, since on camera they appear to be brain-damaged wimps with severe eating disorders. But put them at a police barricade and a miraculous thing hap-pens. They become strong, aggressive, willing and able to shove anything and anyone out of the way and trample them underfoot. It's a bit like the stories about aged mothers lifting trucks when their child is trapped under-neath. The strength comes from some mysterious place – and somehow, when there is gore on the ground, these anorexic creatures can push their way through anything. Without mussing their hair, too.

Luckily for me, one of the uniforms at the barricade recognized me. 'Let him through, folks,' he told the reporters. 'Let him through.'

'Thanks, Julio,' I told the cop. 'Seems like more reporters every year.'

He snorted. 'Somebody must be cloning 'em. They all look the same to me.'

I stepped under the yellow tape and as I straightened on the far side I had the odd sensation that someone was tampering with the oxygen content of Miami's atmosphere. I stood in the broken dirt of a construction site. They were building what would probably be a three-story office building, the kind inhabited by marginal developers. And as I stepped slowly forward, following the activity around the half-built structure, I knew it was not coincidence that we had all been brought here. Nothing was coincidence with this killer. Everything was deliberate, carefully measured for aesthetic impact, explored for artistic necessity.

We were at a construction site because it was necessary. He was making his statement as I had told Deborah he would. *You got the wrong guy,* he was saying. *You locked up a cretin because you are all cretins. You are too stupid to see it unless I rub your noses in it; so here goes.*

But more than that, more than his message to the police and the public, he was talking to me; taunting me, teasing me by quoting a passage from my own hurried work. He had brought the bodies to a construction site because I had taken Jaworski at a construction site. He was playing catch with me, showing all of us just how good he was and telling one of us – me – that he was watching. *I know what you did, and I can do it, too. Better.*

I suppose that should have worried me a little.

It didn't.

It made me feel almost giddy, like a high-school girl watching as the captain of the football team worked up his nerve to ask for a date. You mean me? Little old me? Oh my stars, really? Pardon me while I flutter my eyelashes.

I took a deep breath and tried to remind myself that I was a good girl and I didn't do those things. But I knew *he* did them, and I truly wanted to go out with him. Please, Harry?

Because far beyond simply doing some interesting things with a new friend, I needed to find this killer. I had to see him, talk to him, prove to myself that he was real and that—

That what?

That he wasn't me?

That I was not the one doing such terrible, interesting things?

Why would I think that? It was beyond stupid; it was completely unworthy of the attention of my once-proud brain. Except – now that the idea was actually rattling around in there, I couldn't get the thought to sit down and behave. What if it really was me? What if I had somehow done these things without knowing it? Impossible, of course, absolutely impossible, but—

I wake up at the sink, washing blood off my hands after a 'dream' in which I carefully and gleefully got blood all over my hands doing things I ordinarily only dream about doing. Somehow I know things about the whole string of murders, things I couldn't possibly know unless—

Unless nothing. Take a tranquilizer, Dexter. Start again. Breathe, you silly creature; in with the good air, out with the bad. It was nothing but one more symptom of my recent feeble-mindedness. I was merely going prematurely senile from the strain of all my clean living. Granted I had experienced one or two moments of human stupidity in the last few weeks. So what? It didn't necessarily prove that I was human. Or that I had been creative in my sleep.

No, of course not. Quite right; it meant nothing of the kind. So, um – what did it mean?

I had assumed I was simply going crazy, dropping several handfuls of marbles into the recycle bin. Very comforting – but if I was ready to assume that, why not admit that it was possible I had committed a series of delightful little pranks without remembering them, except as fragmented dreams? Was insanity really easier to accept than unconsciousness? After all, it was just a heightened form of sleepwalking. 'Sleep murder.' Probably very common. Why not? I already gave away the driver's seat of my consciousness on a regular basis when the Dark Passenger went joyriding. It really wasn't such a great leap to accept that the same thing was happening here, now, in a slightly different form. The Dark Passenger was simply borrowing the car while I slept.

How else to explain it? That I was astrally projecting while I slept and just happened to tune my vibrations to the killer's aura because of our connection in a past life? Sure, that might make sense – if this was southern California. In Miami, it seemed a bit thin. And so if I went into this half building and happened to see three bodies arranged in a way that seemed to be speaking to me, I would have to consider the possibility that I had written the message. Didn't that make more sense than believing I was on some kind of subconscious party line?

I had come to the outside stairwell of the building. I stopped there for a moment and closed my eyes, leaning against the bare concrete block of the wall. It was slightly cooler than the air, and rough. I ground my cheek against it, somewhere between pleasure and pain. No matter how much I wanted to go upstairs and see what there was to see, I wanted just as much not to see it at all.

Talk to me, I whispered to the Dark Passenger. *Tell me what you have done.*

But of course there was no answer, beyond the usual cool, distant chuckle. And that was no actual help. I felt a little sick, slightly dizzy, uncertain, and I did not like this feeling of having feelings. I took three long breaths, straightened up and opened my eyes.

Sergeant Doakes stared at me from three feet away, just inside the stairwell, one foot on the first step. His face was a dark carved mask of curious hostility, like a rottweiler that wants to rip your arms off but is mildly interested in knowing first what flavor you might be. And there was something in his expression that I had never seen on anybody's face before, except in the mirror. It was a deep and abiding emptiness that had seen through the comic-strip charade of human life and read the bottom line.

'Who are you talkin' to?' he asked me with his bright hungry teeth showing. 'You got somebody else in there with you?'

His words and the knowing way he said them cut right through me and turned my insides to jelly. Why choose those words? What did he mean by 'in there with me'? Could he possibly know about the Dark Passenger? Impossible! Unless . . .

Doakes knew me for what I was.

Just as I had known Last Nurse.

The Thing Inside calls out across the emptiness when it sees its own kind. Was Sergeant Doakes carrying a Dark Passenger, too? How could it be possible? A homicide sergeant, a Dexter-dark predator? Unthinkable. But how else to explain? I could think of nothing and for much too long I just stared at him. He stared back.

Finally he shook his head, without looking away from me. 'One of these days,' he said. 'You and me.'

'I'll take a rain check,' I told him with all the good cheer I could muster. 'In the meantime, if you'll excuse me . . . ?'

He stood there taking up the entire stairwell and just staring. But finally he nodded slightly and moved to one side. 'One of these days,' he said again as I pushed past him and onto the stairs.

The shock of this encounter had snapped me instantly out of my sniveling little self-involved funk. Of course I wasn't committing unconscious murders. Aside from the pure ridiculousness of the idea, it would be an unthinkable waste to do these things and not remember. There would be some other explanation, something simple and cold. Surely I was not the only one within the sound of my voice capable of this kind of creativity. After all, I was in Miami, surrounded by dangerous creatures like Sergeant Doakes.

I went quickly up the stairs, feeling the adrenaline rushing through me, almost myself again. There was a healthy spring in my step that was only partly because I was escaping the good sergeant. Even more, I was eager to see this most recent assault on the public welfare – natural curiosity, nothing more. I certainly wasn't going to find any of my own fingerprints.

I climbed the stairs to the second floor. Some of the framing had been knocked into place, but most of the floor was still without walls. As I stepped off the landing and onto the main area of the floor, I saw Angel-no-relation squatting in the center of the floor, unmoving. His elbows were planted on his knees, his hands cupped his face, and he was just staring. I stopped and looked at him, startled. It was one of the most remarkable things I had ever seen, a Miami homicide technician swatted into immobility by what he had found at a crime scene.

And what he had found was even more interesting.

It was a scene out of some dark melodrama, a vaudeville for vampires. Just as there had been at the site where I had taken Jaworski, there was a stack of shrink-wrapped drywall. It had been pushed over against a wall and was now flooded with light from the construction lights and a few more the investigating team had set up.

On top of the drywall, raised up like an altar, was a black portable work-bench. It had been neatly centered so the light hit it just right – or rather, so the light illuminated just right the thing that sat on top of the workbench.

It was, of course, a woman's head. Its mouth held the rearview mirror from some car or truck, which stretched the face into an almost comical look of surprise.

Above it and to the left was a second head. The body of a Barbie doll had been placed under its chin so it looked like a huge head with a tiny body.

On the right side was the third head. It had been neatly mounted on a piece of drywall, the ears carefully tacked on with what must be drywall screws. There was no mess of blood puddling around the exhibit. All three heads were bloodless.

A mirror, a Barbie, and drywall.

Three kills.

Bone dry.

Hello, Dexter.

There was absolutely no question about it. The Barbie body was clearly a reference to the one in my freezer. The mirror was from the head left on the causeway, and the drywall referred to Jaworski. Either someone was so far inside my head they might as well be me, or they actually were me.

I took a slow and very ragged breath. I'm quite sure my emotions were not the same as his, but I wanted to squat down in the middle of the floor beside Angel-no-relation. I needed a moment to remember how to think, and the floor seemed a great place to start. Instead, I found myself moving slowly toward the altar, pulled forward as if I was on well-oiled rails. I could not make myself stop or slow down or do anything but move closer. I could only look, marvel, and concentrate on getting the breath to come in and go out in the right place. And all around me I slowly became aware that I was not the only one who couldn't quite believe what he was seeing.

In the course of my job – to say nothing of my hobby – I had been on the scene of hundreds of murders, many of them so gruesome and savage that they shocked even me. And at each and every one of those murders the Miami-Dade team had set up and gone on with their job in a relaxed and professional manner. At each and every one of them someone had been slurp-ing coffee, someone had sent out for *pasteles* or doughnuts, someone was jok-ing or gossiping as she sponged up the gore. At each and every crime scene I had seen a group of people who were so completely unimpressed with the carnage that they might as well have been bowling with the church league.

Until now.

This time the large, bare concrete room was unnaturally quiet. The officers and technicians stood in silent groups of two and three, as if afraid to be alone, and simply looked at what had been displayed at the far end of the room. If anybody accidentally made a small sound, everyone jumped and glared at the noise-maker. The whole scene was so positively comically strange that I certainly would have laughed out loud if I hadn't been just as busy staring as all the other geeks.

Had I done this?

It was beautiful – in a terrible sort of way, of course. But still, the arrangement was perfect, compelling, beautifully bloodless. It showed great wit and a wonderful sense of composition. Somebody had gone to a lot of trouble to make this into a real work of art. Somebody with style, talent, and a morbid sense of playfulness. In my whole life I had only known of one such somebody.

Could that somebody possibly be darkly dreaming Dexter?

20

I stood as close as I could get to the tableau without actually touching it, just looking. The little altar had not been dusted for prints yet; nothing had been done to it at all, although I assumed pictures had been taken. And oh how I wanted a copy of one of those pictures to take home. Poster sized, and in full, bloodless color. If I had done this, I was a much better artist than I had ever suspected. Even from this close the heads seemed to float in space, suspended above the mortal earth in a timeless, bloodless parody of paradise, literally cut off from their bodies—

Their bodies: I glanced around. There was no sign of them, no telltale stack of carefully wrapped packages. There was only the pyramid of heads.

I stared some more. After a few moments Vince Masuoka swam slowly over, his mouth open, his face pale. 'Dexter,' he said, and shook his head.

'Hello, Vince,' I said. He shook his head again. 'Where are the bodies?'

He just stared at the heads for a long moment. Then he looked at me with a face full of lost innocence. 'Somewhere else,' he said.

There was a clatter on the stairs and the spell was broken. I moved away from the tableau as LaGuerta came in with a few carefully selected reporters – Nick Something and Rick Sangre from local TV, and Eric the Viking, a strange and respected columnist from the newspaper. For a moment the room was very busy. Nick and Eric took one look and ran back down the stairs with their hands covering their mouths. Rick Sangre frowned deeply, looked at the lights, and then turned to LaGuerta.

'Is there a power outlet? I gotta get my camera guy,' he said.

LaGuerta shook her head. 'Wait for those other guys,' she said.

'I need pictures,' Rick Sangre insisted.

Sergeant Doakes appeared behind Sangre. The reporter looked around and saw him. 'No pictures,' Doakes said. Sangre opened his mouth, looked at Doakes for a moment, and then closed his mouth again. Once again the sterling qualities of the good sergeant had saved the day. He went back and stood protectively by the displayed body parts, as if it was a science-fair project and he was its guardian.

There was a strained coughing sound at the door, and Nick Something and Eric the Viking returned, shuffling slowly up the stairs and back onto the floor like old men. Eric wouldn't look at the far end of the room. Nick tried not to look, but his head kept drifting around toward the awful sight, and then he would snap it back to face LaGuerta again.

LaGuerta began to speak. I moved close enough to hear. 'I asked you three to come see this thing before we allow any official press coverage,' she said.

'But we can cover it unofficially?' Rick Sangre interrupted.

LaGuerta ignored him. 'We don't want any wild speculation in the press about what has happened here,' she said. 'As you can see, this is a vicious and bizarre crime—' she paused for a moment and then said very carefully, 'Unlike Anything We Have Ever Seen Before.' You could actually hear her capitalize the letters.

Nick Something said, 'Huh,' and looked thoughtful. Eric the Viking got it immediately. 'Whoa, wait a minute,' he said. 'You're saying this is a brand-new killer? A whole different set of murders?'

LaGuerta looked at him with great significance. 'Of course it's too soon to say anything for sure,' she said, sounding sure, 'but let's look at this thing logically, okay? First,' she held up a finger, 'we got a guy who confessed the other stuff. He's in jail, and we didn't let him out to do this. Second, this doesn't look like anything I ever saw, does it? 'Cause there's three and they're stacked up all pretty, okay?' Bless her heart, she had noticed.

'Why can't I get my camera guy?' Rick Sangre asked.

'Wasn't there a mirror found at one of the other murders?' Eric the Viking said weakly, trying very hard not to look.

'Have you identified the, uh—' Nick Something said. His head started to turn toward the display and he caught himself, snapped back around to LaGuerta. 'Are the victims prostitutes, Detective?'

'Listen,' LaGuerta said. She sounded a little annoyed, and a small trace of Cuban accent showed in her voice for just a second. 'Let me *esplain* something. I don't care if they're prostitutes. I don't care if they got a mirror. I don't care about any of that.' She took a breath and went on, much calmer. 'We got the other killer locked up in the jail. We've got a confession. This is a whole new thing, okay? That's the important thing. You can see it – this is different.'

'Then why are you assigned to it?' asked Eric the Viking, very reasonably, I thought.

LaGuerta showed shark teeth. 'I solved the other one,' she said.

'But you're sure this is a brand-new killer, Detective?' Rick Sangre asked.

'There's no question. I can't tell you any details, but I got lab work to back me up.' I was sure she meant me. I felt a small thrill of pride.

'But this is kind of close, isn't it? Same area, same general technique—' Eric the Viking started. LaGuerta cut him off.

'Totally different,' she said. 'Totally different.'

'So you're completely satisfied that McHale committed all those other murders and this one is different,' Nick Something said.

'One hundred percent,' LaGuerta said. 'Besides, I never said McHale did the others.'

For a second, the reporters all forgot the horror of not having pictures. 'What?' Nick Something finally said.

LaGuerta blushed, but insisted, 'I never said McHale did it. McHale said he did it, okay? So what am I supposed to do? Tell him go away, I don't believe you?'

Eric the Viking and Nick Something exchanged a meaningful glance. I would have, too, if only there had been someone for me to look at. So instead I peeked at the central head on the altar. It didn't actually wink at me, but I'm sure it was just as amazed as I was.

'That's nuts,' Eric muttered, but he was overrun by Rick Sangre.

'Are you willing to let us interview McHale?' Sangre demanded. 'With a camera present?'

We were saved from LaGuerta's answer by the arrival of Captain Matthews. He clattered up the stairs and stopped dead as he saw our little art exhibit. 'Jesus Christ,' he said. Then his gaze swung to the group of reporters around LaGuerta. 'What the hell are you guys doing up here?' he asked.

LaGuerta looked around the room, but nobody volunteered anything. 'I let them in,' she said finally. 'Unofficially. Off the record.'

'You didn't say off the record,' Rick Sangre blurted out. 'You just said unofficially.'

LaGuerta glared at him. 'Unofficially *means* off the record.'

'Get out,' Matthews barked. 'Officially and on the record. Out.'

Eric the Viking cleared his throat. 'Captain, do you agree with Detective LaGuerta that this is a brand-new string of murders, a different killer?'

'Out,' Matthews repeated. 'I'll answer questions downstairs.'

'I need footage,' Rick Sangre said. 'It will only take a minute.'

Matthews nodded toward the exit. 'Sergeant Doakes?'

Doakes materialized and took Rick Sangre's elbow. 'Gentlemen,' he said in his soft and scary voice. The three reporters looked at him. I saw Nick Something swallow hard. Then they all three turned without a sound and trooped out.

Matthews watched them go. When they were safely out of earshot he turned on LaGuerta. 'Detective,' he said in a voice so venomous he must have learned it from Doakes, 'if you ever pull this kind of shit again you'll be lucky to get a job doing parking lot security at Wal-Mart.'

LaGuerta turned pale green and then bright red. 'Captain, I just wanted—' she said. But Matthews had already turned away. He straightened his tie, combed his hair back with one hand, and chased down the stairs after the reporters.

I turned to look at the altar again. It hadn't changed, but they were starting to dust for prints now. Then they would take it apart to analyze the pieces. Soon it would all be just a beautiful memory.

I trundled off down the stairs to find Deborah.

Outside, Rick Sangre already had a camera rolling. Captain Matthews stood in the wash of lights with microphones thrusting at his chin, giving his official statement. '. . . always the policy of this department to leave the investigating officer autonomy on a case, until such time as it becomes evident that a series of major errors in judgment call the officer's competence into question. That time has not yet arrived, but I am monitoring the situation closely. With so much at stake for the community—'

I spotted Deborah and moved past them. She stood at the barrier of yellow tape, dressed in her blue patrol uniform. 'Nice suit,' I told her.

'I like it,' she said. 'You saw?'

'I saw,' I told her. 'I also saw Captain Matthews discussing the case with Detective LaGuerta.'

Deborah sucked in her breath. 'What did they say?'

I patted her arm. 'I think I once heard Dad use a very colorful expression that would cover it. He was "reaming her a new asshole." Do you know that one?'

She looked startled, then pleased. 'That's great. Now I really need your help, Dex.'

'As opposed to what I've been doing, of course?'

'I don't know what you think you've been doing, but it isn't enough.'

'So unfair, Deb. And so very unkind. After all, you are actually at a crime site, and wearing your uniform, too. Would you prefer the sex suit?'

She shuddered. 'That's not the point. You've been holding back something about this all along and I want it now.'

For a moment I had nothing to say, always an uncomfortable feeling. I'd had no idea she was this perceptive. 'Why, Deborah—'

'Listen, you think I don't know how this political stuff works, and maybe I'm not as smart about it as you are, but I know they're all going to be busy covering their own asses for a while. Which means nobody is going to be doing any real police work.'

'Which means you see a chance to do some of your own? Bravo, Debs.'

'And it also means I need your help like never before.' She put a hand out and squeezed mine. 'Please, Dexy?'

I don't know what shocked me more – her insight, her hand-squeezing, or her use of the nickname 'Dexy.' I hadn't heard her say that since I was ten years old. Whether she intended it or not, when she called me Dexy she put us both firmly back in Harry Land, a place where family mattered and obligations were as real as headless hookers. What could I say?

'Of course, Deborah,' I said. Dexy indeed. It was almost enough to make me feel emotion.

'Good,' she said, and she was all business again, a wonderfully quick change that I had to admire. 'What's the one thing that really sticks out right now?' she asked with a nod toward the second floor.

'The body parts,' I said. 'As far as you know, is anybody looking for them?'

Deborah gave me one of her new Worldly Cop looks, the sour one. 'As far as I know, there are more officers assigned to keeping the TV cameras out than to doing any actual work on this thing.'

'Good,' I said. 'If we can find the body parts, we might get a small jump on things.'

'Okay. Where do we look?'

It was a fair question, which naturally put me at a disadvantage. I had no idea where to look. Would the limbs be left in the killing room? I didn't think so – it seemed messy to me, and if he wanted to use that same room again, it would be impossible with that kind of nasty clutter lying around.

All right, then I would assume that the rest of the meat had gone somewhere else. But where?

Or perhaps, it slowly dawned on me, the real question should be: Why? The display of the heads was for a reason. What would be the reason for putting the rest of the bodies somewhere else? Simple concealment? No – nothing was simple with this man, and concealment was evidently not a virtue he prized too highly. Especially right now, when he was showing off a bit. That being the case, where would he leave a stack of leftovers?

'Well?' Deborah demanded. 'How about it? Where should we look?'

I shook my head. 'I don't know,' I said slowly. 'Wherever he left the stuff, it's part of his statement. And we're not really sure what his statement is yet, are we?'

'Goddamn it, Dexter—'

'I know he wants to rub our noses in it. He needs to say that we did something incredibly dumb, and even if we hadn't he's still smarter than we are.'

'So far he's right,' she said, putting on her grouper face.

'So . . . wherever he dumped the stuff, it has to continue that statement. That we're stupid— No, I'm wrong. That we DID something stupid.'

'Right. Very important difference.'

'Please, Deb, you'll hurt your face like that. It is important, because he's going to comment on the ACT, and not on the ACTORS.'

'Uh-huh. That's really good, Dex. So we should probably head for the nearest dinner theater and look around for an actor with blood up to his elbows, right?'

I shook my head. 'No blood, Deb. None at all. That's one of the most important things.'

'How can you be so sure?'

'Because there's been no blood at any of the scenes. That's deliberate, and it's vital to what he's doing. And this time, he'll repeat the important parts, but comment on what he's already done, because we've missed it, don't you see?'

'Sure, I see. Makes perfect sense. So why don't we go check Office Depot Center? He's probably got the bodies stacked up in the net again.'

I opened my mouth to make some wonderfully clever reply. The hockey rink was all wrong, completely and obviously wrong. It had been an experiment, something different, but I knew he wouldn't repeat it. I started to explain this to Deb, that the only reason he would ever repeat the rink would be— I stopped dead, my mouth hanging open. *Of course*, I thought. *Naturally*.

'Now who's making a fish face, huh? What is it, Dex?'

For a moment I didn't say anything. I was far too busy trying to catch my whirling thoughts. *The only reason he would repeat the hockey rink was to show us we had the wrong guy locked up.*

'Oh, Deb,' I said at last. 'Of course. You're right, the arena. You are right for all the wrong reasons, but still—'

'Beats the hell out of being wrong,' she said, and headed for her car.

21

'You do understand it's a long shot?' I said. 'Probably we won't find anything at all.'

'I know that,' Deb said.

'And we don't actually have any jurisdiction here. We're in Broward. And the Broward guys don't like us, so—'

'For Christ's sake, Dexter,' she snapped. 'You're chattering like a schoolgirl.'

Perhaps that was true, although it was very unkind of her to say so. And Deborah, on the other hand, appeared to be a bundle of steely, tightly wrapped nerves. As we turned off the Sawgrass Expressway and drove into the parking lot of the Office Depot Center she bit down harder. I could almost hear her jaw creak. 'Dirty Harriet,' I said to myself, but apparently Deb was eavesdropping.

'Fuck off,' she said.

I looked from Deborah's granite profile to the arena. For one brief moment, with the early-morning sunlight hitting it just right, it looked like the building was surrounded by a fleet of flying saucers. Of course it was only the outdoor lighting fixtures that sprouted around the arena like oversized steel toadstools. Someone must have told the architect they were distinctive. 'Youthful and vigorous,' too, most likely. And I'm sure they were, in the right light. I did hope they would find the right light sometime soon.

We drove one time around the arena, looking for signs of life. On the second circuit, a battered Toyota pulled up beside one of the doors. The passenger door was held closed with a loop of rope that ran out the window and around the doorpost. Opening the driver's door as she parked, Deborah was already stepping out of the car while it was still rolling.

'Excuse me, sir?' she said to the man getting out of the Toyota. He was fifty, a squat guy in ratty green pants and a blue nylon jacket. He glanced at Deb in her uniform and was instantly nervous.

'Wha'?' he said. 'I din't do nothin'.'

'Do you work here, sir?'

'Shoor. 'Course, why you think I'm here, eight o'clock in the morning?'

'What's your name, please sir?'

He fumbled for his wallet. 'Steban Rodriguez. I got a ID.'

Deborah waved that off. 'That's not necessary,' she said. 'What are you doing here at this hour, sir?'

He shrugged and pushed his wallet back into the pocket. 'I s'posed to be here earlier most days, but the team is on the road – Vancouver, Ottawa, and L.A. So I get here a little later.'

'Is anyone else here right now, Steban?'

'Naw, jus' me. They all sleep late.'

'What about at night? Is there a guard?'

He waved an arm around. 'The security goes around the parking lot at night, but not too much. I the first one here mos' days.'

'The first one to go inside, you mean?'

'Yeah, tha's right, what I say?'

I climbed out of the car and leaned across the roof. 'Are you the guy who drives the Zamboni for the morning skate?' I asked him. Deb glanced at me, annoyed. Steban peered at me, taking in my natty Hawaiian shirt and gabardine slacks. 'Wha' kinda cop you are, ha?'

'I'm a nerd cop,' I said. 'I just work in the lab.'

'Ooohhh, shoor,' he said, nodding his head as if that made sense.

'Do you run the Zamboni, Steban?' I repeated.

'Yeah, you know. They don' lemme drive her in the games, you know. Tha's for the guys with suits. They like to put a kid, you know. Some celebrity maybe. Ride around and wave, that shit. But I get to do it for the morning skate, you know. When the team is in town. I run the Zamboni just the morning, real early. But they on the road now so I come later.'

'We'd like to take a look inside the arena,' Deb said, clearly impatient with me for speaking out of turn. Steban turned back to her, a crafty gleam lighting up half of one eye.

'Shoor,' he said. 'You got a warrant?'

Deborah blushed. It made a wonderful contrast to the blue of her uniform, but it was possibly not the most effective choice for reinforcing her authority. And because I knew her well, I knew she would realize she had blushed and get mad. Since we did not have a warrant and did not, in fact, have any business here whatsoever that could remotely be considered officially sanctioned, I did not think that getting mad was our best tactical maneuver.

'Steban,' I said before Deb could say anything regrettable.

'Hah?'

'How long have you worked here?'

He shrugged. 'Since the place open. I work at the old arena two year before that.'

'So you were working here last week when they found the dead body on the ice?'

Steban looked away. Under his tan, his face turned green. He swallowed hard. 'I never want to see something like that again, man,' he said. 'Never.'

I nodded with genuine synthetic sympathy. 'I really don't blame you,' I said. 'And that's why we're here, Steban.'

He frowned. 'Wha' you mean?'

I glanced at Deb to make sure she wasn't drawing a weapon or anything. She glared at me with tight-lipped disapproval and tapped her foot, but she didn't say anything.

'Steban,' I said, moving a little closer to the man and making my voice as confidential and manly as I could, 'we think there's a chance that when you open those doors this morning, you might find the same kind of thing waiting for you.'

'Shit!' he exploded. 'I don' want nothin' to do with that.'

'Of course you don't.'

'*Me cago en diez* with that shit,' he said.

'Exactly,' I agreed. 'So why not let us take a peek first? Just to be sure.'

He gaped at me for a moment, then at Deborah, who was still scowling – a very striking look for her, nicely set off by her uniform.

'I could get in trouble,' he said. 'Lose my job.'

I smiled with authentic-looking sympathy. 'Or you could go inside and find a stack of chopped-up arms and legs all by yourself. A lot more of them this time.'

'Shit,' he said again. 'I get in trouble, lose my job, huh? Why I should do that, huh?'

'How about civic duty?'

'Come on, man,' he said. 'Don't fuck with me. What do you care about if I lose my job?'

He did not actually hold out his hand, which I thought was very genteel, but it was clear that he hoped for a small present to insulate him against the possible loss of his job. Very reasonable, considering that this was Miami. But all I had was $5, and I really needed to get a cruller and a cup of coffee. So I just nodded with manly understanding.

'You're right,' I said. 'We hoped you wouldn't have to see all the body parts – did I say there were quite a few this time? But I certainly don't want you to lose your job. Sorry to bother you, Steban. Have a nice day!' I smiled at Deborah. 'Let's go, Officer. We should get back to the other scene and search for the fingers.'

Deborah was still scowling, but at least she had the native wit to play along. She opened her car door as I cheerfully waved to Steban and climbed in.

'Wait!' Steban called. I glanced at him with an expression of polite interest. 'I swear to God, I don' wanna find that shit ever again,' he said. He looked at me for a moment, perhaps hoping I would loosen up and hand him a fistful of Krugerands, but as I said, that cruller was weighing heavily on my mind and I did not relent. Steban licked his lips, then turned away quickly and jammed a key into the lock of the large double door. 'Go 'head. I wait out here.'

'If you're sure—' I said.

'Come on, man, what you want from me? Go 'head!'

I stood up and smiled at Deborah. 'He's sure,' I said. She just shook her head at me, a strange combination of little-sister exasperation and cop sour humor. She walked around the car and led the way in through the door and I followed.

Inside, the arena was cool and dark, which shouldn't have surprised me. It was, after all, a hockey rink early in the morning. No doubt Steban knew where the light switch was, but he had not offered to tell us. Deb unsnapped the large flashlight from her belt and swung the beam around the ice. I held my breath as the light picked out one goalie's net, then the other. She swept back around the perimeter one time, slowly, pausing once or twice, then back to me.

'Nothing,' she said. 'Jack shit.'

'You sound disappointed.'

She snorted at me and headed back out. I stayed in the middle of the rink, feeling the cool radiate up off the ice, and thinking my happy thoughts. Or, more precisely, not quite *my* happy thoughts.

Because as Deb turned to go out I heard a small voice from somewhere over my shoulder; a cool and dry chuckle, a familiar feather touch just under the threshold of hearing. And as dear Deborah departed, I stood motionless there on the ice, closed my eyes and listened to what my ancient friend had to say. It was not much – just a sub-whisper, a hint of unvocal, but I listened. I heard him chuckle and mutter soft and terrible things in one ear, while the other ear let me know that Deborah had told Steban to come in and turn on the lights. Which moments later he did, as the small off-voice whisper rose in a sudden crescendo of rattling jolly humor and good-natured horror.

What is it? I asked politely. My only answer was a surge of hungry amusement. I had no idea what it meant. But I was not greatly surprised when the screaming started.

Steban was really terrible at screaming. It was a hoarse, strangled grunting that sounded more like he was being violently sick than anything else. The man brought no sense of music to the job.

I opened my eyes. It was impossible to concentrate under these circumstances, and anyway there was nothing more to hear. The whispering had stopped when the screaming began. After all, the screams said it all, didn't they? And so I opened my eyes just in time to see Steban catapult out of the little closet at the far end of the arena and vault onto the rink. He went clattering across the ice, slipping and sliding and moaning hoarsely in Spanish and finally hurling headlong into the boards. He scrabbled up and skittered toward the door, grunting with horror. A small splotch of blood smeared the ice where he had fallen.

Deborah came quickly through the door, her gun drawn, and Steban clawed past her, stumbling out into the light of day. 'What is it?' Deborah said, holding her weapon ready.

I tilted my head, hearing one last echo of the final dry chuckle, and now, with the grunting horror still ringing in my ears, I understood.

'I believe Steban has found something,' I said.

22

Police politics, as I had tried so hard to impress on Deborah, was a slippery and many-tentacled thing. And when you brought together two law enforcement organizations that really didn't care for each other, mutual operations tended to go very slowly, very much by the book, and with a good deal of foot-dragging, excuse-making, and veiled insults and threats. All great fun to watch, of course, but it did draw out the proceedings just a trifle more than necessary. Consequently it was several hours after Steban's dreadful yodeling exhibition before the jurisdictional squabbling was straightened out and our team actually began to examine the happy little surprise our new friend Steban had discovered when he opened the closet door.

During that time Deborah stood off to one side for the most part, working very hard at controlling her impatience but not terribly hard at hiding it. Captain Matthews arrived with Detective LaGuerta in tow. They shook hands with their Broward County counterparts, Captain Moon and Detective McClellan. There was a lot of barely polite sparring, which boiled down to this: Matthews was reasonably certain that the discovery of six arms and six legs in Broward was part of his department's investigation of three heads lacking the same pieces in Miami-Dade. He stated, in terms that were far too friendly and simple, that it seemed a bit farfetched to think that he would find three heads without bodies, and then three totally different bodies without heads would turn up here.

Moon and McClellan, with equal logic, pointed out that people found heads in Miami all the time, but in Broward it was a little more unusual, and so maybe they took it a bit more seriously, and anyway there was no way to know for sure they were connected until some preliminary work had been done, which clearly ought to be done by them, since it was in their jurisdiction. Of course they would cheerfully pass on the results.

And of course that was unacceptable to Matthews. He explained carefully that the Broward people didn't know what to look for and might miss something or destroy a piece of key evidence. Not, of course, through incompetence or stupidity; Matthews was quite sure the Broward people were perfectly competent, considering.

This was naturally not taken in a cheerful spirit of cooperation by Moon, who observed with a little bit of feeling that this seemed to imply that his department was full of second-rate morons. By this point Captain Matthews was mad enough to reply much too politely, oh, no, not second-rate at all. I'm sure it would have ended in a fistfight if the gentleman from the Florida Department of Law Enforcement had not arrived to referee.

The FDLE is a sort of state-level FBI. They have jurisdiction anywhere in the state at any time, and unlike the feds they are respected by most of the local cops. The officer in question was a man of average height and build with a shaved head and a close-cropped beard. He didn't really seem out of the ordinary to me, but when he stepped between the two much larger police captains they instantly shut up and took a step back. In short order he had things settled down and organized and we got quickly back to being the neat and well-ordered scene of a multiple homicide.

The man from FDLE had ruled that it was Miami-Dade's investigation unless and until tissue samples proved the body parts here and the heads down there were unrelated. In practical and immediate terms, this meant that Captain Matthews got to have his picture taken first by the mob of reporters already clustering outside.

Angel-no-relation arrived and went to work. I was not at all sure what to make of it, and I don't mean the jurisdictional squabbling. No, I was far more concerned with the event itself, which had left me with a great deal to think about – not merely the fact of the killings and the redistribution of the meat, which was piquant enough. But I had of course managed to sneak a peek into Steban's little closet of horrors earlier, before the troops arrived – can you blame me, really? I had only wanted to sample the carnage and try to understand why my dear unknown business associate had chosen to stack the leftovers there; truly, just a quick look-see.

So immediately after Steban had skidded out the door squealing and grunting like a pig choking on a grapefruit, I had skipped eagerly back to the closet to see what had set him off.

The parts were not wrapped carefully this time. Instead, they were laid out on the floor in four groups. And as I looked closer I realized a wonderful thing.

One leg had been laid straight along the left-hand side of the closet. It was a pale, bloodless blue-white, and around the ankle there was even a small gold chain with a heart-shaped trinket. Very cute, really, unspoiled by awful bloodstains; truly elegant work. Two dark arms, equally well cut, had been bent at the elbow and placed alongside the leg, with the elbow pointing away. Right next to this the remaining limbs, all bent at the joint, had been arranged in two large circles.

It took me a moment. I blinked, and suddenly it swam into focus and I had to frown very hard to keep myself from giggling out loud like the schoolgirl Deb had accused me of being.

Because he had arranged the arms and legs in letters, and the letters spelled out a single small word: BOO.

The three torsos were carefully arranged below the BOO in a quarter-circle, making a cute little Halloween smile.

What a scamp.

But even as I admired the playful spirit this prank exposed, I wondered why he had chosen to put the display here, in a closet, instead of out on the ice where it could gain the recognition of a wider audience. It was a very spacious closet, granted, but still close quarters, just enough room for the display. So why?

And as I wondered, the outer door of the arena swung open with a clatter – the first of the arriving rescue team, no doubt. And the door crashing wide sent, a moment later, a draft of cool air over the ice and onto my back—

The cold air went over my spine and was answered by a flow of warmth moving upward along the same pathway. It ran light-fingered up into the unlit bottom of my consciousness and something changed somewhere deep in the moonless night of my lizard brain and I felt the Dark Passenger agree violently with something that I did not even hear or understand except that it had to do somehow with the primal urgency of cool air and the walls closing in and an attacking sense of—

Rightness. No question about it. Something here was just plain right and made my obscure hitchhiker pleased and excited and satisfied in a way I did not begin to understand. And floating in above all that was the strange notion that this was very familiar. None of it made any sense to me, but there it was. And before I could explore these strange revelations any further I was being urged by a squat young man in a blue uniform to step away and keep my hands in plain sight. No doubt he was the first of the arriving troops, and he was holding his weapon on me in a very convincing way. Since he had only one dark eyebrow running all the way across his face and no apparent forehead, I decided it would be a very good idea to go along with his wishes. He looked to be just the sort of dull-witted brute who might shoot an innocent person – or even me. I stepped away from the closet.

Unfortunately, my retreat revealed the little diorama in the closet, and the young man was suddenly very busy finding someplace to put his breakfast. He made it to a large trash can about ten feet away before commencing his ugly blargging sounds. I stood quite still and waited for him to finish. Nasty habit, hurling half-digested food around like that. So unsanitary. And this was a guardian of public safety, too.

More uniforms trotted in, and soon my simian friend had several buddies sharing the trash can with him. The noise was extremely unpleasant, to say nothing of the smell now wafting my way. But I waited politely for them to finish, since one of the fascinating things about a handgun is that it can be fired almost as well by someone who is throwing up. But one of the uniforms eventually straightened up, wiped his face on his sleeve, and began to question me. I was soon sorted out and pushed over to one side with instructions not to go anywhere or touch anything.

Captain Matthews and Detective LaGuerta had arrived soon after, and when they finally took over the scene I relaxed a bit. But now that I could actually go somewhere and touch something, I simply sat and thought. And the things I thought about were surprisingly troublesome.

Why had the display in the closet seemed familiar?

Unless I was going to return to my idiocy of earlier in the day and persuade myself that I had done this, I was at a loss as to why it should seem so delightfully unsurprising. Of course I hadn't done it. I was already ashamed of the stupidity of that notion. Boo, indeed. It was not even worth taking the time to scoff at the idea. Ridiculous.

So, um – why did it seem familiar?

I sighed and experienced one more new feeling, befuddlement. I simply had no notion of what was going on, except that somehow I was a part of it. This did not seem a terribly helpful revelation, since it matched exactly all my other closely reasoned analytical conclusions so far. If I ruled out the absurd idea that I had done this without knowing it – and I did – then each subsequent explanation became even more unlikely. And so Dexter's summary of the case reads as follows: he is involved somehow, but doesn't even know what that means. I could feel the little wheels in my once-proud brain leaping off their tracks and clattering to the floor. Clang-clang. Whee. Dexter derailed.

Luckily, I was saved from complete collapse by the appearance of dear Deborah. 'Come on,' she said brusquely, 'we're going upstairs.'

'May I ask why?'

'We're going to talk to the office staff,' she said. 'See if they know anything.'

'They must know something if they have an office,' I offered.

She looked at me for a moment, then turned away. 'Come on,' she said.

It may have been the commanding tone in her voice, but I went. We walked to the far side of the arena from where I had been sitting and into the lobby. A Broward cop stood beside the elevator there, and just outside the long row of glass doors I could see several more of them standing at a barrier. Deb marched up to the cop at the elevator and said, 'I'm Morgan.' He nodded and pushed the up button. He looked at me with a lack of expression that said a great deal. 'I'm Morgan, too,' I told him. He just looked at me, then turned his head away to stare out the glass doors.

There was a muted chime and the elevator arrived. Deborah stalked in and slammed her hand against the button hard enough to make the cop look up at her and the door slid shut.

'Why so glum, sis?' I asked her. 'Isn't this what you wanted to do?'

'It's make-work, and everybody knows it,' she snarled.

'But it's detective-type make-work,' I pointed out.

'That bitch LaGuerta stuck her oar in,' she hissed. 'As soon as I'm done spinning my wheels here, I have to go back out on hooker duty.'

'Oh, dear. In your little sex suit?'

'In my little sex suit,' she said, and before I could really formulate any magical words of consolation we arrived at the office level and the elevator doors slid open. Deb stalked out and I followed. We soon found the staff lounge, where the office workers had been herded to wait until the full majesty of the law had the time to get around to them. Another Broward cop stood at the door of the lounge, presumably to make certain that none of the staff made a break for the Canadian border. Deborah nodded to the cop at the door and went into the lounge. I trailed behind her without much enthusiasm and let my mind wander over my problem. A moment later I was startled out of my reverie when Deborah jerked her head at me and led a surly, greasy-faced young man with long and awful hair toward the door. I followed again.

She was naturally separating him from the others for questioning, very good police procedure, but to be perfectly honest it did not light a fire in my heart. I knew without knowing why that none of these people had anything meaningful to contribute. Judging from this first specimen, it was probably safe to apply that generalization to his life as well as to this murder. This was just dull routine make-work that had been doled out to Deb because the captain thought she had done something good, but she was still a pest. So he had sent her away with a piece of real detective drudgery to keep her busy and out of sight. And I had been dragged with her because Deb wanted me along. Possibly she wanted to see if my fantastic ESP powers could help determine what these office sheep had eaten for breakfast. One look at this young gentleman's complexion and I was fairly sure he had eaten cold pizza, potato chips, and a liter of Pepsi. It had ruined his complexion and given him an air of vacuous hostility.

Still, I followed along as Mr. Grumpy directed Deborah to a conference room at the back of the building. There was a long oak table with ten black high-backed chairs in the center of the room, and a desk in the corner with a computer and some audio-visual equipment. As Deb and her pimply young friend sat and began trading frowns, I wandered over to the desk. A small bookshelf sat under the window beside the desk. I looked out the window. Almost directly below me I could see the growing crowd of reporters and squad cars that now surrounded the door where we had gone in with Steban.

I looked at the bookshelf, thinking I would clear a small space and lean there, tastefully away from the conversation. There was a stack of manila folders and perched on top of it was a small gray object. It was squarish and looked to be plastic. A black wire ran from the thing over to the back of the computer. I picked it up to move it.

'Hey!' the surly geek said. 'Don't mess with the webcam!'

I looked at Deb. She looked at me and I swear I saw her nostrils flair like a racehorse at the starting gate. 'The what?' she said quietly.

'I had it focused down on the entrance,' he said. 'Now I gotta refocus it. Man, why do you have to mess with my stuff?'

'He said webcam,' I said to Deborah.

'A camera,' she said to me.

'Yes.'

She turned to young Prince Charming. 'Is it on?'

He gaped at her, still concentrating on maintaining his righteous frown. 'What?'

'The camera,' Deborah said. 'Does it work?'

He snorted, and then wiped his nose with a finger. 'What do you think, I would get all worked up if it didn't? Two hundred bucks. It totally works.'

I looked out the window where the camera had been pointing as he droned on in his surly grumble. 'I got a Web site and everything. Kathouse.com. People can watch the team when they get here and when they leave.'

Deborah drifted over and stood beside me, looking out the window. 'It was pointed at the door,' I said.

'Duh,' our happy pal said. 'How else are people on my Web site gonna see the team?'

Deborah turned and looked at him. After about five seconds he blushed and dropped his eyes to the table. 'Was the camera turned on last night?' she said.

He didn't look up, just mumbled, 'Sure. I mean, I guess so.'

Deborah turned to me. Her computer knowledge was confined to knowing enough to fill out standardized traffic reports. She knew I was a little more savvy.

'How do you have it set up?' I asked the top of the young man's head. 'Do the images automatically archive?'

This time he looked up. I had used archive as a verb, so I must be okay. 'Yeah,' he said. 'It refreshes every fifteen seconds and just dumps to the hard drive. I usually erase in the morning.'

Deborah actually clutched my arm hard enough to break the skin. 'Did you erase this morning?' she asked him.

He glanced away again. 'No,' he said. 'You guys came stomping in and yelling and stuff. I didn't even get to check my e-mail.'

Deborah looked at me. 'Bingo,' I said.

'Come here,' she said to our unhappy camper.

'Huh?' he said.

'Come here,' she repeated, and he stood up slowly, mouth hanging open, and rubbed his knuckles.

'What?' he said.

'Could you please come over here, sir?' Deborah ordered with truly veteran-cop technique, and he stuttered into motion and came over. 'Can we see the pictures from last night, please?'

He gaped at the computer, then at her. 'Why?' he said. Ah, the mysteries of human intelligence.

'Because,' Deborah said, very slowly and carefully. 'I think you might have taken a picture of the killer.'

He stared at her and blinked, then blushed. 'No way,' he said.

'Way,' I told him.

He stared at me, and then at Deb, his jaw hanging open. 'Awesome,' he breathed. 'No shit? I mean – No, really? I mean—' He blushed even harder.

'Can we look at the pictures?' Deb said. He stood still for a second, then plunged into the chair at the desk and touched the mouse. Immediately the screen came to life, and he began typing and mouse-clicking furiously. 'What time should I start?'

'What time did everybody leave?' Deborah asked him.

He shrugged. 'We were empty last night. Everybody gone by, what – eight o'clock?'

'Start at midnight,' I said, and he nodded.

' 'Kay,' he said. He worked quietly for a moment, then, 'Come on,' he mumbled. 'It's only like a six hundred megaherz,' he said. 'They won't update. They keep saying it's fine, but sooooo freaking slow, and it won't— Okay,' he said, breaking off suddenly.

A dark image appeared on the monitor: the empty parking lot below us. 'Midnight,' he said, and stared at the screen. After fifteen seconds, the picture changed to the same picture.

'Do we have to watch five hours of this?' Deborah asked.

'Scroll through,' I said. 'Look for headlights or something moving.'

'Riiiiiight,' he said. He did some rapid point-and-click, and the pictures began to flip past at one per second. They didn't change much at first; the same dark parking lot, one bright light out at the edge of the picture. After about fifty frames had clicked past, an image jumped into view. 'A truck!' Deborah said.

Our pet nerd shook his head. 'Security,' he said, and in the next frame the security car was visible.

He kept scrolling, and the pictures rolled by, eternal and unchanging. Every thirty or forty frames we would see the security truck pass, and then nothing. After several minutes of this, the pattern stopped, and there was a long stretch of nothing. 'Busted,' my greasy new friend said.

Deborah gave him a hard look. 'The camera is broken?'

He looked up at her, blushed again, and looked away. 'The security dudes,' he explained. 'They totally suck. Every night at, like, three? They park over at the other side and go to sleep.' He nodded at the unchanging pictures scrolling past. 'See? Hello! Mr. Security Dude? Hard at work?' He made a wet sound deep in his nose that I had to assume was meant to be laughter. 'Not very!' He repeated the snorting sound and started the pictures scrolling again.

And then suddenly— 'Wait!' I called out.

On-screen, a van popped into view at the door below us. There was another pop as the image changed, and a man stood beside the truck. 'Can you make it go closer?' Deborah asked.

'Zoom in,' I said before he could do more than frown a little. He moved the cursor, highlighted the dark figure on the screen, and clicked the mouse. The picture jumped to a closer look.

'You're not gonna get much more resolution,' he said. 'The pixels—'

'Shut up,' said Deborah. She was staring at the screen hard enough to melt it, and as I stared too I could see why.

It was dark, and the man was still too far away to be certain, but from the few details I could make out, there was something oddly familiar about him; the way he stood frozen in the image on the computer, his weight balanced on both feet, and the overall impression of the profile. Somehow, as vague as it was, it added up to something. And as a very loud wave of sibilant chuckling erupted from deep in the backseat of my brain, it fell on me with the impact of a concert grand piano that, actually, he looked an awful lot like—

'Dexter . . . ?' Deborah said, in a sort of hushed and strangled croak.

Yes indeed.

Just like Dexter.

23

I am pretty sure that Deborah took young Mr. Bad Hair Day back to the lounge, because when I looked up again, she was standing in front of me, alone. In spite of her blue uniform she did not look at all like a cop right now. She looked worried, like she couldn't decide whether to yell or to cry, like a mommy whose special little boy had let her down in a big way.

'Well?' she demanded, and I had to agree that she had a point.

'Not terribly,' I said. 'You?'

She kicked a chair. It fell over. 'Goddamn it, Dexter, don't give me that clever shit! Tell me something. Tell me that wasn't you!' I didn't say anything. 'Well then, tell me it *is* you! Just tell me SOMETHING! Anything at all!'

I shook my head. 'I—' There was really nothing to say, so I just shook my head again. 'I'm pretty sure it isn't me,' I said. 'I mean, I don't think so.' Even to me that sounded like I had both feet firmly planted in the land of lame answers.

'What does that mean, "pretty sure"?' Deb demanded. 'Does that mean you're not sure? That it might be you in that picture?'

'Well,' I said, a truly brilliant riposte, considering. 'Maybe. I don't know.'

'And does "I don't know" mean you don't know whether you're going to tell me, or does it mean that you really don't know if that's you in the picture?'

'I'm pretty sure it isn't me, Deborah,' I repeated. 'But I really don't know for sure. It looks like me, doesn't it?'

'Shit,' she said, and kicked the chair where it lay. It slammed into the table. 'How can you not know, goddamn it?!'

'It *is* a little tough to explain.'

'Try!'

I opened my mouth, but for once in my life nothing came out. As if everything else wasn't bad enough, I seemed to be all out of clever, too. 'I just – I've been having these . . . dreams, but – Deb, I really don't know,' I said, and I may have actually mumbled it.

'Shit shit SHIT!' said Deborah. Kick kick kick.

And it was very hard to disagree with her analysis of the situation.

All my stupid, self-mutilating musings swam back at me with a bright and mocking edge. *Of course it wasn't me – how could it be me? Wouldn't I know it if it was me?* Apparently not, dear boy. Apparently you didn't actually know anything at all. Because our deep dark dim little brains tell us all kinds of things that swim in and out of reality, but pictures do not lie.

Deb unleashed a new volley of savage attacks on the chair, and then straightened up. Her face was flushed very red and her eyes looked more like Harry's eyes than they ever had before. 'All right,' she said. 'It's like this,' and she blinked and paused for a moment as it occurred to both of us that she had just said a Harry thing.

And for a second Harry was there in the room between me and Deborah, the two of us so very different, and yet still both Harry's kids, the two strange fists of his unique legacy. Some of the steel went out of Deb's back and she looked human, a thing I hadn't seen for a while. She stared at me for a long moment, and then turned away. 'You're my brother, Dex,' she said. I was very sure that was not what she had originally intended to say.

'No one will blame you,' I told her.

'Goddamn you, you're my *brother*!' she snarled, and the ferocity of it took me completely by surprise. 'I don't know what went on with you and Dad. The stuff you two never talked about. But I know what he would have done.'

'Turned me in,' I said, and Deborah nodded. Something glittered in the corner of her eye. 'You're all the family I have, Dex.'

'Not such a great bargain for you, is it?'

She turned to me, and I could see tears in both eyes now. For a long moment she just looked at me. I watched the tear run from her left eye and roll down her cheek. She wiped it, straightened up, and took a deep breath, turning away to the window once again.

'That's right,' she said. 'He would've turned you in. Which is what I am going to do.' She looked away from me, out the window, far out to the horizon.

'I have to finish these interviews,' she said. 'I'm leaving you in charge of determining if this evidence is relevant. Take it to your computer at home and figure out whatever you have to figure out. And when I am done here, before I go back out on duty, I am coming to get it, to hear what you have to say.' She glanced at her watch. 'Eight o'clock. And if I have to take you in then, I will.' She looked back at me for a very long moment. 'Goddamn it, Dexter,' she said softly, and she left the room.

I moved over to the window and had a look for myself. Below me the circus of cops and reporters and gawking geeks was swirling, unchanged. Far away, beyond the parking lot, I could see the expressway, filled with cars and trucks blasting along at the Miami speed limit of ninety-five miles per hour. And beyond that in the dim distance was the high-rise skyline of Miami.

And here in the foreground stood dim dazed Dexter, staring out the window at a city that did not speak and would not have told him anything even if it did.

Goddamn it, Dexter.

I don't know how long I stared out the window, but it eventually occurred to me that there were no answers out there. There might be some, though, on Captain Pimple's computer. I turned to the desk. The machine had a CD-RW drive. In the top drawer I found a box of recordable CDs. I put one into the drive, copied the entire file of pictures, and took the CD out. I held it, glanced at it; it didn't have much to say, and I probably imagined the faint chuckling I thought I heard from the dark voice in the backseat. But just to be safe, I wiped the file from the hard drive.

On my way out, the Broward cops on duty didn't stop me, or even speak, but it did seem to me that they looked at me with a very hard and suspicious indifference.

I wondered if this was what it felt like to have a conscience. I supposed I would never really know – unlike poor Deborah, being torn apart by far too many loyalties that could not possibly live together in the same brain. I admired her solution, leaving me in charge of determining if the evidence was relevant. Very neat. It had a very Harry feel to it, like leaving a loaded gun on the table in front of a guilty friend and walking away, knowing that guilt would pull the trigger and save the city the cost of a trial. In Harry's world, a man's conscience couldn't live with that kind of shame.

But as Harry had known very well, his world was long dead – and I did not have any conscience, shame, or guilt. All I had was a CD with a few pictures on it. And of course, those pictures made even less sense than a conscience.

There had to be some explanation that did not involve Dexter driving a truck around Miami in his sleep. Of course, most of the drivers on the road seemed to manage it, but they were at least partially awake when they started out, weren't they? And here I was, all bright-eyed and cheerfully alert and not at all the kind of guy who would ever prowl the city and kill unconsciously; no, I was the kind of guy who wanted to be awake for every moment of it. And to get right down to the bottom line, there was the night on the causeway. It was physically impossible that I could have thrown the head at my own car, wasn't it?

Unless I had made myself believe that I could be in two places at once, which made a great deal of sense – considering that the only alternative I could come up with was believing that I only *thought* I had been sitting there in my car watching someone else throw the head, when in fact I had actually thrown the head at my own car and then—

No. Ridiculous. I could not ask the last few shreds of my brain to believe in this kind of fairy tale. There would be some very simple, logical explanation, and I would find it, and even though I sounded like a man trying to convince himself that there was nothing under the bed, I said it out loud.

'There is a simple, logical explanation,' I said to myself. And because you never know who else is listening, I added, 'And there is nothing under the bed.'

But once again, the only reply was a very meaningful silence from the Dark Passenger.

In spite of the usual cheerful bloodlust of the other drivers, I found no answers on the drive home. Or to be perfectly truthful, I found no answers that made sense. There were plenty of stupid answers. But they all revolved around the same central premise, which was that all was not well inside the skull of our favorite monster, and I found this very hard to accept. Perhaps it was only that I did not feel any crazier than I had ever felt. I did not notice any missing gray tissue, I did not seem to be thinking any slower or more strangely, and so far I'd had no conversations with invisible buddies that I was aware of.

Except in my sleep, of course – and did that really count? Weren't we all crazy in our sleep? What was sleep, after all, but the process by which we dumped our insanity into a dark subconscious pit and came out on the other side ready to eat cereal instead of the neighbor's children?

And aside from the dreams I'd had, everything made sense: someone else had thrown the head at me on the causeway, left a Barbie in my apartment, and arranged the bodies in intriguing ways. Someone else, not me. Someone other than dear dark Dexter. And that someone else was finally captured, right here, in the pictures on this CD. And I would look at the pictures and prove once and for all that—

That it looked very much like the killer might be me?

Good, Dexter. Very good. I told you there was a logical explanation. Someone else who was actually me. Of course. That made wonderful sense, didn't it?

I got home and peeked into my apartment carefully. There did not appear to be anyone waiting for me. There was no reason why there should have been, of course. But knowing that this archfiend who was terrorizing the metropolis knew where I lived was a little unsettling. He had proven he was the kind of monster who might do anything – he could even come in and leave more doll parts at any time. Especially if he was me.

Which of course he was not. Certainly not. The pictures would show some small something to prove that the resemblance was only coincidental – and the fact that I was so strangely attuned to the murders was also coincidental, no doubt. Yes, this was clearly a series of perfectly logical monstrous coincidences. Perhaps I should call the Guinness Book people. I wondered what the world record was for not being sure whether you committed a string of murders?

I put on a Philip Glass CD and sat in my chair. The music stirred the emptiness inside me and after a few minutes something like my usual calm and icy logic returned. I went to my computer and turned it on. I put the CD into the drive and looked at the pictures. I zoomed in and out and did everything I knew how to do in an attempt to clean up the images. I tried things I had only heard about and things that I made up on the spot, and nothing worked. At the end I was no further along than I had been when I started. It was just not possible to get enough resolution to make the face of the man in the picture come clear. Still I stared at the pictures. I moved them around to different angles. I printed them out and held them up to the light. I did everything a normal person would do, and while I was pleased with my imitation, I did not discover anything except that the man in the picture looked like me.

I just could not get a clear impression of anything, even his clothing. He wore a shirt that could have been white, or tan, or yellow, or even light blue. The parking lot light that shone on him was one of the bright Argon anti-crime lights and it cast a pinkish-orange glow; between that and the lack of resolution in the picture it was impossible to tell any more. His pants were long, loosely cut, light-colored. Altogether a standard outfit that anyone might have worn – including me. I had clothing just like it several times over, enough to outfit an entire platoon of Dexter lookalikes.

I did manage to zoom in on the side of the truck enough to make out the letter 'A' and, below it, a 'B,' followed by an 'R' and either a 'C' or an 'O.' But the truck was angled away from the camera and that was all I could see.

None of the other pictures offered me any hints. I watched the sequence again: the man vanished, re-appeared, and then the van was gone. No good angles, no fortuitous accidental glimpses of his license plate – and no reason to say with any authority that either it was or was not deftly dreaming Dexter.

When I finally looked up from the computer night had come and it was dark outside. And I did what a normal person almost certainly would have done several hours ago: I quit. There was nothing else I could do except wait for Deborah. I would have to let my poor tormented sister haul me away to jail. After all, one way or another I was guilty. I really should be locked up. Perhaps I could even share a cell with McHale. He could teach me the rat dance.

And with that thought I did a truly wonderful thing.

I fell asleep.

24

I had no dreams, no sense of traveling outside my body; I saw no parade of ghostly images or headless, bloodless bodies. No visions of sugarplums danced in my head. There was nothing there, not even me, nothing but a dark and timeless sleep. And yet when the telephone woke me up I knew that the call was about Deborah, and I knew that she was not coming. My hand was already sweating as I grabbed up the receiver. 'Yes,' I said.

'This is Captain Matthews,' the voice said. 'I need to speak to Detective Morgan, please.'

'She isn't here,' I said, a small part of me sinking from the thought and what it meant.

'Hmmp. Aahh, well, that's not— When did she leave?'

I glanced at the clock instinctively; it was a quarter after nine and I fell deeper into the sweats. 'She was never here,' I told the captain.

'But she's signed out to your place. She's on duty – she's supposed to be there.'

'She never got here.'

'Well goddamn it,' he said. 'She said you have some evidence we need.'

'I do,' I said. And I hung up the telephone.

I did have some evidence, I was terribly sure of that. I just didn't quite know what it was. But I had to figure it out, and I did not think I had a great deal of time. Or to be more accurate, I did not think Deb had a great deal of time.

And again, I was not aware of how I knew this. I did not consciously say to myself, 'He has Deborah.' No alarming pictures of her impending fate popped into my brain. And I did not have to experience any blinding insights or think, 'Gee, Deb should have been here by now; this is unlike her.' I simply knew, as I had known when I woke up, that Deb had come for me, and she had not made it. And I knew what that meant.

He had her.

He had taken her entirely for my benefit, this I knew. He had been circling closer and closer to me – coming into my apartment, writing small messages with his victims, teasing me with hints and glimpses of what he was doing.

And now he was as close as he could get without being in the same room. He had taken Deb and he was waiting with her. Waiting for me.

But where? And how long would he wait before he became impatient and started to play without me?

And without me, I knew very well who his playmate would be – Deborah. She had turned up at my place dressed for work in her hooker outfit, absolutely gift-wrapped for him. He must have thought it was Christmas. He had her and she would be his special friend tonight. I did not want to think of her like that, taped and stretched tight and watching slow awful pieces of herself disappear forever. But that was how it would be. Under other circumstances, it might make a wonderful evening's entertainment – but not with Deborah. I was pretty sure I didn't want that, didn't want him to do anything permanent and wonderful, not tonight. Later, perhaps, with someone else. When we knew each other a little better. But not now. Not with Deborah.

And with that thought of course everything seemed better. It was just so nice to have that settled. I preferred my sister alive, rather than in small bloodless sections. Lovely, almost human of me. Now that was settled: What next? I could call Rita, perhaps take in a movie, or a walk in the park. Or, let's see – maybe, I don't know . . . save Deborah? Yes, that sounded like fun. But—

How?

I had a few clues, of course. I knew the way he thought – after all, I had been thinking that way myself. And he wanted me to find him. He had been sending that message loud and clear. If I could put all the distracting stupidity out of my head – all the dreams and New Age fairy-chasing and everything else – then I was certain that I could arrive at the logical and correct location. He would not have taken Deb unless he thought he had given me everything a clever monster would need to know in order to find him.

All right then, clever Dexter – find him. Track down the Deb-napper. Let your relentless logic slash across the back trail like an icy wolf pack. Kick the giant brain into high gear; let the wind race across the rocketing synapses of your powerful mind as it speeds to its beautiful, inevitable conclusion. Go, Dexter, go!

Dexter?

Hello? Is anybody in there?

Apparently not. I heard no wind from rocketing synapses. I was as empty as if I had never been. There was no swirl of debilitating emotions, of course, since I didn't have any emotions to swirl. But the result was just as daunting. I was as numb and drained as if I really could feel something. Deborah was gone. She was in terrible danger of becoming a fascinating work of performance art. And her only hope of maintaining any kind of existence beyond a series of still pictures tacked up on a police lab board was her battered, brain-dead brother. Poor dog-dumb Dexter, sitting in a chair with his brain running in circles, chasing its tail, howling at the moon.

I took a deep breath. Of all the times I had ever needed to be me, this was one of the foremost. I concentrated very hard and steadied me, and as a small amount of Dexter returned to fill the echo in my brain cavity, I realized just how human and stupid I had become. There was really no great mystery here. In fact, it was patently obvious. My friend had done everything but send a formal invitation reading, 'The honor of your presence is requested at the vivisection of your sister. Black heart optional.' But even this small blob of logic was wiped out of my throbbing skull by a new thought that wormed its way in, oozing rotten logic.

I had been asleep when Deb disappeared.

Could that mean that once again I had done it without knowing it? What if I had already taken Deb apart somewhere, stacked the pieces in some small, cold storage room and—

Storage room? Where had that come from?

The closed-in feeling . . . the rightness of the closet at the hockey rink . . . the cool air blowing across my spine . . . Why did that matter? Why did I keep coming back to that? Because no matter what else happened, I did; I returned to those same illogical sense memories, and there was no reason for them that I could see. What did it mean? And why did I actually give a single hummingbird's fart what it meant? Because whether it meant something or not, it was all I had to go on. I had to find a place that matched that sense of cool and pressing rightness. There was simply no other way to go: find the box. And there I would find Deb, too, and find either myself or my not-self. Wasn't that simple?

No. It wasn't simple at all, just simpleminded. It made absolutely no sense to pay any attention to the ghostly secret messages floating up at me from my dreams. Dreams had no existence in reality, left no Freddy Krueger-crossover claw marks on our wake-up world. I couldn't very well dash out of the house and drive aimlessly around in a psychic funk. I was a cool and logical being. And so it was in a cool and logical manner that I locked my apartment door and strolled to the car. I still had no idea where I was going, but the need to get there quickly had grabbed the reins and whipped me down to the building's parking area, where I kept my car. But twenty feet away from my trusty vehicle I slammed to a stop as though I had run into an invisible wall.

The dome light was on.

I had certainly not left it on – it had been daylight when I parked, and I could see that the doors were closed tightly. A casual thief would have left the door ajar to avoid the noise from closing it.

I approached slowly, not at all sure what I expected to see or whether I really wanted to see it. From five feet away I could see something in the passenger seat. I circled the car carefully and peered down at it, my nerves tingling, and peeked in. And there it was.

Barbie again. I was getting quite a collection.

This one was dressed in a little sailor hat and a shirt with a bare midriff, and tight pink hot pants. In one hand she clutched a small suitcase that said CUNARD on the side.

I opened the door and picked up the doll. I pulled the little suitcase from Barbie's hand and popped it open. Some small something fell out and rolled onto the floorboard. I picked it up. It looked an awful lot like Deborah's class ring. On the inside of the band was etched D.M., Deborah's initials.

I collapsed onto the seat, clutching Barbie in my sweaty hands. I turned her over. I bent her legs. I waved her arms. And what did you do last night, Dexter? Oh, I played with my dolls while a friend chopped up my sister.

I did not waste any time wondering how Cruise Line Hooker Barbie had gotten into my car. This was clearly a message – or a clue? But clues really ought to hint at something, and this one seemed to lead in the wrong direction. Clearly he had Debbie – but Cunard? How did that fit in with tight cold killing space? I could see no connection. But there was really only one place in Miami where it did fit.

I drove up Douglas and turned right through Coconut Grove. I had to slow down to thread my way through the parade of happy imbeciles dancing between the shops and cafés. They all seemed to have far too much time and money and very few clues beyond that, and it took me much longer than it should have to get through them, but it was hard to be too upset since I didn't actually know where I was going. Onward to somewhere; along Bayfront Drive, over to Brickle, and into downtown. I saw no huge neon signs bedecked with flashing arrows and encouraging words to direct me: 'This way to the dissection!' But I drove on, approaching American Airlines Arena and, just beyond, MacArthur Causeway. In the quick glimpse I got on the near side of the arena, I could see the superstructure of a cruise ship in Government Cut, not a Cunard Lines ship, or course, but I peered anxiously for some sign. It seemed obvious that I was not actually being directed onto a cruise ship; too crowded, too many snooping officials. But somewhere nearby, somewhere related – which of course had to mean what? No further clues. I looked hard enough at the cruise ship to melt the poop deck, but Deborah did not spring from the hold and dance down the gangway.

I looked some more. Beside the ship, cargo cranes reared up into the night sky like abandoned props from *Star Wars*. A little farther and the stacks of cargo boxes were just barely visible in the dark below the cranes, great untidy heaps of them, scattered across the ground as if a gigantic and very bored child had flung out his toy box full of building blocks. Some of the storage boxes were refrigerated. And then beyond these boxes—

Back up just for a moment, dear boy.

Who was that whispering to me, muttering what soft words to all-alone darkly driving Dexter? Who sat behind me now; whose dry chuckling filled the backseat? And why? What message was rattling into my brainless, echo-empty head?

Storage boxes.

Some of them refrigerated.

But why the storage boxes? What possible reason could I have to be interested in a pile of cold, tightly enclosed spaces?

Oh, yes. Well. Since you put it that way.

Could this be the place, the future home of the Dexter's Birthplace Museum? With authentic, lifelike exhibits, including a rare live performance by Dexter's only sister?

I yanked my steering wheel hard, cutting off a BMW with a very loud horn. I extended my middle finger, for once driving like the Miami native I was, and accelerated over the causeway.

The cruise ship was off to the left. The area with all the boxes was on the right, surrounded by a chain-link fence topped with razor wire. I drove around one time on the access road, wrestling a rising tide of certainty and a swelling chorus of what sounded like college fight songs from the Dark Passenger. The road dead-ended at a guard booth well before I got to the containers. There was a gate with several uniformed gentlemen lounging about, and no way through without answering some fairly embarrassing questions. Yes, officer, I wondered if I could come in and look around? You see, I thought it might be a good place for a friend of mine to slice up my sister.

I cut through a line of orange cones in the middle of the road thirty feet from the gate and turned around, back the way I had come. The cruise ship loomed on the right now. I turned left just before I came to the bridge back to the mainland and drove into a large area with a terminal on one end and a chain-link fence on the other. The fence was gaily decorated with signs that threatened dire punishment to anyone who strayed into the area, signed by U.S. Customs.

The fence led back to the main road along a large parking lot, empty at this time of night. I cruised its perimeter slowly, staring at the containers on the far side. These would be from foreign ports, needing to go through customs, access tightly controlled. It would be much too difficult for anyone to get in and out of this area, especially if they were carrying questionable loads of body parts and the like. I would either need to find a different area or admit that chasing vague feelings dredged up from a series of taunting dreams and a scantily clad doll was a waste of time. And the sooner I admitted that, the better my chance of finding Deb. She was not here. There was no reason she should be.

At last, a logical thought. I felt better already, and certainly would have been smug about it – if I had not seen a familiar panel truck parked right up against the inside of the fence, parked to display the lettering on the side that said ALLONZO BROTHERS. My private crowd in the basement of my brain sang too loudly for me to hear myself smirk, so I pulled over and parked. The clever-boy part of me was knocking on the front door of my brain and calling out, 'Hurry! Hurry! Go-go-go!' But around back the lizard slithered up to the window and flicked its cautious tongue, and so I sat for a long moment before I finally climbed out of the car.

I walked to the fence and stood like a bit-part actor in a World War II prison camp movie, my fingers locked in the mesh of the fence, peering hungrily at what lay beyond, only a few impossible yards away. I was sure that there must be a very simple way for a marvelously intelligent creature like me to get in, but it was some indication of the state I was in that I could not seem to fasten one thought onto another. I had to get in, but I could not. And so I stood there clinging to the fence and looking in, knowing full well that everything that mattered was right there, only a few yards away, and I was completely unable to fling my giant brain at the problem and catch a solution as it bounced back. The mind picks some very bad times to take a walk, doesn't it?

My backseat alarm clock went off. I had to move away, and right now. I was standing suspiciously in a well-guarded area, and it was night; any moment one of the guards was certain to take an interest in the handsome young man peering intelligently through the fence. I would have to move on and find some way in as I rolled along in my car. I stepped back from the fence, giving it one last, loving look. Right there where my feet had touched the fence, a break was barely visible. The fence links had been snipped just enough to allow entry for one human being, or even a good copy like me. The flap was pinned in place by the weight of the parked truck so it would not swing out and give itself away. It must have been done recently, this evening, since the truck had arrived.

My final invitation.

I backed away slowly, feeling an automatic hello-there kind of absent-minded smile climb up on my face as a disguise. Hello there, officer, just out for a walk. Lovely evening for a dismemberment, isn't it? I cheerfully scuffed over to my car, looking around at nothing but the moon over the water, whistling a happy tune as I climbed in and drove away. No one seemed to be paying any attention whatsoever – except, of course, for the Hallelujah chorus in my mind. I nudged my car into a parking place over by the cruise ship office, perhaps one hundred yards from my little handmade gate into Paradise. A few other cars were scattered nearby. No one would pay any mind to mine.

But as I parked another car slid into the spot next to me, a light blue Chevy with a woman behind the wheel. I sat still for a moment. So did she. I opened my door and got out.

So did Detective LaGuerta.

25

I have always been very good at awkward social situations, but I must admit that this one had me stumped. I just didn't know what to say, and for a moment I stared at LaGuerta and she looked back at me with her eyes unblinking and her fangs slightly exposed, like a predatory feline trying to decide whether to play with you or eat you. I could think of no remark that did not begin with a stammer, and she seemed interested only in watching me. So we simply stood there for a long moment. At last she broke the ice with a light quip.

'What's in there?' she asked, nodding toward the fence, some one hundred yards away.

'Why, Detective!' I gushed, hoping that she wouldn't notice what she had said, I suppose. 'What are you doing here?'

'I followed you. What's in there?'

'In there?' I said. I know, a really dumb remark, but honestly, I had just about run out of the smart ones and I can't be expected to come up with something good under such circumstances.

She cocked her head to one side and poked her tongue out, letting it run along her bottom lip; slowly to the left, right, left, and back into her mouth again. Then she nodded. 'You must think I'm stupid,' she said. And of course that thought had crossed my mind fleetingly once or twice, but it didn't seem politic to say so. 'But you got to remember,' she went on, 'I'm a full detective, and this is Miami. How do you think I got that, huh?'

'Your looks?' I asked, giving her a dashing smile. It never hurts to compliment a woman.

She showed me her lovely set of teeth, even brighter in the high crime lights that lit up the parking area. 'That's good,' she said, and she moved her lips into a strange half smile that hollowed her cheeks and made her look old. 'That's the kind of shit I used to fall for when I thought you liked me.'

'I do like you, Detective,' I told her, perhaps a little too eagerly. She didn't seem to hear me.

'But then you push me on the floor like I'm some kind of pig, and I wonder what's wrong with me? I got bad breath? And it hits me. It's not me.

It's you. There's something wrong about you.'

Of course she was right, but it still hurt to hear her say so. 'I don't— What do you mean?'

She shook her head again. 'Sergeant Doakes wants to kill you and he does-n't even know why. I should've listened to him. Something is wrong about you. And you're connected to this hooker stuff some way.'

'Connected— What do you mean?'

This time there was an edge of savage glee to the smile she showed me and the trace of accent snuck back into her voice. 'You can save the cute acting for your lawyer. And maybe a judge. 'Cause I think I got you now.' She looked at me for a long hard moment and her dark eyes glittered. She looked as inhu-man as I am and it made a small shiver run across the back of my neck. Had I truly underestimated her? Was she really this good?

'And so you followed me?'

More teeth. 'That's right, yeah,' she said. 'Why are you looking around at the fence? What's in there?'

I am sure that under ordinary circumstances I would have thought of this before, but I plead duress. It truly didn't occur to me until that very moment. But when it did, it was like a small and painful light flashing on. 'When did you pick me up? At my house? At what time?'

'Why do you keep changing the subject? Something's in there, huh?'

'Detective, please – this could be very important. When and where did you start to follow me?'

She studied me for a minute, and I began to realize that I had, in fact, underestimated her. There was a great deal more to this woman than politi-cal instinct. She really did seem to have something extra. I was still not con-vinced that any of it was intelligence, but she did have patience, and sometimes that was more important than smarts in her line of work. She was willing to simply wait and watch me and keep repeating her question until she got an answer. And then she would probably ask the same question a few more times, wait and watch some more, to see what I would do. Ordinarily I could outwit her, but I could not possibly outwait her, not tonight. So I put on my best humble face and repeated myself. 'Please, Detective . . .'

She stuck her tongue out again, and then finally put it away. 'Okay,' she said. 'When your sister was gone for a few hours and no word where, I started to think maybe she's up to something. And I know she can't do anything her-self, so where would she go?' She arched an eyebrow at me, then continued in a triumphant tone. 'To your place, that's where! To talk with you!' She bobbed her head, pleased with her deductive logic. 'And so I think about you for a while. How you're always showing up and looking, even when you don't have to. How you figure out those serial killers sometimes, except this one? And then how you fuck me over with that stupid list, make me look stupid, push me on the fucking floor—' Her face looked harder, a little older again for a moment. Then she smiled and went on. 'I said something out loud, in my office, and Sergeant Doakes says, "I told you about him but you don't listen." And all of a sudden it's your big handsome face all over the place and it shouldn't be.' She shrugged. 'So I went to your place, too.'

'When? At what time, did you notice?'

'Naw,' she said. 'But I'm only there like twenty minutes and then you come out and play with your faggot Barbie doll and then drive over here.'

'Twenty minutes—' So she hadn't been there in time to see who or what had taken Deborah. And quite probably she was telling the truth and had simply followed me to see – to see what?

'But why follow me at all?'

She shrugged. 'You're connected to this thing. Maybe you didn't do it, I don't know. But I'm gonna find out. And some of what I find is gonna stick to you. What's in there, in those boxes? You gonna tell me, or we just going to stand here all night?'

In her own way, she had put her finger right on it. We could not stand here all night. We could not, I was sure, stand here much longer at all before terrible things happened to Deborah. If they hadn't already happened. We had to go, right now, go find him and stop him. But how did I do that with LaGuerta along for the ride? I felt like a comet with a tail I didn't want.

I took a deep breath. Rita had once taken me to a New Age Health Awareness Workshop which had stressed the importance of deep cleansing breaths. I took one. I did not feel any cleaner after my breath, but at least it made my brain whirl into brief action, and I realized I would have to do something I had rarely done before – tell the truth. LaGuerta was still staring at me, waiting for an answer.

'I think the killer is in there,' I told LaGuerta. 'And I think he has Officer Morgan.'

She watched me for a moment without moving. 'Okay,' she said at last. 'And so you come stand at the fence and look in? 'Cause you love your sister so much you want to watch?'

'Because I wanted to get in. I was looking for a way in through the fence.'

'Because you forget that you work for the police?'

Well there it was, of course. She had actually jumped right to the real problem spot, and all by herself, too. I had no good answer for that. This whole business of telling the truth just never seems to work without some kind of awkward unpleasantness. 'I just – I wanted to be sure, before I made a big fuss.'

She nodded. 'Uh-huh. That's really good,' she said. 'But I tell you what I think. Either you did something bad, or you know about it. And you're either hiding it, or you wanna find it by yourself.'

'By myself? But why would I want that?'

She shook her head to show how stupid that was. 'So you get all the credit.

You and that sister of yours. Think I didn't figure that out? I told you I'm not stupid.'

'I'm not your slasher, Detective,' I said, throwing myself on her mercy and now completely confident that she had even less than I did. 'But I think he's in there, in one of the storage boxes.'

She licked her lips. 'Why do you think that?'

I hesitated, but she kept her unblinking lizard stare on me. As uncomfortable as it made me, I had to tell her one more piece of truth. I nodded at the Allonzo Brothers van parked just inside the fence. 'That's his truck.'

'Ha,' she said, and at last she blinked. Her focus left me for a moment and seemed to wander away into some deep place. Her hair? Her makeup? Her career? I couldn't tell. But there were a lot of awkward questions a good detective might have asked here: How did I know that was his truck? How had I found it here? Why was I so sure he hadn't simply dumped the truck and gone somewhere else? But in the final analysis LaGuerta was not a good detective; she simply nodded, licked her lips again, and said, 'How are we gonna find him in there in all that?'

Clearly, I really had underestimated her. She had gone from 'you' to 'we' with no visible transition. 'Don't you want to call for backup?' I asked her. 'This is a very dangerous man.' I admit I was only needling her. But she took it very seriously.

'If I don't catch this guy by myself, in two weeks I'm a meter maid,' she said. 'I got my weapon. Nobody's gonna get away from me. I'll call for backup when I have him.' She studied me without blinking. 'And if he's not in there, I'll give them you.'

It seemed like a good idea to let that go. 'Can you get us through the gate?'

She laughed. ' 'Course I can. I got my badge, get us through anywhere. And then what?'

This was the tricky part. If she went for this, I might well be home free. 'Then we split up and search until we find him.'

She studied me. Again I saw in her face the thing I had seen when she first got out of her car – the look of a predator weighing her prey, wondering when and where to strike, and how many claws to use. It was horrible – I actually found myself warming to the woman. 'Okay,' she said at last, and tilted her head toward her car. 'Get in.'

I got in. She drove us back out onto the road and over to the gate. Even at this hour there was some traffic. Most of it seemed to be people from Ohio looking for their cruise ship, but a few of them wound up at the gate, where the guards sent them back the way they came. Detective LaGuerta cut ahead of them all, bulling her big Chevy to the front of the line. Their Midwest driving skills were no match for a Miami Cuban woman with good medical insurance driving a car she didn't care about. There was a blare of horns and some muffled shouting and we were at the guard booth.

The guard leaned out, a thin, muscular black man. 'Lady, you can't—'

She held up her badge. 'Police. Open the gate.' She said it with such hard-edged authority that I almost jumped out of the car to open the gate myself.

But the guard froze, took a breath through his mouth, and glanced nervously back into the booth. 'What you want with—'

'Open the fucking gate, Rental,' she told him, jiggling her badge, and he finally unfroze.

'Lemme see the badge,' he said. LaGuerta held it up limply, making him take the extra step over to peer at it. He frowned at it and found nothing to object to. 'Uh-huh,' he said. 'Can you tell me what you want in there?'

'I can tell you that if you don't open the gate in two seconds I'm gonna put you in the trunk of my car and take you downtown to a holding cell full of gay bikers and then I'm gonna forget where I put you.'

The guard stood up. 'Just trying to help,' he said, and called over his shoulder, 'Tavio, open the gate!'

The gate went up and LaGuerta gunned her car through. 'Sonnova bitch got something going he doesn't want me to know about,' she said. There was amusement in her voice to go with the rising edge of excitement. 'But I don't care about smuggling tonight.' She looked at me. 'Where we going?'

'I don't know,' I said. 'I guess we should start over where he left his truck.'

She nodded, accelerating down the path between stacks of storage boxes. 'If he's got a body to carry, he probably parked pretty close to wherever he was going.' As we got closer to the fence she slowed down, nosing the car quietly to within fifty feet of the truck and then stopping. 'Let's take a look at the fence,' she said, slamming the transmission into park and sliding out of the car as it rocked to a stop.

I followed. LaGuerta stepped in something she didn't like and lifted her foot to look at her shoe. 'Goddamnit,' she said. I moved past her, feeling my pulse hammering loud and fast, and went to the truck. I walked around it, trying the doors. They were locked, and although there were two small back windows, these were painted over from the inside. I stood on the bumper and tried to peek in anyway, but there were no holes in the paint job. There was nothing more to be seen on this side, but I squatted anyway and looked on the ground. I felt rather than heard LaGuerta slither up behind me.

'What you got?' she asked, and I stood.

'Nothing,' I said. 'The back windows are painted over on the inside.'

'Can you see in the front?'

I went around to the front of the truck. It was bare of any hint as well. Inside the windshield, a pair of the sunscreens so popular in Florida had been unfolded across the dashboard, blocking out any possible view into the cab. I climbed on the front bumper and up onto the hood, crawled along it from right to left, but there were no gaps in the sunscreen. 'Nothing,' I said and climbed down.

'Okay,' LaGuerta said, looking at me with lidded eyes and just the smallest tip of her tongue protruding. 'Which way you wanna go?'

This way, someone whispered deep inside my brain. *Over here.* I glanced to the right, where the chuckling mental fingers had pointed and then back to LaGuerta, who was staring at me with her unblinking hungry tiger stare. 'I'll go left and circle around,' I said. 'Meet you halfway.'

'Okay,' LaGuerta said with a feral smile. 'But I go left.'

I tried to look surprised and unhappy, and I suppose I managed a reasonable facsimile, because she watched me and then nodded. 'Okay,' she repeated, and turned down the first row of stacked shipping containers.

Then I was alone with my shy interior friend. And now what? Now that I had tricked LaGuerta into leaving me the right-hand path, what did I do with it? After all, I had no reason to think it was any better than the left-hand, or for that matter, better than standing by the fence and juggling coconuts. There was only my sibilant internal clamor to direct me, and was that really enough? When you are an icy tower of pure reason as I have always been, you naturally look for logical hints to direct your course of action. Just as naturally, you ignore the nonobjective irrational screeching of loud musical voices from the bottom floor of your brain that try to send you reeling along the path, no matter how urgent they have become in the rippling light of the moon.

And as to the rest, the particulars of where I should go now – I looked around, down the long irregular rows of containers. Off to the side where LaGuerta had gone spike-heeling along, there were several rows of brightly colored truck trailers. And in front of me, stretching off to the right, were the shipping containers.

Suddenly, I was very uncertain. I didn't like the feeling. I closed my eyes. The moment I did, the whispering became a cloud of sound and without knowing why I found myself moving toward a clutter of shipping containers down near the water. I had no conscious notion that these particular containers were any different or better or that this direction was more proper or rewarding. My feet simply jerked into motion and I followed them. It was as if they were tracing some path only the toes could see, or as if some compelling pattern was being sung by the whisper-wail of my internal chorus, and my feet translated and dragged me along.

As they moved the sound grew inside me, a muted hilarious roar, pulling me faster than my feet, yanking me clumsily down the crooked path between boxes with powerful invisible jerks. And yet at the same time a new voice, small and reasonable, was pushing me backward, telling me I did not want to be here of all places, yammering at me to run, go home, get away from this place, and it made no more sense than any of the other voices. I was pulled forward and pushed back at the same time so powerfully that I could not make my legs work properly and I stumbled and fell flat-faced onto the hard rocky ground. I rose to my knees, mouth dry and heart pounding, and paused to finger a rip in my beautiful Dacron bowling shirt. I pushed my fingertip through the hole and wiggled it at myself. Hello, Dexter, where are you going? Hello, Mr. Finger. I don't know, but I'm almost there. I hear my friends calling.

And so I climbed to suddenly unsteady feet and listened. I heard it clearly now, even with my eyes open, and felt it so strongly I could not even walk. I stood for a moment, leaning against one of the containers. A very sobering thought, as if I needed one. Something nameless was born in this place, something that lived in the darkest hidey-hole of the thing that was Dexter, and for the first time that I could remember I was scared. I did not want to be here where horrible things lurked. Yet I had to be here to find Deborah. I was being ripped in half by an invisible tug-of-war. I felt like Sigmund Freud's poster child, and I wanted to go home and go to bed.

But the moon roared in the dark sky above me, the water howled along Government Cut, and the mild night breeze shrieked over me like a convention of banshees, forcing my feet forward. And the singing swelled within me like some kind of gigantic mechanical choir, urging me on, reminding me of how to move my feet, pushing me lock-kneed down the rows of boxes. My heart hammered and yammered, my short gasps of breath were much too loud, and for the first time I could remember I felt weak, woozy, and stupid – like a human being, like a very small and helpless human being.

I staggered along the strangely familiar path on borrowed feet until I could stagger no more and once again I put an arm out to lean against a box, a box with an air-conditioning compressor attached, pounding away at the back and mixing with the shriek of the night, all thumping in my head so loudly now that I could hardly see. And as I leaned against the box the door swung open.

The inside of the box was lit by a pair of battery-powered hurricane lamps. Against the back wall there was a temporary operating table made of packing crates.

And held unmoving in place on the table was my dear sister Deborah.

26

For a few seconds it didn't really seem necessary to breathe. I just looked. Long, slick strands of duct tape wrapped around my sister's arms and legs. She wore gold lamé hot pants and a skimpy silk blouse tied above her navel. Her hair was pulled back tight, her eyes were unnaturally wide, and she breathed rapidly through her nose, since her mouth, too, was held closed by a strip of duct tape that went across her lips and down to the table to hold her head still.

I tried to think of something to say, but realized my mouth was too dry to say it and so I just looked. Deborah looked back. There were many things in her eyes, but the plainest was fear, and that held me there in the doorway. I had never seen that look on her before and I was not sure what to think about it. I took half a step toward Deborah and she flinched against the duct tape. Afraid? Of course – but afraid of me? I was here to rescue her, most likely. Why should she be afraid of me? Unless—

Had I done this?

During my little 'nap' earlier this evening what if Deborah had arrived at my apartment, as scheduled, and found my Dark Passenger behind the wheel of the Dexter-mobile? And unknown to me I had brought her here and taped her so tantalizingly to the table without consciously realizing it – which made absolutely no sense, naturally. Had I raced home and left myself the Barbie doll, then gone upstairs and flopped on the bed and woke up as 'me' again, like I was running some kind of homicidal relay race? Impossible: but . . .

How else had I known to come here?

I shook my head; there was no way I could have picked this one cold box out of all the places in Miami, unless I already knew where it was. And I did. The only way that could be possible was if I had been here before. And if not tonight with Deb, then when and with whom?

'I was almost sure this was the right spot,' a voice said, a voice so very like my own that for a moment I thought I had said it, and I wondered what I meant by that.

The hair went up on the back of my neck and I took another half step toward Deborah – and he came forward out of the shadow. The soft light of the lanterns lit him up and our eyes met; for a moment the room spun back and forth and I did not quite know where I was. My sight shifted between me at the door and him at the small makeshift worktable, and I saw me seeing him, then I saw him seeing me. In a blinding flash I saw me on the floor, sitting still and unmoving, and I did not know what that vision meant. Very unsettling – and then I was myself again, although I was somewhat uncertain what that meant.

'Almost sure,' he said again, a soft and happy voice like Mr. Rogers's troubled child. 'But now here you are, so this must be the right place. Don't you think?'

There is no pretty way for me to say this, but the truth is, I stared at him with my mouth hanging open. I am quite sure I was almost drooling. I just stared. It was him. There was no question about it. Here was the man in the pictures we had found on the webcam, the man both Deb and I had thought might very well be me.

This close I could see that he was not, in fact, me; not quite, and I felt a small wave of gratitude at that realization. Hurray – I was someone else. I was not completely crazy yet. Seriously antisocial, of course, and somewhat sporadically homicidal, nothing wrong with that. But not crazy. There was somebody else, and he was not me. Three cheers for Dexter's brain.

But he was very much like me. Perhaps an inch or two taller, thicker through the shoulders and chest as though he had been doing a great deal of heavy weight lifting. That, combined with the paleness of his face, made me think that he might have been in prison recently. Behind the pallor, though, his face was very similar to mine; the same nose and cheekbones, the same look in the eyes that said the lights were on but nobody was home. Even his hair had the same awkward half wave to it. He did not really look like me, but very similar.

'Yes,' he said. 'It is a little bit of a shock the first time, isn't it?'

'Just a little,' I said. 'Who are you? And why is all this so—' I left it unfinished, because I did not know what all this was.

He made a face, a very Dexter-disappointed face. 'Oh, dear. And I was so sure you had figured it out.'

I shook my head. 'I don't even know how I got here,' I said.

He smiled softly. 'Somebody else driving tonight?' As the hair stood up on the back of my neck he chuckled just a little, a mechanical sound that was not worth mentioning – except that the lizard voice from the underside of my brain matched it note for note. 'And it isn't even a full moon, is it?'

'But not actually an empty moon,' I said. Hardly great wit, but some kind of attempt, which under the circumstances seemed significant. And I realized that I was half drunk with the realization that here at last was someone who *knew*. He was not making idle remarks that coincidentally stabbed into my own personal bull's-eye. It was his bull's-eye, too. He knew. For the first time I could look across the gigantic gulf between my eyes and someone else's and say without any kind of worry, *He is like me.*

Whatever it was that I was, he was one, too.

'But seriously,' I said. 'Who are you?'

His face stretched into a Dexter-the-Cheshire-Cat smile, but because it was so much like my own I could see there was no real happiness behind it. 'What do you remember from before?' he said. And the echo of that question bounced off the container's walls and nearly shattered my brain.

27

What do you remember from before? Harry had asked me.

Nothing, Dad.

Except—

Images tugged at my underbrain. Mental pictures – dreams? memories? – very clear visions, whatever they were. And they were here – this room? No; impossible. This box could not have been here very long, and I had certainly never been in it before. But the tightness of the space, the cool air flowing from the thumping compressor, the dim light – everything called out to me in a symphony of homecoming. Of course it had not been this same box – but the pictures were so clear, so similar, so completely almost-right, except for—

I blinked; an image fluttered behind my eyes. I closed them.

And the inside of a different box jumped back out at me. There were no cartons in this other box. And there were – things over there. Over by . . . Mommy? I could see her face there, and she was somehow hiding and peeking up over the – things – just her face showing, her unwinking unblinking unmoving face. And I wanted to laugh at first, because Mommy had hidden so well. I could not see the rest of her, just her face. She must have made a hole in the floor. She must be hiding in the hole and peeking up – but why didn't she answer me now that I saw her? Why didn't she even wink? And even when I called her really loud she didn't answer, didn't move, didn't do anything but look at me. And without Mommy, I was alone.

But no – not quite alone. I turned my head and the memory turned with me. I was not alone. Someone was with me. Very confusing at first, because it was me – but it was someone else – but it looked like me – but we both looked like me—

But what were we doing here in this box? And why wasn't Mommy moving? She should help us. We were sitting here in a deep puddle, of, of – Mommy should move, get us out of this, this—

'Blood . . . ?' I whispered.

'You remembered,' he said behind me. 'I'm so happy.'

I opened my eyes. My head was pounding hideously. I could almost see the other room superimposed on this one. And in this other room tiny Dexter sat right *there*. I could put my feet on the spot. And the other me sat beside me, but he was not me, of course; he was some other someone, a someone I knew as well as myself, a someone named—

'Biney . . . ?' I said hesitantly. The sound was the same, but the name did not seem quite right.

He nodded happily. 'That's what you called me. At the time you had trouble saying Brian. You said Biney.' He patted my hand. 'That's all right. It's nice to have a nickname.' He paused, his face smiling but his eyes locked onto my face. 'Little brother.'

I sat down. He sat next to me.

'What—' was all I could manage to say.

'Brother,' he repeated. 'Irish twins. You were born only one year after me. Our mother was somewhat careless.' His face twisted into a hideous, very happy smile. 'In more ways than one,' he said.

I tried to swallow. It didn't work. He – Brian – my brother – went on.

'I'm just guessing with some of this,' he said. 'But I had a little time on my hands, and when I was encouraged to learn a useful trade, I did. I got very good at finding things with the computer. I found the old police files. Mommy dearest hung out with a very naughty crowd. In the import business, just like me. Of course, their product was a little more sensitive.' He reached behind him into a carton and pulled out a handful of hats with a springing panther on them. 'My things are made in Taiwan. Theirs came from Colombia. My best guess is that Mumsy and her friends tried a little independent project with some product that strictly speaking did not actually belong to her, and her business associates were unhappy with her spirit of independence and decided to discourage her.'

He put the hats carefully back in the carton and I felt him looking at me, but I could not even turn my head. After a moment he looked away.

'They found us here,' he said. 'Right here.' His hand went to the floor and touched the exact spot where the small other not-me had been sitting in that long-ago other box. 'Two and a half days later. Stuck to the floor in dried blood, an inch deep.' His voice here was grating, horrible; he said that awful word, *blood*, just the way I would have said it, with contemptuous and utter loathing. 'According to the police reports, there were several men here, too. Probably three or four. One or more of them may well have been our father. Of course, the chain saw made identification very difficult. But they are fairly sure there was only one woman. Our dear old mother. You were three years old. I was four.'

'But,' I said. Nothing else came out.

'Quite true,' Brian told me. 'And you were very hard to find, too. They are so fussy with adoption records in this state. But I did find you, little brother. I did, didn't I?' Once again he patted my hand, a strange gesture I had never seen from anyone in my life. Of course, I had never before seen a flesh-and-blood sibling, either. Perhaps hand-patting was something I should practice with my brother, or with Deborah – and I realized with a small flutter of concern that I had forgotten all about Deborah.

I looked over at her, some six feet away, all neatly taped into place.

'She's fine,' my brother said. 'I didn't want to begin without you.'

It may seem a very strange thing for my first coherent question, but I asked him, 'How did you know I would want to?' Which perhaps made it sound as though I truly did want to – and of course I didn't really want to explore Deborah. Certainly not. And yet – here was my big brother, wanting to play, surely a rare enough opportunity. More than our ties of mutual parent, far more, was the fact that he was like me. 'You couldn't really know,' I said, sounding far more uncertain than I would have thought possible.

'I didn't know,' he said. 'But I thought there was a very good chance. The same thing happened to both of us.' His smile broadened and he lifted a fore-finger into the air. 'The Traumatic Event – you know that term? Have you done any reading on monsters like us?'

'Yes,' I said. 'And Harry – my foster father – but he would never say exactly what had happened.'

Brian waved a hand around at the interior of the little box. 'This happened, little brother. The chain saw, the flying body parts, the . . . *blood*—' With that same fearful emphasis again. 'Two and a half days of sitting in the stuff. A wonder we survived at all, isn't it? Almost enough to make you believe in God.' His eyes glittered and, for some reason or other, Deborah squirmed and made a muffled noise. He ignored her. 'They thought you were young enough to recover. I was just a bit over the age limit. But we both suffered a classic Traumatic Event. All the literature agrees. It made me what I am – and I had a thought that it might do the same for you.'

'It did,' I said, 'exactly the same.'

'Isn't that nice,' he said. 'Family ties.'

I looked at him. My brother. That alien word. If I had said it aloud I am sure I would have stuttered. It was utterly impossible to believe – and even more absurd to deny it. He looked like me. We liked the same things. He even had my wretched taste in jokes.

'I just—' I shook my head.

'Yes,' he said. 'It takes a minute to get used to the idea that there are two of us, doesn't it?'

'Perhaps slightly longer,' I said. 'I don't know if I—'

'Oh, dear, are we being squeamish? After what happened? Two and a half days of sitting here, bubba. Two little boys, sitting for two and a half days in *blood*,' he said, and I felt sick, dizzy, heart floundering, head hammering.

'No,' I gagged, and I felt his hand on my shoulder.

'It doesn't matter,' he said. 'What matters is what happens now.'

'What – happens,' I said.

'Yes. What happens. Now.' He made a small, strange, snuffling, gurgling noise that was surely intended to sound like laughter, but perhaps he had not learned to fake it as well as I had. 'I think I should say something like: My whole life has been leading up to this!' He repeated the snuffling sound. 'Of course, neither one of us could manage that with real feeling. After all, we can't actually feel anything, can we? We've both spent our lives playing a part. Moving through this world reciting lines and pretending we belong in a world made for human beings, and never really human ourselves. And always, forever, reaching for a way to *feel* something! Reaching, little brother, for a moment just like this! Real, genuine, unfaked feeling! It takes your breath away, doesn't it?'

And it did. My head was whirling and I did not dare to close my eyes again for fear of what might be waiting there for me. And, far worse, my brother was right beside me, watching me, demanding that I be myself, be just like him. And to be myself, to be his brother, to be who I was, I had to, had to – what? My eyes turned, all by themselves, toward Deborah.

'Yes,' he said, and all the cold happy fury of the Dark Passenger was in his voice now. 'I knew you'd figure it out. This time we do it together,' he said.

I shook my head, but not very convincingly. 'I can't,' I said.

'You have to,' he said, and we were both right. The feather touch on my shoulder again, almost matching the push from Harry that he could never understand and yet seemed every bit as powerful as my brother's hand, as it lifted me to my feet and pushed me forward; one step, two – Deborah's unblinking eyes were locked onto mine, but with that other presence behind me I couldn't tell her that I was certainly not going to—

'Together,' he said. 'One more time. Out with the old. In with the new. Onward, upward, inward—!' Another half step – Deborah's eyes were yelling at me, but—

He was beside me now, standing with me, and something gleamed in his hand, two somethings. 'One for all, both for one— Did you ever read *The Three Musketeers*?' He flipped one knife into the air; it arced up and into his left hand and he held it out toward me. The weak dim light grew on the flat of the blades he held up and burned into me, matched only by the gleam in Brian's eyes. 'Come on, Dexter. Little brother. Take the knife.' His teeth shone like the knives. 'Showtime.'

Deborah in her tightly wrapped tape made a thrashing sound. I looked up at her. There was frantic impatience in her eyes, and a growing madness, too. Come on, Dexter! Was I really thinking of doing this to her? Cut her loose and let's go home. Okay, Dexter? Dexter? Hello, Dexter? It is you, isn't it?

And I didn't know.

'Dexter,' Brian said. 'Of course I don't mean to influence your decision. But ever since I learned I had a brother just like me, this is all I could think about. And you feel the same, I can see it in your face.'

'Yes,' I said, still not taking my eyes off Deb's very anxious face, 'but does it have to be her?'

'Why not her? What is she to you?'

What indeed. My eyes were locked onto Deborah's. She was not actually my sister, not really, not a real relation of any kind, not at all. Of course I was very fond of her, but—

But what? Why did I hesitate? Of course the thing was impossible. I knew it was unthinkable, even as I thought it. Not just because it was Deb, although it was, of course. But such a strange thought came into my poor dismal battered head and I could not bat it away: *What would Harry say?*

And so I stood uncertain, because no matter how much I wanted to begin I knew what Harry would say. He had already said it. It was unchangeable Harry truth: *Chop up the bad guys, Dexter. Don't chop up your sister.* But Harry had never foreseen anything like this – how could he? He had never imagined when he wrote the Code of Harry that I would be faced with a choice like this; to side with Deborah – not my real sister – or to join my authentic 100 percent real live brother in a game that I so very much wanted to play. And Harry could not have conceived that when he set me on my path. Harry had never known that I had a brother who would—

But wait a moment. Hold the phone, please. Harry did know – Harry had been there when it happened, hadn't he? And he had kept it to himself, never told me I had a brother. All those lonely empty years when I thought I was the only me there was – and he knew I was not, knew and had not told me. The most import-ant single fact about me – I was not alone – and he had kept it from me. What did I really owe Harry now, after this fantastic betrayal?

And more to the immediate point, what did I owe this squirming lump of animal flesh quivering beneath me, this creature masquerading as my sibling? What could I possibly owe her in comparison to my bond with Brian, my own flesh, my brother, a living replication of my selfsame precious DNA?

A drop of sweat rolled across Deborah's forehead and into her eye. She blinked at it frantically, making ugly squinting faces in an effort to keep watching me and clear the sweat out of her eye at the same time. She really looked somewhat pathetic, helplessly taped and struggling like a dumb animal; a dumb, human animal. Not at all like me, like my brother; not at all clever clean no-mess bloodless razor-sharp Moondancer snicker-snee Dexter and his very own brother.

'Well?' he said, and I heard impatience, judgment, the beginning of disappointment.

I closed my eyes. The room dove around me, got darker, and I could not move. There was Mommy watching me, unblinking. I opened my eyes. My brother stood so close behind me I could feel his breath on my neck. My sister looked up at me, her eyes as wide and unblinking as Mommy's. And the look she gave me held me, as Mommy's had held me. I closed my eyes; Mommy. I opened my eyes; Deborah.

I took the knife.

There was a small noise and a rush of warm wind came into the cool air of the box. I spun around.

LaGuerta stood in the doorway, a nasty little automatic pistol in her hand.

'I knew you'd try this,' she said. 'I should shoot you both. Maybe all three,' she said, glancing at Deborah, then back at me. 'Hah,' she said, looking at the blade in my hand. 'Sergeant Doakes should see this. He was right about you.' And she pointed the gun toward me, just for half a second.

It was long enough. Brian moved fast, faster than I would have thought possible. Still, LaGuerta got off one shot and Brian stumbled slightly as he slid the blade into LaGuerta's midsection. For a moment they stood like that, and then both of them were on the floor, unmoving.

A small pool of blood began to spread across the floor, the mingled blood of them both, Brian and LaGuerta. It was not deep, it did not spread far, but I shrank away from it, the horrible stuff, with something very near to panic. I only took two backward steps and then I bumped into something that made muffled sounds to match my own panic.

Deborah. I ripped the duct tape off her mouth.

'Jesus Christ that hurt,' she said. 'For God's sake let me out of this shit and quit acting like a fucking lunatic.'

I looked down at Deborah. The tape had left a ring of blood around the outside of her lips, awful red blood that drove me back behind my eyes and into the yesterday box with Mommy. And she lay there – just like Mommy. Just like last time with the cool air of the box lifting the hair on my neck and the dark shadows chattering around us. Just exactly like last time in the way she lay there all taped and staring and waiting like some kind of—

'Goddamn it,' she said. 'Come on, Dex. Snap out of it.'

And yet this time I had a knife, and she was still helpless, and I could change everything now, I could –

'Dexter?' said Mommy.

I mean, Deborah. Of course that's what I meant. Not Mommy at all who had left us here in this same place just like this, left us in this place where it began and now might finally finish, with a burning absolutely must-do-it already on its large dark horse and galloping along under the wonderful moon and the one thousand intimate voices whispering, *Do it – do it now – do it and everything can change – the way it should be – back with—*

'Mommy?' someone said.

'Dexter, come on,' said Mommy. I mean Deborah. But the knife was moving. 'Dexter, for Christ's sake, cut the shit! It's me! Debbie!'

I shook my head and of course it was Deborah, but I could not stop the knife. 'I know, Deb. I'm really very sorry.' The knife crept higher. I could only watch it, couldn't stop it now for anything. One small spiderweb touch of Harry still whipped at me, demanding that I pay attention and get squared away, but it was so small and weak, and the need was big, strong, stronger than it had ever been before, because this was everything, the beginning and the end, and it lifted me up and out of myself and sent me washing away down the tunnel between the boy in the blood and the last chance to make it right. This would change everything, would pay back Mommy, would show her what she had done. Because Mommy should have saved us, and this time had to be different. Even Deb had to see that.

'Put the knife down, Dexter.' Her voice was a little calmer now, but those other voices were so much louder that I could barely hear her. I tried to put the knife down, really I did, but I only managed to lower it a few inches.

'I'm sorry, Deb, I just can't,' I said, fighting to speak at all with the rising howl around me of the storm that had built for twenty-five years – and now with my brother and me brought together like thunderheads on a dark and moony night—

'Dexter!' said wicked Mommy, who wanted to leave us here alone in the awful cold blood, and the voice of my brother inside hissed out with mine, 'Bitch!' and the knife went all the way back up—

A noise came from the floor. LaGuerta? I couldn't tell, and it didn't matter. I had to finish, had to do this, had to let this happen now.

'Dexter,' Debbie said. 'I'm your sister. You don't want to do this to me. What would Daddy say?' And that hurt, I'll admit it, but— 'Put down the knife, Dexter.'

Another sound behind me, and a small gurgle. The knife in my hand went up.

'Dexter, look out!' Deborah said and I turned.

Detective LaGuerta was on one knee, gasping, straining to raise her suddenly very heavy weapon. Up came the barrel, slowly, slowly – pointed at my foot, my knee—

But did it matter? Because this was going to happen now no matter what and even though I could see LaGuerta's finger tighten on the trigger the knife in my hand did not even slow down.

'She's going to shoot you, Dex!' Deb called, sounding somewhat frantic now. And the gun was pointed at my navel, LaGuerta's face was screwing itself into a frown of tremendous concentration and effort and she really was going to shoot me. I half turned toward LaGuerta but my knife was still fighting its way down toward—

'Dexter!' said Mommy/Deborah on the table, but the Dark Passenger called louder and moved forward, grabbing my hand and guiding the knife down—

'Dex—!'

'*You're a good kid, Dex,*' whispered Harry from behind in his feather-hard ghost voice, just enough to twitch the knife so very little up again.

'I can't help it,' I whispered back, so very much growing into the handle of the quivering blade.

'*Choose what . . . or WHO . . . you kill,*' he said with the hard and endless blue of his eyes now watching me from Deborah's same eyes, watching now loud enough to push the knife a full half inch away. '*There are plenty of people who deserve it*,' said Harry so softly above the rising angry yammer of the stampede inside.

The tip of the knife winked and froze in place. The Dark Passenger could not send it down. Harry could not pull it away. And there we were.

Behind me I heard a rasping sound, a heavy thump, and then a moan so very full of emptiness that it crawled across my shoulders like a silk scarf on spider legs. I turned.

LaGuerta lay with her gun hand stretched out, pinned to the floor by Brian's knife, her lower lip trapped between her teeth and her eyes alive with pain. Brian crouched beside her, watching the fear scamper across her face. He was breathing hard through a dark smile.

'Shall we clean up, brother?' he said.

'I . . . can't,' I said.

My brother lurched to his feet and stood in front of me, weaving slightly from side to side. 'Can't?' he said. 'I don't think I know that word.' He pried the knife from my fingers and I could not stop him and I could not help him.

His eyes were on Deborah now, but his voice whipped across me and blasted at the phantom Harry fingers on my shoulder. 'Must, little brother. Absolutely *must*. No other way.' He gasped and bent double for a moment, slowly straightening, slowly raising the knife. 'Do I have to remind you of the importance of family?'

'No,' I said, with both my families, living and dead, crowded around me clamoring for me to do and not do. And with one last whisper from the Harry-blue eyes of my memory, my head began to shake all by itself and I said it again, 'No,' and this time I meant it, 'No. I can't. Not Deborah.'

My brother looked at me. 'Too bad,' he said. 'I'm so disappointed.'

And the knife came down.

EPILOGUE

I know it is a nearly human weakness, and it may be no more than ordinary sentimentality, but I have always loved funerals. For one thing they are so clean, so neat, so completely given over to careful ceremonies. And this was really a very good one. It had rows of blue-uniformed policemen and women, looking solemn and neat and – well, ceremonial. There was the ritual salute with the guns, the careful folding of the flag, all the trimmings – a proper and wonderful show for the deceased. She had been, after all, one of our own, a woman who had served with the few, the proud. Or is that the marines? No matter, she had been a Miami cop, and Miami cops know how to throw a funeral for one of their own. They have had so much practice.

'Oh, Deborah,' I sighed, very softly, and of course I knew she couldn't hear me, but it really did seem like the right thing to do, and I wanted to do this right.

I almost wished I could summon up a tear or two to wipe away. She and I had been very close. And it had been a messy and unpleasant death, no way for a cop to go, hacked to death by a homicidal maniac. Rescue had come too late; it was all over long before anyone could get to her. And yet, by her example of selfless courage, she had helped to show how a cop should live and die. I'm quoting, of course, but that's the gist of it. Really very good stuff, quite moving if one has anything inside that can be moved. Which I don't, but I know it when I hear it and this was the real thing. And very much caught up in the silent bravery of the officers in their clean blues and the weeping of the civilians, I could not help myself. I sighed heavily. 'Oh, Deborah,' I sighed, a little louder this time, almost feeling it. 'Dear, dear Deborah.'

'Quiet, you moron!' she whispered, and poked me hard with her elbow. She looked lovely in her new outfit – a sergeant at last, the least they could do for her after all her hard work identifying and nearly catching the Tamiami Slasher. With the APB out on him, no doubt they would find my poor brother sooner or later – if he didn't find them first, of course. Since I had just been reminded so forcefully that family is important, I did hope he could stay free. And Deborah would come around, now that she had accepted her promotion. She really wanted to forgive me, and she was already more than half convinced of the Wisdom of Harry. We were family, too, and that had shown in the end, hadn't it? It was not such a great leap to accept me as I was after all, was it? Things being what they are. What they have, in fact, always been.

I sighed again. 'Quit it!' she hissed, and nodded at the far end of the line of stiff Miami cops. I glanced where she indicated; Sergeant Doakes glared at me. He had not taken his eyes off me, not once the whole time, even when he had dropped his handful of earth on Detective LaGuerta's coffin. He was so very sure that things were not what they seemed. I knew with a total certainty that he would come for me now, track me like the hound he was, snort at my footsteps and sniff my back trail and hunt me down, bring me to bay for what I had done and what I would quite naturally do again.

I squeezed my sister's hand and with my other hand I fingered the cool hard edge of the glass slide in my pocket, one small drop of dried blood that would not go into the grave with LaGuerta but live forever on my shelf. It gave me comfort, and I did not mind Sergeant Doakes, or whatever he thought or did. How could I mind? He could no more control who he was and what he did than anyone else could. He would come for me. Truly, what else could he do?

What can any of us do? Helpless as we all are, in the grip of our own little voices, what indeed can we do?

I really wished I could shed a tear. It was all so beautiful. As beautiful as the next full moon would be, when I would call on Sergeant Doakes. And things would go on as they were, as they had always been, beneath that lovely bright moon.

The wonderful, fat, musical red moon.

Dearly Devoted Dexter

For Tommie and Gus,
who have certainly waited long enough

Acknowledgements

Nothing is remotely possible without Hilary.

I would also like to thank Julio, the Broccolis, Deacon and Einstein and, as always, Bear, Pook, and Tinky.

Additionally, I am indebted to Jason Kaufman for his steady and wise guiding hand, and to Nick Ellison, who has made all the difference.

1

It's that moon again, slung so fat and low in the tropical night, calling out across a curdled sky and into the quivering ears of that dear old voice in the shadows, the Dark Passenger, nestled snug in the backseat of the Dodge K-car of Dexter's hypothetical soul.

That rascal moon, that loudmouthed leering Lucifer, calling down across the empty sky to the dark hearts of the night monsters below, calling them away to their joyful playgrounds. Calling, in fact, to that monster right there, behind the oleander, tiger-striped with moonlight through the leaves, his senses all on high as he waits for just the right moment to leap from the shadows. It is Dexter in the dark, listening to the terrible whispered suggestions that come pouring down breathlessly into my shadowed hiding place.

My dear dark other self urges me to pounce – now – sink my moonlit fangs into the oh-so-vulnerable flesh on the far side of the hedge. But the time is not right and so I wait, watching cautiously as my unsuspecting victim creeps past, eyes wide, knowing that something is watching but not knowing that I am *here*, only three steely feet away in the hedge. I could so easily slide out like the knife blade I am, and work my wonderful magic – but I wait, suspected but unseen.

One long stealthy moment tiptoes into another and still I wait for just the right time; the leap, the outstretched hand, the cold glee as I see the terror spread across the face of my victim—

But no. Something is not right.

And now it is Dexter's turn to feel the queasy prickling of eyes on his back, the flutter of fear as I become more certain that something is now hunting *me*. Some other night stalker is feeling the sharp interior drool as he watches *me* from somewhere nearby – and I do not like this thought.

And like a small clap of thunder the gleeful hand comes down out of nowhere and onto *me* blindingly fast, and I glimpse the gleaming teeth of a nine-year-old neighbor boy. 'Gotcha! One, two, three on Dexter!' And with the savage speed of the very young the rest of them are there, giggling wildly and shouting at me as I stand in the bushes humiliated. It is over. Six-year-old Cody stares at me, disappointed, as though Dexter the Night God has let down his high priest. Astor, his nine-year-old sister, joins in the hooting of the kids before they skitter off into the dark once more, to new and more complicated hiding places, leaving me so very alone in my shame.

Dexter did not kick the can. And now Dexter is *It*. Again.

You may wonder, how can this be? How can Dexter's night hunt be reduced to this? Always before there has been some frightful twisted predator awaiting the special attention of frightful twisted Dexter – and here I am, stalking an empty Chef Boyardee ravioli can that is guilty of nothing worse than bland sauce. Here I am, frittering away precious time losing a game I have not played since I was ten. Even worse, I am IT.

'One. Two. Three – ' I call out, ever the fair and honest gamesman.

How can this be? How can Dexter the Demon feel the weight of that moon and not be off among the entrails, slicing the life from someone who needs very badly to feel the edge of Dexter's keen judgment? How is it possible on this kind of night for the Cold Avenger to refuse to take the Dark Passenger out for a spin?

'Four. Five. Six.'

Harry, my wise foster father, had taught me the careful balance of Need and Knife. He had taken a boy in whom he saw the unstoppable need to kill – no changing that – and Harry had molded him into a man who only killed the killers; Dexter the no-bloodhound, who hid behind a human-seeming face and tracked down the truly naughty serial killers who killed without code. And I would have been one of them, if not for the Harry Plan. *There are plenty of people who deserve it, Dexter*, my wonderful foster-cop-father had said.

'Seven. Eight. Nine.'

He had taught me how to find these special playmates, how to be sure they deserved a social call from me and my Dark Passenger. And even better, he taught me how to get away with it, as only a cop could teach. He had helped me build a plausible hidey-hole of a life, and drummed into me that I must fit in, always, be relentlessly normal in all things.

And so I had learned how to dress neatly and smile and brush my teeth. I had become a perfect fake human, saying the stupid and pointless things that humans say to each other all day long. No one suspected what crouched behind my perfect imitation smile. No one except my foster sister, Deborah, of course, but she was coming to accept the real me. After all, I could have been much worse. I could have been a vicious raving monster who killed and killed and left towers of rotting flesh in my wake. Instead, here I was on the side of truth, justice, and the American way. Still a monster, of course, but I cleaned up nicely afterward, and I was OUR monster, dressed in red, white, and blue 100 percent synthetic virtue. And on those nights when the moon is loudest I find the others, those who prey on the innocent and do not play by the rules, and I make them go away in small, carefully wrapped pieces.

This elegant formula had worked well through years of happy inhumanity. In between playdates I maintained my perfectly average lifestyle from a persistently ordinary apartment. I was never late to work, I made the right jokes with co-workers, and I was useful and unobtrusive in all things, just as Harry had taught me. My life as an android was neat, balanced, and had real redeeming social value.

Until now. Somehow, here I was on a just-right night playing kick the can with a flock of children, instead of playing Slice the Slasher with a carefully chosen friend. And in a little while, when the game was over, I would take Cody and Astor into their mother, Rita's, house, and she would bring me a can of beer, tuck the kids into bed, and sit beside me on the couch.

How could this be? Was the Dark Passenger slipping into early retirement? Had Dexter mellowed? Had I somehow turned the corner of the long dark hall and come out on the wrong end as Dexter Domestic? Would I ever again place that one drop of blood on the neat glass slide, as I always did – my trophy from the hunt?

'Ten! Ready or not, here I come!'

Yes, indeed. Here I came.

But to what?

It started, of course, with Sergeant Doakes. Every superhero must have an arch-enemy, and he was mine. I had done absolutely nothing to him, and yet he had chosen to hound me, harry me from my good work. Me and my shadow. And the irony of it: me, a hardworking blood-spatter-pattern analyst for the very same police force that employed him – we were on the same team. Was it fair for him to pursue me like this, merely because every now and then I did a little bit of moonlighting?

I knew Sergeant Doakes far better than I really wanted to, much more than just from our professional connection. I had made it my business to find out about him for one simple reason: he had never liked me, in spite of the fact that I take great pride in being charming and cheerful on a world-class level. But it almost seemed like Doakes could tell it was all fake; all my handmade heartiness bounced off him like June bugs off a windshield.

This naturally made me curious. I mean, really; what kind of person could possibly dislike me? And so I had studied him just a little, and I found out. The kind of person who could possibly dislike Debonair Dexter was forty-eight, African American, and held the department's record for the bench press. According to the casual gossip I had picked up, he was an army vet, and since coming to the department had been involved in several fatal shootings, all of which Internal Affairs had judged to be righteous.

But more important than all this, I had discovered first hand that somewhere behind the deep anger that always burned in his eyes there lurked an echo of a chuckle from my own Dark Passenger. It was just a tiny little chime of a very small bell, but I was sure. Doakes was sharing space with something, just like I was. Not the same thing, but something very similar, a panther to my tiger. Doakes was a cop, but he was also a cold killer. I had no real proof of this, but I was as sure as I could be without seeing him crush a jaywalker's larynx.

A reasonable being might think that he and I could find some common ground; have a cup of coffee and compare our Passengers, exchange trade talk and chitchat about dismemberment techniques. But no: Doakes wanted me dead. And I found it difficult to share his point of view.

Doakes had been working with Detective LaGuerta at the time of her somewhat suspicious death, and since then his feelings toward me had grown to be a bit more active than simple loathing. Doakes was convinced that I'd had something to do with LaGuerta's death. This was totally untrue and completely unfair. All I had done was watch – where's the harm in that? Of course I had helped the real killer escape, but what could you expect? What kind of person would turn in his own brother? Especially when he did such neat work.

Well, live and let live, I always say. Or quite often, anyway. Sergeant Doakes could think what he wanted to think, and that was fine with me. There are still very few laws against thinking, although I'm sure they're working hard on that in Washington. No, whatever suspicions the good sergeant had about me, he was welcome to them. But now that he had decided to act on his impure thoughts my life was a shambles. Dexter Derailed was fast becoming Dexter Demented.

And why? How had this whole nasty mess begun? All I had done was try to be myself.

2

There are nights every now and then when the Dark Passenger really must get out to play. It's like walking a dog. You can ignore the barking and scratching at the door for only so long, and then you must take the beast outside.

Not too long after Detective LaGuerta's funeral, there came a time when it seemed reasonable to listen to the whispers from the backseat and start to plan a small adventure.

I had located a perfect playmate, a very plausible real estate salesman named MacGregor. He was a happy, cheerful man who loved selling houses to families with children. Especially young boys – MacGregor was extremely fond of boys between the ages of five and seven. He had been lethally fond of five that I was sure of, and quite likely several more. He was clever and careful, and without a visit from Dark Scout Dexter he would probably stay lucky for a long time. It's hard to blame the police, at least this once. After all, when a young child goes missing, very few people would say, 'Aha! Who sold his family their house?'

But of course, very few people are Dexter. This is generally a good thing, but in this case it came in handy to be me. Four months after reading a story in the paper about a missing boy, I read a similar story. The boys were the same age; details like that always ring a small bell and send a Mister Rogers whisper trickling through my brain: 'Hello, neighbor.'

And so I dug up the first story and compared. I noticed that in both cases the paper milked the grief of the families by mentioning that they had recently moved into new homes; I heard a small chuckle from the shadows, and I looked a little closer.

It really was quite subtle. Detective Dexter had to dig quite a bit, because at first there didn't seem to be any connection. The families in question were in different neighborhoods, which ruled out a great many possibilities. They went to different churches, different schools, and used different moving companies. But when the Dark Passenger laughs, somebody is usually doing something funny. And I finally found the connection; both houses had been listed with the same real estate agency, a small outfit in South Miami, with only one agent, a cheerful and friendly man named Randy MacGregor.

I dug a little more. MacGregor was divorced and lived alone in a small concrete-block house off Old Cutler Road in South Miami. He kept a twenty-six-foot cabin cruiser at Matheson Hammock Marina, which was relatively close to his house. The boat would also be an extremely convenient playpen, a way to get his little chums off alone on the bounding main where he would not be seen or heard while he explored, a real Columbus of pain. And for that matter, it would provide a splendid way to dispose of the messy leftovers; just a few miles out from Miami, the Gulf Stream provided a nearly bottomless dumping ground. No wonder the boys' bodies were never found.

The technique made such good sense that I wondered why I hadn't thought of it to recycle my own leftovers. Silly me; I only used my little boat for fishing and riding around the bay. And here MacGregor had come up with a whole new way to enjoy an evening on the water. It was a very neat idea, and it instantly moved MacGregor right to the top of my list. Call me unreasonable, even illogical since I generally have very little use for humans, but for some reason I care about kids. And when I find someone who preys on children it is very much as if they have slipped the Dark Maître d' twenty dollars to move to the front of the line. I would happily unclip the velvet rope and bring MacGregor right in – assuming he was doing what it looked like he was doing. Of course, I had to be absolutely certain. I had always tried to avoid slicing up the wrong person, and it would be a shame to start now, even with a real estate salesman. It occurred to me that the best way to make sure would be to visit the boat in question.

Happily for me, the very next day it was raining, as it generally rains every day in July. But this had the look of an all-day storm, which made it just what the Dexter ordered. I left my job at the Miami-Dade police forensics lab early and cut over to LeJeune, taking it all the way to Old Cutler Road. I turned left into Matheson Hammock; as I'd hoped, it seemed deserted. But about one hundred yards ahead I knew there was a guard booth, where someone would be waiting eagerly to take four dollars from me for the great privilege of entering the park. It seemed like a good idea not to make an appearance at the guard booth. Of course saving the four dollars was very important, but even more so was that on a rainy day in the middle of the week I might be just a little bit conspicuous, which is something I like to avoid, particularly in the course of my hobby.

On the left side of the road was a small parking lot that served the picnic area. An old coral-rock picnic shelter stood beside a lake on the right. I parked my car and pulled on a bright yellow foul-weather jacket. It made me feel very nautical, just the thing to wear for breaking into a homicidal pedophile's boat. It also made me highly visible, but I was not terribly worried about that. I would take the bicycle path that ran parallel to the road. It was screened in by mangroves, and in the unlikely event that the guard stuck his head out of the booth and into the rain, he would see nothing but a bright yellow blur jogging by. Just a determined runner out for his afternoon trot, come rain or shine.

And trot I did, moving about a quarter of a mile down the path. As I had hoped, there was no sign of life at the guard booth and I jogged to the large parking lot by the water. The last row of docks off to the right was home to a cluster of boats slightly smaller than the big sports fishermen and million-aires' toys tied up closer to the road. MacGregor's modest twenty-six footer, the *Osprey*, was near the end.

The marina was deserted and I went blithely through the gate in the chain-link fence, past a sign that said ONLY BOAT OWNERS PERMITTED ON DOCKS. I tried to feel guilty about violating such an important command, but it was beyond me. The lower half of the sign said NO FISHING OFF DOCKS OR IN MARINA AREA, and I promised myself that I would avoid fishing at all costs, which made me feel better about breaking the other rule.

The *Osprey* was five or six years old and showed only a few signs of wear from the Florida weather. The deck and rails were scrubbed clean and I was careful not to leave scuff marks as I climbed aboard. For some reason the locks on boats are never very complicated. Perhaps sailors are more honest than landlubbers. In any case, it took only a few seconds for me to pick the lock and slip inside the *Osprey*. The cabin did not have the musty smell of baked mildew that so many boats get when they are sealed up even for a few hours in the subtropical sun. Instead there was a faint tang of Pine-Sol in the air, as though someone had scrubbed so thoroughly that no germs or odors could hope to survive.

There was a small table, a galley, and one of those little TV/VCR units on a railed shelf with a stack of movies beside it: *Spider-Man, Brother Bear, Finding Nemo*. I wondered how many boys MacGregor had sent over the side to find Nemo. I dearly hoped that soon Nemo would find him. I stepped to the galley area and began to open drawers. One was filled with candy, the next with plastic action figures. And the third was absolutely crammed with rolls of duct tape.

Duct tape is a wonderful thing, and as I know very well, it can be used for many remarkable and useful things. But I did think that having ten rolls of it stuffed in a drawer on your boat was a bit excessive. Unless, of course, you were using it for some specific purpose that required a great deal of it. Per-haps a science project involving multiple young boys? Just a hunch, of course, based on the way I use it – not on young boys, of course, but on upstanding citizens like, for instance . . . MacGregor. His guilt had started to seem very likely, and the Dark Passenger flicked his dry lizard tongue with anticipation.

I went down the steps into the small forward area the salesman probably called the stateroom. It wasn't a terribly elegant bed, just a thin foam-rubber pad on a raised shelf. I touched the mattress and it crackled under the fabric; a rubber casing. I rolled the mattress to one side. There were four ring bolts screwed into the shelf, one on each corner. I lifted the hatch beneath the mattress.

One might reasonably expect to find a certain amount of chain on a boat. But the accompanying handcuffs did not strike me as being quite so nautical. Of course, there might be a very good explanation. It was possible that MacGregor used them on quarrelsome fish.

Under the chain and handcuffs there were five anchors. That could very well be a good idea on a yacht that was meant to cruise around the world, but it seemed a bit much for a small weekend boat. What on earth could they be for? If I was taking my little boat out into the deep water with a series of small bodies I wished to dispose of cleanly and completely, what would I do with so many anchors? And, of course, when you put it that way, it seemed obvious that the next time MacGregor went cruising with a little friend he would come back with only four anchors under the bunk.

I was certainly gathering enough small details to make a very interesting picture. Still life without children. But so far I had not found anything that could not be explained away as massive coincidence, and I needed to be absolutely sure. I had to have one overwhelmingly conclusive piece of evidence, something so completely unambiguous that it would satisfy the Harry Code.

I found it in a drawer to the right of the bunk.

There were three small drawers built into the bulkhead of the boat. The interior of the bottom one seemed to be a few inches shorter than the other two. It was possible that it was supposed to be, that it was shortened by the curve of the hull. But I have studied humans for many years now, and this has made me deeply suspicious. I pulled the drawer all the way out and, sure enough, there was a small secret compartment on the back end of the drawer. And inside the secret compartment—

Since I am not actually a real human being, my emotional responses are generally limited to what I have learned to fake. So I did not feel shock, outrage, anger, or even bitter resolve. They're very difficult emotions to do convincingly, and there was no audience to do them for, so why bother? But I did feel a slow cold wind from the Dark Backseat sweep up my spine and blow dry leaves over the floor of my lizard brain.

I could identify five different naked boys in the stack of photographs, arranged in a variety of poses, as if MacGregor was still searching for a defining style. And yes indeed, he really was a spendthrift with his duct tape. In one of the pictures, the boy looked like he was in a silver-gray cocoon, with only certain areas exposed. What MacGregor left exposed told me a great deal about him. As I had suspected, he was not the kind of man most parents would wish for a scoutmaster.

The photos were good quality, taken from many different angles. One series in particular stood out. A pale, flabby naked man in a black hood stood beside the tightly taped boy, almost like a trophy shot. From the shape and coloring of the body I was quite sure the man was MacGregor, even though the hood covered his face. And as I flipped through the pictures I had two very interesting thoughts. The first was, Aha! Meaning, of course, that there was absolutely no doubt about what MacGregor had been doing, and he was now the lucky Grand Prize Winner in the Dark Passenger's Clearinghouse Sweepstakes.

And the second thought, somewhat more troubling, was this: Who was taking the pictures?

There were too many different angles for the pictures to have been taken automatically. And as I flipped through them a second time I noticed, in two shots that had been snapped from above, the pointy toe of what looked like a red cowboy boot.

MacGregor had an accomplice. The word sounded so very Court TV, but there it was and I could not think of a better way to say it. He had not done all this alone. Someone had gone along and, if nothing else, had watched and taken pictures.

I blush to admit that I have some modest knowledge and talent in the area of semiregular mayhem, but I had never before run into anything like this. Trophy shots, yes – after all, I had my little box of slides, each with single drop of blood on them, to commemorate every one of my adventures. Perfectly normal to keep some kind of souvenir.

But to have a second person present, watching and taking pictures, turned a very private act into a kind of performance. It was absolutely indecent – the man was a pervert. If only I had been capable of moral outrage, I am quite sure I would have been full of it. As it was, though, I found myself more eager than ever to get viscerally acquainted with MacGregor.

It was stiflingly hot on the boat, and my wonderfully chic foul-weather suit was not helping. I felt like a bright yellow tea bag. I picked several of the clearest pictures and put them in my pocket. I returned the rest to their compartment, tidied the bunk, and went back up into the main cabin. As far as I could tell from peeking out the window – or did I have to call it a porthole? – there was no one lurking about and observing me in a furtive manner. I slipped out the door, making sure it locked behind me, and strolled off through the rain.

From the many movies I have seen over the years, I knew very well that walking in the rain is the correct setting for reflecting on human perfidy, and so I did just that. Oh that wicked MacGregor and his shutterbug friend. How could they be such vile wretches. That sounded about right, and it was all I could come up with; I hoped it was enough to satisfy the formula. Because it was far more fun to reflect on my own perfidy, and how I might feed it by arranging a playdate with MacGregor. I could feel a rising tide of dark delight flooding in from the deepest dungeons of Castle Dexter and building up at the spillways. And soon it would pour out on MacGregor.

There was no longer any room for doubt, of course. Harry himself would acknowledge that the photographs were more than enough proof, and an eager chuckle from the Dark Backseat sanctified the project. MacGregor and I would go exploring together. And then the special bonus of finding his friend in the cowboy boots – he would have to follow MacGregor as soon as possible, of course; no rest for the wicked. It was like a two-for-the-price-of-one sale, absolutely irresistible.

Filled with my happy thoughts, I didn't even notice the rain as I strode manfully and rapidly back to my car. I had a great deal to do.

3

It is always a bad idea to follow a regular routine, particularly if you are a homicidal pedophile who has come to the attention of Dexter the Avenger. Happily for me, no one had ever given MacGregor this vital bit of information, and so it was quite easy for me to find him leaving his office at 6:30 pm, as he did every day. He came out the back door, locked it, and climbed into his big Ford SUV; a perfect vehicle for hauling people around to look at houses, or for carrying bundled-up little boys down to the dock. He pulled out into the traffic and I followed him home to his modest concrete-block house on S.W. 80th Street.

There was quite a bit of traffic going by the house. I turned onto a small side street half a block away and parked unobtrusively where I had a good view. There was a tall, thick hedge running down the far side of MacGregor's lot that would keep the neighbors from seeing anything that went on in his yard. I sat in my car and pretended to look at a map for about ten minutes, just long enough to scheme and be sure that he wasn't going anywhere. When he came out of his house and began to putter around the yard, shirtless and wearing a pair of battered madras shorts, I knew how I would do it. I headed for home to get ready.

In spite of the fact that I normally have a robust and healthy appetite, I always find it difficult to eat before one of my little adventures. My interior associate quivers with rising anticipation, the moon burbles louder and louder in my veins as the night slides over the city, and thoughts of food begin to seem so very ordinary.

And so instead of enjoying a leisurely high-protein dinner, I paced my apartment, eager to begin but still cool enough to wait, letting Daytime Dexter melt quietly into the background and feeling the intoxicating surge of power as the Dark Passenger slowly took the wheel and checked the controls. It was always an exhilarating sensation to allow myself to be pulled into the backseat and let the Passenger drive. Shadows seem to grow sharper edges and the darkness fades into a lively gray that brings everything into much sharper focus. Small sounds become loud and distinct, my skin tingles, my breath roars in and out, and even the air comes alive with smells that were certainly not noticeable during the boring and normal day. I was never more alive than when the Dark Passenger was driving.

I forced myself to sit in my easy chair and I held myself in, feeling the Need roll over me and leave behind a high tide of readiness. Each breath felt like a blast of cold air sweeping through me and pumping me up bigger and brighter until I was like an enormous invincible beacon of steel ready to slash through the now-dark city. And then my chair became a stupid little thing, a hiding place for mice, and only the night was big enough.

And it was time.

Out we went, into the bright night, the moonlight hammering at me and the dead-roses breath of the Miami night blowing across my skin, and in almost no time at all I was there, in the shadows cast by MacGregor's hedge, watching and waiting and listening, just for now, to the caution that curled around my wrist and whispered *patience*. It seemed pathetic that he could not see something that gleamed as brightly as I did, and the thought gave me another surge of strength. I pulled on my white silk mask and I was ready to begin.

Slowly, invisibly, I moved from the darkness of the hedge and placed a child's plastic piano keyboard beneath his window, putting it under a gladiolus bush so it would not be seen immediately. It was bright red and blue, less than a foot long, and only had eight keys, but it would repeat the same four melodies endlessly until the battery died. I switched it on and stepped back into my place in the hedge.

'Jingle Bells' played, and then 'Old MacDonald.' For some reason, a key phrase was missing in each song, but the little toy piped on and into 'London Bridge' in the same cheerfully lunatic tone.

It was enough to make anyone crazy, but it probably had an extra effect on someone like MacGregor who lived for children. At any rate, I certainly hoped so. I had quite deliberately chosen the little keyboard to lure him out, and I sincerely hoped, in fact, that he would think he had been found out – and that a toy had come from Hell to punish him. After all, why shouldn't I enjoy what I do?

It seemed to work. We were only on the third repetition of 'London Bridge' when he came stumbling out of his house with a look of wide-eyed panic. He stood there for a moment, gaping around, his receding reddish hair looking like it had gone through a storm and his pale belly hanging slightly over the waist of his dingy pajama bottoms. He did not look terribly dangerous to me, but of course I was not a five-year-old boy.

After a moment, in which he stood with his mouth open, and scratched himself, and looked like he was modeling for a statue of the Greek god of Stupidity, MacGregor located the source of the sound – 'Jingle Bells' again by now. He stepped over and bent slightly to touch the little plastic keyboard and did not even have the time to be surprised before I had a noose of fifty-pound-test fishing line pulled tight around his throat. He straightened and thought he might struggle for a moment. I pulled tighter and he changed his mind.

'Stop fighting,' we said in our cold and commanding Passenger voice. 'You'll live longer.' And he heard his future in the words and thought he might change it, so I pulled hard on his leash and held it like that until his face turned dark and he dropped to his knees.

Just before he passed out completely I eased the pressure. 'Now do as you're told,' we said. He didn't say anything; he just choked in a few large and painful breaths, so I tweaked the line a touch. 'Understand?' we said, and he nodded so I let him breathe.

He did not try to fight anymore as I frog-marched him into the house for his car keys and then back out into his big SUV. I climbed into the seat behind him, holding the leash in a very tight grip and allowing him only enough breath to stay alive, for now.

'Start the car,' we told him, and he paused.

'What do you want?' he said in a voice that was rough with new-made gravel.

'Everything,' we said. 'Start the car.'

'I have money,' he said.

I pulled hard on his cord. 'Buy me a little boy,' we said. I held it tight for a few seconds, too tight for him to breathe and just long enough to let him know that *we* were in charge, *we* knew what he had done, and *we* would let him breathe only at our pleasure from now on, and when I loosened the line again he had nothing to say.

He drove as we told him to, back up S.W. 80th Street to Old Cutler Road and then south. There was almost no traffic this far out, not at this time of night, and we turned into a new development that had been going up on the far side of Snapper Creek. Construction had halted due to the owner's conviction for money laundering, and we would not be disturbed. We guided MacGregor through a half-built guard booth, around a small traffic circle, east toward the water, and to a halt beside a small trailer, the temporary office of the site, now left to teen thrill seekers and others, like me, who only wanted a little privacy.

We sat for just a moment, enjoying the view – moon over the water, with pedophile in noose in the foreground, very beautiful.

I got out and pulled MacGregor out after me, pulled him hard so that he fell to his knees and clawed at the line around his neck. For a moment I watched him choking and drooling in the dirt, his face turning dark again and his eyes going red. Then I pulled him to his feet and pushed him up the three wooden steps and into the trailer. By the time he had recovered enough to know what was going on, I had him tied to the top of a desk, hands and feet secured with duct tape.

MacGregor tried to speak and just coughed instead. I waited; now there was plenty of time. 'Please,' he said finally, in a voice like sand on glass, 'I'll give you whatever you want.'

'Yes, you will,' we said, and saw the sound of it cut into him, and even though he couldn't see it through my white silk mask we smiled. I took out the photos I had taken from his boat and showed them to him.

He stopped moving completely and his mouth hung open. 'Where did you get those?' he said, sounding rather petulant for someone who was about to be cut into small pieces.

'Tell me who took these pictures.'

'Why should I?' he said.

I used a pair of tin snips and cut off the first two fingers of his left hand. He thrashed and screamed and the blood came, which always makes me angry, so I shoved a tennis ball into his mouth and cut off the first two fingers of his right hand. 'No reason,' I said, and I waited for him to slow down just a little bit.

When he finally did, he rolled an eye to me and his face was filled with that understanding that comes when you have gone beyond pain into knowing that the rest of this was forever. I took the tennis ball out of his mouth.

'Who took the pictures?'

He smiled. 'I hope one of them was yours,' he said, which made the next ninety minutes a lot more rewarding.

4

Normally I feel pleasantly mellow for several days after one of my Nights Out, but the very next morning after MacGregor's hasty exit I was still all aquiver with eagerness. I wanted very badly to find the photographer in the red cowboy boots and make a clean sweep of it. I am a tidy monster, and I do like to finish whatever I begin, and to know that someone was out there clumping around in those ridiculous shoes, carrying a camera that had seen far too much, made me anxious to follow those footprints and wrap up my two-part project.

Perhaps I had been too hasty with MacGregor; I should have given him a little more time and encouragement, and he would have told me everything. But it had seemed like something I could easily find by myself – when the Dark Passenger is driving, I am quite sure I can do anything. So far I have not been wrong, but it had put me in a bit of an awkward spot this time, and I had to find Mr. Boots on my own.

I knew from my earlier research that MacGregor did not have a social life beyond his occasional evening cruises. He belonged to a couple of business organizations, which was to be expected from a realtor, but I had not discovered anyone in particular that he seemed to pal around with. I also knew he had no criminal record, so there was no file to pull and search for known associates. The court records on his divorce simply listed 'irreconcilable differences' and left the rest to my imagination.

And there I was stuck; MacGregor had been a classic loner, and in all my careful study of him I had never seen an indication that he had any friends, companions, dates, mates, or cronies. No poker night with the boys – no boys at all, except for the young ones. No church group, no Elks, no neighborhood bar, no weekly square-dancing society – which might have explained the boots – no nothing, except the photographs with those stupid pointed red toes sticking out.

So who was Cowboy Bob, and how did I find him?

There was really only one place I could go for an answer, and that would have to be soon, before someone noticed that MacGregor was missing. In the distance I heard thunder rumble, and I glanced at the wall clock with surprise. Sure enough, it was 2:15, time for the daily afternoon storm. I had moped all the way through my lunch hour, very unlike me.

Still, the storm would once again give me a little cover, and I could stop for something to eat on the way back. So with my immediate future neatly and pleasantly planned, I headed out to the parking lot, got into my car, and drove south.

The rain had started by the time I got to Matheson Hammock, and so once again I pulled on my sporty yellow foul-weather gear and jogged down the path to MacGregor's boat.

I picked the lock again quite easily and slipped inside the cabin. During my first visit to the boat, I had been looking for signs that MacGregor was a pedophile. Now I was trying to find something a little bit more subtle, some small clue to the identity of MacGregor's photographer friend.

Since I had to start somewhere, I went back down to the sleeping area. I opened the drawer with the false bottom and flipped through the pictures again. This time I checked the back as well as the front. Digital photography has made sleuthing a great deal more difficult, and there were no marks of any kind on the pictures and no empty film packets with traceable serial numbers, either. Any clod in the world could simply download the pictures to his hard drive and print them out at will, even someone with such hideous taste in footgear. It didn't seem fair: Weren't computers supposed to makes things easier?

I closed the drawer and searched through the rest of the area, but there was nothing that I hadn't seen before. Somewhat discouraged, I went back upstairs to the main cabin. There were several drawers there, too, and I flipped through them. Videotapes, action figures, the duct tape – all things I had already noticed, and none of them would tell me anything. I pulled the stack of duct tape out, thinking, perhaps, that there was no sense in letting it go to waste. Idly, I turned over the bottom roll.

And there it was.

It really is better to be lucky than to be good. In a million years I could not have hoped for something this good. Stuck to the bottom of the duct-tape roll was a small scrap of paper, and written on the paper was, 'Reiker,' and under that a telephone number.

Of course there was no guarantee that Reiker was the Red Ranger, or even that he was a human being. It could well be the name of a marine plumbing contractor. But in any case, it was far more of a starting place than I'd had, and I needed to get off the boat before the storm stopped. I stuck the paper inside my pocket, buttoned up my rain slicker, and snuck off the boat and onto the footpath again.

Perhaps I was feeling so happily mellow from the after-effects of my evening out with MacGregor, but as I drove home I found myself humming a catchy little Philip Glass tune from *1000 Airplanes on the Roof*. The key to a happy life is to have accomplishments to be proud of and purpose to look forward to, and at the moment I had both. How wonderful it was to be me.

My good mood lasted only as far as the traffic circle where Old Cutler blends into LeJeune, and then a routine glance in my rearview mirror froze the music on my lips.

Behind me, practically nosing into my backseat, was a maroon Ford Taurus. It looked very much like the sort of car the Miami-Dade Police Department maintained in large numbers for the use of plainclothes personnel.

I did not see how this could possibly be a good thing. A patrol car might follow for no real reason, but someone in a motor-pool car would have some kind of purpose, and it looked like that purpose was to make me aware I was being followed. If so, it was working perfectly. I could not see through the glare of the windshield to know who was driving the other car, but it suddenly seemed very important to know just how long the car had been following me, who was driving, and how much the driver had seen.

I turned down a small side street, pulled over, and parked, and the Taurus parked right behind me. For a moment, nothing happened; we both sat there in our cars, waiting. Was I going to be arrested? If someone had followed me from the marina, it could be a very bad thing for Dashing Dexter. Sooner or later, MacGregor's absence would be noticed, and even the most routine investigation would reveal his boat. Someone would go to see if it was there, and then the fact that Dexter had been there in the middle of the day might seem very significant.

It's little things like this that make for successful police work. Cops look for these funny coincidences, and when they find them they can get very serious with the person who is in too many interesting places by mere happenstance. Even if that person has a police ID and an amazingly charming fake smile.

There really seemed nothing for me to do except bluff my way through: find out who was following me and why, and then convince them it was a silly way to waste time. I put on my very best Official Greeting face, got out of my car, and stepped briskly up to the Taurus. The window rolled down and the always angry face of Sergeant Doakes looked out at me, like an idol for some wicked god, carved from a piece of dark wood.

'Why you leaving work in the middle of the day so much lately?' he asked me. His voice had no real expression in it but still managed to give the impression that whatever I said would be a lie and he would like to hurt me for it.

'Why, Sergeant Doakes!' I said cheerfully. 'What an amazing coincidence. What are you doing here?'

'You got something to do more important than your job?' he said. He really seemed uninterested in maintaining any sort of flow in the conversation, so I shrugged. When faced with people who have very limited conversational skills and no apparent desire to cultivate any, it's always easier simply to go along.

'I, um – I had some personal things to take care of,' I said. Very weak, I agree, but Doakes displayed an unnerving habit of asking the most awkward questions, and with such an understated viciousness, that I found it hard enough not to stutter, let alone come up with something clever.

He looked at me for several endless seconds, the way a starving pit bull looks at raw meat. 'Personal things,' he said without blinking. It sounded even stupider when he repeated it.

'That's right,' I said.

'Your dentist is over in the Gables,' he said.

'Well— '

'Your doctor, too, over on Alameda. Got no lawyer, sister still at work,' he said. 'What kind of *personal things* did I leave out?'

'Actually, um, I, I – ' I said, and I was amazed to hear myself stammer, but nothing else came out, and Doakes just looked at me as though he was begging me to make a run for it so he could practice his wing shot.

'Funny,' he said at last, 'I got *personal things* to do out here, too.'

'Really?' I said, relieved to find that my mouth was once again capable of forming human speech. 'And what would that be, Sergeant?'

It was the first time I had ever seen him smile, and I have to say that I would have greatly preferred it if he had simply jumped out of the car and bitten me. 'I'm watching YOU,' he said. He gave me a moment to admire the high gloss of his teeth, and then the window rolled up and he vanished behind the tinted glass like the Cheshire cat.

5

Given enough time, I am sure I could come up with an entire list of things more unpleasant than having Sergeant Doakes turn into my own personal shadow. But as I stood there in my high-fashion foul-weather gear and thought of Reiker and his red boots slipping away from me, it seemed bad enough, and I was not inspired to think of anything worse. I simply climbed into my car, started the engine, and drove through the rain to my apartment. Ordinarily, the homicidal antics of the other drivers would have comforted me, made me feel right at home, but for some reason the maroon Taurus following so close behind took away the glow.

I knew Sergeant Doakes well enough to know that this was not simply a rainy-day whim on his part. If he was watching me, he would keep watching me until he caught me doing something naughty. Or until he was unable to watch me anymore. Naturally enough, I could readily think of a few intriguing ways to make sure he lost interest. But they were all so permanent, and while I did not actually have a conscience, I did have a very clear set of rules that worked somewhat the same way.

I had known that sooner or later Sergeant Doakes would do something or other to discourage my hobby, and I had thought long and hard about what to do when he did. The best I had come up with, alas, was wait and see.

'Excuse me?' you might say, and you have every right. 'Can we truly ignore the obvious answer here?' After all, Doakes might be strong and lethal, but the Dark Passenger was much more so, and no one could stand against him when he took the wheel. Perhaps just this once . . .

No, said the small soft voice in my ear.

Hello, Harry. Why not? And as I asked, I thought back to the time he had told me.

There are rules, Dexter, Harry had said.

Rules, Dad?

It was my sixteenth birthday. There was never much of a party, since I had not learned yet to be wonderfully charming and chummy, and if I was not avoiding my drooling contemporaries then they were generally avoiding me. I lived my adolescence like a sheepdog moving through a flock of dirty, very stupid sheep. Since then, I had learned a great deal. For example, I was not that far off at sixteen – people really are hopeless! – but it just doesn't do to let on.

So my sixteenth birthday was a rather restrained affair. Doris, my foster mom, had recently died of cancer. But my foster sister, Deborah, made me a cake and Harry gave me a new fishing rod. I blew out the candles, we ate the cake, and then Harry took me into the backyard of our modest Coconut Grove house. He sat at the redwood picnic table that he had built by the brick barbecue oven and motioned me to sit, too.

'Well, Dex,' he said. 'Sixteen. You're almost a man.'

I wasn't sure what that was supposed to mean – me? a man? as in human? – and I did not know what sort of response was expected of me. But I did know that it was usually best not to make clever remarks with Harry, so I just nodded. And Harry gave me a blue-eyed X-ray. 'Are you interested in girls at all?' he asked me.

'Um – in what way?' I said.

'Kissing. Making out. You know. Sex.'

My head whirled at the thought as though a cold dark foot were kicking at the inside of my forehead. 'Not, uh, no. I, um,' I said, silver-tongued even then. 'Not like that.'

Harry nodded as if that made sense. 'Not boys, though,' he said, and I just shook my head. Harry looked at the table, then back at the house. 'When I turned sixteen my father took me to a whore.' He shook his head and a very small smile flickered across his face. 'It took me ten years to get over that.' I could think of absolutely nothing to say to that. The idea of sex was completely alien to me, and to think of *paying* for it, especially for your child, and when that child was *Harry* – well really. It was all too much. I looked at Harry with something close to panic and he smiled.

'No,' said Harry. 'I wasn't going to offer. I expect you'll get more use out of that fishing rod.' He shook his head slowly and looked away, far out over the picnic table, across the yard, down the street. 'Or a fillet knife.'

'Yes,' I said, trying not to sound too eager.

'No,' he said again, 'we both know what you want. But you're not ready.'

Since the first time Harry had talked to me about what I was, on a memorable camping trip a couple of years ago, we had been getting me ready. Getting me, in Harry's words, *squared away*. As a muttonheaded young artificial human I was eager to get started on my happy career, but Harry held me back, because Harry always knew.

'I can be careful,' I said.

'But not perfect,' he said. 'There are rules, Dexter. There have to be. That's what separates you from the other ones.'

'Blend in,' I said. 'Clean up, don't take chances, um . . .'

Harry shook his head. 'More important. You have to be sure before you start that this person really deserves it. I can't tell you the number of times I knew somebody was guilty and I had to let them go. To have the bastard look at you and smirk, and you know and he knows, but you have to hold the door for him and let him go – ' He clenched his jaw and tapped a fist on the picnic table. 'You won't have to. BUT . . . you have to be sure. Dead sure, Dexter. And even if you're absolutely positive – ' He held his hand up in the air, palm facing me. 'Get some proof. It doesn't have to hold up in court, thank God.' He gave a small and bitter laugh. 'You'd never get anywhere. But you need proof, Dexter. That's the most important thing.' He tapped the table with his knuckle. 'You have to have proof. And even then—'

He stopped, an uncharacteristic Harry pause, and I waited, knowing something difficult was coming. 'Sometimes even then, you let them go. No matter how much they deserve it. If they're too . . . *conspicuous*, for example. If it would raise too much attention, let it go.'

Well, there it was. As always, Harry had the answer for me. Whenever I was unsure, I could hear Harry whispering in my ear. I was sure, but I had no proof that Doakes was anything except a very angry and suspicious cop, and chopping up a cop was certainly the sort of thing the city got indignant about. After the recent untimely demise of Detective LaGuerta, the police hierarchy would almost certainly be a little sensitive about a second cop going out in the same way.

No matter how necessary it seemed, Doakes was out of bounds for me. I could look out the window at the maroon Taurus nosed under a tree, but I could do nothing about it except wish for some other solution to spontaneously arise – for example, a piano falling on his head. Sadly enough, I was left hoping for luck.

But there was no luck tonight for poor Disappointed Dexter, and lately there had been a tragic lack of falling pianos in the Miami area. So here I was in my little hovel, pacing the floor with frustration, and every time I casually peeked out the window, there was the Taurus parked across the way. The memory of what I had been so happily contemplating only an hour ago pounded in my head. *Can Dexter come out and play?* Alas, no, dear Dark Passenger. Dexter is in time-out.

There was, however, one constructive thing I could do, even cooped up in my apartment. I took the crumpled piece of paper from MacGregor's boat out of my pocket and smoothed it out, which left my fingers sticky from the leftover gunk off the roll of duct tape to which the paper had been stuck. 'Reiker,' and a phone number. More than enough to feed to one of the reverse directories I could access from my computer, and in just a few minutes I had done so.

The number belonged to a cell phone, which was registered to a Mr. Steve Reiker of Tigertail Avenue in Coconut Grove. A little bit of cross-checking revealed that Mr. Reiker was a professional photographer. Of course, it could have been a coincidence. I am sure that there are many people named Reiker around the world who are photographers. I looked in the Yellow Pages and found that this particular Reiker had a specialty. He had a quarter-page ad that said, 'Remember Them as They Are Now.'

Reiker specialized in pictures of children.

The coincidence theory might have to go.

The Dark Passenger stirred and gave a small chuckle of anticipation, and I found myself planning a trip over to Tigertail for a quick look around. In fact, it wasn't terribly far away. I could drive over now, and—

And let Sergeant Doakes follow along playing Pin the Tail on the Dexter. Splendid idea, old chum. That would save Doakes a great deal of boring investigative work when Reiker finally disappeared some day. He could cut through all the dull routine and just come get me.

And at this rate, when would Reiker disappear? It was terribly frustrating to have a worthwhile goal in sight, and yet to be held in check like this. But after several hours Doakes was still parked across the street and I was still here. What to do? On the plus side, it seemed obvious that Doakes had not seen enough to take any action beyond following me. But leading the way in the very large minus column, if he continued to follow me I would be forced to stay in character as the mild-mannered forensic lab rat, carefully avoiding anything more lethal than rush hour on the Palmetto Expressway. That would never do. I felt a certain pressure, not just from the Passenger but from the clock. Before too much time passed I needed to find some proof that Reiker was the photographer who took MacGregor's pictures, and if he was, have a sharp and pointed chat with him. If he realized MacGregor had gone the way of all flesh he would most likely run for the hills. And if my associates at police headquarters realized it, things could get very uncomfortable for Dashing Dexter.

But Doakes had apparently settled in for a long stay, and at the moment there was nothing I could do about it. It was terribly frustrating to think of Reiker walking around instead of thrashing against the duct tape. Homicidus interruptus. A soft moan and a gnashing of mental teeth came from the Dark Passenger, and I knew just how he felt, but there seemed to be very little I could do except pace back and forth. And even that wasn't very helpful: if I kept it up I would wear a hole in the carpet and then I would never get back my security deposit on the apartment.

My instinct was to do something that would throw Doakes off the track - but he was no ordinary bloodhound. I could think of only one thing that might take the scent out of his quivering, eager snout. It was just barely possible that I could wear him down, play the waiting game, be relentlessly normal for so long that he would have to give it up and return to his real job of catching all the truly horrible residents on the underside of our fair city. Why even now they were out there double parking, littering, and threatening to vote Democratic in the next election. How could he waste time on little old Dexter and his harmless hobby?

All right then: I would be unstintingly ordinary until it made his teeth hurt. It might take weeks rather than days, but I would do it. I would live fully the synthetic life I had created in order to appear human. And since humans are generally ruled by sex, I would start with a visit to my girlfriend Rita.

It's an odd term, 'girlfriend,' particularly for grown persons. And in practice an even odder concept. Generally speaking, in adults it described a woman, not a girl, who was willing to provide sex, not friendship. In fact, from what I had observed it was quite possible for one to actively dislike one's girlfriend, although of course true hatred is reserved for marriage. I had so far been unable to determine what women expect in return from a boyfriend, but apparently I had it as far as Rita was concerned. It certainly wasn't sex, which to me seemed about as interesting as calculating foreign trade deficits.

Luckily, Rita also was uninterested in sex, for the most part. She was the product of a disastrous early marriage to a man whose idea of a good time turned out to be smoking crack and beating her. Later he branched out into infecting her with several intriguing diseases. But when he battered the kids one night Rita's marvelous country-song loyalty ruptured, and she flung the swine out of her life and, happily, into prison.

As a result of all this turmoil, she had been looking for a gentleman who might be interested in companionship and conversation, someone who did not need to indulge the crude animal urges of base passion. A man, in other words, who would value her for her finer qualities and not her willingness to indulge in naked acrobatics. Ecce, Dexter. For almost two years she had been my ideal disguise, a key ingredient of Dexter as the world at large knew him. And in return I had not beaten her, had not infected her with anything, had not forced my animal lust on her, and she actually seemed to enjoy my company.

And as a bonus, I had become quite fond of her children, Astor and Cody. Strange, perhaps, but nonetheless true, I assure you. If everyone else in the world were to mysteriously disappear, I would feel irritated about it only because there would be no one to make me doughnuts. But children are interesting to me and, in fact, I like them. Rita's two kids had been through a traumatic early childhood, and maybe because I had, too, I felt a special attachment to them, an interest that went beyond maintaining my disguise with Rita.

Aside from the bonus of her children, Rita herself was quite presentable. She had short and neat blond hair, a trim and athletic body, and she seldom said things that were outright stupid. I could go in public with her and know that we looked like an appropriately matched human pair, which was really the whole point. People even said we were an attractive couple, although

I was never sure what that meant. I suppose Rita found me attractive some-how, although her track record with men didn't make that too flattering. Still, it's always nice to be around somebody who thinks I am wonderful. It confirms my low opinion of people.

I looked at the clock on my desk. Five thirty-two: within the next fifteen minutes Rita would be home from her job at Fairchild Title Agency, where she did something very complicated involving fractions of percentage points. By the time I got to her house, she should be there.

With a cheerful synthetic smile I headed out the door, waved to Doakes, and drove over to Rita's modest South Miami house. The traffic wasn't too bad, which is to say that there were no fatal accidents or shootings, and in just under twenty minutes I parked my car in front of Rita's bungalow. Sergeant Doakes cruised past to the end of the street and, as I knocked on the front door, he parked across the way.

The door swung open and Rita peered out at me. 'Oh!' she said. 'Dexter.'

'In person,' I said. 'I was in the neighborhood and wondered if you were home yet.'

'Well, I – I just walked in the door. I must look like a mess . . . Um – come on in. Would you like a beer?'

Beer; what a thought. I never touch the stuff – and yet, it was so amazingly normal, so perfectly visit-the-girlfriend-after-work, even Doakes had to be impressed. It was just the right touch. 'I would love a beer,' I said, and I followed her into the relative cool of the living room.

'Have a seat,' she said. 'I'm just going to freshen up a little.' She smiled at me. 'The kids are out back, but I'm sure they'll be all over you when they find out you're here.' And she swished off down the hall, returning a moment later with a can of beer. 'I'll be right back,' she said, and went away to her bedroom at the back of the house.

I sat on the sofa and looked at the beer in my hand. I am not a drinker – really, drinking is not a recommended habit for predators. It slows the reflexes, dulls the perceptions, and knits up the raveled sleeve of care, which always sounded to me like a very bad thing. But here I was, a demon on vacation, attempting the ultimate sacrifice by giving up my powers and becoming human – and so a beer was just the thing for Dipsophobic Dexter.

I took a sip. The taste was bitter and thin, just as I would be if I had to keep the Dark Passenger buckled into his seat belt for very long. Still, I suppose beer is an acquired taste. I took another sip. I could feel it gurgle all the way down and splash into my stomach, and it occurred to me that with all the excitement and frustration of the day I hadn't eaten lunch. But what the hell – it was just a light beer; or as the can proudly proclaimed: LITE BEER. I suppose we should be very grateful they hadn't thought of a cuter way to spell beer.

I took a big sip. It wasn't that bad when you got used to it. By golly, it really WAS relaxing. I, at any rate, felt more relaxed with each swig. Another refreshing sip – I couldn't remember that it had tasted this good when I'd tried it in college. Of course, I was just a boy then, not the manly mature hard-working upright citizen I was now. I tilted the can, but nothing came out.

Well – somehow the can was empty. And yet I was still thirsty. Could this unpleasant situation really be tolerated? I thought not. Absolutely intolerable. In fact, I did not plan to tolerate it. I stood up and proceeded to the kitchen in a firm and unyielding manner. There were several more cans of lite beer in the refrigerator and I took one back to the couch.

I sat. I opened the beer. I took a sip. Much better. Damn that Doakes anyway. Maybe I should take him a beer. It might relax him, get him to loosen up and call the whole thing off. After all, we were on the same side, weren't we?

I sipped. Rita came back wearing a pair of denim shorts and a white tank top with a tiny satin bow at the neckline. I had to admit, she looked very nice. I could really pick a disguise. 'Well,' she said as she slid onto the couch next to me, 'it's nice to see you, out of the blue like this.'

'It certainly must be,' I said.

She cocked her head to one side and looked at me funny. 'Did you have a hard day at work?'

'An awful day,' I said, and took a sip. 'Had to let a bad guy go. Very bad guy.'

'Oh.' She frowned. 'Why did – I mean, couldn't you just . . .'

'I wanted to just,' I said. 'But I couldn't.' I raised the beer can to her. 'Politics.' I took a sip.

Rita shook her head. 'I still can't get used to the idea that, that – I mean, from the outside it seems so cut-and-dried. You find the bad guy, you put him away. But politics? I mean, with – what did he do?'

'He helped to kill some kids,' I said.

'Oh,' she said, and looked shocked. 'My God, there must be something you can do.'

I smiled at her. By gum, she had seen it right away. What a gal. Didn't I say I could pick 'em? 'You have put your finger right on it,' I said, and I took her hand to look at that finger. 'There is something I can do. And very well, too.' I patted her hand, spilling only a little bit of beer. 'I knew you'd understand.'

She looked confused. 'Oh,' she said. 'What kind of – I mean – What will you do?'

I took a sip. Why shouldn't I tell her? I could see she already got the idea. Why not? I opened my mouth, but before I could whisper even one syllable about the Dark Passenger and my harmless hobby, Cody and Astor came racing into the room, stopped dead when they saw me, and stood there looking from me to their mother.

'Hi Dexter,' Astor said. She nudged her brother.

'Hi,' he said softly. He was not a big talker. In fact, he never said much of anything. Poor kid. The whole thing with his father had really messed him up. 'Are you drunk?' he asked me. It was a big speech for him.

'Cody!' Rita said. I waved her off bravely and faced him.

'Drunk?' I said. 'Me?'

He nodded. 'Yeah.'

'Certainly not,' I said firmly, giving him my very best dignified frown. 'Possibly a little bit tipsy, but that's not the same thing at all.'

'Oh,' he said, and his sister chimed in, 'Are you staying for dinner?'

'Oh, I think I should probably be going,' I said, but Rita put a surprisingly firm hand on my shoulder.

'You're not driving anywhere like this,' she said.

'Like what?'

'Tipsy,' said Cody.

'I'm not tipsy,' I said.

'You said you were,' said Cody. I couldn't remember the last time I'd heard him put four words in a row like that, and I was very proud of him.

'You did,' Astor added. 'You said you're not drunk, you're just a little tipsy.'

'I said that?' They both nodded. 'Oh. Well then—'

'Well then,' Rita chimed in, 'I guess you're staying for dinner.'

Well then. I guess I did. I am pretty sure I did, anyway. I do know that at some point I went to the refrigerator for a lite beer and discovered they were all gone. And at some later point I was sitting on the couch again. The television was on and I was trying to figure out what the actors were saying and why an invisible crowd thought it was the most hilarious dialogue of all time.

Rita slid onto the couch next to me. 'The kids are in bed,' she said. 'How do you feel?'

'I feel wonderful,' I said. 'If only I could figure out what's so funny.'

Rita put a hand on my shoulder. 'It really bothers you, doesn't it? Letting the bad guy go. Children . . .' She moved closer and put her arm all the way around me, laying her head on my shoulder. 'You're such a good guy, Dexter.'

'No, I'm not,' I said, wondering why she would say something so very strange.

Rita sat up and looked from my left eye to my right eye and back again. 'But you are, you KNOW you are.' She smiled and nestled her head back down on my shoulder. 'I think it's . . . nice that you came here. To see me. When you were feeling bad.'

I started to tell her that wasn't quite right, but then it occurred to me: I *had* come here when I felt bad. True, it was only to bore Doakes into going away, after the terrible frustration of losing my playdate with Reiker. But it had turned out to be a pretty good idea after all, hadn't it? Good old Rita. She was very warm and she smelled nice. 'Good old Rita,' I said. I pulled her against me as tight as I could and leaned my cheek against the top of her head.

We sat that way for a few minutes, and then Rita wiggled to her feet and pulled me up by the hand. 'Come on,' she said. 'Let's get you to bed.'

Which we did, and when I had flopped down under the top sheet and she crawled in beside me, she was just so nice and smelled so good and felt so warm and comfortable that—

Well. Beer really is amazing stuff, isn't it?

6

I woke up with a headache, a feeling of tremendous self-loathing, and a sense of disorientation. There was a rose-colored sheet against my cheek. My sheets – the sheets I woke up to every day in my little bed – were not rose-colored, and they did not smell like this. The mattress seemed too spacious to be my modest trundle bed, and really – I was quite sure this was not my headache either.

'Good morning, handsome,' said a voice somewhere over my feet. I turned my head and saw Rita standing at the foot of the bed, looking down at me with a happy little smile.

'Ung,' I said in a voice that sounded like a toad's croak and hurt my head even more. But apparently it was an amusing kind of pain, because Rita's smile widened.

'That's what I thought,' she said. 'I'll get you some aspirin.' She leaned over and rubbed my leg. 'Mmm,' she said, and then turned and went into the bathroom.

I sat up. This may have been a strategic mistake, as it made my head pound a great deal more. I closed my eyes, breathed deeply, and waited for my aspirin.

This normal life was going to take a little getting used to.

But oddly enough it didn't, not really. I found that if I limited myself to one or two beers, I could relax just enough to blend in with the slipcover on the couch. And so several nights a week, with ever-faithful Sergeant Doakes in my rearview mirror, I would stop over at Rita's house after work, play with Cody and Astor, and sit with Rita after the kids were in bed. Around ten I would head for the door. Rita seemed to expect to be kissed when I left, so I generally arranged to kiss her standing in the open front door where Doakes could see me. I used all the technique I could muster from the many movies I have seen, and Rita responded happily.

I do like routine, and I settled into this new one to a point where I almost began to believe in it myself. It was so boring that I was putting my real self to sleep. From far away in the backseat of the deepest darkest corner of

Dexterland I could even hear the Dark Passenger starting to snore gently, which was a little scary and made me feel a tiny bit lonesome for the first time. But I stayed the course, making a small game of my visits to Rita to see how far I could push it, knowing that Doakes was watching and, hopefully, beginning to wonder just a little bit. I brought flowers, candy, and pizza. I kissed Rita ever more outlandishly, framed in the open front door to give Doakes the best possible picture. I knew it was a ridiculous display, but it was the only weapon I had.

For days on end Doakes stayed with me. His appearances were unpredictable, which made him seem even more threatening. I never knew when or where he might turn up, and that made me feel like he was always there. If I went into the grocery store, Doakes was waiting by the broccoli. If I rode my bicycle out Old Cutler Road, somewhere along the way I would see the maroon Taurus parked under a banyan tree. A day might go by without a Doakes sighting, but I could feel him out there, circling downwind and waiting, and I did not dare hope that he had given up; if I could not see him, he was either well hidden or waiting to spring another surprise appearance on me.

I was forced into being Daytime Dexter on a full-time basis, like an actor trapped in a movie, knowing that the real world was right there, just beyond the screen, but as unreachable as the moon. And like the moon, the thought of Reiker pulled at me. The thought of him clomping through his unworried life in those absurd red boots was almost more than I could stand.

Of course I knew that even Doakes could not keep this up forever. He was, after all, receiving a handsome salary from the people of Miami for performing a job, and every now and then he had to perform it. But Doakes understood the rising interior tide that battered at me, and he knew that if he kept the pressure on long enough, the disguise would slip, HAD to slip, as the cool whispers from the backseat became more urgent.

And so there we were, balanced on a knife edge that was unfortunately only metaphorical. Sooner or later, I had to be me. But until then I would see an awful lot of Rita. She couldn't hold a candle to my old flame, the Dark Passenger, but I did need my secret identity. And until I escaped Doakes, Rita was my cape, red tights, and utility belt – almost the entire costume.

Very well: I would sit on the couch, can of beer in hand, watching *Survivor* and thinking of an interesting variation of the game that would never make it to the network. If you simply add Dexter to the castaways and interpret the title a bit more literally . . .

It was not all dismal, bleak, and wretched. Several times a week I got to play kick the can with Cody and Astor and the other assorted wild creatures of the neighborhood, which brings us back to where we began: Dexter Dismasted, unable to sail through his normal life, anchored instead to a gaggle of kids and a ravioli can. And on evenings when it was raining, we stayed inside around the dining table, while Rita bustled about doing laundry, washing dishes, and otherwise perfecting the domestic bliss of her little nest.

There are only so many indoor games one can play with two children of such tender ages and damaged spirits as Cody and Astor; most of the board games were uninteresting or incomprehensible to them, and too many of the card games seemed to require a lighthearted simplemindedness that even I could not fake convincingly. But we finally hit on hangman; it was educational, creative, and mildly homicidal, which made everyone happy, even Rita.

If you had asked me pre-Doakes if a life of hangman and Miller Lite sounded like my cup of tea, I would have been forced to confess that Dexter Oolong was somewhat darker. But as the days piled up and I slipped further into the reality of my disguise, I had to ask myself: Was I enjoying the life of Mr. Suburban Householder just a little too much?

Still, it was very comforting somehow to see the predatory zest Cody and Astor brought to something as harmless as hangman. Their enthusiasm for hanging the little stick figures made me feel a bit more like we might all be part of the same general species. As they happily murdered their anonymous hanged men, I felt a certain kinship.

Astor quickly learned to draw the gallows and the lines for the letters. She was, of course, much more verbal about it. 'Seven letters,' she would say, then tucking her upper lip between her teeth add, 'Wait. Six.' As Cody and I missed on our guesses she would pounce and call out, 'An *ARM*! Ha!' Cody would stare at her without expression, and then look down to the doodled figure hanging from its noose. When it was his turn and we missed a guess, he would say in his soft voice, 'Leg,' and look up at us with something that might almost have been triumph in someone who showed emotion. And when the line of dashes under the gallows was finally filled in with the spelled-out word, they would both look at the dangling man with satisfaction, and once or twice Cody even said, 'Dead,' before Astor bounced up and down and said, 'Again, Dexter! My turn!'

All very idyllic. Our perfect little family of Rita, the kids, and Monster makes four. But no matter how many stick figures we executed, it did nothing to kill my worry that time was gurgling rapidly down the drain and soon I would be a white-haired old man, too feeble to lift a carving knife, tottering through my horrifyingly ordinary days, shadowed by an ancient Sergeant Doakes and a sense of missed opportunity.

As long as I couldn't think of a way out, I was in the noose as surely as Cody and Astor's stick figures. Very depressing, and I am ashamed to admit that I almost lost hope, which I never would have done if I had remembered one important thing.

This was Miami.

7

Of course it couldn't last. I should have known that such an unnatural state of affairs had to give way, yield to the natural order of things. After all, I lived in a city where mayhem was like the sunshine, always right behind the next cloud. Three weeks after my first unsettling encounter with Sergeant Doakes, the clouds finally broke.

It was just a piece of luck, really – not quite the falling piano I had been hoping for, but still a happy coincidence. I was having lunch with my sister, Deborah. Excuse me; I should have said, SERGEANT Deborah. Like her father, Harry, Debs was a cop. Owing to the happy outcome of recent events, she had been promoted, pulled out of the prostitute costume she had been forced to wear by her assignment with vice, whisked off the street corner at last and into her very own set of sergeant's stripes.

It should have made her happy. After all, this was what she thought she wanted; an end to her tenure as a pretend hooker. Any young and reasonably attractive female officer assigned to vice would sooner or later find herself in a prostitution sting operation, and Deborah was very attractive. But her lush figure and healthy good looks had never done anything for my poor sister except embarrass her. She hated to wear anything that even hinted at her physical charms, and standing on the street in hot pants and a tube top had been sheer torture for her. She had been in danger of growing permanent frown lines.

Because I am an inhuman monster, I tend to be logical, and I had thought that her new assignment would end her martyrdom as Our Lady of Perpetual Grumpiness. Alas, even her transfer to homicide had failed to bring a smile to her face. Somewhere along the way she had decided that serious law enforcement personnel must reshape their faces until they look like large, mean-spirited fish, and she was still working very hard to accomplish this.

We had come to lunch together in her new motor-pool car, another of the perks of her promotion that really should have brought a small ray of sunshine into her life. It didn't seem to. I wondered if I should worry about her. I watched her as I slid into a booth at Café Relampago, our favorite Cuban restaurant. She called in her location and status and then sat across from me with a frown.

'Well, Sergeant Grouper,' I said as we picked up our menus.

'Is that funny, Dexter?'

'Yes,' I said. 'Very funny. And a little sad, too. Like life itself. Especially your life, Deborah.'

'Fuck you, Charlie,' she said. 'My life is fine.' And to prove it, she ordered a *medianoche* sandwich, the best in Miami, and a *batido de mamey*, a milk shake made from a unique tropical fruit that tastes something like a combination of peach and watermelon.

My life was every bit as fine as hers, so I ordered the same thing. Because we were regulars here, and had been coming here most of our lives, the aging, unshaven waiter snatched away our menus with a face that might have been the role model for Deborah's, and stomped off to the kitchen like Godzilla on his way to Tokyo.

'Everyone is so cheerful and happy,' I said.

'This isn't *Mister Rogers' Neighborhood*, Dex. It's Miami. Only the bad guys are happy.' She looked at me without expression, a perfect cop stare. 'How come you're not laughing and singing?'

'Unkind, Deb. Very unkind. I've been good for months.'

She took a sip of water. 'Uh-huh. And it's making you crazy.'

'Much worse than that,' I said with a shudder. 'I think it's making me normal.'

'Coulda fooled me,' she said.

'Sad but true. I've become a couch potato.' I hesitated, then blurted it out. After all, if a boy can't share his problems with his family, who can he confide in? 'It's Sergeant Doakes,' I said.

She nodded. 'He's got a real hard-on for you,' she said. 'You better keep away from him.'

'I would love to,' I said. 'But HE won't keep away from ME.'

Her cop stare got harder. 'What do you plan to do about it?'

I opened my mouth to deny all the things I had been thinking, but happily for the good of my immortal soul, before I could lie to her we were interrupted by the sound of Deb's radio. She cocked her head to one side, snatched up the radio, and said she was on her way. 'Come on,' she snapped, heading for the door. I followed meekly behind, pausing only to throw some money on the table.

Deborah was already backing out her car by the time I came out of Relampago's. I hurried over and lunged for the door. She was moving forward and out of the parking lot before I even got both feet in. 'Really, Deb,' I said. 'I almost lost a shoe. What's so important?'

Deborah frowned, accelerating through a small gap in traffic that only a Miami driver would have attempted. 'I don't know,' she said as she turned on the siren.

I blinked and raised my voice over the noise. 'Didn't the dispatcher tell you?'

'Have you ever heard the dispatcher stutter, Dexter?'

'Why no, Deb, I haven't. Did this one do that?'

Deb swerved around a school bus and roared up onto 836. 'Yeah,' she said. She turned hard to avoid a BMW full of young men, who all flipped her off. 'I think it's a homicide.'

'You think,' I said.

'Yeah,' she answered, and then she concentrated on driving and I let her. High speeds always remind me of my own mortality, especially on Miami's roads. And as for the Case of the Stuttering Dispatcher – well, Sergeant Nancy Drew and I would find out soon enough, particularly at this speed, and a little excitement is always welcome.

In a very few minutes Deb managed to get us over near the Orange Bowl without causing major loss of life, and we came down onto the surface roads and made a few quick turns before sliding into the curb at a small house on N.W. 4th Street. The street was lined with similar houses, all small and close together and each one with its own wall or chain-link fence. Many of them were brightly colored and had paved yards.

Two patrol cars had already pulled up in front of the house, their lights flashing. A pair of uniformed cops were rolling out the yellow crime-scene tape around the place, and as we got out, I saw a third cop sitting in the front seat of one of the cars, his head in his hands. On the porch of the house a fourth cop stood beside an elderly lady. There were two small steps leading up to the porch and she sat on the top one. She seemed to be alternating weeping with throwing up. Somewhere nearby a dog was howling, the same note over and over.

Deborah marched up to the nearest uniform. He was a square, middle-aged guy with dark hair and a look on his face that said he wished he was sitting in his car with his head in his hands, too. 'What have we got?' Deb asked him, holding up her badge.

The cop shook his head without looking at us and blurted out, 'I'm not going in there again, not if it costs me my pension.' And he turned away, almost walking into the side of a patrol car, rolling out the yellow tape like it could protect him from whatever was in the house.

Deborah stared after the cop, then looked at me. Quite frankly, I could think of nothing really useful or clever to say, and for a moment we just stood there looking at each other. The wind rattled the crime-scene tape, and the dog continued to howl, a kind of weird yodeling sound that did nothing to increase my affection for the canine species. Deborah shook her head. 'Somebody should shut that fucking dog up,' she said, and she ducked under the yellow tape and started up the walk to the house. I followed. After a few steps I realized that the dog sound was getting closer; it was in the house, probably the victim's pet. Quite often an animal reacts badly to its owner's death.

We stopped at the steps and Deborah looked up at the cop, reading his name tag. 'Coronel. Is this lady a witness?'

The cop didn't look at us. 'Yeah,' he said. 'Mrs. Medina. She called it in,' and the old woman leaned over and retched.

Deborah frowned. 'What's with that dog?' she asked him.

Coronel made a sort of barking noise halfway between laughing and gagging, but he didn't answer and he didn't look at us.

I suppose Deborah had had enough, and it's hard to blame her. 'What the fuck is going on here?' she demanded.

Coronel turned his head to look at us. There was no expression at all on his face. 'See for yourself,' he said, and then he turned away again. Deborah thought she was going to say something, but changed her mind. She looked at me instead and shrugged.

'We might as well take a look,' I told her, and I hoped I didn't sound too eager. In truth, I was anxious to see anything that could create this kind of reaction in Miami cops. Sergeant Doakes might very well prevent me from doing anything of my own, but he couldn't stop me from admiring someone else's creativity. After all, it was my job, and shouldn't we enjoy our work?

Deborah, on the other hand, showed uncharacteristic reluctance. She glanced back at the patrol car where the cop still sat unmoving, head in hands. Then she looked back to Coronel and the old lady, then at the front door of the little house. She took a deep breath, blew it out hard, and said, 'All right. Let's have a look.' But she still didn't move, so I slipped past her and pushed open the door.

The front room of the little house was dark, curtains and blinds all pulled closed. There was one easy chair that looked like it had come from a thrift shop. It had a slipcover that was so dirty it was impossible to tell what color it was supposed to be. The chair sat in front of a small TV on a folding card table. Other than that the room was empty. A doorway opposite the front door showed a small patch of light, and that seemed to be where the dog was yowling, so I headed that way, toward the back of the house.

Animals do not like me, which proves they are smarter than we think. They seem to sense what I am, and they disapprove, often expressing their opinion in a very pointed way. So I was a little bit reluctant to approach a dog already so obviously upset. But I moved through the doorway, slowly, calling out hopefully, 'Nice doggie!' It didn't really sound like a very nice doggie; it sounded like a brain-damaged pit bull with rabies. But I do try to put a good face on things, even with our canine friends. With a kind and animal-loving expression on my face, I stepped to the swinging door that led to what was obviously the kitchen.

As I touched the door I heard a soft and uneasy rustling from the Dark Passenger and I paused. *What?* I asked, but there was no reply. I closed my eyes for just a second, but the page was blank; no secret message flashed onto the back of my eyelids. I shrugged, pushed open the door, and stepped into the kitchen.

The upper half of the room was painted a faded, greasy yellow, and the lower half was lined with old, blue pinstriped white tiles. There was a small refrigerator in one corner and a hot plate on the counter. A palmetto bug ran across the counter and dove behind the refrigerator. A sheet of plywood had been nailed across the room's only window, and there was a single dim light-bulb hanging from the ceiling.

Under the lightbulb was a large, heavy old table, the kind with square legs and a white porcelain finish. A large mirror hung on the wall at an angle that allowed it to reflect whatever was on the table. And in that reflection, lying in the middle of the table was a . . . um . . .

Well. I assume it had started life as a human being of some kind, quite probably male and Hispanic. Very difficult to say in its present state which, I admit, left even me a bit startled. Still, in spite of being surprised, I had to admire the thoroughness of the work, and the neatness. It would have made a surgeon very jealous, although it seems likely that very few surgeons would be able to justify this kind of work to an HMO.

I would never have thought, for instance, of cutting off the lips and eyelids like that, and although I pride myself on my neat work, I could never have done so without damage to the eyes, which in this case were rolling wildly back and forth, unable to close or even blink, always returning to that mirror. Just a hunch, but I guessed that the eyelids had been done last, long after the nose and ears had been oh-so-neatly removed. I could not decide, however, if I would have done these before or after the arms, legs, genitals, etc. A diffi-cult series of choices, but from the look of things, it had all been done prop-erly, even expertly, by someone who'd had plenty of practice. We often speak of very neat body work as 'surgical.' But this was actual surgery. There was no bleeding at all, even from the mouth, where the lips and tongue had been removed. Even the teeth; one had to admire such amazing thoroughness. Every cut had been professionally closed; a white bandage was neatly taped to each shoulder where arms had once hung, and the rest of the cuts had already healed, in a way you might hope to find in the very best of hospitals.

Everything on the body had been cut off, absolutely everything. There was nothing left of it but a bare and featureless head attached to an unencum-bered body. I could not imagine how it was possible to do this without killing the thing, and it was certainly far beyond me why anyone would want to. It revealed a cruelty that really made one wonder if the universe was such a good idea after all. Pardon me if this sounds a tad hypocritical coming from Death-head Dexter, but I know very well what I am and it is nothing like this. I do what the Dark Passenger deems necessary, to someone who truly deserves it, and it always ends in death – which I am sure the thing on the table would agree was not such a bad thing.

But this – to do all this so patiently and carefully and leave it alive in front of a mirror . . . I could feel a sense of black wonder drifting up from deep inside, as if for the very first time my Dark Passenger was feeling just a little bit insignificant.

The thing on the table did not appear to register my presence. It just kept making that deranged doggie sound, nonstop, the same horrible wavering note over and over.

I heard Deb scuffle to a halt behind me. 'Oh Jesus,' she said. 'Oh God . . . What is it?'

'I don't know,' I said. 'But at least it's not a dog.'

8

There was a very quiet rush of air, and I looked beyond Deborah to see that Sergeant Doakes had arrived. He glanced once around the room and then his eyes settled on the table. I admit that I had been curious to see what his reaction would be to something this extreme, and it was well worth the wait. When Doakes saw the kitchen's central exhibit his eyes locked onto it and he stopped moving so completely that he could have been a statue. After a long moment he moved toward it, gliding slowly as if pulled on a string. He slid past us without noticing that we were there and came to a stop at the table.

For several seconds he stared down at the thing. Then, still without even blinking, he reached inside his sport coat and drew out his pistol. Slowly, with no expression, he aimed it between the unblinkable eyes of the still-yowling thing on the table. He cocked the pistol.

'Doakes,' said Deborah in a dry croak of a voice, and she cleared her throat and tried again. 'Doakes!'

Doakes did not answer nor look away, but he didn't pull the trigger, which seemed a shame. After all, what were we going to do with this thing? It wasn't going to tell us who had done this. And I had a feeling its days as a useful member of society had come to an end. Why not let Doakes put it out of its misery? And then Deb and I would reluctantly be compelled to report what Doakes had done, he would be fired and even imprisoned, and my problems would be over. It seemed like such a neat solution, but of course it was not the kind of thing Deborah would ever agree to. She can get so fussy and official at times.

'Put away your weapon, Doakes,' she said, and although the rest of him remained absolutely motionless, he swiveled his head to look at her.

'Only thing to do,' he said. 'Believe me.'

Deborah shook her head. 'You know you can't,' she said. They stared at each other for a moment, then his eyes clicked onto me. It was exceptionally hard for me to look back without blurting out something like, 'Oh, what the hell – go for it!' But I managed somehow, and Doakes turned the pistol up into the air. He looked back at the thing, shook his head, and put the pistol away. 'Shit,' he said. 'Shoulda let me.' And he turned, walking rapidly out of the room.

Within the next few minutes the room became crowded with people who tried desperately not to look while they went to work. Camilla Figg, a stocky, short-haired lab tech who had always seemed to be limited in expression to either blushing or staring, was crying quietly as she dusted for fingerprints. Angel Batista, or Angel-no-relation as we called him, since that is how he always introduced himself, turned pale and clamped his jaw tightly shut, but he stayed in the room. Vince Masuoka, a co-worker who normally acted like he was only pretending to be human, trembled so badly he had to go outside and sit on the porch.

I began to wonder if I should pretend to be horrified, too, just to avoid being too noticeable. Perhaps I should go out and sit beside Vince. What did one talk about at such times? Baseball? The weather? Surely one wouldn't talk about the thing we were running from – and yet, I found to my surprise that I would not mind talking about it. In truth, the thing was beginning to raise a mild twitch of interest from a Certain Interior Party. I had always worked so hard to avoid any kind of notice at all, and here was someone doing just the opposite. Clearly this monster was showing off for some reason, and it may have been only a perfectly natural competitive spirit, but that seemed a little irritating, even while it made me want to know more. Whoever did this was unlike anyone else I had ever encountered. Should I move this anonymous predator onto my list? Or should I pretend to swoon with horror and go sit outside on the porch?

As I pondered this difficult choice, Sergeant Doakes brushed past me again, for once barely even pausing to glower at me, and I recalled that because of him I had no chance to work through a list at the moment. It was mildly disconcerting, but it did make the decision seem a little easier. I started composing a properly unsettled facial expression, but got no further than raising my eyebrows. Two paramedics came rushing in, all focused importance, and stopped dead when they saw the victim. One of them immediately ran from the room. The other, a young black woman, turned to me and said, 'What the fuck are *we* supposed to do?' Then she started crying, too.

You have to agree she had a point. Sergeant Doakes's solution was starting to look more practical, even elegant. There seemed very little point in whisking this thing onto a gurney and dashing through Miami traffic to deliver it to a hospital. As the young lady had so elegantly put it, what the fuck were they supposed to do? But clearly somebody had to do something. If we just left it there and stood around like this, eventually someone would complain about all the cops throwing up in the yard, which would be very bad for the department's image.

It was Deborah who finally got things organized. She persuaded the paramedics to sedate the victim and take it away, which allowed the surprisingly squeamish lab techs to come back inside and go to work. The quiet in the little house as the drugs took hold of the thing was close to ecstatic. The paramedics got the thing covered and onto their gurney without dropping it and wheeled it off into the sunset.

And just in time; as the ambulance pulled away from the curb the news trucks started to arrive. In a way it was a shame; I would love to have seen the reaction of one or two of the reporters, Rick Sangre in particular. He had been the area's leading devotee of 'If it bleeds, it leads,' and I had never seen him express any sense of pain or horror, except on camera or if his hair was mussed. But it was not to be. By the time Rick's cameraman was ready to roll, there was nothing left to see other than the little house fenced in by the yellow tape, and a handful of cops with clamped jaws who wouldn't have had much to say to Sangre on a good day, and today probably wouldn't have told him his own name.

There was really not a great deal for me to do. I had come in Deborah's car and so I did not have my kit, and in any case there was no visible blood spatter anywhere that I could see. Since that was my area of expertise, I felt I should find something and be useful, but our surgical friend had been too careful. Just to be sure I looked through the rest of the house, which wasn't much. There was one small bedroom, an even smaller bathroom, and a closet. They all seemed to be empty, except for a bare, battered mattress on the floor of the bedroom. It looked like it had come from the same thrift shop as the living-room chair and had been pounded flat like a Cuban steak. No other furniture or utensils, not even a plastic spoon.

The only thing that showed even the smallest hint of personality was something Angel-no-relation found under the table as I finished my quick tour of the house. 'Hola,' he said, and pulled a small piece of notepaper off the floor with his tweezers. I stepped over to see what it might be. It was hardly worth the effort; nothing but a single small page of white paper, ripped slightly at the top where a little rectangle had been torn away. I looked just above Angel's head and sure enough, there on the side of the table was the missing rectangle of paper, held to the table with a strip of Scotch tape. 'Mira,' I said, and Angel looked. 'Aha,' he said.

As he examined the tape carefully – tape holds fingerprints wonderfully well – he put the paper on the floor and I squatted down to look at it. There were some letters written on it in a spidery hand; I leaned over farther to read them: LOYALTY.

'Loyalty?' I said.

'Sure. Isn't that an important virtue?'

'Let's ask him,' I said, and Angel shuddered hard enough that he almost dropped his tweezers.

'Me cago en diez with that shit,' he said, and reached for a plastic bag to put the paper into. It hardly seemed like something worth watching, and there was really nothing else to see, so I headed for the door.

I certainly am not a professional profiler, but because of my dark hobby I often have a certain amount of insight into other crimes that seem to come from the same neighborhood. This, however, was far outside the bounds of anything I had ever seen or imagined. There was no hint of any kind that pointed toward personality or motivation, and I was intrigued nearly as much as I was irritated. What kind of predator would leave the meat lying around and still wiggling like that?

I went outside and stood on the porch. Doakes was huddled with Captain Matthews, telling him something that had the captain looking worried. Deborah was crouched beside the old lady, talking quietly with her. I could feel a breeze picking up, the squall breeze that comes right before the afternoon thunderstorm, and as I looked up the first hard spatters of rain pelted down on the sidewalk. Sangre, who had been standing at the tape waving his microphone and trying to get the attention of Captain Matthews, looked up at the clouds too and, as the thunder began to rumble, threw his microphone at his producer and lurched into the news van.

My stomach rumbled, too, and I remembered that I had missed my lunch in all the excitement. This would never do; I needed to keep up my strength. My naturally high metabolism needed constant attention: no diet for Dexter. But I had to depend on Deborah for a ride, and I had the feeling, just a hunch, that she would not be sympathetic about any mention of eating at the moment. I looked at her again. She was cradling the old lady, Mrs. Medina, who had apparently given up retching and was concentrating on sobbing.

I sighed and walked to the car through the rain. I didn't really mind getting wet. It looked like I was going to have a long wait to dry off.

It was indeed a long wait, well over two hours. I sat in the car and listened to the radio and tried to picture, bite by bite, what it was like to eat a *medianoche* sandwich: the crackle of the bread crust, so crisp and toasty it scratches the inside of your mouth as you bite down. Then the first taste of mustard, followed by the soothing cheese and the salt of the meat. Next bite – a piece of pickle. Chew it all up; let the flavors mingle. Swallow. Take a big sip of Iron Beer (pronounced Ee-roan Bay-er, and it's a soda). Sigh. Sheer bliss. I would rather eat than do anything else except play with the Passenger. It's a true miracle of genetics that I am not fat.

I was on my third imaginary sandwich when Deborah finally came back to the car. She slid into the driver's seat, closed the door, and just sat there, staring ahead through the rain-splattered windshield. And I knew it wasn't the best thing I could have said, but I couldn't help myself. 'You look beat, Deb. How about lunch?'

She shook her head but didn't say anything.

'Maybe a nice sandwich. Or a fruit salad – get your blood sugar back up? You'll feel so much better.'

Now she looked at me, but it was not a look that showed any real promise of lunch at any time in the near future. 'This is why I wanted to be a cop,' she said.

'The fruit salad?'

'That thing in there – ' she said, and then turned to look out the windshield again. 'I want to nail that – that, whatever it is that could do that to a human being. I want it so bad I can *taste* it.'

'Does it taste like a sandwich, Deborah? Because—'

She smacked the heels of her palms onto the rim of the steering wheel, hard. Then she did it again. 'GodDAMN it,' she said. 'God-fucking-DAMN it!'

I sighed. Clearly long-suffering Dexter was going to be denied his crust of bread. And all because Deborah was having some kind of epiphany from seeing a piece of wiggling meat. Of course it was a terrible thing, and the world would be a much better place without someone in it who could do that, but did that mean we had to miss lunch? Didn't we all need to keep up our strength to catch this guy? Still, it did not seem like the very best time to point this out to Deborah, so I simply sat there with her, watching the rain splat against the windshield, and ate imaginary sandwich number four.

The next morning I had hardly settled into my little cubicle at work when my phone rang. 'Captain Matthews wants to see everybody who was there yesterday,' Deborah said.

'Good morning, Sis. Fine, thanks, and you?'

'Right now,' she said, and hung up.

The police world is made up of routine, both official and unofficial. This is one of the reasons I like my job. I always know what's coming, and so there are fewer human responses for me to memorize and then fake at the appropriate times, fewer chances for me to be caught off guard and react in a way that might call into question my membership in the race.

As far as I knew, Captain Matthews had never before called in 'everybody who was there.' Even when a case was generating a great deal of publicity, it was his policy to handle the press and those above him in the command structure, and let the investigating officer handle the casework. I could think of absolutely no reason why he would violate this protocol, even with a case as unusual as this one. And especially so soon – there had barely been enough time for him to approve a press release.

But 'right now' still meant right now, as far as I could tell, so I tottered down the hall to the captain's office. His secretary, Gwen, one of the most efficient women who had ever lived, sat there at her desk. She was also one of the plainest and most serious, and I found it almost impossible to resist tweaking her. 'Gwendolyn! Vision of radiant loveliness! Fly away with me to the blood lab!' I said as I came into the office.

She nodded at the door at the far end of the room. 'They're in the confer-ence room,' she said, completely stone-faced.

'Is that a no?'

She moved her head an inch to the right. 'That door over there,' she said. 'They're waiting.'

They were indeed. At the head of the conference table Captain Matthews sat with a cup of coffee and a scowl. Ranged around the table were Deborah and Doakes, Vince Masuoka, Camilla Figg, and the four uniformed cops who had been setting the perimeter at the little house of horror when we arrived. Matthews nodded at me and said, 'Is this everybody?'

Doakes stopped glaring at me and said, 'Paramedics.'

Matthews shook his head. 'Not our problem. Somebody will talk to them later.' He cleared his throat and looked down, as though consulting an invis-ible script. 'All right,' he said, and cleared his throat again. 'The, uh, the event of yesterday which occurred at, um, N.W. 4th Street has been interdicted, ah, at the very highest level.' He looked up, and for a moment I thought he was impressed. '*Very* highest,' he said. 'You are all hereby ordered to keep to your-selves what you may have seen, heard, or surmised in connection with this event and its location. No comment, public or private, of any kind.' He looked at Doakes, who nodded, and then he looked around the table at all of us. 'Therefore, ah . . .'

Captain Matthews paused and frowned as he realized that he didn't actu-ally have a 'therefore' for us. Luckily for his reputation as a smooth talker, the door opened. We all turned to look.

The doorway was filled with a very big man in a very nice suit. He wore no tie and the top three buttons of his shirt were undone. A diamond pinkie ring glittered on the little finger of his left hand. His hair was wavy and artfully mussed. He looked to be in his forties, and time had not been kind to his nose. A scar ran across his right eyebrow and another down one side of his chin, but the overall impression was not disfigurement so much as decoration. He looked at us all with a cheerful grin and bright, empty blue eyes, pausing in the door-way for a dramatic moment before he looked to the head of the table and said, 'Captain Matthews?'

The captain was a reasonably large man and masculine in a very well-kept way, but he looked small and even effeminate compared to the man in the doorway, and I believe he felt it. Still, he clenched his manly jaw and said, 'That's right.'

The big man strode in to Matthews and held out his hand. 'Nice to meet you, Captain. I'm Kyle Chutsky. We talked on the phone.' As he shook hands, he glanced around the table, pausing at Deborah before moving back to Matthews. But after only half a second his head snapped back around and he locked stares with Doakes, just for a moment. Neither one of them said anything, moved, twitched, or offered a business card, but I was absolutely positive they knew each other. Without acknowledging this in any way, Doakes looked down at the table in front of him and Chutsky returned his attention to the captain. 'You have a great department here, Captain Matthews. I hear nothing but good things about you guys.'

'Thank you . . . Mr. Chutsky,' Matthews said stiffly. 'Have a seat?'

Chutsky gave him a big, charming smile. 'Thanks, I will,' he said, and slid into the empty seat next to Deborah. She didn't turn to look at him, but from my spot across the table I could see a slow flush climbing up her neck, all the way to her scowl.

And at this point, I could hear a little voice in the back of Dexter's brain clearing its throat and saying, 'Excuse me, just a minute – but what the hell is going on here?' Perhaps someone had slipped some LSD into my coffee, because this entire day was beginning to feel like Dexter in Wonderland. Why were we even here? Who was the battered big guy who made Captain Matthews nervous? How did he know Doakes? And why, for the love of all that is shiny, bright, and sharp, was Deborah's face turning such an unbecoming shade of red?

I often find myself in situations where it seems to me like everyone else has read the instruction book while poor Dexter is in the dark and can't even match tab A with slot B. It usually relates to some natural human emotion, something that is universally understood. Unfortunately, Dexter is from a different universe and does not feel nor understand such things. All I can do is gather a few quick clues to help me decide what kind of face to make while I wait for things to settle back onto the familiar map.

I looked at Vince Masuoka. I was probably closer to him than any of the other lab techs, and not just because we took turns bringing in doughnuts. He always seemed to be faking his way through life, too, as if he had watched a series of videos to learn how to smile and talk to people. He was not quite as talented at pretending as I was, and the results were never as convincing, but I felt a certain kinship.

Right now he looked flustered and intimidated, and he seemed to be trying hard to swallow without any real luck. No clue there.

Camilla Figg was sitting at attention, staring at a spot on the wall in front of her. Her face was pale, but there was a small and very round spot of red color on each cheek.

Deborah, as mentioned, was slumping down in her chair and seemed very busily engaged in turning bright scarlet.

Chutsky slapped the palm of his hand on the table, looked around with a big happy smile, and said, 'I want to thank you all for your cooperation with this thing. It's very important that we keep this quiet until my people can move in on it.'

Captain Matthews cleared his throat. 'Ahem. I, uh, I assume you will want us to continue our routine investigative procedures and the, uh, interrogating of witnesses and so on.'

Chutsky shook his head slowly. 'Absolutely not. I need your people all the way out of the picture immediately. I want this whole thing to cease and desist, disappear – as far as your department is concerned, Captain, I want it never to have happened at all.'

'Are YOU taking over this investigation?' Deborah demanded.

Chutsky looked at her and his smile got bigger. 'That's right,' he said. And he probably would have kept smiling at her indefinitely if not for Officer Coronel, the cop who had sat on the porch with the weeping and retching old lady. He cleared his throat and said, 'Yeah, okay, just a minute here,' and there was a certain amount of hostility in his voice that made his very slight accent a little more obvious. Chutsky turned to look at him, and the smile stayed on his face. Coronel looked flustered, but he met Chutsky's happy stare. 'Are you trying to stop us from doing our jobs here?'

'Your job is to protect and serve,' Chutsky said. 'In this case that means to protect this information and serve me.'

'That's bullshit,' Coronel said.

'It doesn't matter what kind of shit it is,' Chutsky told him. 'You're gonna do it.'

'Who the fuck are you to tell me that?'

Captain Matthews tapped the table with his fingertips. 'That's enough, Coronel. Mr. Chutsky is from Washington, and I have been instructed to render him every assistance.'

Coronel was shaking his head. 'He's no goddamn FBI,' he said.

Chutsky just smiled. Captain Matthews took a deep breath to say something – but Doakes moved his head half an inch toward Coronel and said, 'Shut your mouth.' Coronel looked at him and some of the fight went out of him. 'Don't want to mess with this shit,' Doakes went on. 'Let his people handle it.'

'It isn't right,' said Coronel.

'Leave it,' said Doakes.

Coronel opened his mouth, Doakes raised his eyebrows – and on reflection, looking at the face underneath those eyebrows, perhaps, Officer Coronel decided to leave it.

Captain Matthews cleared his throat in an attempt to take back control. 'Any more questions? All right then – Mr. Chutsky. If there's any other way we can help . . .'

'As a matter of fact, Captain, I would appreciate it if I could borrow one of your detectives for liaison. Somebody who can help me find my way around, dot all the t's, like that.'

All the heads around the table swung to Doakes in perfect unison, except for Chutsky's. He turned to his side, to Deborah, and said, 'How about it, Detective?'

9

I have to admit the surprise ending to Captain Matthews' meeting caught me off guard, but at least I now knew why everyone was acting so much like lab rats thrown into a lion's cage. No one likes to have the Feds come in on a case; the only joy in it is making things as hard as possible for them when they do. But Chutsky was apparently such a very heavy hitter that even this small pleasure would be denied to us.

The significance of Deborah's bright red skin condition was a deeper mystery, but it wasn't my problem. My problem had suddenly become a little bit clearer. You may think that Dexter is a dull boy for not putting it together sooner, but when the nickel finally dropped it was accompanied by a desire to smack myself on the head. Perhaps all the beer at Rita's house had short-sheeted my mental powers.

But clearly this visitation from Washington had been called down upon us by none other than Dexter's personal nemesis, Sergeant Doakes. There had been some vague rumors that his service in the army had been somewhat irregular, and I was starting to believe them. His reaction when he saw the thing on the table had not been shock, outrage, disgust, or anger, but something far more interesting: recognition. Right at the scene he had told Captain Matthews what this was, and who to talk to about it. That particular who had sent Chutsky. And therefore when I had thought Chutsky and Doakes had recognized each other at the meeting, I had been right – because whatever was going on that Doakes knew about, Chutsky knew about it, too, probably even more so, and he had come to squash it. And if Doakes knew about something like this, there had to be a way to use his background against him in some small way, thus flinging the chains off poor Detained Dexter.

It was a brilliant train of pure cool logic; I welcomed the return of my giant brain and mentally patted myself on the head. Good boy, Dexter. Arf arf.

It is always nice to see the synapses clicking in a way that lets you know your opinion of yourself is sometimes justified. But in this particular case, there was just a chance that more was at stake than Dexter's self-esteem. If Doakes had something to hide, I was a step closer to being back in business.

There are several things that Dashing Dexter is good at, and some of them can actually be legally performed in public. One of these things is using a computer to find information. This was a skill I had developed to help me be absolutely sure about new friends like MacGregor and Reiker. Aside from avoiding the unpleasantness of cutting up the wrong person, I like to confront my fellow hobbyists with the evidence of their past indiscretions before I send them off to dreamland. Computers and the Internet were wonderful means of finding this stuff.

So if Doakes had something to hide, I thought I could probably find it, or at least some small thread of it that I could yank on until his whole dark past began to unravel. Knowing him as I did, I was quite sure it would be dismal and Dexter-like. And when I found that certain something . . . Perhaps I was being naïve to think I could use this hypothetical information to get him off my case, but I thought there was a very good chance. Not by confronting him directly and demanding that he cease and desist or else, which might not be entirely wise with someone like Doakes. Besides, that was blackmail, which I am told is very wrong. But information is power, and I would certainly find some small way to use whatever I found – a way to give Doakes something to think about that did not involve shadowing Dexter and curtailing his Crusade for Decency. And a man who discovers his pants are on fire tends to have very little time to worry about somebody else's box of matches.

I went happily down the hall from the captain's office, back to my little cubicle off the forensics lab, and got right to work.

A few hours later I had just about all I could find. There were surprisingly few details in Sergeant Doakes's file. The few that I found left me gasping for breath: Doakes had a first name! It was Albert – had anyone ever really called him that? Unthinkable. I had assumed his name was Sergeant. And he had been born, too – in Waycross, Georgia. Where would the wonders end? There was more, even better; before he had come to the department, Sergeant Doakes had been – Sergeant Doakes! In the army – the Special Forces, of all things! Picturing Doakes in one of those jaunty green beanies marching alongside John Wayne was almost more than I could think about without bursting into military song.

Several commendations and medals were listed, but I could find no mention of any heroic actions that had earned them. Still, I felt much more patriotic just knowing the man. The rest of his record was almost completely empty of details. The only thing that stood out at all was an eighteen-month stretch of something called 'detached service.' Doakes had served it as a military adviser in El Salvador, returned home to a six-month stretch at the Pentagon, and then retired to our fortunate city. Miami's police department had been happy to scoop up a decorated veteran and offer him gainful employment.

But El Salvador – I was not a history buff, but I seemed to recall that it had been something of a horror show. There had been protest marches down on

Brickell Avenue at the time. I didn't remember why, but I knew how to find out. I fired up my computer again and went online, and oh dear – find out I did. El Salvador at the time Doakes was there had been a true three-ring circus of torture, rape, murder, and name-calling. And no one had thought to invite me.

I found an awful lot of information posted by various human rights groups. They were quite serious, almost shrill, in the things they had to say about what had been done down there. Still, as far as I could tell, nothing had ever come of their protests. After all, it was only human rights. It must be terribly frustrating; PETA seems to get much better results. These poor souls had done their research, published their results detailing rapes, electrodes, and cattle prods, complete with photos, diagrams, and the names of the hideous inhuman monsters who reveled in inflicting this suffering on the masses. And the hideous inhuman monsters in question retired to the south of France, while the rest of the world boycotted restaurants for mistreating chickens.

It gave me a great deal of hope. If I was ever caught, perhaps I could simply protest dairy products and they'd let me go.

The El Salvadoran names and historical details I found meant very little to me. Neither did the organizations involved. Apparently it had developed into one of those wonderful free-for-alls where there were no actual good guys, merely several teams of bad guys with the campesinos caught in the middle. The United States had covertly backed one side, however, in spite of the fact that this team seemed just as eager to hammer suspicious poor persons into paste. And it was this side that got my attention. Something had turned the tide in their favor, some terrible threat that was not specified, something that was apparently so awful it left people nostalgic for cattle prods in the rectum.

Whatever it was, it seemed to coincide with the period of Sergeant Doakes's detached service.

I sat back in my rickety swivel chair. Well, well, well, I thought. What an interesting coincidence. At approximately the same time, we had Doakes, hideous unnamed torture, and covert U.S. involvement all buzzing about together. Naturally enough there was no proof that these three things were in any way linked, no reason at all to suspect any kind of connection. Just as naturally, I was as sure as I could be that they were very much three peas in one pod. Because twenty-some years later they had all come back together for a reunion party in Miami: Doakes, Chutsky, and whatever had made the thing on the table. It was starting to look like tab A would fit into slot B after all.

I had found my little string. And if only I could think of a way to pull on it—

Peekaboo, Albert.

Of course, having information to use is one thing. Knowing what it means and how to use it is a different story. And all I really knew was that Doakes had been there when some bad things happened. He probably hadn't done them himself, and in any case they were sanctioned by the government. Covertly, of course – which made one wonder how everyone knew about it.

On the other hand, there was certainly somebody out there who still wanted to keep this quiet. And at the moment, that somebody was represented by Chutsky – who was being chaperoned by my dear sister, Deborah. If I could get her help, I might be able to squeeze a few details out of Chutsky. What I could do then remained to be seen, but at least I could begin.

It sounded too simple, and of course it was. I called Deborah right away, and got her answering machine. I tried her cell phone and it was the same thing. For the rest of the day, Debs was out of the office please leave a message. When I tried her at home that evening it was the same thing. And when I hung up the phone and looked out the window of my apartment, Sergeant Doakes was parked in his favorite spot across the street.

A half-moon came out from behind a tattered cloud and muttered at me, but it was wasting its breath. No matter how much I wanted to slip away and have an adventure named Reiker, I could not; not with that awful maroon Taurus parked there like a discount conscience. I turned away, looking for something to kick. Here it was Friday night, and I was prevented from stepping out and strolling through the shadows with the Dark Passenger – and now I couldn't even get my sister on the phone. What a terrible thing life can be.

I paced around my apartment for a while but accomplished nothing except stubbing my toe. I called Deborah two more times and she was not home two more times. I looked out the window again. The moon had moved slightly; Doakes had not.

All righty then. Back to plan B.

Half an hour later I was sitting on Rita's couch with a can of beer in my hand. Doakes had followed me, and I had to assume he was waiting across the street in his car. I hoped he was enjoying this as much as I was, which was to say not very much at all. Was this what it was like to be human? Were people actually so miserable and brainless that they looked forward to this – to spending Friday night, precious time off from wage slave drudgery, sitting in front of a television with a can of beer? It was mind-numbingly dull, and to my horror, I found that I was getting used to it.

Curses on you, Doakes. You're driving me normal.

'Hey, mister,' Rita said, plunking herself down next to me, where she curled her feet under her, 'why so quiet?'

'I think I'm working too hard,' I told her. 'And enjoying it less.'

She was quiet for a moment, then she said, 'It's that thing with the guy you had to let go, isn't it? The guy who was . . . he killed the kids?'

'That's part of it,' I said. 'I don't like unfinished business.'

Rita nodded, almost as if she actually understood what I was saying. 'That's very . . . I mean, I can tell it's bothering you. Maybe you should – I don't know. What do you usually do to relax?'

It certainly conjured up some funny pictures to think of telling her what I did to relax, but it was probably not a very good idea. So instead I said, 'Well, I like to take my boat out. Go fishing.'

And a small, very soft voice behind me said, 'Me, too.' Only my highly trained nerves of steel prevented me from bumping my head on the ceiling fan; I am nearly impossible to sneak up on, and yet I'd had no idea there was anyone else in the room. But I turned around and there was Cody, looking at me with his large, unblinking eyes. 'You too?' I said. 'You like to go fishing?'

He nodded; two words at a time was close to his daily limit.

'Well, then,' I said. 'I guess it's settled. How about tomorrow morning?'

'Oh,' Rita said, 'I don't think – I mean, he isn't – You don't have to, Dexter.'

Cody looked at me. Naturally enough he didn't say anything, but he didn't need to. It was all there in his eyes. 'Rita,' I said, 'sometimes the boys need to get away from the girls. Cody and I are going fishing in the morning. Bright and early,' I said to Cody.

'Why?'

'I don't know why,' I said. 'But you're supposed to go early, so we will.' Cody nodded, looked at his mother, and then turned around and walked down the hall.

'Really, Dexter,' Rita said. 'You really don't have to.'

And, of course, I knew I didn't have to. But why shouldn't I? It probably wouldn't cause me actual physical pain. Besides that, it would be nice to get away for a few hours. Especially from Doakes. And in any case – again, I don't know why it should be, but kids really do matter to me. I certainly don't get all gooey-eyed at the sight of training wheels on a bicycle, but on the whole I find children far more interesting than their parents.

The next morning, as the sun was coming up, Cody and I were motoring slowly out of the canal by my apartment in my seventeen-foot Whaler. Cody wore a blue-and-yellow life vest and sat very still on the cooler. He slumped down just a little so that his head almost vanished inside the vest, making him look like a brightly colored turtle.

Inside the cooler was soda and a lunch Rita had made for us, a light snack for ten or twelve people. I had brought frozen shrimp for bait, since this was Cody's first trip and I didn't know how he might react to sticking a sharp metal hook into something that was still alive. I rather enjoyed it, of course – the more alive, the better! – but one can't expect sophisticated tastes from a child.

Out the canal, into Biscayne Bay, and I headed across to Cape Florida, steering for the channel that cut past the lighthouse. Cody didn't say anything until we came within sight of Stiltsville, that odd collection of houses built on pilings in the middle of the bay. Then he tugged at my sleeve. I bent down to hear him over the roar of the engine and the wind.

'Houses,' he said.

'Yes,' I yelled. 'Sometimes there are even people in them.'

He watched the houses go by and then, when they began to disappear behind us, he sat back down on the cooler. He turned around once more to look at them when they were almost out of sight. After that he just sat until we got to Fowey Rock and I idled down. I put the motor in neutral and slid the anchor over the bow, waiting to make sure it caught before turning the engine off.

'All right, Cody,' I said. 'It's time to kill some fish.'

He smiled, a very rare event. 'Okay,' he said.

He watched me with unblinking attention as I showed him how to thread the shrimp onto the hook. Then he tried it himself, very slowly and carefully pushing the hook in until the point came out again. He looked at the hook and then up at me. I nodded, and he looked back at the shrimp, reaching out to touch the place where the hook broke through the shell.

'All right,' I said. 'Now drop it in the water.' He looked up at me. 'That's where the fish are,' I said. Cody nodded, pointed his rod tip over the side of the boat, and pushed the release button on his little Zebco reel to drop the bait into the water. I flicked my bait over the side, too, and we sat there rocking slowly on the waves.

I watched Cody fish with his fierce blank concentration. Perhaps it was the combination of open water and a small boy, but I couldn't help but think of Reiker. Even though I could not safely investigate him, I was assuming that he was guilty. When would he know that MacGregor was gone, and what would he do about it? It seemed most likely that he would panic and try to disappear – and yet, the more I thought about it, the more I wondered. There is a natural human reluctance to abandon an entire life and start over somewhere else. Perhaps he would just be cautious for a while. And if so, I could fill my time with the new entry on my rather exclusive social register, whoever had created the Howling Vegetable of N.W. 4th Street, and the fact that this sounded rather like a Sherlock Holmes title made it no less urgent. Somehow I had to neutralize Doakes. Somehow someway sometime soon I had to—

'Are you going to be my dad?' Cody asked suddenly.

Luckily I had nothing in my mouth which might choke me, but for a moment it felt like there was something in my throat, something the approximate size of a Thanksgiving turkey. When I could breathe again, I managed to stammer out, 'Why do you ask?'

He was still watching his rod tip. 'Mom says maybe,' he said.

'Did she?' I said, and he nodded without looking up.

My head whirled. What was Rita thinking? I had been so wrapped up in the hard work of ramming my disguise down Doakes's throat that I had never really thought about what was going on in Rita's head. Apparently, I should have. Could she truly be thinking that, that – it was unthinkable. But I suppose in a strange way it might make sense if one was a human being. Fortunately I am not, and the thought seemed completely bizarre to me. *Mom says maybe?* Maybe I would be Cody's dad? Meaning, um—

'Well,' I said, which was a very good start considering I had absolutely no idea what I might say next. Happily for me, just as I realized nothing resembling a coherent answer was going to come out of my mouth, Cody's rod tip jerked savagely. 'You have a fish!' I said, and for the next few minutes it was all he could do to hang on as the line whirred off his reel. The fish made repeated ferocious, slashing zigzags to the right, the left, under the boat, and then straight for the horizon. But slowly, in spite of several long runs away from the boat, Cody worked the fish closer. I coached him to keep the rod tip up, wind in the line, work the fish in to where I could get a hand on the leader and bring it into the boat. Cody watched it flop on the deck, its forked tail still flipping wildly.

'A blue runner,' I said. 'That is one wild fish.' I bent to release it, but it was bucking too much for me to get a hand on it. A thin stream of blood came from its mouth and onto my clean white deck, which was a bit upsetting. 'Ick,' I said. 'I think he swallowed the hook. We'll have to cut it out.' I pulled my fillet knife from its black plastic sheath and laid it on the deck. 'There's going to be a lot of blood,' I warned Cody. I do not like blood, and I did not want it in my boat, not even fish blood. I took the two steps forward to open the dry locker and get an old towel I kept for cleaning up.

'Ha,' I heard behind me, softly. I turned around.

Cody had taken the knife and stuck it into the fish, watching it struggle away from the blade, and then carefully sticking the point in again. This second time he pushed the blade deep into the fish's gills, and a gout of blood ran out onto the deck.

'Cody,' I said.

He looked up at me and, wonder of wonders, he smiled. 'I like fishing, Dexter,' he said.

10

By Monday morning I still had not gotten in touch with Deborah. I called repeatedly, and although I became so familiar with the sound of the tone that I could hum it, Deborah did not respond. It was increasingly frustrating; here I was with a possible way out of the stranglehold Doakes had put me in, and I could get no further with it than the telephone. It's terrible to have to depend on someone else.

But I am persistent and patient, among my many other Boy Scout virtues. I left dozens of messages, all of them cheerful and clever, and that positive attitude must have done the trick, because I finally got an answer.

I had just settled into my desk chair to finish a report on a double homicide, nothing exciting. A single weapon, probably a machete, and a few moments of wild abandon. The initial wounds on both victims had been delivered in bed, where they had apparently been caught in flagrante delicto. The man had managed to raise one arm, but a little too late to save his neck. The woman made it all the way to the door before a blow to the upper spine sent a spurt of blood onto the wall beside the door frame. Routine stuff, the kind of thing that makes up most of my work, and extremely unpleasant. There is just so very much blood in two human beings, and when somebody decides to let it all out at once it makes a terrible and unattractive mess, which I find deeply offensive. Organizing and analyzing it makes me feel a great deal better, and my job can be deeply satisfying on occasion.

But this one was a real mess. I had found spatter on the ceiling fan, most likely from the machete blade as the killer raised his arm between strokes. And because the fan was on, it flung more spatter to the far corners of the room.

It had been a busy day for Dexter. I was just trying to word a paragraph in the report properly to indicate that it had been what we like to call a 'crime of passion' when my phone rang.

'Hey, Dex,' the voice said, and it sounded so relaxed, even sleepy, that it took me a moment to realize it was Deborah.

'Well,' I said. 'The rumors of your death were exaggerated.'

She laughed, and again the sound of it was downright mellow, unlike her usual hard-edged chuckle. 'Yeah,' she said. 'I'm alive. But Kyle has kept me pretty busy.'

'Remind him of the labor laws, Sis. Even sergeants need their rest.'

'Mm, I don't know about that,' she said. 'I feel pretty good without it.' And she gave a throaty, two-syllable chuckle that sounded as unlike Debs as if she had asked me to show her the best way to cut through living human bone.

I tried to remember when I had heard Deborah say she felt pretty good and actually sound like she meant it at the same time. I came up blank. 'You sound very unlike yourself, Deborah,' I said. 'What on earth has gotten into you?'

This time her laugh was a bit longer, but just as happy. 'The usual,' she said. And then she laughed again. 'Anyway, what's up?'

'Oh, not a thing,' I said, with innocence blooming from my tongue. 'My only sister disappears for days and nights on end without a word and then turns up sounding like she stepped out of *Stepford Sergeants*. So I am naturally curious to know what the hell is going on, that's all.'

'Well, hell,' she said. 'I'm touched. It's almost like having a real human brother.'

'Let's hope it goes no further than almost.'

'How about we get together for lunch?' she said.

'I'm already hungry,' I said. 'Relampago's?'

'Mm, no,' she said. 'How about Azul?'

I suppose her choice of restaurant made as much sense as everything else about her this morning, because it made no sense at all. Deborah was a blue-collar diner, and Azul was the kind of place where Saudi royalty ate when they were in town. Apparently her transformation into an alien was now complete.

'Certainly, Deb, Azul. I'll just sell my car to pay for it and meet you there.'

'One o'clock,' she said. 'And don't worry about the money. Kyle will pick up the tab.' She hung up. And I didn't actually say AHA! But a small light flickered on.

Kyle would pay, would he? Well, well. And at Azul, too.

If the glittery ticky-tack of South Beach is the part of Miami designed for insecure wannabe celebrities, Azul is for people who find the glamour amusing. The little cafés that crowd South Beach compete for attention with a shrill clamor of bright and cheap gaudiness. Azul is so understated by comparison that you wonder if they had ever seen even a single episode of *Miami Vice*.

I left my car with the mandatory valet parking attendant in a small cobble-stone circle out front. I am fond of my car, but I will admit that it did not compare favorably to the line of Ferraris and Rolls-Royces. Even so, the attendant did not actually decline to park it for me, although he must have guessed that it would not result in the kind of tip he was used to. I suppose my bowling shirt and khaki pants were an unmistakable clue that I didn't have even a single bearer bond or Krugerrand for him.

The restaurant itself was dark and cool and so quiet you could hear an American Express Black Card drop. The far wall was tinted glass with a door that led out to a terrace. And there was Deborah, sitting at a small corner table outside, looking out over the water. Across from her, facing back toward the door in to the restaurant, sat Kyle Chutsky, who would pick up the tab. He was wearing very expensive sunglasses, so perhaps he really would. I approached the table and a waiter materialized to pull out a chair that was certainly far too heavy for anyone who could afford to eat here. The waiter didn't actually bow, but I could tell that the restraint was an effort.

'Hey, buddy,' Kyle said as I sat down. He stretched his hand across the table. Since he seemed to believe I was his new best friend, I leaned in and shook hands with him. 'How's the spatter trade?'

'Always plenty of work,' I said. 'And how's the mysterious visitor from Washington trade?'

'Never better,' he said. He held my hand in his just a moment too long. I looked down at it; his knuckles were enlarged, as if he had spent too much time sparring with a concrete wall. He slapped his left hand on the table, and I got a glimpse of his pinkie ring. It was startlingly effeminate, almost an engagement ring. When he finally let go of my hand, he smiled and swiveled his head toward Deborah, although with his sunglasses it was impossible to tell if he was looking at her or just moving his neck around.

Deborah smiled back at him. 'Dexter was worried about me.'

'Hey,' Chutsky said, 'what are brothers for?'

She glanced at me. 'Sometimes I wonder,' she said.

'Why Deborah, you know I'm only watching your back,' I said.

Kyle chuckled. 'Good deal. I got the front,' he said, and they both laughed. She reached across and took his hand.

'All the hormones and happiness are setting my teeth on edge,' I said. 'Tell me, is anybody actually trying to catch that inhuman monster, or are we just going to sit around and make tragic puns?'

Kyle swiveled his head back to me and raised an eyebrow. 'What's your interest in this, buddy?'

'Dexter has a fondness for inhuman monsters,' Deborah said. 'Like a hobby.'

'A hobby,' Kyle said, keeping the sunglasses turned to my face. I think it was supposed to intimidate me, but for all I knew his eyes could be closed. Somehow, I managed not to tremble.

'He's kind of an amateur profiler,' Deborah said.

Kyle didn't move for a moment and I wondered if he had gone to sleep behind his dark lenses. 'Huh,' he finally said, and he leaned back in his chair. 'Well, what do you think about this guy, Dexter?'

'Oh, just the basics so far,' I said. 'Somebody with a lot of training in the medical area and in covert activities who came unhinged and needs to make a statement, something to do with Central America. He'll probably do it again timed for maximum impact, rather than because he feels he *has* to. So he's not really a standard serial type of – What?' I said. Kyle had lost his laid-back smile and was sitting straight up with his fists clenched.

'What do you mean, Central America?'

I was fairly sure we both knew exactly what I meant by Central America, but I thought saying El Salvador might have been a bit too much; it wouldn't do to lose my casual, it's-just-a-hobby credentials. But my whole purpose for coming had been to find out about Doakes, and when you see an opening – well, I admit it had been a little obvious, but it had apparently worked. 'Oh,' I said. 'Isn't that right?' All those years of practice in imitating human expressions paid off for me here as I put on my best innocently curious face.

Kyle apparently couldn't decide if that was right. He worked his jaw muscles and unclenched his fists.

'I should have warned you,' Deborah said. 'He's good at this.'

Chutsky let out a big breath and shook his head. 'Yeah,' he said. With a visible effort he leaned back and flicked on his smile again. 'Pretty good, buddy. How'd you come up with all that?'

'Oh, I don't know,' I said modestly. 'It just seemed obvious. The hard part is figuring out how Sergeant Doakes is involved.'

'Jesus H. Christ,' he said, and clenched his fists again. Deborah looked at me and laughed, not exactly the same kind of laugh she had given Kyle, but still, it felt good to know she could remember now and then that we were on the same team. 'I told you he's good,' she said.

'Jesus Christ,' Kyle said again. He pumped one index finger unconsciously, as if squeezing an invisible trigger, then turned his sunglasses in Deb's direction. 'You're right about that,' he said, and turned back to me. He watched me hard for a moment, possibly to see if I would bolt for the door or start speaking Arabic, and then he nodded. 'What's this about Sergeant Doakes?'

'You're not just trying to drop Doakes in the shit, are you?' Deborah asked me.

'In Captain Matthews's conference room,' I said, 'when Kyle saw Doakes for the first time, there was a moment when I thought they recognized each other.'

'I didn't notice that,' Deborah said with a frown.

'You were busy blushing,' I said. She blushed again, which I thought was a little redundant. 'Besides, Doakes was the one who knew who to call when he saw the crime scene.'

'Doakes knows some stuff,' Chutsky admitted. 'From his military service.'

'What kind of stuff?' I asked. Chutsky looked at me for a long time, or anyway his sunglasses did. He tapped on the table with that silly pinkie ring and the sunlight flashed off the large diamond in the center. When he finally spoke it felt like the temperature at our table had dropped ten degrees.

'Buddy,' he said, 'I don't want to cause you any trouble, but you have to let go of this. Back off. Find a different hobby. Or else you are in a world of shit – and you will get flushed.' The waiter materialized at Kyle's elbow before I could think of something wonderful to say to that. Chutsky kept the sunglasses turned toward me for a long moment. Then he handed the menu to the waiter. 'The bouillabaisse is really good here,' he said.

Deborah disappeared for the rest of the week, which did very little for my self-esteem, because no matter how terrible it was for me to admit it, without her help I was stuck. I could not come up with any sort of alternative plan for ditching Doakes. He was still there, parked under the tree across from my apartment, following me to Rita's house, and I had no answers. My once-proud brain chased its tail and caught nothing but air.

I could feel the Dark Passenger roiling and whimpering and struggling to climb out and take the steering wheel, but there was Doakes looming up through the windshield, forcing me to clamp down and reach for another can of beer. I had worked too hard and too long to achieve my perfect little life and I was not going to ruin it now. The Passenger and I could wait a bit longer. Harry had taught me discipline, and that would have to see me through to happier days.

'Patience,' Harry said. He paused to cough into a Kleenex. 'Patient is more important than smart, Dex. You're already smart.'

'Thank you,' I said. And I meant it politely, really, because I was not at all comfortable sitting there in Harry's hospital room. The smell of medicine and disinfectant and urine mixed with the air of restrained suffering and clinical death made me wish I was almost anywhere else. Of course, as a callow young monster, I never wondered if Harry might not feel the same.

'In your case, you have to be *more* patient, because you'll be thinking you're clever enough to get away with it,' he said. 'You're not. Nobody is.' He paused to cough again, and this time it took longer and seemed to go deeper. To see Harry like this – indestructible, supercop, foster-father Harry, shaking, turning red and weepy-eyed from the strain – was almost too much. I had to look away. When I looked back a moment later, Harry was watching me again.

'I know you, Dexter. Better than you know yourself.' And this was easy to believe until he followed up with, 'You're basically a good guy.'

'No I'm not,' I said, thinking of the wonderful things I had not yet been allowed to do; even wanting to do them pretty much ruled out any kind of association with goodness. There was also the fact that most of the other pimple-headed hormone-churning twinkies my age who were considered good guys were no more like me than an orangutan was. But Harry wouldn't hear it.

'Yes, you are,' he said. 'And you have to believe that you are. Your heart is pretty much in the right place, Dex,' he said, and with that he collapsed into a truly epic fit of coughing. It lasted for what seemed like several minutes, and then he leaned weakly back onto his pillow. He closed his eyes for a moment, but when he opened them again they were steely Harry blue, brighter than ever in the pale green of his dying face. 'Patience,' he said. And he made it sound strong, in spite of the terrible pain and weakness he must have felt. 'You still have a long way to go, and I don't have a whole lot of time, Dexter.'

'Yes, I know,' I said. He closed his eyes.

'That's just what I mean,' he said. 'You're supposed to say no, don't worry, you have plenty of time.'

'But you don't,' I said, not sure where this was going.

'No, I don't,' he said. 'But people pretend. To make me feel better about it.'

'Would you feel better?'

'No,' he said, and opened his eyes again. 'But you can't use logic on human behavior. You have to be patient, watch and learn. Otherwise, you screw up. Get caught and . . . Half my legacy.' He closed his eyes again and I could hear the strain in his voice. 'Your sister will be a good cop. You,' he smiled slowly, a little sadly, 'you will be something else. Real justice. But only if you're patient. If your chance isn't there, Dexter, wait until it is.'

It all seemed so overwhelming to an eighteen-year-old apprentice monster. All I wanted was to do The Thing, very simple really, just go dancing in the moonlight with the bright blade flowing free – such an easy thing, so natural and sweet – to cut through all the nonsense and right down to the heart of things. But I could not. Harry made it complicated.

'I don't know what I'll do when you're dead,' I said.

'You'll do fine,' he said.

'There's so much to remember.'

Harry reached a hand out and pushed the button that hung on a cord beside his bed. 'You'll remember it,' he said. He dropped the cord and it was almost as though it pulled the last of the strength from him as it flopped back down by the bedside. 'You'll remember.' He closed his eyes and for a moment I was all alone in the room. Then the nurse bustled in with a syringe and Harry opened one eye. 'We can't always do what we think we have to do. So when there's nothing else you can do, you wait,' he said, and held out his arm for his shot. 'No matter what . . . pressure . . . you might feel.'

I watched him as he lay there, taking the needle without flinching and knowing that even the relief it brought was temporary, that his end was coming and he could not stop it – and knowing, too, that he was not afraid, and that he would do this the right way, as he had done everything else in his life the right way. And I knew this, too: Harry understood me. No one else ever had, and no one else ever would, through all time in all the world. Only Harry.

The only reason I ever thought about being human was to be more like him.

11

And so I was patient. It was not an easy thing, but it was the Harry thing. Let the bright steely spring inside stay coiled and quiet and wait, watch, hold the hot sweet release locked tight in its cold box until it was Harry-right to let it skitter out and cartwheel through the night. Sooner or later some small opening would show and we could vault through it. Sooner or later I would find a way to make Doakes blink.

I waited.

Some of us, of course, find that harder to do than others, and it was several days later, a Saturday morning, that my telephone rang.

'Goddamn it,' said Deborah without any preamble. It was almost a relief to hear that she was her recognizable cranky self again.

'Fine, thanks, and you?' I said.

'Kyle is making me nuts,' she said. 'He says there's nothing we can do but wait, but he won't tell me what we're waiting for. He disappears for ten or twelve hours and won't tell me where he was. And then we just wait some more. I am so fucking tired of waiting my teeth hurt.'

'Patience is a virtue,' I said.

'I'm tired of being virtuous, too,' she said. 'And I am sick to death of Kyle's patronizing smile when I ask him what we can do to find this guy.'

'Well, Debs, I don't know what I can do except offer my sympathy,' I said. 'I'm sorry.'

'I think you can do a whole hell of a lot more than that, Bro,' she said.

I sighed heavily, mostly for her benefit. Sighs register so nicely on the telephone. 'This is the trouble with having a reputation as a gunslinger, Debs,' I said. 'Everybody thinks I can shoot the eye out of a jack at thirty paces, every single time.'

'I still think it,' she said.

'Your confidence warms my heart, but I don't understand a thing about this kind of adventure, Deborah. It leaves me completely cold.'

'I have to find this guy, Dexter. And I want to rub Kyle's nose in it,' she said.

'I thought you liked him.'

She snorted. 'Jesus, Dexter. You don't know anything about women, do you? Of course I like him. That's *why* I want to rub his nose in it.'

'Oh, good, *now* it makes sense,' I said.

She paused, and then very casually said, 'Kyle said some interesting things about Doakes.'

I felt my long-fanged friend inside stretch just a little and absolutely purr. 'You're getting very subtle all of a sudden, Deborah,' I said. 'All you had to do was ask me.'

'I just asked, and you gave me all that crap about how you can't help,' she said, suddenly good old plain-speaking Debs again. 'So how about it. What have you got?'

'Nothing at the moment,' I said.

'Shit,' said Deborah.

'But I might be able to find something.'

'How soon?'

I admit that I was feeling irked by Kyle's attitude toward me. What had he said? I would be 'in the shit and you will get flushed'? Seriously – who wrote his dialogue? And Deborah's sudden onset of subtlety, which had been my traditional bailiwick, had done nothing to calm me down. So I shouldn't have said it, but I did. 'How about by lunchtime?' I said. 'Let's say I'll have something by one o'clock. Baleen, since Kyle can pick up the check.'

'This I gotta see,' she said, and then added, 'The stuff about Doakes? It's pretty good.' She hung up.

Well, well, I said to myself. Suddenly, I did not mind the thought of working a little bit on a Saturday. After all, the only alternative was to hang out at Rita's and watch moss grow on Sergeant Doakes. But if I found something for Debs, I might at long last have the small opening I had hoped for. I merely had to be the clever boy we all believed I was.

But where to start? There was precious little to go on, since Kyle had pulled the department away from the crime scene before we had done much more than dust for prints. Many times in the past I had earned a few modest brownie points with my police colleagues by helping them track down the sick and twisted demons who lived only to kill. But that was because I understood them, since I am a sick and twisted demon myself. This time, I could not rely on getting any hints from the Dark Passenger, who had been lulled into an uneasy sleep, poor fellow. I had to depend on my own bare-naked native wit, which was also being alarmingly silent at the moment.

Perhaps if I gave my brain some fuel, it would kick into high gear. I went to the kitchen and found a banana. It was very nice, but for some reason it did not launch any mental rockets.

I threw the peel in the garbage and looked at the clock. Well, dear boy, that was five whole minutes gone by. Excellent. And you have already managed to figure out that you can't figure anything out. Bravo, Dexter.

There really were very few places to start. In fact, all I had was the victim and the house. And since I was fairly certain that the victim would not have a lot to say, even if we gave him back his tongue, that left the house. Of course it was possible that the house belonged to the victim. But the decor had such a temporary look to it, I was sure it did not.

Strange to simply walk away from an entire house like that. But he had done so, and with no one breathing down his neck and forcing a hasty and panicked retreat – which meant that he had done it deliberately, as part of his plan.

And that should imply that he had somewhere else to go. Presumably still in the Miami area, since Kyle was here looking for him. It was a starting point, and I thought of it all by myself. Welcome home, Mr. Brain.

Real estate leaves fairly large footprints, even when you try to cover them up. Within fifteen minutes of sitting down at my computer I had found something – not actually a whole footprint, but certainly enough to make out the shape of a couple of toes.

The house on N.W. 4th Street was registered to Ramon Puntia. How he expected to get away with that in Miami, I don't know, but Ramon Puntia was a Cuban joke name, like 'Joe Blow' in English. But the house was paid for and no taxes were due, a sound arrangement for someone who valued privacy as much as I assumed our new friend did. The house had been bought with a single cash payment, a wire transfer from a bank in Guatemala. This seemed a bit odd; with our trail starting in El Salvador and leading through the murky depths of a mysterious government agency in Washington, why take a left turn into Guatemala? But a quick online study of contemporary money laundering showed that it fit very well. Apparently Switzerland and the Cayman Islands were no longer à la mode, and if one wished for discreet banking in the Spanish-speaking world, Guatemala was all the rage.

This raised the interesting question of how much money Dr. Dismember had, and where it came from. But it was a question that led nowhere at the moment. I had to assume that he had enough for another house when he was done with the first one, and probably in the same approximate price range.

All right then. I went back to my Dade County real estate database and looked for other properties recently purchased the same way, from the same bank. There were seven; four of them had sold for more than a million dollars, which struck me as a bit high for disposable property. They had probably been bought by nothing more sinister than run-of-the-mill drug lords and Fortune 500 CEOs on the run.

That left three properties that seemed possible. One of them was in Liberty City, a predominantly black inner-city area of Miami. But on closer inspection, it turned out to be a block of apartments.

Of the two remaining properties, one was in Homestead, within sight of the gigantic dump heap of city garbage known locally as Mount Trashmore. The other was also in the south end of town, just off Quail Roost Drive.

Two houses: I was willing to bet that someone new had just moved in to one of them, and was doing things that might startle the ladies from the welcome wagon. No guarantees, of course, but it certainly seemed likely, and it was, after all, just in time for lunch.

Baleen was a very pricey place that I would not have attempted on my own modest means. It has the kind of oak-paneled elegance that makes you feel the need for a cravat and spats. It also has one of the best views of Biscayne Bay in the city, and if one is lucky there are a handful of tables that take advantage of this.

Either Kyle was lucky or his mojo had bowled over the headwaiter, because he and Deborah were waiting outside at one of these tables working on a bottle of mineral water and a plate of what appeared to be crab cakes. I grabbed one and took a bite as I slid into a chair facing Kyle.

'Yummy,' I said. 'This must be where good crabs go when they die.'

'Debbie says you have something for us,' Kyle said. I looked at my sister, who had always been Deborah or Debs but certainly never Debbie. She said nothing, however, and appeared willing to let this egregious liberty go by, so I turned my attention back to Kyle. He was wearing the designer sunglasses again, and his ridiculous pinkie ring sparkled as he brushed the hair carelessly back from his forehead.

'I hope I have something,' I said. 'But I do want to be careful not to get flushed.'

Kyle looked at me for a long moment, then he shook his head and a reluctant smile moved his mouth perhaps a quarter of an inch upward. 'All right,' he said. 'Busted. But you'd be surprised how often that kind of line really works.'

'I'm sure I'd be flabbergasted,' I said. I passed him the printout from my computer. 'While I catch my breath, you might want to look at this.'

Kyle frowned and unfolded the paper. 'What's this?'

Deborah leaned forward, looking like the eager young police hound she was. 'You found something! I knew you would,' she said.

'It's just two addresses,' said Kyle.

'One of them may very well be the hiding place of a certain unorthodox medical practitioner with a Central American past,' I said, and I told him how I found the addresses. To his credit, he looked impressed, even with the sunglasses on.

'I should have thought of this,' he said. 'That's very good.' He nodded and flicked the paper with a finger. 'Follow the money. Works every time.'

'Of course I can't be positive,' I said.

'Well, I'd bet on it,' he said. 'I think you found Dr. Danco.'

I looked at Deborah. She shook her head, so I looked back at Kyle's sunglasses. 'Interesting name. Is it Polish?'

Chutsky cleared his throat and looked out over the water. 'Before your time, I guess. There was a commercial back then. Danco presents the autoveg-gie. It slices, it dices—' He swiveled his dark lenses back to me. 'That's what we called him. Dr. Danco. He made chopped-up vegetables. It's the kind of joke you like when you're far from home and seeing terrible things,' he said.

'But now we're seeing them close to home,' I said. 'Why is he here?'

'Long story,' Kyle said.

'That means he doesn't want to tell you,' Deborah said.

'In that case, I'll have another crab cake,' I said. I leaned over and took the last one off the plate. They really were quite good.

'Come on, Chutsky,' Deborah said. 'There's a good chance we know where this guy is. Now what are you going to do about it?'

He put a hand on top of hers and smiled. 'I'm going to have lunch,' he said. And he picked up a menu with his other hand.

Deborah looked at his profile for a minute. Then she pulled her hand away. 'Shit,' she said.

The food actually was excellent, and Chutsky tried very hard to be chummy and pleasant, as if he had decided that when you can't tell the truth you might as well be charming. In fairness, I couldn't complain, since I generally get away with the same trick, but Deborah didn't seem very happy. She sulked and poked at her food while Kyle told jokes and asked me if I liked the Dolphins' chances to go all the way this year. I didn't really care if the Dolphins won the Nobel Prize for Literature, but as a well-designed artificial human I had sev-eral authentic-sounding prepared remarks on the subject, which seemed to satisfy Chutsky, and he chattered on in the chummiest way possible.

We even had dessert, which seemed to me to be pushing the distract-them-with-food ploy a little far, particularly since neither Deborah nor I was at all distracted. But it was quite good food, so it would have been barbaric of me to complain.

Of course, Deborah had worked very hard her whole life to become bar-baric, so when the waiter placed an enormous chocolate thing in front of Chutsky, who turned to Debs with two forks and said, 'Well . . .' she took the opportunity to fling a spoon into the center of the table.

'No,' she said to him. 'I don't want another fucking cup of coffee, and I don't want a fucking chocolate foo-foo. I want a fucking answer. When are we going to go get this guy?'

He looked at her with mild surprise and even a certain fondness, as though people in his line of work found spoon-throwing women quite useful and charming, but he thought her timing might be slightly off. 'Can I finish my dessert first?' he said.

12

Deborah drove us south on Dixie Highway. Yes, I did say 'us.' To my surprise, I had become a valuable member of the Justice League and was informed that I was being honored with the opportunity to put my irreplaceable self in harm's way. Although I was far from delighted, one small incident almost made it worthwhile.

As we stood outside the restaurant waiting for the valet to bring Deborah's car, Chutsky had quietly muttered, 'What the fuck . . . ?' and sauntered away down the driveway. I watched him as he walked out to the gate and gestured at a maroon Taurus that had casually parked there beside a palm tree. Debs glared at me as if it was all my fault, and we both watched Chutsky wave at the driver's window, which rolled down to reveal, of course, the ever-watchful Sergeant Doakes. Chutsky leaned on the gate and said something to Doakes, who glanced up the drive to me, shook his head, and then rolled up the window and drove away.

Chutsky didn't say anything when he rejoined us. But he did look at me a little differently before he climbed into the front seat of the car.

It was a twenty-minute drive south to where Quail Roost Drive runs east and west and crosses Dixie Highway, right beside a mall. Just two blocks in, a series of side streets leads into a quiet, working-class neighborhood made up of small, mostly neat houses, usually with two cars in the short driveway and several bicycles scattered across the lawn.

One of these streets bent to the left and led to a cul-de-sac, and it was here, at the end of the street, that we found the house, a pale yellow stucco dwelling with an overgrown yard. There was a battered gray van in the driveway with dark red lettering that said HERMANOS CRUZ LIMPIADORES – Cruz Brothers Cleaners.

Debs drove around the cul-de-sac and up the street about half a block to a house with half a dozen cars parked out front and on the lawn, and loud rap music coming from inside. Debs turned our car around to face our target and parked under a tree. 'What do you think?' she said.

Chutsky just shrugged. 'Uh-huh. Could be,' he said. 'Let's watch a while.' And that was the entire extent of our sparkling conversation for a good half hour. Hardly enough to keep the mind alive, and I found myself mentally drifting off to the small shelf in my apartment, where a little rosewood box holds a number of glass slides, the kind you place under a microscope. Each slide contained a single drop of blood – very well-dried blood, of course. I wouldn't have the nasty stuff in my home otherwise. Forty tiny windows into my shadow other self. One drop from each of my small adventures. There had been First Nurse, so long ago, who had killed her patients by careful overdose, under the guise of easing pain. And the very next slot in the box, the high-school shop teacher who strangled nurses. Wonderful contrast, and I do love irony.

So many memories, and as I stroked each one it made me even more eager to make a new one, number forty-one, even though number forty, MacGregor, was hardly dry. But because it was connected to my next project, and therefore felt incomplete, I was anxious to get on with it. As soon as I could be sure about Reiker and then find some way—

I sat up. Perhaps the rich dessert had clogged my cranial arteries, but I had temporarily forgotten Deborah's bribe. 'Deborah?' I said.

She glanced back at me, with a small frown of concentration on her face. 'What.'

'Here we are,' I said.

'No shit.'

'None whatsoever. A complete lack of shit, in fact – and all thanks to my mighty mental labors. Wasn't there some mention of a few things you were going to tell me?'

She glanced at Chutsky. He was staring straight ahead, still wearing the sunglasses, which did not blink. 'Yeah, all right,' she said. 'In the army Doakes was in Special Forces.'

'I know that. It's in his personnel file.'

'What you don't know, buddy,' said Kyle without moving, 'is that there's a dark side to Special Forces. Doakes was with them.' A very tiny smile creased his face for just a second, so small and sudden I might have imagined it. 'Once you go over to the dark side, it's forever. You can't go back.'

I watched Chutsky sit completely motionless for a moment longer and then I looked at Debs. She shrugged. 'Doakes was a shooter,' she said. 'The army let the guys in El Salvador borrow him, and he killed people for them.'

'Have gun will travel,' Chutsky said.

'That explains his personality,' I said, thinking it also explained a great deal more, like the echo I heard coming from his direction when my Dark Passenger called out.

'You have to understand how it was,' Chutsky said. It was a little eerie to hear his voice coming from a completely unmoving and unemotional face, as if the voice was really coming from a tape recorder somebody had put in his body. 'We believed we were saving the world. Giving up our lives and any hope for something normal and decent, for the cause. Turns out we were just selling our souls. Me, Doakes . . .'

'And Dr. Danco,' I said.

'And Dr. Danco.' Chutsky sighed and finally moved, turning his head briefly to Deborah, then looking forward again. He shook his head, and the movement seemed so large and theatrical after his stillness that I felt like applauding. 'Dr. Danco started out as an idealist, just like the rest of us. He found out in med school there was something missing inside him and he could do things to people and not feel any empathy at all. Nothing at all. It's a lot rarer than you think.'

'Oh, I'm sure it is,' I said, and Debs glared at me.

'Danco loved his country,' Chutsky went on. 'So he switched to the dark side, too. On purpose, to use this talent. And in El Salvador it . . . blossomed. He would take somebody that we brought him and just – ' He paused and took a breath, blew it out slowly. 'Shit. You saw what he does.'

'Very original,' I said. 'Creative.'

Chutsky gave a small snort of laughter that had no humor in it. 'Creative. Yeah. You could say that.' Chutsky swung his head slowly left, right, left. 'I said it didn't bother him to do that stuff – in El Salvador he got to like it. He'd sit in on the interrogation and ask personal questions. Then when he started to – He'd call the person by name, like he was a dentist or something, and say, "Let's try number five," or number seven, whatever. Like there were all these different patterns.'

'What kind of patterns?' I asked. It seemed like a perfectly natural question, showing polite interest and keeping the conversation moving. But Chutsky swiveled around in his seat and looked at me as if I was something that might require a whole bottle of floor cleaner.

'This is funny to you,' he said.

'Not yet,' I said.

He stared at me for what seemed like an awfully long time; then he just shook his head and faced front again. 'I don't know what kind of pattern, buddy. Never asked. Sorry. Probably something to do with what he cut off first. Just something to keep himself amused. And he'd talk to them, call them by name, show them what he was doing.' Chutsky shuddered. 'Somehow that made it worse. You should have seen what it did to the other side.'

'How about what it did to you?' Deborah demanded.

He let his chin fall forward to his chest, then straightened again. 'That too,' he said. 'Anyway, something finally changed at home, the politics, back in the Pentagon. New regime and all that, and they didn't want anything to do with what we had been doing down there. So very quietly the word came that Dr. Danco might buy us a small piece of political accommodation with the other side if we delivered him.'

'You gave up your own guy to be killed?' I asked. It hardly seemed fair –

I mean, I may be untroubled by a sense of morals, but at least I play by the rules.

Kyle was silent for a long moment. 'I told you we sold our souls, buddy,' he said at last. He smiled again, a little longer this time. 'Yeah, we set him up and they took him down.'

'But he's not dead,' Deborah said, always practical.

'We got scammed,' Chutsky said. 'The Cubans took him.'

'What Cubans?' Deborah asked. 'You said El Salvador.'

'Back in the day, anytime there was trouble in the Americas, there were Cubans. They were propping up one side, just like we did with the other. And they wanted our doctor. I told you, he was special. So they took him, tried to turn him. Put him in the Isle of Pines.'

'Is that a resort?' I asked.

Chutsky gave a single small snort of a laugh. 'The last resort, maybe. Isle of Pines is one of the hardest prisons in the world. Dr. Danco spent some real quality time there. They let him know his own side had given him up, and they really put him through it. And a few years later, one of our guys gets caught and turns up like that. No arms or legs, the whole deal. Danco is working for them. And now—' He shrugged. 'Either they turned him loose or he skipped. Doesn't matter which. He knows who set him up, and he's got a list.'

'Is your name on that list?' Deborah demanded.

'Maybe,' Chutsky said.

'Is Doakes's?' I asked. After all, I can be practical, too.

'Maybe,' he said again, which didn't seem very helpful. All the stuff about Danco was interesting, of course, but I was here for a reason. 'Anyway,' Chutsky said, 'that's what we're up against.'

Nobody seemed to have much to say to that, including me. I turned the things I'd heard from side to side, looking for some way to make it help me with my Doakes infestation. I will admit that I saw nothing at the moment, which was humbling. But I did seem to have a slightly better understanding of dear Dr. Danco. So he was empty inside, too, was he? A raptor in sheep's clothing. And he, too, had found a way to use his talent for the greater good – again, just like dear old Dexter. But now he had come off the rails, and he began to seem a little bit more like just another predator, no matter the unsettling direction his technique took him.

And oddly enough, with that insight, another thought nosed its way back into the bubbling cauldron of Dexter's dark underbrain. It had been a passing fancy before – now it began to seem like a very good idea. Why not find Dr. Danco myself, and do a little Dark Dance with him? He was a predator gone bad, just like all the others on my list. No one, not even Doakes, could possibly object to his demise. If I had wondered casually about finding the Doctor before, now it began to take on an urgency that drove away my frustration with missing out on Reiker. So he was like me, was he? We would see about that. A jolt of something cold bristled up my spine and I found that I truly looked forward to meeting the Doctor and discussing his work in depth.

In the distance I heard the first rumble of thunder as the afternoon storm moved in. 'Shit,' said Chutsky. 'Is it going to rain?'

'Every day at this time,' I said.

'That's no good,' he said. 'We gotta do something before it rains. You're up, Dexter.'

'Me?' I said, startled out of my meditations on maverick medical malpractice. I had adjusted to going along for the ride, but to actually have to *do* something was a little more than I had bargained for. I mean, here we had two hardened warriors sitting idly by, while we sent Delicate Dimpled Dexter into danger? Where's the sense in that?

'You,' Chutsky said. 'I need to hang back and see what happens. If it's him, I can take him out better. And Debbie – ' He smiled at her, even though she seemed to be scowling at him. 'Debbie is too much of a cop. She walks like a cop, she stares like a cop, and she might try to write him a ticket. He'd make her from a mile away. So it's you, Dex.'

'It's me doing what?' I asked, and I admit that I was still feeling some righteous indignation.

'Just walk by the house one time, around the cul-de-sac and back. Keep your eyes and ears open, but don't be too obvious.'

'I don't know how to be obvious,' I said.

'Great. Then this should be a piece of cake.'

It was clear that neither logic nor completely justified irritation was going to do any good, so I opened the door and got out, but I couldn't resist a parting shot. I leaned in Deborah's window and said, 'I hope I live to regret this.' And very obligingly, the thunder rumbled again nearby.

I strolled down the sidewalk toward the house. There were leaves underfoot, a couple of crushed juice cartons from some kid's lunch box. A cat rushed out onto a lawn as I passed and sat down very suddenly to lick its paws and stare at me from a safe distance.

At the house with all the cars in front the music changed and someone yelled, 'Whoo!' It was nice to know that somebody was having a good time while I strolled into mortal danger.

I turned left and began to walk the curve around the cul-de-sac. I glanced at the house with the van in front, feeling very proud of the completely nonobvious way I pulled it off. The lawn was shaggy and there were several soggy newspapers in the driveway. There didn't seem to be any visible pile of discarded body parts, and no one rushed out and tried to kill me. But as I passed by I could hear a TV blaring a game show in Spanish. A male voice rose above the hysterical announcer's and a dish clattered. And as a puff of wind brought the first large and hard raindrops, it also carried the smell of ammonia from the house.

I continued on past the house and back to the car. A few more drops of rain pelted down and a rumble of thunder rolled by, but the downpour held off. I climbed back into the car. 'Nothing terribly sinister,' I reported. 'The lawn needs mowing and there's a smell of ammonia. Voices in the house. Either he talks to himself or there's more than one of him.'

'Ammonia,' Kyle said.

'Yes, I think so,' I said. 'Probably just cleaning supplies.'

Kyle shook his head. 'Cleaning services don't use ammonia, the smell's too strong. But I know who does.'

'Who?' Deborah demanded.

He grinned at her. 'I'll be right back,' he said, and got out of the car.

'Kyle!' Deborah said, but he just waved a hand and walked right up to the front door of the house. 'Shit,' Deborah muttered as he knocked and stood glancing up at the dark clouds of the approaching storm.

The front door opened. A short and stocky man with a dark complexion and black hair falling over his forehead stared out. Chutsky said something to him and for a moment neither of them moved. The small man looked up the street, then at Kyle. Kyle slowly pulled a hand from his pocket and showed the dark man something – money? The man looked at whatever it was, looked at Chutsky again, and then held the door open. Chutsky went in. The door slammed shut.

'Shit,' Deborah said again. She chewed on a fingernail, a habit I hadn't seen from her since she was a teenager. Apparently it tasted good, because when it was gone she started on another. She was on her third fingernail when the door to the little house opened and Chutsky came back out, smiling and waving. The door closed and he disappeared behind a wall of water as the clouds finally opened wide. He came pounding up the street to the car and slid into the front seat, dripping wet.

'GodDAMN!' he said. 'I'm totally soaked!'

'What the fuck was that all about?' Deborah demanded.

Chutsky cocked an eyebrow at me and pushed the hair off his forehead. 'Don't she talk elegant?' he said.

'Kyle, goddamn it,' she said.

'The smell of ammonia,' he said. 'No surgical use, and no commercial cleaning crew would use it.'

'We did this already,' Deborah snapped.

He smiled. 'But ammonia IS used for cooking methamphetamine,' he said. 'Which turns out to be what these guys are doing.'

'You just walked right into a meth kitchen?' Deb said. 'What the hell did you do in there?'

He smiled and pulled a Baggie out of his pocket. 'Bought an ounce of meth,' he said.

13

Deborah didn't speak for almost ten minutes, just drove the car and stared ahead with her jaw clamped shut. I could see the muscles flexing along the side of her face and all the way down into her shoulders. Knowing her as I did I was quite sure that an explosion was brewing, but since I knew nothing at all about how Debs in Love might behave, I couldn't tell how soon. The target of her impending meltdown, Chutsky, sat beside her in the front seat, equally silent, but apparently quite happy to sit quietly and look at the scenery.

We were almost to the second address and well into the shadow of Mount Trashmore when Debs finally erupted.

'Goddamn it, that's *illegal!*' she said, smacking the steering wheel with the palm of her hand for emphasis.

Chutsky looked at her with mild affection. 'Yes, I know,' he said.

'I am a sworn fucking officer of the law!' Deborah told him. 'I took an oath to stop this kind of shit – and you— !' She sputtered to a halt.

'I had to be sure,' he said calmly. 'This seemed like the best way.'

'I ought to put the cuffs on *YOU!*' she said.

'That might be fun,' he said.

'You SON of a bitch!'

'At least.'

'I will not cross over to your motherfucking dark side!'

'No, you won't,' he said. 'I won't let you, Deborah.'

The breath whooshed out of her and she turned to look at him. He looked back. I had never seen a silent conversation, and this one was a doozy. Her eyes clicked anxiously from the left side of his face to the right and then left again. He simply looked back, calm and unblinking. It was elegant and fascinating and almost as interesting as the fact that Debs had apparently forgotten she was driving.

'I hate to interrupt,' I said. 'But I believe that's a beer truck right ahead?'

Her head snapped back around and she braked, just in time to avoid turning us into a bumper sticker on a load of Miller Lite. 'I'm calling that address in to vice. Tomorrow,' she said.

'All right,' Chutsky said.

'And you're throwing away that Baggie.'

He looked mildly surprised. 'It cost me two grand,' he said.

'You're throwing it away,' she repeated.

'All right,' he said. They looked at each other again, leaving me to watch for lethal beer trucks. Still, it was nice to see everything settled and harmony restored to the universe so we could get on with finding our hideous inhuman monster of the week, secure in the knowledge that love will always prevail. And so it was a great satisfaction to cruise down South Dixie Highway through the last of the rainstorm, and as the sun broke out of the clouds we turned onto a road that led us into a twisty series of streets, all with a terrific view of the gigantic pile of garbage known as Mount Trashmore.

The house we were looking for was in the middle of what looked like the last row of houses before civilization ended and garbage reigned supreme. It was at the bend of a circular street and we went past it twice before we were sure that we had found it. It was a modest dwelling of the three-bedroom two-mortgage kind, painted a pale yellow with white trim, and the lawn was very neatly cropped. There was no car visible in the driveway or the carport, and a FOR SALE sign on the front lawn had been covered with another that said SOLD! in bright red letters.

'Maybe he hasn't moved in yet,' Deborah said.

'He has to be somewhere,' Chutsky said, and it was hard to argue with his logic. 'Pull over. Have you got a clipboard?'

Deborah parked the car, frowning. 'Under the seat. I need it for my paperwork.'

'I won't smudge it,' he said, and fumbled under the seat for a second before pulling out a plain metal clipboard with a stack of official forms clamped onto it. 'Perfect,' he said. 'Gimme a pen.'

'What are you going to do?' she asked, handing him a cheap white ballpoint with a blue top.

'Nobody ever stops a guy with a clipboard,' Chutsky said with a grin. And before either of us could say anything, he was out of the car and walking up the short driveway in a steady, nine-to-five-bureaucrat kind of pace. He stopped halfway and looked at the clipboard, turning over a couple of pages and reading something before looking at the house and shaking his head.

'He seems very good at this kind of thing,' I said to Deborah.

'He'd goddamned well better be,' she said. She bit another nail and I worried that soon she would run out.

Chutsky continued up the drive, consulting his clipboard, apparently unaware that he was causing a fingernail shortage in the car behind him. He looked natural and unrushed, and had obviously had a lot of experience at either chicanery or skulduggery, depending on which word was better suited for describing officially sanctioned mischief. And he had Debs biting her nails and almost ramming beer trucks. Perhaps he was not a good influence on her after all, although it was nice to have another target for her scowling and her vicious arm punches. I am always willing to let someone else wear the bruises for a while.

Chutsky paused outside the front door and wrote something down. And then, although I did not see how he did it, he unlocked the front door and went in. The door closed behind him.

'Shit,' said Deborah. 'Breaking and entering on top of possession. He'll have me hijacking an airliner next.'

'I've always wanted to see Havana,' I said helpfully.

'Two minutes,' she said tersely. 'Then I call for backup and go in after him.'

To judge from the way her hand was twitching toward the radio, it was one minute and fifty-nine seconds when the front door opened again and Chutsky came back out. He paused in the driveway, wrote something on the clipboard, and returned to the car.

'All right,' he said as he slid into the front seat. 'Let's go home.'

'The house is empty?' Deborah demanded.

'Clean as a whistle,' he said. 'Not a towel or a soup can anywhere.'

'So now what?' she asked as she put the car in gear.

He shook his head. 'Back to plan A,' he said.

'And what the hell is plan A?' Deborah asked him.

'Patience,' he said.

And so in spite of a delightful lunch and a truly original little shopping trip afterward, we were back to waiting. A week passed in the now typically boring way. It didn't seem like Sergeant Doakes would give up before my conversion to a beer-bellied sofa ornament was complete, and I could see nothing else to do except play kick the can and hangman with Cody and Astor, performing outrageously theatrical goodbye kisses with Rita afterward for the benefit of my stalker.

Then came the telephone ringing in the middle of the night. It was Sunday night, and I had to leave for work early the next day; Vince Masuoka and I had an arrangement, and it was my turn to pick up doughnuts. And now here was the telephone, brazenly ringing as if I had no cares in the world and the doughnuts would deliver themselves. I glanced at the clock on my bedside table: 2:38. I admit I was somewhat cranky as I lifted the receiver and said, 'Leave me alone.'

'Dexter. Kyle is gone,' Deborah said. She sounded far beyond tired, totally tense, and unsure whether she wanted to shoot someone or cry.

It took me just a moment to get my powerful intellect up to speed. 'Uh, well Deb,' I said, 'a guy like that, maybe you're better off— '

'He's *gone*, Dexter. Taken. The, the guy has him. The guy who did that thing to the guy,' she said, and although I felt like I was suddenly thrust into an episode of *The Sopranos*, I knew what she meant. Whoever had turned the thing on the table into a yodeling potato had taken Kyle, presumably to do something similar to him.

'Dr. Danco,' I said.

'Yes.'

'How do you know?' I asked her.

'He said it could happen. Kyle is the only one who knows what the guy looks like. He said when Danco found out Kyle was here, he'd make a try. We had a – a signal set up, and – Shit Dexter, just get over here. We have to find him,' she said, and hung up.

It's always me, isn't it? I'm not really a very nice person, but for some reason it's always me that they come to with their problems. *Oh, Dexter, a savage inhuman monster has taken my boyfriend!* Well damn it, I'm a savage inhuman monster, too – didn't that entitle me to some rest?

I sighed. Apparently not.

I hoped Vince would understand about the doughnuts.

14

It was a fifteen-minute drive to Deborah's house from where I lived in the Grove. For once, I did not see Sergeant Doakes following me, but perhaps he was using a Klingon cloaking device. In any case, the traffic was very sparse and I even made the light at U.S. 1. Deborah lived in a small house on Medina in Coral Gables, overgrown with some neglected fruit trees and a crumbling coral-rock wall. I nosed my car in next to hers in the short driveway and was only two steps away when Deborah opened her front door. 'Where have you been?' she said.

'I went to yoga class, and then out to the mall to buy shoes,' I said. In truth, I had actually hurried over, getting there less than twenty minutes after her call, and I was a little miffed at the tone she was taking.

'Get in here,' she said, peering around into the darkness and holding on to the door as if she thought it might fly away.

'Yes, O Mighty One,' I said, and I got in.

Deborah's little house was lavishly decorated in I-have-no-life modern. Her living area generally looked like a cheap hotel room that had been occupied by a rock band and looted of everything except a TV and VCR. There was a chair and a small table by French doors that led out to a patio that was almost lost in a tangle of bushes. She had found another chair somewhere, though, a rickety folding chair, and she pulled it over to the table for me. I was so touched by her hospitable gesture that I risked life and limb by sitting in the flimsy thing. 'Well,' I said. 'How long has he been gone?'

'Shit,' she said. 'About three and a half hours. I think.' She shook her head and slumped into the other chair. 'We were supposed to meet here, and – he didn't show up. I went to his hotel, and he wasn't there.'

'Isn't it possible he just went away somewhere?' I asked – and I'm not proud of it, but I admit I sounded a little hopeful.

Deborah shook her head. 'His wallet and keys were still on the dresser. The guy has him, Dex. We gotta find him before— ' She bit her lip and looked away.

I was not at all sure what I could do to find Kyle. As I said, this was not the kind of thing I generally had any insight into, and I had already given it my best shot tracking down the real estate. But since Deborah was already saying 'we' it seemed that I didn't have a lot of choice in the matter. Family ties and all that. Still, I tried to make a little bit of wiggle room. 'I'm sorry if this sounds stupid, Debs, but did you report this?'

She looked up with a half snarl. 'Yeah, I did. I called Captain Matthews. He sounded relieved. He told me not to get hysterical, like I'm some kind of old lady with the vapors.' She shook her head. 'I asked him to put out an APB, and he said, "For what?" ' She hissed out her breath. 'For what . . . Goddamn it, Dexter, I wanted to strangle him, but . . .' She shrugged.

'But he was right,' I said.

'Yeah. Kyle is the only one who knows what the guy looks like,' she said. 'We don't know what he's driving or what his real name is or – Shit, Dexter. All I know is he's got Kyle.' She took a ragged breath. 'Anyway, Matthews called Kyle's people in Washington. Said that was all he could do.' She shook her head and looked very bleak. 'They're sending somebody Tuesday morning.'

'Well then,' I said hopefully. 'I mean, we know that this guy works very slowly.'

'Tuesday morning,' she said. 'Almost two days. Where do you think he starts, Dex? Does he take a leg off first? Or an arm? Will he do them both at the same time?'

'No,' I said. 'One at a time.' She looked at me hard. 'Well, it just makes sense, doesn't it?'

'Not to me,' she said. 'Nothing about this makes sense.'

'Deborah, cutting off the arms and legs is not *what* this guy wants to do. It's just *how* he does it.'

'Goddamn it, Dexter, talk English.'

'What he *wants* to do is totally destroy his victims. Break them inside and out, way beyond repair. Turn them into musical beanbags that will never again have a moment of anything except total endless insane horror. Cutting off limbs and lips is just the way he – What?'

'Oh, Jesus, Dexter,' Deborah said. Her face had screwed up into something I hadn't seen since our mom died. She turned away, and her shoulders began to shake. It made me just a little uneasy. I mean, I do not feel emotions, and I know Deborah quite often does. But she was not the kind of person who showed them, unless irritation is an emotion. And now she was making wet snuffly sounds, and I knew that I should probably pat her shoulder and say, 'There there,' or something equally profound and human, but I couldn't quite make myself do it. This was Deb, my sister. She would know I was faking it and—

And what? Cut off my arms and legs? The worst she would do would be to tell me to stop it, and go back to being Sergeant Sourpuss again. Even that would be a great improvement over her wilting-lily act. In any case, this was clearly one of those times where some human response was called for, and since I knew from long study what a human would do, I did it. I stood up and stepped over to her. I put my arm on her shoulder, patted her, and said, 'All right, Deb. There there.' It sounded even stupider than I had feared, but she leaned against me and snuffled, so I suppose it was the right thing to do after all.

'Can you really fall in *love* with somebody in a week?' she asked me.

'I don't think I can do it at all,' I said.

'I can't take this, Dexter,' she said. 'If Kyle gets killed, or turned into – Oh, God, I don't know what I'll do.' And she collapsed against me again and cried.

'There there,' I said.

She gave a long hard snuffle, and then blew her nose on a paper towel from the table beside her. 'I wish you'd stop saying that,' she said.

'I'm sorry,' I said. 'I don't know what else to tell you.'

'Tell me what this guy is up to. Tell me how to find him.'

I sat back down in the wobbly little chair. 'I don't think I can, Debs. I don't really have much of a feel for what he's doing.'

'Bullshit,' she said.

'Seriously. I mean, technically speaking, he hasn't actually killed anybody, you know.'

'Dexter,' she said, 'you already understand more about this guy than Kyle did, and he knows who it is. We've got to find him. We've GOT to.' She bit her lower lip, and I was afraid she would start blubbering again, which would have left me totally helpless since she had already told me I couldn't say 'There there' again. But she pulled it together like the tough sergeant sister she was and merely blew her nose again.

'I'll try, Deb. Can I assume that you and Kyle have done all the basic work? Talked to witnesses and so on?'

She shook her head. 'We didn't need to. Kyle knew – ' She paused at that past tense, and then went on, very determined. 'Kyle KNOWS who did it, and he KNOWS who should be next.'

'Excuse me. He knows who's next?'

Deborah frowned. 'Don't sound like that. Kyle said there are four guys in Miami who are on the list. One of them is missing, Kyle figured he was already taken, but that gave us a little time to set up surveillance on the other three.'

'Who are these four guys, Deborah? And how does Kyle know them?'

She sighed. 'Kyle didn't tell me their names. But they were all part of a team of some kind. In El Salvador. Along with this . . . Dr. Danco guy. So – ' She spread her hands and looked helpless, a new look for her. And although it gave her a certain little-girl charm, the only thing it did for me was to make me feel even more put-upon. The whole world goes spinning merrily along, getting itself into the most God-awful trouble, and then it's all up to Dashing Dexter to tidy things up again. It didn't seem fair, but what can you do?

More to the point – what could I do now? I didn't see any way to find Kyle before it was too late. And although I am fairly sure I didn't say that out loud, Deborah reacted as if I had. She slapped one hand on the table and said, 'We have to find him before he starts on Kyle. Before he even STARTS, Dexter. Because – I mean, am I supposed to hope Kyle will only lose an arm before we get there? Or a leg? Either way, Kyle is . . .' She turned away without finishing, looking out into the darkness through the French doors by the little table.

She was right, of course. It looked like there was very little we could do to get Kyle back intact. Because with all the luck in the world, even my dazzling intellect couldn't possibly lead us to him before the work started. And then – how long could Kyle hold out? Presumably he'd had some sort of training in dealing with this sort of thing, and he knew what was coming, so—

But wait a moment. I closed my eyes and tried to think about it. Dr. Danco would know that Kyle was a pro. And as I had already told Deborah, the whole purpose was to shatter the victim into screaming unfixable pieces. Therefore . . .

I opened my eyes. 'Deb,' I said. She looked at me. 'I am in the rare position of having some hope to offer.'

'Spill it,' she said.

'This is only a guess,' I said. 'But I think Dr. Demented will probably keep Kyle around for a while, without working on him.'

She frowned. 'Why would he do that?'

'To make it last longer, and to soften him up. Kyle knows what's coming. He's braced for it. But now, imagine he's just left lying in the dark, tied up, so his imagination goes to work. And so I think maybe,' I added as it occurred to me, 'there's another victim ahead of him. The guy who's missing. So Kyle hears it – the saws and scalpels, the moans and whispers. He even smells it, knows it's coming but doesn't know when. He'll be half crazy before he even loses a toenail.'

'Jesus,' she said. 'That's your version of hope?'

'Absolutely. It gives us a little extra time to find him.'

'Jesus,' she said again.

'I could be wrong,' I said.

She looked back out the window. 'Don't be wrong, Dex. Not this time,' she said.

I shook my head. This was going to be pure drudgery, no fun at all. I could only think of two things to try, and neither of them were possible until the morning. I glanced around for a clock. According to the VCR, it was 12:00. 12:00. 12:00. 'Do you have a clock?' I asked.

Deborah frowned. 'What do you want a clock for?'

'To find out what time it is,' I said. 'I think that's the usual purpose.'

'What the hell difference does that make?' she demanded.

'Deborah. There is very little to go on here. We will have to go back and do all the routine stuff that Chutsky pulled the department away from. Luckily, we can use your badge to barge around and ask questions. But we will have to wait until morning.'

'Shit,' she said. 'I hate waiting.'

'There there,' I said. Deborah gave me a very sour look, but didn't say anything.

I didn't like waiting either, but I had done so much of it lately that perhaps it came easier to me. In any case, wait we did, dozing in our chairs until the sun came up. And then, since I was the domestic one lately, I made coffee for the two of us – one cup at a time, since Deborah's coffeemaker was one of those single-cup things for people who don't expect to be entertaining a great deal and don't actually have a life. There was nothing in the refrigerator remotely worth eating, unless you were a feral dog. Very disappointing: Dexter is a healthy boy with a high metabolism, and facing what was sure to be a difficult day on an empty stomach was not a happy thought. I know family comes first, but shouldn't that mean after breakfast?

Ah, well. Dauntless Dexter would make the sacrifice once again. Pure nobility of spirit, and I could expect no thanks, but one does what one must.

15

Dr. Mark Spielman was a large man who looked more like a retired linebacker than an ER physician. But he had been the physician on duty when the ambulance delivered The Thing to Jackson Memorial Hospital, and he was not at all happy about it. 'If I ever have to see something like that again,' he told us, 'I will retire and raise dachshunds.' He shook his head. 'You know what the ER at Jackson is like. One of the busiest. All the crazy stuff comes here, from one of the craziest cities in the world. But this— ' Spielman knocked twice on the table in the mild green staff lounge where we sat with him. 'Something else,' he said.

'What's the prognosis?' Deborah asked him, and he looked at her sharply.

'Is that a joke?' he said. 'There's no prognosis, and there's not going to be one. Physically, there's not enough left to do anything but sustain life, if you want to call it that. Mentally?' He put both hands palm up and then dropped them on the table. 'I'm not a shrink, but there's nothing left in there and no way that he'll ever have a single lucid moment, ever again. The only hope he has is that we keep him so doped up he doesn't know who he is, until he dies. Which for his sake we should all hope is soon.' He looked at his watch, a very nice Rolex. 'Is this going to take long? I am on duty, you know.'

'Were there traces of any drugs in the blood?' Deborah asked.

Spielman snorted. 'Traces, hell. The guy's blood is a cocktail sauce. I've never seen such a mix before. All designed to keep him awake, but deaden the physical pain so the shock of the multiple amputations didn't kill him.'

'Was there anything unusual about the cuts?' I asked him.

'The guy's had training,' Spielman said. 'They were all done with very good surgical technique. But any medical school in the world could have taught him that.' He blew out a breath and an apologetic smile flickered quickly across his face. 'Some of them were already healed.'

'What kind of time frame does that give us?' Deborah asked him.

Spielman shrugged. 'Four to six weeks, start to finish,' he said. 'He took at least a month to surgically dismember this guy, one small piece at a time. I can't imagine anything more horrible.'

'He did it in front of a mirror,' I said, ever-helpful. 'So the victim had to watch.'

Spielman looked appalled. 'My God,' he said. He just sat there for a minute, and then said, 'Oh, my God.' Then he shook his head and looked at his Rolex again. 'Listen, I'd like to help out here, but this is . . .' He spread his hands and then dropped them on the table again. 'I don't think there's really anything I can tell you that's going to do any good. So let me save you some time here. That Mister, uh – Chesney?'

'Chutsky,' Deborah said.

'Yes, that was it. He called in and suggested I might get an ID with a retinal scan at, um, a certain database in Virginia.' He raised an eyebrow and pursed his lips. 'Anyway. I got a fax yesterday, with a positive identification of the victim. I'll get it for you.' He stood up and disappeared into the hall. A moment later he returned with a sheet of paper. 'Here it is. Name is Manuel Borges. A native of El Salvador, in the import business.' He put the paper down in front of Deborah. 'I know it's not much, but believe me, that's it. The shape he's in . . .' He shrugged. 'I didn't think we'd get this much.'

A small intercom speaker in the ceiling muttered something that might have come from a TV show. Spielman cocked his head, frowned, and said, 'Gotta go. Hope you catch him.' And he was out the door and down the hall so quickly that the fax paper he had dropped on the table fluttered.

I looked at Deborah. She did not seem particularly encouraged that we had found the victim's name. 'Well,' I said. 'I know it isn't much.'

She shook her head. 'Not much would be a big improvement. This is nothing.' She looked at the fax, read it through one time. 'El Salvador. Connected to something called FLANGE.'

'That was our side,' I said. She looked up at me. 'The side the United States supported. I looked it up on the Internet.'

'Swell. So we just found out something we already knew.' She got up and headed for the door, not quite as quickly as Dr. Spielman but fast enough that I had to hurry and I didn't catch up until she was at the door to the parking lot.

Deborah drove rapidly and silently, with her jaw clenched, all the way to the little house on N.W. 4th Street where it had all started. The yellow tape was gone, of course, but Deborah parked haphazardly anyway, cop fashion, and got out of the car. I followed her up the short walkway to the house next door to the one where we had found the human doorstop. Deborah rang the bell, still without speaking, and a moment later it swung open. A middle-aged man wearing gold-rimmed glasses and a tan guayabera shirt looked out at us inquiringly.

'We need to speak to Ariel Medina,' Deborah said, holding up her badge.

'My mother is resting now,' he said.

'It's urgent,' Deborah said.

The man looked at her, then at me. 'Just a moment,' he said. He closed the door. Deborah stared straight ahead at the door, and I watched her jaw muscles working for a couple of minutes before the man opened the door again and held it wide. 'Come in,' he said.

We followed him into a small dark room crowded with dozens of end tables, each one festooned with religious articles and framed photographs. Ariel, the old lady who had discovered the thing next door and cried on Deb's shoulder, sat on a large overstuffed sofa with doilies on the arms and across the back. When she saw Deborah she said, 'Aaahhh,' and stood up to give her a hug. Deborah, who really should have been expecting an *abrazo* from an elderly Cuban lady, stood stiffly for a moment before awkwardly returning the embrace with a few pats on the woman's back. Deborah backed off as soon as she decently could. Ariel sat back down on the couch and patted the cushion beside her. Deborah sat.

The old lady immediately launched into a very rapid stream of Spanish. I speak some Spanish, and often I can even understand Cuban, but I was getting only one word in ten of Ariel's harangue. Deborah looked at me helplessly; for whatever quixotic reasons, she had chosen to study French in school, and as far as she was concerned the woman might as well have been speaking ancient Etruscan.

'Por favor, Señora,' I said. 'Mi hermana no habla español.'

'Ah?' Ariel looked at Deborah with a little less enthusiasm and shook her head. 'Lázaro!' Her son stepped forward, and as she resumed her monologue with barely a pause, he began to translate for her. 'I came here from Santiago de Cuba in 1962,' Lázaro said for his mother. 'Under Batista I saw some terrible things. People disappeared. Then Castro came and for a while I had hope.' She shook her head and spread her hands. 'Believe it or not, but this is what we thought at the time. Things would be different. But soon it was the same thing again. Worse. So I came here. To the United States. Because here, people don't disappear. People are not shot in the street or tortured. That's what I thought. And now this.' She waved an arm toward the house next door.

'I need to ask you a few questions,' Deborah said, and Lázaro translated.

Ariel simply nodded and went right on with her riveting tale. 'Even with Castro, they would never do a thing like that,' she said. 'Yes, they kill people. Or they put you in the Isle of Pines. But never a thing like this. Not in Cuba. Only in America,' she said.

'Did you ever see the man next door?' Deborah interrupted. 'The man who did this?' Ariel studied Deborah for a moment. 'I need to know,' Deb said. 'There's going to be another one if we can't find him.'

'Why is it you who asks me?' Ariel said through her son. 'This is no job for you. A pretty woman like you, you should have a husband. A family.'

'El victimo proximo es el novio de mi hermana,' I said. *The next victim is my sister's sweetheart.* Deborah glared at me, but Ariel said, 'Aaahhh,' clucked her tongue, and nodded her head. 'Well, I don't know what I can tell you. I did see the man, maybe two times.' She shrugged and Deborah leaned forward impatiently. 'Always at night, never very close. I can say, the man was small, very short. And skinny as well. With big glasses. More than this, I don't know. He never came out, he was very quiet. Sometimes we would hear music.' She smiled just a little and added, 'Tito Puente.' And Lázaro echoed unnecessarily, 'Tito Puente.'

'Ah,' I said, and they all looked at me. 'It would hide the noise,' I said, a little embarrassed at all the attention.

'Did he have a car?' Deborah asked, and Ariel frowned.

'A van,' she said. 'He drove an old white van with no windows. It was very clean, but had many rust spots and dents. I saw it a few times, but he usually kept it in his garage.'

'I don't suppose you saw the license plate?' I asked her, and she looked at me.

'But I did,' she said through her son, and held up one hand, palm outward. 'Not to get the number, that only happens in the old movies. But I know it was a Florida license plate. The yellow one with the cartoon of a child,' she said, and she stopped talking and glared at me, because I was giggling. It's not at all dignified, and certainly not something I practice on a regular basis, but I was actually giggling and I could not help myself.

Deborah glared at me, too. 'What is so goddamned funny?' she demanded.

'The license plate,' I said. 'I'm sorry, Debs, but my God, don't you know what the yellow Florida plate is? And for this guy to have one and do what he does . . .' I swallowed hard to keep from laughing again, but it took all my self-control.

'All right, damn it, what's so funny about the yellow license plate?'

'It's a specialty plate, Deb,' I said. 'The one that says, CHOOSE LIFE.'

And then, picturing Dr. Danco carting around his wriggling victims, filling them with chemicals and cutting so very perfectly to keep them alive through it all, I'm afraid I giggled again. 'Choose life,' I said.

I really wanted to meet this guy.

We walked back to the car in silence. Deborah got in and called in the description of the van to Captain Matthews, and he agreed that he could probably put out an APB. While she talked to the captain, I looked around. Neatly manicured yards, mostly consisting of colored rocks. A few children's bicycles chained to the front porch, and the Orange Bowl looming in the background. A nice little neighborhood to live in, work in, raise a family in – or chop off somebody's arms and legs.

'Get in,' said Deborah, interrupting my rustic reverie. I got in and we drove off. At one point, stopped at a red light, Deb glanced at me and said, 'You pick a funny time to start laughing.'

'Really, Deb,' I said. 'This is the first hint of personality we've got from the guy. We know he has a sense of humor. I think that's a big step forward.'

'Sure. Maybe we'll catch him at a comedy club.'

'We will catch him, Deb,' I said, although neither one of us believed me. She just grunted; the light changed and she stomped on the gas as if she was killing a poisonous snake.

We moved through the traffic back to Deb's house. The morning rush hour was coming to an end. At the corner of Flagler and 34th a car had run up onto the sidewalk and smacked into a light pole in front of a church. A cop stood beside the car between two men who were screaming at each other. A little girl sat on the curb crying. Ah, the enchanting rhythms of another magical day in paradise.

A few moments later we turned down Medina and Deborah parked her car beside mine in the driveway. She switched off the engine and for a moment we both just sat there listening to the ticking of the cooling motor. 'Shit,' she said.

'I agree.'

'What do we do now?' she said.

'Sleep,' I said. 'I'm too tired to think.'

She pounded both hands on the steering wheel. 'How can I sleep, Dexter? Knowing that Kyle is . . .' She hit the wheel again. 'Shit,' she said.

'The van will turn up, Deb. You know that. The database will spit out every white van with a CHOOSE LIFE tag, and with an APB out it's just a matter of time.'

'Kyle doesn't have time,' she said.

'Human beings need sleep, Debs,' I said. 'And so do I.'

A courier's van squealed around the corner and clunked to a halt in front of Deborah's house. The driver jumped out with a small package and approached Deb's front door. She said, 'Shit,' one last time and got out of the car to collect the package.

I closed my eyes and sat for just a moment longer, pondering, which is what I do instead of thinking when I am very tired. It really seemed like wasted effort; nothing came to me except to wonder where I'd left my running shoes. With my new sense of humor apparently still idling, that seemed funny to me and, to my great surprise I heard a very faint echo from the Dark Passenger. *Why is that funny?* I asked. *Is it because I left the shoes at Rita's?* Of course it didn't answer. The poor thing was probably still sulking. And yet it had chuckled. *Is it something else altogether that seems funny?* I asked. But again there was no answer; just a faint sense of anticipation and hunger.

The courier rattled and roared away. Just as I was about to yawn, stretch, and admit that my finely tuned cerebral powers were on hiatus, I heard a kind of retching moan. I opened my eyes and looked up to see Deborah stagger forward a step and then sit down hard on her front walk. I got out of the car and hurried over to her.

'Deb?' I said. 'What is it?'

She dropped the package and hid her face in her hands, making more unlikely noises. I squatted beside her and picked up the package. It was a small box, about the right size to hold a wristwatch. I pried the end up. Inside was a ziplock bag. And inside the bag was a human finger.

A finger with a big, flashy pinkie ring.

16

It took a very great deal more than patting Deborah on the shoulder and saying 'There there' to get her calmed down this time. In fact I had to force-feed her a large glass of peppermint schnapps. I knew that she needed some kind of chemical help to relax and even sleep if possible, but Debs had nothing in her medicine chest stronger than Tylenol, and she was not a drinker. I finally found the schnapps bottle under her kitchen sink, and after making sure it wasn't actually drain cleaner I made her chug down a glass of it. From the apparent taste, it might as well have been drain cleaner. She shuddered and gagged but she drank it, too bone weary and brain numb to fight.

While she slumped in her chair I threw a few changes of her clothing into a grocery bag and dropped it by the front door. She stared at the bags and then at me. 'What are you doing,' she said. Her voice was slurred and she sounded uninterested in the answer.

'You're staying at my place for a few days,' I said.

'Don't want to,' she said.

'It doesn't matter,' I said. 'You have to.'

She shifted her gaze to the bag of clothing by the door. 'Why.'

I walked over to her and squatted beside her chair. 'Deborah. He knows who you are and where you are. Let's try to make it just a little bit of a challenge for him, all right?'

She shuddered again, but she didn't say anything more as I helped her to her feet and out the door. Half an hour and one more slug of peppermint schnapps later she was in my bed, snoring lightly. I left her a note to call me when she woke up, and then I took her little surprise package with me and headed in to work.

I didn't expect to find any important clues from running the finger through a lab check, but since I do forensics for a living it seemed like I really ought to give it a professional once-over. And because I take all my obligations very seriously, I stopped on the way and bought doughnuts. As I approached my second-floor cubbyhole, Vince Masuoka came down the hall from the opposite direction. I bowed humbly and held up the bag. 'Greetings, Sensei,' I said. 'I bring gifts.'

'Greetings, Grasshopper,' he said. 'There is a thing called time. You must explore its mysteries.' He held up his wrist and pointed to his watch. 'I'm on my way to lunch, and now you bring me my breakfast?'

'Better late than never,' I said, but he shook his head.

'Nah,' he said. 'My mouth has already changed gears. I'm gonna go get some *ropa vieja* and *plátanos*.'

'If you spurn my gift of food,' I said, 'I will give you the finger.' He raised an eyebrow, and I handed him Deb's package. 'Can I have half an hour of your time before lunch?'

He looked at the small box. 'I don't think I want to open this on an empty stomach, do I?' he said.

'Well then, how about a doughnut?'

It took more than half an hour, but by the time Vince left for lunch we had learned that there was nothing to learn from Kyle's finger. The cut was extremely clean and professional, done with a very sharp instrument that left no trace behind in the wound. There was nothing under the fingernail except a little dirt that could have come from anywhere. I removed the ring, but we found no threads or hairs or telltale fabric swatches, and Kyle had somehow failed to etch an address or phone number onto the inside of the ring. Kyle's blood type was AB positive.

I put the finger into cold storage, and slipped the ring into my pocket. That wasn't exactly standard procedure, but I was fairly sure that Deborah would want it if we didn't get Kyle back. As it was, it looked like if we did get him back it would be by messenger, one piece at a time. Of course, I'm not a sentimental person, but that didn't seem like something that would warm her heart.

By now I was very tired indeed, and since Debs hadn't called yet I decided that I was well within my rights to head for home and take a nap. The afternoon rain started as I climbed into my car. I shot straight down LeJeune in the relatively light traffic and got home after being screamed at only one time, which was a new record. I dashed in through the rain and found Deborah gone. She had scribbled a note on a Post-it saying she would call later. I was relieved, since I had not been looking forward to sleeping on my half-size couch. I crawled right into my own bed and slept without interruption until a little after six o'clock in the evening.

Naturally, even the mighty machine that is my body needs a certain amount of maintenance, and when I sat up in bed I felt very much in need of an oil change. The long night with so little sleep, the missed breakfast, the tension and suspense of trying to think of something besides 'There there' to say to Deborah – all these things had taken their toll. I felt as though someone had snuck in and packed my head with beach sand, even including the bottle caps and cigarette butts.

There is only one solution to this occasional condition, and that is exercise.

But as I decided that what I really needed was a pleasant two- or three-mile jog, I remembered again that I had misplaced my running shoes. They were not in their usual spot by the door, and they were not in my car. This was Miami, so it was possible that someone had broken into my apartment and stolen them; they were, after all, very nice New Balance shoes. But I thought it more likely that I had left them over at Rita's. For me, to decide is to act. I toddled down to my car and drove over to Rita's house.

The rain was long gone – it seldom lasts even an hour – and the streets were already dry and filled with the usual cheerfully homicidal crowd. My people. The maroon Taurus showed up behind me at Sunset, and stayed with me all the way. It was nice to see Doakes back on the job. I had felt just a little bit neglected. Once again he parked across the street as I knocked on the door. He had just turned off the engine when Rita opened the door. 'Well,' she said. 'What a surprise!' She lifted her face for a kiss.

I gave her one, putting a little extra English on it to entertain Sergeant Doakes. 'There's no easy way to say this,' I said, 'but I've come for my running shoes.'

Rita smiled. 'Actually, I just put mine on. Care to get sweaty together?' And she held the door wide for me.

'That's the best invitation I've had all day,' I said.

I found my shoes in her garage beside the washing machine, along with a pair of shorts and a sleeveless sweatshirt, laundered and ready to go. I went into the bathroom and changed clothes, leaving my work clothes folded neatly on the toilet seat. In just a few minutes Rita and I were trotting up the block together. I waved to Sergeant Doakes as we went by. We ran down the street, turned right for a few blocks, and then around the perimeter of the nearby park. We had run this route together before, had even measured it out at just under three miles, and we were used to each other's pace. And so about half an hour later, sweaty and once again willing to face the challenges of another evening of life on Planet Earth, we stood at the front door of Rita's house.

'If you don't mind, I'll take the first shower,' she said. 'That way I can start dinner while you clean up.'

'Absolutely,' I said. 'I'll just sit out here and drip.'

Rita smiled. 'I'll get you a beer,' she said. A moment later she handed me one and then went in and closed the door. I sat on the step and sipped my beer. The last few days had gone by in a savage blur, and I had been so entirely upended from my normal life that I actually enjoyed the moment of peaceful contemplation, calmly sitting there and drinking a beer while somewhere in the city Chutsky was shedding spare parts. Life whirled on around me with its sundry slashings, strangulations, and dismemberings, but in Dexter's Domain it was Miller Time. I raised the can in a toast to Sergeant Doakes.

Somewhere in the house I heard a commotion. There was shouting and a little bit of squealing, as if Rita had just discovered the Beatles in her bathroom. Then the front door slammed open and Rita grabbed me around the neck in a stranglehold. I dropped my beer and gasped for air. 'What? What did I do?' I said. I saw Astor and Cody watching from just inside the door. 'I'm terribly sorry, and I'll never do it again,' I added, but Rita kept squeezing.

'Oh, Dexter,' she said, and now she was crying. Astor smiled at me and clasped her hands together under her chin. Cody just watched, nodding a little bit. 'Oh, Dexter,' Rita said again.

'Please,' I said, struggling desperately to get some air, 'I promise it was an accident and I didn't mean it. What did I do?' Rita finally relented and loosened her death grip.

'Oh, Dexter,' she said one more time, and she put her hands on my face and looked at me with a blinding smile and a faceful of tears. 'Oh, YOU!' she said, although to be honest it didn't seem very much like me at the moment. 'I'm sorry, it was an accident,' she said, snuffling now. 'I hope you didn't have anything really special planned.'

'Rita. Please. What is going on?'

Her smile got bigger and bigger. 'Oh, Dexter. I really – it was just – Astor needed to use the toilet, and when she picked up your clothes, it just fell out onto the floor and – Oh, Dexter, it's so beautiful!' She had now said Oh Dexter so many times that I began to feel Irish, but I still had no idea what was going on.

Until Rita lifted up her hand in front of her. Her left hand. Now with a large diamond ring sparkling on her ring finger.

Chutsky's ring.

'Oh, Dexter,' she said again, and then buried her face in my shoulder. 'Yes yes YES! Oh, you've made me so happy!'

'All right,' Cody said softly.

And after that, what can you say except congratulations?

The rest of the evening passed in a blur of disbelief and Miller Lite. I knew very well that hovering somewhere out in space was a perfect, calm, logical series of words that I could put together and say to Rita to make her understand that I had not actually proposed to her, and we would all have a good laugh and say good night. But the harder I searched for that magical elusive sentence, the faster it ran away from me. And I found myself reasoning that perhaps one more beer would unlock the doors of perception, and after several cans Rita went up to the corner store and returned with a bottle of champagne. We drank the champagne and everyone seemed so very happy, and one thing led to another and somehow I ended up in Rita's bed once again, witness to some exceedingly unlikely and undignified events.

And once again I found myself wondering, as I drifted off to stunned and unbelieving sleep: *How do these terrible things always happen to me?*

Waking up after a night like that is never very pleasant. Waking up in the middle of the night and thinking, *Oh God – Deborah!* is even worse. You may think I was guilty or uneasy about neglecting someone who depended on me, in which case you would be very wrong. As I have said, I don't really feel - emotions. I can, however, experience fear, and the idea of Deborah's potential rage pulled the trigger. I hurried into my clothes and managed to slip out to my car without waking anyone. Sergeant Doakes was no longer in his position across the street. It was nice to know that even Doakes needed to sleep   sometime. Or perhaps he had thought that someone who just got engaged deserved a little privacy. Knowing him as I did, however, this didn't seem likely. It was far more likely that he had been elected pope and had to fly off to the Vatican.

I drove home quickly, and checked my answering machine. There was one automated message urging me to buy a new set of tires before it was too late, which seemed ominous enough, but no message from Debs. I made coffee and waited for the thump of the morning paper against my door. There was a sense of unreality to the morning that was not entirely caused by the after-effects of the champagne. Engaged, was I? Well well. I wished that I could scold myself and demand to know what I thought I had been doing. But the truth was that, unfortunately, I hadn't been doing anything wrong; I was entirely clothed in virtue and diligence. And I had done nothing that could be called spectacularly stupid – far from it. I had been proceeding with life in a noble and even exemplary manner, minding my own business and trying to help my sister recover her boyfriend, exercising, eating plenty of green vegetables, and not even slicing up other monsters. And somehow all this pure and decent behavior had snuck around behind me and bitten me on the ass. Never a good deed goes unpunished, as Harry used to say.

And what could I do about it now? Surely Rita would come to her senses. I mean, really: *ME?* Who could possibly want to marry *ME?!* There had to be better alternatives, like becoming a nun, or joining the Peace Corps. This was Dexter we were talking about. In a city the size of Miami, couldn't she find somebody who was at least human? And what was her rush to get married again anyway? It hadn't worked out terribly well for her the first time, but she was apparently willing to plunge right back into it again. Were women really this desperate to get married?

Of course there were the children to think about. Conventional wisdom would say they needed a father, and there was something to that, because where would I have been without Harry? And Astor and Cody had looked so happy. Even if I made Rita see that a comical mistake had happened, would the kids ever understand?

I was on my second cup of coffee when the paper came. I glanced through the main sections, relieved to find that terrible things were still happening almost everywhere. At least the rest of the world hadn't gone crazy.

By seven o'clock I thought it would be safe to call Deborah on her cell phone. There was no answer; I left a message, and fifteen minutes later she called back. 'Good morning, Sis,' I said, and I marveled at the way I managed to sound cheerful. 'Did you get some sleep?'

'A little,' she grumbled. 'I woke up around four yesterday. I traced the package to a place in Hialeah. I drove around the area most of the night looking for the white van.'

'If he dropped the package way up in Hialeah, he probably drove in from Key West to do it,' I said.

'I know that, goddamn it,' she snapped. 'But what the hell else am I supposed to do?'

'I don't know,' I admitted. 'But doesn't the guy from Washington get here today?'

'We don't know anything about him,' she said. 'Just because Kyle is good, doesn't mean this guy will be.'

She apparently didn't remember that Kyle had not shown himself to be particularly good, at least in public. He'd done nothing at all, in fact, except get himself captured and have his finger nipped off. But it didn't seem politic for me to comment on how good he was, so I simply said, 'Well, we have to assume the new guy knows something about this that we don't know.'

Deborah snorted. 'That wouldn't be too hard,' she said. 'I'll call you when he gets in.' She hung up, and I got ready for work.

17

At 12:30 Deb stalked into my modest retreat off the forensics lab and threw a cassette tape on my desk. I looked up at her; she didn't seem happy, but that really wasn't much of a novelty. 'From my answering machine at home,' she said. 'Listen to it.'

I lifted the hatch on my boom box and put in the tape Deb had flung at me. I pushed play: the tape beeped loudly, and then an unfamiliar voice said, 'Sergeant, um, Morgan. Right? This is Dan Burdett, from uh – Kyle Chutsky said I should call you. I'm on the ground at the airport, and I'll call you about getting together when I get to my hotel, which is – ' There was a rustling sound and he obviously moved the cell phone away from his mouth, since his voice got fainter. 'What? Oh, hey, that's nice. All right, thanks.' His voice got louder again. 'I just met your driver. Thanks for sending somebody. All right, I'll call from the hotel.'

Deborah reached across my desk and switched off the machine. 'I didn't send anybody to the fucking airport,' she said. 'And Captain Matthews damn sure didn't either. Did you send somebody to the fucking airport, Dexter?'

'My limo was out of gas,' I said.

'Well then GOD*DAMN* it!' she said, and I had to agree with her analysis.

'Anyway,' I said, 'at least we found out how good Kyle's replacement is.'

Deborah slumped into the folding chair by my desk. 'Square fucking one,' she said. 'And Kyle is . . .' She bit her lip and didn't finish the sentence.

'Did you tell Captain Matthews about this yet?' I asked her. She shook her head. 'Well, he has to call them. They'll send somebody else.'

'Sure, great. They send somebody else, who might make it all the way to baggage claim this time. Shit, Dexter.'

'We have to tell them, Debs,' I said. 'By the way, who are *them*? Did Kyle ever tell you exactly who he works for?'

She sighed. 'No. He joked about working for the OGA, but he never said why that was funny.'

'Well, whoever they are, they need to know,' I said. I pried the cassette out of my boom box and put it on the desk in front of her. 'There has to be something they can do.'

Deborah didn't move for a moment. 'Why do I get the feeling they've already done it, and Burdett was it?' she said. Then she scooped up the tape and trudged out of my office.

I was sipping coffee and digesting my lunch with the help of a jumbo chocolate-chip cookie when the call came to report to the scene of a homicide in the Miami Shores area. Angel-no-relation and I drove over to where a body had been found in the shell of a small house on a canal that was being ripped apart and rebuilt. Construction had been temporarily halted while the owner and the contractor sued each other. Two teenaged boys skipping school had snuck into the house and found the body. It was laid out on heavy plastic on top of a sheet of plywood which had been placed over two sawhorses. Someone had taken a power saw and neatly lopped off the head, legs, and arms. The whole thing had been left like that, with the trunk in the middle and the pieces simply trimmed off and moved a few inches away.

And although the Dark Passenger had chuckled and whispered little dark nothings in my ear, I put it down to pure envy and went on with my work. There was certainly plenty of blood spatter for me to work with, still very fresh, and I probably would have spent a cheerfully efficient day finding and analyzing it if I hadn't happened to overhear the uniformed officer who had been first on the scene talking with a detective.

'The wallet was right there by the body,' Officer Snyder was saying. 'Got a Virginia driver's license in the name of Daniel Chester Burdett.'

Oh, well then, I said to the happy chattering voice in the backseat of my brain. *That would certainly explain a lot, wouldn't it?* I looked again at the body. Although the removal of the head and limbs had been fast and savage, there was a neatness to the arrangement that I could now recognize as slightly familiar, and the Dark Passenger chuckled happily in agreement. Between the trunk and each part, the gap was as precise as if it had been measured, and the whole presentation was arranged almost like an anatomy lesson. The hip bone disconnected from the leg bone.

'Got the two boys who found it in the squad car,' Snyder said to the detective. I glanced back at the two of them, wondering how to tell them my news. Of course, it was possible that I was wrong, but—

'Sonamabeech,' I heard someone mutter. I looked back to where Angel-no-relation was squatting on the far side of the body. Once again he was using his tweezers to hold up a small piece of paper. I stepped behind him and looked over his shoulder.

In a clear and spidery hand, someone had written 'POGUE,' and crossed it out with a single line. 'Whassa pogue?' Angel asked. 'His name?'

'It's somebody who sits behind a desk and orders around the real troops,' I told him.

He looked at me. 'How you know all this shit?' he asked.

'I see a lot of movies,' I said.

Angel glanced back down at the paper. 'I think the handwriting is the same,' he said.

'Like the other one,' I said.

'The one that never happened,' he said. 'I know, I was there.'

I straightened up and took a breath, thinking how nice it was to be right. 'This one never happened, either,' I said, and walked over to where Officer Snyder was chatting with the detective.

The detective in question was a pear-shaped man named Coulter. He was sipping from a large plastic bottle of Mountain Dew and looking out at the canal that ran by the backyard. 'What do you think a place like this goes for?' he asked Snyder. 'On a canal like that. Less than a mile from the bay, huh? Figure maybe what. Half a million? More?'

'Excuse me, Detective,' I said. 'I think we have a situation here.' I'd always wanted to say that, but it didn't seem to impress Coulter.

'A situation. You been watching *CSI* or something?'

'Burdett is a federal agent,' I said. 'You have to call Captain Matthews right away and tell him.'

'I *have* to,' Coulter said.

'This is connected to something we're not supposed to touch,' I said. 'They came down from Washington and told the captain to back off.'

Coulter took a swig from his bottle. 'And did the captain back off?'

'Like a rabbit in reverse,' I said.

Coulter turned and looked at Burdett's body. 'A fed,' he said. He took one more swig as he stared at the severed head and limbs. Then he shook his head. 'Those guys always come apart under pressure.' He looked back out the window and pulled out his cell phone.

Deborah got to the scene just as Angel-no-relation was putting his kit back in the van, which was three minutes before Captain Matthews. I don't mean to seem critical of the captain. To be perfectly fair, Debs didn't have to put on a fresh spray of Aramis, and he did, and redoing the knot in his tie must have taken some time, too. Just moments behind Matthews came a car I had come to know as well as my own; a maroon Ford Taurus, piloted by Sergeant Doakes. 'Hail, hail, the gang's all here,' I said cheerfully. Officer Snyder looked at me like I had suggested we dance naked, but Coulter just pushed his index finger into the mouth of his soda bottle and let it dangle as he walked away to meet the captain.

Deborah had been looking the scene over from the outside and directing Snyder's partner to move the perimeter tape back a little. By the time she finally walked over to talk to me, I had reached a startling conclusion. It had started as an exercise in ironic whimsy, but it grew into something that I couldn't argue with, as much as I tried. I stepped over to Coulter's expensive window and stared out, leaning on the wall and looking hard at the idea. For some reason, the Dark Passenger found the notion hugely amusing and began whispering frightful counterpoint. And finally, feeling like I was selling nuclear secrets to the Taliban, I realized it was all we could do. 'Deborah,' I said as she stalked over to where I stood by the window, 'the cavalry isn't coming this time.'

'No shit, Sherlock,' she said.

'We are all there is, and we are not enough.'

She pushed a lock of hair away from her face and blew out a deep breath. 'What have I been saying?'

'But you didn't take the next step, Sis. Since we are not enough, we need help, somebody who knows something about this— '

'For Christ's sake, Dexter! We've been *feeding* people like that to this guy!'

'Which means the only remaining candidate at the moment is Sergeant Doakes,' I said.

It might not be fair to say that her jaw dropped. But she did stare at me with her mouth open before turning to look at Doakes, where he stood beside Burdett's body, talking to Captain Matthews.

'Sergeant Doakes,' I repeated. 'Formerly *Sergeant* Doakes. Of the Special Forces. On detached service in El Salvador.'

She looked back at me, and then at Doakes again.

'Deborah,' I said, 'if we want to find Kyle, we need to know more about this. We need to know the names on Kyle's list and we need to know what kind of team it was and why all this is happening. And Doakes is the only one I can think of who knows any of it.'

'Doakes wants you dead,' she said.

'No working situation is ever ideal,' I said with my best smile of cheerful perseverance. 'And I think he wants this to go away as badly as Kyle does.'

'Probably not as much as Kyle,' Deborah said. 'Not as much as I do, either.'

'Well then,' I said. 'This looks like your best shot.'

Deborah still didn't look convinced for some reason. 'Captain Matthews won't want to lose Doakes for this. We'd have to clear it with him.'

I pointed to where that very same captain was conferring with Doakes. 'Behold,' I said.

Deborah chewed her lip for a moment before she finally said, 'Shit. It might work.'

'I can't think of anything else that might,' I said.

She took another breath, and then as if someone had clicked a switch, she stepped toward Matthews and Doakes with her jaw clenched. I trailed along behind, trying hard to blend in with the bare walls so Doakes wouldn't pounce and rip out my heart.

'Captain,' Deborah said, 'we need to get proactive with this.'

Even though 'proactive' was one of his favorite words, Matthews stared at her like she was a cockroach in the salad. 'What we need,' he said, 'is for these . . . *people* . . . in Washington to send somebody competent to clean up this situation.'

Deborah pointed at Burdett. 'They sent him,' she said.

Matthews glanced down at Burdett and pushed his lips out thoughtfully. 'What do you suggest?'

'We have a couple of leads,' she said, nodding toward me. I really wished she hadn't, since Matthews swung his head in my direction and, much worse, so did Doakes. If his hungry-dog expression was any indication, he apparently hadn't mellowed in his feelings toward me.

'What is your involvement with this?' Matthews asked me.

'He's providing forensic assistance,' Deborah said, and I nodded modestly.

'Shit,' Doakes said.

'There's a time factor here,' Deborah said. 'We need to find this guy before he – before more of these turn up. We can't keep a lid on it forever.'

'I think the term "media feeding frenzy" might be appropriate,' I offered, always helpful. Matthews glared at me.

'I know the overall shape of what Kyle – of what Chutsky was trying to do,' Deborah went on. 'But I can't go on with it because I don't know any background details.' She stuck her chin out in the direction of Doakes. 'Sergeant Doakes does.'

Doakes looked surprised, which was obviously an expression he hadn't practiced enough. But before he could speak Deborah plowed ahead. 'I think the three of us together can catch this guy before another fed gets on the ground and catches up to what's happened so far.'

'Shit,' Doakes said again. 'You want me to work with *him*?' He didn't need to point to let everyone know he meant me, but he did anyway, pushing a muscular, knobby index finger at my face.

'Yeah, I do,' Deborah said. Captain Matthews was chewing on his lip and looking undecided, and Doakes said, 'Shit,' again. I did hope that his conversational skills would improve if we were going to work together.

'You said you know something about this,' Matthews said to Doakes, and the sergeant reluctantly turned his glare away from me and onto the captain.

'Uh-huh,' said Doakes.

'From your, uh – From the army,' Matthews said. He didn't seem terribly frightened by Doakes's expression of petulant rage, but perhaps that was just the habit of command.

'Uh-huh,' Doakes said again.

Captain Matthews frowned, looking as much as he possibly could like a man of action making an important decision. The rest of us managed to control our goose bumps.

'Morgan,' Captain Matthews finally said. He looked at Debs, and then he paused. A van that said Action News on the side pulled up in front of the little house and people began to get out. 'Goddamn it,' Matthews said. He glanced at the body and then at Doakes. 'Can you do it, Sergeant?'

'They're not going to like it in Washington,' Doakes said. 'And I don't much like it here.'

'I'm beginning to lose interest in what they like in Washington,' Matthews said. 'We have our own problems. Can you handle this?'

Doakes looked at me. I tried to look serious and dedicated, but he just shook his head. 'Yeah,' he said. 'I can do this.'

Matthews clapped him on the shoulder. 'Good man,' he said, and he hurried away to talk to the news crew.

Doakes was still looking at me. I looked back. 'Think how much easier it's going to be to keep track of me,' I said.

'When this is over,' he said. 'Just you and me.'

'But not until it's over,' I said, and he finally nodded, just once.

'Until then,' he said.

18

Doakes took us to a coffee shop called Ocho, just across the street from a car dealership. He led us to a small table in the back corner and sat down facing the door. 'We can talk here,' he said, and he made it sound so much like a spy movie that I wished I had brought sunglasses. Still, perhaps Chutsky's would come in the mail. Hopefully without his nose attached.

Before we could actually talk, a man came from the back room and shook Doakes's hand. 'Alberto,' he said. 'Como estas?' And Doakes answered him in very good Spanish – better than mine, to be honest, although I do like to think that my accent is better. 'Luis,' he said. 'Mas o menos.' They chattered away for a minute, and then Luis brought us all tiny cups of horribly sweet Cuban coffee and a plate of *pastelitos*. He nodded once at Doakes and then disappeared into the back room.

Deborah watched the whole performance with growing impatience, and when Luis finally left us she opened up. 'We need the names of everybody from El Salvador,' she blurted out.

Doakes just looked at her and sipped his coffee. 'Be a big list,' he said.

Deborah frowned. 'You know what I mean,' she said. 'Goddamn it, Doakes, he's got Kyle.'

Doakes showed his teeth. 'Yeah, Kyle getting old. Never would have got him in his prime.'

'What exactly were *you* doing down there?' I asked him. I know it was a bit off message, but my curiosity about how he would answer got the best of me.

Still smiling, if that's what it was, Doakes looked at me and said, 'What do you think?' And just underneath the threshold of hearing there came a quiet rumble of savage glee, answered right away from deep inside my dark backseat, one predator calling across a moonlit night to another. And really and truly, what else could he have been doing? Just as Doakes knew me, I knew Doakes for what he was: a cold killer. Even without what Chutsky had said, it was very clear what Doakes would have been doing in a homicidal carnival like El Salvador. He would have been one of the ringmasters.

'Cut the staring contest,' Deborah said. 'I need some names.'

Doakes picked up one of the *pastelitos* and leaned back. 'Why don't you all bring me up to date?' he said. He took a bite, and Deborah tapped a finger on the table before deciding that made sense.

'All right,' she said. 'We got a rough description of the guy who's doing this, and his van. A white van.'

Doakes shook his head. 'Don't matter. We *know* who's doing this.'

'We also got an ID on the first victim,' I said. 'A man named Manuel Borges.'

'Well, well,' Doakes said. 'Old Manny, huh? Really should've let me shoot him.'

'A friend of yours?' I asked, but Doakes ignored me.

'What else you got?' he said.

'Kyle had a list of names,' Deborah said. 'Other men from the same unit. He said one of them would be the next victim. But he didn't tell me the names.'

'No, he wouldn't,' Doakes said.

'So we need you to tell us,' she said.

Doakes appeared to think this over. 'If I was a hotshot like Kyle, I'd pick one of these guys and stake him out.' Deborah pursed her lips and nodded. 'Problem is, I am *not* a hotshot like Kyle. Just a simple cop from the country.'

'Would you like a banjo?' I asked, but for some reason he didn't laugh.

'I only know about one guy from the old team here in Miami,' he said, after a quick and savage glance at me. 'Oscar Acosta. Saw him at Publix two years ago. We could run him down.' He pointed his chin at Deborah. 'Two other names I can think of. You look 'em up, see if they're here.' He spread his hands. 'About all I got. I could maybe call some old buddies in Virginia, but no telling what that might stir up.' He snorted. 'Anyway, take them two days to decide what I was really asking and what they ought to do about it.'

'So what do we do?' Deborah said. 'We stake this guy out? The one you saw? Or do we talk to him?'

Doakes shook his head. 'He remembered me. I can talk to him. You try to watch him, he'll know it and probably disappear.' He looked at his watch. 'Quarter of three. Oscar be home in a couple of hours. You-all wait for my call.' And then he gave me his 150-watt I'm-watching-you smile, and said, 'Why don't you go wait with your pretty fiancée?' And he got up and walked out, leaving us with the check.

Deborah stared at me. 'Fiancée?' she said.

'It's not really definite,' I said.

'You're *engaged*!?'

'I was going to tell you,' I said.

'When? On your third anniversary?'

'When I know how it happened,' I said. 'I still don't really believe it.'

She snorted. 'I don't either.' She stood up. 'Come on. I'll take you back to work. Then you can go wait with your *fiancée*,' she said. I left some money on the table and followed meekly.

Vince Masuoka was passing by in the hall when Deborah and I got off the elevator. 'Shalom, boy-chick,' he said. 'How's by you?'

'He's engaged,' Deborah said before I could speak. Vince looked at her like she had said I was pregnant.

'He's *what*?' he said.

'Engaged. About to be married,' she said.

'*Married*? Dexter?' His face seemed to struggle with finding the right expression, which was not an easy task since he always seemed to be faking it, one of the reasons I got along with him; two artificial humans, like plastic peas in a real pod. He finally settled on what looked like delighted surprise – not very convincing, but still a sound choice. 'Mazel tov!' he said, and gave me an awkward hug.

'Thank you,' I said, still feeling completely baffled by the whole thing and wondering if I would actually have to go through with it.

'Well then,' he said, rubbing his hands together, 'we can't let this go unpunished. Tomorrow night at my house?'

'For what?' I asked.

He gave me his very best phony smile. 'Ancient Japanese ritual, dating back to the Tokugawa shogunate. We get smashed and watch dirty movies,' he said, and then he turned to leer at Deborah. 'We can get your sister to jump out of a cake.'

'How about if you jump up your ass instead?' Debs said.

'That's very nice, Vince, but I don't think— ' I said, trying to avoid anything that made my engagement more official, and also trying to stop the two of them from trading their clever put-downs before I got a headache. But Vince wouldn't let me finish.

'No, no,' he said, 'this is highly necessary. A matter of honor, no escape. Tomorrow night, eight o'clock,' he said, and, looking at Deborah as he walked away, he added, 'and you only have twenty-four hours to practice twirling your tassels.'

'Go twirl your own tassel,' she said.

'Ha! Ha!' he said with his terrible fake laugh, and he disappeared down the hall.

'Little freak,' Deborah muttered, and she turned to go in the other direction. 'Stick with your *fiancée* after work. I'll call you when I hear from Doakes.'

There wasn't a great deal left of the workday. I filed a few things, ordered a case of Luminol from our supplier, and acknowledged receiving half a dozen memos that had piled up in my e-mail in-box. And with a feeling of real accomplishment, I headed down to my car and drove through the soothing carnage of rush hour. I stopped at my apartment for a change of clothes; Debs was nowhere to be seen, but the bed was unmade so I knew she had been here. I stuffed my things into a carry-on bag and headed for Rita's.

It was fully dark by the time I got to Rita's house. I didn't really want to go there, but was not quite sure what else to do. Deborah expected me to be there if she needed to find me, and she was using my apartment. So I parked in Rita's driveway and got out of my car. Purely from reflex, I glanced across the street to Sergeant Doakes's parking spot. It was empty, of course. He was occupied talking with Oscar, his old army buddy. And the sudden realization grew on me that I was free, away from the unfriendly bloodhound eyes that had for so long now kept me from being me. A slow, swelling hymn of pure dark joy rose up inside me and the counterpoint thumped down from a sudden moon oozing out from a low cloud bank, a lurid, guttering three-quarter moon still low and huge in the dark sky. And the music blared from the loudspeakers and climbed into the upper decks of Dexter's Dark Arena, where the sly whispers grew into a roaring cheer to match the moon music, a rousing chant of *Do it, do it, do it*, and my body quivered from the inside out as I came up on point and thought, *Why not?*

Why not indeed? I could slip away for a few happy hours – taking my cell phone with me, of course, I wouldn't want to be irresponsible about it. But why not take advantage of the Doakes-less moony night and slide away into the dark breeze? The thought of those red boots pulled at me like a spring tide. Reiker lived just a few miles from here. I could be there in ten minutes. I could slip in and find the proof I needed, and then – I suppose I would have to improvise, but the voice just under the edge of sound was full of ideas tonight and we could certainly come up with something to lead to the sweet release we both needed so much. *Oh, do it, Dexter*, the voices howled and as I paused on tiptoe to listen and think again *Why not?* and came up with no reasonable answer . . .

. . . the front door of Rita's house swung wide and Astor peered out. 'It's him!' she called back into the house. 'He's here!'

And so I was. Here, instead of there. Reeling in to the couch instead of dancing away into darkness. Wearing the weary mask of Dexter the Sofa Spud instead of the bright silver gleam of the Dark Avenger.

'Come on in, you,' Rita said, filling the doorway with such warm good cheer that I felt my teeth grind together, and the crowd inside howled with disappointment but slowly filed out of the stadium, game over, because after all, what could we do? Nothing, of course, which was what we did, trailing meekly into the house behind the happy parade of Rita, Astor, and ever-quiet Cody. I managed not to whimper, but really: Wasn't this pushing the envelope a tiny bit? Weren't we all taking advantage of Dexter's cheerful good nature just a trifle too much?

Dinner was annoyingly pleasant, as if to prove to me that I was buying into a lifetime of happiness and pork chops, and I played along even though my heart was not in it. I cut the meat into small chunks, wishing I was cutting something else and thinking of the South Pacific cannibals who referred to humans as 'long pork.' It was appropriate, really, because it was that other pork I truly longed to slice into and not this tepid mushroom soup-covered thing on my plate. But I smiled and stabbed the green beans and made it all the way through to coffee somehow. Ordeal by pork chop, but I survived.

After dinner, Rita and I sipped our coffee as the kids ate small portions of frozen yogurt. Although coffee is supposed to be a stimulant, it gave me no help in thinking of a way out of this – not even a way to slip out for a few hours, let alone avoid this lifelong bliss that had snuck up behind me and grabbed me around the neck. I felt like I was slowly fading away at the edges and melting into my disguise, until eventually the happy rubber mask would meld with my actual features and I would truly become the thing I had been pretending to be, taking the kids to soccer, buying flowers when I drank too many beers, comparing detergents and cutting costs instead of flensing the wicked of their unneeded flesh. It was a very depressing line of thought, and I might have grown unhappy if the doorbell had not rung just in time.

'That must be Deborah,' I said. I'm fairly sure I kept most of the hope for rescue out of my voice. I got up and went to the front door, swinging it open to reveal a pleasant-looking, overweight woman with long blond hair.

'Oh,' she said. 'You must be, ahm – Is Rita here?'

Well, I suppose I was ahm, although until now I hadn't been aware of it. I called Rita to the door and she came, smiling. 'Kathy!' she said. 'So nice to see you. How are the boys? Kathy lives next door,' she explained to me.

'Aha,' I said. I knew most of the kids in the area, but not their parents. But this one was apparently the mother of the faintly sleazy eleven-year-old boy next door, and his nearly always-absent older brother. Since that meant she was probably not carrying a car bomb or a vial of anthrax, I smiled and went back to the table with Cody and Astor.

'Jason's at band camp,' she said. 'Nick is lounging around the house trying to reach puberty so he can grow a mustache.'

'Oh Lord,' Rita said.

'Nicky is a creep,' Astor whispered. 'He wanted me to pull down my pants so he could see.' Cody stirred his frozen yogurt into a frozen pudding.

'Listen, Rita, I'm sorry to bother you at dinnertime,' Kathy said.

'We just finished. Would you like some coffee?'

'Oh, no, I'm down to one cup a day,' she said. 'Doctor's orders. But it's about our dog – I just wanted to ask if you had seen Rascal? He's been missing for a couple of days now, and Nick is so worried.'

'I haven't seen him. Let me ask the kids,' Rita said. But as she turned to ask, Cody looked at me, got up without a sound, and walked out of the room. Astor stood up, too.

'We haven't seen him,' she said. 'Not since he knocked over the trash last week.' And she followed Cody out of the room. They left their desserts on the table, still only half eaten.

Rita watched them go with her mouth open, and then turned back to her neighbor. 'I'm sorry, Kathy. I guess nobody's seen him. But we'll keep an eye open, all right? I'm sure he'll turn up, tell Nick not to worry.' She prattled on for another minute with Kathy, while I looked at the frozen yogurt and wondered what I had just seen.

The front door closed and Rita came back to her cooling coffee. 'Kathy's a nice person,' she said. 'But her boys can be a handful. She's divorced, her ex bought a place in Islamorada, he's a lawyer? But he stays down there, so Kathy's had to raise the boys alone and I don't think she's very firm sometimes. She's a nurse with a podiatrist over by the university.'

'And her shoe size?' I asked.

'Am I blathering?' Rita asked. She bit her lip. 'I'm sorry. I guess I was just worrying a little bit . . . I'm sure it's just . . .' She shook her head and looked at me. 'Dexter. Did you—'

I never got to find out if I did, because my cell phone chirped. 'Excuse me,' I said, and I went over to the table by the front door where I had left it.

'Doakes just called,' Deborah said to me without even saying hello. 'The guy he went to talk to is running. Doakes is following to see where he goes, but he needs us for backup.'

'Quickly, Watson, the game's afoot,' I said, but Deborah was not in a literary mood.

'I'll pick you up in five minutes,' she said.

19

I left Rita with a hurried explanation and went outside to wait. Deborah was as good as her word, and in five and a half minutes we were heading north on Dixie Highway.

'They're out on Miami Beach,' she told me. 'Doakes said he approached the guy, Oscar, and told him what's up. Oscar says, let me think about it, Doakes says okay, I'll call you. But he watches the house from up the street, and ten minutes later the guy is out the door and into his car with an overnight bag.'

'Why would he run now?'

'Wouldn't you run if you knew Danco was after you?'

'No,' I said, thinking happily of what I might actually do if I came face-to-face with the Doctor. 'I would set some kind of trap for him, and let him come.' *And then*, I thought, but did not say aloud to Deborah.

'Well, Oscar isn't you,' she said.

'So few of us are,' I said. 'Where is he headed?'

She frowned and shook her head. 'Right now he's just cruising around, and Doakes is tailing him.'

'Where do we think he's going to lead us?' I asked.

Deborah shook her head and cut around an old ragtop Cadillac loaded with yelling teenagers. 'It doesn't matter,' she said, and headed up the on-ramp onto the Palmetto Expressway with the pedal to the floor. 'Oscar is still our best chance. If he tries to leave the area we'll pick him up, but until then we need to stick with him to see what happens.'

'Very good, a really terrific idea – but what exactly do we think might happen?'

'I don't know, Dexter!' she snapped at me. 'But we know this guy is a target sooner or later, all right? And now he knows it, too. So maybe he's just trying to see if he's being followed before he runs. Shit,' she said, and swerved around an old flatbed truck loaded with crates of chickens. The truck was going possibly thirty-five miles per hour, had no taillights, and three men sat on top of the load, hanging on to battered hats with one hand and the load with the other. Deborah gave them a quick blast of the siren as she pulled around them. It didn't seem to have any effect. The men on top of the load didn't even blink.

'Anyway,' she said as she straightened out the wheel and accelerated again, 'Doakes wants us on the Miami side for backup. So Oscar can't get too fancy. We'll run parallel along Biscayne.'

It made sense; as long as Oscar was on Miami Beach, he couldn't escape in any other direction. If he tried to dash across a causeway or head north to the far side of Haulover Park and cross, we were there to pick him up. Unless he had a helicopter stashed, we had him cornered. I let Deborah drive, and she headed north rapidly without actually killing anyone.

At the airport we swung east on the 836. The traffic picked up a little here, and Deborah wove in and out, concentrating fiercely. I kept my thoughts to myself and she displayed her years of training with Miami traffic by winning what amounted to a nonstop free-for-all high-speed game of chicken. We made it safely through the interchange with I-95 and slid down onto Biscayne Boulevard. I took a deep breath and let it out carefully as Deborah eased back into street traffic and down to normal speed.

The radio crackled once and Doakes's voice came over the speaker. 'Morgan, what's your twenty?'

Deborah lifted the microphone and told him. 'Biscayne at the MacArthur Causeway.'

There was a short pause, and then Doakes said, 'He's pulled over by the drawbridge at the Venetian Causeway. Cover it on your side.'

'Ten-four,' Deborah said.

And I couldn't help saying, 'I feel so *official* when you say that.'

'What does that mean?' she said.

'Nothing, really,' I said.

She glanced at me, a serious cop look, but her face was still young and for just a moment it felt like we were kids again, sitting in Harry's patrol car and playing cops and robbers – except that this time, I got to be a good guy, a very unsettling feeling.

'This isn't a game, Dexter,' she said, because of course she shared that same memory. 'Kyle's life is at stake here.' And her features dropped back into her Serious Large-Fish Face as she went on. 'I know it probably doesn't make sense to you, but I care about that man. He makes me feel so – Shit. You're getting *married* and you still won't ever get it.' We had come to the traffic light at N.E. 15th Street and she turned right. What was left of the Omni Mall loomed up on the left and ahead of us was the Venetian Causeway.

'I'm not very good at feeling things, Debs,' I said. 'And I really don't know at all about this marriage thing. But I don't much like it when you're unhappy.'

Deborah pulled off opposite the little marina by the old Herald building and parked the car facing back toward the Venetian Causeway. She was quiet for a moment, and then she hissed out her breath and said, 'I'm sorry.'

That caught me a bit off guard, since I admit that I had been preparing to say something very similar, just to keep the social wheels greased. Almost certainly I would have phrased it in a slightly more clever way, but the same essence. 'For what?'

'I don't mean to – I know you're different, Dex. I'm really trying to get used to that and – But you're still my brother.'

'Adopted,' I said.

'That's horseshit and you know it. You're my brother. And I know you're only here because of me.'

'Actually, I was hoping I'd get to say "ten-four" on the radio later.'

She snorted. 'All right, be an asshole. But thanks anyway.'

'You're welcome.'

She picked up the radio. 'Doakes. What's he doing?'

After a brief pause, Doakes replied, 'Looks like he's talking on a cell phone.'

Deborah frowned and looked at me. 'If he's running, who's he going to talk to on the phone?'

I shrugged. 'He might be arranging a way out of the country. Or— '

I stopped. The idea was far too stupid to think about, and that should have kept it out of my head automatically, but somehow there it was, bouncing off the gray matter and waving a small red flag.

'What?' Deborah demanded.

I shook my head. 'Not possible. Stupid. Just a wild thought that won't go away.'

'All right. How wild?'

'What if – Now I did say this was stupid.'

'It's a lot stupider to dick around like this,' she snapped. 'What's the idea?'

'What if Oscar is calling the good Doctor and trying to bargain his way out?' I said. And I was right; it did sound stupid.

Debs snorted. 'Bargain with what?'

'Well,' I said, 'Doakes said he's carrying a bag. So he could have money, bearer bonds, a stamp collection. I don't know. But he probably has something that might be even more valuable to our surgical friend.'

'Like what?'

'He probably knows where everybody else from the old team is hiding.'

'Shit,' she said. 'Give up everybody else in exchange for his life?' She chewed on her lip as she thought that over. After a minute she shook her head. 'That's pretty far-fetched,' she said.

'Far-fetched is a big step up from stupid,' I said.

'Oscar would have to know how to get in touch with the Doctor.'

'One spook can always find a way to get to another. There are lists and databases and mutual contacts, you know that. Didn't you see *Bourne Identity*?'

'Yeah, but how do we know Oscar saw it?' she said.

'I'm just saying it's possible.'

'Uh-huh,' she said. She looked out the window, thinking, then made a face and shook her head. 'Kyle said something – that after a while you'd forget what team you were on, like baseball with free agency. So you'd get friendly with guys on the other side, and – Shit, that's stupid.'

'So whatever side Danco is on, Oscar *could* find a way to reach him.'

'So fucking what. We can't,' she said.

We were both quiet for a few minutes after that. I suppose Debs was thinking about Kyle and wondering if we would find him in time. I tried to imagine caring about Rita the same way and came up blank. As Deborah had so astutely pointed out, I was engaged and still didn't get it. And I never would, either, which I usually regard as a blessing. I have always felt that it was preferable to think with my brain, rather than with certain other wrinkled parts located slightly south. I mean, seriously, don't people ever *see* themselves, staggering around drooling and mooning, all weepy-eyed and weak-kneed and rendered completely idiotic over something even animals have enough sense to finish quickly so they can get on with more sensible pursuits, like finding fresh meat?

Well, as we all agreed, I didn't get it. So I just looked out across the water to the subdued lights of the homes on the far side of the causeway. There were a few apartment buildings close to the toll booth, and then a scattering of houses almost as big. Maybe if I won the lottery I could get a real estate agent to show me something with a small cellar, just big enough for one homicidal photographer to fit in snugly under the floor. And as I thought it a soft whisper came from my personal backseat voice, but of course there was nothing I could do about that, except perhaps applaud the moon that hung over the water. And across that same moon-painted water floated the sound of a clanging bell, signaling that the drawbridge was about to go up.

The radio crackled. 'He's moving,' Doakes said. 'Gonna run the drawbridge. Watch for him – white Toyota 4Runner.'

'I see him,' Deborah said into the radio. 'We're on him.'

The white SUV came across the causeway and onto 15th Street just moments before the bridge went up. After a slight pause to let him get ahead, Deborah pulled out and followed. At Biscayne Boulevard he turned right and a moment later we did, too. 'He's headed north on Biscayne,' she said into the radio.

'Copy that,' Doakes said. 'I'll follow out here.'

The 4Runner moved at normal speed through moderate traffic, keeping to a mere five miles per hour above the speed limit, which in Miami is considered tourist speed, slow enough to justify a blast of the horn from the drivers who passed him. But Oscar didn't seem to mind. He obeyed all the traffic signals and stayed in the right lane, cruising along as if he had no particular place to go and was merely out for a relaxing after-dinner drive.

As we came up on the 79th Street Causeway, Deborah picked up the radio. 'We're passing 79th Street,' she said. 'He's in no hurry, proceeding north.'

'Ten-four,' Doakes said, and Deborah glanced at me.

'I didn't say anything,' I said.

'You thought the hell out of it,' she said.

We moved on north, stopping twice at traffic signals. Deborah was careful to stay several cars behind, no mean feat in Miami traffic, with most of the cars trying to go around, over, or through all the others. A fire engine went wailing past in the other direction, blasting its horn at the intersections. For all the effect it had on the other drivers, it might have been a lamb bleating. They ignored the siren and clung to their hard-won places in the scrambled line of traffic. The man behind the wheel of the fire engine, being a Miami driver himself, simply wove in and out with the horn and siren playing: Duet for Traffic.

We reached 123d Street, the last place to cross back to Miami Beach before 826 ran across at North Miami Beach, and Oscar kept heading north. Deborah told Doakes by radio as we passed it.

'Where the hell is he going?' Deborah muttered as she put down the radio.

'Maybe he's just driving around,' I said. 'It's a beautiful night.'

'Uh-huh. You want to write a sonnet?'

Under normal circumstances, I would have had a splendid comeback for that, but perhaps due to the thrilling nature of our chase, nothing occurred to me. And anyway, Debs looked like she could use a victory, however small.

A few blocks later, Oscar suddenly accelerated into the left lane and turned left across oncoming traffic, raising an entire concerto of angry horns from drivers moving in both directions.

'He's making a move,' Deborah told Doakes, 'west on 135th Street.'

'I'm crossing behind you,' Doakes said. 'On the Broad Causeway.'

'What's on 135th Street?' Debs wondered aloud.

'Opa-Locka Airport,' I said. 'A couple of miles straight ahead.'

'Shit,' she said, and picked up the radio. 'Doakes – Opa-Locka Airport is out this way.'

'On my way,' he said, and I could hear his siren cutting on before his radio clicked off.

Opa-Locka Airport had long been popular with people in the drug trade, as well as with those in covert operations. This was a handy arrangement, considering that the line between the two was often quite blurry. Oscar could very easily have a small plane waiting there, ready to whisk him out of the country and off to almost anyplace in the Caribbean or Central or South America – with connections to the rest of the world, of course, although I doubted he would be headed for the Sudan, or even Beirut. Someplace in the Caribbean was more likely, but in any case fleeing the country seemed like a reasonable move under the circumstances, and Opa-Locka Airport was a logical place to start.

Oscar was going a little faster now, although 135th Street was not as wide and well traveled as Biscayne Boulevard. We came up over a small bridge across a canal and as Oscar came down the far side he suddenly accelerated, squealing through traffic around an S curve in the road.

'Goddamn it, something spooked him,' Deborah said. 'He must have spotted us.' She sped up to stay with him, still keeping two or three cars back, even though there seemed little point now to pretending we weren't following him.

Something had indeed spooked him, because Oscar was driving wildly, dangerously close to slamming into the traffic or running up onto the sidewalk, and naturally enough, Debs was not going to let herself lose this kind of pissing contest. She stayed with him, swerving around cars that were still trying to recover from their encounters with Oscar. Just ahead he swung into the far left lane, forcing an old Buick to spin away, hit the curb, and crash through a chain-link fence into the front yard of a light blue house.

Would the sight of our little unmarked car be enough to cause Oscar to behave this way? It was nice to think so and made me feel very important, but I didn't believe it – so far, he had acted in a cool and controlled way. If he wanted to ditch us it seemed more likely that he would have made some kind of sudden and tricky move, like going over the drawbridge as it went up. So why had he suddenly panicked? Just for something to do, I leaned forward and looked into the side mirror. The block letters on the surface of the mirror told me that objects were closer than they appeared. Things being what they were, this was a very unhappy thought, because only one object appeared in the mirror at the moment.

It was a battered white van.

And it was following us, and following Oscar. Matching our speed, moving in and out of traffic. 'Well,' I said, 'not stupid after all.' And I raised my voice to go over the squeal of tires and the horns of the other motorists.

'Oh, Deborah?' I said. 'I don't want to distract you from your driving chores, but if you have a moment, could you look in your rearview mirror?'

'What the fuck is that supposed to mean,' she snarled, but she flicked her eyes to the mirror. It was a piece of good luck that we were on a straight stretch of road, because for just a second she almost forgot to steer. 'Oh, shit,' she whispered.

'Yes, that's what I thought,' I said.

The I-95 overpass stretched across the road directly ahead, and just before he passed under it Oscar swerved violently to the right across three lanes and turned down a side street that ran parallel to the freeway. Deborah swore and wrenched her car around to follow. 'Tell Doakes!' she said, and I obediently picked up the radio.

'Sergeant Doakes,' I said. 'We are not alone.'

The radio hissed once. 'The fuck does that mean?' Doakes said, almost as if he had heard Deborah's response and admired it so much he had to repeat it.

'We have just turned right on 6th Avenue, and we are being followed by a white van.' There was no answer, so I said again, 'Did I mention that the van is white?' and this time I had the great satisfaction of hearing Doakes grunt, 'Motherfucker.'

'That's exactly what we thought,' I said.

'Let the van in front and stay with him,' he said.

'No shit,' Deborah muttered through clenched teeth, and then she said something much worse. I was tempted to say something similar, because as Doakes clicked off his radio, Oscar headed up the on-ramp onto I-95 with us following, and at the very last second he yanked his car back down the paved slope and onto 6th Avenue. His 4Runner bounced as it hit the road and teetered drunkenly to the right for a moment, then accelerated and straightened up. Deborah hit the brakes and we spun through half a turn; the white van slid ahead of us, bounced down the slope, and closed the gap with the 4Runner. After half a second, Debs straightened us out of our slide and followed them down onto the street.

The side road here was narrow, with a row of houses on the right and a high yellow-cement embankment on the left with I-95 on top. We ran along for several blocks, picking up speed. A tiny old couple holding hands paused on the sidewalk to watch our strange parade rocket past. It may have been my imagination, but they seemed to flutter in the wind from Oscar's car and the van going by.

We closed the gap just a little, and the white van closed on the 4Runner, too. But Oscar picked up the pace; he ran a stop sign, leaving us to veer around a pickup truck that was spinning in a circle in its attempt to avoid the 4Runner and the van. The truck wobbled through a clumsy doughnut turn and slammed into a fire hydrant. But Debs just clamped her jaw tight and squealed around the truck and through the intersection, ignoring the horns and the fountain of water from the ruptured hydrant, and closing the gap again in the next block.

Several blocks ahead of Oscar I could see the red light of a major cross street. Even from this far I could see a steady stream of traffic moving through the intersection. Of course nobody lives forever, but this was really not the way I would choose to die if given a vote. Watching TV with Rita suddenly seemed a lot more attractive. I tried to think of a polite but very convincing way to persuade Deborah to stop and smell the roses for a moment, but just when I needed it the most my powerful brain seemed to shut down, and before I could get it going again Oscar was approaching the traffic light.

Quite possibly Oscar had been to church this week, because the light turned green as he rocketed through the intersection. The white van followed close behind, braking hard to avoid a small blue car trying to beat the light, and then it was our turn, with the light fully green now. We swerved around the van and almost made it through – but this was Miami, after all, and a cement truck ran the red light behind the blue car, right in front of us. I swallowed hard as Deborah stood on the brake pedal and spun around the truck. We thumped hard against the curb, running the two left wheels up onto the sidewalk for just a moment before bouncing down onto the road again. 'Very nice,' I said as Deborah accelerated once again. And quite possibly, she might have taken the time to thank me for my compliment, if only the white van had not chosen that moment to take advantage of our slow-down to drop back beside our car and swerve into us. The rear end of our car slewed around to the left, but Deborah fought it back around again.

The van popped us again, harder, right behind my door, and as I lurched away from the blow the door sprung open. Our car swerved and Deborah braked – perhaps not the best strategy, since the van accelerated at the same moment and this time clipped my door so hard that it came loose and bounced away, hitting the van a solid smack near the rear wheel before spinning off like a deformed wheel, spitting sparks.

I saw the van wobble slightly, and heard the slack rattling sound of a blown tire. Then the wall of white slammed into us one more time. Our car bucked violently, lurched to the left, hopped the curb and burst through a chain-link fence separating the side road from the ramp leading down off I-95. We twirled around as if the tires were made of butter. Deborah fought the wheel with her teeth showing, and we very nearly made it across the off-ramp. But of course, I had *not* been to church this week, and as our two front wheels hit the curb on the far side of the off-ramp, a large red SUV banged into our rear fender. We spun up onto the grassy area of the freeway intersection that surrounded a large pond. I had only a moment to notice that the cropped grass seemed to be switching places with the night sky. Then the car bounced hard and the passenger air bag exploded into my face. It felt like I had been in a pillow fight with Mike Tyson; I was still stunned as the car flipped onto its roof, hit the pond, and began to fill with water.

20

I am not shy about admitting my modest talents. For example, I am happy to admit that I am better than average at clever remarks, and I also have a flair for getting people to like me. But to be perfectly fair to myself, I am ever-ready to confess my shortcomings, too, and a quick round of soul-searching forced me to admit that I had never been any good at all at breathing water. As I hung there from the seat belt, dazed and watching the water pour in and swirl around my head, this began to seem like a very large character flaw.

The last look I had at Deborah before the water closed over her head was not encouraging, either. She was hanging from her seat belt unmoving, with her eyes closed and her mouth open, just the opposite of her usual state, which was probably not a good sign. And then the water flooded up around my eyes, and I could see nothing at all.

I also like to think that I react well to the occasional unexpected emergency, so I'm quite sure my sudden stunned apathy was the result of being rattled around and then smacked with an air bag. In any case, I hung there upside down in the water for what seemed like quite a long time, and I am ashamed to admit that for the most part, I simply mourned my own passing. Dear Departed Dexter, so much potential, so many dark fellow travelers still to dissect, and now so tragically cut short in his prime. Alas, Dark Passenger, I knew him well. And the poor boy was finally just about to get married, too. How more than sad – I pictured Rita in white, weeping at the altar, two small children wailing at her feet. Sweet little Astor, her hair done up in a bouffant bubble, a pale green bridesmaid dress now soaked with tears. And quiet Cody in his tiny tuxedo, staring at the back of the church and waiting, thinking of our last fishing trip and wondering when he would ever get to push the knife in again and twist it so slowly, watching the bright red blood burble out onto the blade and smiling, and then—

Slow down, Dexter. Where did that thought come from? Rhetorical question, of course, and I did not need the low rumble of amusement from my old interior friend to give me the answer. But with his prompting I put together a few scattered pieces into half a puzzle and realized that Cody—

Isn't it odd what we think about when we're dying? The car had settled

282

onto its flattened roof, moving with no more than a gentle rocking now and completely filled with water so thick and mucky that I could not have seen a flare gun firing from the end of my nose. And yet I could see Cody perfectly clearly, more clearly now than the last time we had been in the same room together; and standing behind this sharp image of his small form towered a gigantic dark shadow, a black shape with no features that somehow seemed to be laughing.

Could it be? I thought again about the way he had put the knife so happily into his fish. I thought about his strange reaction to the neighbor's missing dog – much like mine when I had been asked as a boy about a neighborhood dog I had taken and experimented with. And I remembered that he, too, had gone through a traumatic event like I had, when his biological father had attacked him and his sister in a terrifying drug-induced rage and beat them with a chair.

It was a totally unthinkable thing to think. A ridiculous thought, but – All the pieces were there. It made perfect, poetic sense.

I had a son.

Someone Just Like Me.

But there was no wise foster father to guide his first baby steps into the world of slice and dice; no all-seeing Harry to teach him how to be all he could be, to help change him from an aimless child with a random urge to kill into a caped avenger; no one to carefully and patiently steer him past the pitfalls and into the gleaming knife blade of the future – no one at all for Cody, not if Dexter died here and now.

It would sound far too melodramatic for me to say, 'The thought spurred me to furious action,' and I am only melodramatic on purpose, when there is an audience. However, as the realization of Cody's true nature hit me, I also heard, almost like an echo, a deep unbodied voice saying, 'Undo the seat belt, Dexter.' And somehow I managed to make my suddenly huge and clumsy fingers move to the belt's lock and fumble with the release. It felt like trying to thread a needle with a ham, but I poked and pushed and finally felt something give. Of course this meant that I bumped down onto the ceiling on my head, a little hard considering that I was under water. But the shock of getting thumped on the head cleared away a few more cobwebs, and I righted myself and reached for the opening where the car's door had been knocked away. I managed to pull myself through and face-first into several inches of muck on the bottom of the pond.

I righted myself and kicked hard for the surface. It was a fairly feeble kick, but quite good enough since the water was only about three feet deep. The kick sent me shooting up to my knees and then staggering to my feet, and I stood there in the water for just a moment retching and sucking in the wonderful air. A marvelous and underrated thing, air. How true it was that we never appreciate things until we must do without them. What a terrible thought to picture all the poor people of this world who must do without air, people like . . .

. . . Deborah?

A real human being might have thought of his drowning sister much sooner, but really, let's be fair, one can only expect so much from an imitation after what I had been through. And I did actually think of her now, possibly still in time to do something meaningful. But although I was not really reluctant to rush to the rescue, I couldn't help thinking that we were asking a bit much of Dutifully Dashing Dexter this evening, weren't we? No sooner out of it than I had to go right back in again.

Still, family was family, and complaining had never done me a bit of good. I took a deep breath and slid back under the muddy water, feeling my way through the doorway and into the front seat of Deborah's topsy-turvy car. Something smacked me across the face and then grabbed me brutally by the hair – Debs herself, I hoped, since anything else moving around in the water would surely have much sharper teeth. I reached up and tried to pry apart her fingers. It was hard enough to hold my breath and fumble around blindly without receiving an impromptu haircut at the same time. But Deborah held tight – which was a good sign, in a way, since it meant she was still alive, but it left me wondering whether my lungs or my scalp would give out first. This would never do; I put both my hands on the job and managed to pry her fingers away from my poor tender hairdo. Then I followed her arm up to the shoulder and felt across her body until I found the strap of the seat belt. I slid my hand down the strap to the buckle and pushed the release.

Well of course it was jammed. I mean, we already knew it was one of those days, didn't we? It was one thing after another, and really, it would have been far too much to hope that even one small thing might go right. Just to underline the point, something went *blurp* in my ear, and I realized that Deborah had run out of time and was now trying her luck at breathing water. It was possible that she would be better at it than I was, but I didn't think so.

I slid lower in the water and braced my knees against the roof of the car, wedging my shoulder against Deb's midsection and pushing up to take her weight off the seat belt. Then I pulled as much slack as I could get down to the buckle and slid it through, making the belt very floppy and loose. I braced my feet and pulled Deborah through the belt and toward the door. She seemed a bit loose and floppy herself; perhaps after all my valiant effort I was too late. I squeezed through the door and pulled her after me. My shirt caught on something in the doorway and ripped, but I pulled myself through anyway, staggering upright once again into the night air.

Deborah was dead weight in my arms and a thin stream of mucky water dribbled from the corner of her mouth. I hoisted her onto my shoulder and sloshed through the muck to the grass. The muck fought back every step of the way, and I lost my left shoe before I got more than three steps from the car.

But shoes are, after all, much easier to replace than sisters, so I soldiered on until I could climb up onto the grass and dump Deborah on her back on the solid earth.

In the near distance a siren wailed, and was almost immediately joined by another. Joy and bliss: help was on the way. Perhaps they would even have a towel. In the meantime, I was not certain it would arrive in time to do Deborah any good. So I dropped down beside her, slung her facedown over my knee, and forced out as much water as I could. Then I rolled her onto her back, cleared a finger-load of mud from her mouth, and began to give her mouth-to-mouth resuscitation.

At first my only reward was another gout of mucky water, which did nothing to make the job more pleasant. But I kept at it, and soon Debs gave a convulsive shudder and vomited a great deal more water – most of it on me, unfortunately. She coughed horribly, took a breath that sounded like rusty door hinges swinging open, and said, 'Fuck . . .'

For once, I truly appreciated her hard-boiled eloquence. 'Welcome back,' I said. Deborah rolled weakly onto her face and tried to push herself up onto her hands and knees. But she collapsed onto her face again, gasping with pain.

'Oh, God. Oh, shit, something's broken,' she moaned. She turned her head to the side and threw up a little more, arching her back and sucking in great ratcheting breaths in between spasms of nausea. I watched her, and I admit I felt a little pleased with myself. Dexter the Diving Duck had come through and saved the day. 'Isn't throwing up great?' I asked her. 'I mean, considering the alternative?' Of course a really biting reply was beyond the poor girl in her weakened condition, but I was pleased to see that she was strong enough to whisper, 'Fuck you.'

'Where does it hurt?' I asked her.

'Goddamn it,' she said, sounding very weak, 'I can't move my left arm. The whole arm – ' She broke off and tried to move the arm in question and succeeded only in causing herself what looked like a great deal of pain. She hissed in a breath, which set her coughing weakly again, and then just flopped over onto her back and gasped.

I knelt beside her and probed gently at the upper arm. 'Here?' I asked her. She shook her head. I moved my hand up, over the shoulder joint and to the collarbone, and I didn't have to ask her if that was the place. She gasped, her eyes fluttered, and even through the mud on her face I could see her turn several shades paler. 'Your collarbone is broken,' I said.

'It can't be,' she said with a weak and raspy voice. 'I have to find Kyle.'

'No,' I said. 'You have to go to the emergency room. If you go stumbling around like this you'll end up right next to him, all tied and taped, and that won't do anyone any good.'

'I *have* to,' she said.

'Deborah, I just pulled you out of an underwater car, ruining a very nice bowling shirt. Do you want to waste my perfectly good heroic rescue?'

She coughed again, and grunted from the pain of her collarbone as it moved with her spasmodic breathing. I could tell that she wasn't finished arguing yet, but it was starting to register with her that she was in a great deal of pain. And since our conversation was going nowhere, it was just as well that Doakes arrived, followed almost immediately by a pair of paramedics.

The good sergeant looked hard at me, as if I had personally shoved the car into the pond and flipped it on its back. 'Lost 'em, huh,' he said, which seemed terribly unfair.

'Yes, it turned out to be much harder than I thought to follow him when we were upside down and under water,' I said. 'Next time you try that part and we'll stand here and complain.'

Doakes just glared at me and grunted. Then he knelt beside Deborah and said, 'You hurt?'

'Collarbone,' she said. 'It's broken.' The shock was wearing off rapidly and she was fighting the pain by biting her lip and taking ragged breaths. I hoped the paramedics had something a little more effective for her.

Doakes said nothing; he just lifted his glare up to me. Deborah reached out with her good arm and grabbed his arm. 'Doakes,' she said, and he looked back at her. 'Find him,' she said. He just watched her as she gritted her teeth and gasped through another wave of pain.

'Coming through here,' one of the paramedics said. He was a wiry young guy with a spiky haircut, and he and his older, thicker partner had maneuvered their gurney through the chain-link fence where Deb's car had torn a gap. Doakes tried to stand to let them get to Deborah, but she pulled on his arm with surprising strength.

'Find him,' she said again. Doakes just nodded, but it was enough for her. Deborah let go of his arm and he stood up to give the paramedics room. They swooped in and gave Debs a once-over, and they moved her onto their gurney, raised it up, and began to wheel her toward the waiting ambulance. I watched her go, wondering what had happened to our dear friend in the white van. He had a flat tire – how far could he get? It seemed likely that he would try to switch to a different vehicle, rather than stop and call AAA to help him change the tire. So somewhere nearby, we would be very likely to find the abandoned van and a missing car.

Out of an impulse that seemed extremely generous, considering his attitude toward me, I moved over to tell Doakes my thoughts. But I only made it a step and a half in his direction when I heard a commotion coming our way. I turned to look.

Running at us up the middle of the street was a chunky middle-aged guy in a pair of boxer shorts and nothing else. His belly hung over the band of his shorts and wobbled wildly as he came and it was clear that he had not had much practice at running, and he made it harder on himself by waving his arms around over his head and shouting, 'Hey! Hey! Hey!' as he ran. By the time he crossed the ramp from I-95 and got to us he was breathless, gasping too hard to say anything coherent, but I had a pretty good idea what he wanted to say.

'De bang,' he gasped out, and I realized that his breathlessness and his Cuban accent had combined, and he was trying to say, 'The van.'

'A white van? With a flat tire? And your car is gone,' I said, and Doakes looked at me.

But the gasping man was shaking his head. 'White van, sure. I hear I thought it's a dog inside, maybe hurt,' he said, and paused to breathe deeply so he could properly convey the full horror of what he had seen. 'And then—'

But he was wasting his precious breath. Doakes and I were already sprinting up the street in the direction he had come from.

21

Sergeant Doakes apparently forgot he was supposed to be following me, because he beat me to the van by a good twenty yards. Of course he had the very large advantage of having both shoes, but still, he moved quite well. The van was run up on the sidewalk in front of a pale orange house surrounded by a coral-rock wall. The front bumper had thumped a rock corner post and toppled it, and the rear of the vehicle was skewed around to face the street so we could see the bright yellow of the Choose Life license plate.

By the time I caught up with Doakes he already had the rear door open and I heard the mewling noise coming from inside. It really didn't sound quite so much like a dog this time, or maybe I was just getting used to it. It was a slightly higher pitch than before, and a little bit choppier, more of a shrill gurgle than a yodel, but still recognizable as the call of one of the living dead.

It was strapped to a backless car seat that had been turned sideways, so it ran the length of the interior. The eyes in their lidless sockets were rolling wildly back and forth, up and down, and the lipless, toothless mouth was frozen into a round O and it was squirming the way a baby squirms, but without arms and legs it couldn't manage any significant movement.

Doakes was crouched over it, looking down at the remainder of its face with an intense lack of expression. 'Frank,' he said, and the thing rolled its eyes to him. The yowling paused for just a moment, and then resumed on a higher note, keening with a new agony that seemed to be begging for something.

'You recognize this one?' I asked.

Doakes nodded. 'Frank Aubrey,' he said.

'How can you tell?' I asked. Because really, you would think that all former humans in this condition would be awfully hard to tell apart. The only distinguishing mark I could see was forehead wrinkles.

Doakes kept looking at it, but he grunted once and nodded at the side of the neck. 'Tattoo. It's Frank.' He grunted again, leaning forward and flicking a small piece of notepaper taped to the bench. I leaned in for a look: in the same spidery hand I had seen before Dr. Danco had written HONOR.

'Get the paramedics,' Doakes said.

I hurried over to where they were just closing the back doors of the ambulance. 'Do you have room for one more?' I asked. 'He won't take up a lot of space, but he'll need heavy sedation.'

'What kind of condition is he in?' the spike-haired one asked me.

It was a very good question for someone in his profession to ask, but the only answers that occurred to me seemed a little flippant, so I just said, 'I think you may want heavy sedation, too.'

They looked at me like they thought I was kidding and didn't really appreciate the seriousness of the situation. Then they looked at each other and shrugged. 'Okay, pal,' the older one said. 'We'll squeeze him in.' The spike-haired paramedic shook his head, but he turned and opened the back door of the ambulance again and began pulling out the gurney.

As they wheeled down the block to Danco's crashed van I climbed in the back of the ambulance to see how Debs was doing. Her eyes were closed and she was very pale, but she seemed to be breathing easier. She opened one eye and looked up at me. 'We're not moving,' she said.

'Dr. Danco crashed his van.'

She tensed and tried to sit up, both eyes wide open. 'You got him?'

'No, Debs. Just his passenger. I think he was about to deliver it, because it's all done.'

I had thought she was pale before, but she almost vanished now. 'Kyle,' she said.

'No,' I told her. 'Doakes says it's someone named Frank.'

'Are you sure?'

'Apparently positive. There's a tattoo on his neck. It's not Kyle, Sis.'

Deborah closed her eyes and drifted back down onto the cot as if she was a deflating balloon. 'Thank God,' she said.

'I hope you don't mind sharing your cab with Frank,' I said.

She shook her head. 'I don't mind,' she said, and then her eyes opened again. 'Dexter. No fucking around with Doakes. Help him find Kyle. Please?'

It must have been the drugs working on her, because I could count on one finger the number of times I had heard her ask anything so plaintively. 'All right, Debs. I'll do my best,' I said, and her eyes fluttered closed again.

'Thanks,' she said.

I got back to Danco's van just in time to see the older paramedic straighten up from where he had obviously been vomiting, and turn to talk to his partner, who was sitting on the curb mumbling to himself over the sounds that Frank was still making inside. 'Come on, Michael,' the older guy said. 'Come on, buddy.'

Michael didn't seem interested in moving, except for rocking back and forth as he repeated, 'Oh God. Oh Jesus. Oh God.' I decided he probably didn't need my encouragement, and went around to the driver's door of the van. It was sprung open and I peeked in.

Dr. Danco must have been in a hurry, because he had left behind a very pricey-looking scanner, the kind that police groupies and newshounds use to monitor emergency radio traffic. It was very comforting to know that Danco had been tracking us with this and not some kind of magic powers.

Other than that, the van was clean. There was no telltale matchbook, no slip of paper with an address or a cryptic word in Latin scribbled on the back. Nothing at all that could give us any kind of clue. There might turn out to be fingerprints, but since we already knew who had been driving that didn't seem very helpful.

I picked up the scanner and walked around to the rear of the van. Doakes was standing beside the open back door as the older paramedic finally got his partner onto his feet. I handed Doakes the scanner. 'It was in the front seat,' I said. 'He's been listening.'

Doakes just glanced at it and put it down inside the back door of the van. Since he didn't seem terribly chatty I asked, 'Do you have any ideas about what we should do next?'

He looked at me and didn't say anything and I looked back expectantly, and I suppose we could have stood like that until the pigeons began to nest on our heads, if it hadn't been for the paramedics. 'Okay, guys,' the senior one said, and we moved aside to let them get to Frank. The stocky paramedic seemed to be perfectly all right now, as if he was here to put a splint on a boy with a twisted ankle. His partner still looked quite unhappy, however, and even from six feet away I could hear his breathing.

I stood beside Doakes and watched them slide Frank onto the gurney and then wheel him away. When I looked back at Doakes he was staring at me again. Once more he gave me his very unpleasant smile. 'Down to you and me,' he said. 'And I don't know about you.' He leaned against the battered white van and crossed his arms. I heard the paramedics slam the ambulance door, and a moment later the siren started up. 'Just you and me,' Doakes said again, 'and no more referee.'

'Is this more of your simple country wisdom?' I said, because here I was, having sacrificed an entire left shoe and a very nice bowling shirt, to say nothing of my hobby, Deborah's collarbone, and a perfectly good motor-pool car – and there he stood without so much as a wrinkle in his shirt, making cryptically hostile remarks. Really, the man was too much.

'Don't trust you,' he said.

I thought it was a very good sign that Sergeant Doakes was opening up to me by sharing his doubts and feelings. Still, I felt like I should try to keep him focused. 'That doesn't matter. We're running out of time,' I said. 'With Frank finished and delivered, Danco will start on Kyle now.'

He cocked his head to one side and then shook it slowly. 'Don't matter about Kyle,' he said. 'Kyle knew what he was getting into. What matters is catching the Doctor.'

'Kyle matters to my sister,' I said. 'That's the only reason I'm here.'

Doakes nodded again. 'Pretty good,' he said. 'Could almost believe that.'

For some reason, it was then that I had an idea. I admit that Doakes was monumentally irritating – and it wasn't just because he had kept me from my important personal research, although that was clearly bad enough. But now he was even critiquing my acting, which was beyond the boundaries of all civilized behavior. So perhaps irritation was the mother of invention; it doesn't seem all that poetic, but there it is. In any case, a little door opened up in Dexter's dusty cranium and a small light came shining out; a genuine piece of mental activity. Of course, Doakes might not think much of it, unless I could help him to see what a good idea it actually was, so I gave it a shot. I felt a little bit like Bugs Bunny trying to talk Elmer Fudd into something lethal, but the man had it coming. 'Sergeant Doakes,' I said, 'Deborah is my only family, and it is not right for you to question my commitment. Particularly,' I said, and I had to fight the urge to buff my fingernails, Bugs-style, 'since so far you have not done doodley-squat.'

Whatever else he was, cold killer and all, Sergeant Doakes was apparently still capable of feeling emotion. Perhaps that was the big difference between us, the reason he tried to keep his white hat so firmly cemented to his head and fight against what should have been his own side. In any case, I could see a surge of anger flicker across his face, and deep down inside there was an almost audible growl from his interior shadow. 'Doodley-squat,' he said. 'That's good, too.'

'Doodley-squat,' I said firmly. 'Deborah and I have done all the legwork and taken all the risks, and you know it.'

For just a moment his jaw muscles popped straight out as if they were going to leap out of his face and strangle me, and the muted interior growl surged into a roar that echoed down to my Dark Passenger, which sat up and answered back, and we stood like that, our two giant shadows flexing and facing off invisibly in front of us.

Quite possibly, there might have been ripped flesh and pools of blood in the street if a squad car hadn't chosen that moment to screech to a halt beside us and interrupt. A young cop jumped out and Doakes reflexively took out his badge and held it toward them without looking away from me. He made a shooing motion with his other hand, and the cop backed off and stuck his head into the car to consult with his partner.

'All right,' Sergeant Doakes said to me, 'you got something in mind?'

It wasn't really perfect. Bugs Bunny would have made him think of it himself, but it was good enough. 'As a matter of fact,' I said, 'I do have an idea. But it's a little risky.'

'Uh-huh,' he said. 'Thought it might be.'

'If it's too much for you, come up with something else,' I said. 'But I think it's all we can do.'

I could see him thinking it over. He knew I was baiting him, but there was just enough truth to what I had said, and enough pride or anger in him that he didn't care.

'Let's have it,' he said at last.

'Oscar got away,' I said.

'Looks like it.'

'That only leaves one person we can be sure Dr. Danco might be interested in,' I said, and I pointed right at his chest. 'You.'

He didn't actually flinch, but something twitched on his forehead and he forgot to breathe for a few seconds. Then he nodded slowly and took a deep breath. 'Slick motherfucker,' he said.

'Yes, I am,' I admitted. 'But I'm right, too.'

Doakes picked up the scanner radio and moved it to one side so he could sit on the open back gate of the van. 'All right,' he said. 'Keep talking.'

'First, I'm betting he'll get another scanner,' I said, nodding at the one beside Doakes.

'Uh-huh.'

'So if we know he's listening, we can let him hear what we want him to hear. Which is,' I said with my very best smile, 'who you are, and where you are.'

'And who am I?' he said, and he didn't seem impressed by my smile.

'You are the guy who set him up to get taken by the Cubans,' I said.

He studied me for a moment, then shook his head. 'You really putting my pecker on the chopping block, huh?'

'Absolutely,' I said. 'But you're not worried, are you?'

'He got Kyle, no trouble.'

'You'll know he's coming,' I said. 'Kyle didn't. Besides, aren't you supposed to be just a little bit better than Kyle at this kind of thing?'

It was shameless, totally transparent, but he went for it. 'Yes, I am,' he said. 'You're a good ass-kisser, too.'

'No ass-kissing at all,' I said. 'Just the plain, simple truth.'

Doakes looked at the scanner beside him. Then he looked up and away over the freeway. The streetlights made an orange flare off a drop of sweat that rolled across his forehead and down into one eye. He wiped at it unconsciously, still staring away over I-95. He had been staring at me without blinking for so long that it was a little bit unsettling to be in his presence and have him look somewhere else. It was almost like being invisible.

'All right,' he said as he looked back at me at last, and now the orange light was in his eyes. 'Let's do it.'

22

Sergeant Doakes drove me back to headquarters. It was a strange and unsettling experience to sit so close to him, and we found very little to say to each other. I caught myself studying his profile out of the corner of my eye. What went on in there? How could he be what I knew he was without actually doing something about it? Holding back from one of my playdates was setting my teeth on edge, and yet Doakes apparently didn't have any such trouble. Perhaps he had gotten it all out of his system in El Salvador. Did it feel any different to do it with the official blessings of the government? Or was it simply easier, not having to worry about being caught?

I could not know, and I certainly could not see myself asking him. Just to underline the point, he came to a halt at a red light and turned to look at me. I pretended not to notice, staring straight ahead through the windshield, and he faced back around when the light changed to green.

We drove right to the motor pool and Doakes put me in the front seat of another Ford Taurus. 'Gimme fifteen minutes,' he said, nodding at the radio. 'Then call me.' Without another word, he got back into his car and drove away.

Left to my own devices, I pondered the last few surprise-filled hours. Deborah in the hospital, me in league with Doakes – and my revelation about Cody during my near-death experience. Of course, I could be totally wrong about the boy. There might be some other explanation for his behavior at the mention of the missing pet, and the way he shoved the knife so eagerly into his fish could have been perfectly normal childish cruelty. But oddly enough, I found myself wanting it to be true. I wanted him to grow up to be like me – mostly, I realized, because I wanted to shape him and place his tiny feet onto the Harry Path.

Was this what the human reproductive urge was like, a pointless and powerful desire to replicate wonderful, irreplaceable me, even when the me in question was a monster who truly had no right to live among humans? That would certainly explain how a great many of the monumentally unpleasant cretins I encountered every day came to be. Unlike them, however, I was perfectly aware that the world would be a better place without me in it – I simply cared more about my own feelings in the matter than whatever the world might think. But now here I was eager to spawn more of me, like Dracula creating a new vampire to stand beside him in the dark. I knew it was wrong – but what fun it would be!

And what a total muttonhead I was being! Had my interval on Rita's sofa really turned my once-mighty intellect into such a quivering heap of sentimental mush? How could I be thinking such absurdities? Why wasn't I trying to devise a plan to escape marriage instead? No wonder I couldn't get away from Doakes's cloying surveillance – I had used up all my brain cells and was now running on empty.

I glanced at my watch. Fourteen minutes of time wasted on absurd mental blather. It was close enough: I lifted the radio and called Doakes.

'Sergeant Doakes, what's your twenty?'

There was a pause, then a crackle. 'Uh, I'd rather not say just now.'

'Say again, Sergeant?'

'I have been tracking a perp, and I'm afraid he made me.'

'What kind of perp?'

There was a pause, as though Doakes was expecting me to do all the work and hadn't figured out what to say. 'Guy from my army days. He got captured in El Salvador, and he might think it was my fault.' Pause. 'The guy is dangerous,' he said.

'Do you want backup?'

'Not yet. I'm going to try to dodge him for now.'

'Ten-four,' I said, feeling a little thrill at getting to say it at last.

We repeated the basic message a few times more, just to be sure it would get through to Dr. Danco, and I got to say 'ten-four' each time. When we called it a night around 1:00 AM, I was exhilarated and fulfilled. Perhaps tomorrow I would try to work in 'That's a copy' and even 'Roger that.' At last, something to look forward to.

I found a squad car headed south and persuaded the cop driving to drop me at Rita's. I tiptoed over to my car, got in, and drove home.

When I got back to my little bunk and saw it in a state of terrible disarray, I remembered that Debs should have been here but was, instead, in the hospital. I would go see her tomorrow. In the meantime, I'd had a memorable but exhausting day; chased into a pond by a serial limb-barber, surviving a car crash only to be nearly drowned, losing a perfectly good shoe, and on top of all that, as if that wasn't bad enough, forced to buddy up with Sergeant Doakes. Poor Drained Dexter. No wonder I was so tired. I fell into bed and went to sleep at once.

Early the next day Doakes pulled his car in beside mine in the parking lot at headquarters. He got out carrying a nylon gym bag, which he set down on the hood of my car. 'You brought your laundry?' I asked politely. Once again my lighthearted good cheer went right by him.

'If this works at all, either he gets me or I get him,' he said. He zipped open the bag. 'If I get him, it's over. If he gets me . . .' He took out a GPS receiver and placed it on the hood. 'If he gets me, you're my backup.' He showed me a few dazzling teeth. 'Think how good that makes me feel.' He took out a cell phone and placed it next to the GPS unit. 'This is my insurance.'

I looked at the two small items on the hood of my car. They did not seem particularly menacing to me, but perhaps I could throw one and then hit someone on the head with the other. 'No bazooka?' I asked.

'Don't need it. Just this,' he said. He reached into the gym bag one more time. 'And this,' he said, holding out a small steno notebook, flipped open to the first page. It seemed to have a string of numbers and letters on it and a cheap ballpoint was shoved through the spiral.

'The pen is mightier than the sword,' I said.

'This one is,' he said. 'Top line is a phone number. Second line is an access code.'

'What am I accessing?'

'You don't need to know,' he said. 'You just call it, punch in the code, and give 'em my cell phone number. They give you a GPS fix on my phone. You come get me.'

'It sounds simple,' I said, wondering if it really was.

'Even for you,' he said.

'Who will I be talking to?'

Doakes just shook his head. 'Somebody owes me a favor,' he said, and pulled a handheld police radio out of the bag. 'Now the easy part,' he said. He handed me the radio and got back into his car.

Now that we had clearly laid out the bait for Dr. Danco, step two was to get him to a specific place at the right time, and the happy coincidence of Vince Masuoka's party was too perfect to ignore. For the next few hours we drove around the city in our separate cars and repeated the same message back and forth a couple of times with subtle variations, just to be sure. We had also enlisted a couple of patrol units Doakes said just possibly might not fuck it up. I took that to be his understated wit, but the cops in question did not seem to get the joke and, although they did not actually tremble, they did seem to go a little overboard in anxiously assuring Sergeant Doakes that they would not, in fact, fuck it up. It was wonderful to be working with a man who could inspire such loyalty.

Our little team spent the rest of the day pumping the airwaves full of chatter about my engagement party, giving directions to Vince's house and reminding people of the time. And just after lunch, our coup de grâce. Sitting in my car in front of a Wendy's, I used the handheld radio and called Sergeant Doakes one last time for a carefully scripted conversation.

'Sergeant Doakes, this is Dexter, do you copy?'

'This is Doakes,' he said after a slight pause.

'It would mean a lot to me if you could come to my engagement party tonight.'

'I can't go anywhere,' he said. 'This guy is too dangerous.'

'Just come for one drink. In and out,' I wheedled.

'You saw what he did to Manny, and Manny was just a grunt. I'm the one gave this guy to some bad people. He gets his hands on me, what's he gonna do to me?'

'I'm getting married, Sarge,' I said. I liked the Marvel Comics flavor of calling him Sarge. 'That doesn't happen every day. And he's not going to try anything with all those cops around.'

There was a long dramatic pause in which I knew Doakes was counting to seven, just as we had written it down. Then the radio crackled again. 'All right,' he said. 'I'll come by around nine o'clock.'

'Thanks, Sarge,' I said, thrilled to be able to say it again, and just to complete my happiness, I added, 'This really means a lot to me. Ten-four.'

'Ten-four,' he said.

Somewhere in the city I hoped that our little radio drama was playing out to our target audience. As he scrubbed up for his surgery, would he pause, cock his head, and listen? As his scanner crackled with the beautiful mellow voice of Sergeant Doakes, perhaps he'd put down a bone saw, wipe his hands, and write the address on a scrap of paper. And then he would go happily back to work – on Kyle Chutsky? – with the inner peace of a man with a job to do and a full social calendar when he was done for the day.

Just to be absolutely sure, our squad-car friends would breathlessly repeat the message a few times, and without fucking it up; that Sergeant Doakes himself would be at the party tonight, live and in person, around nine o'clock.

And for my part, with my work done for a few hours, I headed for Jackson Memorial Hospital to look in on my favorite bird with a broken wing.

Deborah was wrapped in an upper-body cast, sitting in bed in a sixth-floor room with a lovely view of the freeway, and although I was sure they were giving her some kind of painkiller, she did not look at all blissful when I walked into her room. 'Goddamn it, Dexter,' she greeted me, 'tell them to let me the hell out of here. Or at least give me my clothes so I can leave.'

'I'm glad to see you're feeling better, sister dear,' I said. 'You'll be on your feet in no time.'

'I'll be on my feet the second they give me my goddamn clothes,' she said. 'What the hell is going on out there? What have you been doing?'

'Doakes and I have set a rather neat trap, and Doakes is the bait,' I said. 'If Dr. Danco bites, we'll have him tonight at my, um, party. Vince's party,' I added, and I realized I wanted to distance myself from the whole idea of being engaged and it was a silly way to do it, but I felt better anyway – which apparently brought no comfort to Debs.

'Your engagement party,' she said, and then snarled. 'Shit. You got Doakes to set himself up for you.' And I admit it sounded kind of elegant when she said it, but I didn't want her thinking such things; unhappy people heal slower.

'No, Deborah, seriously,' I said in my best soothing voice. 'We're doing this to catch Dr. Danco.'

She glared at me for a long time and then, amazingly, she sniffled and fought back a tear. 'I have to trust you,' she said. 'But I hate this. All I can think about is what he's doing to Kyle.'

'This will work, Debs. We'll get Kyle back.' And because she was, after all, my sister, I did not add, 'or most of him anyway.'

'Christ, I hate being stuck here,' she said. 'You need me there for backup.'

'We can handle this, Sis,' I said. 'There will be a dozen cops at the party, all armed and dangerous. And I'll be there, too,' I said, feeling just a little miffed that she so undervalued my presence.

But she continued to do so. 'Yeah. And if Doakes gets Danco, we get Kyle back. If Danco gets Doakes, you're off the hook. Real slick, Dexter. You win either way.'

'That had never occurred to me,' I lied. 'My only thought is to serve the greater good. Besides, Doakes is supposed to be very experienced at this sort of thing. And he knows Danco.'

'Goddamn it, Dex, this is killing me. What if— ' She broke off and bit her lip. 'This better work,' she said. 'He's had Kyle too long.'

'This will work, Deborah,' I said. But neither one of us really believed me.

The doctors quite firmly insisted on keeping Deborah for twenty-four hours, for observation. And so with a hearty hi-ho to my sister, I galloped off into the sunset, and from there to my apartment for a shower and change of clothes. What to wear? I could think of no guidelines on what we were wearing this season to a party forced on you to celebrate an unwanted engagement that might turn into a violent confrontation with a vengeful maniac. Clearly brown shoes were out, but beyond that nothing really seemed de rigueur. After careful consideration I let simple good taste guide me, and selected a lime green Hawaiian shirt covered with red electric guitars and pink hot rods. Simple but elegant. A pair of khaki pants and some running shoes, and I was ready for the ball.

But there was still an hour left before I had to be there, and I found my thoughts turning again to Cody. Was I right about him? If so, how could he deal with his awakening Passenger on his own? He needed my guidance, and I found that I was eager to give it to him.

I left my apartment and drove south, instead of north to Vince's house. In fifteen minutes I was knocking at Rita's door and staring across the street at the empty spot formerly occupied by Sergeant Doakes in his maroon Taurus. Tonight he was no doubt at home preparing, girding his loins for the coming conflict and polishing his bullets. Would he try to kill Dr. Danco, secure in the knowledge that he had legal permission to do so? How long had it been since he killed something? Did he miss it? Did the Need come roaring over him like a hurricane, blowing away all the reason and restraints?

The door opened. Rita beamed and lunged at me, wrapping me in a hug and kissing me on the face. 'Hey, handsome,' she said. 'Come on in.'

I hugged back briefly for form's sake and then disengaged myself. 'I can't stay very long,' I said.

She beamed bigger. 'I know,' she said. 'Vince called and told me. He was so cute about the whole thing. He promised he would keep an eye on you so you wouldn't do anything too crazy. Come inside,' she said, and dragged me in by the arm. When she closed the door she turned to me, suddenly serious. 'Listen Dexter. I want you to know that I am not the jealous type and I trust you. You just go and have fun.'

'I will, thank you,' I said, although I doubted that I would. And I wondered what Vince had said to her to make her think that the party would be some kind of dangerous pit of temptation and sin. For that matter, it might well be. Since Vince was largely synthetic, he could be somewhat unpredictable in social situations, as shown by his bizarre duels of sexual innuendo with my sister.

'It was sweet of you to stop here before the party,' Rita said, leading me to the couch where I had spent so much of my recent life. 'The kids wanted to know why they couldn't go.'

'I'll talk to them,' I said, eager to see Cody and try to discover if I had been right.

Rita smiled, as if thrilled to learn that I would actually talk to Cody and Astor. 'They're out back,' she said. 'I'll go get them.'

'No, stay here,' I said. 'I'll go out.'

Cody and Astor were in the yard with Nick, the surly clot from next door who had wanted to see Astor naked. They looked up as I slid the door open, and Nick turned away and scurried back to his own yard. Astor ran over to me and gave me a hug, and Cody trailed behind, watching, no emotion at all on his face. 'Hi,' he said, in his quiet voice.

'Greetings and salutations, young citizens,' I said. 'Shall we put on our formal togas? Caesar calls us to the senate.'

Astor cocked her head to one side and looked at me as if she had just seen me eat a raw cat. Cody merely said, 'What,' very quietly.

'Dexter,' Astor said, '*why* can't we go to the party with you?'

'In the first place,' I told her, 'it's a school night. And in the second place, I am very much afraid this is a grown-up party.'

'Does that mean there will be naked girls there?' she asked.

'What kind of a person do you think I am?' I said, scowling fiercely. 'Do you really think I would *ever* go to a party with no naked girls?'

'Eeeeeewwww,' she said, and Cody whispered, 'Ha.'

'But more important, there will also be stupid dancing and ugly shirts, and these are not good for you to see. You would lose all your respect for grown-ups.'

'What respect?' Cody said, and I shook him by the hand.

'Well said,' I told him. 'Now go to your room.'

Astor finally giggled. 'But we want to go to the party,' she said.

'I'm afraid not,' I said. 'But I brought you a piece of treasure so you won't run away.' I handed her a roll of Necco wafers, our secret currency. She would split it evenly with Cody later, out of sight of all prying eyes. 'Now then, young persons,' I said. They looked up at me expectantly. But at that point I was stuck, all aquiver with eagerness to know the answer but not at all sure where or even how to start asking. I could not very well say, 'By the way, Cody, I was wondering if you like to kill things?' That, of course, was exactly what I wanted to know, but it didn't really seem like the kind of thing you could say to a child – especially Cody, who was generally about as talkative as a coconut.

His sister, Astor, though, often seemed to speak for him. The pressures of spending their early childhood together with a violent ogre for a father had created a symbiotic relationship so close that when he drank soda she would burp. Whatever might be going on inside Cody, Astor would be able to express it.

'Can I ask something very serious?' I said, and they exchanged a look that contained an entire conversation, but said nothing to anyone else. Then they nodded to me, almost as if their heads were mounted together on a Foosball rod.

'The neighbor's dog,' I said.

'Told you,' Cody said.

'He was always knocking over the garbage,' Astor said. 'And pooping in our yard. And Nicky tried to make him bite us.'

'So Cody took care of him?' I asked.

'He's the boy,' said Astor. 'He likes to do that stuff. I just watch. Are you going to tell Mom?'

There it was. *He likes to do that stuff.* I looked at the two of them, watching me with no more worry than if they had just said they liked vanilla ice cream better than strawberry. 'I won't tell your mom,' I said. 'But you can't tell anybody else in the world, not ever. Just the three of us, nobody else, understand?'

'Okay,' Astor said, with a glance at her brother. 'But why, Dexter?'

'Most people won't understand,' I said. 'Not even your mom.'

'You do,' said Cody in his husky near-whisper.

'Yes,' I said. 'And I can help.' I took a deep breath and felt an echo rolling through my bones, down across the years from Harry so long ago to me right now, under the same Florida nightscape Harry and I had stood under when he said the same thing to me. 'We have to get you squared away,' I said, and Cody looked at me with large blinkless eyes and nodded.

'Okay,' he said.

23

Vince Masuoka had a small house in north Miami, at the end of a dead-end street off N.E. 125th Street. It was painted pale yellow with pastel purple trim, which really made me question my taste in associates. There were a few very well-barbered bushes in the front yard and a cactus garden by the front door, and he had a row of those solar-powered lamps lighting the cobblestone walk-way to his front door.

I had been there once before, a little more than a year ago, when Vince had decided for some reason to have a costume party. I had taken Rita, since the whole purpose of having a disguise is to be seen wearing it. She had gone as Peter Pan, and I was Zorro, of course; the Dark Avenger with a ready blade. Vince had answered the door in a body-hugging satin gown with a basket of fruit on his head.

'J. Edgar Hoover?' I asked him.

'You're very close. Carmen Miranda,' he had said before leading us in to a fountain of lethal fruit punch. I had taken one sip and decided to stick with the sodas, but of course that had been before my conversion to a beer-swill-ing red-blooded male. There had been a nonstop soundtrack of monotonous techno-pop music turned up to a volume designed to induce voluntary self-performed brain surgery, and the party had gotten exceedingly loud and hilar-ious.

As far as I knew, Vince had not entertained since then, at least not on that scale. Still, the memory apparently lingered, and Vince had no trouble in gath-ering an enthusiastic crowd to join in my humiliation with only twenty-four-hours' notice. True to his word, there were dirty movies playing all over the house on a number of video monitors he had set up, even out back on his patio. And, of course, the fruit-punch fountain was back.

Because the rumors of that first party were still fresh on the grapevine, the place was packed with rowdy people, mostly male, who attacked the punch like they had heard there was a prize for the first one to achieve permanent brain damage. I even knew a few of the partiers. Angel Batista-no-relation was there from work, along with Camilla Figg and a handful of other foren-sic lab geeks, and a few cops I knew, including the four who had not fucked it up for Sergeant Doakes. The rest of the crowd seemed to be pulled off South Beach at random, chosen for their ability to make a loud, high-pitched WHOO! sound when the music changed or the video monitor showed something particularly undignified.

It didn't take long at all for the party to settle into something we would all regret for a very long time. By a quarter of nine I was the only one left who could still stand upright unassisted. Most of the cops had camped out by the fountain in a grim clot of rapidly bending elbows. Angel-no-relation was lying under the table sound asleep with a smile on his face. His pants were gone and someone had shaved a bare streak down the center of his head.

Things being as they were, I thought this would be an ideal time to slip outside undetected to see if Sergeant Doakes had arrived yet. As it turned out, however, I was wrong. I had taken no more than two steps toward the door when a great weight came down on me from behind. I spun around quickly to find that Camilla Figg was attempting to drape herself across my back. 'Hi,' she said with a very bright and somewhat slurred smile.

'Hello,' I said cheerfully. 'Can I get you a drink?'

She frowned at me. 'Don't need drink. Jus wanna say hello.' She frowned harder. 'Jeez Christ you're cute,' she said. 'Always wand to tell you that.'

Well, the poor thing was obviously drunk, but even so – Cute? Me? I suppose too much alcohol can blur the sight, but come on – what could possibly be cute about someone who would rather cut you open than shake your hand? And in any case, I was already way over my limit for women with one, Rita. As far as I could recall, Camilla and I had rarely said more than three words to each other. She had never before mentioned my alleged cuteness. She had seemed to avoid me, in fact, preferring to blush and look away rather than say a simple good morning. And now she was practically raping me. Did that make sense?

In any case, I had no time to waste on deciphering human behavior. 'Thank you very much,' I said as I tried to undrape Camilla without causing any serious injuries to either of us. She had locked her hands around my neck and I pried at them, but she clung like a barnacle. 'I think you need some fresh air, Camilla,' I said, hoping that she might take the hint and wander away out back. Instead she lunged closer, mashing her face against mine as I frantically backpedaled away.

'I'll take my fresh air right here,' she said. She squeezed her lips into a pouty kissy-face and pushed me back until I bumped into a chair and nearly fell over.

'Ah – would you like to sit down?' I asked hopefully.

'No,' she said, pulling me downward toward her face with what felt like at least twice her actual weight, 'I would like to screw.'

'Ah, well,' I stammered, overcome by the absolute shocking effrontery and absurdity of it – were all human women crazy? Not that the men were any better. The party around me looked like it had been arranged by Hieronymus Bosch, with Camilla ready to drag me behind the fountain where no doubt a gang with bird beaks was waiting to help her ravish me. But it hit me that I now had the perfect excuse to avoid ravishment. 'I am getting married, you know.' As difficult as it was to admit, it was only fair that it come in handy once in a while.

'Bassurd,' Camilla said. 'Beautiful bassurd.' She slumped suddenly and her arms flopped off my neck. I barely managed to catch her and keep her from falling to the floor.

'Probably so,' I said. 'But in any case I think you need to sit down for a few minutes.' I tried to ease her into the chair, but it was like pouring honey onto a knife blade, and she flowed off onto the floor.

'Beautiful bassurd,' she said, and closed her eyes.

It's always nice to learn that you are well regarded by your co-workers, but my romantic interlude had used up several minutes and I very much needed to get out front and check in with Sergeant Doakes. And so leaving Camilla to slumber sweetly amid her dewy dreams of love, I headed for the front door once again.

And once again I was waylaid, this time by a savage attack on my upper arm. Vince himself grabbed my bicep and pulled me away from the door and back into surrealism. 'Hey!' he yodeled. 'Hey, party boy! Where ya going?'

'I think I left my keys in my car,' I said, trying to disengage from his death grip. But he just yanked at me harder.

'No, no, no,' he said, pulling me toward the fountain. 'It's your party, you're not going anywhere.'

'It's a wonderful party, Vince,' I said. 'But I really need to— '

'Drink,' he said, splashing a cup into the fountain and pushing it at me so it slopped onto my shirt. 'That's what you need. Banzai!' He held his own cup up in the air and then drained it. Happily for all concerned, the drink sent him into a coughing fit, and I managed to slip away as he doubled over and struggled for air.

I made it all the way out the front door and partway down the walk before he appeared at the door. 'Hey!' he yelled at me. 'You can't leave yet, the strippers are coming!'

'I'll be right back,' I called. 'Fix me another drink!'

'Right!' he said with his phony smile. 'Ha! Banzai!' And he went back in to the party with a cheery wave. I turned to look for Doakes.

He had been parked right across the street from wherever I was for so long that I should have spotted him immediately, but I didn't. When I finally saw the familiar maroon Taurus, I realized what a clever thing he had done. He was parked up the street under a large tree, which blocked any light from the streetlights. It was the kind of thing a man trying to hide might do, but at the same time it would allow Dr. Danco to feel confident that he could get close without being seen.

I walked over to the car and as I approached the window slid down. 'He's not here yet,' Doakes said.

'You're supposed to come in for a drink,' I said.

'I don't drink.'

'You obviously don't go to parties, either, or you would know that you can't do them properly sitting across the street in your car.'

Sergeant Doakes didn't say anything, but the window rolled up and then the door opened and he stepped out. 'What're you gonna do if he comes now?' he asked me.

'Count on my charm to save me,' I said. 'Now come on in while there's still someone conscious in there.'

We crossed the street together, not actually holding hands, but it seemed so odd under the circumstances that we might as well have. Halfway across a car turned the corner and came down the street toward us. I wanted to run and dive into a row of oleanders, but was very proud of my icy control when instead I merely glanced at the oncoming car. It cruised slowly along, and Sergeant Doakes and I were all the way across the street by the time it got to us.

Doakes turned to look at the car, and I did, too. A row of five sullen teen faces looked out at us. One of them turned his head and said something to the others, and they laughed. The car rolled on by.

'We better get inside,' I said. 'They looked dangerous.'

Doakes didn't respond. He watched the car turn around at the end of the street and then continued on his way to Vince's front door. I followed along behind, catching up with him just in time to open the front door for him.

I had only been outside for a few minutes, but the body count had grown impressively. Two of the cops beside the fountain were stretched out on the floor, and one of the South Beach refugees was throwing up into a Tupperware container that had held Jell-O salad a few minutes ago. The music was pounding louder than ever, and from the kitchen I heard Vince yelling, 'Banzai!' joined by a ragged chorus of other voices. 'Abandon all hope,' I said to Sergeant Doakes, and he mumbled something that sounded like, 'Sick motherfuckers.' He shook his head and went in.

Doakes did not take a drink and he didn't dance, either. He found a corner of the room with no unconscious body in it and just stood there, looking like a cut-rate Grim Reaper at a frat party. I wondered if I should help him get into the spirit of the thing. Perhaps I could send Camilla Figg over to seduce him.

I watched the good sergeant stand in his corner and look around him, and I wondered what he was thinking. It was a lovely metaphor: Doakes standing silent and alone in a corner while all around him human life raged riotously on. I probably would have felt a wellspring of sympathy for him bubbling up, if only I could feel. He seemed completely unaffected by the whole thing, not even reacting when two of the South Beach gang ran past him naked. His eyes fell on the nearest monitor, which was portraying some rather startling and original images involving animals. Doakes looked at it without interest or emotion of any kind; just a look, then his gaze moved on to the cops on the floor, Angel under the table, and Vince leading a conga line in from the kitchen. His gaze traveled all the way over to me and he looked at me with the exact same lack of expression. He crossed the room and stood in front of me.

'How long we got to stay?' he asked.

I gave him my very best smile. 'It is a bit much, isn't it? All this happiness and fun – it must make you nervous.'

'Makes me want to wash my hands,' he said. 'I'll wait outside.'

'Is that really a good idea?' I asked.

He tilted his head at Vince's conga line, which was collapsing in a heap of spastic hilarity. 'Is that?' he said. And of course he had a point, although in terms of sheer lethal pain and terror a conga line on the floor couldn't really compete with Dr. Danco. Still, I suppose one has to consider human dignity, if it truly exists somewhere. At the moment, looking around the room, that didn't seem possible.

The front door swung open. Both Doakes and I turned to face it, all our reflexes up on tiptoe, and it was a good thing we were ready for danger because otherwise we might have been ambushed by two half-naked women carrying a boom box. 'Hello?' they called out, and were rewarded with a ragged high-pitched roar of 'WHOOOO!' from the conga line on the floor. Vince struggled out from under the pile of bodies and swayed to his feet. 'Hey!' he shouted. 'Hey everybody! Strippers are here! Banzai!' There was an even louder 'WHOOOO!' and one of the cops on the floor struggled to his knees, swaying gently and staring as he mouthed the word, 'Strippers . . .'

Doakes looked around the room and back at me. 'I'll be outside,' he said, and turned for the door.

'Doakes,' I said, thinking it really wasn't a good idea. But I got no more than one step after him when once again I was savagely ambushed.

'Gotcha!' Vince roared out, holding me in a clumsy bear hug.

'Vince, let me go,' I said.

'No way!' he chortled. 'Hey, everybody! Help me out with the blushing bridegroom!' There was a surge of ex-conga liners from the floor and the last standing cop by the fountain and I was suddenly at the center of a mini-mosh pit, the press of bodies heaving me toward the chair where Camilla Figg had passed out and rolled onto the floor. I struggled to get away, but it was no use. There were too many of them, too filled with Vince's rocket juice. I could do nothing but watch as Sergeant Doakes, with a last molten-stone glare, went through the front door and out into the night.

They levered me into the chair and stood around me in a tight half-circle and it was obvious that I was going nowhere. I hoped Doakes was as good as he thought he was, because he was clearly on his own for a while.

The music stopped, and I heard a familiar sound that made the hairs on my arms stand up straight: it was the ratchet of duct tape spooling off the roll, my own favorite prelude to a Concerto for Knife Blade. Someone held my arms and Vince wrapped three big loops of tape around me, fastening me to the chair. It was not tight enough to hold me, but it would certainly slow me enough to allow the crowd to keep me in the chair.

'All righty then!' Vince called out, and one of the strippers turned on her boom box and the show began. The first stripper, a sullen-looking black woman, began to undulate in front of me while removing a few unnecessary items of clothing. When she was almost naked, she sat on my lap and licked my ear while wiggling her butt. Then she forced my head between her breasts, arched her back, and leaped backward, and the other stripper, a woman with Asian features and blond hair, came forward and repeated the whole process. When she had wiggled around on my lap for a few moments, she was joined by the first stripper, and the two of them sat together, one on each side of me. Then they leaned forward so that their breasts rubbed my face, and began to kiss each other.

At this point, dear Vince brought them each a large glass of his murderous fruit punch, and they drank it off, still wiggling rhythmically. One of them muttered, 'Whoo. Good punch.' I couldn't tell which one of them said it, but they both seemed to agree. The two women began to writhe a great deal more now and the crowd around me began to howl like it was full moon at a rabies convention. Of course, my view was somewhat obscured by four very large and unnaturally hard breasts – two in each shade – but at least it sounded like everyone except me was having a great deal of fun.

Sometimes you have to wonder if there is some kind of malign force with a sick sense of humor running our universe. I knew enough about human males to know that most of them would happily trade their excess body parts to be where I was. And yet, all I could think of was that I would be equally pleased to trade a body part or two to get out of this chair and away from the naked squirming women. Of course, I would have preferred it to be somebody else's body part, but I would cheerfully collect it.

But there was no justice; the two strippers sat there on my lap, bouncing to the music and sweating all over my beautiful rayon shirt and each other, while around us the party raged on. After what seemed like an endless spell in purgatory, broken only by Vince bringing the strippers two more drinks, the two roiling women finally moved off my lap and danced around the circling crowd. They touched faces, sipped from the partyers' drinks, and grabbed at an occasional crotch. I used the distraction to free my hands and remove the duct tape, and it was only then that I noticed that no one was paying any attention at all to Dimpled Dexter, the theoretical Man of the Hour. One quick look around showed me why: everyone in the room was standing in a slack-jawed circle watching the two strippers as they danced, completely naked now, glistening with sweat and spilled drinks. Vince looked like a cartoon the way he stood there with his eyes almost bulged out of his head, but he was in good company. Everyone who was still conscious was in a similar pose, staring without breathing, swaying slightly from side to side. I could have barreled through the room blasting away on a flaming tuba and no one would have paid me any attention.

I stood up, walked carefully around behind the crowd, and slipped out the front door. I had thought that Sergeant Doakes would wait somewhere near the house, but he was nowhere to be seen. I walked across the street and looked in his car. It was empty, too. I looked up and down the street and it was the same. There was no sign of him.

Doakes was gone.

24

There are many aspects of human existence that I will never understand, and I don't just mean intellectually. I mean that I lack the ability to empathize, as well as the capacity to feel emotion. To me it doesn't seem like much of a loss, but it does put a great many areas of ordinary human experience completely outside my comprehension.

However, there is one almost overwhelmingly common human experience I feel powerfully, and that is temptation. And as I looked at the empty street outside Vince Masuoka's house and realized that somehow Dr. Danco had taken Doakes, I felt it wash over me in dizzying, nearly suffocating waves. *I was free.* The thought surged around me and pummeled me with its elegant and completely justified simplicity. It would be the easiest thing in the world just to walk away. Let Doakes have his reunion with the Doctor, report it in the morning, and pretend that I'd had too much to drink – my engagement party, after all! – and I wasn't really sure what had happened to the good sergeant. And who would contradict me? Certainly no one inside at the party could say with anything approaching realistic certainty that I was not watching the peep show with them the whole time.

Doakes would be gone. Whisked away forever into a final haze of lopped off limbs and madness, never to lighten my dark doorway again. Liberty for Dexter, free to be me, and all I had to do was absolutely nothing. Even I could handle that.

So why not walk away? For that matter, why not take a slightly longer stroll, down to Coconut Grove, where a certain children's photographer had been waiting for my attentions much too long? So simple, so safe – why, indeed, not? A perfect night for dark delight with a downbeat, the moon nearly full and that small missing edge lending the whole thing a casual, informal air. The urgent whispers agreed, rising in a hissed insistent chorus.

It was all there. Time and target and most of a moon and even an alibi, and the pressure had been growing for so long now that I could close my eyes and let it happen all by itself, walk through the whole happy thing on autopilot. And then the sweet release again, the afterglow of buttery muscles with all the knots drained out, the happy coasting into my first complete sleep of far too long now. And in the morning, rested and relieved, I would tell Deborah . . .

Oh. Deborah. There was that, wasn't there?

I would tell Deborah that I had taken the sudden opportunity of a no-Doakes zone and gone dashing into the darkness with a Need and a Knife as the last few fingers of her boyfriend trickled away into a trash heap? Somehow, even with my inner cheerleaders insisting that it would be all right, I didn't think she would go for it. It had the feel of something final in my relationship with my sister, a small lapse in judgment, perhaps, but one she would find a bit hard to forgive, and even though I am not capable of feeling actual love, I did want to keep Debs relatively happy with me.

And so once again I was left with virtuous patience and a feeling of long-suffering rectitude. Dour Dutiful Dexter. *It will come*, I told my other self. *Sooner or later, it will come. Has to come; it will not wait forever, but this must come first.* And there was some grumbling, of course, because it had not come in far too long, but I soothed the growls, rattled the bars with false good cheer one time, and pulled out my cell phone.

I dialed the number Doakes had given me. After a moment there was a tone, and then nothing, just a faint hiss. I punched in the long access code, heard a click, and then a neutral female voice said, 'Number.' I gave the voice Doakes's cell number. There was a pause, and then it read me some coordinates; I hurriedly scribbled them down on the pad. The voice paused, and then added, 'Moving due west, 65 miles per hour.' The line went dead.

I never claimed to be an expert navigator, but I do have a small GPS unit that I use on my boat. It comes in handy for marking good fishing spots. So I managed to put in the coordinates without bumping my head or causing an explosion. The unit Doakes had given me was a step up from mine and had a map on the screen. The coordinates on the map translated to Interstate 75, heading for Alligator Alley, the corridor to the west coast of Florida.

I was mildly surprised. Most of the territory between Miami and Naples is Everglades, swamp broken up by small patches of semidry land. It was filled with snakes, alligators, and Indian casinos, which did not seem at all like the kind of place to relax and enjoy a peaceful dismemberment. But the GPS could not lie, and supposedly neither could the voice on the phone. If the coordinates were wrong, it was Doakes's doing, and he was lost anyway. I had no choice. I felt a little guilty about leaving the party without thanking my host, but I got into my car and headed for I-75.

I was up on the interstate in just a few minutes, then quickly north to I-75. As you head west on 75 the city gradually thins away. Then there is one final furious explosion of strip malls and houses just before the toll booth for Alligator Alley. At the booth I pulled over and called the number again. The same neutral female voice gave me a set of coordinates and the line went dead. I took it to mean that they were no longer moving.

According to the map, Sergeant Doakes and Dr. Danco were now settling comfortably into the middle of an unmarked watery wilderness about forty miles ahead of me. I didn't know about Danco, but I didn't think Doakes would float very well. Perhaps the GPS could lie after all. Still, I had to do something, so I pulled back onto the road, paid my toll, and continued westward.

At a spot parallel to the location on the GPS, a small access road branched off to the right. It was nearly invisible in the dark, especially since I was traveling at seventy miles per hour. But as I saw it whiz past I braked to a stop on the shoulder of the road and backed up to peer at it. It was a one-lane dirt road that led nowhere, up over a rickety bridge and then straight as an arrow into the darkness of the Everglades. In the headlights of the passing cars I could only see about fifty yards down the road, and there was nothing to see. A patch of knee-high weeds grew up in the center of the road between the two deeply rutted tire tracks. A clump of short trees hung over the road at the edge of darkness, and that was it.

I thought about getting out and looking for some kind of clue, until I realized how silly that was. Did I think I was Tonto, faithful Indian guide? I couldn't look at a bent twig and tell how many white men had been past in the last hour. Perhaps Dexter's dutiful but uninspired brain pictured him as Sherlock Holmes, able to examine the wheel ruts and deduce that a left-handed hunchback with red hair and a limp had gone down the road carrying a Cuban cigar and a ukelele. I would find no clues, not that it mattered. The sad truth was, this was either it or I was all done for the night, and Sergeant Doakes was done for considerably longer.

Just to be absolutely sure – or at any rate, absolutely free of guilt – I called Doakes's top secret telephone number again. The voice gave me the same coordinates and hung up; wherever they were, they were still there, down this dark and dirty little road.

I was apparently out of choices. Duty called, and Dexter must answer. I turned the wheel hard and started down the road.

According to the GPS, I had about five and a half miles to travel before I got to whatever was waiting for me. I put my headlights on low and drove slowly, watching the road carefully. This gave me plenty of time to think, which is not always a good thing. I thought about what might be there at the end of the road, and what I would do when I got there. And although it was a rather bad time for this to occur to me, I realized that even if I found Dr. Danco at the end of this road I had no idea what I was going to do about it. 'Come get me,' Doakes had said, and it sounded simple enough until you were driving into the Everglades on a dark night with no weapon more threatening than a steno pad. And Dr. Danco had apparently not had much trouble with any of the others he had taken, in spite of the fact that they were rough, well-armed customers. How could poor, helpless Docile Dexter hope to thwart him when the Mighty Doakes had gone down so fast?

And what would I do if he got me? I did not think I would make a very good yodeling potato. I was not sure if I could go crazy, since most authorities would most likely say that I already was. Would I snap anyway and go burbling out of my brain to the land of the eternal scream? Or because of what I am, would I remain aware of what was happening to me? Me, precious me, strapped to a table and offering a critique of the dismemberment technique? The answer would certainly tell me a great deal about what I was, but I decided that I didn't really want to know the answer that badly. The very thought was almost enough to make me feel real emotion, and not the kind that one is grateful for.

The night had closed in around me, and not in a good way. Dexter is a city boy, used to the bright lights that leave dark shadows. The farther along this road I went, the darker it seemed to get, and the darker it got the more this whole thing began to seem like a hopeless, suicidal trip. This situation clearly called for a platoon of Marines, not an occasionally homicidal forensic lab geek. Who did I really think I was? Sir Dexter the Valiant, galloping to the rescue? What could I possibly hope to do? For that matter, what could anyone do except pray?

I don't pray, of course. What would something like me pray to, and why should It listen to me? And if I found Something, whatever It was, how could It keep from laughing at me, or flinging a lightning bolt down my throat? It would have been very comforting to be able to look to some kind of higher power, but of course, I only knew one higher power. And even though it was strong and swift and clever, and very good at stalking silently through the nightscape, would even the Dark Passenger be enough?

According to the GPS unit I was within a quarter of a mile of Sergeant Doakes, or at least his cell phone, when I came to a gate. It was one of those wide gates made of aluminum that they use on dairy farms to keep the cows in. But this was no dairy farm. A sign that hung on the gate said:

BLALOCK GATOR FARM
Trespassers Will Be Eaten

This seemed like a very good place for a gator farm, which did not necessarily make it the kind of place I wanted to be. I am ashamed to admit that even though I have lived my entire life in Miami, I know very little about gator farms. Did the animals roam freely through watery pastures, or were they penned in somehow? It seemed like a very important question at the moment. Could alligators see in the dark? And how hungry were they, generally? All good questions, and very relevant.

I switched off my headlights, stopped the car, and got out. In the sudden silence I could hear the engine ticking, the keening of mosquitoes, and, in the distance, music was playing on a tinny speaker. It sounded like Cuban music. Possibly Tito Puente.

The Doctor was in.

I approached the gate. The road on the far side still ran straight, up to an old wooden bridge and then into a grove of trees. Through the branches I could see a light. I did not see any alligators basking in the moonlight.

Well, Dexter, here we are. And what would you like to do tonight? At the moment, Rita's couch didn't seem like such a bad place to be. Especially compared to standing here in the nighttime wild. On the far side of this gate were a maniacal vivisectionist, hordes of ravenous reptiles, and a man I was supposed to rescue even though he wanted to kill me. And in this corner, wearing dark trunks, the Mighty Dexter.

I certainly seemed to be asking this an awful lot lately, but why was it always me? I mean, really. Me, braving all this to rescue Sergeant Doakes of all people? Hello? Isn't there something wrong with this picture? Like the fact that I am in it?

Nevertheless, I was here, and might as well go through with it. I climbed over the gate and headed toward the light.

The normal night sounds started to return a few at a time. At least I assumed they were normal for out here in the savage primeval forest. There were clicks and hums and buzzes from our insect friends, and a mournful sort of shriek that I very much hoped was only some kind of owl; a small one, please. Something rattled the shrubbery off to my right and then went completely silent. And happily for me, instead of getting nervous or scared like a human being, I found myself slipping into nightstalker mode. Sounds shifted down, movement around me slowed, and all my senses seemed to come slightly more alive. The darkness bleached out a little lighter; details sprang into focus from the night around me, and a slow cold careful silent chuckle began to grow just under the surface of my awareness. Was poor misunderstood Dexter feeling out of his element and over his head? Then let the Passenger take the wheel. He would know what to do, and he would do it.

And why, after all, not? At the end of this driveway and over the bridge, Dr. Danco was waiting for us. I had been wanting to meet him, and now I would. Harry would approve of anything I did to this one. Even Doakes would have to admit that Danco was fair game – he would probably thank me for it. It was dizzying; this time I had permission. And even better, it had poetry to it. For so very long Doakes had kept my genie trapped in its bottle. There would be a certain justice if his rescue were to let it out again. And I would rescue him, certainly, of course I would. Afterward . . .

But first.

I crossed the wooden bridge. Halfway over a board creaked and I froze for a moment. The night sounds did not change, and from up ahead I heard Tito Puente say, 'Aaaaaahh-YUH!' before returning to his melody. I moved on.

On the far side of the bridge the road widened into a parking area. To the left was a chain-link fence and straight ahead was a small, one-story building with a light shining in the window. It was old and battered and needed paint, but perhaps Dr. Danco wasn't as thoughtful of appearances as he should have been. Off to the right a chickee hut moldered quietly beside a canal, chunks of its palm-frond roof dangling like tattered old clothes. An airboat was tied to a dilapidated dock jutting out into the canal.

I slid into the shadows cast by a row of trees and felt a predator's cool poise take control of my senses. I circled carefully around the parking area, to the left, along the chain-link fence. Something grunted at me and then splashed into the water, but it was on the other side of the fence so I ignored it and moved on. The Dark Passenger was driving and did not stop for such things.

The fence ended in a right-angle turn away from the house. There was one last stretch of emptiness, no more than fifty feet, and one last stand of trees. I moved to the last tree for a good long look at the house, but as I paused and placed my hand on the trunk something crashed and fluttered in the branches above me and a horribly loud bugling shriek split the night. I jumped back as whatever it was smashed down through the leaves of the tree and onto the ground.

Still making a sound like an insane over-amplified trumpet, the thing faced me. It was a large bird, bigger than a turkey, and it was apparent from the way he hissed and hooted that he was angry at me. It strutted a step forward, whisking a massive tail across the ground, and I realized that it was a peacock. Animals do not like me, but this one seemed to have formed an extreme and violent hatred. I suppose it did not understand that I was much bigger and more dangerous. It seemed intent on either eating me or driving me away, and since I needed the hideous caterwauling din to stop as quickly as possible I obliged him with a dignified retreat and hurried back along the fence to the shadows by the bridge. Once I was safely tucked into a quiet pool of darkness I turned to look at the house.

The music had stopped, and the light was out.

I stood frozen in my shadow for several minutes. Nothing happened, except that the peacock quit its bugling and, with a final mean-spirited mutter in my direction, fluttered back up into his tree. And then the night sounds came back again, the clicks and whines of the insects and another snort and splash from the alligators. But no more Tito Puente. I knew that Dr. Danco was watching and listening just as I was, that each of us was waiting for the other to make some move, but I could wait longer. He had no idea what might be out there in the dark – for all he could tell it might be either a SWAT team or the Delta Rho Glee Club – and I knew that there was only him. I knew where he was, and he could not know if there was someone on the roof or even if he was surrounded. And so he would have to do something first, and there were just two choices. Either he had to attack, or—

At the far end of the house there came the sudden roar of an engine and as I tensed involuntarily the airboat leaped away from the dock. The engine revved higher and the boat raced off down the canal. In less than a minute it was gone, around a bend and away into the night, and with it went Dr. Danco.

25

For a few minutes I just stood and watched the house, partly because I was being cautious. I had not actually seen the driver of the airboat, and it was possible that the Doctor was still lurking inside, waiting to see what would happen. And to be honest, I did not wish to be savaged by any more gaudy predatory chickens, either.

But after several minutes when nothing at all happened, I knew I had to go into the house and take a look. And so, circling widely around the tree where the evil bird roosted, I approached the house.

It was dark inside, but not silent. As I stood outside next to the battered screen door that faced the parking area, I heard a kind of quiet thrashing coming from somewhere inside, followed after a moment by a rhythmic grunting and an occasional whimper. It did not seem like the kind of noise someone would make if they were hiding in a lethal ambush. Instead, it was very much the kind of sound somebody might make if they were tied up and trying to escape. Had Dr. Danco fled so quickly that he had left Sergeant Doakes behind?

Once again I found the entire cellar of my brain flooded with ecstatic temptation. Sergeant Doakes, my nemesis, tied up inside, gift-wrapped and delivered to me in the perfect setting. All the tools and supplies I could want, no one around for miles – and when I was done I only had to say, 'Sorry, I got there too late. Look what that awful Dr. Danco did to poor old Sergeant Doakes.' The idea was intoxicating, and I believe I actually swayed a little as I tasted it. Of course it was just a thought, and I would certainly never do anything of the kind, would I? I mean, would I really? Dexter? Hello? Why are you salivating, dear boy?

Certainly not, not me. Why, I was a moral beacon in the spiritual desert of South Florida. Most of the time. I was upright, scrubbed clean, and mounted on a Dark Charger. Sir Dexter the Chaste to the rescue. Or at any rate, probably to the rescue. I mean, all things considered. I pulled open the screen door and went in.

Immediately inside the door I flattened against the wall, just to be cautious, and felt for a light switch. I found one right where it should be and flipped it up.

Like Danco's first den of iniquity, this one was sparsely furnished. Once again, the main feature of the place was a large table in the center of the room. A mirror hung on the opposite wall. Off to the right a doorway without a door led to what looked like the kitchen, and on the left a closed door, probably a bedroom or bathroom. Directly across from where I stood was another screen door leading outside, presumably the way Dr. Danco had made his escape.

And on the far side of the table, now thrashing more furiously than ever, was something dressed in a pale orange coverall. It looked relatively human, even from across the room. 'Over here, oh please, help me, help me,' it said, and I crossed the room and knelt beside it.

His arms and legs were bound with duct tape, naturally, the choice of every experienced, discriminating monster. As I cut the tape I examined him, listening but not really hearing his constant blubbering of, 'Oh thank God, oh please, oh God, get me loose, buddy, hurry hurry for God's sake. Oh Christ, what took you so long, Jesus, thank you, I knew you'd come,' or words to that effect. His skull was completely shaved, even the eyebrows. But there was no mistaking the rugged manly chin and the scars festooning his face. It was Kyle Chutsky.

Most of him, anyway.

As the tape came off and Chutsky was able to wiggle up to a sitting position, it became apparent that he was missing his left arm up to the elbow and his right leg up to the knee. The stumps were wrapped with clean white gauze, nothing leaking through; again, very nice work, although I did not think Chutsky would appreciate the care Danco had used in taking his arm and leg. And how much of Chutsky's mind was also missing was not yet clear, although his constant wet yammering did nothing to convince me that he was ready to sit at the controls of a passenger jet.

'Oh, God, buddy,' he said. 'Oh Jesus. Oh thank God, you came,' and he leaned his head onto my shoulder and wept. Since I had some recent experience with this, I knew just what to do. I patted him on the back and said, 'There there.' It was even more awkward than when I had done it with Deborah, since the stump of his left arm kept thumping against me and that made it much harder to fake sympathy.

But Chutsky's crying jag lasted only a few moments, and when he finally pulled away from me, struggling to stay in an upright position, my beautiful Hawaiian shirt was soaked. He gave a huge snuffle, a little too late for my shirt. 'Where's Debbie?' he said.

'She broke her collarbone,' I told him. 'She's in the hospital.'

'Oh,' he said, and he snuffled again, a long wet sound that seemed to echo somewhere inside him. Then he glanced quickly behind him and tried to struggle to his feet. 'We better get out of here. He might come back.'

It hadn't occurred to me that Danco might come back, but it was true. It's a time-honored predator's trick to run off and then circle back to see who's sniffing your spoor. If Dr. Danco did that, he would find a couple of fairly easy targets. 'All right,' I said to Chutsky. 'Let me have a quick look around.'

He snaked a hand out – his right hand, of course – and grabbed my arm. 'Please,' he said. 'Don't leave me alone.'

'I'll just be a second,' I said and tried to pull away. But he tightened his grip, still surprisingly strong considering what he had gone through.

'Please,' he repeated. 'At least leave me your gun.'

'I don't have a gun,' I said, and his eyes got much bigger.

'Oh, God, what the hell were you thinking? Christ, we've got to get out of here.' He sounded close to panic, as though any second now he would begin to cry again.

'All right,' I said. 'Let's get you up on your, ah, foot.' I hoped he didn't catch my glitch; I didn't mean to sound insensitive, but this whole missing-limbs thing was going to require a bit of retooling in the area of vocabulary. But Chutsky said nothing, just held out his arm. I helped him up, and he leaned against the table. 'Just give me a few seconds to check the other rooms,' I said. He looked at me with moist, begging eyes, but he didn't say anything and I hurried off through the little house.

In the main room, where Chutsky was, there was nothing to be seen beyond Dr. Danco's working equipment. He had some very nice cutting instruments, and after carefully considering the ethical implications, I took one of the nicest with me, a beautiful blade designed for cutting through the stringiest flesh. There were several rows of drugs; the names meant very little to me, except for a few bottles of barbiturates. I didn't find any clues at all, no crumpled matchbook covers with phone numbers written in them, no dry-cleaning slips, nothing.

The kitchen was practically a duplicate of the kitchen at the first house. There was a small and battered refrigerator, a hot plate, a card table with one folding chair, and that was it. Half a box of doughnuts sat on the counter, with a very large roach munching on one of them. He looked at me as if he was willing to fight for the doughnut, so I left him to it.

I came back in to the main room to find Chutsky still leaning on the table. 'Hurry up,' he said. 'For Christ's sake let's go.'

'One more room,' I said. I crossed the room and opened the door opposite the kitchen. As I had expected, it was a bedroom. There was a cot in one corner, and on the cot lay a pile of clothing and a cell phone. The shirt looked familiar, and I had a thought about where it might have come from. I pulled out my own phone and dialed Sergeant Doakes's number. The phone on top of the clothing began to ring.

'Oh, well,' I said. I pushed disconnect and went to get Chutsky.

He was right where I had left him, although he looked like he would have run away if he could have. 'Come on, for Christ's sake, hurry up,' he said. 'Jesus, I can almost feel his breath on my neck.' He twisted his head to the back door and then over to the kitchen and, as I reached to support him, he turned and his eyes snapped onto the mirror that hung on the wall.

For a long moment he stared at his reflection and then he slumped as if all the bones had been pulled out of him. 'Jesus,' he said, and he started to weep again. 'Oh, Jesus.'

'Come on,' I said. 'Let's get moving.'

Chutsky shuddered and shook his head. 'I couldn't even move, just lying there listening to what he was doing to Frank. He sounded so happy – "What's your guess? No? All right, then – an arm." And then the sound of the saw, and—'

'Chutsky,' I said.

'And then when he got me up there and he said, "Seven," and "What's your guess." And then—'

It's always interesting to hear about someone else's technique, of course, but Chutsky seemed like he was about to lose whatever control he had left, and I could not afford to let him snuffle all over the other side of my shirt. So I stepped close and grabbed him by the good arm. 'Chutsky. Come on. Let's get out of here,' I said.

He looked at me like he didn't know where he was, eyes as wide as they could go, and then turned back to the mirror. 'Oh Jesus,' he said. Then he took a deep and ragged breath and stood up as if he was responding to an imaginary bugle. 'Not so bad,' he said. 'I'm alive.'

'Yes, you are,' I said. 'And if we can get moving we might both stay that way.'

'Right,' he said. He turned his head away from the mirror decisively and put his good arm around my shoulder. 'Let's go.'

Chutsky had obviously not had a great deal of experience at walking with only one leg, but he huffed and clumped along, leaning heavily on me between each hopping step. Even with the missing parts, he was still a big man, and it was hard work for me. Just before the bridge he paused for a moment and looked through the chain-link fence. 'He threw my leg in there,' he said, 'to the alligators. He made sure I was watching. He held it up so I could see it and then he threw it in and the water started to boil like . . .' I could hear a rising note of hysteria in his voice, but he heard it, too, and stopped, inhaled shakily, and said, somewhat roughly, 'All right. Let's get out of here.'

We made it back to the gate with no more side trips down memory lane, and Chutsky leaned on a fence post while I got the gate open. Then I hopped him around to the passenger seat, climbed in behind the wheel, and started the car. As the headlights flicked on, Chutsky leaned back in his seat and closed his eyes. 'Thanks, buddy,' he said. 'I owe you big-time. Thank you.'

'You're welcome,' I said. I turned the car around and headed back toward Alligator Alley. I thought Chutsky had fallen asleep, but halfway along the little dirt road he began to talk.

'I'm glad your sister wasn't here,' he said. 'To see me like this. It's – Listen, I really have to pull myself together before – ' He stopped abruptly and didn't say anything for half a minute. We bumped along the dark road in silence. The quiet was a pleasant change. I wondered where Doakes was and what he was doing. Or perhaps, what was being done to him. For that matter, I wondered where Reiker was and how soon I could take him somewhere else. Someplace quiet, where I could contemplate and work in peace. I wondered what the rent might be on the Blalock Gator Farm.

'Might be a good idea if I don't bother her anymore,' Chutsky said suddenly, and it took me a moment to realize he was still talking about Deborah. 'She's not going to want anything to do with me the way I am now, and I don't need anybody's pity.'

'Nothing to worry about,' I said. 'Deborah is completely without pity.'

'You tell her I'm fine, and I went back to Washington,' he said. 'It's better that way.'

'It might be better for you,' I said. 'But she'll kill me.'

'You don't understand,' he said.

'No, *you* don't understand. She told me to get you back. She's made up her mind and I don't dare disobey. She hits very hard.'

He was silent for a while. Then I heard him sigh heavily. 'I just don't know if I can do this,' he said.

'I could take you back to the gator farm,' I said cheerfully.

He didn't say anything after that, and I pulled onto Alligator Alley, made the first U-turn, and headed back toward the orange glow of light on the horizon that was Miami.

26

We rode in silence all the way back to the first real clump of civilization, a housing development and a row of strip malls on the right, a few miles past the toll booth. Then Chutsky sat up and stared out at the lights and the buildings. 'I have to use a phone,' he said.

'You can use my phone, if you'll pay the roaming charges,' I said.

'I need a land line,' he said. 'A pay phone.'

'You're out of touch with the times,' I said. 'A pay phone might be a little hard to find. Nobody uses them anymore.'

'Take this exit here,' he said, and although it was not getting me any closer to my well-earned good night's sleep, I drove down the off-ramp. Within a mile we found a mini-mart that still had a pay phone stuck to the wall beside the front door. I helped Chutsky hop over to the phone and he leaned up against the shield around it and lifted the receiver. He glanced at me and said, 'Wait over there,' which seemed a little bit bossy for somebody who couldn't even walk unassisted, but I went back to my car and sat on the hood while Chutsky chatted.

An ancient Buick chugged into the parking spot next to me. A group of short, dark-skinned men in dirty clothes got out and walked toward the store. They stared at Chutsky standing there on one leg with his head so very shaved, but they were too polite to say anything. They went in and the glass door whooshed behind them and I felt the long day rolling over me; I was tired, my neck muscles felt stiff, and I hadn't gotten to kill anything. I felt very cranky, and I wanted to go home and go to bed.

I wondered where Dr. Danco had taken Doakes. It didn't really seem important, just idle curiosity. But as I thought about the fact that he had indeed taken him somewhere and would soon begin doing rather permanent things to the sergeant, I realized that this was the first good news I'd had in a long time, and I felt a warm glow spread through me. I was free. Doakes was gone. One small piece at a time he was leaving my life and releasing me from the involuntary servitude of Rita's couch. I could live again.

'Hey, buddy,' Chutsky called. He waved the stump of his left arm at me and I stood up and walked over to him. 'All right,' he said. 'Let's get going.'

'Of course,' I said. 'Going where?'

He looked off in the distance and I could see the muscles along the side of his jaw tighten. The security lights of the mini-mart's parking lot lit up his coveralls and gleamed off his head. It's amazing how different a face looks if you shave off the eyebrows. There's something freakish to it, like the makeup in a low-budget science-fiction movie, and so even though Chutsky should have looked tough and decisive as he stared at the horizon and clenched his jaw, he instead looked like he was waiting for a blood-curdling command from Ming the Merciless. But he just said, 'Take me back to my hotel, buddy. I got work to do.'

'What about a hospital?' I asked, thinking that he couldn't be expected to cut a walking stick from a sturdy yew tree and stump on down the trail. But he shook his head.

'I'm okay,' he said. 'I'll be okay.'

I looked pointedly at the two patches of white gauze where his arm and leg used to be and raised an eyebrow. After all, the wounds were still fresh enough to be bandaged, and at the very least Chutsky had to be feeling somewhat weak.

He looked down at his two stumps, and he did seem to slump just a little and become slightly smaller for a moment. 'I'll be fine,' he said, and he straightened up a bit. 'Let's get going.' And he seemed so tired and sad that I didn't have the heart to say anything except, 'All right.'

He hopped back to the passenger door of my car, leaning on my shoulder, and as I helped ease him into the seat the passengers of the old Buick trooped out carrying beer and pork rinds. The driver smiled and nodded at me. I smiled back and closed the door. 'Crocodilios,' I said, nodding at Chutsky.

'Ah,' the driver said back. 'Lo siento.' He got behind the wheel of his car, and I walked around to get into mine.

Chutsky had nothing at all to say for most of the drive. Right after the interchange onto I-95, however, he began to tremble badly. 'Oh fuck,' he said. I looked over at him. 'The drugs,' he said. 'Wearing off.' His teeth began to chatter and he snapped them shut. His breath hissed out and I could see sweat begin to form on his bald face.

'Would you like to reconsider the hospital?' I asked.

'Do you have anything to drink?' he asked, a rather abrupt change of subject, I thought.

'I think there's a bottle of water in the backseat,' I said helpfully.

'Drink,' he repeated. 'Some vodka, or whiskey.'

'I don't generally keep any in the car,' I said.

'Fuck,' he said. 'Just get me to my hotel.'

I did that. For reasons known only to Chutsky, he was staying at the Mutiny in Coconut Grove. It had been one of the first luxury high-rise hotels in the area and had once been frequented by models, directors, drug runners, and other celebrities. It was still very nice, but it had lost a little bit of its cachet as the once-rustic Grove became overrun with luxury high-rises. Perhaps Chutsky had known it in its heyday and stayed there now for sentimental reasons. You really had to be deeply suspicious of sentimentality in a man who had worn a pinkie ring.

We came down off 95 onto Dixie Highway, and I turned left on Unity and rolled on down to Bayshore. The Mutiny was a little ways ahead on the right, and I pulled up in front of the hotel. 'Just drop me here,' Chutsky said.

I stared at him. Perhaps the drugs had affected his mind. 'Don't you want me to help you up to your room?'

'I'll be fine,' he said. That may have been his new mantra, but he didn't look fine. He was sweating heavily now and I could not imagine how he thought he would get up to his room. But I am not the kind of person who would ever intrude with unwanted help, so I simply said, 'All right,' and watched as he opened the door and got out. He held on to the roof of the car and stood unsteadily on his one leg for a minute before the bell captain saw him swaying there. The captain frowned at this apparition with the orange jumpsuit and the gleaming skull. 'Hey, Benny,' Chutsky said. 'Gimme a hand, buddy.'

'Mr. Chutsky?' he said dubiously, and then his jaw dropped as he noticed the missing parts. 'Oh, Lord,' he said. He clapped his hands three times and a bellboy ran out.

Chutsky looked back at me. 'I'll be fine,' he said.

And really, when you're not wanted there's not much you can do except leave, which is what I did. The last I saw of Chutsky he was leaning on the bell captain as the bellboy pushed a wheelchair toward them out the front door of the hotel.

It was still a little bit shy of midnight as I drove down Main Highway and headed for home, which was hard to believe considering all that had happened tonight. Vince's party seemed like several weeks ago, and yet he probably hadn't even unplugged his fruit-punch fountain yet. Between my Trial by Stripper and rescuing Chutsky from the gator farm, I had earned my rest tonight, and I admit that I was thinking of little else except crawling into my bed and pulling the covers over my head.

But of course, there's no rest for the wicked, which I certainly am. My cell phone rang as I turned left on Douglas. Very few people call me, especially this late at night. I glanced at the phone; it was Deborah.

'Greetings, sister dear,' I said.

'You asshole, you said you'd call!' she said.

'It seemed a little late,' I said.

'Did you really think I could fucking SLEEP?!' she yelled, loud enough to cause pain to people in passing cars. 'What happened?'

'I got Chutsky back,' I said. 'But Dr. Danco got away. With Doakes.'

'Where is he?'

'I don't know, Debs, he got away in an airboat and—'

'Kyle, you idiot. Where is Kyle? Is he all right?'

'I dropped him at the Mutiny. He's, um . . . He's almost all right,' I said.

'What the fuck does that mean?!?' she screamed at me, and I had to switch my phone to the other ear.

'Deborah, he's going to be okay. He's just – he lost half of his left arm and half the right leg. And all his hair,' I said. She was quiet for several seconds.

'Bring me some clothes,' she said at last.

'He's feeling very uncertain, Debs. I don't think he wants—'

'Clothes, Dexter. Now,' she said, and she hung up.

As I said, no rest for the wicked. I sighed heavily at the injustice of it all, but I obeyed. I was almost back to my apartment, and Deborah had left some things there. So I ran in and, although I paused to look longingly at my bed, I gathered a change of clothing for her and headed for the hospital.

Deborah was sitting on the edge of her bed tapping her feet impatiently when I came in. She held her hospital gown closed with the hand that protruded from her cast, and clutched her gun and badge with the other. She looked like Avenging Fury after an accident.

'Jesus Christ,' she said, 'where the hell have you been? Help me get dressed.' She dropped her gown and stood up.

I pulled a polo shirt over her head, working it awkwardly around the cast. We just barely had the shirt in place when a stout woman in a nurse's uniform hurried into the room. 'What you think you're doing?' she said in a thick Bahamian accent.

'Leaving,' Deborah said.

'Get back in that bed or I will call doctor,' the nurse said.

'Call him,' Deborah said, now hopping on one foot as she struggled into her pants.

'No you don't,' the nurse said. 'You get back in the bed.'

Deborah held up her shield. 'This is a police emergency,' she said. 'If you impede me I am authorized to arrest you for obstruction of justice.'

The nurse thought she was going to say something very severe, but she opened her mouth, looked at the shield, looked at Deborah, and changed her mind. 'I will have to tell doctor,' she said.

'Whatever,' Deborah said. 'Dexter, help me close my pants.' The nurse watched disapprovingly for another few seconds, then turned and whisked away down the hall.

'Really, Debs,' I said. 'Obstruction of justice?'

'Let's go,' she said, and marched out the door. I trailed dutifully behind.

Deborah was alternately tense and angry on the drive back over to the Mutiny. She would chew on her lower lip, and then snarl at me to hurry up, and then as we came close to the hotel, she got very quiet. She finally looked out her window and said, 'What's he like, Dex? How bad is it?'

'It's a very bad haircut, Debs. It makes him look pretty weird. But the other stuff . . . He seems to be adjusting. He just doesn't want you to feel sorry for him.' She looked at me, again chewing her lip. 'That's what he said,' I told her. 'He wanted to go back to Washington rather than put up with your pity.'

'He doesn't want to be a burden,' she said. 'I know him. He has to pay his own way.' She looked back out the window again. 'I can't even imagine what it was like. For a man like Kyle to lie there so helpless as— ' She shook her head slowly, and a single tear rolled down her cheek.

Truthfully, I could imagine very well what it had been like, and I had done so many times already. What I was having difficulty with was this new side of Deborah. She had cried at her mother's funeral, and at her father's, but not since then, as far as I knew. And now here she was practically flooding the car over what I had come to regard as an infatuation with someone who was a little bit of an oaf. Even worse, he was now a disabled oaf, which should mean that a logical person would move on and find somebody else with all the proper pieces still attached. But Deborah seemed even more concerned with Chutsky now that he was permanently damaged. Could this be love after all? Deborah in love? It didn't seem possible. I knew that theoretically she was capable of it, of course, but – I mean, after all, she was my sister.

It was pointless to wonder. I knew nothing at all about love and I never would. It didn't seem like such a terrible lack to me, although it does make it difficult to understand popular music.

Since there was nothing else I could possibly say about it, I changed the subject. 'Should I call Captain Matthews and tell him that Doakes is gone?' I said.

Deborah wiped a tear off her cheek with one fingertip and shook her head. 'That's for Kyle to decide,' she said.

'Yes, of course, but Deborah, under the circumstances— '

She slammed a fist onto her leg, which seemed pointless as well as painful. 'GodDAMN it, Dexter, I won't lose him!'

Every now and then I feel like I am only receiving one track of a stereo recording, and this was one such time. I had no idea what – well, to be honest, I didn't even have an idea what to have an idea about. What did she mean? What did it have to do with what I had said, and why had she reacted so violently? And how can so many fat women think they look good in a belly shirt?

I suppose some of my confusion must have showed on my face, because Deborah unclenched her fist and took a deep breath. 'Kyle is going to need to stay focused, keep working. He needs to be in charge, or this will finish him.'

'How can you know that?'

She shook her head. 'He's always been the best at what he does. That's his whole – it's who he is. If he gets to thinking about what Danco did to him— ' She bit her lip and another tear rolled down her cheek. 'He has to stay who he is, Dexter. Or I'll lose him.'

'All right,' I said.

'I can't lose him, Dexter,' she said again.

There was a different doorman on duty at the Mutiny, but he seemed to recognize Deborah and simply nodded as he held the door open for us. We walked silently to the elevator and rode up to the twelfth floor.

I have lived in Coconut Grove my entire life, so I knew very well from gushing newspaper accounts that Chutsky's room was done in British Colonial. I never understood why, but the hotel had decided that British Colonial was the perfect setting to convey the ambience of Coconut Grove, although as far as I knew there had never been a British colony here. So the entire hotel was done in British Colonial. But I find it hard to believe that either the interior decorator or any Colonial British had ever pictured something like Chutsky flopped onto the king size bed of the penthouse suite Deborah led me to.

His hair had not grown back in the last hour, but he had at least changed out of the orange coverall and into a white terry-cloth robe and he was lying there in the middle of the bed shaved, shaking, and sweating heavily with a half-empty bottle of Skyy Vodka lying beside him. Deborah didn't even slow down at the door. She charged right over to the bed and sat beside him, taking his only hand in her only hand. Love among the ruins.

'Debbie?' he said in a quavery old-man voice.

'I'm here now,' she said. 'Go to sleep.'

'I guess I'm not as good as I thought I was,' he said.

'Sleep,' she said, holding his hand and settling down next to him.

I left them like that.

27

I slept late the next day. after all, hadn't I earned it? And although I arrived at work around ten o'clock, I was still there well before Vince, Camilla, or Angel-no-relation, who had apparently all called in deathly ill. One hour and forty-five minutes later Vince finally came in, looking green and very old. 'Vince!' I said with great good cheer and he flinched and leaned against the wall with his eyes closed. 'I want to thank you for an epic party.'

'Thank me quietly,' he croaked.

'Thank you,' I whispered.

'You're welcome,' he whispered back, and staggered softly away to his cubicle.

It was an unusually quiet day, by which I mean that, besides the lack of new cases, the forensics area was silent as a tomb, with the occasional pale-green ghost floating by suffering silently. Luckily there was also very little work to do. By five o'clock I had caught up on my paperwork and arranged all my pencils. Rita had called at lunchtime to ask me to come for dinner. I think she might have wanted to make sure I had not been kidnapped by a stripper, so I agreed to come after work. I did not hear from Debs, but I did-n't really need to. I was quite sure she was with Chutsky in his penthouse. But I was a little bit concerned, since Dr. Danco knew where to find them and might come looking for his missing project. On the other hand, he had Sergeant Doakes to play with, which should keep him busy and happy for several days.

Still, just to be safe, I called Deborah's cell phone number. She answered on the fourth ring. 'What,' she said.

'You do remember that Dr. Danco had no trouble getting in there the first time,' I said.

'*I* wasn't here the first time,' she said. And she sounded so very fierce that I had to hope she wouldn't shoot someone from room service.

'All right,' I said. 'Just keep your eyes open.'

'Don't worry,' she said. I heard Chutsky muttering something cranky in the background, and Deborah said, 'I have to go. I'll call you later.' She hung up.

Evening rush hour was in full swing as I headed south to Rita's house, and

I found myself humming cheerfully as a red-faced man in a pickup truck cut me off and gave me the finger. It was not just the ordinary feeling of belonging I got from being surrounded by the homicidal Miami traffic, either; I felt like a great burden had been removed from my shoulders. And, of course, it had been. I could go to Rita's and there would be no maroon Taurus parked across the street. I could go back to my apartment, free of my clinging shadow. And even more important, I could take the Dark Passenger out for a spin and we would be alone together for some badly needed quality time. Sergeant Doakes was gone, out of my life – and soon, presumably, out of his own life, too.

I felt absolutely giddy as I wheeled down South Dixie and made the turn to Rita's house. I was free – and free of obligation, too, since one really had to believe that Chutsky and Deborah would stay put to recuperate for a while. As for Dr. Danco – it is true that I had felt a certain twinge of interest in meeting him, and even now I would gladly take a few moments out of my busy social schedule for some real quality bonding time with him. But I was quite sure that Chutsky's mysterious Washington agency would send someone else to deal with him, and they would certainly not want me hovering around and offering advice. With that ruled out, and with Doakes out of the picture, I was back to plan A and free to assist Reiker into early retirement. Whoever would now have to deal with the problem of Dr. Danco, it would not be Delightfully Discharged Dexter.

I was so happy that I kissed Rita when she answered the door, even though no one was watching. And after dinner, while Rita cleaned up, I went out into the backyard once again, playing kick the can with the neighborhood children. This time, though, there was a special edge to it with Cody and Astor, our own small secret adding a touch more zest. It was almost fun to watch them stalking the other children, my own little predators in training.

After half an hour of stalking and pouncing, however, it became apparent that we were severely outnumbered by even stealthier predators – mosquitoes, several billion of the disgusting little vampires, all ravenously hungry. And so, weak from loss of blood, Cody, Astor, and I staggered back into the house and reconvened around the dining table for a session of hangman.

'I'll go first,' Astor announced. 'It's my turn anyway.'

'Mine,' said Cody, frowning.

'Nuh-uh. Anyway, I got one,' she told him. 'Five letters.'

'C,' said Cody.

'No! Head! Ha!' she howled in triumph, and drew the little round head.

'You should ask the vowels first,' I said to Cody.

'What,' he said softly.

'A, E, I, O, U, and sometimes Y,' Astor told him. 'Everybody knows that.'

'Is there an E?' I asked her, and some of the wind went out of her sails.

'Yes,' Astor said, sulkily, and she wrote the E on the middle blank line.

'Ha,' said Cody.

We played for almost an hour before their bedtime. All too soon my magical evening drew to a close and I was once again on the couch with Rita. But this time, free as I was from spying eyes, it was an easy matter for me to disengage myself from her tentacles and head for home, and my own little bed, with well-meaning excuses of having partied too hard at Vince's and a big day of work tomorrow. And then I was off, all alone in the night, just my echo, my shadow, and me. It was two nights until the full moon, and I would make this one well worth my wait. This full moon I would spend not with Miller Lite but with Reiker Photography, Inc. In two nights I would turn loose the Passenger at last, slide into my true self, and fling the sweat-stained costume of Dearly Devoted Dexter into the garbage heap.

Of course I needed to find proof first, but somehow I was quite confident that I would. After all, I had a whole day for that, and when the Dark Passenger and I work together everything seems to fall right into place.

And filled with such cheerful thoughts of dark delights I motored back to my comfy apartment, and climbed into bed to sleep the deep and dreamless sleep of the just.

The next morning my offensively cheerful mood continued. When I stopped for doughnuts on the way to work I gave in to impulse and bought a full dozen, including several of the cream-filled ones with chocolate icing, a truly extravagant gesture that was not lost on Vince, who had finally recovered. 'Oh, my,' he said with raised eyebrows. 'You have done well, O mighty hunter.'

'The gods of the forest have smiled upon us,' I said. 'Cream-filled or raspberry jelly?'

'Cream-filled, of course,' he said.

The day passed quickly, with only one trip out to a homicide scene, a routine dismemberment with garden equipment. It was strictly amateur work; the idiot had tried to use an electric hedge clipper and succeeded only in making a great deal of extra work for me, before finishing off his wife with the pruning shears. A truly nasty mess, and it served him right that they caught him at the airport. A well-done dismemberment is *neat*, above all, or so I always say. None of this puddled blood and caked flesh on the walls. It shows a real lack of class.

I finished up at the scene just in time to get back to my little cubbyhole off the forensics lab and leave my notes on my desk. I would type them up and finish the report on Monday, no hurry. Neither the killer nor the victim was going anywhere.

And so there I was, out the door to the parking lot and into my car, free to roam the land as I pleased. No one to follow me or feed me beer or force me to do things I would rather avoid. No one to shine the unwanted light into Dexter's shadows. I could be me again, Dexter Unchained, and the thought was far more intoxicating than all Rita's beer and sympathy. It had been too long since I felt this way, and I promised myself I would never again take it for granted.

A car was on fire at the corner of Douglas and Grand, and a small but enthusiastic crowd had gathered to watch. I shared their good cheer as I eased through the traffic jam caused by the emergency vehicles and headed for home.

At home I sent out for a pizza and made some careful notes on Reiker; where to look for proof, what sort of thing would be enough – a pair of red cowboy boots would certainly be a good start. I was very nearly certain that he was the one; pedophile predators tend to find ways to combine business and pleasure, and child photography was a perfect example. But 'very nearly' was not certain enough. And so I organized my thoughts into a neat little file – nothing incriminating, of course, and it would all be carefully destroyed before showtime. By Monday morning there would be no hint at all of what I had done except a new glass slide in the box on my shelf. I spent a happy hour planning and eating a large pizza with anchovies and then, as the nearly full moon began to mutter through the window, I got restless. I could feel the icy fingers of moonlight stroking me, tickling at my spine, urging me into the night to stretch the predator's muscles that had been dormant for too long.

And why not? It would do no harm to slide out into the chuckling evening and steal a look or two. To stalk, to watch unseen, to cat-foot down Reiker's game trails and sniff the wind — it would be prudent as well as fun. Dark Scout Dexter must Be Prepared. Besides, it was Friday night. Reiker might very well leave the house for some social activity — a visit to the toy store, for instance. If he was out, I could slip into his house and look around.

And so I dressed in my best dark nightstalker clothes and took the short drive from my apartment, up Main Highway and through the Grove to Tiger-tail Avenue and down to the modest house where Reiker lived. It was in a neighborhood of small concrete-block houses and his seemed no different from all the others, set back from the road just far enough for a short drive-way. His car was parked there, a little red Kia, which gave me a surge of hope. Red, like the boots; it was his color, a sign that I was on track.

I drove by the house twice. On my second pass the dome light in his car was on and I was just in time to catch a glimpse of his face as he climbed into the car. It was not a very impressive face: thin, nearly chinless, and partly hidden by long bangs and large-frame glasses. I could not see what he was wearing on his feet, but from what I could see of the rest of him he might well wear cowboy boots to make himself seem a little taller. He got into the car and closed the door, and I went on by and around the block.

When I came by again, his car was gone. I parked a few blocks away on a small side street and went back, slowly slipping into my night skin as I walked. The lights were all out at a neighbor's house and I cut through the yard. There was a small guesthouse behind Reiker's place, and the Dark Passenger whispered in my inner ear, *studio*. It was indeed a perfect place for a photographer to set up, and a studio was exactly the right kind of place to find incriminating photographs. Since the Passenger is seldom wrong about these things, I picked the lock and went in.

The windows were all boarded over on the inside, but in the dimness from the open door I could see the outline of darkroom equipment. The Passenger had been right. I closed the door and flipped up the light switch. A murky red light flooded the room, just enough to see by. There were the usual trays and bottles of chemicals over by a small sink, and to the left of that a very nice computer workstation with digital equipment. A four-drawer filing cabinet stood against the far wall and I decided to start there.

After ten minutes of flipping through pictures and negatives, I had found nothing more incriminating than a few dozen photos of naked babies posed on a white fur rug, pictures that would generally be regarded as 'cute' even by people who think Pat Robertson is too liberal. There were no hidden compartments in the filing cabinet as far as I could tell, and no other obvious place to hide pictures.

Time was short; I could not take the chance that Reiker had simply gone to the store to buy a quart of milk. He might come back at any minute and decide to poke through his files and gaze fondly at the dozens of dear little pixies he had captured on film. I moved to the computer area.

Next to the monitor there was a tall CD rack and I went through the disks one at a time. After a handful of program disks and others hand-lettered GREENFIELD or LOPEZ, I found it.

'It' was a bright pink jewel case. Across the front of the case in very neat letters it said, NAMBLA 9/04.

It may well be that NAMBLA is a rare Hispanic name. But it also stands for North American Man/Boy Love Association, a warm and fuzzy support group that helps pedophiles maintain a positive self-image by assuring them that what they do is perfectly natural. Well, of course it is — so are cannibalism and rape, but really. One mustn't.

I took the CD with me, turned out the light, and slid back into the night.

Back at my apartment it took only a few minutes to discover that the disk was a sales tool, presumably carried to a NAMBLA gathering of some kind and offered around to a select list of discriminating ogres. The pictures on it were arranged in what are called 'thumbnail galleries,' miniature series of shots almost like the picture decks that Victorian dirty old men used to flip through. Each picture had been strategically blurred so you could imagine but not quite see the details.

And oh, yes: several of the shots were professionally cropped and edited versions of the ones I had discovered on MacGregor's boat. So while I had not actually found the red cowboy boots, I had found quite enough to satisfy the Harry Code. Reiker had made the A-list. With a song in my heart and a smile on my lips, I trundled off to bed, thinking happy thoughts about what Reiker and I would be doing tomorrow night.

The next morning, Saturday, I got up a little late and went for a run through my neighborhood. After a shower and a hearty breakfast I went shopping for a few essentials — a new roll of duct tape, a razor-sharp fillet knife, just the basic necessities. And because the Dark Passenger was flexing and stretching to wakefulness, I stopped at a steak house for a late lunch. I ate a sixteen-ounce New York strip, well done of course, so there was absolutely no blood. Then I drove by Reiker's one more time to see the place again in daylight. Reiker himself was mowing his lawn. I slowed for a casual look; alas, he was wearing old sneakers, not red boots. He was shirtless and on top of scrawny, he looked flabby and pale. No matter: I would put a little color into him soon enough.

It was a very satisfying and productive day, my Day Before. And I was sitting quietly back in my apartment wrapped in my virtuous thoughts when the telephone rang.

'Good afternoon,' I said into the receiver.

'Can you get over here?' Deborah said. 'We have some work to finish up.'

'What sort of work?'

'Don't be a jerk,' she said. 'Come on over,' and she hung up. This was more than a little bit irritating. In the first place, I didn't know of any kind of unfinished work, and in the second, I was not aware of being a jerk — a monster, yes, certainly, but on the whole a very pleasant and well-mannered monster. And to top it all off, the way she hung up like that, simply assuming I had heard and would tremble and obey. The nerve of her. Sister or not, vicious arm punch or no, I trembled for no one.

I did, however, obey. The short drive to the Mutiny took longer than usual, this being Saturday afternoon, a time when the streets in the Grove flood with aimless people. I wove slowly through the crowd, wishing for once that I could simply pin the gas pedal to the floorboard and smash into the wandering horde. Deborah had spoiled my perfect mood.

She didn't make it any better when I knocked on the penthouse door at the Mutiny and she opened it with her on-duty-in-a-crisis face, the one that made her look like a bad-tempered fish. 'Get in here,' she said.

'Yes master,' I said.

Chutsky was sitting on the sofa. He still didn't look British Colonial — maybe it was the lack of eyebrows — but he did at least look like he had decided to live, so apparently Deborah's rebuilding project was going well. There was a metal crutch leaning against the wall beside him, and he was sipping coffee. A platter of Danish sat on the end table next to him. 'Hey, buddy,' he called out, waving his stump. 'Grab a chair.'

I took a British Colonial chair and sat, after snagging a couple of Danish as well. Chutsky looked at me like he was going to object, but really, it was the very least they could do for me. After all, I had waded through flesh-eating alligators and an attack peacock to rescue him, and now here I was giving up my Saturday for who-knows-what kind of awful chore. I deserved an entire cake.

'All right,' Chutsky said. 'We have to figure where Henker is hiding, and we have to do it fast.'

'Who?' I asked. 'You mean Dr. Danco?'

'That's his name, yeah. Henker,' he said. 'Martin Henker.'

'And we have to *find* him?' I asked, filled with a sense of ominous foreboding. I mean, why were they looking at me and saying 'we'?

Chutsky gave a small snort as if he thought I was joking and he got it. 'Yeah, that's right,' he said. 'So where are you thinking he might be, buddy?'

'Actually, I'm not thinking about it at all,' I said.

'Dexter,' Deborah said with a warning tone in her voice.

Chutsky frowned. It was a very strange expression without eyebrows. 'What do you mean?' he said.

'I mean, I don't see why it's my problem anymore. I don't see why I or even *we* have to find him. He got what he wanted — won't he just finish up and go home?'

'Is he kidding?' Chutsky asked Deborah, and if he'd only had eyebrows they would have been raised.

'He doesn't like Doakes,' Deborah said.

'Yeah, but listen, Doakes is one of our guys,' Chutsky said to me.

'Not one of mine,' I said.

Chutsky shook his head. 'All right, that's your problem,' he said. 'But we still have to find this guy. There's a political side to this whole thing, and it's deep doo-doo if we don't collar him.'

'Okay,' I said. 'But why is it my problem?' And it seemed like a very reasonable question to me, although to see his reaction you would have thought I wanted to fire bomb an elementary school.

'Jesus Christ,' he said, and he shook his head in mock admiration. 'You really are a piece of work, buddy.'

'Dexter,' Deborah said. 'Look at us.' I did look, at Deb in her cast and Chutsky with his twin stumps. To be honest, they did not look terribly fierce. 'We need your help,' she said.

'But Debs, really.'

'Please, Dexter,' she said, knowing full well that I found it very hard to refuse her when she used that word.

'Debs, come on,' I said. 'You need an action hero, somebody who can kick down the door and storm in with guns blazing. I'm just a mild-mannered forensics geek.'

She crossed the room and stood in front of me, inches away. 'I know what you are, Dexter,' she said softly. 'Remember? And I know you can do this.' She put her hand on my shoulder and lowered her voice even farther, almost whispering. 'Kyle *needs* this, Dex. Needs to catch Danco. Or he'll never feel like a man again. That's important to me. Please, Dexter?'

And after all, what can you do when the big guns come out? Except summon your reserves of goodwill and wave the white flag gracefully.

'All right, Debs,' I said.

Freedom is such a fragile, fleeting thing, isn't it?

28

However reluctant I had been, I had given my word to help, and so poor Dutiful Dexter instantly attacked the problem with all the resourceful cunning of his powerful brain. But the sad truth was that my brain seemed to be off-line; no matter how diligently I typed in clues, nothing dropped into the out-box.

Of course it was possible that I needed more fuel to function at the highest possible level, so I wheedled Deborah into sending down for more Danish. While she was on the phone with room service Chutsky focused a sweaty, slightly glazed smile on me and said, 'Let's get to it, okay, buddy?' Since he asked so nicely — and after all, I had to do something while I waited for the Danish — I agreed.

The loss of his two limbs had removed some kind of psychic lock from Chutsky. In spite of being just a little bit shaky, he was far more open and friendly, and actually seemed eager to share information in a way that would have been unthinkable to the Chutsky with four complete limbs and a pair of expensive sunglasses. And so out of what was really no more than an urge to be tidy and know as many details as possible, I took advantage of his new good cheer by getting the names of the El Salvador team from him.

He sat with a yellow legal pad balanced precariously on his knee, holding it still with his wrist while he scrawled the names with his right, and only, hand. 'Manny Borges you know about,' he said.

'The first victim,' I said.

'Uh-huh,' Chutsky said without looking up. He wrote the name and then drew a line through it. 'And then there was Frank Aubrey?' He frowned and actually stuck the tip of his tongue out of the corner of his mouth as he wrote and then crossed out. 'He missed Oscar Acosta. God knows where he is now.' He wrote the name anyway and put a question mark beside it. 'Wendell Ingraham. Lives on North Shore Drive, out on Miami Beach.' The pad slipped to the floor as he wrote the name, and he grabbed at it as it fell, missing badly. He stared at the pad where it lay for a moment, then leaned over and retrieved it. A drop of sweat rolled off his hairless head and onto the floor. 'Fucking drugs,' he said. 'Got me a little woozy.'

'Wendell Ingraham,' I said.

'Right. Right.' He scribbled the rest of the name and without pausing went on with, 'Andy Lyle. Sells cars now, up in Davie.' And in a furious burst of energy he went right on and triumphantly scrawled the last name. 'Two other guys dead, one guy still in the field, that's it, the whole team.'

'Don't any of these guys know Danco is in town?'

He shook his head. Another drop of sweat flew off and narrowly missed me. 'We're keeping a pretty tight lid on this thing. Need-to-know only.'

'They don't need to know that somebody wants to convert them to squealing pillows?'

'No, they don't,' he said, clamping his jaw and looking like he was going to say something tough again; perhaps he would offer to flush them. But he glanced up at me and thought better of it.

'Can we at least check and see which one is missing?' I asked, without any real hope.

Chutsky started shaking his head before I even finished speaking. Two more drops of sweat flew off, left, right. 'No. Uh-uh, no way. These guys always have an ear to the ground. Somebody starts asking around about them, they'll know. And I can't risk having them run. Like Oscar did.'

'Then how do we find Dr. Danco?'

'That's what you're going to figure out,' he said.

'What about the house by Mount Trashmore?' I asked hopefully. 'The one you checked out with the clipboard.'

'Debbie had a patrol car drive by. Family has moved in. No,' he said, 'we're putting all our chips on you, buddy. You'll think of something.'

Debs rejoined us before I could think of anything meaningful to say to that, but in truth, I was too surprised at Chutsky's official attitude toward his former comrades. Wouldn't it have been the nice thing to do, to give his old friends a running start or at least a heads-up? I certainly don't pretend to be a paragon of civilized virtue, but if a deranged surgeon was after Vince Masuoka, for instance, I like to think I might find a way to drop a hint into casual conversation by the coffee machine. Pass that sugar, please. By the way — there's a medical maniac after you who wants to lop off all your limbs. Would you like the creamer?

But apparently that wasn't the way the game was played by the guys with the big manly chins, or at least not by their representative Kyle Chutsky. No matter; I had a list of names, at least, which was a place to start, although nothing else. I had no idea where to begin turning my starting point into some kind of actual helpful information, and Kyle did not seem to be doing quite as well with creativity as he had done with sharing. Deborah was little help. She was totally wrapped up in fluffing Kyle's pillow, mopping his fevered brow, and making sure he took his pills, a matronly kind of behavior that I would have thought impossible for her, but there it was.

It became apparent that little real work would be accomplished here in the hotel penthouse. The only thing I could suggest was that I return to my computer and see what I could turn up. And so after prying two final Danish out of Kyle's remaining hand I headed for home and my trusty computer. There were no guarantees that I would come up with anything, but I was committed to trying. I would give it my best effort, poke around at the problem for a few hours and hope that someone might wrap a secret message around a rock and throw it through my window. Perhaps if the rock hit me on the head, it would jar loose some kind of idea.

My apartment was just as I'd left it, which was comforting. The bed was even made, since Deborah was no longer in residence. I soon had my computer humming and began to search. I checked the real estate database first, but there were no new purchases that fit the pattern of the others. Still, it was obvious that Dr. Danco had to be somewhere. We had run him out of his prepared hidey-holes and yet I was quite sure that he would not wait to begin on Doakes and whoever else from Chutsky's list might have caught his attention.

How did he decide the order of his victims anyway? By seniority? By how much they pissed him off? Or was it random? If I knew that, it was at least possible that I could find him. He had to go somewhere, and his operations were not the sort of thing one would do in a hotel room. So where would he go?

It was not a rock crashing through the window and bouncing off my head after all, but a very small idea began to trickle onto the floor of Dexter's brain. Danco had to go somewhere to work on Doakes, obviously, and he couldn't wait to set up another safe house. Wherever he went had to be in the Miami area, close to his victims, and he could not afford to risk all the variables of grabbing a place at random. A seemingly empty house might suddenly be overrun by prospective buyers, and if he snatched an occupied place he could not know when Cousin Enrico might drop in for a visit. So — why not simply use the home of his next victim? He had to believe that Chutsky, the only one who knew the list until now, was out of action for a while and would not pursue him. By moving in on the next name on the list he could amputate two limbs with one scalpel, as it were, by using his next victim's house to finish Doakes and then make a leisurely start on the happy homeowner.

It made a certain amount of sense and was a more definite starting point than the list of names. But even if I was right, which of the men would be next?

The thunder rumbled outside. I looked again at the list of names and sighed. Why wasn't I somewhere else? Even playing hangman with Cody and Astor would be a big improvement over this kind of frustrating drudgery. I had to keep after Cody to find the vowels first. Then the rest of the word would start to swim into focus. And when he mastered that, I could start to teach him other, more interesting things. Very strange to have child instruction to look forward to, but I was actually kind of eager to begin. A shame he had already taken care of the neighbor's dog – it would have been a perfect place to start learning security as well as technique. The little scamp had so much to learn. All the old Harry lessons, passed on to a new generation.

And as I thought of helping Cody along, I realized that the price tag was accepting my engagement to Rita. Could I really go through with it? Fling away my carefree bachelor ways and settle into a life of domestic bliss? Oddly enough, I thought I might be able to pull it off. Certainly the kids were worth a little bit of sacrifice, and making Rita a permanent disguise would actually lower my profile. Happily married men are not as likely to do the kind of thing I live for.

Maybe I could go through with it. We would see. But of course, this was procrastination. It was getting me no closer to my evening out with Reiker, and no closer to finding Danco. I called my scattered senses back and looked at the list of names: Borges and Aubrey done. Acosta, Ingraham, and Lyle still to go. Still unaware that they had an appointment with Dr. Danco. Two down, three more to go, not including Doakes, who must be feeling the blade now, with Tito Puente playing his dance music in the background and the Doctor leaning over with his so-bright scalpel and leading the sergeant through his dance of dismemberment. Dance with me, Doakes. Baila conmigo, amigo, as Tito Puente would put it. A little bit harder to dance with no legs, of course, but well worth the effort.

And in the meantime, here I was dancing in circles just as surely as if the good Doctor had removed one of my legs.

All right: let's assume Dr. Danco was at the house of his current victim, not counting Doakes. Of course, I didn't know who that might be. So where did that leave me? When scientific inquiry was eliminated, that left lucky guess. Elementary, dear Dexter. Eeny meeny miney mo—

My finger landed on the notepad on Ingraham's name. Well then, that was definite, wasn't it? Sure it was. And I was King Olaf of Norway.

I got up and walked to the window where I had so many times peered out at Sergeant Doakes parked across the street in his maroon Taurus. He wasn't there. Soon he wouldn't actually be anywhere unless I found him. He wanted me dead or in prison, and I would be happier if he simply disappeared – one small piece at a time, or all at once, it made no difference. And yet here I was working overtime, pushing Dexter's mighty mental machinery through its awesome paces, in order to rescue him – so he could kill or imprison me. Is it any wonder I find the whole idea of life overrated?

Perhaps stirred by the irony, the almost-perfect moon snickered through the trees. And the longer I stared out, the more I felt the weight of that wicked old moon, sputtering softly just under the horizon and already puffing hot and cold at my spine, urging me into action, until I found myself picking up my car keys and heading for the door. After all, why not just go check it out? It would take no more than an hour, and I wouldn't have to explain my thinking to Debs and Chutsky.

I realized that the idea seemed appealing to me partly because it was quick and easy and if it paid off it would return me to my hard-won liberty in time for tomorrow night's playdate with Reiker – and even more, I was beginning to develop a small hankering for an appetizer. Why not warm up a little on Dr. Danco? Who could fault me for doing unto him what he oh-so-readily did unto others? If I had to save Doakes in order to get Danco, well, no one ever said life was perfect.

And so there I was, headed north on Dixie Highway and then up onto I-95, taking it all the way to the 79th Street Causeway and then straight over to the Normandy Shores area of Miami Beach, where Ingraham lived. It was night by the time I turned down the street and drove slowly past. A dark green van was parked in the driveway, very similar to the white one Danco had crashed only a few days ago. It was parked next to a newish Mercedes, and looked very much out of place in this tony neighborhood. Well, then, I thought. The Dark Passenger began to mutter words of encouragement but I kept going through the bend in the road past the house and on to a vacant lot before I stopped. Just around the corner I pulled over.

The green van did not belong there, judging by the type of neighborhood this was. Of course, it could be that Ingraham was having some plastering work done and the workers had decided to stay until the job was done. But I didn't think so, and neither did the Dark Passenger. I took out my cell phone to call Deborah.

'I may have found something,' I told her when she answered.

'What took you so long?' she said.

'I think Dr. Danco is working out of Ingraham's house on Miami Beach,' I said.

There was a short pause in which I could almost see her frown. 'Why do you think that?'

The idea of explaining to her that my guess was only a guess was not terribly appealing, so I just said, 'It's a long story, Sis. But I think I'm right.'

'You think,' she said. 'But you're not sure.'

'I will be in a few minutes,' I said. 'I'm parked around the corner from the house, and there's a van parked in front that looks a little out of place in this neighborhood.'

'Stay put,' she said. 'I'll call you back.' She hung up and left me looking at the house. It was an awkward angle to watch from and I could not really look without developing a severe knot in my neck. So I turned the car around and faced down the street toward the bend where the house sat sneering at me and as I did – there it was. Poking its bloated head through the trees, guttering bleary beams of light down onto the rancid landscape. That moon, that always laughing lighthouse of a moon. There it was.

I could feel the cold fingers of moonlight poking at me, prodding and teasing and urging me on to some foolish and wonderful something, and it had been so very long since I had listened that the sounds came twice as loud as ever, washing over my head and down my spine and in truth, what harm could it do to be absolutely sure before Deborah called back? Not to do anything stupid, of course, but just to ease out of the car and down the street past the house, just a casual stroll in the moonlight along a quiet street of houses. And if by chance the opportunity arose to play a few small games with the Doctor—

It was mildly upsetting to notice that my breath was slightly shaky as I climbed out of my car. Shame on you, Dexter. Where's that famous icy control? Perhaps it had slipped from being under wraps too long, and perhaps it was just that the same hiatus had made me a little too eager, but this would never do. I took a long, deep breath to steady myself and headed up the street, just a casual monster out for an evening stroll past an impromptu vivisection clinic. Hello, neighbor, beautiful night to remove a leg, isn't it?

With each step closer to the house I felt That Something growing taller and harder inside me, and at the same time the old cold fingers clamping down to hold it in place. I was fire and ice, alive with moonlight and death, and as I came even with the house the whispers inside began to well up as I heard the faint sounds from the house, a chorus of rhythm and saxophones that sounded very much like Tito Puente and I did not need the rising whispers to tell me that I was right, this was indeed the place where the Doctor had set up his clinic.

He was here, and he was at work.

And now, what did I do about that? Of course the wise thing to do would be to stroll back to my car and wait for Deborah's call – but was this really a night for wisdom, with that lyrically sneering moon so low in the sky and ice pouring through my veins and urging me onward?

And so when I had walked on past the house, I slipped into the shadows around the house next door and slid carefully through the backyard until I could see the back of Ingraham's house. There was a very bright light showing in the back window and I stalked into the yard in the shadow of a tree, closer and closer. A few more cat-footed steps and I could almost see in the window. I moved a little closer, just outside the line that light cast on the ground.

From where I now stood I could at last see in the window, upward at a slight angle, inside, to the ceiling of the room. And there was the mirror Danco seemed so fond of using, showing me half the table—

– and slightly more than half of Sergeant Doakes.

He was strapped securely in place, motionless, even his newly shaved head clamped tight to the table. I could not see too many details, but from what I could see, both his hands were gone at the wrist. The hands first? Very interesting, a totally different approach from the one he had used on Chutsky. How did Dr. Danco decide what was right for each individual patient?

I found myself increasingly intrigued by the man and his work; there was a quirky sense of humor in motion here and as silly as it is, I wanted to know just a little bit more about how it worked. I moved half a step closer.

The music paused and I paused with it, and then as the mambo beat picked up again I heard a metallic cough behind me and felt something flick my shoulder, stinging and tingling, and I turned around to see a small man with large, thick glasses looking at me. He was holding in his hand what looked like a paintball gun, and I just had time to feel indignant that it was aimed at me before somebody removed all the bones from my legs and I melted down into the dew-smeared moonlit grass where it was all dark and full of dreams.

29

I was cutting happily away at a very bad person who I had taped securely and strapped to a table but somehow the knife was made of rubber and only wobbled from side to side. I reached up and grabbed a giant bone saw instead and laid it into the alligator on the table, but the real joy would not come to me and instead there was pain and I saw that I was slicing away at my own arms. My wrists burned and bucked but I could not stop cutting and then I hit an artery and the awful red spewed out everywhere and blinded me with a scarlet mist and then I was falling, falling forever through the darkness of dim empty me where the awful shapes twisted and yammered and pulled at me until I fell through and hit the dreadful red puddle there on the floor beside where two hollow moons glared down at me and demanded: Open your eyes, you are awake—

And it all came back into focus on the two hollow moons that were actually the pair of thick lenses set in large black frames and wedged onto the face of a small, wiry man with a mustache who was bending over me with a syringe in his hand.

Dr. Danco, I presume?

I didn't think I had said it out loud, but he nodded and said, 'Yes, they called me that. And who are you?' His accent was slightly strained, as if he had to think a little too hard about each word. There was a trace of Cuban to it, but not like Spanish was his native tongue. For some reason his voice made me very unhappy, as if it had an odor of Dexter Repellant to it. But deep inside my lizard brain an old dinosaur lifted its head and roared back and so I did not cringe away from him as I had at first wanted to. I tried to shake my head, but found that very hard to do for some reason.

'Don't try to move yet,' he said. 'It won't work. But don't worry, you'll be able to see everything I do to your friend on the table. And soon enough it will be your turn. You can see yourself, then, in the mirror.' He blinked at me, and a light touch of whimsy came into his voice. 'It's a wonderful thing about mirrors. Did you know that if someone is standing outside the house looking into a mirror, you can see them from inside the house?'

He sounded like an elementary-school teacher explaining a joke to a student he was fond of, but who might be too dumb to get it. And I felt just dumb enough for that to make sense, because I had walked right into this with no thought deeper than, *Gee, that's interesting*. My own moon-driven impatience and curiosity had made me careless and he had seen me peeping in. Still, he was gloating, and that was annoying, so I felt compelled to say something, however feeble.

'Why yes, I knew that,' I said. 'And did you know that this house has a front door, too? And no peacocks on guard this time.'

He blinked. 'Should I be alarmed?' he said.

'Well, you never know who might come barging in uninvited.'

Dr. Danco moved the left corner of his mouth upward perhaps a quarter of an inch. 'Well,' he said, 'if your friend on the operating table is a fair sample, I think I may be all right, don't you?' And I had to admit that he had a point. The first-team players had not been impressive; what did he have to fear from the bench? If only I wasn't still a little dopey from whatever drugs he had used on me, I'm quite sure I would have said something far more clever, but in truth I was still in a little bit of a chemical fog.

'I do hope I'm not supposed to believe that help is on the way?' he said.

I was wondering the same thing, but it didn't seem entirely smart to say so. 'Believe what you like,' I said instead, hoping that was ambiguous enough to give him pause, and cursing the slowness of my normally swift mental powers.

'All right then,' he said. 'I believe you came here alone. Although I am curious about why.'

'I wanted to study your technique,' I said.

'Oh, good,' he said. 'I'll be happy to show you – firsthand.' He flickered his tiny little smile at me again and added, 'And then feet.' He waited for a moment, probably to see if I would laugh at his hilarious pun. I felt very sorry to disappoint him, but perhaps later it might seem funnier, if I got out of this alive.

Danco patted my arm and leaned in just a bit. 'We'll have to have your name, you know. No fun without it.'

I pictured him speaking to me by name as I lay strapped to the table, and it was not a cheerful image.

'Will you tell me your name?' he asked.

'Rumplestiltskin,' I said.

He stared at me, his eyes huge behind the thick lenses. Then he reached down to my hip pocket and worked my wallet out. He flipped it open and found my driver's license. 'Oh. So YOU'RE Dexter. Congratulations on your engagement.' He dropped my wallet beside me and patted my cheek. 'Watch and learn, because all too soon I will be doing the same things to you.'

'How wonderful for you,' I said.

Danco frowned at me. 'You really should be more frightened,' he said. 'Why aren't you?' He pursed his lips. 'Interesting. I'll increase the dosage next time.' And he stood up and moved away.

I lay in a dark corner next to a bucket and a broom and watched him bustle about the kitchen. He made himself a cup of instant Cuban coffee and stirred in a huge amount of sugar. Then he moved back to the center of the room and stared down at the table, sipping thoughtfully.

'Nahma,' the thing on the table that had once been Sergeant Doakes pleaded. 'Nahana. Nahma.' Of course his tongue had been removed – obvious symbology for the person Danco believed had squealed on him.

'Yes, I know,' Dr. Danco said. 'But you haven't guessed a single one yet.' He almost seemed to be smiling as he said that, although his face did not look like it was formed to make any expression beyond thoughtful interest. But it was enough to set Doakes off into a fit of yammering and trying to thrash his way out of his bonds. It didn't work very well, and didn't seem to concern Dr. Danco, who moved away sipping his coffee and humming along off-key to Tito Puente. As Doakes flopped about I could see that his right foot was gone, as well as his hands and tongue. Chutsky had said his entire lower leg had been removed all at once. The Doctor was obviously making this one last a little longer. And when it was my turn – how would he decide what to take and when?

Piece by small dim piece my brain was clearing itself of fog. I wondered how long I had been unconscious. It didn't seem like the kind of thing I could discuss with the Doctor.

The dosage, he had said. He had been holding a syringe as I woke up, been surprised that I was not more frightened – Of course. What a wonderful idea, to inject his patients with some kind of psychotropic drug to increase their sense of helpless terror. I wished I knew how to do that. Why hadn't I gotten medical training? But, of course, it was a little late to worry about that. And in any case, it sounded very much like the dosage was adjusted just right for Doakes.

'Well, Albert,' said the Doctor to the sergeant, in a very pleasant and conversational voice, slurping his coffee, 'what's your guess?'

'Nahana! Nah!'

'I don't think that's right,' said the Doctor. 'Although perhaps if you had a tongue, it might have been. Well, in any case,' he said, and he bent to the edge of the table and made a small mark on a piece of paper, almost like he was crossing something out. 'It is rather a long word,' he said. 'Nine letters. Still, you have to take the good with the bad, don't you?' And he put down his pencil and picked up a saw, and as Doakes bucked wildly against his bonds the Doctor sawed off Doakes's left foot, just above the ankle. He did it very quickly and neatly, placing the severed foot beside Doakes's head as he reached over to his array of instruments and picked up what looked a large soldering iron. He applied this to the new wound and a wet hiss of steam billowed up as he cauterized the stump for minimal blood flow. 'There now,' he said. Doakes made a strangled noise and went limp as the smell of seared flesh drifted through the room. With any luck at all he would be unconscious for a while.

And I, happily, was a little more conscious all the time. As the chemicals from the Doctor's dart gun seeped out of my brain, a sort of muddy light began to trickle in.

Ah, memory. Isn't it a lovely thing? Even when we are in the middle of the worst of times, we have our memories to cheer us. I, for example, lay there helpless, able only to watch as dreadful things happened to Sergeant Doakes, knowing that soon it would be my turn. But even so, I had my memories.

And what I remembered now was something Chutsky had said when I rescued him. 'When he got me up there,' he had said, 'he said, "Seven," and "What's your guess?"' At the time I had thought it a rather strange thing to say, and wondered if Chutsky had imagined it as a side effect of the drugs.

But I had just heard the Doctor say the same things to Doakes: 'What's your guess?' followed by, 'Nine letters.' And then he had made a mark on the piece of paper taped to the table.

Just as there had been a piece of paper taped near each victim we had found, each time with a single word on it, the letters crossed out one at a time. HONOR. LOYALTY. Irony, of course: Danco reminding his former comrades of the virtues they had forsaken by turning him over to the Cubans. And poor Burdett, the man from Washington whom we found in the shell of the house in Miami Shores. He had been worth no real mental effort. Just a quick five letters, POGUE. And his arms, legs, and head had been quickly cut off and separated from his body. P-O-G-U-E. Arm, leg, leg, arm, head.

Was it really possible? I knew that my Dark Passenger had a sense of humor, but it was quite a bit darker than this – this was playful, whimsical, and even silly.

Much like the Choose Life license plate had been. And like everything else I had observed about the Doctor's behavior.

It seemed so completely unlikely, but—

Doctor Danco was playing a little game as he sliced and diced. Perhaps he had played it with others in those long years inside the Cuban prison at the Isle of Pines, and maybe it had come to seem like just the right thing to serve his whimsical revenge. Because it certainly seemed like he was playing it now – with Chutsky, and with Doakes and the others. It was quite absurd, but it was also the only thing that made sense.

Doctor Danco was playing hangman.

'Well,' he said, squatting beside me again. 'How do you think your friend is doing?'

'I think you have him stumped,' I said.

He cocked his head to one side and his small, dry tongue flicked out and over his lips as he stared at me, his eyes large and unblinking through his thick glasses. 'Bravo,' he said, and he patted my arm again. 'I don't think you really believe this will happen to you,' he said. 'Perhaps a ten will persuade you.'

'Does it have an E in it?' I asked, and he rocked back slightly as if some offensive odor had drifted up to him from my socks.

'Well,' he said, still without blinking, and then something that may have been related to a smile twitched at the corner of his mouth. 'Yes, there are two E's. But of course, you guessed out of turn, so . . .' He shrugged, a tiny gesture.

'You could count it as a wrong guess – for Sergeant Doakes,' I suggested, quite helpfully, I thought.

He nodded. 'You don't like him. I see,' he said, and he frowned a little. 'Even so, you really should be more afraid.'

'Afraid of what?' I said. Sheer bravado, of course, but how often does one get a chance to banter with an authentic villain? And the shot seemed to go home; Danco stared at me for a long moment before he finally gave his head a very slight shake.

'Well, Dexter,' he said, 'I can see we're going to have our work cut out for us.' And he gave me his tiny, almost invisible smile. 'Among other things,' he added, and a cheerful black shadow reared up behind him as he spoke, thundering a happy challenge to my Dark Passenger, which slid forward and bellowed back. For a moment we faced off like that, and then he finally blinked, just once, and stood up. He walked back over to the table where Doakes slumbered so peacefully, and I sank back in my homey little corner and wondered what sort of miracle the Great Dexterini might come up with for this, his greatest escape.

Of course, I knew that Deborah and Chutsky were on their way, but I found that more worrisome than anything else. Chutsky would insist on restoring his damaged manhood by charging in on his crutch waving a gun in his only hand, and even if he allowed Deborah to back him up, she was wearing a large cast that made movement difficult. Hardly a rescue team to inspire confidence. No, I had to believe that my little corner of the kitchen was simply going to become crowded, and with all three of us taped and doped there would be no help coming for any of us.

And truthfully, in spite of my brief spatter of heroic dialogue, I was still somewhat woozy from whatever had been in Danco's sleepy dart. So I was doped, tightly bound, and all alone. But there's always some positive to every situation, if you just look hard enough, and after trying to think of one for a moment, I realized that I had to admit that so far I had not been attacked by rabid rats.

Tito Puente swung into a new tune, something a bit softer, and I grew more philosophical. We all have to go sometime. Even so, this would not make my list of top ten preferred ways to perish. Falling asleep and not waking up was number one on my list, and it got rapidly more distasteful after that.

What would I see when I died? I can't really bring myself to believe in the soul, or Heaven and Hell, or any of that solemn nonsense. After all, if human beings have souls, wouldn't I have one, too? And I can assure you, I don't. Being what I am, how could I? Unthinkable. It's hard enough just to be me. To be me with a soul and a conscience and the threat of some kind of after-life would be impossible.

But to think of wonderful, one-of-a-kind me going away forever and never coming back – very sad. Tragic, really. Perhaps I should consider reincarna-tion. No control there, of course. I could come back as a dung beetle, or even worse, come back as another monster like me. There was certainly nobody who would grieve over me, especially if Debs went out at the same time. Self-ishly, I hoped I would go first. Just get it over with. This whole charade had gone on long enough. Time to end it. Perhaps it was just as well.

Tito started a new song, very romantic, singing something about 'Te amo,' and now that I thought of it, it might very well be that Rita would grieve over me, the idiot. And Cody and Astor, in their damaged way, would surely miss me. Somehow I had been picking up an entire train of emotional attachments lately. How could this keep happening to me? And hadn't I been thinking much the same thoughts far too recently, as I hung upside down underwater in Deborah's flipped car? Why was I spending so much time dying lately, and not getting it right? As I knew only too well, there really wasn't much to it.

I heard Danco rattling around on a tray of tools and turned my head to look. It was still very difficult to move, but it seemed to be getting a little eas-ier and I managed to get him into focus. He had a large syringe in his hand and approached Sergeant Doakes with the instrument held up as if he wanted it to be seen and admired. 'Time to wake up, Albert,' he said cheerfully and jammed the needle into Doakes's arm. For a moment, nothing happened; then Doakes twitched awake and gave out a gratifying series of groans and yammers, and Dr. Danco stood there watching him and enjoying the moment, syringe once again held aloft.

There was a thud of some kind from the front of the house and Danco spun around and grabbed for his paintball gun just as the large and bald form of Kyle Chutsky filled the door to the room. As I had feared, he was leaning on his crutch and holding a gun in what even I could tell was a sweaty and unsteady hand. 'Son of a bitch,' he said, and Dr. Danco shot him with the paintball gun once, twice. Chutsky stared at him, slack-jawed, and Danco lowered his weapon as Chutsky began to slide to the floor.

And right behind Chutsky, invisible until he slumped to the floor, was my dear sister, Deborah, the most beautiful thing I had ever seen, next to the Glock pistol she held in her steady right fist. She did not pause to sweat or call Danco names. She simply tightened down her jaw muscles and fired two quick shots that took Dr. Danco in the middle of the chest and lifted him off his feet to spill backward over the frantically squealing Doakes.

Everything was very quiet and motionless for a long moment, except for the relentless Tito Puente. Then Danco slipped off the table, and Debs knelt beside Chutsky and felt for a pulse. She eased him down to a more comfy position, kissed his forehead, and finally turned to me. 'Dex,' she said. 'Are you all right?'

'I'll be fine, Sis,' I said, feeling somewhat light-headed, 'if you'll just turn off that horrible music.'

She crossed to the battered boom box and yanked the plug from the wall, looking down at Sergeant Doakes in the sudden huge silence and trying not to show too much on her face. 'We'll get you out of here now, Doakes,' she said. 'It's going to be all right.' She put a hand on his shoulder as he blubbered, and then turned suddenly away and came over to me with the tears starting down her face. 'Jesus,' she whispered as she cut me loose. 'Doakes is a mess.'

But as she ripped the last of the tape off my wrists it was hard for me to feel any distress about Doakes, because I was free at last, all the way free, of the tape and the Doctor and doing favors and yes, it looked like I might finally be free of Sergeant Doakes, too.

I stood up, which was not as easy as it sounds. I stretched my poor cramped limbs as Debs pulled out her radio to summon our friends on the Miami Beach police force. I walked over to the operating table. It was a little thing, but my curiosity had gotten the best of me. I reached down and grabbed the piece of paper taped to the edge of the table.

In those familiar, spidery block letters, Danco had written, 'TREACHERY.' Five of the letters were crossed out.

I looked at Doakes. He looked back at me, wide-eyed and broadcasting a hate that he would never be able to speak.

So you see, sometimes there really are happy endings.

EPILOGUE

It is a very beautiful thing to watch the sun come up over the water in the stillness of South Florida's subtropical morning. It is far more beautiful when that great yellow full moon hangs so low on the opposite horizon, slowly paling to silver before it slides below the waves of the open ocean and lets the sun take over the sky. And it is even more beautiful still to watch all this out of sight of land, from the deck of a twenty-six-foot cabin cruiser as you stretch the last knots from your neck and arms, tired but fulfilled and oh-so-very happy at last, from a night of work that had waited just a bit too long.

Soon I would step into my own little boat, towing behind us now, and I would throw off the tow line and head back in the direction the moon had gone, motoring sleepily home to a brand-new life as a soon-to-be-married man. And the *Osprey*, the twenty-six-foot borrowed cabin cruiser, would motor slowly in the opposite direction, toward Bimini, out into the Gulf Stream, the great blue bottomless river that runs through the ocean so conveniently near Miami. The *Osprey* would not make it to Bimini, would not even make it across the Gulf Stream. Long before I closed my happy eyes in my little bed, its engines would stall, flooded with water, and then the boat would slowly fill with water, too, rocking sluggishly in the waves before it slid under, down into the endless crystal clear depths of the Gulf Stream.

And perhaps somewhere far below the surface it would finally settle onto the bottom among the rocks and giant fish and sunken ships, and it was whimsically wonderful to think that somewhere nearby was a neatly bound package swaying gently in the current as the crabs nibbled it down to the bones. I had used four anchors on Reiker after wrapping the pieces with rope and chain, and the neat, bloodless bundle with two awful red boots firmly chained to the bottom had sunk quickly out of sight, all of it except one tiny drop of rapidly drying blood on the glass slide in my pocket. The slide would go in the box on my shelf, right behind MacGregor's, and Reiker would feed the crabs and life would at last go on again, with its happy rhythms of pretending and then pouncing.

And a few years from now I would bring Cody along and show him all the wonders that unfold in a Night of the Knife. He was far too young now, but he would start small, learn to plan, and move slowly upward. Harry had taught me that, and now I would teach it to Cody. And someday, perhaps he would follow in my shadowy footsteps and become a new Dark Avenger, carrying the Harry Plan forward against a new generation of monsters. Life, as I said, goes on.

I sighed, happy and content and ready for all of it. So beautiful. The moon was gone now and the sun had begun to burn away the cool of the morning. It was time to go home.

I stepped into my own boat, started the engine, and cast off the tow line. Then I turned my boat around and followed the moon home to bed.

Dexter in the Dark

For Hilary, as always

Acknowledgements

It is impossible to write in a vacuum. The air for this book was provided by Bear, Pookie, and Tink. My gratitude to Jason Kaufman and his aide-de-camp, Caleb, for their enormous help in shaping the manuscript.

And as ever, special thanks to Nick Ellison, who made it all happen.

IN THE BEGINNING

IT remembered a sense of surprise, and then falling, but that was all. Then IT just waited.

IT waited a very long time, but IT could wait easily because there was no memory and nothing had screamed yet. And so IT did not know IT was waiting. IT did not know it was anything at that point. IT just was, with no way to mark time, with no way even to have the idea of time.

So IT waited, and IT watched. There was not a great deal to see at first; fire, rocks, water, and eventually some little crawly things, which began to change and get bigger after a while. They didn't do very much except to eat each other and reproduce. But there was nothing to compare that to, so for a while that was enough.

Time passed. IT watched as the big things and the little things killed and ate one another aimlessly. There was no real joy in watching that, since there was nothing else to do and there were plenty more of them. But IT didn't seem able to do anything but watch. And so IT began to wonder: Why am I watching this?

IT could see no real point to anything that happened and there was nothing IT could do, and yet there IT was, watching. IT thought about this a very long time, but came to no conclusions. There was still no way to think any of this through; the whole idea of purpose wasn't quite there yet. There was just IT and them.

There were lots of them, more all the time, busily killing and eating and copulating. But there was only one of IT, and IT did none of those things, and IT began to wonder why that was, too. Why was IT different? Why was IT so unlike everything else? What was IT, and if IT actually was something, was IT supposed to do something, too?

More time passed. The countless changing crawly things slowly got bigger and better at killing each other. Interesting at first, but only because of the subtle differences. They crawled, hopped, and slithered to kill one another – one actually flew through the air to kill. Very interesting – but so what?

IT began to feel uncomfortable with all this. What was the point? Was IT supposed to be a part of what IT watched? If not, then why was IT here watching?

IT became determined to find the reason IT was here, whatever that was. So now when IT studied the big things and the little things, IT studied the ways IT was different from them. All the other things needed to eat and drink or they died. And even if they ate and drank, they eventually died anyway. IT didn't die. IT just went on and on. IT didn't need to eat or drink. But gradually IT became aware that IT did need . . . something – but what? IT could feel that somewhere there was a need, and the need was growing, but IT could not tell what it was; there was just the sense that something was missing.

No answers came as ages of scales and egg clutches paraded by. Kill and eat, kill and eat. What is the point here? Why do I have to watch all this when I can't do anything about it? IT began to feel just a little bit sour about the whole thing.

And then suddenly one day there was a brand-new thought: Where did I come from?

IT had figured out long ago that the eggs the others hatched from came from copulation. But IT had not come from an egg. Nothing at all had copulated to bring IT into existence. There had been nothing there to copulate when IT first became aware. IT had been there first and, seemingly, forever, except for the vague and disturbing memory of falling. But everything else had been hatched or born. IT had not. And with this thought the wall between IT and them seemed to grow vastly higher, stretching up impossibly tall, separating IT from them completely and eternally. IT was alone, completely alone forever, and that hurt. IT wanted to be a part of something. There was only one of IT – shouldn't there be a way for IT to copulate and make more, too?

And that began to seem infinitely more important, that thought: MORE of IT. Everything else made more. IT wanted to make more, too.

It suffered, watching the mindless things in their roiling riotous living. Resentment grew, turned into anger, and finally the anger turned into rage toward the stupid, pointless things and their endless, inane, insulting existence. And the rage grew and festered until one day IT couldn't stand it any longer. Without a pause to think what IT was doing, IT rose up and rushed at one of the lizards, wanting somehow to crush it. And a wonderful thing happened.

IT was inside the lizard.

Seeing what the lizard saw, feeling what it felt.

For a long while IT forgot rage altogether.

The lizard did not appear to notice it had a passenger. It went about its business of killing and copulating, and IT rode along. It was very interesting to be on board when the lizard killed one of the littler ones. As an experiment, IT moved into one of the little ones. Being in the one that killed was far more fun, but not enough to lead to any real purposeful ideas. Being in the one that died was very interesting and did lead to some ideas, but not very happy ones.

IT enjoyed these new experiences for a while. But although IT could feel their simple emotions, they never went beyond confusion. They still didn't notice IT, didn't have any idea that – well, they simply didn't have any idea. They didn't seem capable of having an idea. They were just so limited – and yet they were alive. They had life and didn't know it, didn't understand what to do with it. It didn't seem fair. And soon IT was bored once more, and growing angry all over again.

And finally one day the monkey things started to show up. They didn't seem like much at first. They were small and cowardly and loud. But one tiny difference finally caught IT's attention: they had hands that let them do some amazing things. IT watched as they became aware of their hands, too, and began to use them. They used them for a great variety of brand-new things: masturbating, maiming one another, and taking food from the smaller of their own kind.

IT was fascinated and watched more closely. IT watched them hit each other and then run away and hide. IT watched them steal from one another, but only when no one was looking. IT watched them do horrible things to each other and then pretend that nothing had happened. And as IT watched, for the first time, something wonderful happened: IT laughed.

And as IT laughed, a thought was born, and grew into clarity wrapped in glee.

IT thought: I can work with this.

1

What kind of moon is this? Not the bright, gleaming moon of slashing happiness, no indeed. Oh, it pulls and whines and shines in a cheap and guttering imitation of what it should do, but there is no edge to it. This moon has no wind in it to sail carnivores across the happy night sky and into slash-and-slice ecstasy. Instead this moon flickers shyly through a squeaky-clean window, onto a woman who perches all cheerful and perky on the edge of the couch and talks about flowers, canapés, and Paris.

Paris?

Yes, with moon-faced seriousness, Paris is what she is talking about in that far-spreading syrupy tone. She is talking about Paris. Again.

So what kind of moon can this possibly be, with its near-breathless smile and smirking lace around the edges? It batters feebly at the window, but it can't quite get in past all the sickly-sweet warbling. And what kind of Dark Avenger could simply sit across the room, as poor Dazed Dexter does now, pretending to listen while mooning blearily on his chair?

Why, this moon must be a honeymoon – unfurling its marital banner across the living-room night, signaling for all to rally round, sound the charge, once more into the church, dear friends – because Dexter of the Deadly Dimples is getting married. Hitched to the wagon of bliss pulled by the lovely Rita, who has turned out to have a lifelong passion to see Paris.

Married, honeymoon in Paris . . . Do these words really belong in the same sentence as any reference at all to our Phantom Flenser?

Can we really see a suddenly sober and simpering slasher at the altar of an actual church, in Fred Astaire tie and tails, slipping the ring onto a white-wrapped finger while the congregation sniffles and beams? And then Demon Dexter in madras shorts, gawking at the Eiffel Tower and snarfing café au lait at the Arc de Triomphe? Holding hands and trundling giddily along the Seine, staring vacantly at every gaudy trinket in the Louvre?

Of course, I suppose I could make a pilgrimage to the Rue Morgue, a sacred site for serial slashers.

But let us be just a tiny bit serious for a moment: Dexter in Paris? For starters, are Americans still allowed to go to France? And for finishers,

Dexter in Paris? On a *honeymoon*? How can someone of Dexter's midnight persuasions possibly consider anything so ordinary? How can someone who considers sex as interesting as deficit accounting enter into marriage? In short, how by all that is unholy, dark, and deadly can Dexter really mean to do this?

All wonderful questions, and very reasonable. And in truth, somewhat difficult to answer, even to myself. But here I am, enduring the Chinese water torture of Rita's expectations and wondering how Dexter can possibly go through with this.

Well then. Dexter can go through with this because he must, in part to maintain and even upgrade his necessary disguise, which prevents the world at large from seeing him for what he is, which is at best not something one would really like to have sitting across the table when the lights go out – especially if there is silverware present. And quite naturally, it takes a great deal of careful work to make sure it is not generally known that Dexter is driven by his Dark Passenger, a whispery-silk voice in the shaded backseat that from time to time climbs into the front seat to take the wheel and drive us to the Theme Park of the Unthinkable. It would never do to have the sheep see that Dexter is the wolf among them.

And so work we do, the Passenger and I, work very hard at our disguise. For the past several years we have had Dating Dexter, designed to present a cheerful and above all normal face to the world. This charming production featured Rita as the Girlfriend, and it was in many ways an ideal arrangement, since she was as uninterested in sex as I am, and yet wanted the companionship of an Understanding Gentleman. And Dexter really does understand. Not humans, romance, love, and all that gabble. No. What Dexter understands is the lethally grinning bottom line, how to find the utterly deserving among Miami's oh-so-many candidates for that final dark election to Dexter's modest Hall of Fame.

This does not absolutely guarantee that Dexter is a charming companion; the charm took years of practice, and it is the pure artificial product of great laboratory skill. But alas for poor Rita – battered by a terribly unfortunate and violent first marriage – she can't seem to tell the margarine from the butter.

All well and good. For two years Dexter and Rita cut a brilliant swathe across the Miami social scene, noticed and admired everywhere. But then, through a series of events that might well leave an enlightened observer somewhat skeptical, Dexter and Rita had become accidentally engaged. And the more I pondered on how to extricate myself from this ridiculous fate, the more I realized that it was a logical next step in the evolution of my disguise. A married Dexter – a Dexter with two ready-made children! – is surely a great deal further from seeming to be anything at all like what he really is. A quantum leap forward, onto a new level of human camouflage.

And then there are the two children.

It may seem strange that someone whose only passion is for human vivisection should actually enjoy Rita's children, but he does. I do. Mind you, I don't get all weepy-eyed at the thought of a lost tooth, since that would require the ability to feel emotion, and I am quite happily without any such mutation. But on the whole, I find children a great deal more interesting than their elders, and I get particularly irritable with those who cause them harm. In fact, I occasionally search them out. And when I track these predators down, and when I am very sure that they have actually done what they have been doing, I make sure they are quite unable to do it ever again – and with a very happy hand, unspoiled by conscience.

So the fact that Rita had two children from her disastrous first marriage was far from repellent, particularly when it became apparent that they needed Dexter's special parenting touch to keep their own fledgling Dark Passengers strapped into a safe, snug Dark Car Seat until they could learn how to drive for themselves. For presumably as a result of the emotional and even physical damage inflicted on Cody and Astor by their drug-addled biological father, they too had turned to the Dark Side, just like me. And now they were to be my children, legally as well as spiritually. It was almost enough to make me feel that there was some guiding purpose to life after all.

And so there were several very good reasons for Dexter to go through with this – but Paris? I don't know where it came from, this idea that Paris is romantic. Aside from the French, has anyone but Lawrence Welk ever thought an accordion was sexy? And wasn't it by now clear that they don't like us there? And they insist on speaking French, of all things?

Perhaps Rita had been brainwashed by an old movie, something with a perky-plucky blonde and a romantic dark-haired man, modernist music playing as they pursue each other around the Eiffel Tower and laugh at the quaint hostility of the dirty, Gauloise-smoking man in the beret. Or maybe she had heard a Jacques Brel record once and decided it spoke to her soul. Who can say? But somehow Rita had the notion firmly welded into her steel-trap brain that Paris was the capital of sophisticated romance, and the idea would not come out without major surgery.

So on top of the endless debates about chicken versus fish and wine versus cash bar, a series of monomaniacal rambling monologues about Paris began to emerge. Surely we could afford a whole week, that would give us time to see the Jardin des Tuileries and the Louvre – and maybe something by Molière at the Comédie-Française. I had to applaud the depth of her research. For my part, my interest in Paris had faded away completely long ago when I learned that it was in France.

Luckily for us, I was saved from the necessity of finding a politic way of telling her all this when Cody and Astor made their subtle entrance. They don't barrel into a room with guns blazing as most children of seven and ten do. As I have said, they were somewhat damaged by their dear old biological dad, and one consequence is that you never see them come and go: they enter the room by osmosis. One moment they are nowhere to be seen and the next they are standing quietly beside you, waiting to be noticed.

'We want to play kick the can,' Astor said. She was the spokesperson for the pair; Cody never put more than four words together in a single day. He was not stupid, very far from it. He simply preferred not to speak most of the time. Now he just looked at me and nodded.

'Oh,' said Rita, pausing in her reflections on the land of Rousseau, Candide, and Jerry Lewis, 'well then, why don't you—'

'We want to play kick the can with *Dexter*,' Astor added, and Cody nodded very loudly.

Rita frowned. 'I guess we should have talked about this before, but don't you think Cody and Astor – I mean, shouldn't they start to call you something more, I don't know – but just Dexter? It seems kind of—'

'How about mon papere?' I asked. 'Or Monsieur le Comte?'

'How about, I don't think so?' muttered Astor.

'I just think—' said Rita.

'Dexter is fine,' I said. 'They're used to it.'

'It doesn't seem respectful,' she said.

I looked down at Astor. 'Show your mother you can say "Dexter" respectfully,' I told her.

She rolled her eyes. 'Puh-*leeeeeze*,' she said.

I smiled at Rita. 'See? She's ten years old. She can't say *anything* respectfully.'

'Well, yes, but—' Rita said.

'It's okay. They're okay,' I said. 'But Paris—'

'Let's go outside,' said Cody, and I looked at him with surprise. Four entire syllables – for him it was practically an oration.

'All right,' said Rita. 'If you really think—'

'I almost never think,' I said. 'It gets in the way of the mental process.'

'That doesn't make any sense,' Astor said.

'It doesn't have to make sense. It's true,' I said.

Cody shook his head. 'Kick the can,' he said. And rather than break in on his talking jag, I simply followed him out into the yard.

2

Of course, even with Rita's glorious plans unfolding, life was not all jubilation and strawberries. There was real work to do, too. And because Dexter is nothing if not conscientious, I had been doing it. I had spent the past two weeks dabbing on the last few brushstrokes of a brand-new canvas. The young gentleman who served as my inspiration had inherited a great deal of money, and he had apparently been using it for the kind of dreadful homicidal escapades that made me wish I was rich, too. Alexander Macauley was his name, though he called himself 'Zander,' which seemed somewhat preppy to me, but perhaps that was the point. He was a dyed-in-the-wool trust-fund hippie, after all, someone who had never done any real work, devoting himself entirely to lighthearted amusement of the kind that would have made my hollow heart go pitter-pat, if only Zander had shown slightly better taste in choosing his victims.

The Macauley family's money came from vast hordes of cattle, endless citrus groves, and dumping phosphates into Lake Okeechobee. Zander came frequently to the poor areas of town to pour out his largesse across the city's homeless. And the favored few he really wished to encourage he reportedly brought back to the family ranch and gave employment, as I learned from a teary-eyed and admiring newspaper article.

Of course Dexter always applauds the charitable spirit. But in general, I am so very much in favor of it because it is nearly always a warning sign that something nefarious, wicked, and playful is going on behind the Mother Teresa mask. Not that I would ever doubt that somewhere in the depths of the human heart there really and truly does live a spirit of kind and caring charity, mingled with the love of fellow man. Of course it does. I mean, I'm sure it must be in there somewhere. I've just never seen it. And since I lack both humanity and real heart, I am forced to rely on experience, which tells me that charity begins at home, and almost always ends there, too.

So when I see a young, wealthy, handsome, and otherwise normal-appearing young man lavishing his resources on the vile downtrodden of the earth, I find it difficult to accept the altruism at face value, no matter how beautifully presented. After all, I am fairly good at presenting a charming and innocent picture of myself, and we know how accurate that is, don't we?

Happily for my consistent worldview, Zander was no different – just a lot richer. And his inherited money had made him a little bit sloppy. Because in the meticulous tax records I uncovered, the family ranch appeared to be unoccupied and idle, which clearly meant that wherever he was taking his dear dirty friends, it was not to a healthy and happy life of country labor.

Even better for my purposes, wherever they went with their new friend Zander, they were going barefoot. Because in a special room at his lovely Coral Gables home, guarded by some very cunning and expensive locks that took me almost five full minutes to pick, Zander had saved some souvenirs. It's a foolish risk for a monster to take; I know this full well, since I do it myself. But if someday a hardworking investigator comes across my little box of memories, he will find no more than some glass slides, each with a single drop of blood preserved upon it, and no way ever to prove that any of them is anything sinister at all.

Zander was not quite so clever. He had saved a shoe from each of his victims, and counted on too much money and a locked door to keep his secrets safe.

Well really. No wonder monsters get such a bad reputation. It was just too naive for words – and shoes? Seriously, shoes, by all that's unholy? I try to be tolerant and understanding of the foibles of others, but this was a bit much. What could possibly be the attraction in a sweaty, slime-encrusted, twenty-year-old sneaker? And then to leave them right out in the open like that, too. It was almost insulting.

Of course, Zander probably thought that if he was ever caught he could count on buying the best legal care in the world, who would surely get him off with only community service – a little ironic, since that was how it had all started. But one thing he had not counted on was being caught by Dexter instead of the police. And his trial would take place in the Traffic Court of the Dark Passenger, in which there are no lawyers – although I certainly hope to catch one someday soon – and the verdict is always absolutely final.

But was a shoe really enough proof? I had no doubt of Zander's guilt. Even if the Dark Passenger hadn't been singing arias the entire time I looked at the shoes, I knew very well what the collection meant – left to his own devices, Zander would collect more shoes. I was quite sure that he was a bad man, and I wanted very much to have a moonlight discussion with him and give him some pointed comments. But I had to be absolutely sure – that was the Harry Code.

I had always followed the careful rules laid down by Harry, my cop foster father, who taught me how to be what I am with modesty and exactness. He had shown me how to leave a crime scene clean as only a cop can, and he had taught me to use the same kind of thoroughness in selecting my partner for the dance. If there was any doubt at all, I could not call Zander out to play.

And now? No court in the world would convict Zander of anything beyond unsanitary fetishism based on his display of footwear – but no court in the world had the expert testimony of the Dark Passenger, either, that soft, urgent inner voice that demanded action and was never wrong. And with that sibilance mounting in my interior ear it was difficult to stay calm and impartial. I wanted to claim Zander for the Final Dance the way I wanted my next breath.

I wanted, I was sure – but I knew what Harry would say. It wasn't enough. He taught me that it's good to see bodies in order to be certain, and Zander had managed to hide all of them well enough to keep me from finding them. And without a body, no amount of wanting it would make it right.

I went back to my research to find out where he might be stashing a short row of pickled corpses. His home was out of the question. I had been in it and had not had a hint of anything other than the shoe museum, and the Dark Passenger is normally quite good at nosing out cadaver collections. Besides, there was no place to put them at the house – there are no basements in Florida, and it was a neighborhood where he could not dig in the yard or carry in bodies without being observed. And a short consultation with the Passenger convinced me that someone who mounted his souvenirs on walnut plaques would certainly dispose of the leftovers neatly.

The ranch was an excellent possibility, but a quick trip to the old place revealed no traces at all. It had clearly been abandoned for some time; even the driveway was overgrown.

I dug deeper: Zander owned a condo in Maui, but that was much too far away. He had a few acres in North Carolina – possible, but the thought of driving twelve hours with a body in the car made it seem unlikely. He owned stock in a company that was trying to develop Toro Key, a small island south of Cape Florida. But a corporate site was certainly out of the question – too many people might wander in and poke around. In any case, I remembered trying to land on Toro Key when I was younger, and it had armed guards strolling about to keep people away. It had to be somewhere else.

Among his many portfolios and assets, the only thing that made any sense at all was Zander's boat, a forty-five-foot Cigarette. I knew from my experience with a previous monster that a boat provided wonderful opportunities for disposing of leftovers. Simply wire the body to a weight, flip it over the rail, and wave bye-bye. Neat, clean, tidy; no fuss, no muss, no evidence.

And no way for me to get my proof, either. Zander kept his boat at the most exclusive private marina in Coconut Grove, the Royal Bay Yacht Club. Their security was very good, too good for Dexter to sneak in with a lock pick and a smile. It was a full-service marina for the terminally rich, the kind of place where they cleaned and polished your bowline when you brought the boat in. You didn't even have to fuel up your own boat; just call ahead and it would be ready for you, down to chilled champagne in the cockpit. And happily smiling armed guards infested the grounds night and day, tipping their hats at the Quality and shooting anyone who climbed the fence.

The boat was unreachable. I was as certain as I could be that Zander was using it to dispose of the bodies, and so was the Dark Passenger, which counts for even more. But there was no way to get to it.

It was annoying, even frustrating, to picture Zander with his latest trophy – probably bundled neatly into a gold-plated ice chest – calling cheerfully ahead to the dockmaster and ordering the boat fueled, and then strolling non-chalantly down the dock while two grunting Wackenhuts put the chest on board his boat and waved a respectful good-bye. But I could not get to the boat and prove it. Without this final proof, the Harry Code would not allow me to proceed.

Certain as I was, what did that leave me? I could try to catch Zander in the act the next time. But there was no way to be sure when that would be, and I couldn't watch him all the time. I did have to show up at work now and then, and make my token appearances at home, and go through all the motions of maintaining a normal-seeming life. And so at some point in the next weeks or so if the pattern held, Zander would call the dockmaster and order his boat prepared, and—

And the dockmaster, because he was an efficient employee at a rich man's club, would make a note of exactly what he did to the boat and when: how much fuel he put in, what kind of champagne, and how much Windex he used on the windscreen. He would put all that in the file marked 'Macauley,' and store it on his computer.

And suddenly we were back in Dexter's world again, with the Passenger hissing certainty and urging me to the keyboard.

Dexter is modest, even self-effacing, and certainly aware of the limits of his considerable talent. But if there was a limit to what I could discover on the computer, I had not found it yet. I sat back down and went to work.

It took me less than half an hour to hack into the club's computers and find the records. Sure enough, there was a thorough service record. I checked it against the meetings of the board of Zander's favorite charity, One World Mission of Divine Light, which was on the edge of Liberty City. On 14 February, the board was delighted to announce that Wynton Allen would be moving out of the den of iniquity that is Miami and onto Zander's ranch to be rehabilitated by honest labor. And on 15 February, Zander had taken a boat trip that used thirty-five gallons of fuel.

On March 11, Tyrone Meeks had been granted similar happiness. And on 12 March, Zander took a boat ride.

And so it went; each time some lucky homeless person was chosen for a life of bucolic joy, Zander placed a service order on his boat within twenty-four hours.

This was not seeing the bodies – but the Harry Code had been set up to operate in the cracks of the system, in the shadow areas of perfect justice rather than perfect law. I was sure, the Passenger was sure, and this was enough proof to satisfy all of us.

Zander would go on a different kind of moonlight cruise, and not all of his money would keep him afloat.

3

So on a night like many others, when the moon flung down chords of manic melody onto its happily bloodthirsty children, I was humming along and preparing to go out for a sharp frolic. All the work was done and it was play-time now for Dexter. It should have been a matter of mere moments to gather my simple toys and head out the door for my appointment with the trust-fund troublemaker. But of course, with marriage looming, nothing at all was simple anymore. I began to wonder, in fact, if anything would ever be simple again.

Of course, I was building a perfect and nearly impenetrable facade of gleaming antiseptic steel and glass to cement onto the front of the Gothic horror of Castle Dexter. So I was very willing to cooperate in retiring the Old Dexter, and therefore I had been in the process of 'consolidating our lives,' as Rita put it. In this case that meant moving out of my comfy little nook on the edge of Coconut Grove and into Rita's three-bedroom house farther south, as this was the 'sensible' thing to do. Of course, aside from being sensible it was also a Monster Inconvenience. Under the new regime there was no way I could keep anything even slightly private if I should want to. Which of course I did. Every dedicated, responsible ogre has his secrets, and there were things that I did not wish to see the light of day in anyone's hands but my own.

There was, for example, a certain amount of research on potential play-mates; and there was also the small wooden box, very dear to me, that con-tained forty-one glass slides, each with a single drop of dried blood preserved in the center, each drop representing a single less-than-human life that had ended at my hands – the entire scrapbook of my inner life. Because I do not leave great heaps of decaying flesh lying about. I am not a slovenly, slipshod, madly slashing fiend. I am an extremely tidy, madly slashing fiend. I am always very careful indeed to get rid of my leftovers, and even some cruel implacable foe bent on proving me the vile ogre that I am would be hard-pressed to say what my little slides really were.

Still, explaining them might raise questions that could eventually prove awkward, even to a doting wife – and even more so to some fearsome neme-sis passionately devoted to my destruction. There had been one such recently, a Miami cop named Sergeant Doakes. And although he was technically still alive, I had begun to think of him in the past tense, since his recent misadventures had cost him both his feet and hands, as well as his tongue. He was certainly in no shape to bring me to well-deserved justice. But I knew enough to know that if there had been one like him, there would sooner or later be another.

And so privacy seemed important – not that I had ever been a show-off where my personal affairs were concerned. As far as I knew, no one had ever seen into my little slide box. But I had never had a fiancée cleaning up for me, nor two very inquisitive kids sniffing around my things so they could learn to be much more like Dark Daddy Dexter.

Rita seemed to appreciate my need for a bit of personal space, if not the reasons for it, and she had sacrificed her sewing room, turning it into something she called Dexter's study. Eventually this would house my computer and my few books and CDs and, I suppose, my little rosewood box of slides. But how could I possibly leave it in here? I could explain it to Cody and Astor easily enough – but what to tell Rita? Should I try to hide it? Build a secret passage behind a fake bookcase leading down a winding stairway to my dark lair? Put the box in the bottom of a fake can of shaving cream, perhaps? It was something of a problem.

So far I had avoided needing to find a solution by hanging on to my apartment. But I still kept a few simple things in my study, like my fillet knives and duct tape, which could readily be explained away by my love for fishing and air-conditioning. The solution could come later. Right now I felt icy fingers prodding and tickling at my spine, and I had an urgent need to keep an appointment with a spoiled young man.

And so into my study I went, in search of a navy blue nylon gym bag I had been saving for a formal occasion, to hold my knife and tape. I pulled it from the closet, a sharp taste of anticipation building on my tongue, and put in my party toys: a new roll of duct tape, a fillet knife, gloves, my silk mask, and a coil of nylon rope for emergencies. All set. I could feel my veins gleaming with steely excitement, the wild music rising in my inner ears, the roaring of the Passenger's pulse urging me on, out, into it. I turned to go—

And ran into a matched pair of solemn children, staring up at me with expectation.

'He wants to go,' Astor said, and Cody nodded, looking at me with large unblinking eyes.

I honestly believe that those who know me would say I have a glib tongue and a ready wit, but as I mentally played back what Astor had said and tried again to find a way to make it mean something else, all I could manage was a very human sound, something like, 'He muh whu hoo?'

'With you,' Astor said patiently, as if speaking to a mentally challenged chambermaid. 'Cody wants to go with you tonight.'

In retrospect, it's easy to see that this problem would come up sooner or later. And to be perfectly fair to me, which I think is very important, I had expected it – but later. Not now. Not on the edge of my Night of Need. Not when every hair on my neck was standing straight up and screeching with the pure and urgent compulsion to slither into the night in cold, stainless-steel fury—

The situation clearly called for some serious pondering, but all my nerves were clamoring for me to leap out the window and be off into the night – but there they were, and so somehow I took a deep breath and pondered the two of them.

The sharp and shiny tin soul of Dexter the Avenger was forged from a childhood trauma so violent that I had blocked it out completely. It had made me what I am, and I am sure I would sniffle and feel unhappy about that if I was able to feel at all. And these two, Cody and Astor, had been scarred the same way, beaten and savaged by a violent drug-addicted father until they, too, were turned forever away from sunlight and lollipops. As my wise foster father had known in raising me, there was no way to take that away, no way to put the serpent back in the egg.

But it could be trained. Harry had trained me, shaped me into something that hunted only the other dark predators, the other monsters and ghouls who dressed in human skin and prowled the game trails of the city. I had the indelible urge to kill, unchangeable and forever, but Harry had taught me to find and dispose of only those who, by his rigorous cop standards, truly needed it.

When I discovered that Cody was the same way, I had promised myself that I would carry on the Harry Way, pass on what I had learned to the boy, raise him up in Dark Righteousness. But this was an entire galaxy of complications, explanations, and teachings. It had taken Harry nearly ten years to cram it all into me before he allowed me to play with anything more complicated than stray animals. I had not even started with Cody – and although it made me feel like I was trying to be a Jedi Master, I could not possibly start with him now. I knew that Cody must someday come to terms with being like me, and I truly meant to help him – but not tonight. Not with the moon calling so playfully just outside the window, pulling at me like a soft yellow freight train hitched to my brain.

'I'm not, uh—' I started to say, meaning to deny everything. But they looked up at me with such an endearing expression of cold certainty that I stopped. 'No,' I said at last. 'He's much too young.'

They exchanged a quick glance, no more, but there was an entire conversation in it. 'I told him you would say that,' Astor said.

'You were right,' I said.

'But Dexter,' she said, 'you said you would show us stuff.'

'I will,' I said, feeling the shadowy fingers crawl slowly up my spine and prodding for control, urging me out the door, 'but not now.'

'When?' Astor demanded.

I looked at the two of them and felt the oddest combination of wild impatience to be off and cutting mixed with an urge to wrap them both in a soft blanket and kill anything that came near them. And nibbling at the edges, just to round out the blend, a desire to smack their thick little heads together.

Was this fatherhood at last?

The entire surface of my body was tingling with cold fire from my need to be gone, to begin, to do the mighty unmentionable, but instead I took a very deep breath and put on a neutral face. 'This is a school night,' I said, 'and it is almost your bedtime.'

They looked at me as if I had betrayed them, and I supposed I had by changing the rules and playing Daddy Dexter when they thought they were talking to Demon Dexter. Still, it was true enough. One really can't take small children along on a late-night evisceration and expect them to remember their ABCs the next day. It was hard enough for me to show up at work the morning after one of my little adventures, and I had the advantage of all the Cuban coffee I wanted. Besides, they really were much too young.

'Now you're just being a grown-up,' Astor said with a withering ten-year-old sneer.

'But I am a grown-up,' I said. 'And I am trying to be the right one for you.' Even though I said it with my teeth hurting from fighting back the rising need, I meant it – which did nothing at all to soften the identical looks of bleak contempt I got from both of them.

'We thought you were different,' she said.

'I can't imagine how I could be any more different and still look human,' I said.

'Not fair,' Cody said, and I locked eyes with him, seeing a tiny dark beast raise its head and roar at me.

'No, it's not fair,' I said. 'Nothing in life is fair. Fair is a dirty word and I'll thank you not to use that language around me.'

Cody looked hard at me for a moment, a look of disappointed calculation I had never seen from him before, and I didn't know if I wanted to swat him or give him a cookie.

'Not fair,' he repeated.

'Listen,' I said, 'this is something I know about. And this is the first lesson. Normal children go to bed on time on school nights.'

'Not normal,' he said, sticking his lower lip out far enough to hold his schoolbooks.

'Exactly the point,' I told him. 'That's why you always have to *look* normal, *act* normal, make everyone else think you *are* normal. And the other thing you have to do is exactly what I tell you, or I won't do this.' He didn't look quite convinced, but he was weakening. 'Cody,' I said. 'You have to trust me, and you have to do it my way.'

'*Have* to,' he said.

'Yes,' I said. 'Have to.'

He looked at me for a very long moment, then switched his stare to his sister, who looked back at him. It was a marvel of subvocal communication; I could tell that they were having a long, very intricate conversation, but they didn't make a sound until Astor shrugged and turned back to me. 'You have to promise,' she said to me.

'All right,' I said. 'Promise what?'

'That you'll start teaching us,' she said, and Cody nodded. 'Soon.'

I took a deep breath. I had never really had any chance of going to what I consider a very hypothetical heaven, even before this. But to go through with this, agreeing to turn these ragged little monsters into neat, well-schooled little monsters – well, I would certainly hope I was right about the hypothetical part. 'I promise,' I said. They looked at each other, looked at me, and left.

And there I was with a bag full of toys, a pressing engagement, and a somewhat shriveled sense of urgency.

Is family life like this for everyone? If so, how does anyone survive it? Why do people have more than one child, or any at all? Here I was with an important and fulfilling goal in front of me, and suddenly I get blindsided by something no soccer mom ever had to face and it was nearly impossible to remember what I was thinking only moments ago. Even with an impatient growl from the Dark Passenger – strangely muted, as if just a little confused – it took me several moments to pull myself together, from Dazed Daddy Dexter back to the Cold Avenger once again. I found it difficult to call back the icy edge of readiness and danger; it was difficult, in fact, to remember where I had left my car keys.

Somehow I found them and stumbled out of my study, and after mumbling some heartfelt nothing to Rita, I was out the door and into the night at last.

4

I had followed Zander long enough to know his routine, and since this was Thursday night, I knew exactly where he would be. He spent every Thursday evening at One World Mission of Divine Light, presumably inspecting the livestock. After about ninety minutes of smiling at the staff and listening to a brief service he would write a check for the pastor, a huge black man who had once played in the NFL. The pastor would smile and thank him, and Zander would slip quietly out the back door to his modest SUV and drive humbly to his house, all aglow with the virtuous feeling that comes only from true good works.

But tonight, he would not drive alone.

Tonight Dexter and his Dark Passenger would go along for the ride and steer him to a brand-new kind of journey.

But first the cold and careful approach, the payoff to the weeks of stealthy stalking.

I parked my car only a few miles from Rita's house at a large old shopping area called Dadeland and walked to the nearby Metrorail station. The train was seldom crowded, even at rush hour, but there were enough people around that no one paid any attention to me. Just a nice man in fashionably dark clothes carrying a gym bag.

I got off one stop past downtown and walked six blocks to the mission, feeling the keen edge sharpening itself within me, moving me back to the readiness I needed. We would think about Cody and Astor later. Right now, on this street, I was all hard, hidden brightness. The blinding orange-pink glare of the special crime-fighting streetlights could not wash away the darkness I wrapped tighter around me as I walked.

The mission sat on the corner of a medium-busy street, in a converted storefront. There was a small crowd gathered in front – no real surprise, since they gave out food and clothing, and all you had to do to get it was to spend a few moments of your rum-soaked time listening to the good reverend explain why you were going to hell. It seemed like a pretty good bargain, even to me, but I wasn't hungry. I moved on past, around back to the parking lot.

Although it was slightly dimmer here, the parking lot was still far too bright for me, almost too bright even to see the moon, although I could feel it there in the sky, smirking down on our tiny squirming fragile life, festooned as it was with monsters who lived only to take that life away in large, pain-filled mouthfuls. Monsters like me, and like Zander. But tonight there would be one less.

I walked one time around the perimeter of the parking lot. It appeared to be safe. There was no one in sight, no one sitting or dozing in any of the cars. The only window with a view into the area was a small one, high up on the back wall of the mission, fitted with opaque glass – the restroom. I circled closer to Zander's car, a blue Dodge Durango nosed in next to the back door, and tried the door handle – locked. Parked next to it was an old Chrysler, the pastor's venerable ride. I moved to the far side of the Chrysler and began my wait.

From my gym bag I pulled a white silk mask and dropped it over my face, settling the eyeholes snugly. Then I took out a loop of fifty-pound-test fishing line and I was ready. Very soon now it would begin, the Dark Dance. Zander strolling all unknowing into a predator's night, a night of sharp surprises, a final and savage darkness pierced with fierce fulfillment. So very soon, he would amble calmly out of his life and into mine. And then—

Had Cody remembered to brush his teeth? He had been forgetting lately, and Rita was reluctant to get him out of bed once he was settled in. But it was important to set him on the path of good habits now, and brushing was important.

I flicked my noose, letting it settle onto my knees. Tomorrow was photo day at Astor's school. She was supposed to wear her Easter dress from last year to look nice for the picture. Had she set it out so she wouldn't forget in the morning? Of course she wouldn't smile for the picture, but she should at least wear the good dress.

Could I really be crouched here in the night, noose in hand and waiting to pounce, and thinking about such things? How was it possible for my anticipation to be filled with these thoughts instead of the fang-sharpening eagerness of turning the Dark Passenger loose on an oh-so-deserving playmate? Was this a foretaste of Dexter's shiny new married life?

I breathed in carefully, feeling a great sympathy for W. C. Fields. I couldn't work with kids, either. I closed my eyes, felt myself fill with dark night air, and let it out again, feeling the frigid readiness return. Slowly Dexter receded and the Dark Passenger took back the controls.

And not a moment too soon.

The back door clattered open and we could hear the sound of horrible animal noises blatting and bleating away inside, a truly awful rendering of 'Just a Closer Walk with Thee,' the sound of it enough to send anyone back to the bottle. And enough to propel Zander out the door. He paused in the doorway, turned to give the room a cheery wave and a smirk, and then the door slammed shut and he came around his car to the driver's side and he was ours.

Zander fumbled for his keys and the lock clicked open and we were around the car and behind him. Before he knew what was happening the noose whistled through the air and slipped around his neck and we yanked hard enough to pull him off his feet, hard enough to bring him to his knees with his breath stopped and his face turning dark and it was good.

'Not a sound,' we said, cold and perfect. 'Do exactly as we say, not a single word or sound, and you will live a little longer,' we told him, and we tightened the noose just a bit to let him know he belonged to us and must do as we said.

Zander responded in a most gratifying way by slipping forward onto his face and he was not smirking now. Drool leaked from the corner of his mouth and he clawed at the noose, but we held it far too tight for him to get a finger under the line. When he was very close to passing out we eased the pressure, just enough to let him crackle in a single painful breath. 'On your feet now,' we said gently, pulling upward on the noose so he would do as he was told. And slowly, clawing his way up the side of his car, Zander obeyed.

'Good,' we said. 'Get in the car.' We switched the noose to my left hand and opened the door of the car, then reached around the door post and took it again in my right as we climbed in the backseat behind him. 'Drive,' we said in our dark and icy command voice.

'Where?' Zander said in his voice, now a hoarse whisper from our little reminders with the noose.

We pulled the line tight again to remind him not to talk out of turn. When we thought he had received the message we loosened it again. 'West,' we said. 'No more talk. Drive.'

He put the car in gear and, with a few small tugs on the noose, I steered him west and up onto the Dolphin Expressway. For a while Zander did exactly as we said. He would look at us in the mirror from time to time, but a very slight twitch of the noose kept him extremely cooperative until we took him onto the Palmetto Expressway and north.

'Listen,' he said suddenly, as we drove past the airport, 'I am like really rich. I can give you whatever you want.'

'Yes, you can,' we said, 'and you will,' and he did not understand what we wanted, because he relaxed just a little bit.

'Okay,' he said, voice still rough from the noose, 'so how much do you want?'

We locked eyes with him in the mirror and slowly, very slowly so he would begin to understand, we tightened the line around his neck. When he could barely breathe, we held it like that for a moment. 'Everything,' we said. 'We will have everything.' We loosened the noose, just a little. 'Drive,' we said.

Zander drove. He was very quiet the rest of the way, but he did not seem as frightened as he should have been. Of course, he must believe that this was not really happening to him, could not possibly happen, not to him, living forever in his impenetrable cocoon of money. Everything had a price, and he could always afford it. Soon he would negotiate. Then he would buy his way out.

And he would. Eventually he would buy his way out. But not with money. And never out of this noose.

It was not a terribly long drive and we were quiet all the way to the Hialeah exit we had chosen. But when Zander slowed for the off-ramp, he glanced at me in the mirror with fear in his eyes, the climbing terror of a monster in a trap, ready to chew off his leg to escape, and the tangible bite of his panic sparked a warm glow in the Dark Passenger and made us very glad and strong. 'You don't – there, there isn't – where are we going?' he stammered, weak and pitiful and sounding more human all the time, which made us angry and we yanked too hard until he swerved onto the shoulder momentarily and we had to grant him some slack in the noose. Zander steered back onto the road and the bottom of the ramp.

'Turn right,' we said, and he did, the unlovely breath rasping in and out through his spit-flecked lips. But he did just as we told him to do, all the way down the street and left onto a small, dark lane of old warehouses.

He parked his car where we told him, by the rusty door of a dark unused building. A partially rotted sign with the end lopped off still said JONE PLASTI. 'Park,' we said, and as he fumbled the gear lever into park we were out the door and yanking him after us and onto the ground, pulling tight and watching him thrash for a moment before we jerked him up to his feet. The spit had caked around his mouth, and there was some small bit of belief in his eyes now as he stood there ugly and disgusting in the lovely moonlight, all atremble with some terrible mistake I had made against his money, and the growing notion that perhaps he was no different from the ones he had done exactly this to washed over him and left him weak. We let him stand and breathe for just a moment, then pushed him toward the door. He put one hand out, palm against the concrete-block wall. 'Listen,' he said, and there was a quaver of pure human in his voice now. 'I can get you a ton of money. Whatever you want.'

We said nothing. Zander licked his lips. 'All right,' he said, and his voice now was dry, shredded, and desperate. 'So what do you want from me?'

'Exactly what you took from the others,' we said with an extra-sharp twitch of the noose. 'Except the shoe.'

He stared and his mouth sagged and he peed in his pants. 'I didn't,' he said. 'That's not—'

'You did,' we told him. 'It is.' And pulling back hard on the leash we pushed him forward and through the door, into the carefully prepared space. There were a few shattered clumps of PVC pipe swept off to the sides and, more important for Zander, two fifty-gallon drums of hydrochloric acid, left behind by Jone Plasti when they had gone out of business.

It was easy enough for us to get Zander up onto the work space we had cleared for him, and in just a few moments we had him taped and tied into place and we were very eager to begin. We cut the noose off and he gasped as the knife nicked his throat.

'Jesus!' he said. 'Listen, you're making a big mistake.'

We said nothing; there was work to do and we prepared for it, slowly cutting away his clothing and dropping it carefully into one of the drums of acid.

'Oh, fuck, please,' he said. 'Seriously, it's not what you think – you don't know what you're about to do.'

We were ready and we held up the knife for him to see that actually we knew very well what we were doing, and we were about to do it.

'Dude, please,' he said. The fear in him was far beyond anything he thought possible, beyond the humiliation of wetting his pants and begging, beyond anything he had ever imagined.

And then he grew surprisingly still. He looked right into my eyes with an uncalled-for clarity and in a voice I had not heard from him before he said, 'He'll find you.'

We stopped for a moment to consider what this meant. But we were quite sure that it was his last hopeful bluff, and it blunted the delicious taste of his terror and made us angry and we taped his mouth shut and went to work.

And when we were done there was nothing left except for one of his shoes. We thought about having it mounted, but of course that would be untidy, so it went into the barrel of acid with the rest of Zander.

This was not good, the Watcher thought. They had been inside the abandoned warehouse far too long, and there could be no doubt that whatever they were doing in there, it was not a social occasion.

Nor was the meeting he had been scheduled to have with Zander. Their meetings had always been strictly business, although Zander obviously thought of them in different terms. The awe on his face at their rare encounters spoke volumes on what the young fool thought and felt. He was so proud of the small contribution he made, so eager to be near the cold, massive power.

The Watcher did not regret anything that might happen to Zander – he was easy enough to replace: the real concern was why this was happening tonight, and what it might mean.

And he was glad now that he had not interfered, had simply hung back and followed. He could easily have moved in and taken the brash young man who had taken Zander, crushed him completely. Even now he felt the vast power murmuring within himself, a power that could roar out and sweep away anything that stood before it – but no.

The Watcher also had patience, and this, too, was a strength. If this other was truly a threat, it was better to wait and to watch, and when he knew enough about the danger, he would strike – swiftly, overwhelmingly, and finally.

So he watched. It was several hours before the other came out and got into Zander's car. The Watcher stayed well back, with his headlights off at first, tailing the blue Durango easily in the late-night traffic. And when the other parked the car in the lot at a Metrorail station and got on the train, he stepped on, too, just as the doors slid closed, and sat at the far end, studying the reflection of the face for the first time.

Surprisingly young and even handsome. An air of innocent charm. Not the sort of face you might expect, but they never were.

The Watcher followed when the other got off at Dadeland and walked toward one of the many parked cars. It was late and there were no people in the lot. He knew he could make it happen now, so easily, just slip up behind the other and let the power flow through him, out into his hands, and release the other into the darkness. He could feel the slow, majestic rise of the strength inside as he closed the distance, almost taste the great and silent roar of the kill—

And then he stopped suddenly in his tracks and slowly moved away down a different aisle.

Because the other's car had a very noticeable placard lying on the dashboard.

A police parking permit.

He was very glad he had been patient. If the other was with the police . . . This could be a much bigger problem than he had expected. Not good at all. This would take some careful planning. And a great deal more observation.

And so the Watcher slipped quietly back into the night to prepare, and to watch.

5

Somebody once said that there's no rest for the wicked, and they were almost certainly talking about me, because for several days after I sent dear little Zander on to his just reward poor Dogged Dexter was very busy indeed. Even as Rita's frenetic planning kicked into high gear, my job followed suit. We seemed to have hit one of those periodic spells Miami gets every now and then in which murder just seems like a good idea, and I was up to my eyeballs in blood spatter for three days.

But on the fourth day, things actually got a little bit worse. I had brought in doughnuts, as is my habit from time to time – especially in the days following my playdates. For some reason, not only do I feel more relaxed for several days after the Passenger and I have a night encounter, but I also feel quite hungry. I'm sure that fact is filled with deep psychological significance, but I am far more interested in making sure I get one or two of the jelly doughnuts before the savage predators in Forensics shred them all to pieces. Significance can wait when doughnuts are on the line.

But this morning I barely managed to grab one raspberry-filled doughnut – and I was lucky not to lose a finger in the process. The whole floor was buzzing with preparation for a trip to a crime scene, and the tone of the buzz let me know that it was a particularly heinous one, which did not please me. That meant longer hours, stuck somewhere far from civilization and Cuban sandwiches. Who knew what I would end up with for lunch? Considering that I had been short-changed on the doughnuts, lunch could prove to be a very important meal, and for all I knew I would be forced to work right through it.

I grabbed my handy blood-spatter kit and headed out the door with Vince Masuoka, who despite his small size had somehow grabbed two of the very valuable filled doughnuts – including the Bavarian cream with the chocolate frosting. 'You have done a little too well, Mighty Hunter,' I told him with a nod at his plundered loot.

'The gods of the forest have been good,' he said, and took a large bite. 'My people will not starve this season.'

'No, but I will,' I said.

He gave me his terrible phony smile, which looked like something he had learned to do by studying a government manual on facial expressions. 'The ways of the jungle are hard, Grasshopper,' he said.

'Yes, I know,' I said. 'First you must learn to think like a doughnut.'

'Ha,' Vince said. His laugh was even phonier than his smile, sounding like he was reading aloud from a phonetic spelling of laughter. 'Ah, ha ha ha!' he said. The poor guy seemed to be faking everything about being human, just like me. But wasn't as good at it as I was. No wonder I was comfortable with him. That and the fact that he quite often took a turn bringing the doughnuts.

'You need better camouflage,' he said, nodding at my shirt, a bright pink-and-green Hawaiian pattern complete with hula girls. 'Or at least better taste.'

'It was on sale,' I said.

'Ha,' he said again. 'Well, pretty soon Rita will be picking your clothes.' And then abruptly dropping his terrible artificial jollity, he said, 'Listen, I think I have found the perfect caterer.'

'Does he do jelly doughnuts?' I said, truthfully hoping that the whole subject of my impending matrimonial bliss would simply go away. But I had asked Vince to be my best man, and he was taking the job seriously.

'The guy is very big,' Vince said. 'He did the MTV Awards, and all those showbiz parties and stuff.'

'He sounds delightfully expensive,' I said.

'Well, he owes me a favor,' Vince said. 'I think we can get him down on the price. Maybe like a hundred and fifty bucks a plate.'

'Actually, Vince, I had hoped we could afford more than one plate.'

'He was in that South Beach magazine,' he said, sounding a little hurt. 'You should at least talk to him.'

'To be honest,' I said, which of course meant I was lying, 'I think Rita wants something simple. Like a buffet.'

Vince was definitely sulking now. 'At least talk to him,' he repeated.

'I'll talk to Rita about it,' I said, wishing that would make the whole thing go away. And during the trip to the crime scene Vince said no more about it, so maybe it had.

The scene turned out to be a lot easier for me than I had anticipated, and I cheered up quite a bit when I got there. In the first place, it was on the University of Miami campus, which was my dear old alma mater, and in keeping with my lifelong attempt to appear human, I always tried to remember to pretend I felt a warm, fuzzy fondness for the place when I was there. Secondly, there was apparently very little raw blood to deal with, which might mean that I could be done with it in a reasonable amount of time. It also meant freedom from the nasty wet red stuff – I really don't like blood, which may seem odd, but there it is. I do, however, find great satisfaction in organizing it at a crime scene, forcing it to fit a decent pattern and behave itself. In this case, from what I learned on the way there, that would hardly be a challenge.

And so it was with my usual cheerful good spirits that I sauntered over toward the yellow crime-scene tape, certain of a charming interlude in a hectic workday—

And came to a dead stop with one foot just inside the tape.

For a moment the world turned bright yellow and there was a sickening sensation of lurching weightless through space. I could see nothing except the knife-edged glare. There was a silent sound from the dark backseat, the feeling of subliminal nausea mixed with the blind panic of a butcher's knife squealing across a chalkboard. A skittering, a nervousness, a wild certainty that something was very badly wrong, and no hint of what or where it was.

My sight came back and I looked around me. I saw nothing I didn't expect to see at a crime scene: a small crowd gathered at the yellow tape, some uniforms guarding the perimeter, a few cheap-suited detectives, and my team, the forensic geeks, scrabbling through the bushes on their hands and knees. All perfectly normal to the naked eye. And so I turned to my infallible fully clothed interior eye for an answer.

What is it? I asked silently, closing my eyes again and searching for some answer from the Passenger to this unprecedented display of discomfort. I was accustomed to commentary from my Dark Associate, and quite often my first sight of a crime scene would be punctuated by sly whispers of admiration or amusement, but this – it was clearly a sound of distress, and I did not know what to make of it.

What? I asked again. But there was no answer beyond the uneasy rustle of invisible wings, so I shook it off and walked over to the site.

The two bodies had clearly been burned somewhere else, since there was no sign of any barbecue large enough to bake two medium-size females quite so thoroughly. They had been dumped beside the lake that runs through the UM campus, just off the path that ran around it, and discovered by a pair of early-morning joggers. It was my opinion from the state of the small amount of blood evidence I found that the heads had been removed after the two had burned to death.

One small detail gave me pause. The bodies were laid out neatly, almost reverently, with the charred arms folded across the chests. And in place of the severed heads, a ceramic bull's head had been carefully placed at the top of each torso.

This is exactly the kind of loving touch that always brings some type of comment from the Dark Passenger – generally speaking, an amused whisper, a small chuckle, even a twinge of jealousy. But this time, as Dexter said to himself, *Aha, a bull's head! What do we think about that?*, the Passenger responded immediately and forcefully with—

Nothing?

Not a whisper, not a sigh?

I sent an irritated demand for answers, and got no more than a worried scuttling, as if the Passenger were ducking down behind anything that might provide cover, and hoping to ride out the storm without being noticed.

I opened my eyes, as much from startlement as anything else. I could not remember any time when the Passenger had nothing to say on some example of our favorite subject, and yet here he was, not merely subdued but hiding.

I looked back at the two charred bodies with new respect. I had no clue as to what this might mean, but since it had never happened before, it seemed like a good idea to find out.

Angel Batista-no-relation was on his hands and knees on the far side of the path, very carefully examining things I couldn't see and didn't really care about. 'Did you find it yet?' I asked him.

He didn't look up. 'Find what?' he said.

'I don't have any idea,' I said. 'But it must be here somewhere.'

He reached out with a pair of tweezers and plucked a single blade of grass, staring hard at it and then stuffing it into a plastic baggie as he spoke. 'Why,' he said, 'would somebody put a ceramic bull head there?'

'Because chocolate would melt,' I said.

He nodded without looking up. 'Your sister thinks it's a Santeria thing.'

'Really,' I said. That possibility had not occurred to me, and I felt a little miffed that it hadn't. After all, this was Miami; anytime we encountered something that looked like a ritual and involved animal heads, Santeria should have been the first thing all of us thought. An Afro-Cuban religion that combined Yoruba animism with Catholicism, Santeria was widespread in Miami. Animal sacrifice and symbolism were common for its devotees, which would explain the bull heads. And although a relatively small number of people actually practiced Santeria, most homes in the city had one or two small saint candles or cowrie-shell necklaces bought at a botanica. The prevailing attitude around town was that even if you didn't believe in it, it didn't hurt to pay it some respect.

As I said, it should have occurred to me at once. But my foster sister, now a full sergeant in homicide, had thought of it first, even though I was supposed to be the clever one.

I had been relieved to learn that Deborah was assigned to the case, since it meant that there would be a minimum of bone-numbing stupidity. It would also, I hoped, give her something better to do with her time than she had appeared to have lately. She had been spending all hours of the day and night hovering around her damaged boyfriend, Kyle Chutsky, who had lost one or two minor limbs in his recent encounter with a deranged freelance surgeon who specialized in turning human beings into squealing potatoes – the same villain who had artfully trimmed away so many unnecessary parts from Sergeant Doakes. He had not had the time to finish with Kyle, but Debs had taken the whole thing rather personally and, after fatally shooting the good

doctor, she had devoted herself to nursing Chutsky back to vigorous manhood.

I'm sure she had racked up numberless points on the ethical scoreboard,
no matter who was keeping track, but in truth all the time off had done her
no good with the department, and even worse, poor lonely Dexter had felt
keenly the uncalled-for neglect from his only living relative.

So it was very good news all around to have Deborah assigned to the case,
and on the far side of the path she was talking to her boss, Captain Matthews,
no doubt giving him a little ammunition for his ongoing war with the press,
who simply refused to take his picture from his good side.

The press vans were, in fact, already rolling up and spewing out crews to
tape background shots of the area. A couple of the local bloodhounds were
standing there, solemnly clutching their microphones and intoning mournful sentences about the tragedy of two lives so brutally ended. As always, I felt
reverently grateful to live in a free society, where the press had a sacred right
to show footage of dead people on the evening news.

Captain Matthews carefully smoothed his already perfect hair with the
heel of his hand, clapped Deborah on the shoulder, and marched over to talk
to the press. And I marched over to my sister.

She stood where Matthews had left her, watching his back as he began to
speak to Rick Sangre, one of the true gurus of if-it-bleeds-it-leads reporting.
'Well, Sis,' I said. 'Welcome back to the real world.'

She shook her head. 'Hip hooray,' she said.

'How is Kyle doing?' I asked her, since my training told me that was the
right thing to ask about.

'Physically?' she said. 'He's fine. But he just feels *useless* all the time. And
those assholes in Washington won't let him go back to work.'

It was difficult for me to judge Chutsky's ability to get back to work, since
no one had ever said exactly what work he did. I knew it was vaguely connected to some part of the government and was also something clandestine,
but beyond that I didn't know. 'Well,' I said, searching for the proper cliché,
'I'm sure it just needs some time.'

'Yeah,' she said. 'I'm sure.' She looked back at the place where the two
charred bodies lay. 'Anyhow, this is a great way to get my mind off it.'

'The rumor mill tells me you think it's Santeria,' I said, and her head
swiveled rapidly around to face me.

'You think it's *not*?' she demanded.

'Oh, no, it might well be,' I said.

'But?' she said sharply.

'No buts at all,' I said.

'Damn it, Dexter,' she said. 'What do you know about this?' And it was
probably a fair question. I had been known on occasion to offer a pretty fair
guess about some of the more gruesome murders we worked on. I had gained

a small reputation for my insight into the way the twisted homicidal sickos thought and operated – natural enough, since, unknown to everyone but Deborah, I was a twisted homicidal sicko myself.

But even though Deborah had only recently become aware of my true nature, she had not been shy about taking advantage of it to help her in her work. I didn't mind; glad to help. What else is family for? And I didn't really care if my fellow monsters paid their debt to society in Old Sparky – unless, of course, it was somebody I was saving for my own innocent pleasure.

But in this case, I had nothing whatsoever to tell Deborah. I had, in fact, been hoping she might have some small crumb of information to give to me, something that might explain the Dark Passenger's peculiar and uncharacteristic shrinking act. That, of course, was not the sort of thing I really felt comfortable telling Deborah about. But no matter what I said about this burned double offering, she wouldn't believe me. She would be sure I had information and some kind of angle that made me want to keep it all to myself. The only thing more suspicious than a sibling is a sibling who happens to be a cop.

Sure enough, she was convinced I was holding out on her. 'Come on, Dexter,' she said. 'Out with it. Tell me what you know about this.'

'Dear Sis, I am at a total loss,' I said.

'Bullshit,' she said, apparently unaware of the irony. 'You're holding something back.'

'Never in life,' I said. 'Would I lie to my only sister?'

She glared at me. 'So it isn't Santeria?'

'I have no idea,' I said, as soothingly as possible. 'It seems like a really good place to start. But—'

'I knew it,' she snapped. 'But what?'

'Well,' I started. And truly it had just occurred to me, and probably it meant nothing at all, but here I was in mid-sentence already, so I went on with it. 'Have you ever heard of a *santero* using ceramics? And bulls – don't they have a thing for *goat* heads?'

She looked at me very hard for a minute, then shook her head. 'That's it? That's what you got?'

'I told you, Debs, I don't got anything. It was only a thought, something that just now came to me.'

'Well,' she said. 'If you're telling me the truth—'

'Of course I am,' I protested.

'Then, you've got doodly-squat,' she said and looked away, back to where Captain Matthews was answering questions with his solemn, manly jaw jutting out. 'Which is only slightly less than the horsepucky I got,' she said.

I had never before grasped that doodly-squat was less than horsepucky, but it's always nice to learn something new. And yet even this startling revelation did very little to answer the real question here: Why had the Dark

Passenger pulled a duck and cover? In the course of my job and my hobby
I have seen some things that most people can't even imagine, unless they have
watched several of those movies they show at traffic school for driving drunk.
And in every case I had ever encountered, no matter how grisly, my shadow
companion had some kind of pithy comment on the proceedings, even if it
was only a yawn.

But now, confronted by nothing more sinister than two charred bodies
and some amateur pottery, the Dark Passenger chose to scuttle away like a
scared spider and leave me without guidance – a brand-new feeling for me,
and I discovered I did not like it at all.

Still, what was I to do? I knew of no one I could talk to about something
like the Dark Passenger; at least, not if I wanted to stay at liberty, which I very
much did. As far as I was aware, there were no experts on the subject, other
than me. But what did I really know about my boon companion? Was I really
that knowledgeable, merely because I had shared space with it for so long?
The fact that it had chosen to scuttle into the cellar was making me very edgy,
as if I found myself walking through my office with no pants on. When it
came down to the nub of things, I had no idea what the Dark Passenger was
or where it came from, and that had never seemed all that important.

For some reason, now it did.

A modest crowd had gathered by the yellow tape barrier the police had put
up. Enough people so that the Watcher could stand in the middle of the group
without sticking out in any way.

He watched with a cold hunger that did not show on his face – nothing
showed on his face; it was merely a mask he wore for the time being, a way to
hide the coiled power stored inside. Yet somehow the people around him
seemed to sense it, glancing his way nervously from time to time, as if they
had heard a tiger growling nearby.

The Watcher enjoyed their discomfort, enjoyed the way they stared in stupid fear at what he had done. It was all part of the joy of this power, and part
of the reason he liked to watch.

But he watched with a purpose right now, carefully and deliberately, even
as he watched them scrabble around like ants and felt the power surge and flex
inside him. *Walking meat,* he thought. *Less than sheep, and we are the shepherd.*

As he gloated at their pathetic reaction to his display he felt another presence tickle at the edge of his predator's senses. He turned his head slowly
along the line of yellow tape—

There. That was him, the one in the bright Hawaiian shirt. He really was
with the police.

The Watcher reached a careful tendril out toward the other, and as it
touched he watched the other stop cold in his tracks and close his eyes, as if
asking a silent question – yes. It all made sense now. The other had felt the

subtle reach of senses; he was powerful, that was certain.

But what was his purpose?

He watched as the other straightened up, looked around, and then seemingly shrugged it off and crossed the police line.

We are stronger, he thought. *Stronger than all of them. And they will discover this, to their very great sorrow.*

He could feel the hunger growing – but he needed to know more, and he would wait until the right time. Wait and watch.

For now.

6

A homicide scene with no blood splattered should have been a real holiday outing for me, but somehow I couldn't get into the lighthearted frame of mind to enjoy it. I lurked around for a while, going in and out of the taped-off area, but there was very little for me to do. And Deborah seemed to have said all she had to say to me, which left me somewhat alone and unoccupied.

A reasonable being might very well be pardoned for sulking just a tiny bit, but I had never claimed to be reasonable, and that left me with very few options. Perhaps the best thing to do would be to get on with life and think about the many important things that demanded my attention – the kids, the caterer, Paris, lunch . . . Considering my laundry list of things to worry about, it was no wonder the Passenger was proving a wee bit shy.

I looked at the two overcooked bodies again. They were not doing anything sinister. They were still dead. But the Dark Passenger was still silent.

I wandered back over to where Deborah stood, talking to Angel-no-relation. They both looked at me expectantly, but I had no readily available wit to offer, which was very much out of character. Happily for my world-famous reputation for permanently cheerful stoicism, before I could really turn gloomy, Deborah looked over my shoulder and snorted. 'About fucking time.'

I followed her gaze to a patrol car that had just pulled up and watched a man dressed all in white climb out.

The official City of Miami *babalao* had arrived.

Our fair city exists in a permanent blinding haze of cronyism and corruption that would make Boss Tweed jealous, and every year millions of dollars are thrown away on imaginary consulting jobs, cost overruns on projects that haven't begun because they were awarded to someone's mother-in-law, and other special items of great civic importance, like new luxury cars for political supporters. So it should be no surprise at all that the city pays a Santeria priest a salary and benefits.

The surprise is that he earns his money.

Every morning at sunrise, the *babalao* arrives at the courthouse, where he usually finds one or two small animal sacrifices left by people with important legal cases pending. No Miami citizen in his right mind would touch these things, but of course it would be very bad form to leave dead animals littered about Miami's great temple of justice. So the *babalao* removes the sacrifices, cowrie shells, feathers, beads, charms, and pictures in a way that will not offend the *orishas*, the guiding spirits of Santeria.

He is also called upon from time to time to cast spells for other important civic items, like blessing a new overpass built by a low-bid contractor or putting a curse on the New York Jets. And he had apparently been called upon this time by my sister, Deborah.

The official city *babalao* was a black man of about fifty, six feet tall with very long fingernails and a considerable paunch. He was dressed in white pants, a white guayabera, and sandals. He came plodding over from the patrol car that had brought him, with the cranky expression of a minor bureaucrat whose important filing work had been interrupted. As he walked he polished a pair of black horn-rimmed glasses on the tail of his shirt. He put them on as he approached the bodies and, when he did, what he saw stopped him dead.

For a long moment he just stared. Then, with his eyes still glued to the bodies, he backed away. At about thirty feet away, he turned around and walked back to the patrol car and climbed in.

'What the fuck,' Deborah said, and I agreed that she had summed things up nicely. The *babalao* slammed the car door and sat there in the front seat, staring straight ahead through the windshield without moving. After a moment Deborah muttered, 'Shit,' and went over to the car. And because like all inquiring minds I want to know, I followed.

When I got to the car Deborah was tapping on the glass of the passenger-side window and the *babalao* was still staring straight ahead, jaw clenched, grimly pretending not to see her. Debs knocked harder; he shook his head. 'Open the door,' she said in her best police-issue put-down-the-gun voice. He shook his head harder. She knocked on the window harder. 'Open it!' she said.

Finally he rolled down the window. 'This is nothing to do with me,' he said.

'Then what is it?' Deborah asked him.

He just shook his head. 'I need to get back to work,' he said.

'Is it Palo Mayombe?' I asked him, and Debs glared at me for interrupting, but it seemed like a fair question. Palo Mayombe was a somewhat darker offshoot of Santeria, and although I knew almost nothing about it, there had been rumors of some very wicked rituals that had piqued my interest.

But the *babalao* shook his head. 'Listen,' he said. 'There's stuff out there, you guys got no idea, and you don't wanna know.'

'Is this one of those things?' I asked.

'I dunno,' he said. 'Might be.'

'What can you tell us about it?' Deborah demanded.

'I can't tell you nothing 'cause I don't know nothing,' he said. 'But I don't like it and I don't want anything to do with it. I got important stuff to do today – tell the cop I gotta go.' And he rolled the window up again.

'Shit,' Deborah said, and she looked at me accusingly.

'Well I didn't do anything,' I said.

'Shit,' she said again. 'What the hell does that mean?'

'I am completely in the dark,' I said.

'Uh-huh,' she said, and she looked entirely unconvinced, which was a little ironic. I mean, people believe me all the time when I'm being somewhat less than perfectly truthful – and yet here was my own foster flesh and blood, refusing to believe that I was, in fact, completely in the dark. Aside from the fact that the *babalao* seemed to be having the same reaction as the Passenger – and what should I make of that?

Before I could pursue that fascinating line of thought, I realized that Deborah was still staring at me with an exceedingly unpleasant expression on her face.

'Did you find the heads?' I asked, quite helpfully I thought. 'We might get a feel for the ritual if we saw what he did to the heads.'

'No, we haven't found the heads. I haven't found anything except a brother who's holding out on me.'

'Deborah, really, this permanent air of nasty suspicion is not good for your face muscles. You'll get frown lines.'

'Maybe I'll get a killer, too,' she said, and walked back to the two charred bodies.

Since my usefulness was apparently at an end, at least as far as my sister was concerned, there was really not a great deal more for me to do on-site. I finished up with my blood kit, taking small samples of the dried black stuff caked around the two necks, and headed back to the lab in plenty of time for a late lunch.

But alas, poor Dauntless Dexter obviously had a target painted on his back, because my troubles had barely begun. Just as I was tidying up my desk and getting ready to take part in the cheerfully homicidal rush-hour traffic, Vince Masuoka came skipping into my office. 'I just talked to Manny,' he said. 'He can see us tomorrow morning at ten.'

'That's wonderful news,' I said. 'The only thing that could possibly make it any better would be to know who Manny is and why he wants to see us.'

Vince actually looked a little hurt, one of the few genuine expressions I had ever seen on his face. 'Manny Borque,' he said. 'The caterer.'

'The one from MTV?'

'Yeah, that's right,' Vince said. 'The guy that's won all the awards, and he's been written up in *Gourmet* magazine.'

'Oh, yes,' I said, stalling for time in the hope that some brilliant flash of inspiration would hit to help me dodge this terrible fate. 'The award-winning caterer.'

'Dexter, this guy is big. He could make your whole wedding.'

'Well, Vince, I think that's terrific, but—'

'Listen,' he said, with an air of firm command that I had never heard from him before, 'you said you would talk to Rita about this and let her decide.'

'I said that?'

'Yes, you did. And I am not going to let you throw away a wonderful opportunity like this, not when it's something that I know Rita would really love to have.'

I wasn't sure how he could be so positive about that. After all, I was actually engaged to the woman, and I had no idea what sort of caterer might fill her with shock and awe. But I didn't think this was the time to ask him how he knew what Rita would and would not love. Then again, a man who dressed up as Carmen Miranda for Halloween might very well have a keener insight than mine into my fiancée's innermost culinary desires.

'Well,' I said, at last deciding that procrastinating long enough to escape was the best answer, 'in that case, I'll go home and talk to Rita about it.'

'Do that,' he said. And he did not storm out, but if there had been a door to slam, he might have slammed it.

I finished tidying up and trundled on out into the evening traffic. On the way home a middle-aged man in a Toyota SUV got right behind me and started honking the horn for some reason. After five or six blocks he pulled around me and, as he flipped me off, juked his steering wheel slightly to frighten me into running up on the sidewalk. Although I admired his spirit and would have loved to oblige him, I stayed on the road. There is never any point in trying to make sense of the way Miami drivers go about getting from one place to another. You just have to relax and enjoy the violence – and of course, that part was never a problem for me. So I smiled and waved, and he stomped on his accelerator and disappeared into traffic at about sixty miles per hour over the speed limit.

Normally I find the chaotic mayhem of the evening drive home to be the perfect way to end the day. Seeing all the anger and lust to kill relaxes me, makes me feel at one with my hometown and its spritely inhabitants. But tonight I found it difficult to summon up any good cheer at all. I never for a moment thought it could ever happen, but I was worried.

Worse still, I didn't know what I was actually worried about, only that the Dark Passenger had used the silent treatment on me at a scene of creative homicide. This had never happened, and I could only believe that something unusual and possibly Dexter-threatening had caused it now. But what? And how could I be sure, when I didn't really know the first thing about the Passenger itself, except that it had always been there to offer happy insight and commentary. We had seen burned bodies before, and pottery aplenty, with never a twitch or a tweet. Was it the combination? Or something specific to these two bodies? Or was it entirely coincidental and had nothing whatever to do with what we had seen?

The more I thought about it, the less I knew, but the traffic swirled around me in its soothing homicidal patterns, and by the time I got to Rita's house I had almost convinced myself that there was really nothing to worry about.

Rita, Cody, and Astor were already home when I got there. Rita worked much closer to the house than I did, and the kids were in an after-school program at a nearby park, so they had all been waiting for at least half an hour for the opportunity to torment me out of my hard-won peace of mind.

'It was on the news,' Astor whispered as I opened the door, and Cody nodded and said, 'Gross,' in his soft, hoarse voice.

'What was on the news?' I said, struggling to get past them and into the house without trampling on them.

'You *burned* them!' Astor hissed at me, and Cody looked at me with a complete lack of expression that somehow conveyed disapproval.

'I what? Who did I—'

'Those two people they found at the college,' she said. 'We don't want to learn *that*,' she added emphatically, and Cody nodded again.

'At the – you mean at the university? I didn't—'

'A university is a college,' Astor said with the underlined certainty of a ten-year-old girl. 'And we think burning is just gross.'

It began to dawn on me what they had seen on the news – a report from the scene where I had spent my morning collecting dry-roasted blood samples from two charred bodies. And somehow, merely because they knew I had been out to play the other night, they had decided that this was how I had spent my time. Even without the Dark Passenger's strange retreat, I agreed that it was completely gross, and I found it highly annoying that they thought I was capable of something like that. 'Listen,' I said sternly, 'that was not—'

'Dexter? Is that you?' Rita yodeled from the kitchen.

'I'm not sure,' I called back. 'Let me check my wallet.'

Rita bustled in beaming and before I could protect myself she wrapped herself around me, apparently intent on squeezing hard enough to interfere with my breathing. 'Hi, handsome,' she said. 'How was your day?'

'Gross,' muttered Astor.

'Absolutely wonderful,' I said, fighting for breath. 'Plenty of corpses for everybody today. And I got to use my cotton swabs, too.'

Rita made a face. 'Ugh. That's – I don't know if you should talk like that around the children. What if they get bad dreams?'

If I had been a completely honest person, I would have told her that her children were far more likely to cause someone else bad dreams than to get them, but since I am not hampered by any need to tell the truth, I just patted her and said, 'They hear worse than that on the cartoons every day. Isn't that right, kids?'

'No,' said Cody softly, and I looked at him with surprise. He rarely said anything, and to have him not only speak but actually contradict me was disturbing. In fact, the whole day was turning out to be wildly askew, from the panicked flight of the Dark Passenger this morning and continuing on through Vince's catering tirade – and now this. What in the name of all that is dark and dreadful was going on? Was my aura out of balance? Had the moons of Jupiter aligned against me in Sagittarius?

'Cody,' I said. And I do hope some hurt showed in my voice. 'You're not going to have bad dreams about this, are you?'

'He doesn't have bad dreams,' Astor said, as if everyone who was not severely mentally challenged ought to know that. 'He doesn't have any dreams at *all*.'

'Good to know,' I said, since I almost never dream myself, either, and for some reason it seemed important to have as much as possible in common with Cody. But Rita was having none of it.

'Really, Astor, don't be silly,' she said. 'Of course Cody has dreams. Every-body has dreams.'

'I don't,' Cody insisted. Now he was not only standing up to both of us, he was practically breaking his own record for chattiness at the same time. And even though I didn't have a heart, except for circulatory purposes, I felt an affection for him and wanted to come down on his side.

'Good for you,' I said. 'Stick with it. Dreams are very overrated. Interfere with getting a good night's sleep.'

'Dexter, really,' Rita said. 'I don't think we should encourage this.'

'Of course we should,' I said, winking at Cody. 'He's showing fire, spunk, and imagination.'

'Am not,' he said, and I absolutely marveled at his verbal outpouring.

'Of course you're not,' I said to him, lowering my voice. 'But we have to say stuff like that to your mom, or she gets worried.'

'For Pete's sake,' Rita said. 'I give up with you two. Run outside and play, kids.'

'We wanna play with Dexter,' Astor pouted.

'I'll be along in a few minutes,' I said.

'You better,' she said darkly. They vanished down the hall toward the back door, and as they left I took a deep breath, happy that the vicious and unwar-ranted attacks against me were over for now. Of course, I should have known better.

'Come in here,' Rita said, and she led me by the hand to the sofa. 'Vince called a little while ago,' she said as we settled onto the cushions.

'Did he?' I said, and a sudden thrill of danger ripped through me at the idea of what he might have said to Rita. 'What did he say?'

She shook her head. 'He was very mysterious. He said to let him know as soon as we had talked it over. And when I asked him talked what over he wouldn't say. He just said you would tell me.'

I barely managed to stop myself from the unthinkable conversational blunder of saying, 'Did he?' again. In my defense, I have to admit that my brain was whirling, not only with the panicked notion that I had to flee to some place of safety but also with the thought that before I fled I needed to find time to visit Vince with my little bag of toys. But before I could mentally choose the correct blade, Rita went on.

'Honestly, Dexter, you're very lucky to have a friend like Vince. He really does take his duties as best man seriously, and he has wonderful taste.'

'Wonderfully expensive, too,' I said – and perhaps I was still recovering from my near-gaffe with almost repeating 'Did he?' but I knew the moment it was out of my mouth that it was absolutely the wrong thing to say. And sure enough, Rita lit up like a Christmas tree.

'Really?' she said. 'Well, I suppose he would, after all. I mean, it most often goes together, doesn't it? You really do get what you pay for, usually.'

'Yes, but it's a question of how much you have to pay,' I said.

'How much for what?' Rita said, and there it was. I was stuck.

'Well,' I said, 'Vince has this crazy idea that we should hire this South Beach caterer, a very pricey guy who does a lot of celebrity events and things.'

Rita clapped her hands under her chin and looked radiantly happy. 'Not Manny Borque!' she cried. 'Vince knows Manny Borque?'

Of course it was all over right there, but Dauntless Dexter does not go down without a fight, no matter how feeble. 'Did I mention that he's very expensive?' I said hopefully.

'Oh, Dexter, you can't worry about money at a time like this,' she said.

'I can too. I am.'

'Not if there's a chance to get Manny Borque,' she said, and there was a surprisingly strong note in her voice that I had never heard before except when she was angry with Cody and Astor.

'Yes, but Rita,' I said, 'it doesn't make sense to spend a ton of money just for the caterer.'

'Sense has nothing to do with it,' she said, and I admit that I agreed with her there. 'If we can get Manny Borque to cater our wedding, we'd be crazy not to do it.'

'But,' I said, and there I stopped, because beyond the fact that it seemed idiotic to pay a king's ransom for crackers with endives hand-painted with rhubarb juice and sculpted to look like Jennifer Lopez, I could not think of any other objection. I mean, wasn't that enough?

Apparently not. 'Dexter,' she said. 'How many times will we get married?' And to my great credit I was still alert enough to clamp down on the urge to say, 'At least twice, in your case,' which I think was probably very wise.

I quickly changed course, diving straight into tactics learned from pretending to be human for so many years. 'Rita,' I said, 'the important part of the wedding is when I slip the ring on your finger. I don't care what we eat afterward.'

'That's so sweet,' she said. 'Then you don't mind if we hire Manny Borque?'

Once again I found myself losing an argument before I even knew which side I was on. I became aware of a dryness in my mouth – caused, no doubt, by the fact that my mouth was hanging open as my brain struggled to make sense of what had just happened, and then to find something clever to say to get things back onto dry land.

But it was far too late. 'I'll call Vince back,' she said, and she leaned over to give me a kiss on the cheek. 'Oh, this is so exciting. Thank you, Dexter.'

Well, after all, isn't marriage about compromise?

7

Naturally enough, Manny Borque lived in South Beach. He was on the top floor of one of the new high-rise buildings that spring up around Miami like mushrooms after a heavy rain. This one sat on what was once a deserted beach where Harry used to take Debs and me beachcombing early on Saturday mornings. We would find old life preservers, mysterious wooden chunks of some unfortunate boat, lobster-pot buoys, pieces of fishnet, and on one thrilling morning, an exceedingly dead human body rolling in the surf. It was a treasured boyhood memory, and I resented extremely that someone had built this shiny flimsy tower on the site.

The next morning at ten Vince and I left work together and drove over to the horrible new building that had replaced the scene of my youthful joy. I rode the elevator to the top in silence, watching Vince fidget and blink. Why he should be nervous about facing someone who sculpted chopped liver for a living, I don't know, but he clearly was. A drop of sweat rolled down his cheek and he swallowed convulsively, twice.

'He's a caterer, Vince,' I told him. 'He isn't dangerous. He can't even revoke your library card.'

Vince looked at me and swallowed again. 'He's got a real temper,' he said. 'He can be very demanding.'

'Well, then,' I said with great good cheer, 'let's go find somebody else more reasonable.'

He set his jaw like a man facing a firing squad and shook his head. 'No,' he said bravely, 'we're going to go through with this.' And the elevator door slid open, right on cue. He squared his shoulders, nodded, and said, 'Come on.'

We went down to the end of the hall, and Vince stopped in front of the last door. He took a deep breath, raised his fist, and, after a slight hesitation, knocked on the door. After a long moment in which nothing happened, he looked at me and blinked, his hand still raised. 'Maybe,' he said.

The door opened. 'Hello Vic!' the thing in the doorway warbled, and Vince responded by blushing and stammering, 'I only hi.' Then he shifted his weight from one foot to the other, stammered something that sounded like, 'Er wellah,' and took a half step backward.

It was a remarkable and thoroughly engaging performance, and I was not the only one who seemed to enjoy it. The manikin who had answered the door watched with a smile that suggested he might enjoy being in the audience for any kind of human suffering, and he let Vince squirm for several long moments before he finally said, 'Well come *in!*'

Manny Borque, if this was really him and not some strange hologram from *Star Wars*, stood a full five foot six inches tall, from the bottom of his embroidered high-heeled silver boots to the top of his dyed orange head. His hair was cut short, except for black bangs which parted on his forehead like a swallow's tail and draped down over a pair of enormous rhinestone-studded eyeglasses. He was dressed in a long, bright-red dashiki, and apparently nothing else, and it swirled around him as he stepped back from the door to motion us in, and then walked in rapid little steps toward a huge picture window that looked out on the water.

'Come over here and we'll have a little talk,' he said, sidestepping a pedestal holding an enormous object that looked like a giant ball of animal vomit dipped in plastic and spray-painted with Day-Glo graffiti. He led the way to a glass table by the window, around which sat four things that were probably supposed to be chairs but could easily have been mistaken for bronze camel saddles welded onto stilts. 'Sit,' he said, with an expansive wave of his hand, and I took the chair-thing nearest the window. Vince hesitated for a moment, then sat next to me, and Manny hopped up onto the seat directly across from him. 'Well,' he said. 'How have you been, Vic? Would you like some coffee?' and without waiting for an answer he swiveled his head to his left and called, 'Eduardo!'

Beside me Vince took a ragged breath, but before he could do anything with it Manny whipped back around and faced me. 'And you must be the blushing bridegroom!' he said.

'Dexter Morgan,' I said. 'But I'm not a very good blusher.'

'Oh, well, I think Vic is doing enough for both of you,' he said. And sure enough, Vince obligingly turned just as scarlet as his complexion would allow him to do. Since I was still more than a little peeved at being subjected to this ordeal, I decided not to come to his aid by offering Manny a withering remark, or even correcting him on the subject of Vince's actual identity as 'Vince,' not 'Vic.' I was sure he knew the right name quite well and was simply tormenting Vince. And that was fine with me: let Vince squirm – it served him right for going over my head to Rita and getting me into this.

Eduardo bustled in holding a vintage Fiestaware coffee service in several bright colors, balanced on a clear plastic tray. He was a stocky young man about twice the size of Manny, and he, too, seemed very anxious to please the little troll. He set a yellow cup in front of Manny, and then moved to put the blue one in front of Vince when he was stopped by Manny, who laid a finger on his arm.

'Eduardo,' he said in a silky voice, and the boy froze. 'Yellow? Don't we remember? Manny gets the blue cup.'

Eduardo practically fell over himself grinding into reverse, nearly dropping the tray in his haste to remove the offensive yellow coffee cup and replace it with the proper blue one.

'Thank you, Eduardo,' Manny said, and Eduardo paused for a moment, apparently to see if Manny really meant it or if he had done something else wrong. But Manny just patted him on the arm and said, 'Serve our guests now, please,' and Eduardo nodded and moved around the table.

As it turned out, I got the yellow cup, which was fine with me, although I wondered if it meant that they didn't like me. When he had poured the coffee, Eduardo hustled back to the kitchen and returned with a small plate holding half a dozen *pastelitos*. And although they were not, in fact, shaped like Jennifer Lopez's derriere, they might as well have been. They looked like little cream-filled porcupines – dark brown lumps bristling with quills that were either chocolate or taken from a sea anemone. The center was open, revealing a blob of orange-colored custardy-type stuff, and each blob had a dab of green, blue, or brown on top.

Eduardo put the plate in the center of the table, and we all just looked at it for a moment. Manny seemed to be admiring them, and Vince was apparently feeling some kind of religious awe, as he swallowed a few more times and made a sound that may have been a gasp. For my part, I wasn't sure if we were supposed to eat the things or use them for some bizarre, bloody Aztec ritual, so I simply studied the plate, hoping for a clue.

It was finally provided by Vince. 'My God,' he blurted.

Manny nodded. 'They're wonderful, aren't they?' he said. 'But so-o-o-o last year.' He picked one up, the one with the blue top, and gazed at it with a kind of aloof fondness. 'The color palette really got tired, and that horrible old hotel over by Indian Creek started to copy them. Still,' he said with a shrug, and he popped it into his mouth. I was glad to see that it didn't seem to cause any major bleeding. 'One does grow fond of one's own little tricks.' He turned and winked at Eduardo. 'Perhaps a little too fond sometimes.' Eduardo went pale and fled to the kitchen, and Manny turned back to us with a huge crocodile smile. 'Do try one, though, won't you?'

'I'm afraid to bite one,' Vince said. 'They're so *perfect*.'

'And I'm afraid they might bite back,' I said.

Manny showed off a few dozen teeth. 'If I could teach them that,' he said, 'I would never be lonely.' He nudged the plate in my direction. 'Go ahead,' he said.

'Would you serve these at my wedding?' I asked, thinking perhaps somebody ought to find some kind of point in all this.

Vince elbowed me, hard, but it was apparently too late. Manny's eyes had narrowed to little slits, although his impressive dental work was still on display. 'I do not serve,' he said. 'I *present*. And I present whatever seems best to *me*.'

'Shouldn't I have some idea ahead of time what that might be?' I asked, 'I mean, suppose the bride is allergic to wasabi-basted arugula aspic?'

Manny tightened his fists so hard I could hear the knuckles creak. For a moment I had a small thrill of hope at the thought that I might have clevered myself out of a caterer. But then Manny relaxed and laughed. 'I like your friend, Vic,' he said. 'He's very brave.'

Vince favored us both with a smile and started to breathe again, and Manny began to doodle with a pad and paper, and that is how I ended up with the great Manny Borque agreeing to cater my wedding at the special discounted price of only $250 a plate.

It seemed a bit high. But after all, I had been specifically instructed not to worry about money. I was sure Rita would think of some way to make it work, perhaps by inviting only two or three people. In any case, I didn't get a great deal of time to worry about mere finances, as my cell phone began its happy little dirge almost immediately, and when I answered I heard Deborah say, without even attempting to match my cheery hello, 'I need you here right away.'

'I'm awfully busy with some very important canapés,' I told her. 'Can I borrow twenty thousand dollars?'

She made a noise in her throat and said, 'I don't have time for bullshit, Dexter. The twenty-four hours starts in twenty minutes and I need you there for it.' It was the custom in Homicide to convene everybody involved in a case twenty-four hours after the work began, to make sure everything was organized and everyone was on the same page. And Debs obviously felt that I had some kind of shrewd insight to offer – very thoughtful really, but untrue. With the Dark Passenger apparently still on hiatus, I didn't think the great light of insight would come flooding in anytime soon.

'Debs, I really don't have any thought at all on this one,' I said.

'Just get over here,' she told me, and hung up.

8

The traffic on the 836 was backed up for half a mile right after the 395 from Miami Beach poured into it. We inched forward between exits until we could see the problem: a truckload of watermelons had emptied out onto the highway. There was a streak of red-and-green goo six inches thick across the road, dotted with a sprinkling of cars in various stages of destruction. An ambulance went past on the shoulder, followed by a procession of cars driven by people too important to wait in a traffic jam. Horns honked all along the line, people yelled and waved their fists, and somewhere ahead I heard a single gunshot. It was good to be back to normal life.

By the time we fought our way through the traffic and onto surface streets, we had lost fifteen minutes and it took another fifteen to get back to work. Vince and I rode the elevator to the second floor in silence, but as the doors slid open and we stepped out, he stopped me. 'You're doing the right thing,' he said.

'Yes, I am,' I said. 'But if I don't do it quickly Deborah will kill me.'

He grabbed my arm. 'I mean about Manny,' he said. 'You're going to love what he does. It will really make a difference.'

I was already aware that it would really make a difference in my bank account, but beyond that I still didn't see the point. Would everyone truly have a better time if they were served a series of apparently alien objects of uncertain use and origin instead of cold cuts? There is a great deal I don't understand about human beings, but this really seemed to take the cake – assuming we would have a cake at all, which in my opinion was not a sure thing.

There was one thing I understood quite well, however, and that was Deborah's attitude about punctuality. It was handed down from our father, and it said that lateness was disrespect and there were no excuses. So I pried Vince's fingers off my arm and shook his hand. 'I'm sure we're all going to be very happy with the food,' I said.

He held on to my hand. 'It's more than that,' he said.

'Vince—'

'You're making a statement about the rest of your life,' he said. 'A really *good* statement, that your and Rita's life together—'

'My life is in danger if I don't go, Vince,' I said.

'I'm really happy about this,' he said, and it was so unnerving to see him display an apparently authentic emotion that there was actually a little bit of panic to my flight away from him and down the hall to the conference room.

The room was full, since this was becoming a somewhat high-profile case after the hysterical news stories of the evening before about two young women found burned and headless. Deborah glared at me as I slipped in and stood by the door, and I gave her what I hoped was a disarming smile. She cut off the speaker, one of the patrolmen who had been first on the scene.

'All right,' she said. 'We know we're not going to find the heads on the scene.'

I had thought that my late entrance and Deborah's vicious glare at me would certainly win the award for Most Dramatic Entrance, but I was dead wrong. Because just as Debs tried to get the meeting moving again, I was upstaged as thoroughly as a candle at a firebombing.

'Come on, people,' Sergeant Sister said. 'Let's have some ideas about this.'

'We could drag the lake,' Camilla Figg said. She was a thirty-five-year-old forensics geek and usually kept quiet, and it was rather surprising to hear her speak. Apparently some people preferred it that way, because a thin, intense cop named Corrigan jumped on her right away.

'Bullshit,' said Corrigan. 'Heads float.'

'They don't float – they're solid bone,' Camilla insisted.

'Some of 'em are,' Corrigan said, and he got his little laugh.

Deborah frowned, and was about to step in with an authoritative word or two, when a noise in the hall stopped her.

CLUMP.

Not that loud, but somehow it commanded all the attention there was in the room.

CLUMP.

Closer, a little louder, for all the world approaching us now like something from a low-budget horror movie . . .

CLUMP.

For some reason I couldn't hope to explain, everyone in the room seemed to hold their breath and turn slowly toward the door. And if only because I wanted to fit in, I began to turn for a peek into the hall myself, when I was stopped by the smallest possible interior tickle, just a hint of a twitch, and so I closed my eyes and listened. *Hello?* I said mentally, and after a very short pause there was a small, slightly hesitant sound, almost a clearing of the mental throat, and then—

Somebody in the room muttered, 'Holy sweet Jesus,' with the kind of reverent horror that was always guaranteed to pique my interest, and the small not-quite-sound within purred just a bit and then subsided. I opened my eyes.

I can only say that I had been so happy to feel the Passenger stirring in the dark backseat that for a moment I had tuned out everything around me. This is always a dangerous slip, especially for artificial humans like me, and the point was driven home with an absolutely stunning impact when I opened my eyes.

It was indeed low-budget horror, *Night of the Living Dead*, but in the flesh and not a movie at all, because standing in the doorway, just to my right, staring at me, was a man who was really supposed to be dead.

Sergeant Doakes.

Doakes had never liked me. He seemed to be the only cop on the entire force who suspected that I might be what, in fact, I was. I had always thought he could see through my disguise because he was somewhat the same thing himself, a cold killer. He had tried and failed to prove that I was guilty of almost anything, and that failure had also failed to endear me to him.

The last time I had seen Doakes the paramedics had been loading him into an ambulance. He had been unconscious, partly as the result of the shock and pain of having his tongue, feet, and hands removed by a very talented amateur surgeon who thought Doakes had done him wrong. Now it was true that I had gently encouraged that notion with the part-time doctor, but I had at least had the decency to persuade Doakes first to go along with the plan, in order to catch the inhuman fiend. And I had also very nearly saved Doakes at considerable risk to my own precious and irreplaceable life and limbs. I hadn't quite pulled off the dashing and timely rescue I'm sure Doakes had hoped for, but I had tried, and it was really and truly not my fault that he had been more dead than alive when they hauled him away.

So I didn't think it was asking too much for some small acknowledgment of the great hazard I had exposed myself to on his behalf. I didn't need flowers, or a medal, or even a box of chocolates, but perhaps something along the lines of a hearty clap on the back and a murmured, 'Thanks, old fellow.' Of course he would have some trouble murmuring coherently without a tongue, and the clap on the back with one of his new metal hands could prove painful, but he might at least try. Was that so unreasonable?

Apparently it was. Doakes stared at me as if he was the hungriest dog in the world and I was the very last steak. I had thought that he used to look at me with enough venom to lay low the entire endangered species list. But that had been the gentle laughter of a tousle-haired child on a sunny day compared to the way he was looking at me now. And I knew what had made the Dark Passenger clear its throat – it had been the scent of a familiar predator. I felt the slow flex of interior wings, coming back to full roaring life, rising to the challenge in Doakes's eyes. And behind those dark eyes his own inner monster snarled and spat at mine. We stood like that for a long moment, on the outside simply staring but on the inside two predatory shadows screeching out a challenge.

Someone was speaking, but the world had narrowed to just me and Doakes and the two black shadows inside us calling for battle, and neither one of us heard a word, just an annoying drone in the background.

Deborah's voice cut through the fog at last. 'Sergeant Doakes,' she said, somewhat forcefully. Finally Doakes turned to face her and the spell was broken. And feeling somewhat smug in the power – joy and bliss! – of the Passenger, as well as the petty victory of having Doakes turn away first, I faded into the wallpaper, taking a small step back to survey the leftovers of my once-mighty nemesis.

Sergeant Doakes still held the department record for bench press, but he did not look like he would defend his record anytime soon. He was gaunt and, except for the fire smoldering behind his eyes, he looked almost weak. He stood stiffly on his two prosthetic feet, his arms hanging straight down by his sides, with gleaming silver things that looked like a complicated kind of vise grip protruding from each wrist.

I could hear the others in the room breathing, but aside from that there was not a sound. Everyone simply stared at the thing that had once been Doakes, and he stared at Deborah, who licked her lips, apparently trying to think of something coherent to say, and finally came up with, 'Have a seat, Doakes. Um. I'll bring you up to date?'

Doakes looked at her for a long moment. Then he turned awkwardly around, glared at me, and clumped out of the room, his strange, measured footsteps echoing down the hall until they were gone.

On the whole, cops don't like to give the impression that they are ever impressed or intimidated, so it was several seconds before anyone risked giving away any unwanted emotion by breathing again. Naturally enough, it was Deborah who finally broke the unnatural silence. 'All right,' she said, and suddenly everyone was clearing their throats and shifting in their chairs.

'All right,' she repeated, 'so we won't find the heads at the scene.'

'Heads don't float,' Camilla Figg insisted scornfully, and we were back to where we had been before the sudden semi-appearance of Sergeant Doakes. And they droned on for another ten minutes or so, tirelessly fighting crime by arguing about who was supposed to fill out the paperwork, when we were rudely interrupted once again by the door beside me swinging open.

'Sorry to interrupt,' Captain Matthews said. 'I've got some – ah – really great news, I think.' He looked around the room frowning, which even I could have told him was not the proper face for delivering great news. 'It's, uh, ahem. Sergeant Doakes has come back, and he's, uh – It's important for you people to realize that he's been badly, uh, damaged. He has only a couple of years left before he's eligible for full pension, so the lawyers, ah – we thought, under the circumstances, um . . .' He trailed off and looked around the room. 'Did somebody already tell you people?'

'Sergeant Doakes was just here,' Deborah said.

'Oh,' Matthews said. 'Well, then—' He shrugged. 'That's fine. All right then. I'll let you get on with the meeting then. Anything to report?'

'No real progress yet, Captain,' Deborah said.

'Well, I'm sure you'll get this thing wrapped up before the press— I mean, in a timely fashion.'

'Yes, sir,' she said.

'All right then,' he said again. And he looked around the room once, squared his shoulders, and left the room.

'Heads don't float,' somebody else said, and a small snort of laughter went around the room.

'Jesus,' Deborah said. 'Can we focus on this, please? We got two bodies here.'

And more to come, I thought, and the Dark Passenger quivered slightly, as if trying very bravely not to run away, but that was all, and I thought no more about it.

9

I don't dream. I mean, I'm sure that at some point during my normal sleep, there must be images and fragments of nonsense parading through my sub-conscious. After all, they tell me that happens with everyone. But I never seem to remember dreams if I do have them, which they tell me happens to nobody at all. So I assume that I do not dream.

It was therefore something of a shock to discover myself late that night, cradled in Rita's arms, shouting something I could not quite hear; just the echo of my own strangled voice coming back at me out of the cottony dark, and Rita's cool hand on my forehead, her voice murmuring, 'All right, sweet-heart, I won't leave you.'

'Thank you very much,' I said in a croaking voice. I cleared my throat and sat up.

'You had a bad dream,' she told me.

'Really? What was it?' I still didn't remember anything but my shouting and a vague sense of danger crowding in on me, and me all alone.

'I don't know,' Rita said. 'You were shouting, "Come back! Don't leave me alone."' She cleared her throat. 'Dexter – I know you're feeling some stress about our wedding—'

'Not at all,' I said.

'But I want you to know. I will never leave you.' She reached for my hand again. 'This is forever with me, big man. I am holding on to you.' She scooted over and put her head on my shoulder. 'Don't worry. I won't ever leave you, Dexter.'

Even though I lack experience with dreams, I was fairly sure that my sub-conscious was not terribly worried about Rita leaving me. I mean, it hadn't occurred to me that she would, which was not really a sign of trust on my part. I just hadn't thought about it. Truly, I had no idea why she wanted to hang on to me in the first place, so any hypothetical leave-taking was just as mysterious.

No, this was my subconscious. If it was crying out in pain at the threat of abandonment, I knew exactly what it feared losing: the Dark Passenger. My bosom buddy, my constant companion on my journey through life's sorrows and sharp pleasures. That was the fear behind the dream: losing the thing that had been so very much a part of me, had actually defined me, for my whole life.

When it scuttled into hiding at the university crime scene it had clearly shaken me badly, more than I had known at the time. The sudden and very scary reappearance of 65 percent of Sergeant Doakes supp-lied the sense of danger, and the rest was easy. My subconscious had kicked in and supplied a dream on the subject. Perfectly clear – Psych 101, a textbook case, nothing to worry about.

So why was I still worrying?

Because the Passenger had never even flinched before, and I still didn't know why it had chosen now. Was Rita right about the stress of the approaching wedding? Or was there really something about the two headless bodies by the university lake that just plain scared the Dark out of me?

I didn't know – and, since it seemed like Rita's ideas about comforting me had begun to take a more active turn, it did not look like I was going to find out anytime soon.

'Come here, baby,' Rita whispered.

And after all, there really isn't any place to run in a queen-size bed, is there?

The next morning found Deborah obsessed with finding the missing heads from the two bodies at the university. Somehow word had leaked out to the press that the department was interested in finding a couple of skulls that had wandered away. This was Miami, and I really would have thought that a missing head would get less press coverage than a traffic tie-up on I-95, but something about the fact that there were two of them, and that they apparently belonged to young women, created quite a stir. Captain Matthews was a man who knew the value of being mentioned in the press, but even he was not pleased with the note of surly hysteria that attached itself to this story.

And so pressure came down on all of us from above; from the captain to Deborah, who wasted no time passing it on down to the rest of us. Vince Masuoka became convinced that he could provide Deborah with the key to the whole matter by finding out which bizarre religious sect was responsible. This led to him sticking his head in my door that morning and, without any kind of warning, giving me his best fake smile and saying, firmly and distinctly, 'Candomblé.'

'Shame on you,' I said. 'This is no time for that kind of language.'

'Ha,' he said, with his terrible artificial laugh. 'But it is, I'm sure of it. Candomblé is like Santeria, but it's Brazilian.'

'Vince, I have no reason to doubt you on that. My question is, what the hell are you talking about?'

He came two steps into the room in a kind of prance, as if his body wanted to take off and he couldn't quite fight it down. 'They have a thing about animal heads in some of their rituals,' he said. 'It's on the Internet.'

'Really,' I said. 'Does it say on the Internet that this Brazilian thing barbecues humans, cuts off their heads, and replaces them with ceramic bulls' heads?'

Vince wilted just a bit. 'No,' he admitted, and he raised his eyebrows hopefully. 'But they use animals.'

'How do they use them, Vince?' I asked.

'Well,' he said, and he looked around my little room, possibly for another topic of conversation. 'Sometimes they, you know, offer a part to the gods, and then they eat the rest.'

'Vince,' I said, 'are you suggesting that somebody ate the missing heads?'

'No,' he said, turning sullen, almost like Cody and Astor might have done. 'But they could have.'

'It would be very crunchy, wouldn't it?'

'All right,' he said, exceedingly sulky now. 'I'm just trying to help.' And he stalked away, without even a small fake smile.

But the chaos had only begun. As my unwanted trip to dreamland indicated, I was already under enough pressure without the added strain of a rampaging sister. But only a few minutes later, my small oasis of peace was ripped asunder once again, this time by Deborah, who came roaring into my office as if pursued by killer bees.

'Come on,' she snarled at me.

'Come on where?' I asked, quite a reasonable question, I thought, but you would have thought I had asked her to shave her head and paint her skull blue.

'Just get in gear, and come on!' she said, so I came on and followed her down to the parking lot and into her car.

'I swear to God,' she fumed as she hammered her car through the traffic, 'I have never seen Matthews this pissed before. And now it's my fault!' She banged on the horn for emphasis and swerved in front of a van that said PALMVIEW ASSISTED LIVING on the side. 'All because some asshole leaked the heads to the press.'

'Well, Debs,' I said, with all the reasonable soothing I could muster, 'I'm sure the heads will turn up.'

'You're goddamned right they will,' she said, narrowly missing a fat man on a bicycle that had huge saddlebags stuffed with scrap metal. 'Because I am going to find out which cult the son of a bitch belongs to, and then I'm going to nail the bastard.'

I paused in mid-soothe. Apparently my dear demented sister, just like Vince, had gotten hold of the idea that finding the appropriate alternative religion would yield a killer. 'Ah, all right,' I said. 'And where are we going to do that?'

She slid the car out onto Biscayne Boulevard and into a parking space at the curb without answering, and got out of the car. And so I found myself patiently following her into the Center for Inner Enhancement, a clearing-house for all the wonderfully useful things that have the words 'holistic,' 'herbal,' or 'aura' in them.

The Center was a small and shabby building in an area of Biscayne Boulevard that had apparently been designated by treaty as a kind of reservation for prostitutes and crack dealers. There were enormous bars on the storefront windows and more of them on the door, which was locked. Deborah pounded on it and after a moment it gave an annoying buzz. She pushed, and finally it clicked and swung open.

We stepped in. A suffocating cloud of sickly sweet incense rolled over me, and I could tell that my inner enhancement had begun with a complete overhaul of my lungs. Through the smoke I could dimly see a large yellow silk banner hung along one wall that stated WE ARE ALL ONE. It did not say one of what. A recording played softly, the sound of someone who seemed to be fighting off an overdose of downers by occasionally ringing a series of small bells. A waterfall murmured in the background and I am sure that my spirit would have soared, if only I had one. Since I didn't, I found the whole thing just a bit irritating.

But of course, we weren't here for pleasure, or even inner enhancement. And Sergeant Sister was, of course, all business all the time. She marched over to the counter, where there stood a middle-aged woman wearing a full-length tie-dyed dress that seemed to be made out of old crêpe paper. Her graying hair radiated out from her head in a kind of random mess, and she was frowning. Of course, it may have been a beatific frown of enlightenment.

'Can I help you?' she said, in a gravelly voice that seemed to suggest we were beyond help.

Deborah held up her badge. Before she could say anything the woman reached over and plucked it from her hand.

'All right, Sergeant Morgan,' the woman said, tossing the badge on the counter. 'It seems to be genuine.'

'Couldn't you just read her aura and tell that?' I suggested. Neither of them seemed ready to give that remark any of the appreciation it deserved, so I shrugged and listened as Deborah began her grueling interrogation.

'I'd like to ask you a few questions, please,' Deborah said, leaning forward to scoop up her badge.

'About what?' the woman demanded. She frowned even harder, and Deborah frowned back, and it began to look like we were in for a good old-fashioned country frown-off, with the winner getting free Botox treatments to freeze her face into a permanent scowl.

'There have been some murders,' Deborah said, and the woman shrugged.

'What's that got to do with me?' she asked.

I applauded her reasoning, but after all, I did have to play for my own team now and then.

'It's because we are all one,' I said. 'That's the basis of all police work.'

She swiveled her frown to me and blinked at me in a very aggressive way. 'Who the hell are you?' she demanded. 'Lemme see your badge.'

'I'm her backup,' I said. 'In case she's attacked by bad karma.'

The woman snorted, but at least she didn't shoot me. 'Cops in this town,' she said, 'are *swimming* in bad karma. I was at the FTAA rally, and I know what you people are like.'

'Maybe we are,' Deborah said, 'but the other side is even worse, so could you just answer a few questions?'

The woman looked back at Deborah, still frowning, and shrugged. 'Okay, I guess,' she said. 'But I don't see how I can help. And I call my lawyer if you get out of line.'

'Fine,' Deborah said. 'We're looking for a lead on somebody who might be connected to a local alternative religious group that has a thing for bulls.'

For a second I thought the woman was almost going to smile, but she caught herself just in time. 'Bulls? Jesus, who doesn't have a thing for bulls. Goes all the way back to Sumer, Crete, all those old cradle-of-civilization places. Lots of people have worshipped them. I mean, aside from the huge cocks, they're very powerful.'

If the woman thought she was going to embarrass Deborah, she didn't know as much about Miami cops as she thought she did. My sister didn't even blink. 'Do you know of any group in particular that might be local?' Debs said.

'I dunno,' she said. 'What kind of group?'

'Candomblé?' I said, briefly grateful to Vince for supplying a word. 'Palo Mayombe? Or even Wicca.'

'The Spanish stuff, you gotta go over to Eleggua on Eighth Street. I wouldn't know about that. We sell some stuff to the Wicca people, but I'm not gonna tell you about it without a warrant. Anyway, they don't do bulls.' She snorted. 'They just stand around in the Everglades naked, waiting for their power to come.'

'Is there anybody else?' Debs insisted.

The woman just shook her head. 'I dunno. I mean, I know about most of the groups in town, and nothing like that I can think of.' She shrugged. 'Maybe the Druids, they got a spring event coming up. They used to do human sacrifice.'

Deborah frowned even more intensely. 'When was that?' she said.

This time the woman actually did smile, just a little, with one corner of her mouth. 'About two thousand years ago. You're a little late on that one, Sherlock.'

'Is there anything else you can think of that might help?' Deborah asked.

The woman shook her head. 'Help with what? There might be some psycho loser out there who read Aleister Crowley and lives on a dairy farm.

How would I know?'

Deborah looked at her for a moment, as if trying to decide if she had been offensive enough to arrest, and then apparently decided against it. 'Thank you for your time,' she said, and she flipped her business card on the counter. 'If you think of anything that might be helpful, please give me a call.'

'Yeah, sure,' the woman said, without even glancing at the card. Deborah glared at her for a moment longer and then stalked out of the door. The woman stared at me and I smiled.

'I really like vegetables,' I said. Then I gave the woman the peace sign and followed my sister out.

'That was a stupid idea,' Deborah said as we walked rapidly back to her car.

'Oh, I wouldn't say that,' I said. And it was quite true, I wouldn't say it. Of course, it really was a stupid idea, but to say so would have been to invite one of Debs's vicious arm punches. 'If nothing else, we eliminated a few possibilities.'

'Sure,' she said sourly. 'We know it probably wasn't a bunch of naked fruits, unless they did it two thousand years ago.'

She did have a point, but I see it as my job in life to help all those around me maintain a positive attitude. 'It's still progress,' I said. 'Shall we check out the place on Eighth Street? I'll translate for you.' In spite of being a Miami native, Debs had whimsically insisted on studying French in school, and she could barely order lunch in Spanish.

She shook her head. 'Waste of time,' she said. 'I'll tell Angel to ask around, but it won't go anywhere.'

And she was right. Angel came back late that afternoon with a very nice candle that had a prayer to St. Jude on it in Spanish, but other than that his trip to the place on Eighth Street was a waste of time, just as Debs had predicted.

We were left with nothing, except two bodies, no heads, and a very bad feeling.

That was about to change.

10

The next day passed uneventfully and we got no closer to any kind of hint about the two murders at the university. And life being the kind of lopsided, grotesque affair that it is, Deborah blamed our lack of progress on me. She was still convinced that I had special magical powers and had used them to see straight into the dark heart of the killings, and that I was keeping vital information from her for petty personal reasons.

Very flattering, but totally untrue. The only insight I had into the matter was that something about it had scared the Dark Passenger, and I did not want that to happen again. I decided to stay away from the case, and since there was almost no blood work involved, that should have been easy in a logical and well-ordered universe.

But alas, we do not live in any such place. Our universe is ruled by random whim, inhabited by people who laugh at logic. At the moment, the chief of these was my sister. Late the following morning she cornered me in my little cubbyhole and dragged me away to lunch with her boyfriend, Kyle Chutsky. I had no real objections to Chutsky, other than his permanent attitude of knowing the real truth about everything. Aside from that, he was just as pleasant and amiable as a cold killer can be, and it would have been hypocritical for me to object to his personality on those grounds. And since he seemed to make my sister happy, I did not object on any other grounds, either.

So off I went to lunch, since in the first place she was my sister, and in the second, the mighty machine that is my body needs almost constant fuel.

The fuel it craves most often is a *medianoche* sandwich, usually with a side of fried *plátanos* and a *mamey* milk shake. I don't know why this simple, hearty meal plays such a transcendent chord on the strings of my being, but there is nothing else like it. Prepared properly, it takes me as close to ecstasy as I can get. And no one prepares it quite as properly as Café Relampago, a storefront place not far from police HQ, where the Morgans have been eating since time out of mind. It was so good even Deborah's perpetual grumpiness couldn't spoil it.

'Goddamn it!' she said to me through a mouthful of sandwich. It was certainly far from a novel phrase coming from her, but she said it with a viciousness that left me lightly spattered with bread crumbs. I took a sip of my excellent *batido de mamey* and waited for her to expand on her argument, but instead she simply said it again. 'Goddamn it!'

'You're covering up your feelings again,' I said. 'But because I am your brother, I can tell something is bothering you.'

Chutsky snorted as he sawed at his Cuban steak. 'No shit,' he said. He was about to say more, but the fork clamped in his prosthetic left hand slipped sideways. 'Goddamn it,' he said, and I realized that they had a great deal more in common than I had thought. Deborah leaned over and helped him straighten the fork. 'Thanks,' he said, and shoveled in a large bite of the pounded-flat meat.

'There, you see?' I said brightly. 'All you needed was something to take your mind off your own problems.'

We were sitting at a table where we had probably eaten a hundred times. But Deborah was rarely troubled by sentiment; she straightened up and slapped the battered Formica tabletop hard enough to make the sugar bowl jump.

'I want to know who talked to that asshole Rick Sangre!' she said. Sangre was a local TV reporter who believed that the gorier a story was, the more vital it was for people to have a free press that could fill them in on as many gruesome details as possible. From the tone of her voice, Deborah was apparently convinced that Rick was my new best friend.

'Well, it wasn't me,' I said. 'And I don't think it was Doakes.'

'Ouch,' said Chutsky.

'*And,*' she said, 'I want to find those fucking heads!'

'I don't have them, either,' I said. 'Did you check lost and found?'

'You know something, Dexter?' she said. 'Come on, why are you holding out on me?'

Chutsky looked up and swallowed. 'Why should he know something you don't?' he asked. 'Was there a lot of spatter?'

'No spatter at all,' I said. 'The bodies were cooked, nice and dry.'

Chutsky nodded and managed to scoop some rice and beans onto his fork. 'You're a sick bastard, aren't you?'

'He's worse than sick,' Deborah said. 'He's holding out on something.'

'Oh,' Chutsky said through a mouthful of food. 'Is this his amateur profiling thing again?' It was a small fiction; we had told him that my hobby was actually analytical, rather than hands-on.

'It is,' Deborah said. 'And he won't tell me what he's figured out.'

'It might be hard to believe, Sis, but I know nothing about this. Just . . .' I shrugged, but she was already pouncing.

'What! Come on, please?'

I hesitated again. There was no good way to tell her that the Dark Passenger had reacted to these killings in a brand-new and totally unsettling way.

'I just get a feeling,' I said. 'Something is a little off with this one.'

She snorted. 'Two burned headless bodies, and he says something's a little off. Didn't you used to be smart?'

I took a bite of my sandwich as Deborah frittered away her precious eating time by frowning. 'Have you identified the bodies yet?' I asked.

'Come on, Dexter. There're no heads, so we got no dental records. The bodies were burned, so there're no fingerprints. Shit, we don't even know what color their hair was. What do you want me to do?'

'I could probably help, you know,' Chutsky said. He speared a chunk of fried *maduras* and popped it into his mouth. 'I have a few resources I can call on.'

'I don't need your help,' she said and he shrugged.

'You take Dexter's help,' he said.

'That's different.'

'How is that different?' he asked, and it seemed like a reasonable question.

'Because he gives me *help*,' she said. 'You want to solve it for me.'

They locked eyes and didn't speak for a long moment. I'd seen them do it before, and it was eerily reminiscent of the nonverbal conversations Cody and Astor had. It was nice to see them so clearly welded together as a couple, even though it reminded me that I had a wedding of my own to worry about, complete with an apparently insane high-class caterer. Happily, just before I could begin to gnash my teeth, Debs broke the eerie silence.

'I won't be one of those women who needs help,' she said.

'But I can get you information that you can't get,' he said, putting his good hand on her arm.

'Like what?' I asked him. I'll admit I had been curious for some time about what Chutsky was, or had been before his accidental amputations. I knew that he had worked for some government agency which he referred to as the OGA, but I still didn't know what that stood for.

He turned to face me obligingly. 'I have friends and sources in a lot of places,' he said. 'Something like this might have left some kind of trail somewhere else, and I could call around and find out.'

'You mean call your buddies at the OGA?' I said.

He smiled. 'Something like that,' he said.

'For Christ's sake, Dexter,' Deborah said. 'OGA just means other government agency. There's no such agency, it's an in-joke.'

'Nice to be in at last,' I said. 'And you can still get access to their files?'

He shrugged. 'Technically I'm on convalescent leave,' he said.

'From doing what?' I asked.

He gave me a mechanical smile. 'You don't really want to know,' he said. 'The point is, they haven't decided yet whether I'm any fucking good anymore.' He looked at the fork clamped in his steel hand, turning his arm over to see it move. 'Shit,' he said.

And because I could feel that one of those awkward moments was upon us, I did what I could to move things back onto a sociable footing. 'Didn't you find anything at the kiln?' I asked. 'Some kind of jewelry or something?'

'What the fuck is that?' she said.

'The kiln,' I said. 'Where the bodies were burned.'

'Haven't you been paying attention? We haven't found where the bodies were burned.'

'Oh,' I said. 'I assumed it was done right there on campus, in the ceramic studio.'

By the suddenly frozen look on her face, I realized that either she was experiencing massive indigestion or she did not know about the ceramic studio. 'It's just half a mile from the lake where the bodies were found,' I said. 'You know, the kiln. Where they make pottery?'

Deborah stared at me for a moment longer, and then jumped up from the table. I thought it was a wonderfully creative and dramatic way to end a conversation, and it took a moment before I could do more than blink after her.

'I guess she didn't know about that,' Chutsky said.

'That's my first guess,' I said. 'Shall we follow?'

He shrugged and speared the last chunk of his steak. 'I'm gonna have some flan, and a *cafecita*. Then I'll get a cab, since I'm not allowed to help,' he said. He scooped up some rice and beans and nodded at me. 'You go ahead, unless you want to walk back to work.'

I did not, in fact, have any desire to walk back to work. On the other hand, I still had almost half a milk shake and I did not want to leave that, either. I stood up and followed, but I softened the blow by grabbing the uneaten half of Deborah's sandwich and taking it with me as I lurched out the door after her.

Soon we were rolling through the front gate of the university campus. Deborah spent part of the ride talking on the radio and arranging for people to meet us at the kilns, and the rest of the ride clenching her teeth and muttering.

We turned left after the gate and headed down the winding road that leads to the ceramic and pottery area. I had taken a class in pottery there my junior year in an effort to widen my horizons, and found out that I was good at making very regular-looking vases but not terribly successful at creating original works of art, at least not in that medium. In my own area, I flatter myself that I can be creative, as I had recently demonstrated with Zander.

Angel-no-relation was already there, carefully and patiently looking through the first kiln for any sign of practically anything. Deborah went over and squatted beside him, leaving me alone with the last three bites of her sandwich. I took the first bite. A crowd was beginning to gather by the yellow tape. Perhaps they were hoping to see something too terrible to look at: I never knew why they gathered like that, but they always did.

Deborah was now on the ground beside Angel, who had his head inside the first of the kilns. This would probably be a long wait.

I had barely put the last bite of sandwich into my mouth when I became aware that I was being watched. Of course I was being *looked* at, anyone on the business side of the yellow tape always was. But I was also being *watched* – the Dark Passenger clamored at me that I had been singled out by something with an unhealthy interest in special wonderful me, and I did not like the feeling. As I swallowed the last of the sandwich and turned to look, the whisper inside me hissed something that sounded like confusion . . . and then settled into silence.

And as it did I felt again the wave of panicked nausea and the bright yellow edge of blindness, and I stumbled for a moment, all my senses crying out that there was danger but my ability to do anything about it completely gone. It lasted only a second. I fought my way back to the surface and looked harder at my surroundings – nothing had changed. A handful of people stood looking on, the sun shone brightly, and a gentle wind riffled through the trees. Just another perfect Miami day, but somewhere in paradise the snake had reared its head. I closed my eyes and listened hard, hoping for some hint about the nature of the menace, but there was nothing but the echo of clawed feet scrabbling away.

I opened my eyes and looked around again. There was a crowd of perhaps fifteen people pretending not to be fascinated by the hope of seeing gore, but none of them stood out in any way. None of them were skulking or staring evilly or trying to hide a bazooka under their shirt. In any normal time, I might have expected my Passenger to see a dark shadow around an obvious predator, but there was no such assistance now. As far as I could see, nothing sinister loomed in the crowd. So what had set off the Passenger's fire alarm? I knew so little about it; it was just there, a presence filled with wicked amusement and sharp suggestions. It had never showed confusion before, not until it saw the two bodies by the lake. And now it was repeating its vague uncertainty, only half a mile from the first spot.

Was it something in the water? Or was there some connection to the two burned bodies here at the kilns?

I wandered over to where Deborah and Angel-no-relation were working. They didn't seem to be finding anything particularly alarming, and there were no jolts of panic roiling out from the kiln to the place where the Dark Passenger was hiding.

If this second retreat was not caused by something in front of me, then what caused it? What if it was some kind of weird interior erosion? Perhaps my new status of impending husbandhood and stepfatherness was overwhelming my Passenger. Was I becoming too nice to be a proper host? This would be a fate worse than someone else's death.

I became aware that I was standing just inside the yellow crime-scene tape, and a large form was lurking in front of me.

'Uh, hello?' he said. He was a big, well-muscled young specimen with longish, lank hair and the look of someone who believed in breathing through the mouth.

'How can I help you, citizen?' I said.

'Are you, uh, you know,' he said, 'like a cop?'

'A little bit like one,' I said.

He nodded and thought about that for a moment, looking around behind him as if there might be something there he could eat. On the back of his neck was one of those unfortunate tattoos that have become so popular, an Oriental character of some kind. It probably spelled out 'slow learner.' He rubbed the tattoo as if he could hear me thinking about it, then turned around to me and blurted out, 'I was wondering about Jessica.'

'Of course you were,' I said. 'Who wouldn't?'

'Do they know if it's her?' he said. 'I'm like her boyfriend.'

The young gentleman had now succeeded in grabbing my professional attention. 'Is Jessica missing?' I asked him.

He nodded. 'She was, you know, supposed to work out with me? Like every morning, you know. Around the track, and then some abs. But yesterday she doesn't show up. And same thing this morning. So I started thinking, uh . . .' He frowned, apparently at the effort of thinking, and his speech trickled to a halt.

'What's your name?' I asked him.

'Kurt,' he said. 'Kurt Wagner. What's yours?'

'Dexter,' I said. 'Wait here a moment, Kurt.' I hurried over to Deborah before the strain of trying to think again proved too much for the boy.

'Deborah,' I said, 'we may have a small break here.'

'Well, it isn't your damned pot ovens,' she snarled. 'They're too small for a body.'

'No,' I said. 'But the young man over there is missing a girlfriend.'

Her head jerked up and she rose to standing almost on point like a hunting dog. She stared over at Jessica's like-boyfriend, who looked back and shifted his weight from foot to foot. 'About fucking time,' she said, and she headed for him.

I looked at Angel. He shrugged and stood up. For a moment, he looked like he was going to say something. But then he shook his head, dusted off his hands, and followed Debs over to hear what Kurt had to say, leaving me really and truly all alone with my dark thoughts.

Just to watch; sometimes it was enough. Of course there was the sure knowledge that watching would lead inevitably to the surging heat and glorious flow of blood, the overwhelming pulse of emotions throbbing from the victims, the rising music of the ordered madness as the sacrifice flew into wonderful death . . . All this would come. For now, it was enough for the Watcher to observe and soak in the delicious feeling of anonymous, ultimate power. He could feel the unease of the other. That unease would grow, rising through the musical range into fear, then panic, and at last full-fledged terror. It would all come in good time.

The Watcher saw the other scanning the crowd, flailing about for some clue to the source of the blossoming sense of danger that tickled at his senses. He would find nothing, of course. Not yet. Not until he determined that the time was right. Not until he had run the other into dull mindless panic. Only then would he stop watching and begin to take final action.

And until then – it was time to let the other begin to hear the music of fear.

11

Her name was Jessica Ortega. she was a junior and lived in one of the nearby residence halls. We got the room number from Kurt, and Deborah left Angel to wait at the kilns until a squad car arrived to take over.

I never knew why they were called residence halls instead of dormitories. Perhaps it was because they looked so much like hotels nowadays. There were no ivy-covered walls bedecking the hallowed halls here, the lobby had lots of glass and potted plants, and the halls were carpeted and clean and new-looking.

We stopped at the door of Jessica's room. It had a small, neat card taped at eye level that read ARIEL GOLDMAN & JESSICA ORTEGA. Below that in smaller print it said INTOXICANTS REQUIRED FOR ENTRY. Someone had underlined 'Entry' and scrawled below it YOU THINK?

Deborah raised an eyebrow at me. 'Party girls,' she said.

'Somebody has to do it,' I said.

She snorted and knocked on the door. There was no answer, and Debs waited a full three seconds before knocking again, much harder.

I heard a door open behind me and turned to see a reed-thin girl with short blond hair and glasses looking at us. 'They're not here,' she said with clear disapproval. 'For like a couple of days. First quiet I've had all semester.'

'Do you know where they went?' Deborah asked her.

The girl rolled her eyes. 'Must be a major kegger somewhere,' she said.

'When was the last time you saw them?' Deborah said.

The girl shrugged. 'With those two it's not seeing them, it's hearing them. Loud music and laughing all night, okay? Major pain in the butt for some-body who actually studies and goes to class.' She shook her head, and her short hair riffled around her face. 'I mean, please.'

'So when was the last time you heard them?' I asked her.

She looked at me. 'Are you like cops or something? What did they do now?'

'What have they done before?' Debs asked.

She sighed. 'Parking tickets. I mean, lots of them. DUI once. Hey, I don't want to sound like I'm ratting them out or something.'

'Would you say it's unusual for them to be away like this?' I said.

'What's unusual is if they show up to class. I don't know how they pass anything. I mean,' she gave us half a smirk, 'I can probably guess how they pass, but . . .' She shrugged. She did not share her guess with us, unless you counted her smirk.

'What classes do they have together?' Deborah asked.

The girl shrugged again and shook her head. 'You'd have to check like the registrar,' she said.

It was not a terribly long walk to see like the registrar, especially at the pace Deborah set. I managed to keep up with her and still have enough breath to ask her a pointed question or two. 'Why does it matter what classes they had together?'

Deborah made an impatient gesture with her hand. 'If that girl is right, Jessica and her roommate—'

'Ariel Goldman,' I said.

'Right. So if they are trading sex for good grades, that makes me want to talk to their professors.'

On the surface, that made sense. Sex is one of the most common motives for murder, which does not seem to fit in with the fact that it is often rumored to be connected to love. But there was one small thing that did not make sense. 'Why would a professor cook them and cut off their heads like that? Why not just strangle them and throw the bodies in a Dumpster?'

Deborah shook her head. 'It's not important how he did it. What matters is whether he did.'

'All right,' I said. 'And how sure are we that these two are the victims?'

'Sure enough to talk to their teachers,' she said. 'It's a start.'

We arrived at the registrar's office, and when Debs flashed her badge we were shown right in. But it was a good thirty minutes of Deborah pacing and muttering while I went through the computer records with the registrar's assistant. Jessica and Ariel were, in fact, in several of the same classes, and I printed out the names, office numbers, and home addresses of the professors. Deborah glanced at the list and nodded. 'These two guys, Bukovich and Halpern, have office hours now,' she said. 'We can start with them.'

Once again Deborah and I stepped out into the muggy day for a stroll across campus.

'It's nice to be back on campus, isn't it?' I said, in my always futile effort to keep a pleasant flow of conversation going.

Deborah snorted. 'What's nice is if we can get a definite ID on the bodies and maybe move a little closer to grabbing the guy who did this.'

I did not think that identifying the bodies would really move us closer to identifying the killer, but I have been wrong before, and in any case police work is powered by routine and custom, and one of the proud traditions of our craft is that it's good to know the dead person's name. So I willingly trundled along with Deborah to the office building where the two professors waited.

Professor Halpern's office was on the ground floor just inside the main entrance, and before the outer door could swing shut Debs was already knocking on his door. There was no answer. Deborah tried the knob. It was locked, so she thumped on the door again with the same lack of result.

A man came strolling along the hall and stopped at the office next door, glancing at us with a raised eyebrow. 'Looking for Jerry Halpern?' he said. 'I don't think he's in today.'

'Do you know where he is?' Deborah said.

He gave us a slight smile. 'I imagine he's home, at his apartment, since he's not here. Why do you ask?'

Debs pulled out her badge and showed it to him. He didn't seem impressed. 'I see,' he said. 'Does this have anything to do with the two dead bodies across campus?'

'Do you have any reason to think it would?' Deborah said.

'N-n-n-o,' he said, 'not really.'

Deborah looked at him and waited, but he didn't say anything more. 'Can I ask your name, sir?' she said at last.

'I'm Dr. Wilkins,' he said, nodding toward the door he stood in front of. 'This is my office.'

'Dr. Wilkins,' Deborah said. 'Could you please tell me what your remark about Professor Halpern means?'

Wilkins pursed his lips. 'Well,' he said, hesitating, 'Jerry's a nice enough guy, but if this is a murder investigation . . .' He let it hang for a moment. So did Deborah. 'Well,' he said at last, 'I believe it was last Wednesday I heard a disturbance in his office.' He shook his head. 'These walls are not terribly thick.'

'What kind of disturbance?' Deborah asked.

'Shouting,' he said. 'Perhaps a little bit of scuffling? Anyway, I peeked out the door and saw a student, a young woman, stagger out of Halpern's office and run away. She was, ah – her shirt was torn.'

'By any chance did you recognize the young woman?' Deborah asked.

'Yes,' Wilkins said. 'I had her in a class last semester. Her name is Ariel Goldman. Lovely girl, but not much of a student.'

Deborah glanced at me and I nodded encouragingly. 'Do you think Halpern tried to force himself on Ariel Goldman?' Deborah said.

Wilkins tilted his head to one side and held up one hand. 'I couldn't say for sure. That's what it looked like, though.'

Deborah looked at Wilkins, but he didn't have anything to add, so she nodded and said, 'Thank you, Dr. Wilkins. You've been very helpful.'

'I hope so,' he said, and he turned away to open his door and enter his office. Debs was already looking at the printout from the registrar.

'Halpern lives just a mile or so away,' she said, and headed toward the doors. Once again I found myself hurrying to catch up to her.

'Which theory are we giving up?' I asked her. 'The one that says Ariel tried to seduce Halpern? Or that he tried to rape her?'

'We're not giving up anything,' she said. 'Not until we talk to Halpern.'

12

Dr. Jerry Halpern had an apartment less than two miles from the campus, in a two-story building that had probably been very nice forty years ago. He answered the door right away when Deborah knocked, blinking at us as the sunlight hit his face. He was in his mid-thirties and thin without looking fit, and he hadn't shaved for a few days. 'Yes?' he said, in a querulous tone of voice that would have been just right for an eighty-year-old scholar. He cleared his throat and tried again. 'What is it?'

Deborah held up her badge and said, 'Can we come in, please?'

Halpern goggled at the badge and seemed to sag a little. 'I didn't – what, what – why come in?' he said.

'We'd like to ask you a few questions,' Deborah said. 'About Ariel Goldman.'

Halpern fainted.

I don't get to see my sister look surprised very often – her control is too good. So it was quite rewarding to see her with her mouth hanging open as Halpern hit the floor. I manufactured a suitable matching expression, and bent over to feel for a pulse.

'His heart is still going,' I said.

'Let's get him inside,' Deborah said, and I dragged him into the apartment.

The apartment was probably not as small as it looked, but the walls were lined with overflowing bookshelves, a worktable stacked high with papers and more books. In the small remaining space there was a battered, mean-looking two-seater couch and an overstuffed chair with a lamp behind it. I managed to heft Halpern up and onto the couch, which creaked and sank alarmingly under him.

I stood up and nearly bumped into Deborah, who was already hovering and glaring down at Halpern. 'You better wait for him to wake up before you intimidate him,' I said.

'This son of a bitch knows something,' she said. 'Why else would he flop like that?'

'Poor nutrition?' I said.

'Wake him up,' she said.

420

I looked at her to see if she was kidding, but of course she was dead serious. 'What would you suggest?' I said. 'I forgot to bring smelling salts.'

'We can't just stand around and wait,' she said. And she leaned forward as if she was going to shake him, or maybe punch him in the nose.

Happily for Halpern, however, he chose just that moment to return to consciousness. His eyes fluttered a few times and then stayed open, and as he looked up at us his whole body tensed. 'What do you want?' he said.

'Promise not to faint again?' I said. Deborah elbowed me aside.

'Ariel Goldman,' she said.

'Oh God,' Halpern whined. 'I knew this would happen.'

'You were right,' I said.

'You have to believe me,' he said, struggling to sit up. 'I didn't do it.'

'All right,' Debs said. 'Then who did it?'

'She did it herself,' he said.

Deborah looked at me, perhaps to see if I could tell her why Halpern was so clearly insane. Unfortunately, I could not, so she looked back at him. 'She did it herself,' she said, her voice loaded with cop doubt.

'Yes,' he insisted. 'She wanted to make it look like I did it, so I would have to give her a good grade.'

'She burned herself,' Deborah said, very deliberately, like she was talking to a three-year-old. 'And then she cut off her own head. So you would give her a good grade.'

'I hope you gave her at least a B for all that work,' I said.

Halpern goggled at us, his jaw hanging open and jerking spasmodically, as if it was trying to close but lacked a tendon. 'Wha,' he said finally. 'What are you talking about?'

'Ariel Goldman,' Debs said. 'And her roommate, Jessica Ortega. Burned to death. Heads cut off. What can you tell us about that, Jerry?'

Halpern twitched and didn't say anything for a long time. 'I, I – are they dead?' he finally whispered.

'Jerry,' said Deborah, 'their heads were cut off. What do you think?'

I watched with great interest as Halpern's face slid through a whole variety of expressions portraying different kinds of blankness, and finally, when the nickel dropped, it settled on the unhinged-jaw look again. 'You – you think I – you can't—'

'I'm afraid I can, Jerry,' Deborah said. 'Unless you can tell me why I shouldn't.'

'But that's – I would never,' he said.

'Somebody did,' I said.

'Yes, but, my God,' he said.

'Jerry,' Deborah said, 'what did you think we wanted to ask about?'

'The, the rape,' he said. 'When I didn't rape her.'

Somewhere there's a world where everything makes sense, but obviously we were not in it. 'When you *didn't* rape her,' Deborah said.

'Yes, that's – she wanted me to, ah,' he said.

'She wanted you to rape her?' I said.

'She, she,' he said, and he began to blush. 'She offered me, um, sex. For a good grade,' he said, looking at the floor. 'And I refused.'

'And that's when she asked you to rape her?' I said. Deborah hit me with her elbow.

'So you told her no, Jerry?' Deborah said. 'A pretty girl like that?'

'That's when she, um,' he said, 'she said she'd get an A one way or the other. And she reached up and ripped her own shirt and then started to scream.' He gulped, but he didn't look up.

'Go on,' said Deborah.

'And she waved at me,' he said, holding up his hand and waving bye-bye. 'And then she ran out into the hall.' He looked up at last. 'I'm up for tenure this year,' he said. 'If word about something like this got around, my career would be over.'

'I understand,' Debs said very understandingly. 'So you killed her to save your career.'

'What? No!' he sputtered. 'I didn't kill her!'

'Then who did, Jerry?' Deborah asked.

'I don't know!' he said, and he sounded almost petulant, as if we had accused him of taking the last cookie. Deborah just stared at him, and he stared back, flicking his gaze from her to me and back again. 'I didn't!' he insisted.

'I'd like to believe you, Jerry,' Deborah said. 'But it's really not up to me.'

'What do you mean?' he said.

'I'm going to have to ask you to come with me,' she said.

'You're *arresting* me?' he said.

'I'm taking you down to the station to answer a few questions, that's all,' she said reassuringly.

'Oh my God,' he said. 'You're arresting me. That's – no. No.'

'Let's do this the easy way, Professor,' Deborah said. 'We don't need the handcuffs, do we?'

He looked at her for a long moment and then suddenly jumped to his feet and ran for the door. But unfortunately for him and his masterful escape plan, he had to get past me, and Dexter is widely and justly praised for his lightning reflexes. I stuck a foot in the professor's way, and he went down onto his face and slid headfirst into the door.

'Ow,' he said.

I smiled at Deborah. 'I guess you do need the cuffs,' I said.

13

I am not really paranoid. I don't believe that I am surrounded by mysterious enemies who seek to trap me, torture me, kill me. Of course, I know very well that if I allow my disguise to slip and reveal me for what I am, then this entire society will join together in calling for my slow and painful death, but this is not paranoia – this is a calm, clearheaded view of consensus reality, and I am not frightened by it. I simply try to be careful so it doesn't happen.

But a very large piece of my carefulness had always been listening to the subtle whisperings of the Dark Passenger, and it was still being strangely shy about sharing its thoughts. And so I faced a new and unsettling inner silence, and that made me very edgy, sending out a little ripple of uneasiness. It had started with that feeling of being watched, even stalked, at the kilns. And then, as we drove back to headquarters, I could not shake the idea that a car seemed to be following us. Was it really? Did it have sinister intent? And if so, was it toward me or Deborah, or was it just random Miami driver spookiness?

I watched the car, a white Toyota Avalon, in the side mirror. It stayed with us all the way until Deborah turned into the parking lot, and then it simply drove by without slowing or the driver appearing to stare, but I could not lose my ridiculous notion that it had indeed been following us. Still, I could not be sure unless the Passenger told me, which it did not – it merely gave a sort of sibilant throat-clearing, and so it seemed beyond stupid for me to say anything to Deborah about it.

And then later, when I came out of the building to my own car to go home for the night, I had the same feeling once again, that someone or something was watching – but it was a *feeling*. Not a warning, not an interior whisper from the shadows, not a get-ready flutter of invisible black wings – a *feeling*. And that made me nervous. When the Passenger speaks, I listen. I act. But it was not speaking now, merely squirming, and I had no idea what to do given that message. So in the absence of any more definite idea, I kept my eyes on my rearview mirror as I headed south for home.

Was this what it was like to be human? To walk through life with the perpetual feeling that you were meat on the hoof, stumbling down the game trail with tigers sniffing at your heels? If so, it would certainly go a long way toward explaining human behavior. As a predator myself, I knew very well the powerful feeling of strolling in disguise through the herds of potential prey, knowing that I could at any moment cut one of them from the herd. But without any word from the Passenger I did not merely blend in; I was actually part of the herd, vulnerable. I was prey, and I did not like it. It made me a great deal more watchful.

And when I came down off the expressway, my watching revealed a white Toyota Avalon following me.

Of course there are lots of white Toyota Avalons in the world. After all, the Japanese lost the war and that gives them the right to dominate our car market. And certainly many of these Avalons could reasonably be heading for home along the same crowded route I took. Logically speaking, there are only so many directions in which to go, and it made perfect sense for a white Avalon to go in any one of them. And it was not logical to assume that anyone would want to follow me. What had I done? I mean, that anybody could prove?

And so it was perfectly illogical of me to feel that I was being followed, which does not explain why I made a sudden right turn off U.S. 1 and down a side street.

It also does not explain why the white Avalon followed.

The car kept well back, as any predator would do to avoid spooking its chosen prey – or as any normal person might do if they just happened to take the same turn by coincidence. And so with the same uncharacteristic lack of logic, I zigged again, this time to the left, down a small residential street.

A moment later the other car followed.

As mentioned, Dashing Dexter does not know the meaning of fear. That would have to mean that the roaring thump of my heart, the parching of my mouth, and the sweat pouring out of my hands was no more than massive uneasiness.

I did not enjoy the feeling. I was no longer the Knight of the Knife. My blade and my armor were in some subbasement of the castle, and I was on the field of battle without them, a suddenly soft and tasty victim, and for no reason I could name I was sure that something had my scent in its ravening nostrils.

I turned right again – and noticed only as I went by it the sign that said NO OUTLET.

I had turned down a cul-de-sac. I was trapped.

For some reason, I slowed and waited for the other car to follow me. I suppose I just wanted to be sure that the white Avalon was really there. It was. I continued to the end of the street, where the road widened into a small circle for turning around. There were no cars in the driveway of the house at the top of the circle. I pulled in and stopped my engine, waiting, amazed by the crashing of my heart and my inability to do anything more than sit and wait for the inevitable teeth and claws of whatever was chasing me.

The white car came closer. It slowed as it reached the circle, slowed as it approached me . . .

And it went past me, around the circle, back up the street, and into the Miami sunset.

I watched it go, and as its taillights disappeared around the corner I suddenly remembered how to breathe. I took advantage of this rediscovered knowledge, and it felt very good. Once I had restored my oxygen content and settled back into being me, I began to feel like a very stupid me. What, after all, had really happened? A car had appeared to follow me. Then it had gone away. There were a million reasons why it might have taken the same route as I had, most of them summed up by the one word: coincidence. And then, as poor Dithering Dexter sat sweating in his seat, what had the big bad car done? It had gone past. It had not paused to stare, snarl, or throw a hand grenade. It had just gone by and left me in a puddle of my own absurd fear.

There was a knock on my window and I bumped my head on the ceiling of the car.

I turned to look. A middle-aged man with a mustache and bad acne scars was bent over, looking in at me. I had not noticed him until now, further proof that I was alone and unprotected.

I rolled down the window. 'Can I help you with something?' the man said.

'No, thank you,' I told him, somewhat puzzled as to what help he thought he could offer. But he did not keep me guessing.

'You're in my driveway,' he said.

'Oh,' I said, and it occurred to me that I probably was and some explanation was called for. 'I was looking for Vinny,' I said. Not brilliant, but serviceable under the circumstances.

'You got the wrong place,' the man said with a certain mean triumph that almost cheered me up again.

'Sorry,' I said. I rolled up the window and backed out of the driveway, and the man stood and watched me go, presumably to be sure that I did not suddenly leap out and attack him with a machete. In just a few moments I was back in the bloodthirsty chaos of U.S. 1. And as the routine violence of the traffic closed around me like a warm blanket, I felt myself slowly sinking back into myself. Home again, behind the crumbling walls of Castle Dexter, vacant basement and all.

I had never felt so stupid – which is to say, I felt as close to being a real human being as it was possible for me to feel. What on earth had I been thinking? I had not, in truth, been thinking at all, merely reacting to a bizarre twitch of panic. It was all too ridiculous, too patently human and laughable, if only I had been a real human who could really laugh. Ah, well. At least I was really ridiculous.

I drove the last few miles thinking of insulting things to call myself for such a timid overreaction, and by the time I pulled into the driveway at Rita's house I was thoroughly soaked in my own abuse, which made me feel much better. I got out of my car with something very close to a real smile on my face, generated by my joy in the true depth of Dexter Dunderhead. And as I took one step away from the car, half turning to head for the front door, a car drove slowly by.

A white Avalon, of course.

If there is such a thing in the world as justice, then this was surely one of the moments it had arranged just for me. Because many times I had enjoyed the sight of a person standing with their mouth hanging open, completely incapacitated by surprise and fear, and now here was Dexter in the same stupid pose. Frozen in place, unable to move even to wipe away my own drool, I watched the car drive slowly past, and the only thought I could muster was that I must look very, very stupid.

Naturally, I would have looked a great deal stupider if whoever was in the white car did anything other than drive past slowly, but happily for the many people who know and love me – at least two, including myself – the car went by without pausing. For a moment I thought I could see a face looking at me from the driver's seat. And then he accelerated, turning slightly away into the middle of the street so that the light gleamed for an instant off the silver bull's head Toyota emblem, and the car was gone.

And I could think of nothing at all to do but eventually close my mouth, scratch my head, and stumble into the house.

There was a soft but very deep and powerful drumbeat, and gladness surged up, born from relief and anticipation of what was to come. And then the horns sounded, and it was very close now, only a matter of moments before it came and then everything would begin and happen again at last, and as the gladness rose into a melody that climbed until it seemed to come from everywhere, I felt my feet taking me to where the voices promised bliss, filling everything with that joy that was on the way, that overwhelming fulfillment that would lift us into ecstasy—

And I woke up with my heart pounding and a sense of relief that was certainly not justified and that I did not understand at all. Because it was not merely the relief of a sip of water when you are thirsty or resting when you are tired, although it was those things, too.

But – far beyond puzzling, deep into disturbing – it was also the relief that comes after one of my playdates with the wicked; the relief that says you have fulfilled the deep longings of your innermost self and now you may relax and be content for a while.

And this could not be. It was impossible for me to feel that most private and personal of feelings while lying in bed asleep.

I looked at the clock beside the bed: five minutes past midnight, not a time for Dexter to be up and about, not on a night when he had planned only to sleep.

On the other side of the bed Rita snored softly, twitching slightly like a dog who dreamed of chasing a rabbit.

And on my side of the bed, one terribly confused Dexter. Something had come into my dreamless night and made waves across the tranquil sea of my soulless sleep. I did not know what that something was, but it had made me very glad for no reason I could name, and I did not like that at all. My moon-light hobby made me glad in my own emotionless way and that was all. Noth-ing else had ever been allowed into that corner of the dark subbasement of Dexter. That was the way I preferred it to be. I had my own small, well-guarded space inside, marked off and locked down, where I felt my own par-ticular joy – on those nights only and at no other time. Nothing else made sense for me.

So what had invaded, knocked down the door, and flooded the cellar with this uncalled-for and unwanted feeling? What in all the world possibly *could* climb in with such overwhelming ease?

I lay down, determined to go back to sleep and prove to myself that I was still in charge here, that nothing had happened, and certainly wouldn't hap-pen again. This was Dexterland, and I was king. Nothing else was permitted inside. And I closed my eyes and turned for confirmation to the voice of authority on the inside, the inarguable master of the shadowy corners of all that is me, the Dark Passenger, and I waited for it to agree, to hiss a soothing phrase to put the jangling music and its geyser of feeling into its place, out of the dark and into the outside. And I waited for it to say something, anything, and it did not.

And I poked at it with a very hard and irritated thought, thinking, *Wake up! Show some teeth in there!*

And it said nothing.

I hurried myself into all the corners of me, hollering with increasing con-cern, calling for the Passenger, but the place it had been was empty, swept clean, room to rent. It was gone as if it had never been there at all.

In the place where it used to be I could still hear an echo of the music, bouncing off the hard walls of an unfurnished apartment and rolling through a sudden, very painful emptiness.

The Dark Passenger was gone.

14

I spent the next day in a lather of uncertainty, hoping that the Passenger would return and somehow sure it would not. And as the day wore on, this dreary certainty got bigger and bleaker.

There was a large, brittle empty spot inside me and I had no real way to think about it or cope with the gaping hollowness that I had never felt before. I would certainly not claim to feel anguish, which has always struck me as a very self-indulgent thing to experience, but I was acutely uneasy and I lived the whole day in a thick syrup of anxious dread.

Where had my Passenger gone, and why? Would it come back? And these questions pulled me inevitably down into even more alarming speculation: What was the Passenger and why had it come to me in the first place?

It was somewhat sobering to realize just how deeply I had defined myself by something that was not actually me – or was it? Perhaps the entire persona of the Dark Passenger was no more than the sick construct of a damaged mind, a web spun to catch tiny glimmers of filtered reality and protect me from the awful truth of what I really am. It was possible. I am well aware of basic psychology, and I have assumed for quite some time that I am some-where off the charts. That's fine with me; I get along very well without any shred of normal humanity to my name.

Or I had until now. But suddenly I was all alone in there, and things did not seem quite so hard-edged and certain. And for the first time, I truly needed to know.

Of course, few jobs provide paid time off for introspection, even on a topic as important as missing Dark Passengers. No, Dexter must still lift that bale. Especially with Deborah cracking the whip.

Happily, it was mostly routine. I spent the morning with my fellow geeks combing through Halpern's apartment for some concrete residue of his guilt. Even more happily, the evidence was so abundant that very little real work was necessary.

In the back of his closet we found a sock with several drops of blood on it. Under the couch was a white canvas shoe with a matching blotch on top. In a plastic bag in the bathroom was a pair of pants with a singed cuff and even more blood, small dots of spray that had been heat-hardened.

It was probably a good thing that there was so much of it out in the open, because Dexter was truly not his usual bright and eager self today. I found myself drifting in an anxious gray mist and wondering if the Passenger was coming home, only to jerk back to the present, standing there in the closet holding a dirty, blood-spattered sock. If any real investigation had been necessary, I am not sure I could have performed up to my own very high standards.

Luckily, it wasn't needed. I had never before seen such an outpouring of clear and obvious evidence from somebody who had, after all, had several days to clean up. When I indulge in my own little hobby I am neat and tidy and forensically innocent within minutes; Halpern had let several days go by without taking even the most elementary precautions. It was almost too easy, and when we checked his car I dropped the 'almost.' Clearly displayed on the central armrest of the front seat was a thumbprint of dried blood.

Of course, it was still possible that our lab work would show that it was chicken blood, and Halpern had simply been indulging in an innocent pastime, perhaps as an amateur poultry butcher. Somehow, I doubted it. It seemed overwhelmingly clear that Halpern had done something truly unkind to someone.

And yet, the small nagging thought tugged at me that it was, just as overwhelmingly so, too easy. Something was not quite right here. But since I had no Passenger to point me in the right direction, I kept it to myself. It would have been cruel, in any case, to burst Deborah's happy balloon. She was very nearly glowing with satisfaction as the results came in and Halpern looked more and more like our demented catch of the day.

Deborah was actually humming when she dragged me along to interview Halpern, which took my unease to a new level. I watched her as we went into the room where Halpern was waiting. I could not remember the last time she had seemed so happy. She even forgot to wear her expression of perpetual disapproval. It was very unsettling, a complete violation of natural law, as if everyone on I-95 suddenly decided to drive slowly and carefully.

'Well, Jerry,' she said cheerfully as we settled into chairs facing Halpern. 'Would you like to talk about those two girls?'

'There's nothing to talk about,' he said. He was very pale, almost greenish, but he looked a lot more determined than he had when we brought him in. 'You've made a mistake,' he said. 'I didn't do anything.'

Deborah looked at me with a smile and shook her head. 'He didn't do anything,' she said happily.

'It's possible,' I said. 'Somebody else might have put the bloody clothes in his apartment while he was watching Letterman.'

'Is that what happened, Jerry?' she said. 'Did somebody else put those bloody clothes in your place?'

If possible, he looked even greener. 'What – bloody – what are you talking about?'

She smiled at him. 'Jerry. We found a pair of your pants with blood on 'em. It matches the victims' blood. We found a shoe and a sock, same story. And we found a bloody fingerprint in your car. Your fingerprint, their blood.' Deborah leaned back in her chair and folded her arms. 'Does that jog your memory at all, Jerry?'

Halpern had started shaking his head while Deborah was talking, and he continued to do so, as if it was some kind of weird reflex and he didn't know he was doing it. 'No,' he said. 'No. That isn't even – No.'

'No, Jerry?' Deborah said. 'What does that mean, no?'

He was still shaking his head. A drop of sweat flew off and plopped on the table and I could hear him trying very hard to breathe. 'Please,' he said. 'This is crazy. I didn't do anything. Why are you – This is pure Kafka, I didn't do anything.'

Deborah turned to me and raised an eyebrow. 'Kafka?' she said.

'He thinks he's a cockroach,' I told her.

'I'm just a dumb cop, Jerry,' she said. 'I don't know about Kafka. But I know solid evidence when I see it. And you know what, Jerry? I'm seeing it all over your apartment.'

'But I didn't *do* anything,' he pleaded.

'Okay,' said Deborah with a shrug. 'Then help me out here. How did all that stuff get into your place?'

'Wilkins did it,' he said, and he looked surprised, as if someone else had said it.

'Wilkins?' Deborah said, looking at me.

'The professor in the office next door?' I said.

'Yes, that's right,' Halpern said, suddenly gathering steam and leaning forward. 'It was Wilkins – it had to be.'

'Wilkins did it,' Deborah said. 'He put on your clothes, killed the girls, and then put the clothes back in your apartment.'

'Yes, that's right.'

'Why would he do that?'

'We're both up for tenure,' he said. 'Only one of us will get it.'

Deborah stared at him as if he had suggested dancing naked. 'Tenure,' she said at last, and there was wonder in her voice.

'That's right,' he said defensively. 'It's the most important moment in any academic career.'

'Important enough to kill somebody?' I asked.

He just stared at a spot on the table. 'It was Wilkins,' he said.

Deborah stared at him for a full minute, with the expression of a fond aunt watching her favorite nephew. He looked at her for a few seconds, and then blinked, glanced down at the table, over to me, and back down to the table again. When the silence continued, he finally looked back up at Deborah. 'All right, Jerry,' she said. 'If that's the best you can do, I think it might be time for you to call your lawyer.'

He goggled at her, but seemed unable to think of anything to say, so Deborah stood up and headed for the door, and I followed.

'Got him,' she said in the hallway. 'That son of a bitch is cooked. Game, set, point.'

And she was so positively sunny that I couldn't help saying, 'If it was him.'

She absolutely beamed at me. 'Of course it was him, Dex? Jesus, don't knock yourself. You did some great work here, and for once we got the right guy first time out.'

'I guess so,' I said.

She cocked her head to one side and stared at me, still smirking in a completely self-satisfied way. 'Whatsa matter, Dex?' she said. 'Got your shorts in a knot about the wedding?'

'Nothing's the matter,' I said. 'Life on earth has never before been so completely harmonious and satisfying. I just—' And here I hesitated, because I didn't really know what I just. There was only this unshakable and unreasonable feeling that something was not right.

'I know, Dex,' she said in a kindly voice that somehow made it feel even worse. 'It seems way too easy, right? But think of all the shit we go through every day, with every other case. It stands to reason that now and then we get an easy one, doesn't it?'

'I don't know,' I said. 'This just doesn't *feel* right.'

She snorted. 'With the amount of hard evidence we got on this guy, nobody's going to give a shit how it *feels*, Dex,' she said. 'Why don't you lighten up and enjoy a good day's work?'

I'm sure it was excellent advice, but I could not take it. Even though I had no familiar whisper to feed me my cues, I had to say something. 'He doesn't act like he's lying,' I said, rather feebly.

Deborah shrugged. 'He's a nut job. Not my problem. He did it.'

'But if he's psychotic in some way, why would it just burst out all of a sudden? I mean, he's thirty-something years old, and this is the first time he's done anything? That doesn't fit.'

She actually patted my shoulder and smiled again. 'Good point, Dex. Why don't you get on your computer and check his background? I bet we find something.' She glanced at her watch. 'You can do that right after the press conference, okay? Come on, can't be late.'

And I followed along dutifully, wondering how I always seemed to volunteer for extra work.

Deborah had, in fact, been granted the priceless boon of a press conference, something Captain Matthews did not give out lightly. It was her first as lead detective on a major case with its own media frenzy, and she had clearly studied up on how to look and speak for the evening news. She lost her smile and any other visible trace of emotion and spoke flat sentences of perfect cop-ese. Only someone who knew her as well as I did could tell that great and uncharacteristic happiness was burbling behind her wooden face.

So I stood at the back of the room and watched as my sister made a series of radiantly mechanical statements adding up to her belief that she had arrested a suspect in the heinous murders at the university, and as soon as she knew if he was guilty her dear friends in the media would be among the first to know it. She was clearly proud and happy and it had been pure meanness on my part even to hint that something was not quite righteous with Halpern's guilt, especially since I did not know what that might be – or even if.

She was almost certainly right – Halpern was guilty and I was being stu-pid and grumpy, thrown off the trolley of pure reason by my missing Passen-ger. It was the echo of its absence that made me uneasy, and not any kind of doubt about the suspect in a case that really meant absolutely nothing to me anyway. Almost certainly—

And there was that almost again. I had lived my life until now in absolutes – I had no experience with 'almost,' and it was unsettling, deeply disturbing not to have that voice of certainty to tell me what was what with no dither-ing and no doubt. I began to realize just how helpless I was without the Dark Passenger. Even in my day job, nothing was simple anymore.

Back in my cubicle I sat in my chair and leaned back with my eyes closed. *Anybody there?* I asked hopefully. Nobody was. Just an empty spot that was beginning to hurt as the numb wonder wore off. With the distraction of work over, there was nothing to keep me from self-absorbed self-pity. I was alone in a dark, mean world full of terrible things like me. Or at least, the me I used to be.

Where had the Passenger gone, and why had it gone there? If something had truly scared it away, what could that something be? What could frighten a thing that lived for darkness, that really came to life only when the knives were out?

And this brought a brand-new thought that was most unwelcome: If this hypothetical something had scared away the Passenger, had it followed it into exile? Or was it still sniffing at my trail? Was I in danger with no way left to protect myself – with no way of knowing whether some lethal threat was right behind me until its drool actually fell on my neck?

I have always heard that new experiences are a good thing, but this one was pure torture. The more I thought about it, the less I understood what was happening to me, and the more it hurt.

Well, there was one sure remedy for misery, and that was good hard work on something completely pointless. I swiveled around to face my computer and got busy.

In only a few minutes I had opened up the entire life and history of

Dr. Gerald Halpern, Ph.D. Of course, it was a little trickier than simply searching Halpern's name on Google. There was, for example, the matter of the
sealed court records, which took me almost five full minutes to open. But
when I did, it was certainly worth the effort, and I found myself thinking,
Well, well, well . . . And because at the moment I was tragically alone on the
inside, with no one to hear my pensive remarks, I said it aloud, too. 'Well,
well, well,' I said.

The foster-care records would have been interesting enough – not because
I felt any bond with Halpern from my own parentless past. I had been more
than adequately provided with a home and family by Harry, Doris, and Deborah, unlike Halpern, who had flitted from foster home to foster home until
finally landing at Syracuse University.

Far more interesting, however, was the file that no one was supposed to
open without a warrant, a court order, and a stone tablet direct from the hand
of God. And when I had read through it a second time, my reaction was even
more profound. 'Well, well, well, well,' I said, mildly unsettled at the way the
words bounced off the walls of my empty little office. And since profound
revelations are always more dramatic with an audience, I reached for the
phone and called my sister.

In just a few minutes she pushed into my cubicle and sat on the folding
chair. 'What did you find?' she said.

'Dr. Gerald Halpern has A Past,' I said, carefully pronouncing the capital
letters so she wouldn't leap across the desk and hug me.

'I knew it,' she said. 'What did he do?'

'It's not so much what he did,' I said. 'At this point, it's more like what was
done to him.'

'Quit screwing around,' she said. 'What is it?'

'To begin with, he's apparently an orphan.'

'Come on, Dex, cut to the chase.'

I held up a hand to try to calm her down, but it clearly didn't work very
well, because she started tapping her knuckles on the desktop. 'I am trying to
paint a subtle canvas here, Sis,' I said.

'Paint faster,' she said.

'All right. Halpern went into the foster-care system in upstate New York
when they found him living in a box under the freeway. They found his parents, who were unfortunately dead of recent and unpleasant violence. It seems
to have been very well-deserved violence.'

'What the fuck does that mean?'

'His parents were pimping him out to pedophiles,' I said.

'Jesus,' Deborah said, and she was clearly a little shocked. Even by Miami
standards, this was a bit much.

'And Halpern doesn't remember any of that part. He gets blackouts under
stress, the file says. It makes sense. The blackouts were probably a conditioned

response to the repeated trauma,' I said. 'That can happen.'

'Well, fuck,' Deborah said, and I inwardly applauded her elegance. 'So he forgets shit. You have to admit that fits. The girl tries to frame him for rape, and he's already worried about tenure – so he gets stressed and kills her without knowing it.'

'A couple of other things,' I said, and I admit that I enjoyed the drama of the moment perhaps a little more than was necessary. 'To begin with, the death of his parents.'

'What about it?' she said, quite clearly lacking any theatrical pleasure at all.

'Their heads were cut off,' I said. 'And then the house was torched.'

Deborah straightened up. 'Shit,' she said.

'I thought so, too.'

'Goddamn, that's *great*, Dex,' she said. 'We have his ass.'

'Well,' I said, 'it certainly fits the pattern.'

'It sure as hell does,' she said. 'So did he kill his parents?'

I shrugged. 'They couldn't prove anything. If they could, Halpern would have been committed. It was so violent that nobody could believe a kid had done it. But they're pretty sure that he was there, and at least saw what happened.'

She looked at me hard. 'So what's wrong with that? You still think he didn't do it? I mean, you're having one of your hunches here?'

It stung a lot more than it should have, and I closed my eyes for a moment. There was still nothing there except dark and empty. My famous hunches were, of course, based on things whispered to me by the Dark Passenger, and in its absence I had nothing to go on. 'I'm not having hunches lately,' I admitted. 'There's just something that bothers me about this. It just—'

I opened my eyes and Deborah was staring at me. For the first time today there was something in her expression beyond bubbly happiness, and for a moment I thought she was going to ask me what that meant and was I all right. I had no idea what I would say if she did, since the Dark Passenger was not something I had ever talked about, and the idea of sharing something that intimate was very unsettling.

'I don't know,' I said weakly. 'It doesn't seem right.'

Deborah smiled gently. I would have felt more at ease if she had snarled and told me to fuck off, but she smiled and reached a hand across the desk to pat mine. 'Dex,' she said softly, 'the hard evidence is more than enough. The background fits. The motive is good. You admit you're not having one of your . . . hunches.' She cocked her head to the side, still smiling, which made me even more uneasy. 'This one is righteous, Bro. Whatever is bothering you, don't pin it on this. He did it, we got him, that's it.' She let go of my hand before either one of us could burst into tears. 'But I'm a little worried about you.'

'I'm fine,' I said, and it sounded false even to me.

Deborah looked at me for a long moment, and then stood up. 'All right,' she said. 'But I'm here for you if you need me.' And she turned and walked away.

Somehow I slogged through the gray soup of the rest of the day and made it all the way home to Rita's at the end of the day, where the soup gelled into an aspic of sensory deprivation. I don't know what we had for dinner, or what anyone might have said. The only thing I could bring myself to listen for was the sound of the Passenger rushing back in, and this sound did not come. And so I swam through the evening on automatic pilot and finally went to bed, still completely wrapped up in Dull Empty Dexter.

It surprised me a great deal to learn it, but sleep is not automatic for humans, not even for the semi-human I was becoming. The old me, Dexter of the Darkness, had slept perfectly, with great ease, simply lying down, closing his eyes, and thinking, 'One two three GO.' Presto, sleep-o.

But the New Model Dexter had no such luck.

I tossed, I turned, I commanded my pitiful self to go immediately to sleep with no further dithering, and all to no avail. I could not sleep. I could only lie there wide-eyed and wonder why.

And as the night dragged on, so did the terrible, dreary introspection. Had I been misleading myself my entire life? What if I was not Dashing Slashing Dexter and his Canny Sidekick the Passenger? What if I was, in fact, actually only a Dark Chauffeur, allowed to live in a small room at the big house in exchange for driving the master on his appointed rounds? And if my services were no longer required, what could I possibly be now that the boss had moved away? Who was I if I was no longer me?

It was not a happy thought, and it did not make me happy. It also did not help me sleep. Since I had already tossed and turned exhaustively, without getting exhausted, I now concentrated on rolling and pitching, with much the same result. But finally, at around 3:30 a.m., I must have hit on the right combination of pointless movement and I dropped off at last into a shallow uncomfortable sleep.

The sound and smell of bacon cooking woke me up. I glanced at the clock – it was 8:32, later than I ever sleep. But of course it was Saturday morning. Rita had allowed me to doze on in my miserable unconsciousness. And now she would reward my return to the land of the waking with a bountiful breakfast. Yahoo.

Breakfast did, in fact, take some of the sourness out of me. It is very hard to maintain a really good feeling of utter depression and total personal worthlessness when you are full of food, and I gave up trying halfway through an excellent omelet.

Cody and Astor had naturally been awake for hours – Saturday morning was their unrestricted television time, and they usually took advantage of it to watch a series of cartoon shows that would certainly have been impossible before the discovery of LSD. They did not even notice me when I staggered past them on my way to the kitchen, and they stayed glued to the image of a talking kitchen utensil while I finished my breakfast, had a final cup of coffee, and decided to give life one more day to get its act together.

'All better?' Rita asked as I put down my coffee mug.

'It was a very nice omelet,' I said. 'Thank you.'

She smiled and lunged up out of her chair to give me a peck on the cheek before flinging all the dishes in the sink and starting to wash them. 'Remember you said you'd take Cody and Astor somewhere this morning,' she said over the sound of running water.

'I said that?'

'Dexter, you know I have a fitting this morning. For my wedding gown. I told you that weeks ago, and you said fine, you would take care of the kids while I went over to Susan's for the fitting, and then I really need to go to the florist's and see about some arrangements, even Vince offered to help me with that, he says he has a friend?'

'I doubt that,' I said, thinking of Manny Borque. 'Not Vince.'

'But I said no thanks. I hope that was all right?'

'Fine,' I said. 'We have only one house to sell to pay for things.'

'I don't want to hurt Vince's feelings and I'm sure his friend is wonderful, but I have been going to Hans for flowers since forever, and he would be brokenhearted if I went somewhere else for the wedding.'

'All right,' I said. 'I'll take the kids.'

I had been hoping for a chance to devote some serious time to my own personal misery and find a way to start on the problem of the absent Passenger. Failing that, it would have been nice just to relax a little bit, perhaps even catch up on some of the precious sleep I had lost the night before, as was my sacred right.

It was, after all, a Saturday. Many well-regarded religions and labor unions have been known to recommend that Saturdays are for relaxation and personal growth; for spending time away from the hectic hurly-burly, in well-earned rest and recreation. But Dexter was more or less a family man nowadays, which changes everything, as I was learning. And with Rita spinning around making wedding preparations like a tornado with blond bangs, it was a clear imperative for me to scoop up Cody and Astor and take them away from the pandemonium to the shelter of some activity sanctioned by society as appropriate for adult-child bonding time.

After a careful study of my options, I chose the Miami Museum of Science and Planetarium. After all, it would be crowded with other family groups, which would maintain my disguise – and start them on theirs as well. Since they were planning to embark on the Dark Trail, they needed to begin right away to understand the notion that the more abnormal one is, the more important it is to appear normal.

And going to the museum with Doting Daddy Dexter was supremely normal-appearing for all three of us. It had the added cachet of being something that was officially Good for Them, a very big advantage, no matter how much that notion made them squirm.

So I loaded the three of us into my car and headed north on U.S. 1, promising the whirling Rita that we would return safely for dinner. I drove us through Coconut Grove and just before the Rickenbacker Causeway turned into the parking lot of the museum in question. We did not go gentle into that good museum, however. In the parking lot, Cody got out of the car and simply stood there. Astor looked at him for a moment, and then turned to me. 'Why do we have to go in there?' she said.

'It's educational,' I told her.

'Ick,' she said, and Cody nodded.

'It's important for us to spend time together,' I said.

'At a *museum*?' Astor demanded. 'That's *pathetic*.'

'That's a lovely word,' I said. 'Where did you get it?'

'We're *not* going in there,' she said. 'We want to *do* something.'

'Have you ever been to this museum?'

'No,' she said, drawing the word out into three contemptuous syllables as only a ten-year-old girl can.

'Well, it might surprise you,' I said. 'You might actually learn something.'

'That's not what we want to learn,' she said. 'Not at a *museum*.'

'What is it you think you want to learn?' I said, and even I was impressed by how very much like a patient adult I sounded.

Astor made a face. 'You know,' she said. 'You said you'd show us stuff.'

'How do you know I'm not?' I said.

She looked at me uncertainly for a moment, then turned to Cody. Whatever it was they said to each other, it didn't require words. When she turned back to me a moment later, she was all business, totally self-assured. 'No way,' she said.

'What do you know about the stuff I'm going to show you?'

'Dexter,' she said. 'Why else did we ask you to show us?'

'Because you don't know anything about it and I do.'

'Duh-uh.'

'Your education begins in that building,' I said with my most serious face. 'Follow me and learn.' I looked at them for a moment, watched their uncertainty grow, then I turned and headed for the museum. Maybe I was just cranky from a night of lost sleep, and I was not sure they would follow, but I had to set down the ground rules right away. They had to do it my way, just as I had come to understand so long ago that I had to listen to Harry and do it his way.

15

Being fourteen years old is never easy, even for artificial humans. It's the age where biology takes over, and even when the fourteen-year-old in question is more interested in clinical biology than the sort more popular with his class-mates at Ponce de Leon Junior High, it still rules with an iron hand.

One of the categorical imperatives of puberty that applies even to young monsters is that nobody over the age of twenty knows anything. And since Harry was well over twenty at this point, I had gone into a brief period of rebellion against his unreasonable restraints on my perfectly natural and wholesome desires to hack my school chums into little bits.

Harry had laid out a wonderfully logical plan to get me squared away, which was his term for making things – or people – neat and orderly. But there is nothing logical about a fledgling Dark Passenger flexing its wings for the first time and beating them against the bars of the cage, yearning to fling itself into the free air and fall on its prey like a sharp steel thunderbolt.

Harry knew so many things I needed to learn to become safely and quietly me, to turn me from a wild, blossoming monster into the Dark Avenger: how to act human, how to be certain and careful, how to clean up afterward. He knew all these things as only an old cop could know them. I understood this, even then – but it all seemed so dull and unnecessary.

And Harry couldn't really know everything, after all. He could not know, for example, about Steve Gonzalez, a particularly charming example of pubes-cent humanity who had earned my attention.

Steve was larger than me, and at a year or two older; he already had some-thing on his upper lip that he referred to as a mustache. He was in my PE class and felt it his God-given duty to make my life miserable whenever pos-sible. If he was right, God must have been very pleased with the effort he put into it.

This was long before Dexter became the Living Ice Cube, and a certain amount of heated and very hard feeling built up inside. This seemed to please Steve and urge him on to greater heights of creativity in his persecution of the simmering young Dexter. We both knew this could end only one way, but alas for him, it was not the way Steve had in mind.

And so one afternoon an unfortunately industrious janitor stumbled into the biology lab at Ponce de Leon to find Dexter and Steve sorting out their personality conflict. It was not quite the classical middle-school face-off of filthy words and swinging fists, although I believe that might have been what Steve had in mind. But he had not reckoned with confronting the young Dark Passenger, and so the janitor found Steve securely taped to the table with a swatch of gray duct tape over his mouth, and Dexter standing above him with a scalpel, trying to remember what he had learned in biology class the day they dissected the frog.

Harry came to get me in his police cruiser, in uniform. He listened to the outraged assistant principal, who described the scene, quoted the student handbook, and demanded to know what Harry was going to do about it. Harry just looked at the assistant principal until the man's words dribbled away into silence. He looked at him a moment longer, for effect, and then he turned his cold blue eyes on me.

'Did you do what he says you did, Dexter?' he asked me.

There was no possibility of evasion or falsehood in the grip of that stare. 'Yes,' I said, and Harry nodded.

'You see?' the assistant principal said. He thought he was going to say more, but Harry turned the look back on him and he fell silent again.

Harry looked back at me. 'Why?' he said.

'He was picking on me.' That sounded somewhat feeble, even to me, so I added, 'A lot. All the time.'

'And so you taped him to a table,' he said, with very little inflection.

'Uh-huh.'

'And you picked up a scalpel.'

'I wanted him to stop,' I said.

'Why didn't you tell somebody?' Harry asked me.

I shrugged, which was a large portion of my working vocabulary in those days.

'Why didn't you tell me?' he asked.

'I can take care of it,' I said.

'Looks like you didn't take care of it so well,' he said.

There seemed to be very little I could do, so naturally enough I chose to look at my feet. They apparently had very little to add to the discussion, however, so I looked up again. Harry still watched me, and somehow he no longer needed to blink. He did not seem angry, and I was not really afraid of him, and that somehow made it even more uncomfortable.

'I'm sorry,' I said at last. I wasn't sure if I meant it – for that matter, I'm still not sure I can really be sorry for anything I do. But it seemed like a very politic remark, and nothing else burbled up in my teenaged brain, simmering as it was with an oatmeal-thick sludge of hormones and uncertainty. And although I am sure Harry didn't believe that I was sorry, he nodded again.

'Let's go,' he said.

'Just a minute,' the assistant principal said. 'We still have things to discuss.'

'You mean the fact that you let a known bully push my boy to this kind of confrontation because of poor supervision? How many times has the other boy been disciplined?'

'That's not the point—' the assistant principal tried to say.

'Or are we talking about the fact that you left scalpels and other dangerous equipment unsecured and easily available to students in an unlocked and unsupervised classroom?'

'Really, Officer—'

'I tell you what,' Harry said. 'I promise to overlook your extremely poor performance in this matter, if you agree to make a real effort to improve.'

'But this boy—' he tried to say.

'I will deal with this boy,' Harry said. 'You deal with fixing things so I don't have to call in the school board.'

And that, of course, was that. There was never any question of contradicting Harry, whether you were a murder suspect, the president of the Rotary Club, or a young errant monster. The assistant principal opened and closed his mouth a few more times, but no actual words came out, just a sort of sputtering sound combined with throat-clearing. Harry watched him for a moment, and then turned to me. 'Let's go,' he said again.

Harry was silent all the way out to the car, and it was not a chummy silence. He did not speak as we drove away from the school and turned north on Dixie Highway – instead of heading around the school in the other direction, Granada to Hardee and over to our little house in the Grove. I looked at him as he made his turn, but he still had nothing to say, and the expression on his face did not seem to encourage conversation. He looked straight ahead at the road, and drove – fast, but not so fast he had to turn on the siren.

Harry turned left on 17th Avenue, and for a few moments I had the irrational thought that he was taking me to the Orange Bowl. But we passed the turnoff for the stadium and kept going, over the Miami River and then right on North River Drive, and now I knew where we were going but I didn't know why. Harry still hadn't said a word or looked in my direction, and I was beginning to feel a certain oppression creeping into the afternoon that had nothing to do with the storm clouds that were beginning to gather on the horizon.

Harry parked the cruiser and at last he spoke. 'Come on,' he said. 'Inside.' I looked at him, but he was already climbing out of the car, so I got out, too, and followed him meekly into the detention center.

Harry was well known here, as he was everywhere a good cop might be known. He was followed by calls of 'Harry!' and 'Hey, Sarge!' all the way through the receiving area and down the hall to the cell block. I simply trudged behind him as my sense of grim foreboding grew. Why had Harry brought me to the jail? Why wasn't he scolding me, telling me how disappointed he was, devising harsh but fair punishment for me?

Nothing he did or refused to say offered me any clues. So I trailed along behind. We were stopped at last by one of the guards. Harry took him to one side and spoke quietly; the guard looked over at me, nodded, and led us to the end of the cell block. 'Here he is,' the guard said. 'Enjoy yourself.' He nodded at the figure in the cell, glanced at me briefly, and walked away, leaving Harry and me to resume our uncomfortable silence.

Harry did nothing to break the silence at first. He turned and stared into the cell, and the pale shape inside moved, stood up, and came to the bars. 'Why it's Sergeant Harry!' the figure said happily. 'How are you, Harry? So *nice* of you to drop by.'

'Hello, Carl,' Harry said. At last he turned to me and spoke. 'This is Carl, Dexter.'

'What a handsome lad you are, Dexter,' Carl said. 'Very pleased to meet you.'

The eyes Carl turned on me were bright and empty, but behind them I could almost see a huge dark shadow, and something inside me twitched and tried to slink away from the larger and fiercer thing that lived there beyond the bars. He was not in himself particularly large or fierce-looking – he was even pleasant in a very superficial way, with his neat blond hair and regular features – but there was something about him that made me very uneasy.

'They brought Carl in yesterday,' Harry said. 'He's killed eleven people.'

'Oh, well,' Carl said modestly, 'more or less.'

Outside the jail, the thunder crashed and the rain began. I looked at Carl with real interest; now I knew what had unsettled my Dark Passenger. We were just starting out, and here was somebody who had already been there and back, on eleven occasions, more or less. For the first time I understood how my classmates at Ponce might feel when they came face-to-face with an NFL quarterback.

'Carl enjoys killing people,' Harry said matter-of-factly. 'Don't you, Carl?'

'It keeps me busy,' Carl said happily.

'Until we caught you,' Harry said bluntly.

'Well, yes, there is that of course. Still . . .' he shrugged and gave Harry a very phony-looking smile, 'it was fun while it lasted.'

'You got careless,' Harry said.

'Yes,' Carl said. 'How could I know the police would be so very thorough?'

'How do you do it?' I blurted out.

'It's not so hard,' Carl said.

'No, I mean – Um, like *how*?'

Carl looked at me searchingly, and I could almost hear a purring coming from the shadow just past his eyes. For a moment our eyes locked and the world was filled with the black sound of two predators meeting over one small, helpless prey. 'Well, well,' Carl said at last. 'Can it really be?' He turned to Harry just as I was beginning to squirm. 'So I'm supposed to be an object lesson, is that it, Sergeant? Frighten your boy onto the straight and narrow path to godliness?'

Harry stared back, showing nothing, saying nothing.

'Well, I'm afraid I have to tell you that there is no way off this particular path, poor dear Harry. When you are on it, you are on it for life, and possibly beyond, and there is nothing you or I or the dear child here can do about it.'

'There's one thing,' Harry said.

'Really,' Carl said, and now a slow black cloud seemed to be rising up around him, coalescing on the teeth of his smile, spreading its wings out toward Harry, and toward me. 'And what might that be, pray tell?'

'Don't get caught,' Harry said.

For a moment the black cloud froze, and then it drew back and vanished. 'Oh my God,' Carl said. 'How I wish I knew how to laugh.' He shook his head slowly, from side to side. 'You're serious, aren't you? Oh my God. What a wonderful dad you are, Sergeant Harry.' And he gave us such a huge smile that it almost looked real.

Harry turned his full ice-blue gaze on me now.

'He got caught,' Harry said to me, 'because he didn't know what he was doing. And now he will go to the electric chair. Because he didn't know what the *police* were doing. Because,' Harry said without raising his voice at all and without blinking, 'he had no training.'

I looked at Carl, watching us through the thick bars with his too-bright dead empty eyes. Caught. I looked back at Harry. 'I understand,' I said.

And I did.

That was the end of my youthful rebellion.

And now, so many years later – wonderful years, filled with slicing and dicing and not getting caught – I truly knew what a remarkable gamble Harry had taken by introducing me to Carl. I could never hope to measure up to his performance – after all, Harry did things because he had *feelings* and I never would – but I could follow his example and make Cody and Astor toe the line. I would gamble, just as Harry had.

They would follow or not.

16

They followed.

The museum was crowded with groups of curious citizens in search of knowledge – or a bathroom, apparently. Most of them were between the ages of two and ten, and there seemed to be about one adult for every seven children. They moved like a great colorful flock of parrots, swooping back and forth through the exhibits with a loud cawing sound that, in spite of the fact that it was in at least three languages, all sounded the same. The international language of children.

Cody and Astor seemed slightly intimidated by the crowd and stayed close to me. It was a pleasant contrast to the spirit of Dexter-less adventure that seemed to rule them the rest of the time, and I tried to take advantage of it by steering them immediately to the piranha exhibit.

'What do they look like?' I asked them.

'Very bad,' Cody said softly, staring unblinking at the many teeth the fish displayed.

'Those are piranha,' Astor said. 'They can eat a whole cow.'

'If you were swimming and you saw piranha, what would you do?' I asked them.

'Kill them,' said Cody.

'There's too many,' Astor said. 'You should run away from them, and not go anywhere near.'

'So anytime you see these wicked-looking fish you will either try to kill them or run away from them?' I said. They both nodded. 'If the fish were really smart, like people, what would they do?'

'Wear a disguise,' Astor giggled.

'That's right,' I said, and even Cody smiled. 'What kind of disguise would you recommend? A wig and a beard?'

'Dex-ter,' Astor said. 'They're fish. Fish don't wear beards.'

'Oh,' I said. 'So they would still want to look like fish?'

'Of course,' she said, as if I was too stupid to understand big words.

'What kind of fish?' I said. 'Great big ones? Like sharks?'

'Normal,' Cody said. His sister looked at him for a moment, and then nodded.

'Whatever there's lots of in the area,' she said. 'Something that won't scare away what they want to eat.'

'Uh-huh,' I said.

They both looked at the fish in silence for a moment. It was Cody who first got it. He frowned and looked at me. I smiled encouragingly. He whispered something to Astor, who looked startled. She opened her mouth to say something, and then stopped.

'Oh,' she said.

'Yes,' I said. 'Oh.'

She looked at Cody, who looked up again from the piranha. Again, they didn't say anything aloud, but there was an entire conversation. I let it run its course, until they looked up at me. 'What can we learn from piranha?' I said.

'Don't look ferocious,' Cody said.

'Look like something normal,' Astor said grudg-ingly. 'But Dexter, fish aren't people.'

'That's exactly right,' I said. 'Because people survive by recognizing things that look dangerous. And fish get caught. We don't want to.' They looked at me solemnly, then back at the fish. 'So what else have we learned today?' I asked after a moment.

'Don't get caught,' Astor said.

I sighed. At least it was a start, but there was much work yet to do. 'Come on,' I said. 'Let's see some of the other exhibits.'

I was not really very familiar with the museum, perhaps because until recently I'd had no children to drag in there. So I was definitely improvising, looking for things that might get them started toward thinking and learning the right things. The piranha had been a stroke of luck, I admit – they had simply popped into view and my giant brain had supplied the correct lesson. Finding the next piece of happy coincidence was not as easy, and it was half an hour of trudging grimly through the murderous crowd of kids and their vicious parents before we came to the lion exhibit.

Once again, the ferocious appearance and reputation proved irresistible to Cody and Astor, and they came to a halt in front of the exhibit. It was a stuffed lion, of course, what I think they call a diorama, but it held their attention. The male lion stood proudly over the body of a gazelle, mouth wide and fangs gleaming. Beside him were two females and a cub. There was a two-page explanation that went with the exhibit, and about halfway down the second page I found what I needed.

'Well now,' I said brightly. 'Aren't we glad we're not lions?'

'No,' said Cody.

'It says here,' I said, 'that when a male lion takes over a lion family—'

'It's called a *pride*, Dexter,' Astor said. 'It was in *Lion King*.'

'All right,' I said. 'When a new daddy lion takes over a pride, he kills all the cubs.'

'That's horrible,' Astor said.

I smiled to show her my sharp teeth. 'No, it's perfectly natural,' I said. 'To protect his own and make sure that it's *his* cubs that rule the roost. Lots of predators do that.'

'What does that have to do with us?' Astor said. 'You're not going to kill us when you marry Mom, are you?'

'Of course not,' I said. 'You are my cubs now.'

'Then so what?' she said.

I opened my mouth to explain to her and then felt all the air rush out of me. My mouth hung open but I couldn't speak, because my brain was whirling with a thought so far-fetched that I didn't even bother to deny it. *Lots of predators do that*, I heard myself say. *To protect his own*, I had said.

Whatever made me a predator, its home was in the Dark Passenger. And now something had scared away the Passenger. Was it possible that, that—

That what? A new daddy Passenger was threatening my Passenger? I had run into many people in my life who had the shadow of something similar to mine hung over them, and nothing had ever happened with them except mutual recognition and a bit of inaudible snarling. This was too stupid even to think about – Passengers didn't have daddies.

Did they?

'Dexter,' Astor said. 'You're scaring us.'

I admit that I was scaring me, too. The thought that the Passenger could have a parent stalking it with lethal intentions was appallingly stupid – but then, after all, where had the Passenger really come from? I was reasonably sure that it was more than a psychotic figment of my disordered brain. I was not schizophrenic – both of us were sure of that. The fact that it was now gone proved that it had an independent existence.

And this meant that the Passenger had come from somewhere. It had existed before me. It had a source, whether you called it a parent or anything else.

'Earth to Dexter,' Astor said, and I realized that I still stood in front of them frozen in my unlikely, foolish openmouthed pose like a pedantic zombie.

'Yes,' I said stupidly, 'I was just thinking.'

'Did it hurt a lot?' she said.

I closed my mouth and looked at her. She was facing me with her look of ten-year-old disgust at how dumb grown-ups can be, and this time I agreed with her. I had always taken the Passenger for granted, so much so that I had never really wondered where it had come from, or how it had come to be. I had been smug, fatuously content to share space with it, simply glad to be me and not some other, emptier mortal, and now, when a little self-knowledge might have saved the day, I was struck dumb. Why had I never thought of any of these things before? And why did I have to choose now as the first time, in the presence of a sarcastic child? I had to devote some time and thought to this – but of course, this was neither the time nor the place.

'Sorry,' I said. 'Let's go see the planetarium.'

'But you were going to tell us why lions are important,' she said.

In truth, I could no longer remember why lions were important. But happily for my image, my cell phone began to chatter before I could admit it. 'Just a minute,' I said, and I pulled the phone from its holster. I glanced at it and saw that it was Deborah. And after all, family is family, so I answered.

'They found the heads,' she said.

It took me a moment to figure out what she meant, but Deborah was hissing in my ear and I realized some sort of response was called for. 'The heads? From the two bodies over at the university?' I said.

Deborah made an exasperated hissing noise and said, 'Jesus, Dex, there aren't that many missing heads in town.'

'Well, there's city hall,' I said.

'Get your ass over here, Dexter. I need you.'

'But Deborah, it's Saturday, and I'm in the middle of—'

'Now,' she said, and hung up.

I looked at Cody and Astor and pondered my quandary. If I took them home it would be at least an hour before I got back to Debs, and in addition we would lose our precious Saturday quality time together. On the other hand, even I knew that taking children to a homicide scene might be considered a little bit eccentric.

But it would also be educational. They needed to be impressed with just how thorough the police are when dead bodies turn up, and this was as good an opportunity as any. On balance, even taking into consideration that my dear sister might have a semi-ballistic reaction, I decided it would be best simply to pile into the car and take them to their first investigation.

'All right,' I said to them as I reholstered my phone. 'We have to go now.'

'Where?' Cody said.

'To help my sister,' I said. 'Will you remember what we learned today?'

'Yes, but this is just a *museum*,' Astor said. 'It's not what we want to learn.'

'Yes, it is,' I said. 'And you have to trust me, and do it my way, or I'm not going to teach you.' I leaned down to where I could look them both in the eyes. 'Not doodly-squat,' I said.

Astor frowned. 'Dex-terrrr,' she said.

'I mean it. It has to be my way.'

Once again she and Cody locked glances. After a moment he nodded, and she turned back to me. 'All right,' she said. 'We promise.'

'We'll wait,' Cody said.

'We understand,' Astor said. 'When can we start the cool stuff?'

'When I say,' I said. 'Anyway, right now we have to go.'

She switched immediately back to snippy ten-year-old. 'Now where do we have to go?'

'I have to go to work,' I said. 'So I'm taking you with me.'

'To see a *body*?' she asked hopefully.

I shook my head. 'Just the head,' I said.

She looked at Cody and shook her head. 'Mom won't like it.'

'You can wait in the car if you want to,' I said.

'Let's go,' said Cody, just about his longest speech all day.

We went.

17

Deborah was waiting at a modest $2 million house on a private cul-de-sac in Coconut Grove. The street was sealed off from just inside the guard booth to the house itself, about halfway down on the left, and a crowd of indignant residents stood around on their carefully manicured lawns and walkways, fuming at the swarm of low-rent social undesirables from the police department who had invaded their little paradise. Deborah was in the street instructing a videographer in what to shoot and from what angles. I hurried over to join her, with Cody and Astor trailing along right behind.

'What the hell is that?' Deborah demanded, glaring from the kids to me.

'They are known as children,' I told her. 'They are often a by-product of marriage, which may be why you are unfamiliar with them.'

'Are you off your fucking nut bringing them here?' she snapped.

'You're not supposed to say that word,' Astor told Deborah with a glare. 'You owe me fifty cents for saying it.'

Deborah opened her mouth, turned bright red, and closed it again. 'You gotta get them outta here,' she finally said. 'They shouldn't see this.'

'We want to see it,' Astor said.

'Hush,' I told them. 'Both of you.'

'Jesus Christ, Dexter,' Deborah said.

'You told me to come right away,' I said. 'I came.'

'I can't play nursemaid to a couple of kids,' Deborah said.

'You don't have to,' I said. 'They'll be fine.'

Deborah stared at the two of them; they stared back. Nobody blinked, and for a moment I thought my dear sister would chew off her lower lip. Then she shook herself. 'Screw it,' she said. 'I don't have time for a hassle. You two wait over there.' She pointed to her car, which was parked across the street, and grabbed me by the arm. She dragged me toward the house where all the activity was humming. 'Lookit,' she said, and pointed at the front of the house.

On the phone, Deborah had told me they found the heads, but in truth it would have taken a major effort to miss them. In front of the house, the short driveway curled through a pair of coral-rock gateposts before puddling into a small courtyard with a fountain in the middle. On top of each gatepost was an ornate lamp. Chalked on the driveway between the posts was something that looked like the letters MLK, except that it was in a strange script that I did not recognize. And to make sure that no one spent too long puzzling out the message, on top of each gatepost—

Well. Although I had to admit the display had a certain primitive vigor and an undeniable dramatic impact, it was really far too crude for my taste. Even though the heads apparently had been carefully cleaned, the eyelids were gone and the mouths had been forced into a strange smile by the heat, and it was not pleasant. Certainly no one on-site asked my opinion, but I have always felt that there should be no leftovers. It's untidy, and it shows a lack of a real workmanlike spirit. And for these heads to be left so conspicuously – this was mere showing off, and demonstrated an unrefined approach to the problem. Still, there's no accounting for taste. I'm always willing to admit that my technique is not the only way. And as always in aesthetic matters, I waited for some small sibilant whisper of agreement from the Dark Passenger – but of course, there was nothing.

Not a murmur, not a twitch of the wing, not a peep. My compass was gone, leaving me in the very unsettling position of needing to hold my own hand.

Of course, I was not completely alone. There was Deborah beside me, and I became aware that as I was pondering the matter of my shadow companion's disappearance, she was speaking to me.

'They were at the funeral this morning,' she said. 'Came back and this was waiting for them.'

'Who are they?' I asked, nodding at the house.

Deborah jabbed me in the ribs with her elbow. It hurt. 'The family, ass-hole. The Ortega family. What did I just say?'

'So this happened in daylight?' For some reason, that made it seem a little more disturbing.

'Most of the neighbors were at the funeral, too,' she said. 'But we're still looking for somebody who might have seen something.' She shrugged. 'We might get lucky. Who knows.'

I did not know, but for some reason I did not think that anything connected to this would bring us luck. 'I guess this creates a little doubt about Halpern's guilt,' I said.

'It damned well does not,' she said. 'That asshole is guilty.'

'Ah,' I said. 'So you think that somebody else found the heads, and, uh . . .'

'Fucking hell, I don't know,' she said. 'Somebody must be working with him.'

I just shook my head. That didn't make any sense at all, and we both knew it. Somebody capable of conceiving and performing the elaborate ritual of the two murders would almost have to do it alone. Such acts were so highly personal, each small step the acting out of some unique inner need, that the idea of two people sharing the same vision was almost pure nonsense. In a weird way, the ceremonial display of the heads fit in with the way the bodies had been left – two pieces of the same ritual.

'That doesn't seem right,' I said.

'Well then, what does?'

I looked at the heads, perched so carefully atop the lamps. They had of course been burned in the fire that had toasted the bodies, and there were no traces of blood visible. The necks appeared to have been cut very neatly. Other than that, I had no keen insight into anything at all – and yet there was Deborah, staring at me expectantly. It's difficult to have a reputation for being able to see into the still heart of the mystery when all that notoriety rests on the shadowy guidance of an interior voice that was, at the moment, somewhere else altogether. I felt like a ventriloquist's dummy, suddenly called upon to perform the whole act alone.

'Both the heads are here,' I said, since I clearly had to say something. 'Why not at the other girl's house? The one with the boyfriend?'

'Her family lives in Massachusetts,' Deborah said. 'This was easier.'

'And you checked him out, right?'

'Who?'

'The dead girl's boyfriend,' I said slowly and carefully. 'The guy with the tattoo on his neck.'

'Jesus Christ, Dexter, of course we're checking him out. We're checking out everybody who came within half a mile of these girls in their whole fucking sad little lives, and you—' She took a deep breath, but it didn't seem to calm her down very much. 'Listen, I don't really need any help with the basic police work, okay? What I need help with is the weird creepy shit you're supposed to know about.'

It was nice to confirm my identity as the Weird Creepy Shit King, but I did have to wonder how long it would last without my Dark Crown. Still, with my reputation on the line I had to venture some kind of insightful opinion, so I took a small bloodless stab at it.

'All right,' I said. 'Then from a weird creepy point of view, it doesn't make sense to have two different killers with the same ritual. So either Halpern killed 'em and somebody found the heads and thought, what the hell, I'll hang 'em up – or else the wrong guy is in jail.'

'Fuck that,' she said.

'Which part?'

'All of it, goddamn it!' she said. 'Neither one of those choices is any better.'

'Well, shit,' I said, surprising us both. And since I felt cranky beyond endurance with Deborah, and with myself, and with this whole burned-and-headless thing, I took the only logical, reasonable course. I kicked a coconut.

Much better. Now my foot hurt, too.

'I'm checking Goldman's background,' she said abruptly, nodding at the house. 'So far, he's just a dentist. Owns an office building in Davie. But this – it smells like the cocaine cowboys. And that doesn't make sense, either. Goddamn it, Dexter,' she said. 'Give me something.'

I looked at Deborah with surprise. Somehow she had brought it around so it was back in my lap again, and I had absolutely nothing beyond a very strong hope that Goldman would turn out to be a drug lord who was only disguised as a dentist. 'I have come up empty,' I said, which was sad but far too true.

'Aw, crap,' she said, looking past me to the edge of the gathering crowd. The first of the news vans had arrived, and even before the vehicle had come to a full stop the reporter leaped out and began poking at his cameraman, prodding him into position for a long shot. 'Goddamn it,' Deborah said, and hurried over to deal with them.

'That guy is scary, Dexter,' said a small voice behind me, and I turned quickly around. Once again, Cody and Astor had snuck up on me unobserved. They stood together, and Cody inclined his head toward the small crowd that had gathered on the far side of the crime-scene tape.

'Which guy is scary?' I said, and Astor said, 'There. In the orange shirt. Don't make me point, he's *looking*.'

I looked for an orange shirt in the crowd and saw only a flash of color at the far end of the cul-de-sac as someone ducked into a car. It was a small blue car, not a white Avalon – but I did notice a familiar dab of additional color dangling from the rearview mirror as the car moved out onto the main road. And although it was difficult to be sure, I was relatively confident that it was a University of Miami faculty parking pass.

I turned back to Astor. 'Well, he's gone now,' I said. 'Why did you say he was scary?'

'*He* says so,' Astor said, pointing to Cody, and Cody nodded.

'He was,' Cody said, barely above a whisper. 'He had a big shadow.'

'I'm sorry he scared you,' I said. 'But he's gone now.'

Cody nodded. 'Can we look at the heads?'

Children are so interesting, aren't they? Here Cody had been frightened by something as insubstantial as somebody's shadow, and yet he was as eager as I'd ever seen him to get a closer look at a concrete example of murder, terror, and human mortality. Of course I didn't blame him for wanting a peek, but I didn't think I could openly allow it. On the other hand, I had no idea how to explain all of this to them, either. I am told that the Turkish language, for example, has subtleties far beyond what I can imagine, but English was definitely not adequate for a proper response.

Happily for me, Deborah came back just then, muttering, 'I will never complain about the captain again.' That seemed highly unlikely, but it did not seem politic to say so. 'He can *have* those bloodsucking bastards from the press.'

'Maybe you're just not a people person,' I said.

'Those assholes aren't people,' she said. 'All they want is to get some goddamned pictures of their perfect fucking haircuts standing in front of the heads, so they can send their tape to the network. What kind of animal wants to see this?'

Actually, I knew the answer to that one, since I was shepherding two of them at the moment and, truth be told, might be considered one myself. But it did seem like I should avoid this question and try to keep our focus on the problem at hand. So I pondered whatever it was that had made Cody's scary guy seem scary, and the fact that he'd had what looked very much like a university parking permit.

'I've had a thought,' I said to Deborah, and the way her head snapped around you might have thought I'd told her she was standing on a python. 'It doesn't really fit with your dentist-as-drug-lord theory,' I warned her.

'Out with it,' she said through her teeth.

'Somebody was here, and he scared the kids. He took off in a car with a faculty parking tag.'

Deborah stared at me, her eyes hard and opaque. 'Shit,' she said softly. 'The guy Halpern said, what's his name?'

'Wilkins,' I said.

'No,' she said. 'Can't be. All because the kids say somebody scared them? No.'

'He has a motive,' I said.

'To get tenure, for Christ's sake? Come on, Dex.'

'We don't have to think it's important,' I said. 'They do.'

'So to get tenure,' she said, shaking her head, 'he breaks into Halpern's apartment, steals his clothes, kills two girls—'

'And then steers us to Halpern,' I said, remembering how he had stood there in the hall and suggested it.

Deborah's head jerked around to face me. 'Shit,' she said. 'He did do that, didn't he? Told us to go see Halpern.'

'And however feeble tenure might seem as a motive,' I said, 'it makes more sense than Danny Rollins and Ted Bundy getting together on a little project, doesn't it?'

Deborah smoothed down the back of her hair, a surprisingly feminine gesture for someone I had come to think of as Sergeant Rock. 'It might,' she said finally. 'I don't know enough about Wilkins to say for sure.'

'Shall we go talk to him?'

She shook her head. 'First I want to see Halpern again,' she said.

'Let me get the kids,' I said.

Naturally, they were not anywhere near where they should have been. But I found them easily enough; they had wandered over to get a better look at the two heads, and it may have been my imagination, but I thought I could see a small gleam of professional appreciation in Cody's eyes.

'Come on,' I told them, 'we have to get going.' They turned away and followed me reluctantly, but I did hear Astor muttering under her breath, 'Better than a stupid museum anyway.'

From the far edge of the group that had gathered to see the spectacle he had watched, careful to be just one of the staring crowd, no different from all the rest of them, and unobserved in any specific way. It was a risk for the Watcher to be there at all – he could well be recognized, but he was willing to take the chance. And of course, it was gratifying to see the reaction to his work; a small vanity but one he allowed himself.

Besides, he was curious to see what they would make of the one simple clue he had left. The other was clever – but so far he had ignored it, walking right past and allowing his coworkers to photograph it and examine it. Perhaps he should have been a little more blatant – but there was time to do this right. No hurry at all, and the importance of getting the other ready, taking him when it was all just right – that outweighed everything else.

The Watcher moved a little closer, to study the other, perhaps see some sign as to how he was reacting so far. Interesting to bring those children with him. They didn't seem particularly disturbed by the sight of the two heads. Perhaps they were used to such things, or—No. It was not possible.

Moving with the greatest possible care, he edged closer, still trying to work his way near with the natural ebb and flow of the onlookers, until he got to the yellow tape at a point as close to the children as he could get.

And when the boy looked up and their eyes met, there was no longer any possibility of mistake.

For a moment their gaze locked and all sense of time was lost in the whir of shadowy wings. The boy simply stood there and stared at him with recognition – not of who he was but of what, and his small dark wings fluttered in panicked fury. The Watcher could not help himself; he moved closer, allowing the boy to see him and the nimbus of dark power he carried. The boy showed no fear – simply looked back at him and showed his own power. Then the boy turned away and took his sister's hand, and the two of them trotted over to the other.

Time to leave. The children would certainly point him out, and he did not want his face seen, not yet. He hurried back to the car and drove away, but not with anything like worry. Not at all. If anything, he was more pleased than he had a right to be.

It was the children, of course. Not just that they would tell the other, and move him a few small steps further into the necessary fear. But also because he really liked children. They were wonderful to work with, they broadcast emotions that were so very powerful, and raised the whole energy of the event to a higher plane.

Children – wonderful.

This was actually starting to be enjoyable.

For a while, it was enough to ride in the monkey-things and help them kill. But even this grew dull with the simple repetition, and every now and then IT felt again that there had to be something more. There was that tantalizing twitch of something indefinable at the moment of the kill, the sense that something stirred toward waking and then settled back down again, and IT wanted to know what that was.

But no matter how many times, no matter how many different monkey-things, IT could never get any closer to that feeling, never push in far enough to find out what it was. And that made IT want to know all the more.

A great deal of time went by, and IT began to turn sour again. The monkey-things were just too simple, and whatever IT did with them was not enough. IT began to resent their stupid, pointless, endlessly repeating existence. IT lashed out at them once or twice, wanting to punish them for their dumb, unimaginative suffering, and IT drove IT's host to kill entire families, whole tribes of the things. And as they all died, that wonderful hint of something else would hang there just out of reach and then settle back down again into slumber.

It was furiously frustrating; there had to be a way to break through, find out what that elusive something was and pull it into existence.

And then at last, the monkey-things began to change. It was very slow at first, so slow that IT didn't even realize what was happening until the process was well under way. And one wonderful day, when IT went into a new host, the thing stood up on its back legs and, as IT still wondered what was happening, the thing said, 'Who are you?'

The extreme shock of this moment was followed by an even more extreme pleasure.

IT was no longer alone.

18

The ride to the detention center went smoothly, but with Deborah driving that merely meant that no one was severely injured. She was in a hurry, and she was first and foremost a Miami cop who had learned to drive from Miami cops. And that meant she believed that traffic was fluid in nature and she sliced through it like a hot iron in butter, sliding into gaps that weren't really there, and making it clear to the other drivers that it was either move or die.

Cody and Astor were very pleased, of course, from their securely seat-belted position in the backseat. They sat as straight as possible, craning upward to see out. And rarest of all, Cody actually smiled briefly when we narrowly missed smashing into a 350-pound man on a small motorcycle.

'Put on the siren,' Astor demanded.

'This isn't a goddamned game,' Deborah snarled.

'Does it have to be a goddamned game for the siren?' Astor said, and Deborah turned bright red and yanked the wheel hard to bring us off U.S. 1, just barely missing a battered Honda riding on four doughnut tires.

'Astor,' I said, 'don't say that word.'

'She says it all the time,' Astor said.

'When you are her age, you can say it, too, if you want to,' I said. 'But not when you're ten years old.'

'That's stupid,' she said. 'If it's a bad word it doesn't matter how old you are.'

'That's very true,' I said. 'But I can't tell Sergeant Deborah what to say.'

'That's stupid,' Astor repeated, and then switched directions by adding, 'Is she really a sergeant? Is that better than a policeman?'

'It means she's the boss policeman,' I said.

'She can tell the ones in the blue suits what to do?'

'Yes,' I said.

'And she gets to have a gun, too?'

'Yes.'

Astor leaned forward as far as the seat belt would let her, and stared at Deborah with something approaching respect, which was not an expression I saw on her face very often. 'I didn't know girls could have a gun and be the boss policeman,' she said.

'Girls can do any god – anything boys can do,' Deborah snapped. 'Usually better.'

Astor looked at Cody, and then at me. 'Anything?' she said.

'Almost anything,' I said. 'Professional football is probably out.'

'Do you shoot people?' Astor asked Deborah.

'For Christ's sake, Dexter,' Deborah said.

'She shoots people sometimes,' I told Astor, 'but she doesn't like to talk about it.'

'Why not?'

'Shooting somebody is a very private thing,' I said, 'and I think she feels that it isn't anybody else's business.'

'Stop talking about me like I'm a lamp, for Christ's sake,' Deborah snapped. 'I'm sitting right here.'

'I know that,' Astor said. 'Will you tell us about who you shot?'

For an answer, Deborah squealed the car through a sharp turn, into the parking lot, and rocked to a stop in front of the center. 'We're here,' she said, and jumped out as if she was escaping a nest of fire ants. She hurried into the building and as soon as I got Cody and Astor unbuckled, we followed at a more leisurely pace.

Deborah was still speaking with the sergeant on duty at the desk, and I steered Cody and Astor to a pair of battered chairs. 'Wait here,' I said. 'I'll be back in a few minutes.'

'Just wait?' Astor said, with outrage quivering in her voice.

'Yes,' I said. 'I have to go talk to a bad guy.'

'Why can't we go?' she demanded.

'It's against the law,' I said. 'Now wait here like I said. Please.'

They didn't look terribly enthusiastic, but at least they didn't leap off the chairs and charge down the hallway screaming. I took advantage of their cooperation and joined Deborah.

'Come on,' she said, and we headed to one of the interview rooms down the hall. In a few minutes a guard brought Halpern in. He was handcuffed, and he looked even worse than he had when we brought him in. He hadn't shaved and his hair was a rat's nest, and there was a look in his eyes that I can only describe as haunted, no matter how clichéd that sounds. He sat in the chair where the guard nudged him, perching on the edge of the seat and staring at his hands as they lay before him on the table.

Deborah nodded to the guard, who left the room and stood in the hall outside. She waited for the door to swing closed and then turned her attention to Halpern. 'Well, Jerry,' she said, 'I hope you had a good night's rest.'

His head jerked as if it had been yanked upward by a rope, and he goggled at her. 'What – what do you mean?' he said.

Debs raised her eyebrows. 'I don't mean anything, Jerry,' she said mildly. 'Just being polite.'

He stared at her for a moment and then dropped his head again. 'I want to go home,' he said in a small, shaky voice.

'I'm sure you do, Jerry,' Deborah said. 'But I can't let you go right now.'

He just shook his head, and muttered something inaudible.

'What's that, Jerry?' she asked in the same kind, patient voice.

'I said, I don't think I did anything,' he said, still without looking up.

'You don't think so?' she asked him. 'Shouldn't we be kind of sure about that before we let you go?'

He raised his head to look at her, very slowly this time. 'Last night . . .' he said. 'Something about being in this place . . .' He shook his head. 'I don't know. I don't know,' he said.

'You've been in a place like this before, haven't you, Jerry? When you were young,' Deborah said, and he nodded. 'And this place made you remember something?'

He jerked as if she'd spit in his face. 'I don't – it isn't a memory,' he said. 'It was a dream. It had to be a dream.'

Deborah nodded very understandingly. 'What was the dream about, Jerry?'

He shook his head and stared at her with his jaw hanging open.

'It might help you to talk about it,' she said. 'If it's just a dream, what can it hurt?' He kept shaking his head. 'What was the dream about, Jerry?' she said again, a little more insistently, but still very gently.

'There's a big statue,' he said, and he stopped shaking his head and looked surprised that words had come out.

'All right,' Deborah said.

'It – it's really big,' he said. 'And there's a . . . a . . . it has a fire burning in its belly.'

'It has a belly?' Deborah said. 'What kind of statue is it?'

'It's so big,' he said. 'Bronze body, with two arms held out, and the arms are moving down, to . . .' He trailed off, and then mumbled something.

'What did you say, Jerry?'

'He said it has a bull's head,' I said, and I could feel all the hairs on the back of my neck standing straight out.

'The arms come down,' he said. 'And I feel . . . really happy. I don't know why. Singing. And I put the two girls into the arms. I cut them with a knife, and they go up to the mouth, and the arms dump them in. Into the fire . . .'

'Jerry,' Debs said, even more gently, 'your clothes had blood on them, and they'd been singed.' He didn't say anything, and she went on. 'We know you have blackouts when you're feeling too much stress,' she said. He stayed quiet. 'Isn't it just possible, Jerry, that you had one of these blackouts, killed the girls, and came home? Without knowing it?'

He began shaking his head again, slowly and mechanically.

'Can you give me a better suggestion?' she said.

'Where would I find a statue like that?' he said. 'That's – how could I, what, find the statue, and build the fire inside it, and get the girls there, and – how could that be possible? How could I do all that and not know it?'

Deborah looked at me, and I shrugged. It was a fair point. After all, there must surely be some practical limit to what you can do while sleepwalking, and this did seem to go a little beyond that.

'Then where did the dream come from, Jerry?' she said.

'Everybody has dreams,' he said.

'And how did the blood get on your clothes?'

'Wilkins did it,' he said. 'He had to, there's no other answer.'

There was a knock on the door and the sergeant came in. He bent over and spoke softly into Deborah's ear, and I leaned closer to hear. 'This guy's lawyer is making trouble,' he said. 'He says now that the heads turned up while his client is in here, he has to be innocent.' The sergeant shrugged. 'I can't keep him outta here,' he said.

'All right,' Debs said. 'Thanks, Dave.' He shrugged again, straightened, and left the room.

Deborah looked at me. 'Well,' I said, 'at least it doesn't seem too easy any-more.'

She turned back to Halpern. 'All right, Jerry,' she said. 'We'll talk some more later.' She stood up and walked out of the room and I followed.

'What do we think about that?' I asked her.

She shook her head. 'Jesus, Dex, I don't know. I need a major break here.' She stopped walking and turned to face me. 'Either the guy really did this in one of his blackouts, which means he set the whole thing up without really knowing, which is impossible.'

'Probably,' I said.

'Or else somebody else went to a shitload of trouble to set it up and frame him, and timed it just right to match one of his blackouts.'

'Which is also impossible,' I said helpfully.

'Yeah,' she said. 'I know.'

'And the statue with the bull's head and the fire in its belly?'

'Fuck,' she said. 'It's just a dream. Has to be.'

'So where were the girls burned?'

'You want to show me a giant statue with a bull's head and a built-in bar-becue? Where do you hide that? You find it and I'll believe it's real,' she said.

'Do we have to release Halpern now?' I asked.

'No, goddamn it,' she snarled. 'I still got him on resisting arrest.' And she turned away and walked back toward the receiving area.

Cody and Astor were sitting with the sergeant when we got back out to the entryway, and even though they had not remained where I told them to, I was so grateful that they had not set anything on fire that I let it go. Deborah watched impatiently while I collected them, and we all headed out the door together. 'Now what?' I said.

'We have to talk to Wilkins, of course,' Deborah said.

'And do we ask him if he has a statue with a bull's head in his backyard?' I asked her.

'No,' she said. 'That's bullshit.'

'That's a bad word,' said Astor. 'You owe me fifty cents.'

'It's getting late,' I said. 'I have to get the kids home before their mother barbecues me.'

Deborah looked at Cody and Astor for a long moment, then up at me. 'All right,' she said.

19

I did manage to get the kids home before Rita went over the edge, but it was a very close call that was not made any easier when she found out that they had been to see severed heads. Still, they were obviously unbothered and even excited about their day, and Astor's new determination to be a Mini-Me to my sister Deborah seemed to distract Rita from anything approaching actual wrath. After all, an early career choice could save a lot of time and bother later.

It was clear that Rita had a full head of steam and we were in for Babble-fest. Normally I would simply smile and nod and let her run on. But I was in no mood for anything that smacked of normal. For the last two days I had wanted nothing but a quiet place and time to try to figure out where my Passenger had gone, and I had instead been pulled in every other direction possible by Deborah, Rita, the kids, even my job, of all things. My disguise had taken over from the thing it was supposed to be hiding, and I did not like it. But if I could make it past Rita and out the door, I would finally have some time to myself.

And so, pleading important case work that could not wait for Monday morning, I slid out the door and drove in to the office, enjoying the relative peace and calm of Miami traffic on a Saturday night.

For the first fifteen minutes of the drive I could not lose the feeling that I was being followed. Ridiculous, I know, but I had no experience with being alone in the night and it made me feel very vulnerable. Without the Passenger I was a tiger with a dull nose and no fangs. I felt slow and stupid, and the skin on my back would not stop crawling. It was an overall feeling of impending creepiness, the sense that I needed to circle around and sniff the back trail, because something was lurking there hungrily. And tickling at the edges of all that was an echo of that strange dream music, making my feet twitch in an involuntary way, as if they had someplace to go without me.

It was a terrible feeling, and if only I had been capable of empathy, I'm sure I might have had a moment of awful revelation, wherein I flung a hand to my forehead and sank to the ground, murmuring anguished regrets over all the times I had done the stalking and caused this dreadful feeling in others. But I am not built for anguish – at least, not my own – and so all I could think about was my very large problem. My Passenger was gone, and I was empty and defenseless if somebody really was tailing me.

It had to be mere imagination. Who would stalk Dutiful Dexter, plodding through his completely normal artificial existence with a happy smile, two children, and a new mortgage to a caterer? Just to be sure, I glanced into the rearview mirror.

No one of course; no one lurking with an ax and a piece of pottery with Dexter's name on it. I was turning stupid in my lonely dotage.

A car was on fire on the shoulder of the Palmetto Expressway, and most of the traffic was dealing with the congestion by either roaring around it on the left shoulder or leaning on the horn and shouting. I got off and drove past the warehouses near the airport. At a storage place just off 69th Avenue a burglar alarm was clattering endlessly, and three men were loading boxes into a truck without any appearance of haste. I smiled and waved; they ignored me.

It was a feeling I was getting used to – everyone was ignoring poor empty Dexter lately, except, of course, whoever it was that had either been following me or not really following me at all.

But speaking of empty, the way I had weaseled out of a confrontation with Rita, smooth as it had been, had left me without dinner, and this is not something I willingly tolerate. Right now I wanted to eat almost as much as I wanted to breathe.

I stopped at a Pollo Tropical and picked up half a chicken to take with me. The smell instantly filled the car, and the last couple of miles it was all I could do to keep the car on the road instead of screeching to a halt and ripping at the chicken with my teeth.

It finally overwhelmed me in the parking lot, and as I walked in the door I had to fumble out my credentials with greasy fingers, nearly dropping the beans in the process. But by the time I settled in at my computer, I was a much happier boy and the chicken was no more than a bag of bones and a pleasant memory.

As always, with a full stomach and a clean conscience I found it much easier to shift my powerful brain into high gear and think about the problem. The Dark Passenger was missing; that seemed to imply that it had some kind of independent existence without me. That meant it must have come from somewhere and, quite possibly, gone back there. So my first problem was to learn what I could about where it came from.

I knew very well that mine was not the only Passenger in the world. Over the course of my long and rewarding career I had encountered several other predators wrapped in the invisible black cloud that indicated a hitchhiker like mine. And it stood to reason that they had originated somewhere and sometime, and not just with me and in my own time. Shamefully enough, I had never wondered why, or where these inner voices came from. Now, with the whole night stretching ahead of me in the peace and quiet of the forensics lab, I could rectify this tragic oversight.

And so without any thought of my own personal safety, I dashed fearlessly onto the Internet. Of course, there was nothing helpful when I searched 'Dark Passenger.' That was, after all, my private term. I tried it anyway, just to be safe, and found nothing more than a few online games and a couple of blogs that someone really should report to the proper authorities, whoever was in charge of policing teenage angst.

I searched for 'interior companion,' 'inside friend,' and even 'spirit guide.' Once again there were some very interesting results that made one wonder what this tired old world was coming to, but nothing that illuminated my problem. But as far as I know there has never been only one of anything, and the odds were that I was simply failing to come up with the correct search terms to find what I needed.

Very well: 'Inner guide.' 'Internal adviser.' 'Hidden helper.' I went through as many combinations of these as I could think of, switching around the adjectives, running through lists of synonyms, and always marveling at how New Age pseudo-philosophy had taken over the Internet. And still I came up with nothing more sinister than a way to tap my powerful subconscious to make a killing in real estate.

There was, however, one very interesting reference to Solomon, of biblical fame, which claimed that the old wise guy had made secret references to some kind of inner king. I searched for a few tidbits of information on Solomon. Who would have guessed that this Bible stuff was interesting and relevant? But apparently when we think of him as being a wise, jolly old guy with a beard who offered to cut a baby in half just for laughs, we are missing out on all the good parts.

For example, Solomon built a temple to something called Moloch, apparently one of the naughty elder gods, and he killed his brother because 'wickedness' was found inside him. I could certainly see that, from a biblical perspective, interior wickedness might be a fine description of a Dark Passenger. But if there was a connection here, did it really make sense that someone with an 'inner king' would kill somebody inhabited by wickedness?

It was making my head spin. Was I to believe that King Solomon himself actually had a Dark Passenger of his own? Or because he was supposedly one of the Bible's good guys, should I interpret it to mean that he found one in his brother and killed him because of it? And contrary to what we had all been led to believe, did he really mean it when he offered to cut the baby in half?

Most important of all, did it really matter what had happened several thousand years ago on the far side of the world? Even supposing that King Solomon had one of the original Dark Passengers, how did that help me get back to being lovable deadly me? What did I actually do with all this fascinating historical lore? None of it told me where the Passenger came from, what it was, or how to get it back.

I was at a loss. All right, then, it was clearly time to give up, accept my fate, throw myself on the mercy of the court, assume the role of Dexter, quiet family man and former Dark Avenger. Resign myself to the idea that I would never again feel the hard cool touch of the moonlight on my electrified nerve endings as I slid through the night like the avatar of cold, sharp steel.

I tried to think of something to inspire me to even greater heights of mental effort in my investigation, but all I came up with was a piece of a Rudyard Kipling poem: 'If you can keep your head when all about you are losing theirs,' or words to that effect. It didn't seem like it was enough. Perhaps Ariel Goldman and Jessica Ortega should have memorized Kipling. In any case, my search had taken me no place helpful.

Fine. What else could someone call the Passenger? 'Sardonic commentator,' 'warning system,' 'inside cheerleader.' I checked them all. Some of the results for inside cheerleader were really quite startling, but had nothing to do with my search.

I tried 'watcher,' 'interior watcher,' 'dark watcher,' 'hidden watcher.'

One last long shot, possibly having to do with the fact that my thoughts were once again turning toward food, but quite justified nevertheless: 'hungry watcher.'

Again, the results were mostly New Age blather. But one blog caught my eye, and I clicked on it. I read the opening paragraph and, although I did not actually say 'Bingo,' that was certainly the gist of what I thought.

'Once again into the night with the Hungry Watcher,' it began. 'Stalking the dark streets that teem with prey, riding slowly through the waiting feast and feeling the pull of the tide of blood that will soon rise to cover us with joy . . .'

Well. The prose was somewhat purple, perhaps. And the part about the blood was a little bit icky. But that aside, it was a pretty good description of how I felt when I went off on one of my adventures. It seemed likely that I had found a kindred spirit.

I read on. It was all consistent with the experience as I knew of it, cruising through the night with hungry anticipation as a sibilant inner voice whispered guidance. But then, when the narrative came to the point where I would have pounced and slashed, this narrator instead made a reference to 'the others,' followed by three figures from some alphabet I didn't recognize.

Or did I?

Feverishly, I scrabbled across my desk for the folder holding the file for the two headless girls. I yanked out the stack of photographs, flipped through them – and there it was.

Chalked on the driveway at Dr. Goldman's house, the same three letters, looking like a misshapen MLK.

I glanced up at my computer screen: it was a match, no question about it. This was way too much to be a coincidence. It clearly meant something very important; perhaps it was even the key to understanding the entire mess. Yes, highly significant, with just one small footnote: Significant of what? What did it mean?

On top of everything else, why was this particular clue afflicting me? I had come here to work on my own personal problem of a missing Passenger – had come late at night so I would not be harried by my sister or other demands of work. And now, apparently, if I wanted to solve my problem I would have to do it by working on Deborah's case. How come nothing was fair anymore?

Well, if there was any real reward for complaining I hadn't seen it so far, in a life filled with suffering and verbal skill. So I might as well take what was offered and see where it led.

First, what language was the script? I was reasonably certain it wasn't Chinese or Japanese – but what about some other Asian alphabet I knew nothing about? I pulled up an online atlas and began checking off countries: Korea, Cambodia, Thailand. None of them had an alphabet that was even close. What did that leave? Cyrillic? Easy enough to check. I pulled up a page containing the whole alphabet. I had to stare at it for a long time; some of the letters seemed close, but in the end I concluded that it was not a match.

What then? What did that leave? What would somebody really smart do next, somebody like who I had once been, or even somebody like that all-time champion of bright guys, King Solomon?

A small beeping sound began to chirp in the back of my brain, and I listened to it for a moment before I answered it. Yes, that's right, I said King Solomon. The guy from the Bible with an inner king. What? Oh, really? A connection, you say? You think so?

A long shot, but easy enough to check, and I did. Solomon would have spoken ancient Hebrew, of course, which was simple to find on the Web. And it looked very little like the characters I had found. So that was that, and there was no connection: ipso facto, or some other equally compelling Latin saying.

But hold on: Didn't I remember that the original language of the Bible was not Hebrew but something else? I beat my gray cells brutally, and they finally came out with it. Yes, it had been something I remembered from that unimpeachable scholarly source, *Raiders of the Lost Ark*. And the language I was looking for was Aramaic.

Once again, it was easy to find a Web site eager to teach us all to write Aramaic. And as I looked at it, I became eager to learn, because there was no doubt about it – the three letters were an exact match. And they were, in fact, the Aramaic counterparts of MLK, just the way they looked.

I read on. Aramaic, like Hebrew, did not use vowels. Instead, you had to supply them yourself. Very tricky, really, because you had to know what the word was before you could read it. Therefore, MLK could be milk or milik or malik or any other combination, and none of them made sense. At least not to me, which seemed like the important thing. But I doodled anyway, trying to make sense of the letters. Milok. Molak. Molek—

Once again something flickered in the back of my brain and I grabbed at it, pulled it forward into the light, and looked it over. It was King Solomon again. Just before the part where he killed his brother for having wickedness inside, he had built a temple to Moloch. And of course, the preferred alternative spelling for Moloch was Molek, known as the detestable god of the Ammonites.

This time I searched 'Moloch worship,' scanning through a dozen irrelevant Web sites before hitting a few that told me the same things: the worship was characterized by an ecstatic loss of control and ended with a human sacrifice. Apparently the people were whipped into a frenzy until they didn't realize that little Jimmy had somehow been killed and cooked, not necessarily in that order.

Well, I don't really understand ecstatic loss of control, even though I have been to football games at the Orange Bowl. So I admit I was curious: How did they work that trick? I read a little closer, and found that apparently there was music involved, music so compelling that the frenzy was almost automatic. How this happened was a little ambiguous – the clearest reading I found, from an Aramaic text translated with lots of footnotes, was that 'Moloch sent music unto them.' I supposed that meant a band of his priests would march through the streets with drums and trumpets . . .

Why drums and trumpets, Dexter?

Because that was what I was hearing in my sleep. Drums and trumpets rising into a glad chorus of singing and the feeling that pure eternal joy was right outside the door.

Which seemed like a pretty good working definition of ecstatic loss of control, didn't it?

All right, I reasoned: just for the sake of argument, let's say Moloch has returned. Or maybe he never went away. So a three-thousand-year-old detestable god from the Bible was sending music in order to, um – what, exactly? Steal my Dark Passenger? Kill young women in Miami, the modern Gomorrah? I even dragged in my earlier insight from the museum and tried to fit it into the puzzle: so Solomon had the original Dark Passenger, which had now come to Miami, and, like a male lion taking over a pride, was therefore trying to kill the Passengers already here, because, um . . . Why exactly?

Or was I really supposed to believe that an Old Testament bad guy was coming out of time to get me? Wouldn't it make more sense simply to reserve myself a rubber room right now?

I pushed at it from every side and still came up with nothing. Possibly my brain was starting to fall apart, too, along with the rest of my life. Maybe I was just tired. Whatever the case, none of it made sense. I needed to know more about Moloch. And because I was sitting in front of the computer, I wondered if Moloch had his own Web site.

It took only a moment to find out, so I typed it in, went down the list of self-important self-pitying blogs, online fantasy games, and arcane paranoid fantasies until I found one that looked likely. When I clicked on the link, a picture began to form very slowly, and as it did—

The deep, powerful beat of the drum, insistent horns rising behind the pulsing rhythm to a point that swells until it can no longer hold back the voices which break out in anticipation of a gladness beyond knowing – it was the music I had heard in my sleep.

Then the slow blossom of a smoldering bull's head, there in the middle of the page, with two upraised hands beside it and the same three Aramaic letters above.

And I sat and stared and blinked with the cursor, still feeling the music crash through me and lift me toward the hot glorious heights of an unknown ecstasy that promised me all the blinding delight ever possible in a world of hidden joy. For the first time in my memory, as these passionate strange sensations washed over and through me and finally out and away – for the first time ever I felt something new, different, and unwelcome.

I was afraid.

I could not say why, or of what, which made it much worse, a lonely unknown fear that roiled through me and echoed off the empty places and drove away everything but the picture of that bull's head and the fear.

This is nothing, Dexter, I told myself. *An animal picture and some random notes of not terribly good music.* And I agreed with myself completely – but I could not make my hands listen to reason and move off my lap. Something about this crossover between the supposedly unconnected worlds of sleep and waking made telling them apart impossible, as if anything that could show up in my sleep and then appear on my screen at work was too powerful to resist and I had no chance of fighting it, had simply to watch as it dragged me down and under into the flames.

There was no black, mighty voice inside me to turn me into steel and fling me like a spear at whatever this was. I was alone, afraid, helpless, and clueless; Dexter in the dark, with the bogeyman and all his unknown minions hiding under the bed and getting ready to pull me out of this world and into the burning land of shrieking, terror-filled pain.

With a motion that was far from graceful I lunged across my desk and yanked the computer's power cord from the wall and, breathing rapidly and looking like someone had attached electrodes to my muscles, I jerked backward into my chair again, so quick and clumsy that the plug on the end of the cord whipped back and snapped me on the forehead just above the left eyebrow.

For several minutes I did nothing but breathe and watch as the sweat rolled off my face and plopped onto my desk. I had no idea why I had leaped off my chair like a gaffed barracuda and yanked the cord out of the wall, beyond the fact that for some reason it had felt like I had to do it or die, and I couldn't understand where that notion came from, either, but come it had, barreling out of the new darkness between my ears and crushing me with its urgency.

And so I sat in my quiet office and gaped at a dead screen, wondering who I was and what had just happened.

I was never afraid. Fear was an emotion and Dexter did not have them. To be afraid of a Web site was so far beyond stupid and pointless that there were no adjectives for it. And I did not act irrationally, except when imitating human beings.

So why had I pulled the plug, and why were my hands trembling, all from a cheerful little tune and a cartoon cow?

There were no answers, and I was no longer sure I wanted to find them.

I drove home, convinced that I was being followed, even though the rearview mirror stayed empty the whole way.

The other really was quite special, resilient in a way that the Watcher had not seen in quite some time. This was proving to be far more interesting than some of the ones in the past. He began to feel something that might even be called kinship with the other. Sad, really. If only things had worked out differently. But there was a kind of beauty to the inevitable fate of the other, and that was good, too.

Even this far behind the other's car, he could see the signs of nerves starting to fray: speeding up and slowing down, fiddling with the mirrors. Good. Uneasy was just the beginning. He needed to move the other far beyond uneasy, and he would. But first it was essential to make sure the other knew what was coming. And so far, in spite of the clues, he did not seem to have figured it out.

Very well, then. The Watcher would simply repeat the pattern until the other recognized just what sort of power was after him. After that, the other would have no choice. He would come like a happy lamb to the slaughter.

Until then, even the watching had purpose. Let him know he was watched. It would do him no good, even if he saw the face watching him.

Faces can change. But the watching would not.

20

Of course there was no sleep for me that night. The next day, Sunday, passed in a haze of fatigue and anxiety. I took Cody and Astor to a nearby park and sat on a bench while I tried to make sense of the pile of uncooperative information and conjecture I had come up with so far. The pieces refused to come together into any kind of picture that made sense. Even if I hammered them into a semi-coherent theory, it told me nothing that would help me understand how to find my Passenger.

The best I could come up with was a sort of half-formed notion that the Dark Passenger and others like it had been hanging around for at least three thousand years. But why mine should flee from any other was impossible to say – especially since I had encountered others before with no more reaction than raised hackles. My notion of the new daddy lion seemed particularly far-fetched in the pleasant sunlight of the park, against the background of the children twittering threats at one another. Statistically speaking, about half of them had new daddies, based on the divorce rate, and they seemed to be thriving.

I let despair wash over me, a feeling that seemed slightly absurd in the lovely Miami afternoon. The Passenger was gone, I was alone, and the only solution I could come up with was to take lessons in Aramaic. I could only hope that a chunk of frozen wastewater from a passing airplane would fall on my head and put me out of my misery. I looked up hopefully, but there, too, I was out of luck.

Another semi-sleepless night, broken only by a recurrence of the strange music that came into my sleep and woke me as I sat up in bed to go to it. I had no idea why it seemed like such a good idea to follow the music, and even less idea where it wanted to take me, but apparently I was going anyway. Clearly I was falling apart, sliding rapidly downhill into gray, empty madness.

Monday morning a dazed and battered Dexter staggered into the kitchen, where I was immediately and violently assaulted by Hurricane Rita, who charged at me waving a huge stack of papers and CDs. 'I need to know what you think,' she said, and it struck me that this was something she definitely did *not* need to know, considering the deep bleakness of my thoughts. But before I could summon even a mild objection she had hurled me into a kitchen chair and began flinging the documents around.

468

'These are the flower arrangements that Hans wants to use,' she started, showing me a series of pictures that were, in fact, floral in nature. 'This is for the altar. And it's maybe a little too, oh, I don't know,' she said desperately. 'Is anybody going to make jokes about too much white?'

Although I am known for a finely tuned sense of humor, very few jokes based on the color white sprang to mind, but before I could reassure her on the subject, Rita was already flipping the pages.

'Anyway,' she said, 'this is the individual table setting. Which hopefully goes with what Manny Borque is doing. Maybe we should get Vince to check it with him?'

'Well,' I said.

'Oh good lord, look at the time,' she said, and before I could speak even one more syllable she had dropped a pile of CDs in my lap. 'I've narrowed it down to six bands,' she said. 'Can you listen to these today and let me know what you think? Thanks, Dex,' she went on relentlessly, leaning to plant a kiss on my cheek and then heading for the door, already moving on to the next item on her checklist. 'Cody?' she called. 'It's time to go, sweetie. Come on.'

There was another three minutes of commotion, the highlights of which were Cody and Astor sticking their heads in the kitchen door to say good-bye, and then the front door slammed and all was silent.

And in the silence I thought I could almost hear, as I had heard in the night, the faint echo of the music. I knew I should leap from my chair and charge out the door with my saber clamped firmly between my teeth – charge into the bright light of day and find this thing, whatever it was, beard it in its den and slay it – but I could not.

The Moloch Web site had stuck its fear into me, and even though I knew it was foolish, wrong, counter-productive, totally non-Dexter in every way, I could not fight it. Moloch. Just a silly ancient name. An old myth that had disappeared thousands of years ago, torn down with Solomon's temple. It was nothing, a figment from prehistoric imaginations, less than nothing – except that I was afraid of it.

There seemed nothing else to do except to stumble through the day with my head down and hope that it didn't get me, whatever it was. I was bone tired, and maybe that was adding to my sense of helplessness. But I didn't think so. I had the feeling that a very bad thing was circling closer with its nose full of my scent, and I could already feel its sharp teeth in my neck. All I could hope for was to make its sport last a little longer, but sooner or later I would feel its claws on me and then I, too, would bleat, beat my heels in the dust, and die. There was no fight left in me; there was, in fact, almost nothing at all left in me, except a kind of reflex humanity that said it was time to go to work.

I picked up Rita's stack of CDs and slogged out the door. And as I stood in the doorway of the house, turning the key to lock the front door, a white

Avalon very slowly pulled away from the curb and drove off with a lazy insolence that cut through all my fatigue and despair and sliced right into me with a jolt of sheer terror that rocked me back against the door as the CDs slipped from my fingers and crashed onto the walk.

The car motored slowly up the street to the stop sign. I watched, nerveless and numb. And as its brake lights flicked off and it started up and through the inter-section, a small piece of Dexter woke up, and it was very angry.

It might have been the absolute bold uncaring disrespect of the Avalon's behavior, and it might have been that all I really needed was the jolt of adrenaline to supplement my morning coffee. Whatever it was, it filled me with a sense of righteous indignation, and before I could even decide what to do I was already doing it, running down the driveway to my car and leaping into the driver's seat. I jammed the key into the ignition, fired up the engine, and raced after the Avalon.

I ignored the stop sign, accelerated through the intersection, and caught sight of the car as it turned right a few blocks ahead. I went much faster than I should have and saw him turn left toward U.S. 1. I closed the gap and sped up, frantic to catch him before he got lost in the rush-hour traffic.

I was only a block or so back when he turned north on U.S. 1 and I followed, ignoring the squealing brakes and the deafening chord of horn music from the other motorists. The Avalon was about ten cars ahead of me now, and I used all my Miami driving skills to get closer, concentrating only on the road and ignoring the lines that separated the lanes, even failing to enjoy the wonderful creativity of the language that followed me from the surrounding cars. The worm had turned, and although it might not have all its teeth, it was ready for battle, however it was that worms fought. I was angry – another novelty for me. I had been drained of all my darkness and pushed into a bright drab corner where all the walls were closing in, but enough was enough. It was time for Dexter to fight back. And although I did not really know what I planned to do when I caught up with the other car, I was absolutely going to do it.

I was half a block back when the Avalon's driver became aware of me and sped up immediately, slipping into the far left lane into a space so tight that the car behind him slammed on its brakes and spun sideways. The two cars behind it smashed into its exposed side and a great roar of horns and brakes hammered at my ears. I found just enough room to my right to squeak through around the crash and then over to the left again in the now-open far lane. The Avalon was a block ahead and picking up speed, but I put the pedal down and followed.

For several blocks the gap between us stayed about the same. Then the Avalon caught up with the traffic that was ahead of the accident and I got a bit closer, until I was only two cars behind, close enough to see a pair of large sunglasses looking back at me in the side mirror. And as I surged up to within one car length of his bumper, he suddenly yanked his steering wheel hard to the left, bouncing his car up onto the median strip and sliding sideways down into traffic on the other side. I was past him before I could even react. I could almost hear mocking laughter drifting back at me as he trundled off toward Homestead.

But I refused to let him go. It was not that catching the other car might give me some answers, although that was probably true. And I was not thinking of justice or any other abstract concept. No, this was pure indignant anger, rising from some unused interior corner and flowing straight out of my lizard brain and down to my knuckles. What I really wanted to do was pull this guy out of his rotten little car and smack him in the face. It was an entirely new sensation, this idea of inflicting bodily harm in the heat of anger, and it was intoxicating, strong enough to shut down any logical impulses that might be left in me and it sent me across the median in pursuit.

My car made a terrible crunching noise as it bounced up onto the median and then down on the other side, and a large cement truck missed flattening me by only about four inches, but I was off again, heading after the Avalon in the lighter southbound traffic.

Far ahead of me there were several spots of moving white color, any one of which might have been my target. I stomped down on the gas and followed.

The gods of traffic were kind to me, and I zipped through the steadily moving cars for almost half a mile before I hit my first red light. There were several cars in each lane halted obediently at the intersection and no way around them – except to repeat my car-crunching trick of banging up onto the median strip. I did. I came down off the narrow end of the median and into the intersection just in time to cause severe inconvenience to a bright yellow Hummer that was foolishly trying to use the roads in a rational way. It gave a manic lurch to avoid me, and very nearly succeeded; there was only the lightest of thuds as I bounced neatly off its front bumper, through the intersection, and onward, followed by yet another blast of horn music and yelling.

The Avalon would be a quarter of a mile ahead if it was still on U.S. 1, and I did not wait for the distance to grow. I chugged on in my trusty, banged-up little car, and after only half a minute I was in sight of two white cars directly ahead of me – one of them a Chevy SUV and the other a minivan. My Avalon was nowhere to be seen.

I slowed just for a moment – and out of the corner of my eye I saw it again, edging around behind a grocery store in a strip mall parking lot off to the right. I slammed my foot down onto the gas pedal and slewed across two lanes of traffic and into the parking lot. The driver of the other car saw me coming; he sped up and pulled out onto the street running perpendicular to U.S. 1, racing away to the east as fast as he could go. I hurried through the parking lot and followed.

He led me through a residential area for a mile or so, then around another corner and past a park where a day-care program was in full swing. I got a little closer – just in time to see a woman holding a baby and leading two other children step into the road in front of us.

The Avalon accelerated up and onto the sidewalk and the woman continued to move slowly across the road looking at me as if I was a billboard she couldn't read. I swerved to go behind her, but one of her children suddenly darted backward right in front of me and I stood on the brake. My car went into a skid, and for a moment it looked as if I would slide right into the whole slow, stupid cluster of them as they stood there in the road, watching me with no sign of interest. But my tires bit at last, and I managed to spin the wheel, give it a little bit of gas, and skid through a quick circle on the lawn of a house across the street from the park. Then I was back onto the road in a cloud of crabgrass, and after the Avalon, now farther ahead.

The distance stayed about the same for several more blocks before I got my lucky break. Ahead of me the Avalon roared through another stop sign, but this time a police cruiser pulled out after it, turned on the siren, and gave chase. I wasn't sure if I should be glad of the company or jealous of the competition, but in any case it was much easier to follow the flashing lights and siren, so I continued to slog along in the rear.

The two other cars went through a quick series of turns, and I thought I might be getting a little closer, when suddenly the Avalon disappeared and the cop car slid to a halt. In just a few seconds I was up beside the cruiser and getting out of my car.

In front of me the cop was running across a close-cropped lawn marked with tire tracks that led around behind a house and into a canal. The Avalon was settling down into the water by the far side and, as I watched, a man climbed out of the car through the window and swam the few yards to the opposite bank of the canal. The cop hesitated on our side and then jumped in and swam to the half-sunk car. As he did, I heard the sound of heavy tires braking fast behind me. I turned to look.

A yellow Hummer rocked to a stop behind my car and a red-faced man with sandy hair jumped out and started to yell at me. 'You cocksucker son of a bitch!' he hollered. 'You dinged up my car! What the hell you think you're doing?'

Before I could answer, my cell phone rang. 'Excuse me,' I said, and oddly enough the sandy-haired man stood there quietly as I answered the phone.

'Where the hell are you?' Deborah demanded.

'Cutler Ridge, looking at a canal,' I said.

It gave her pause for a full second before she said, 'Well, dry off and get your ass over to the campus. We got another body.'

21

It took me a few minutes to disengage myself from the driver of the yellow Hummer, and I might have been there still if not for the cop who had jumped into the canal. He finally climbed out of the water and came over to where I stood listening to a nonstop stream of threats and obscenities, none very original. I tried to be polite about it – the man obviously had a great deal to get off his chest, and I certainly didn't want him to sustain psychological damage by repressing it – but I did have some urgent police business to attend to, after all. I tried to point that out, but apparently he was one of those individuals who could not yell and listen to reason at the same time.

So the appearance of an unhappy and extremely wet cop was a welcome interruption to a conversation that was verging on tedious and one-sided. 'I would really like to know what you find out about the driver of that car,' I said to the cop.

'I bet you would,' he said. 'Can I see some ID, please?'

'I have to get to a crime scene,' I said.

'You're at one,' he told me. So I showed him my credentials and he looked at them very carefully, dripping canal water onto the laminated picture. Finally he nodded and said, 'Okay, Morgan, you're out of here.'

From the Hummer driver's reaction you might have thought the cop had suggested setting the Pope on fire. 'You can't let that son of a bitch just go like that!' he screeched. 'That goddamn asshole dinged up my car!'

And the cop, bless him, simply stared at the man, dripped a little more water, and said, 'May I see your license and registration, sir?' It seemed like a wonderful exit line, and I took advantage of it.

My poor battered car was making very unhappy noises, but I put it on the road to the university anyway – there really was no other choice. No matter how badly damaged it was, it would have to get me there. And it made me feel a certain kinship with my car. Here we were, two splendidly built pieces of machinery, hammered out of our original beautiful condition by circumstances beyond our control. It was a wonderful theme for self-pity, and I indulged it for several minutes. The anger I had felt only a few minutes ago had leeched away, dripped onto the lawn like canal water off the cop. Watching the Avalon's driver swim to the far side, climb out, and walk away had been in the same spirit as everything else lately; get a little bit close and then have the rug pulled out from under your feet.

And now there was a new body, and we hadn't even figured out what to do about the others yet. It was making us look like the greyhounds at a dog track, chasing after a fake rabbit that is always just a little bit too far ahead, jerked tantalizingly away every time the poor dog thinks he's about to get it in his teeth.

There were two squad cars at the university ahead of me, and the four officers had already cordoned off the area around the Lowe Art Museum and pushed back the growing crowd. A squat, powerful-looking cop with a shaved head came over to meet me, and pointed toward the back of the building.

The body was in a clump of vegetation behind the gallery. Deborah was talking to someone who looked like a student, and Vince Masuoka was squatting beside the left leg of the body and poking carefully with a ballpoint pen at something on the ankle. The body could not be seen from the road, but even so you could not really say it had been hidden. It had obviously been roasted like the others, and it was laid out just like the first two, in a stiff formal position, with the head replaced by a ceramic bull's head. And once again, as I looked at it I waited by reflex for some reaction from within. But I heard nothing except the gentle tropical wind blowing through my brain. I was still alone.

As I stood in huffish thought, Deborah came roaring over to me at full volume. 'Took you long enough,' she snarled. 'Where have you been?'

'Macramé class,' I said. 'It's just like the others?'

'Looks like it,' she said. 'What about it, Masuoka?'

'I think we got a break this time,' Vince said.

'About fucking time,' Deborah said.

'There's an ankle bracelet,' Vince said. 'It's made of platinum, so it didn't melt off.' He looked up at Deborah and gave her his terribly phony smile. 'It says Tammy on it.'

Deborah frowned and looked over to the side door of the gallery. A tall man in a seersucker jacket and bow tie stood there with one of the cops, looking anxiously at Deborah. 'Who's that guy?' she asked Vince.

'Professor Keller,' he told her. 'Art history teacher. He found the body.'

Still frowning, Deborah stood up and beckoned the uniformed cop to bring the professor over.

'Professor . . . ?' Deborah said.

'Keller. Gus Keller,' the professor said. He was a good-looking man in his sixties with what looked like a dueling scar on his left cheek. He didn't appear to be about to faint at the sight of the body.

'So you found the body here,' Deb said.

'That's right,' he said. 'I was coming over to check on a new exhibit – Mesopotamian art, actually, which is interesting – and I saw it here in the shrubbery.' He frowned. 'About an hour ago, I guess.'

Deborah nodded as if she already knew all that, even the Mesopotamian part, which was a standard cop trick designed to make people eager to add new details, especially if they might be a little bit guilty. It didn't appear to work on Keller. He simply stood and waited for another question, and Deborah stood and tried to think of one. I am justly proud of my hard-earned artificial social skills, and I didn't want the silence to turn awkward, so I cleared my throat, and Keller looked at me.

'What can you tell us about the ceramic head?' I asked him. 'From the artistic point of view.' Deborah glared at me, but she may have been jealous that I thought of the question instead of her.

'From the artistic point of view? Not much,' Keller said, looking down at the bull's head by the body. 'It looks like it was done in a mold, and then baked in a fairly primitive kiln. Maybe even just a big oven. But historically, it's much more interesting.'

'What do you mean interesting?' Deborah snapped at him, and he shrugged.

'Well, it's not perfect,' Keller said. 'But somebody tried to re-create a very old stylized design.'

'How old?' Deborah said. Keller raised an eyebrow and shrugged, as if to say she had asked the wrong question, but he answered.

'Three or four thousand years old,' he said.

'That's very old,' I offered helpfully, and they both looked at me, which made me think I ought to add something halfway clever, so I said, 'And what part of the world would it be from?'

Keller nodded. I was clever again. 'Middle East,' he said. 'We see a similar motif in Babylonia, and even earlier around Jerusalem. The bull head appears to be attached to the worship of one of the elder gods. A particularly nasty one, really.'

'Moloch,' I said, and it hurt my throat to say that name.

Deborah glared at me, absolutely certain now that I had been holding out on her, but she looked back at Keller as he continued to talk.

'Yes, that's right,' he said. 'Moloch liked human sacrifice. Especially children. It was the standard deal: sacrifice your child and he would guarantee a good harvest, or victory over your enemies.'

'Well, then, I think we can look forward to a very good harvest this year,' I said, but neither one of them appeared to think that was worth even a tiny smile. Ah well, you do what you can to bring a little cheer into this dreary world, and if people refuse to respond to your efforts it's their loss.

'What's the point of burning the bodies?' Deborah demanded.

Keller smiled briefly, kind of a professorial thanks-for-asking smile. 'That's the whole key to the ritual,' he said. 'There was a huge bull-headed statue of Moloch that was actually a furnace.'

I thought of Halpern and his 'dream.' Had he known about Moloch beforehand, or had it come to him the way the music came to me? Or was Deborah right all along and he had actually been to the statue and killed the girls – as unlikely as that seemed now?

'A furnace,' said Deborah, and Keller nodded. 'And they toss the bodies in there?' she said, with an expression that indicated she was having trouble believing it, and it was all his fault.

'Oh, it gets much better than that,' Keller said. 'They delivered the miracle in the ritual. Very sophisticated flummery, in fact. But that's why Moloch had such lasting popularity – it was convincing, and it was exciting. The statue had arms that stretched out to the congregation. When you placed the sacrifice in his arms, Moloch would appear to come to life and eat the sacrifice – the arms would slowly raise up the victim and place it in his mouth.'

'And into the furnace,' I said, not wanting to be left out any longer, 'while the music played.'

Deborah looked at me strangely, and I realized that no one else had mentioned music, but Keller shrugged it off and answered.

'Yes, that's right. Trumpets and drums, singing, all very hypnotic. Climaxing as the god lifted the body up to its mouth and dropped it. Into the mouth and you fall down into the furnace. Alive. It can't have been much fun for the victim.'

I believed what Keller said – I heard the soft throb of the drums in the distance, and it wasn't much fun for me, either.

'Does anybody still worship this guy?' Deborah asked.

Keller shook his head. 'Not for two thousand years, as far as I know,' he said.

'Well then, what the hell,' Deborah said. 'Who's doing this?'

'It isn't any kind of secret,' Keller said. 'It's a pretty well-documented part of history. Anybody could have done a little research and found out enough to do something like this.'

'But why would they?' Deborah said.

Keller smiled politely. 'I'm sure I don't know,' he said.

'So what the hell good does any of that do me?' she said, with a tone that suggested it was Keller's job to come up with an answer.

He gave her a kindly professor smile. 'It never hurts to know things,' he said.

'For instance,' I said, 'we know that somewhere there must be a big statue of a bull with a furnace inside.'

Deborah snapped her head around so that she faced me.

I leaned close to her and said softly, 'Halpern.' She blinked at me and I could see she hadn't thought of that yet.

'You think it wasn't a dream?' she demanded.

'I don't know what to think,' I said. 'But if somebody is doing this Moloch thing for real, why wouldn't he do it with all the proper equipment?'

'Goddamn it,' Deborah said. 'But where could you hide something like that?'

Keller coughed with a certain delicacy. 'I'm afraid there's more to it than that,' he said.

'Like what?' Deborah demanded.

'Well, you'd have to hide the smell, too,' he said. 'The smell of cooking human bodies. It lingers, and it's rather unforgettable.' He sounded a little bit embarrassed and he shrugged.

'So we're looking for a gigantic *smelly* statue with a furnace inside,' I said cheerfully. 'That shouldn't be too hard to find.'

Deborah glared at me, and once again I had to feel a little disappointed at her heavy-handed approach to life – especially since I would almost certainly join her as a permanent resident in the Land of Gloom if the Dark Passenger refused to behave and come out of hiding.

'Professor Keller,' she said, turning away from me and completing the abandonment of her poor brother, 'is there anything else about this bull shit that might help us?'

It was certainly a clever enough remark to be encouraging, and I almost wished I had said it, but it appeared to have no effect on Keller, nor even on Deborah herself, who looked as though she was unaware that she had said something notable. Keller merely shook his head.

'It's not really my area, I'm afraid,' he said. 'I know just a little background stuff that affects the art history. You might check with somebody in philosophy or comparative religion.'

'Like Professor Halpern,' I whispered again, and Deborah nodded, still glaring.

She turned to go and luckily remembered her manners just in time; she turned back to Keller and said, 'You've been very helpful, Dr. Keller. Please let me know if you think of anything else.'

'Of course,' he said, and Debs grabbed my arm and propelled me onward.

'Are we going back to the registrar's office?' I asked politely as my arm went numb.

'Yeah,' she said. 'But if there's a Tammy enrolled in one of Halpern's classes, I don't know what I'm going to do.'

I pulled the tattered remnants of my arm from her grip. 'And if there isn't?'

She just shook her head. 'Come on,' she said.

But as I passed by the body once more, something clutched at the leg of my pants, and I looked down.

'Ahk,' Vince said to me. He cleared his throat. 'Dexter,' he said, and I raised an eyebrow. He flushed and let go of my pants. 'I have to talk to you,' he said.

'By all means,' I said. 'Can it wait?'

He shook his head. 'It's pretty important,' he said.

'Well, all right then.' I took the three steps back to where he was still squatting beside the body. 'What is it?'

He looked away, and as unlikely as it was that he would show real emotion, his face flushed even more. 'I talked to Manny,' he said.

'Wonderful. And yet you still have all your limbs,' I said.

'He, ahm,' Vince said. 'He wants to make a few changes. Ahm. In the menu. Your menu. For the wedding.'

'Aha,' I said, in spite of how corny it sounds to say 'Aha' when you are standing beside a dead body. I just couldn't help myself. 'By any chance, are these expensive changes?'

Vince refused to look up at me. He nodded his head. 'Yes,' he said. 'He said he's had an inspiration. Something really new and different.'

'I think that's terrific,' I said, 'but I don't think I can afford inspiration. We'll have to tell him no.'

Vince shook his head again. 'You don't understand. He only called because he *likes* you. He says the contract allows him to do whatever he wants.'

'And he wants to raise the price a wee bit?'

Vince was definitely blushing now. He mumbled a few syllables and tried to look away even further. 'What?' I asked him. 'What did you say?'

'About double,' he said, very quietly, but at least audible.

'Double,' I said.

'Yes.'

'That's $500 a plate,' I said.

'I'm sure it will be very nice,' said bright-red Vince.

'For $500 a plate it had better be more than nice. It had better park the cars, mop the floor, and give all the guests a back rub.'

'This is cutting-edge stuff, Dexter. You'll probably get your wedding in a magazine.'

'Yes, and it will probably be *Bankruptcy Today*. We have to talk to him, Vince.'

He shook his head and continued to look at the grass. 'I can't,' he said.

Humans are wonderful combinations of silly, ignorant, and dumb, aren't they? Even the ones who are pretending most of the time, like Vince. Here he was, a fearless forensic tech, actually within inches of a gruesomely murdered body that had no more effect on him than a tree stump, and yet he was paralyzed with terror at the thought of facing a tiny man who sculpted chocolate for a living.

'All right,' I said. 'I'll talk to him myself.'

He looked up at me at last. 'Be careful, Dexter,' he said.

22

I caught up with Deborah as she was turning her car around, and happily, she paused long enough for me to climb in for a ride to the registrar's office. She had nothing to say on the short drive over, and I was too preoccupied with my own problems to care.

A quick search of the records with my new friend at the registrar's office turned up no Tammy in any of Halpern's classes. But Deborah, who had been pacing back and forth while she waited, was ready for that. 'Try last semester,' she said. I did; again nothing.

'All right,' she said with a frown. 'Then try Wilkins's classes.'

It was a lovely idea, and to prove it, I got an immediate hit: Ms. Connor was in Wilkins's seminar on situational ethics.

'Right,' Deborah said. 'Get her address.'

Tammy Connor lived in a residential hall that was only moments away, and Deborah wasted no time in getting us over there and parking illegally in front of it. She was out of the car and marching toward the front door before I could even get my door open, but I followed along as quickly as I could.

The room was on the third floor. Deborah chose to vault up the stairs two at a time rather than waste time pushing the button for an elevator, and since this left me with not enough breath to complain about it, I didn't. I got there just in time to see the door to Tammy's room swing open to reveal a stocky girl with dark hair and glasses. 'Yes?' she said, frowning at Deborah.

Debs showed her badge and said, 'Tammy Connor?'

The girl gasped and put a hand to her throat. 'Oh, God, I knew it,' she said.

Deborah nodded. 'Are you Tammy Connor, miss?'

'No. No, of course not,' the girl said. 'Allison, her roommate.'

'Do you know where Tammy is, Allison?'

The girl inhaled her lower lip and chewed it while shaking her head vigorously. 'No,' she said.

'How long has she been gone?' Deborah asked.

'Two days.'

'Two days?' Deborah said, raising her eyebrows. 'Is that unusual?'

Allison looked like she was going to chew her lip off, but she kept gnawing on it, pausing only long enough to blurt out, 'I'm not supposed to say anything.'

Deborah stared at her for a long moment before finally saying, 'I think you're going to have to say something, Allison. We think Tammy may be in a lot of trouble.'

That seemed to me a very understated way of saying that we thought she was dead, but I let it go by, since it was obviously having a profound effect on Allison.

'Oh,' she said, and started jiggling up and down. 'Oh, oh, I just knew this would happen.'

'What is it that you think happened?' I asked her.

'They got caught,' she said. 'I told her.'

'I'm sure you did,' I said. 'So why not tell us, too?'

She hopped a little faster for a moment. 'Oh,' she said again and then warbled, 'she's having an affair with a professor. Oh, God, she'll *kill* me for this!'

Personally, I didn't think Tammy would be killing anybody, but just to be sure I said, 'Did Tammy wear any jewelry?'

She looked at me like I was crazy. 'Jewelry?' she said, as if the word was in some foreign language – Aramaic, perhaps.

'Yes, that's right,' I said encouragingly. 'Rings, bracelets – anything like that?'

'You mean like her platinum anklet?' Allison said, very obligingly, I thought.

'Yes, exactly like that,' I said. 'Did it have any markings on it?'

'Uh-huh, her name,' she said. 'Oh, God, she'll be so pissed at me.'

'Do you know which professor she was having an affair with, Allison?' Deborah said.

Allison went back to shaking her head. 'I really shouldn't tell,' she said.

'Was it Professor Wilkins?' I said, and even though Deborah glared at me, Allison's reaction was much more gratifying.

'Oh God,' she said. 'I swear I never said.'

One call on the cell phone got us the address in Coconut Grove where Dr. Wilkins made his humble home. It was in a section called The Moorings, which meant that either my alma mater was paying professors a great deal more than they used to, or else Professor Wilkins had independent means. As we turned onto the street, the afternoon rain started, blowing across the road in slanted sheets, then slowing to a trickle, then picking up again.

We found the house easily. The number was on the yellow seven-foot wall that surrounded the house. A wrought-iron gate blocked off the driveway. Deborah pulled up in front and parked in the street, and we climbed out and looked through the gate. It was a rather modest home, no more than 4,000 square feet, and situated at least seventy-five yards from the water, so perhaps Wilkins wasn't really all that wealthy.

As we peeked in, looking for some way to signal the house that we had arrived and wished to enter, the front door swung open and a man came out, wearing a bright yellow rain suit. He headed for the car parked in the drive, a blue Lexus.

Deborah raised her voice and called out, 'Professor? Professor Wilkins?'

The man looked up at us from under the hood of his rain suit. 'Yes?'

'Can we speak to you for a moment, please?' Deborah said.

He walked toward us slowly, head cocked at Deborah on a slight angle. 'That depends. Who is us?'

Deborah reached into her pocket for her badge and Professor Wilkins paused cautiously, no doubt worried that she might pull out a hand grenade.

'Us is the police,' I reassured him.

'Is we?' he said, and he turned toward me with a half smile that froze when he saw me, flickered, and then resumed as a very poor fake smile. Since I am an expert on faking emotions and expressions I was in absolutely no doubt about it – the sight of little old me had startled him somehow, and he was covering it by pretending to smile. But why? If he was guilty, surely the thought of police at the gate would be worse than Dexter at the door. But instead he looked at Deborah and said, 'Oh, yes, we met once before, outside my office.'

'That's right,' said Deborah as she finally fished out her badge.

'I'm sorry, will this take long? I'm kind of in a hurry,' he said.

'We have just a couple of questions, Professor,' Deborah said. 'It will take only a minute.'

'Well,' he said, looking from the badge to my face and then quickly away again. 'All right.' He opened the gate and held it wide. 'Would you like to come in?'

Even though we were already soaked to the skin, it seemed like a pretty good idea to get out of the rain, and we followed Wilkins through the gate, up the driveway, and into his house.

The interior of the house was done in a style I recognized as classic Coconut Grove Rich Person Casual. I had not seen an example like this since I was a boy, when Miami Vice Modern took over as the area's dominant decorative pattern. But this was old school, bringing back the memory of when the area was called Nut Grove because of its loose, Bohemian flavor.

The floors were reddish-brown tile and shiny enough to shave in, and there was a conversation area consisting of a leather couch and two matching chairs off to the right beside a large picture window. Next to the window was a wet bar with a large, glassed-in, temperature-controlled wine cabinet and an abstract painting of a nude on the wall next to it.

Wilkins led us past a pair of potted plants and over to the couch, and hesitated a couple of steps in front of it. 'Ah,' he said, pushing back the hood from his rain jacket, 'we're kind of wet for the leather furniture. Can I offer you a barstool?' He gestured toward the bar.

I looked at Deborah, who shrugged. 'We can stand,' she said. 'This will only take a minute.'

'All right,' Wilkins said. He folded his arms and smiled at Deborah. 'What's so important that they send someone like you, in this weather?' he said.

Deborah flushed slightly, whether from irritation or something else I couldn't tell. 'How long have you been sleeping with Tammy Connor?' Deborah said.

Wilkins lost his happy expression and for a moment there was a very cold, unpleasant look on his face. 'Where did you hear that?' he said.

I could see that Deborah was trying to push him off-balance just a bit, and since that is one of my specialties I chimed in. 'Will you have to sell this place if you don't get tenure?' I said.

His eyes snapped to mine, and there was nothing at all pleasant about the look he gave me. He kept his tongue in his mouth, too. 'I should have known,' he said. 'So this was Halpern's jailhouse confession, was it? Wilkins did it.'

'So you didn't have an affair with Tammy Connor?' Deborah said.

Wilkins looked back to her again and, with a visible effort, regained his relaxed smile. He shook his head. 'I'm sorry,' he said. 'I can't get used to you as the tough one. I guess that's a pretty successful technique for you two, hmm?'

'Not so far,' I said. 'You haven't answered any of the questions.'

He nodded. 'All right,' he said. 'And did Halpern tell you he broke into my office? I found him hiding under my desk. God knows what he was doing there.'

'Why do you think he broke into your office?' Deborah asked.

Wilkins shrugged. 'He said I sabotaged his paper.'

'Did you?'

He looked at her, and then over to me for an unpleasant moment, then back to Deborah. 'Officer,' he said, 'I am trying very hard to cooperate here. But you've accused me of so many different things I'm not sure which one I'm supposed to answer.'

'Is that why you haven't answered any of them?' I asked.

Wilkins ignored me. 'If you can tell me how Halpern's paper and Tammy Connor fit together, I'll be happy to help any way I can. But otherwise, I've got to get going.'

Deborah looked at me, whether for advice or because she was tired of looking at Wilkins, I couldn't tell, so I gave her my very best shrug, and she looked back at Wilkins. 'Tammy Connor is dead,' she said.

'Oh, my,' Wilkins said. 'How did it happen?'

'The same way as Ariel Goldman,' Debs said.

'And you knew them both,' I added helpfully.

'I imagine that dozens of people knew them both. Including Jerry Halpern,' he said.

'Did Professor Halpern kill Tammy Connor, Professor Wilkins?' Deborah asked him. 'From the detention center?'

He shrugged. 'I'm only saying that he knew them, too.'

'And did he have an affair with her, too?' I asked.

Wilkins smirked. 'Probably not. Not with Tammy, anyway.'

'What does that mean, Professor?' Deborah asked.

Wilkins shrugged. 'Just rumors, you know. The kids talk. Some of them think Halpern is gay.'

'Less competition for you,' I said. 'Like with Tammy Connor.'

Wilkins scowled at me and I'm sure I would have been intimidated if I was a university sophomore. 'You need to make up your mind whether I killed my students or screwed them,' he said.

'Why not both?'

'Did you go to college?' he demanded.

'Why yes, I did,' I said.

'Then you ought to know that a certain type of girl sexually pursues her professors. Tammy was over eighteen, and I'm not married.'

'Isn't it a little bit unethical to have sex with a student?' I said.

'Ex-student,' he snapped. 'I dated her after the class last semester. There's no law against dating an ex-student. Especially if she throws herself at you.'

'Nice catch,' I said.

'Did you sabotage Professor Halpern's paper?' Deborah said.

Wilkins looked back at Deborah and smiled again. It was wonderful to watch somebody almost as good as I am at switching emotions so quickly. 'Detective, do you see a pattern here?' he said. 'Listen, Jerry Halpern is a brilliant guy, but . . . not exactly stable? And with all the pressure on him right now, he's just decided that I am a whole conspiracy to get him, all by myself.' He shrugged. 'I don't think I'm quite that good,' he said with a little smile. 'At least, not at conspiracy.'

'So you think Halpern killed Tammy Connor and the others?' Deborah said.

'I didn't say that,' he said. 'But hey, he's the psycho. Not me.' He made a step toward the door and raised an eyebrow at Deborah. 'And now, if you don't mind, I really have to get going.'

Deborah handed him a business card. 'Thank you for your time, Professor,' she said. 'If you think of anything that might help, please give me a call.'

'I certainly will,' he said, giving her the kind of smile that killed disco and placing a hand on her shoulder. She managed not to flinch. 'I really hate to throw you back out into the rain, but . . .'

Deborah moved, very willingly I thought, out from under his hand and toward the door. I followed. Wilkins herded us out the door and through the gate, and then climbed into his car, backed out of the driveway, and drove away. Debs stood in the rain and watched him go, which I am sure she intended to make Wilkins nervous enough to leap from the car and confess, but considering the weather it struck me as excessive zeal. I got into the car and waited for her.

When the blue Lexus had vanished Deborah finally got in beside me. 'Guy gives me the fucking creeps,' she said.

'Do you think he's the killer?' I asked. It was a strange feeling for me, not knowing, and wondering if somebody else had seen behind the predator's mask.

She shook her head with irritation. Water flew off her hair and hit me. 'I think he's a fucking creep,' she said. 'What do you think?'

'I'm pretty sure you're right,' I said.

'He didn't mind admitting his affair with Tammy Connor,' she said. 'So why lie and say she was in his class *last* semester?'

'Reflex?' I said. 'Because he's up for tenure?'

She drummed her fingers on the steering wheel, and then leaned forward decisively and started the car. 'I'm putting a tail on him,' she said.

23

A copy of an incident report lay on my desk when I finally got to work, and I realized that someone expected me to be a productive drone today, in spite of it all. So much had happened in the last few hours that it was hard to adjust to the idea that most of the workday was still looming over me with its long sharp teeth, so I went for a cup of coffee before submitting to servitude. I had half hoped that someone might have brought in some doughnuts or cookies, but of course it was a foolish thought. There was nothing but a cup and a half of burned, very dark coffee. I poured some into a cup – leaving the rest for someone truly desperate – and slogged back to my desk.

I picked up the report and began to read. Apparently someone had driven a vehicle belonging to a Mr. Darius Starzak into a canal and then fled the scene. Mr. Starzak himself was thus far unavailable for questioning. It took me several long moments of blinking and sipping the vile coffee to realize that this was the report of my incident this morning, and several minutes longer to decide what to do about it.

To have the name of the car's owner was little enough to go on – almost nothing, since the odds were good that the car was stolen. But to assume that and do nothing was worse than trying it and coming up empty, so I went to work once again on my computer.

First, the standard stuff: the car's registration, which showed an address off Old Cutler Road in a somewhat pricey neighborhood. Next, the police records: traffic stops, outstanding warrants, child support payments. There was nothing. Mr. Starzak was apparently a model citizen who'd had no contact at all with the long arm of the law.

All right then; the name itself, 'Darius Starzak.' Darius was not a common name – at least, not in the United States. I checked immigration records. And surprisingly, I got a hit right away.

First of all, it was Dr. Starzak, not Mister. He held a Ph.D. in religious philosophy from Heidelberg University, and until a few years ago had been a tenured professor at the University of Kraków. A little more digging revealed that he had been fired for some kind of uncertain scandal. Polish is not really one of my stronger languages, although I can say *kielbasa* when ordering lunch at a deli. But unless the translation was completely off, Starzak had been fired for membership in an illegal society.

The file did not mention why a European scholar who had lost his job for such an obscure reason would want to follow me and then drive his car into a canal. It seemed like a significant omission. Nevertheless, I printed the picture of Starzak from the immigration file. I squinted at the photo, trying to imagine it half hidden by the large sunglasses I had seen in the Avalon's side mirror. It could have been him. It could also have been Elvis. And as far as I knew, Elvis had just as much reason to follow me as Starzak.

I went a little deeper. It isn't easy for a forensics wonk to access Interpol without an official reason, even when he is charming and clever. But after playing my online version of dodgeball for a few minutes, I got into the central records, and here things became more interesting.

Dr. Darius Starzak was on a special watch list in four countries, not including the States, which explained why he was here. Although there was no proof that he had done anything, there were suspicions that he knew more than he would say about the traffic in war orphans from Bosnia. And the file casually mentioned that, of course, it is impossible to account for the whereabouts of such children. In the language of official police documents, that meant that somebody thought he might be killing them.

I should have filled up with a great thrill of cold glee as I read this, a wicked gleam of sharp anticipation – but there was nothing, not the dullest echo of the smallest spark. Instead, I felt a very small return of the human-style anger I had felt this morning when Starzak was following me. It was not an adequate replacement for the surge of dark, savage certainty from the Passenger that I had been used to, but at least it was something.

Starzak had been doing bad things to children, and he – or someone using his car, at least – had tried to do them to me. All right then. So far I had been battered back and forth like a Ping-Pong ball, and I had been content to take it, passively and without complaint, sucked into a vacuum of miserable submission because I had been deserted by the Dark Passenger. But here was something I could understand and, better, act upon.

The Interpol file told me that Starzak was a bad man, exactly the kind of person I normally tried to find in pursuit of my hobby. Someone had followed me in his car, and then gone to the extreme measure of driving his car into a canal to escape. It was possible that someone had stolen the car and Starzak was completely innocent. I didn't think so, and the Interpol report argued against it. But just to be sure I checked the stolen vehicle reports. There was no listing for Starzak or his car.

All right: I was sure it had been him, and this confirmed his guilt. I knew what to do about this: Just because I was alone inside, did that have to mean I couldn't do it?

The warm glow of certainty flickered under the anger and brought it to a slow, confident simmer. It was not the same as the gold-standard sureness I had always received from the Passenger, but it was certainly more than a hunch. This was right, I was sure. If I did not have the kind of solid proof I usually had, too bad. Starzak had escalated the situation to a point where I had no doubt, and he had moved himself to the top of my list. I would find him and turn him into a bad memory and a drop of dried blood in my little rosewood box.

And since I was running on emotion for the first time anyway, I allowed a small feeble flicker of hope to bloom. It might well be that dealing with Starzak and doing all the things I had never before done alone might bring back the Dark Passenger. I knew nothing about how these things worked, but it made a certain kind of sense, didn't it? The Passenger had always been there urging me on – wouldn't it just possibly show up if I created the kind of situation it needed? And wasn't Starzak right in front of me and practically begging to be dealt with?

And if the Passenger didn't come back, why shouldn't I begin to be me by myself? I was the one who did the heavy lifting – couldn't I carry on with my vocation, even in my empty state?

All the answers clicked up an angry red 'yes.' And for a moment I paused and waited automatically for the accustomed answering hiss of pleasure from the shadowy inside corner – but of course, it did not come.

Never mind. I could do this alone.

I had been working at night a good deal lately, so there was no surprise at all on Rita's face when I told her after dinner that I had to go back to the office. Of course, I was not off the hook with Cody and Astor, who wanted to come with me and do something interesting, or at least stay home and play kick the can. But after some minor wheedling and a few vague threats I plucked them off me and slid out the door into the night. My night, my last remaining friend, with its feeble half-moon flickering in a dull soggy sky.

Starzak lived in an area with a gate, but a minimum-wage guard in a little hut is really much better at raising property values than it is at keeping out someone with Dexter's experience and hunger. And even though it meant a little bit of a hike after I left my car up the road from the guardhouse, the exercise was welcome. I'd had too many late nights, too many sour mornings lately, and it felt good to be up on my legs and moving toward a worthwhile goal.

I circled slowly through the neighborhood, finding Starzak's address and moving on past as if I was no more than a neighbor out for an evening constitutional. There was a light on in the front room and a single car in the driveway; it had a Florida plate that said Manatee County on the bottom. There are only 300,000 people living in Manatee County, and at least twice that many cars on the road that claim to be from there. It's a rental-car trick, designed to disguise the fact that the driver has rented a car and is therefore a tourist and a legitimate target for any predator with a yen for easy prey.

I felt a small surge of hot anticipation. Starzak was home, and the fact that he had a rental car made it more likely that he was the one who had driven his car into the canal. I moved past the house, alert for any sign that I had been seen. I saw nothing, and heard only the faint sound of a TV somewhere nearby.

I circled the block and found a house with no lights on and hurricane shutters up, a very good sign that no one was home. I moved through the darkened yard and up to the tall hedge that separated it from Starzak's house. I slipped into a gap in the shrubbery, slid the clean mask over my face, pulled on gloves, and waited as my eyes and ears adjusted. And as I did it occurred to me just how ridiculous I would look if someone saw me. I had never worried about that before; the Passenger's radar is excellent and always gave me warning of unwanted eyes. But now, without any interior help, I felt naked. And as that feeling washed over me, it left another in its wake: sheer, helpless stupidity.

What was I doing? I was violating nearly every rule I had lived by, coming here spontaneously, without my usual careful preparation, without any real proof, and without the Passenger. It was madness. I was just asking to be discovered, locked up, or hacked to bits by Starzak.

I closed my eyes and listened to the novel emotions gurgling through me. Feeling – what authentic human fun. Next I could join a bowling league. Find a chat room online and talk about New Age self-help and alternative herbal medicine for hemorrhoids. Welcome to the human race, Dexter, the endlessly futile and pointless human race. We hope you will enjoy your short and painful stay.

I opened my eyes. I could give up, accept the fact that Dexter's day was done. Or – I could go through with this, whatever the risks, and reassert the thing that had always been me. Take action that would either bring back the Passenger or start me on the path to living without it. If Starzak was not an absolute certainty, he was close, I was here, and this was an emergency.

At least it was a clear choice, something I hadn't had in quite some time. I took a deep breath and moved as silently as I could through the hedge and into Starzak's yard.

I kept to the shadows and got to the side of the house where a door opened into the garage. It was locked – but Dexter laughs at locks, and I did not need any help from the Passenger to open this one and step into the dark garage, quietly closing the door behind me. There was a bicycle along the far wall, and a workbench with a very neat set of hanging tools. I made a mental note and crossed the garage to the door that led into the house and paused there for a long moment with my ear against the door.

Above the faint hum of air-conditioning, I heard a TV and nothing else. I listened a little longer to be sure, and then very carefully eased open the door.

It was unlocked and opened smoothly and without sound, and I was into Starzak's house as silent and dark as one of the shadows.

I slipped down a hallway toward the purple glow of the TV, keeping myself pressed against the wall, painfully aware that if he was behind me for some reason I was brilliantly backlit. But as I came in sight of the TV, I saw a head rising above the back of a sofa and I knew I had him.

I held my noose of fifty-pound-test fishing line ready in my hand and stepped closer. A commercial came on and the head moved slightly. I froze, but he moved his head back to center again and I was across the room and on him, my noose whistling around his neck and sliding tight just above his Adam's apple.

For a moment he thrashed in a very gratifying way, which only pulled the noose tighter. I watched him flop and grab at his throat, and while it was enjoyable I did not feel the same cold, savage glee that I was used to at such moments. Still, it was better than watching the commercial, and I let him go on until his face started to turn purple and the thrashing subsided into a helpless wobble.

'Be still and be quiet,' I said, 'and I will let you breathe.'

It was very much to his credit that he understood at once and stopped his feeble floundering. I eased off on the noose just a bit and listened while he forced in a breath. Just one – and then I tightened up again and pulled him to his feet. 'Come,' I said, and he came.

I stood behind him, keeping the pressure on the line just tight enough so that he could breathe a little if he tried really hard, and I led him down the hall to the back of the house and into the garage. As I pushed him to the workbench he went down to one knee, either a stumble or a foolish attempt to escape. Either way, I was in no mood for it, and I pulled hard enough to make his eyes bulge out and watched as his face got dark and he slumped over on the floor, unconscious.

Much easier for me. I got his dead weight up onto the workbench and duct-taped securely into place while he still wallowed in gape-mouthed unconsciousness. A thin stream of drool ran from one corner of his mouth and his breath came very rough, even after I loosened the noose. I looked down at Starzak, taped to the table with his unlovely face hanging open, and I thought, as I never had before, this is what we all are. This is what it comes to. A bag of meat that breathes, and when that stops, nothing but rotting garbage.

Starzak began to cough, and more phlegm dribbled from his mouth. He pushed against the duct tape, found he could not move, and fluttered open his eyes. He said something incomprehensible, composed of far too many consonants, and then rolled his eyes back and saw me. Of course he could not see my face through my mask, but I got the very unsettling feeling that he recognized me anyway. He moved his mouth a few times, but said nothing until he finally rolled his eyes back down to point at his feet and said in a dry and raspy voice with a Central European accent, but very little of the expected emotion in it, 'You are making a very large mistake.'

I searched for an automatic sinister reply, and found nothing.

'You will see,' he said in his terrible flat and raw voice. 'He will get you anyway, even without me. It is too late for you.'

And there it was. As close to a confession as I needed that he had been following me with sinister intent. But all I could think to say was, 'Who is he?'

He forgot he was taped to the bench and tried to shake his head. It didn't work, but it didn't seem to bother him much, either. 'They will find you,' he repeated. 'Soon enough.' He twitched a little, as if he was trying to wave a hand, and said, 'Go ahead. Kill me now. They will find you.'

I looked down at him, so passively taped and ready for my special attentions, and I should have been filled with icy delight at the job ahead of me – and I was not. I was not filled with anything except emptiness, the same feeling of hopeless futility that had come over me while I waited outside the house.

I shook myself out of the funk and taped Starzak's mouth shut. He flinched a little, but other than that he continued to look straight away, with no show of any kind of emotion.

I raised my knife and looked down at my unmoving and unmoved prey. I could still hear his awful wet breath rattling in and out through his nostrils and I wanted to stop it, turn out his lights, shut down this noxious thing, cut it into pieces and seal them into neat, dry garbage bags, unmoving chunks of compost that would no longer threaten, no longer eat and excrete and flail around in the patternless maze of human life—

And I could not.

I called silently for the familiar rush of dark wings to sweep out of me and light up my knife with the wicked gleam of savage purpose, and nothing came. Nothing moved within me at the thought of doing this sharp and necessary thing I had done so happily so many times. The only thing that welled up inside me was emptiness.

I lowered the knife, turned away, and walked out into the night.

24

Somehow I pulled myself out of bed and went in to work the next day, in spite of the gnawing sense of dull despair that bloomed in me like a brittle garden of thorns. I felt wrapped in a fog of dull pain that hurt only enough to remind me that it, too, was without purpose, and there seemed no point to going through the empty motions of breakfast, the long slow drive to work, no reason at all beyond the slavery of habit. But I did it, allowing muscle memory to push me all the way into the chair at my desk, where I sat, turned on the computer, and let the day drag me off into gray drudgery.

I had failed with Starzak. I was no longer me, and had no idea who or what I was.

Rita was waiting for me at the door when I got home with a look of anxious annoyance on her face.

'We need to decide about the band,' she said. 'They may already be booked.'

'All right,' I said. Why not decide about bands? It was as meaningful as anything else.

'I picked up all the CDs from where you dropped them yesterday,' she said, 'and sorted them by price.'

'I'll listen to them tonight,' I said, and although Rita still seemed peeved, eventually the evening routine took over and calmed her down, and she settled into cooking and cleaning while I listened to a series of rock bands playing 'Chicken Dance' and 'Electric Slide.' I'm sure that ordinarily it would have been as much fun as a toothache, but since I couldn't think of anything else in the world worth doing, I labored through the whole stack of CDs and soon it was time for bed again.

At 1 a.m. the music came back to me, and I don't mean 'Chicken Dance.' It was the drums and trumpets, and a chorus of voices came with them and rolled through my sleep, lifting me up into the heavens, and I woke up on the floor with the memory of it still echoing in my head.

I lay on the floor for a long time, unable to form any truly coherent thought about what it meant, but afraid to go to sleep in case it should come back again. Eventually I did get into bed, and I suppose I even slept, since I opened my eyes to sunlight and sound coming from the kitchen.

It was a Saturday morning, and Rita made blueberry pancakes, a very welcome nudge back to everyday life. Cody and Astor piled into the pancakes with enthusiasm, and on any normal morning I would not have held back either. But today was not a normal morning.

It is difficult to understate how large the shock must be to put Dexter off his feed. I have a very fast metabolism, and require constant fuel in order to maintain the wonderful device that is me, and Rita's pancakes fully qualify as high-test unleaded. And yet, time and again I found myself staring at the fork as it wavered halfway between the plate and my mouth, and I was unable to muster the necessary enthusiasm for completing the motion and putting in food.

Soon enough, everyone else was finished with the meal, and I was still staring at half a plate of food. Even Rita noticed that all was not well in Dexter's Domain.

'You've hardly touched your food,' she said. 'Is something wrong?'

'It's this case I'm working on,' I said, at least half truthfully. 'I can't stop thinking about it.'

'Oh,' she said. 'You're sure that . . . I mean, is it very violent?'

'It's not that,' I said, wondering what she wanted to hear. 'It's just . . . very puzzling.'

Rita nodded. 'Sometimes if you stop thinking about something for a while, the answer comes to you,' she said.

'Maybe you're right,' I said, which was probably stretching the truth.

'Are you going to finish your breakfast?' she said.

I stared down at my plate with its pile of half-eaten pancakes and congealed syrup. Scientifically speaking, I knew they were still delicious, but at the moment they seemed about as appealing as old wet newspaper. 'No,' I said.

Rita looked at me with alarm. When Dexter does not finish his breakfast, we are in uncharted territory. 'Why don't you take your boat out?' she said. 'That always helps you relax.' She came over and put a hand on me with aggressive concern, and Cody and Astor looked up with the hope of a boat ride written on their faces, and it was suddenly like being in quicksand.

I stood up. It was all too much. I could not even meet my own expectations, and to be asked to deal with all theirs too was suffocating. Whether it was my failure with Starzak, the pursuing music, or being sucked down into family life, I could not say. Maybe it was the combination of all of them, pulling me apart with wildly opposite gravities and sucking the pieces into a whirlpool of clinging normalcy that made me want to scream, and at the same time left me unable even to whimper. Whatever it was, I had to get out of here.

'I have an errand I have to run,' I said, and they all looked at me with wounded surprise.

'Oh,' Rita said. 'What kind of errand?'

'Wedding business,' I blurted out, without any idea what I was going to say next, but trusting the impulse blindly. And happily for me, at least one thing went right, because I remembered my conversation with the blushing, groveling Vince Masuoka. 'I have to talk to the caterer.'

Rita lit up. 'You're going to see Manny Borque? Oh,' she said. 'That's really— '

'Yes, it is,' I assured her. 'I'll be back later.' And so at the reasonable Saturday morning time of fifteen minutes before ten o'clock, I bid a fond farewell to dirty dishes and domesticity, and climbed into my car. It was an unusually calm morning on the roads, and I saw no violence or crime of any kind as I drove to South Beach, which was almost like seeing snow at the Fontainebleau. Things being what they were for me lately, I kept an eye on the rearview mirror. For just a minute I thought that a little red Jeep-style car was following me, but when I slowed down it went right past me. The traffic stayed light, and it was still only ten fifteen when I had parked my car, rode up in the elevator, and knocked on Manny Borque's door.

There was a very long spell of utter silence, and I knocked again, a little more enthusiastically this time. I was about to try a truly rousing salute on the door when it swung open and an exceedingly bleary and mostly naked Manny Borque blinked up at me. 'Jesus' tits,' he croaked. 'What time is it?'

'Ten fifteen,' I said brightly. 'Practically time for lunch.'

Perhaps he wasn't really awake, or perhaps he thought it was so funny it was worth saying again, but in any case he repeated himself: 'Jesus' tits.'

'May I come in?' I asked him politely, and he blinked a few more times and then pushed the door open all the way.

'This better be good,' he said, and I followed him in, past the hideous artthing in his foyer and on to his perch by the window. He hopped up onto his stool, and I sat on the one opposite.

'I need to talk to you about my wedding,' I said, and he shook his head very grumpily and squealed out, '*Franky!*' There was no answer and he leaned on one tiny hand and tapped the other on the table. 'That little bitch had better – Goddamn it, *Franky!*' he called out in something like a very high-pitched bellow.

A moment later there was a scurrying sound from the back of the apartment, and then a young man came out, pulling a robe closed as he hurried in and brushing back his lank brown hair as he came to a halt in front of Manny. 'Hi,' he said. 'I mean, you know. Good morning.'

'Get coffee very quickly,' Manny said without looking up at him.

'Um,' Franky said. 'Sure. Okay.' He hesitated for half a second, just long enough to give Manny time to fling out his minuscule fist and shriek, 'Now, goddamn it!' Franky gulped and lurched away toward the kitchen, and Manny went back to leaning his full eighty-five pounds of towering grumpiness on his fist and closing his eyes with a sigh, as though he were tormented by numberless hordes of truly idiotic demons.

Since it seemed obvious that there could be no possibility of conversation without coffee, I looked out the window and enjoyed the view. There were three large freighters on the horizon, sending up plumes of smoke, and closer in to shore a good scattering of pleasure boats, ranging from the multimillion-dollar playtoys headed for the Bahamas all the way down to a cluster of windsurfers in close to the beach. A bright yellow kayak was offshore, apparently heading out to meet the freighters. The sun shone, the gulls flew by searching for garbage, and I waited for Manny to receive his transfusion.

There was a shattering crash from the kitchen, and Franky's muted wail of 'Oh, *shit*.' Manny tried to close his eyes tighter, as if he could seal out all the agony of being surrounded by terrible stupidity. And only a few minutes later, Franky arrived with the coffee service, a silver semi-shapeless pot and three squat stoneware cups, perched on a transparent platter shaped like an artist's palette.

With trembling hands Franky placed a cup in front of Manny and poured it full. Manny took a tiny sip, sighed heavily without any sense of relief, and opened his eyes at last. 'All right,' he said. And turning to Franky, he added, 'Go clean up your hideous mess, and if I step on broken glass later, I swear to *God* I will disembowel you.' Franky stumbled away, and Manny took another microscopic sip before turning his bleary glare on me. 'You want to talk about your wedding,' he said as if he couldn't really believe it.

'That's right,' I said, and he shook his head.

'A nice-looking man like you,' he said. 'Why on earth would you want to get married?'

'I need the tax break,' I said. 'Can we talk about the menu?'

'At the crack of dawn, on a Saturday? No,' he said. 'It's a horrible, pointless, primitive ritual,' and I assumed he was talking about the wedding rather than the menu, although with Manny one really couldn't be sure. 'I am truly appalled that anyone would *willingly* go through with it. But,' he said, waving his hand dismissively, 'at least it gives me a chance to experiment.'

'I wonder if it might be possible to experiment a little cheaper.'

'It might be,' he said and for the first time he showed his teeth, but it could only be called a smile if you agree that torturing animals is funny, 'but it just won't happen.'

'Why not?'

'Because I've already decided what I want to do, and there's nothing you can do to stop me.'

To be perfectly truthful there were several things I could think of to stop him, but none of them – enjoyable as they might be – would pass the strict guidelines of the Harry Code, and so I could not do them. 'I don't suppose sweet reason would have any effect?' I asked hopefully.

He leered at me. 'How sweet did you have in mind?' he said.

'Well, I was going to say please and smile a lot,' I said.

'Not good enough,' he said. 'Not by a great deal.'

'Vince said you were guessing five hundred dollars a plate?'

'I don't *guess*,' he snarled. 'And I don't give a *shit* about counting your fuck-ing pennies.'

'Of course not,' I said, trying to soothe him a bit. 'After all, they're not your pennies.'

'Your girlfriend signed the fucking contract,' he said. 'I can charge you any-thing I fucking feel like.'

'But there must be something I can do to get the price down a little?' I said hopefully.

His snarl loosened into his patented leer again. 'Not in a chair,' he said.

'Then what can I do?'

'If you mean what can you do to get me to change my mind, nothing. Not a thing in the world. I have people lined up around the block trying to hire me – I am booked two years in advance, and I am doing you a very large favor.' His leer widened into something almost supernatural. 'So prepare yourself for a miracle. And a very hefty bill.'

I stood up. The little gnome was obviously not going to bend in the least, and there was nothing I could do about it. I really wanted to say something like 'You haven't heard the last of me,' but there didn't seem much point to that either. So I just smiled back, said, 'Well then,' and walked out of the apart-ment. As the door closed behind me, I could hear him, already squealing at Franky, 'For Christ's sake move your big ass and get all that shit off my fuck-ing *floor*.'

As I walked toward the elevator I felt an icy steel finger brush the back of my neck and for just a moment I felt a faint stirring, as if the Dark Passenger had put one toe in the water and run away after seeing that it was too cold. I stopped dead and slowly looked around me in the hallway.

Nothing. Down at the far end a man was fumbling with the newspaper in front of his door. Otherwise, the hall was empty. I closed my eyes for just a moment. *What?* I asked. But there was no answer. I was still alone. And unless somebody was glaring at me through a peephole in one of the doors, it had been a false alarm. Or, more likely, wishful thinking.

I got in the elevator and went down.

As the elevator door slid shut the Watcher straightened up, still holding the newspaper from where he had taken it off the mat. It was a good piece of camouflage, and it might work again. He stared down the hall and wondered what was so interesting in that other apartment, but it didn't really matter. He would find out. Whatever the other had been doing, he would find out.

He counted slowly to ten and then sauntered down the hallway to the apartment the other had visited. It would only take a moment to find out why he had gone in there. And then—

The Watcher had no real idea what was really going through the other's mind right now, but it was not happening fast enough. It was time for a real push, something to break the other out of his passivity. He felt a rare pulse of playfulness welling up through the dark cloud of power, and he heard the flutter of dark wings inside.

25

In my lifelong study of human beings, I have found that no matter how hard they might try, they have found no way yet to prevent the arrival of Monday morning. And they do try, of course, but Monday always comes, and all the drones have to scuttle back to their dreary workaday lives of meaningless toil and suffering.

That thought always cheers me up, and because I like to spread happiness wherever I go, I did my small part to cushion the blow of unavoidable Monday morning by arriving at work with a box of doughnuts, all of which vanished in what can only be called an extremely grumpy frenzy before I reached my desk. I doubted very seriously that anyone had a better reason than I did for feeling surly, but you would not have known it to watch them all snatching at my doughnuts and grunting at me.

Vince Masuoka seemed to be sharing in the general feeling of low-key anguish. He stumbled into my cubbyhole with a look of horror and wonderment on his face, an expression that must have indicated something very moving because it looked almost real. 'Jesus, Dexter,' he said. 'Oh, Jesus Christ.'

'I tried to save you one,' I said, thinking that with that much anguish he could only be referring to the calamity of facing an empty doughnut box. But he shook his head.

'Oh, Jesus, I can't believe it. He's dead!'

'I'm sure it had nothing to do with the doughnuts,' I said.

'My God, and you were going to see him. Did you?'

There comes a point in every conversation where at least one of the people involved has to know what is being talked about, and I decided that point had arrived.

'Vince,' I said, 'I want you to take a deep breath, start all over from the top, and pretend you and I speak the same language.'

He stared at me as if he was a frog and I was a heron. 'Shit,' he said. 'You don't know yet, do you? Holy shit.'

'Your language skills are deteriorating,' I said. 'Have you been talking to Deborah?'

'He's *dead*, Dexter. They found the body late last night.'

'Well, then, I'm sure he'll stay dead long enough for you to tell me what in the hell you're talking about.'

Vince blinked at me, his eyes suddenly huge and moist. 'Manny Borque,' he breathed. 'He was murdered.'

I will admit to having mixed reactions. On the one hand, I was certainly not sorry to have somebody else take the little troll out of the picture in a way I was unable to do for ethical reasons. But on the other hand, now I needed to find another caterer – and oh, yes, I would probably have to give a statement of some kind to the detective in charge. Annoyance fought it out with relief, but then I remembered that the doughnuts were gone, too.

And so the reaction that won out was irritation at all the bother this was going to cause. Still, Harry had schooled me well enough to know that this is not really an acceptable reaction to display when one hears of the death of an acquaintance. So I did my best to push my face into something resembling shock, concern, and distress. 'Wow,' I said. 'I had no idea. Do they know who did it?'

Vince shook his head. 'The guy had no enemies,' he said, and he didn't seem aware of how unlikely his statement sounded to anyone who had ever met Manny. 'I mean, everybody was just in awe of him.'

'I know,' I said. 'He was in magazines and everything.'

'I can't believe anybody would do that to him,' he said.

In truth, I couldn't believe it had taken so long for somebody to do that to him, but it didn't seem like the politic thing to say. 'Well, I'm sure they'll figure it out. Who's assigned to the case?'

Vince looked at me like I had asked him if he thought the sun might come up in the morning. 'Dexter,' he said wonderingly, 'his head was cut off. It's just like the three over at the university.'

When I was young and trying hard to fit in, I played football for a while, and one time I had been hit hard in the stomach and couldn't breathe for a few minutes. I felt a little bit like that now.

'Oh,' I said.

'So naturally they've given it to your sister,' he said.

'Naturally.' A sudden thought hit me, and because I am a lifelong devotee of irony, I asked him, 'He wasn't cooked, too, was he?'

Vince shook his head. 'No,' he said.

I stood up. 'I better go talk to Deborah,' I said.

Deborah was not in any mood to talk when I arrived at Manny's apartment. She was bending over Camilla Figg, who was dusting for prints around the legs of the table by the window. She didn't look up, so I peeked into the kitchen, where Angel-no-relation was bent over the body.

'Angel,' I said, and I found some difficulty believing my eyes, so I asked him, 'Is that really a girl's head there?'

He nodded and poked at the head with a pen. 'Your sister says, prolly the girl from the Lowe Museum,' he said. 'They put it here because this guy is such a *bugero*.'

I looked down at the two cuts, one just above the shoulders, the other just below the chin. The one on the head matched what we had seen before, done with neatness and care. But the one on the body that was presumably Manny was much rougher, as if it had been hurried. The edges of the two cuts were pushed together carefully, but of course they did not quite mesh. Even on my own, with no dark interior muttering, I could tell that this was different some-how, and one small cold finger crawling across the back of my neck suggested that the difference might be very important – maybe even to my current trou-bles – but beyond that vague and unsatisfying ghost of a hint, there was noth-ing for me here but uneasiness.

'Is there another body?' I asked him, remembering poor bullied Franky.

Angel shrugged without looking up. 'In the bedroom,' he said. 'Just with a butcher knife stuck in him. They left his head.' He sounded a little offended that someone would go to all that trouble and leave the head, but other than that he seemed to have nothing to tell me, so I walked away, over to where my sister was now squatting beside Camilla.

'Good morning, Debs,' I said, with a cheerfulness I did not feel at all, and I was not the only one, because she didn't even look up at me.

'Goddamn it, Dexter,' she said. 'Unless you have something really good for me, stay the fuck away.'

'It isn't all that good,' I said. 'But the guy in the bedroom is named Franky. This one here is Manny Borque, who has been in a number of magazines.'

'How the fuck would you know that?' she said.

'Well, it's a little awkward,' I said, 'but I may have been one of the last peo-ple to see this guy alive.'

She straightened up. 'When?' she asked.

'Saturday morning. Around ten thirty. Right here.' And I pointed to the coffee cup that was still on top of the table. 'Those are my prints.'

Deborah was looking at me with disbelief and shaking her head. 'You *knew* this guy,' she said. 'He was a friend of yours?'

'I hired him to cater my wedding,' I said. 'He was supposed to be very good at it.'

'Uh-huh,' she said. 'So what were you doing here on a Saturday morning?'

'He raised the price on me,' I said. 'I wanted to talk him down.'

She looked around the apartment and glanced out the window at the million-dollar view. 'What was he charging?' she said.

'Five hundred dollars a plate,' I said.

Her head snapped around to face me again. 'Jesus fuck,' she said. 'For what?'

I shrugged. 'He wouldn't tell me, and he wouldn't lower the price.'

'Five hundred dollars a *plate*?' she said.

'It is a little high, isn't it? Or should I say, it was.'

Deborah chewed on her lip for a long moment without blinking, and then she grabbed me by the arm and pulled me away from Camilla. I could still see one small foot sticking out of the kitchen door where the dear departed had met his untimely end, but Deborah led me away from it and over to the far end of the room.

'Dexter,' she said, 'promise me you didn't kill this guy.'

As I have mentioned before, I do not have real emotions. I have practiced long and hard to react the way human beings would react in almost every possible situation – but this one caught me by surprise. What is the correct facial expression for being accused of murder by your sister? Shock? Anger? Disbelief? As far as I knew, this wasn't covered in any of the textbooks.

'Deborah,' I said. Not tremendously clever, but it was all I could think of.

'Because you don't get a free pass with me,' she said. 'Not for something like this.'

'I would never,' I said. 'This is not . . .' I shook my head, and it really seemed so unfair. First the Dark Passenger left me, and now my sister and my wits had apparently fled, too. All the rats were swimming away as the good ship Dexter slid slowly under the waves.

I took a deep breath and tried to organize the crew to bail out a little. Deborah was the only person on earth who knew what I really was, and even though she was still getting used to the idea, I had thought she understood the very careful boundaries set up by Harry, and understood, too, that I would never cross them. Apparently I was wrong. 'Deborah,' I said. 'Why would I—'

'Cut the crap,' she snapped. 'We both know you could have done it. You were here at the right time. And you have a pretty good motive, to get out of paying him like fifty grand. It's either that or I believe some guy in jail did it.'

Because I am an artificial human, I am also extremely clearheaded most of the time, uncluttered by emotions. But I felt as if I was trying to see through quicksand. On the one hand, I was surprised and a little disappointed that she thought I might have done something this sloppy. On the other hand, I wanted to reassure her that I hadn't. And I wanted to say that if I had done this, she would never have found out about it, but that didn't seem quite diplomatic. So I took another deep breath and settled for, 'I promise.'

My sister looked at me long and hard. 'Really,' I said.

She finally nodded. 'All right,' she said. 'You better be telling me the truth.'

'I am,' I said. 'I didn't do this.'

'Uh-huh,' she said. 'Then who did?'

It really isn't fair, is it? I mean, this whole life thing. Here I was, still defending myself from an accusation of murder – from my own foster flesh and blood! – and at the same time being asked to solve the crime. I had to admire the mental agility that allowed Deborah to perform that kind of cerebral tumbling act, but I also had to wish she would direct her creative thinking at somebody else.

'I don't know who did this,' I said. 'And I don't – I'm not getting any, um, ideas about it.'

She stared at me very hard indeed. 'Why should I believe that, either?' she said.

'Deborah,' I said, and I hesitated. Was this the time to tell her about the Dark Passenger and its present absence? There was a very uncomfortable series of sensations sloshing through me, somewhat like the onset of the flu. Could these be emotions, pounding at the defenseless coastline of Dexter, like huge tidal waves of toxic sludge? If so, it was no wonder humans were such miserable creatures. This was an awful experience.

'Listen, Deborah,' I said again, trying to think of a way to start.

'I am listening, for Christ's sake,' she said. 'But you're not saying anything.'

'It's hard to say,' I said. 'I've never said it before.'

'This would be a great time to start.'

'I, uh – I have this thing inside me,' I said, aware that I sounded like a complete idiot and feeling a strange heat rising into my cheeks.

'What do you mean,' she demanded. 'You've got cancer?'

'No, no, it's – I hear, um – It tells me things,' I said. For some reason I had to look away from Deborah. There was a photograph of a naked man's torso on the wall; I looked back to Deborah.

'Jesus,' she said. 'You mean you hear voices? Jesus Christ, Dex.'

'No,' I said. 'It's not like hearing voices. Not exactly.'

'Well then, what the fuck?' she said.

I had to look at the naked torso again, and then blow out a large breath before I could look back at Deborah. 'When I get one of my hunches about, you know . . . At a crime scene,' I said. 'It's because this . . . thing is telling me.' Deborah's face was frozen over, completely immobile, as if she was listening to a confession of terrible deeds; which she was, of course.

'So it *tells* you what?' she said. 'Hey, somebody who thinks he's Batman did this.'

'Kind of,' I said. 'Just, you know. The little hints I used to get.'

'Used to get,' she said.

I really had to look away again. 'It's gone, Deborah,' I said. 'Something about all this Moloch stuff scared it away. That's never happened before.'

She didn't say anything for a long time, and I saw no reason to say it for her.

'Did you ever tell Dad about this voice?' she said at last.

'I didn't have to,' I said. 'He already knew.'

'And now your voices are gone,' she said.

'Just one voice.'

'And that's why you're not telling me anything about all this.'

'Yes.'

Deborah ground her teeth together loud enough for me to hear them. Then she released a large breath without unlocking her jaw. 'Either you're lying to me because you did this,' she hissed at me, 'or you're telling the truth and you're a fucking psycho.'

'Debs—'

'Which one do you think I want to believe, Dexter? Huh? Which one?'

I don't believe I have felt real anger since I was an adolescent, and it may be that even then I was not able to feel the real thing. But with the Dark Passenger gone and me slipping down the slope into genuine humanity, all the old barriers between me and normal life were fading, and I felt something now that must have been very close to the real thing. 'Deborah,' I said, 'if you don't trust me and you want to think I did this, then I don't give a rat's ass which one you believe.'

She glared at me, and for the very first time, I glared back.

Finally she spoke. 'I still have to report this,' she said. 'Officially, you can't come anywhere near this for now.'

'Nothing would make me happier,' I said. She stared at me for a moment longer, then made her mouth very small and returned to Camilla Figg. I watched her back for a moment, and then headed for the door.

There was really no point in hanging around, especially since I had been told, officially and unofficially, that I was not welcome. It would be nice to say that my feelings were hurt, but surprisingly, I was still too angry to feel miffed. And in truth, I have always been so shocked that anyone could really like me that it was almost a relief to see Deborah taking a sensible attitude for once.

It was all good all the time for Dexter, but for some reason, it didn't really feel like a very large victory as I headed for the door and exile.

I was waiting for the elevator to arrive when I was blindsided by a hoarse shout of 'Hey!'

I turned and saw a grim, very angry old man racing at me wearing sandals and black socks that came up almost to his knobby old knees. He also wore baggy shorts and a silk shirt and an expression of completely righteous wrath. 'Are you the police?' he demanded.

'Not all of them,' I said.

'What about my goddamn paper?' he said.

Elevators are so slow, aren't they? But I do try to be polite when it is unavoidable, so I smiled reassuringly at the old lunatic. 'You didn't like your paper?' I asked.

'I didn't *get* my goddamn paper!' he shouted at me, turning a light purple from the effort. 'I called and I told you people and the colored girl on the phone said to call the newspaper! I watch the kid steal it, and she hangs up on me!'

'A kid stole your newspaper?' I said.

'What the hell did I just say?' he said, and he was getting a little bit shrill now, which did nothing to make waiting for the elevator any more enjoyable. 'Why the hell do I pay my taxes, to hear her say that? And she laughs at me, goddamn it!'

'You could get another paper,' I said soothingly.

It didn't seem to soothe him. 'What the hell is that, get another paper? Saturday morning, in my pajamas, and I should get another paper? Why can't you people just catch the criminals?'

The elevator made a muted *ding* sound to announce its arrival at last, but I was no longer interested, because I had a thought. Every now and then I do have thoughts. Most of them never make it all the way to the surface, probably because of a lifetime of trying to seem human. But this one came slowly up and, like a gas bubble bursting through mud, popped brightly in my brain. 'Saturday morning?' I said. 'Do you remember what time?'

'Of course I remember what time! I told them when I called, ten thirty on a Saturday morning, and the kid is stealing my paper!'

'How do you know it was a kid?'

'I watched through the peephole, that's how!' he yelled at me. 'I should go out in the hall without looking, the job you people do? Forget it!'

'When you say "kid,"' I said, 'how old do you mean?'

'Listen, mister,' he said, 'to me, everybody under seventy is a kid. But this kid was maybe twenty, and he had a backpack on like they all wear.'

'Can you describe this kid?' I asked.

'I'm not blind,' he said. 'He stands up with my paper, he's got one of those goddamn tattoos they all have now, right on the back of his neck!'

I felt little metal fingers flutter across the back of my neck and I knew the answer, but I asked anyway. 'What kind of tattoo?'

'Stupid thing, one of those Jap symbols. We beat the crap out of the Japs so we could buy their cars and tattoo their goddamn scribbles on our kids?'

He seemed to be only warming up, and while I really admired the fact that he had such terrific stamina at his age, I felt it was time to turn him over to the proper authorities as constituted by my sister, which lit up in me a small glow of satisfaction, since it not only gave her a suspect better than poor Disenfranchised Dexter but also inflicted this beguiling old poop on her as a small measure of punishment for suspecting me in the first place. 'Come with me,' I said to the old man.

'I'm not going anywhere,' he said.

'Wouldn't you like to talk to a real detective?' I said, and the hours of practice I had spent on my smile must have paid off, because he frowned, looked around him, and then said, 'Well, all right,' and followed me all the way back to where Sergeant Sister was snarling at Camilla Figg.

'I told you to stay away,' she said, with all the warmth and charm I had come to expect from her.

'Okay,' I said. 'Shall I take the witness away with me?'

Deborah opened her mouth, then closed and opened it a few more times, as if she was trying to figure out how to breathe like a fish.

'You can't – it isn't – Goddamn it, Dexter,' she said at last.

'I can, it is, and I'm sure he will,' I said. 'But in the meantime, this nice old gentleman has something interesting to tell you.'

'Who the hell are you to call me old?' he said.

'This is Detective Morgan,' I told him. 'She's in charge here.'

'A girl?' he snorted. 'No wonder they can't catch anybody. A girl detective.'

'Be sure to tell her about the backpack,' I told him. 'And the tattoo.'

'What tattoo?' she demanded. 'What the hell are you talking about?'

'The mouth on you,' the old man said. 'Shame!'

I smiled at my sister. 'Have a nice chat,' I said.

26

I could not be sure that I was officially invited back to the party, but I didn't want to go so far away that I missed the chance to graciously accept my sister's apology. So I went to loiter just inside the front door of the former Manny Borque's apartment, where I could be noticed at the appropriate time. Unfortunately, the killer had not stolen the giant artistic ball of animal vomit on the pedestal by the door. It was still there, right in the middle of my loitering grounds, and I was forced to look at it while I waited.

I was wondering how long it would take Deborah to ask the old man about the tattoo and then make the connection. Even as I wondered, I heard her raise her voice in official ritual words of dismissal, thanking the old man for his help and instructing him to call if he thought of anything else. And then the two of them came toward the door, Deborah holding the old man firmly by the elbow and steering him out of the apartment.

'But what about my paper, miss?' he protested as she opened the door.

'It's Sergeant Miss,' I told him, and Deborah glared at me.

'Call the paper,' she told him. 'They'll give you a refund.' And she practically hurled him out the door, where he stood for a moment trembling with anger.

'The bad guys are winning!' he shouted, and then, happily for us, Deborah closed the door.

'He's right, you know,' I said to her.

'Well, you don't have to look so goddamned happy about it,' she said.

'And you, on the other hand, might try looking a lot happier,' I said. 'It's him, the boyfriend, what's his name.'

'Kurt Wagner,' she said.

'Very good,' I said. 'Due diligence. Kurt Wagner it is, and you know it.'

'I don't know shit,' she said. 'It could still be a coincidence.'

'Sure, it could be,' I said. 'And there's even a mathematical chance that the sun will come up in the west, but it's not very likely. And who else do you have?'

'That fucking creep, Wilkins,' she said.

'Somebody's been watching him, right?'

She snorted. 'Yeah, but you know what these guys are like. They take a nap, or take a dump, and swear the guy was never out of their sight. Meantime, the guy they're supposed to watch is out chopping up cheerleaders.'

'So you really still think he could be the killer? Even when this kid was here at exactly the same time Manny was killed?'

'You were here at the same time,' she said. 'And this one's not like the others. More like a cheap copy.'

'Then how did Tammy Connor's head get here?' I said. 'Kurt Wagner is doing this, Debs, he has to be.'

'All right,' she said. 'He probably is.'

'Probably?' I said, and I really was surprised. Everything pointed to the kid with the neck tattoo, and Deborah was dithering.

She looked at me for a long moment, and it was not a look of warm, loving filial affection. 'It still might be you,' she said.

'By all means, arrest me,' I said. 'That would be the smart thing to do, wouldn't it? Captain Matthews will be happy because you made an arrest, and the media will love you for busting your brother. Terrific solution, Deborah. It will even make the real killer happy.'

Deborah said nothing, just turned and walked away. After thinking about it for a moment, I realized what a good idea that was. So I did it, too, and walked away in the opposite direction, out of the apartment and back to work.

The rest of my day was far more fulfilling. Two bodies, male, Caucasian, had been found in a BMW parked on the shoulder of the Palmetto Expressway. When somebody tried to steal the car, they found the bodies and phoned it in – after removing the sound system and the airbags. The apparent cause of death was multiple gunshot wounds. The newspapers are fond of using the phrase 'gangland style' for killings that show a certain neatness and economy. We would not be searching for any gangs this time. The two bodies and the inside of the car had been quite literally hosed with lead and spurting blood, as though the killer had trouble figuring out which end of the gun to hold on to. Judging from the bullet holes in the windows, it was a miracle that no passing motorists had been shot as well.

A busy Dexter should be a happy Dexter, and there was enough awful dried blood in the car and on the surrounding pavement to keep me occupied for hours, but not surprisingly I was still not happy. I had such a large number of hideous things happening to me, and now there was this disagreement with Debs. It was not really accurate to say that I loved Deborah, since I am incapable of love, but I was used to her, and I would rather have her around and reasonably content with me.

Other than a few ordinary sibling squabbles when we were younger, Deborah and I had rarely had any serious disagreements, and I was a bit surprised to find out that this one bothered me a great deal. In spite of the fact that I am a soulless monster who enjoys killing, it stung to have her think of me that way, especially since I had given my word of honor as an ogre that I was entirely innocent, at least in this case.

I wanted to get along with my sister, but I was also miffed that she seemed a little too enthusiastic about her role as a representative of the Full Majesty of the Law, and not quite willing enough as my sidekick and confidante.

Of course it made sense for me to be wasting my perfectly good indignation on this, since there was nothing else at all to occupy my attention at the time – things like weddings, mysterious music, and missing Passengers always sort themselves out, right? And blood spatter is a simple craft that requires minimal concentration. To prove it, I let my thoughts wander as I mentally wallowed in my sad state, and because of it I slipped in the congealed blood and went down on one knee on the roadside by the BMW.

The shock of contact with the road was immediately echoed by an interior shock, a jolt of fear and cold air going through me, rising up from the awful sticky mess and straight into my empty self, and it was a long moment before I could breathe again. Steady, Dexter, I thought. This is just a small, painful reminder of who you are and where you came from, brought on by stress. It has nothing to do with operatic cattle.

I managed to stand up without whimpering, but my pants were torn, my knee hurt, and one leg of the pants was covered with the vile half-dry blood.

I really don't like blood. And to look down and see it actually on my clothes, actually *touching* me, and on top of the complete turmoil my life had become and the great empty Passengerless pit I had fallen into – the blood completed the circuit. These were definitely emotions I was feeling now, and they were not pleasant. I felt myself shudder and I nearly shouted, but I managed, just barely, to contain myself, clean up, and soldier on.

I did not feel much better, but I made it through the day by changing into the extra set of clothing that wise blood-spatter techs keep handy, and it was finally time to head home.

As I drove south to Rita's on Old Cutler a little red Geo got on my bumper and would not back off. I watched in the mirror, but I could not see the driver's face, and I wondered if I had done something I wasn't aware of to make him or her angry. I was very tempted to step on the brakes and let the chips fall where they might, but I was not yet so completely frazzled as to believe that wrecking my car would make anything better. I tried to ignore the other car, just one more semi-insane Miami driver with a mysterious hidden agenda.

But it stayed with me, inches away, and I began to wonder what that agenda might be. I sped up. The Geo sped up and stayed right on my bumper.

I slowed down; so did the Geo.

I moved across two lanes of traffic, leaving a chorus of angry horns and upraised fingers in my wake. The Geo followed.

Who was it? What did they want with me? Was it possible that Starzak knew that it was me who had taped him up, and now he was coming after me in a different car, determined to revenge himself on me? Or was it someone else this time – and if so, who? Why? I could not bring myself to believe that Moloch was driving the car behind me. How could an ancient god even get a learner's permit? But somebody was back there, clearly planning to stay with me for a while, and I had no idea who. I found myself flailing for an answer, reaching for something that was no longer there, and the sense of loss and emptiness amplified my uncertainty and anger and uneasiness, and I realized my breath was hissing in and out between clenched teeth and my hands were clenched on the wheel and covered with a chilly sheen of sweat, and I thought, that's enough.

And as I mentally prepared myself to slam on the brakes and leap out of the car to smash this other driver's face into a red pulp, the red Geo suddenly slid off my bumper and turned right, vanishing down a side street into the Miami night.

It had been nothing after all, just a perfectly normal rush-hour psychosis. Another average crazed Miami driver, killing the boredom of the long drive home by playing tag with the car in front.

And I was nothing more than a dazed, battered, paranoid former monster with his hands clenched and his teeth grinding together.

I went home.

The Watcher dropped away and then circled back. He moved through the traffic invisible to the other now, and turned down the street to the house well behind the other. He had enjoyed tailing him so closely, forcing a display of mild panic. He had provoked the other in order to gauge his readiness, and what he found was very satisfying. It was a finely balanced process, to push the other precisely into the right frame of mind. He had done it many times before, and he knew the signs. Jumpy, but not quite on the ragged edge where he needed to be, not yet.

It was clearly time to accelerate things.

Tonight would be very special.

27

Dinner was ready when I got to Rita's house. Considering what I had gone through and what I was thinking about it, you might have thought that I would never eat again. But as I walked in the front door I was assaulted by the aroma; Rita had made roast pork, broccoli, and rice and beans, and there are very few things in this world that compare to Rita's roast pork. And so it was a somewhat mollified Dexter who finally pushed the plate away and rose from the table. And in truth, the rest of the evening was mildly soothing as well. I played kick the can with Cody and Astor and the other neighborhood children until it was bedtime, and then Rita and I sat on the couch and watched a show about a grumpy doctor before turning in for the night.

Normality wasn't all bad, not with Rita's roast pork in it, and Cody and Astor to keep me interested. Perhaps I could live vicariously through them, like an old baseball player who becomes a coach when his playing days are over. They had so much to learn, and in teaching them I could relive my fading days of glory. Sad, yes, but it was at least a small compensation.

And as I drifted off to sleep, in spite of the fact that I really do know better, I caught myself thinking that maybe things weren't that bad after all.

That foolish notion lasted until midnight, when I woke up to see Cody standing at the foot of the bed. 'Somebody's outside,' he said.

'All right,' I said, feeling half asleep and not at all curious about why he needed to tell me that.

'They want in,' he said.

I sat up. 'Where?' I said.

Cody turned and headed into the hallway and I followed. I was half convinced that he had simply had a bad dream, but after all, this was Miami and these things have been known to happen, although certainly seldom more than five or six hundred times on any given night.

Cody led me to the door to the backyard. About ten feet from the door he stopped dead, and I stopped with him.

'There,' Cody said softly.

There indeed. It was not a bad dream, or at least not the kind you need to be asleep to have.

The doorknob was moving, wiggling as someone on the outside tried to turn it.

'Wake up your mom,' I whispered to Cody. 'Tell her to call 9-1-1.' He looked up at me as if he was disappointed that I wasn't going to charge out the door with a hand grenade and take care of things myself, but then he turned and walked back down the hall toward the bedroom.

I approached the door, quietly and cautiously. On the wall beside it was a switch that turned on a floodlight which illuminated the backyard. As I reached for the switch, the doorknob stopped turning. I turned the light on anyway.

Immediately, as if the switch had caused it to happen, something began to thump on the front door.

I turned and ran for the front of the house – and halfway there Rita stepped into the hall and crashed into me. 'Dexter,' she said. 'What – Cody said—'

'Call the cops,' I told her. 'Someone is trying to break in.' I looked behind her at Cody. 'Get your sister and all of you get into the bathroom. Lock the door.'

'But who would – we're not—' Rita said.

'Go,' I told her, and pushed past her to the front door.

Once again I flipped on the outside light, and once again the sound stopped immediately.

Only to start up again down the hall, apparently on the kitchen window.

And naturally enough when I ran into the kitchen the sound had already stopped, even before I turned on the overhead light.

I slowly approached the window over the sink and carefully peeked out.

Nothing. Just the night and the hedge and the neighbor's house and nothing else whatsoever.

I straightened up and stood there for a moment, waiting for the noise to start up again at some other corner of the house. It didn't. I realized I was holding my breath, and I let it out. Whatever it was, it had stopped. It was gone. I unclenched my fists and took a deep breath.

And then Rita screamed.

I turned around fast enough to twist my ankle, but still hobbled for the bathroom as quickly as I could. The door was locked, but from inside I could hear something scrabbling at the window. Rita shouted, 'Go away!'

'Open the door,' I said, and a moment later Astor opened it wide.

'It's at the window,' she said, rather calmly I thought.

Rita was standing in the middle of the bathroom with her clenched fists raised to her mouth. Cody stood in front of her protectively holding the toilet plunger, and they were both staring at the window.

'Rita,' I said.

She turned to me with her eyes wide and filled with fear. 'But what do they want?' she demanded, as if she thought I could tell her. And perhaps I could have, in the ordinary course of things – 'ordinary' being defined as the entire previous portion of my life, when I had my Passenger to keep me company and whisper terrible secrets. But as it was, I only knew they wanted in and I did not know why.

I also did not know what they wanted, but it didn't seem quite as important at the moment as the fact that they obviously wanted something and thought we had it. 'Come on,' I said. 'Everybody out of here.' Rita turned to look at me, but Cody stood his ground. 'Move,' I said, and Astor took Rita by the hand and hurried through the door. I put a hand on Cody's shoulder and pushed him after his mother, gently prying the plunger from his hands, and then I turned to face the window.

The noise continued, a hard scratching that sounded like someone was trying to claw through the glass. Without any real conscious thought I stepped forward and whacked the window with the rubber head of the toilet plunger.

The sound stopped.

For a long moment there was no sound except for my breathing, which I realized was somewhat fast and ragged. And then, not too far away, I heard a police siren cutting through the silence. I backed out of the bathroom, watching the window.

Rita sat on the bed with Cody on one side of her and Astor on the other. The children seemed quite calm, but Rita was clearly on the edge of hysteria. 'It's all right,' I said. 'The cops are almost here.'

'Will it be Sergeant Debbie?' Astor asked me, and she added hopefully, 'Do you think she'll shoot somebody?'

'Sergeant Debbie is in bed, asleep,' I said. The siren was near now, and with a squeal of tires it came to a stop in front of our house and wound its way down through the scale to a grumbling halt. 'They're here,' I told them, and Rita lunged up off the bed and grabbed the children by the hand.

The three of them followed me out of the bedroom, and by the time we got to the front door there was already a knock sounding on the wood, polite but firm. Still, life teaches us caution, so I called out, 'Who is it?'

'This is the police,' a stern masculine voice said. 'We have a report of a possible break-in.' It sounded authentic, but just to be sure, I left the chain on as I opened the door and looked out. Sure enough, there were two uniformed cops standing there, one looking at the door and one turned away, looking out into the yard and the street.

I closed the door, took the chain off, and reopened it. 'Come in, Officer,' I said. His name tag said Ramirez, and I realized I knew him slightly. But he made no move to enter the house; he simply stared down at my hand.

'What kind of emergency is this, chief?' he said, nodding at my hand. I looked and realized I was still holding the toilet plunger.

'Oh,' I said. I put the plunger behind the door in the umbrella stand. 'Sorry. That was for self-defense.'

'Uh-huh,' Ramirez said. 'Guess it would depend what the other guy had.' He stepped forward into the house, calling over his shoulder to his partner, 'Take a look around the yard, Williams.'

'Yo,' said Williams, a wiry black man of about forty. He walked down into the yard and disappeared around the corner of the house.

Ramirez stood in the center of the room, looking at Rita and the kids. 'So, what's the story here?' he asked, and before I could answer he squinted at me. 'I know you from somewhere?' he said.

'Dexter Morgan,' I said. 'I work in forensics.'

'Right,' he said. 'So what happened here, Dexter?'

I told him.

28

The cops stayed with us for about forty minutes. They looked around the yard and the surrounding neighborhood and found nothing, which did not seem to surprise them, and which truthfully was not a great shock to me, either. When they were done looking Rita made them coffee and fed them some oatmeal cookies she had made.

Ramirez was certain it had been a couple of kids trying to get some kind of reaction from us, and if so they had certainly succeeded. Williams tried very hard to be reassuring, telling us it was just a prank and now it was over, and as they were leaving Ramirez added that they would drive by a few times the rest of the night. But even with these soothing words still fresh, Rita sat in the kitchen with a cup of coffee for the rest of the night, unable to get back to sleep. For my part, I tossed and turned for more than three minutes before I drifted back to slumberland.

And as I flew down the long black mountain into sleep, the music started up again. And there was a great feeling of gladness and then heat on my face . . .

And somehow I was in the hallway, with Rita shaking me and calling my name. 'Dexter, wake up,' she said. 'Dexter.'

'What happened?' I said.

'You were sleepwalking,' she said. 'And singing. Singing in your sleep.'

And so rosy-fingered dawn found both of us sitting at the kitchen table, drinking coffee. When the alarm finally went off in the bedroom, she got up to turn it off and came back and looked at me. I looked back, but there did-n't seem to be anything to say, and then Cody and Astor came into the kitchen, and there was nothing more we could do except stumble through the morning routine and head for work, automatically pretending that everything was exactly the way it should be.

But of course it wasn't. Someone was trying to get into my head, and they were succeeding far too well. And now they were trying to get into my house, and I didn't even know who it was, or what they wanted. I had to assume that somehow it was all connected to Moloch, and the absence of my Presence.

The bottom line was that somebody was trying to do something to me, and they were getting closer and closer to doing it.

I found myself unwilling to consider the idea that a real live ancient god was trying to kill me. To begin with, they don't exist. And even if they did, why would one bother with me? Clearly some human being was using the whole Moloch thing as a costume in order to feel more powerful and important, and to make his victims believe he had special magical powers.

Like the ability to invade my sleep and make me hear music, for instance? A human predator couldn't do that. And it couldn't scare away the Dark Passenger, either.

The only possible answers were impossible. Maybe it was just the crippling fatigue, but I couldn't think of any others that weren't.

When I arrived at work that morning, I had no chance to think of anything better, because there was an immediate call to a double homicide in a quiet marijuana house in the Grove. Two teenagers had been tied up, cut up, and then shot several times each, just for good measure. And although I am certain that I should have considered this a terrible thing, I was actually very grateful for the opportunity to view dead bodies that were not cooked and beheaded. It made things seem normal, even peaceful, for just a little while. I sprayed my luminol hither and yon, almost happy to perform a task that made the hideous music recede for a little while.

But it also gave me time to ponder, and this I did. I saw scenes like this every day, and nine times out of ten the killers said things like 'I just snapped' or 'By the time I knew what I was doing it was too late.' All grand excuses, and it had seemed a bit amusing to me, since I always knew what I was doing, which was why I did it.

And at last a thought wandered in – I had found myself unable to do anything at all to Starzak without my Dark Passenger. This meant that my talent was in the Passenger, not in me by myself. Which could mean that all these others who 'snapped' were temporarily playing host to something similar, couldn't it?

Until now, mine had never left me; it was permanently at home with me, not wandering around in the streets hitchhiking with the first bad-tempered wretch that wandered by.

All right, put that aside for the time being. Let's just assume that some Passengers wander and some of them nest. Could this account for what Halpern had described as a dream? Could something go into him, make him kill two girls, and then take him home and tuck him into bed before leaving?

I didn't know. But I did know that if that idea held water, I was in a lot deeper than I had imagined.

By the time I got back to my office it was past time for lunch, and there was a call waiting from Rita to remind me that I had a 2:30 appointment with her minister. And by 'minister' I don't mean the kind with a position in the cabinet of a foreign government. As unlikely as it seems, I mean the kind of minister you will find in a church, if you are ever compelled to visit one for some reason. For my part, I have always assumed that if there is any kind of God at all He would never let something like me flourish. And if I am wrong, the altar might crack and fall if I went inside a church.

But my sensible avoidance of religious buildings was at an end now, since Rita wanted her very own minister to perform our wedding ceremony, and apparently he needed to check my human credentials before agreeing to the assignment. Of course, he hadn't done a very good job of it the first time, since Rita's first husband had been a crack addict who regularly beat her, and the reverend had somehow failed to detect that. And if the minister had missed something that obvious before, the odds of him doing better with me were not very good at all.

Still, Rita set great store by the man, so away we went to an ancient coral-rock church on an overgrown lot in the Grove, only half a mile from the homicide scene I had worked that morning. Rita had been confirmed there, she told me, and had known the minister for a very long time. Apparently that was important, and I supposed it should be, considering what I knew about several men of God who had come to my attention through my hobby. My former hobby, that is.

Reverend Gilles was waiting for us in his office – or is it called a cloister, or a retreat, or something like that? Rectory always sounded to me like a place where you would find a proctologist. Perhaps it was a sacristy – I admit that I am not up on my terminology here. My foster mother, Doris, did try to get me to church when I was young, but after a couple of regrettable incidents it became apparent that it wasn't going to stick, and Harry intervened.

The reverend's study was lined with books that had improbable titles offering no doubt very sound advice on dealing with things God would really prefer you to avoid. There were also a few that offered insight into a woman's soul, although it did not specify which woman, and information on how to make Christ work for you, which I hoped did not mean at minimum wage. There was even one on Christian chemistry, which seemed to me to be stretching the point, unless it gave a recipe for the old water-into-wine trick.

Much more interesting was a book with Gothic script on the binding. I turned my head to read the title; mere curiosity, but when I read it I felt a jolt go through me as if my esophagus had suddenly filled with ice.

Demonic Possession: Fact or Fancy? it said, and as I read the title I distinctly heard the far-off sound of a nickel dropping.

It would be very easy for an outside observer to shake his head and say, Yes, obviously, Dexter is a dull boy if he has never thought of that. But the truth is, I had not. Demon has so many negative connotations, doesn't it? And as long as the Presence was present, there seemed no need to define it in those arcane terms. It was only now that it was gone that I required some explanation. And why not this one? It was a bit old-fashioned, but its very hoariness seemed to argue that there might be something to it, some connection that went back to the nonsense with Solomon and Moloch and all the way up to what was happening to me today.

Was the Dark Passenger really a demon? And did the Passenger's absence mean it had been cast out? If so, by what? Something overwhelmingly good? I could not recall encountering anything like that in the last, oh, lifetime or so. Just the opposite, in fact.

But could something very very bad cast out a demon? I mean, what could be worse than a demon? Perhaps Moloch? Or could a demon cast itself out for some reason?

I tried to comfort myself with the thought that at least I had some good questions now, but I didn't feel terribly comforted, and my thoughts were interrupted when the door opened and the Right Reverend Gilles breezed in, beaming and muttering, 'Well, well.'

The reverend was about fifty and seemed well fed, so I suppose the tithing business was working. He came right to us and gave Rita a hug and a peck on the cheek, before turning to offer me a hearty masculine handshake.

'Well,' he said, smiling cautiously at me. 'So you're Dexter.'

'I suppose I am,' I said. 'I just couldn't help it.'

He nodded, almost as if I had made sense. 'Sit down, please, relax,' he said, and he moved around behind the desk and sat in a large swivel chair.

I took him at his word and leaned back in the red leather chair opposite his desk, but Rita perched nervously on the edge of her identical seat.

'Rita,' he said, and he smiled again. 'Well, well. So you're ready to try again, are you?'

'Yes, I – that's just – I mean, I think so,' Rita said, blushing furiously. 'I mean, yes.' She looked at me with a bright red face and said, 'Yes, I'm ready.'

'Good, good,' he said, and he switched his expression of fond concern over to me. 'And you, Dexter. I would really like to know a little bit about you.'

'Well, to begin with, I'm a murder suspect,' I said modestly.

'Dexter,' Rita said, and impossibly turned even redder.

'The police think you killed somebody?' Reverend Gilles asked.

'Oh, they don't all think that,' I said. 'Just my sister.'

'Dexter works in forensics,' Rita blurted out. 'His sister is a detective. He just – he was only kidding about the other part.'

Once again he nodded at me. 'A sense of humor is a big help in any relationship,' he said.

He paused for a moment, looked very thoughtful and even more sincere, and then said, 'How do you feel about Rita's children?'

'Oh, Cody and Astor *adore* Dexter,' Rita said, and she looked very happy that we were no longer talking about my status as a wanted man.

'But how does Dexter feel about *them*?' he insisted gently.

'I like them,' I said.

Reverend Gilles nodded and said, 'Good. Very good. Sometimes children can be a burden. Especially when they're not yours.'

'Cody and Astor are very good at being a burden,' I said. 'But I don't really mind.'

'They're going to need a lot of mentoring,' he said, 'after all they went through.'

'Oh, I mentor them,' I said, although I thought it was probably a good idea not to be too specific, so I just added, 'They're very eager to be mentored.'

'All right,' he said. 'So we'll see those kids here at Sunday school, right?' It seemed to me to be a bald-faced attempt to blackmail us into providing future recruits to fill his collection basket, but Rita nodded eagerly, so I went along with it. Besides, I was reasonably sure that whatever anyone might say, Cody and Astor would find their spiritual comfort somewhere else.

'Now, the two of you,' he said, leaning back in his chair and rubbing the back of one hand with the palm of the other. 'A relationship in today's world needs a strong foundation in faith,' he said, looking at me expectantly. 'Dexter? How about it?'

Well, there it was. You have to believe that sooner or later a minister will find a way to twist things around so they fall into his area. I don't know if it's worse to lie to a minister than to anyone else, but I did want to get this interview over quickly and painlessly, and could that possibly happen if I told the truth? Suppose I did and said something like, Yes, I have a great deal of faith, Reverend – in human greed and stupidity, and in the sweetness of sharp steel on a moonlit night. I have faith in the dark unseen, the cold chuckle from the shadows inside, the absolute clarity of the knife. Oh, yes, I have faith, Reverend, and beyond faith – I have certainty, because I have seen the bleak bottom line and I know it is real; it's where I live.

But really, that was hardly calculated to reassure the man, and I surely didn't need to worry about going to hell for telling a lie to a minister. If there actually is a hell, I already have a front-row seat. So I merely said, 'Faith is very important,' and he seemed to be happy with that.

'Great, okay,' he said, and he glanced covertly at his watch. 'Dexter, do you have any questions about our church?'

A fair question, perhaps, but it took me by surprise, since I had been thinking of this interview as my time for answering questions, not asking them. I was perfectly ready to be evasive for at least another hour – but really, what was there to ask about? Did they use grape juice or wine? Was the collection basket metal or wood? Was dancing a sin? I was just not prepared. And yet he seemed like he was truly interested in knowing. So I smiled reassuringly back at Reverend Gilles and said, 'Actually, I'd love to know what you think about demonic possession.'

'Dexter!' Rita gulped with a nervous smile. 'That's not – You can't really—'

Reverend Gilles raised a hand. 'It's all right, Rita,' he said. 'I think I know where Dexter's coming from.' He leaned back in the chair and nodded, favoring me with a pleasant and knowing smile. 'Been quite a while since you've been to church, Dexter?'

'Well, actually, it has,' I said.

'I think you'll find that the new church is quite a good fit for the modern world. The central truth of God's love doesn't change,' he said. 'But sometimes our understanding of it can.' And then he actually winked at me. 'I think we can agree that demons are for Halloween, not for Sunday service.'

Well, it was nice to have an answer, even if it wasn't the one I was looking for. I hadn't really expected Reverend Gilles to pull out a grimoire and cast a spell, but I admit it was a little disappointing. 'All right, then,' I said.

'Any other questions?' he asked me with a very satisfied smile. 'About our church, or anything about the ceremony?'

'Why, no,' I said. 'It seems very straightforward.'

'We like to think so,' he said. 'As long as we put Christ first, everything else falls into place.'

'Amen,' I said brightly. Rita gave me a bit of a look, but the reverend seemed to accept it.

'All right, then,' he said, and he stood up and held out his hand, 'June twenty-fourth it is.' I stood up, too, and shook his hand. 'But I expect to see you here before then,' he said. 'We have a great contemporary service at ten o'clock every Sunday.' He winked and gave my hand an extra-manly squeeze. 'Gets you home in time for the football game.'

'That's terrific,' I said, thinking how nice it is when a business anticipates the needs of its customers.

He dropped my hand and grabbed Rita, wrapping her up in a full embrace. 'Rita,' he said. 'I'm so happy for you.'

'Thank you,' Rita sobbed into his shoulder. She leaned against him for a moment longer and snuffled, and then stood upright again, rubbing her nose and looking at me. 'Thank you, Dexter,' she said. For what I don't know, but it's always nice to be included.

29

For the first time in quite a while I was actually anxious to get back to my cubicle. Not because I was pining for blood spatter – but because of the idea that had descended on me in Reverend Gilles's study. Demonic possession. It had a certain ring to it. I had never really felt possessed, although Rita was certainly staking her claim. But it was at least some kind of explanation with a degree of history attached, and I was very eager to pursue it.

First I checked my answering machine and e-mail: no messages except a routine departmental memo on cleaning up the coffee area. No abject apology from Debs, either. I made a few careful calls and found that she was out trying to round up Kurt Wagner, which was a relief, since it meant she wasn't following me.

Problem solved and conscience clear, I began looking into the question of demonic possession. Once again, good old King Solomon figured prominently. He had apparently been quite cozy with a number of demons, most of whom had improbable names with several z's in them. And he had ordered them about like indentured servants, forcing them to fetch and tote and build his great temple, which was a bit of a shock, since I had always heard that the temple was a good thing, and surely there must have been some kind of law in place about demon labor. I mean, if we get so upset about illegal immigrants picking the oranges, shouldn't all those God-fearing patriarchs have had some kind of ordinance against demons?

But there it was in black and white. King Solomon had consorted with them quite comfortably, as their boss. They didn't like being ordered around, of course, but they put up with it from him. And that raised the interesting thought that perhaps someone else was able to control them, and was trying to do so with the Dark Passenger, who had therefore fled from involuntary servitude. I paused and thought about that.

The biggest problem with that theory was that it did not fit in with the overwhelming sense of mortal danger that had flooded through me from the very first, even when the Passenger had still been on board. I can understand reluctance to do unwanted work as easily as the next guy, but that had nothing to do with the lethal dread that this had raised in me.

Did that mean the Passenger was not a demon? Did it mean that what was happening to me was mere psychosis? A totally imagined paranoid fantasy of pursuing bloodlust and approaching horror?

And yet, every culture in the world throughout history seemed to believe that there was something to the whole idea of possession. I just couldn't get it to connect in any way to my problem. I felt like I was onto something, but no great thought emerged.

Suddenly it was five thirty, and I was more than usually anxious to flee from the office and head for the dubious sanctuary of home.

The next afternoon I was in my cubicle, typing up a report on a very dull multiple killing. Even Miami gets ordinary murders, and this was one of them – or three and a half of them, to be precise, since there were three bodies in the morgue and one more in intensive care at Jackson Memorial. It was a simple drive-by shooting in one of the few areas of the city with low property values. There was really no point in spending a great deal of my time on it, since there were plenty of witnesses and they all agreed that someone named 'Motherfucker' had done the deed.

Still, forms must be observed, and I had spent half a day on the scene making sure that no one had jumped out of a doorway and hacked the victims with a hedge clipper while they were being shot from a passing car. I was trying to think of an interesting way to say that the blood spatter was consistent with gunfire from a moving source, but the boredom of it all was making my eyes cross, and as I stared vacantly at the screen, I felt a ringing rise in my ears and change to the clang of gongs and the night music came again, and the plain white of the word-processing page seemed suddenly to wash over with awful wet blood and spill out across me, flood the office, and fill the entire visible world. I jumped out of my chair and blinked a few times until it went away, but it left me shaking and wondering what had just happened.

It was starting to come at me in the full light of day, even sitting at my desk at police headquarters, and I did not like that at all. Either it was getting stronger and closer, or I was going right off the deep end and into complete madness. Schizophrenics heard voices – did they ever hear music, too? And did the Dark Passenger qualify as a voice? Had I been completely insane all this time and was just now coming to some kind of crazy final episode in the artificial sanity of Dubious Dexter?

I didn't think that was possible. Harry had gotten me squared away, made sure that I fit in just right – Harry would have known if I was crazy, and he had told me I was not. Harry was never wrong. So it was settled and I was fine, just fine, thank you.

So why did I hear that music? Why was my hand shaking? And why did I need to cling to a ghost to keep from sitting on the floor and flipping my lips with an index finger?

Clearly no one else in the building heard anything – it was just me.

Otherwise the halls would be filled with people either dancing or screaming. No, fear had crawled into my life, slinking after me faster than I could run, filling the huge empty space inside me where the Passenger had once snuggled down.

I had nothing to go on; I needed some outside information if I hoped to understand this. Plenty of sources believed that demons were real – Miami was filled with people who worked hard to keep them away every day of their lives. And even though the babalao had said he wanted nothing to do with this whole thing, and had walked away from it as rapidly as he could, he had seemed to know what it was. I was fairly sure that Santeria allowed for possession. But never mind: Miami is a wonderful and diverse city, and I would certainly find some other place to ask the question and get an entirely different answer – perhaps even the one I was looking for. I left my cubicle and headed for the parking lot.

The Tree of Life was on the edge of Liberty City, an area of Miami that is not a good place for tourists from Iowa to visit late at night. This particular corner had been taken over by Haitian immigrants, and many of the buildings had been painted in several bright colors, as if there was not enough of one color to go around. On some of the buildings there were murals depicting Haitian country life. Roosters seemed to be prominent, and goats.

Painted on the outside wall of the Tree of Life there was a large tree, appropriately enough, and under it was an elongated image of two men pounding on some tall drums. I parked right in front of the shop and went in through a screen door that rang a small bell and then banged behind me. In the back, behind a curtain of hanging beads, a woman's voice called out something in Creole, and I stood by the glass counter and waited. The store was lined with shelves that contained numerous jars filled with mysterious things, liquid, solid, and uncertain. One or two of them seemed to be holding things that might once have been alive.

After a moment, a woman pushed through the beads and came into the front of the store. She appeared to be about forty and reed thin, with high cheekbones and a complexion like sun-bleached mahogany. She wore a flowing red-and-yellow dress, and her head was wrapped in a matching turban. 'Ah,' she said with a thick Creole accent. She looked me over with a very doubtful expression and shook her head slightly. 'How I can help you, sir?'

'Ah, well,' I said, and I more or less stumbled to a halt. How, after all, did one begin? I couldn't really say that I thought I used to be possessed and wanted to get the demon back – the poor woman might throw chicken blood at me.

'Sir?' she prompted impatiently.

'I was wondering,' I said, which was true enough, 'do you have any books on possession by demons? Er – in English?'

She pursed her lips with great disapproval and shook her head vigorously. 'It is not the demons,' she said. 'Why do you ask this – are you a reporter?'

'No,' I said. 'I'm just, um, interested. Curious.'

'Curious about the *voudoun*?' she said.

'Just the possession part,' I said.

'Huh,' she said, and if possible her disapproval grew even more. 'Why?'

Someone very clever must already have said that when all else fails, try the truth. It sounded so good that I was sure I was not the first to think of it, and it seemed like the only thing I had left. I gave it a shot.

'I think,' I said, 'I mean, I'm not sure. I think I may have been possessed. A while ago.'

'Ha,' she said. She looked at me long and hard, and then shrugged. 'May be,' she said at last. 'Why do you say so?'

'I just, um . . . I had the feeling, you know. That something else was, ah. Inside me? Watching?'

She spat on the floor, a very strange gesture from such an elegant woman, and shook her head. 'All you blancs,' she said. 'You steal us and bring us here, take everythin' from us. And then when we make somethin' from the nothin' you give us, now you want to be part of that, too. Ha.' She shook her finger at me, for all the world like a second-grade teacher with a bad student. 'You listen, blanc. If the spirit enters you, you would know. This is not somethin' like in a movie. It is a very great blessing, and,' she said with a mean smirk, 'it does not happen to the blancs.'

'Well, actually,' I said.

'Non,' she said. 'Unless you are willing, unless you ask for the blessing, it does not come.'

'But I am willing,' I said.

'Ha,' she said. 'It never come to you. You waste my time.' And she turned around and walked through the bead curtains to the back of the store.

I saw no point in waiting around for her to have a change of heart. It didn't seem likely to happen – and it didn't seem likely that voodoo had any answers about the Dark Passenger. She had said it only comes when called, and it was a blessing. At least that was a different answer, although I did not remember ever calling the Dark Passenger to come in – it was just always there. But to be absolutely sure, I paused at the curb outside the store and closed my eyes. *Please come back in*, I said.

Nothing happened. I got in my car and went back to work.

What an interesting choice, the Watcher thought. Voodoo. There was a certain logic to the idea, of course, he could not deny that. But what was really interesting was what it showed about the other. *He was moving in the right direction – and he was very close.*

And when his next little clue turned up, the other would be that much closer. The boy had been so panicky, he had almost wriggled away. But he had not; he had been very helpful and he was now on his way to his dark reward.

Just like the other was.

30

I had barely settled back into my chair when Deborah came into my little cubicle and sat in the folding chair across from my desk.

'Kurt Wagner is missing,' she said.

I waited for more, but nothing came, so I just nodded. 'I accept your apology,' I said.

'Nobody's seen him since Saturday afternoon,' she said. 'His roommate says he came in acting all freaked out, but wouldn't say anything. He just changed his shoes, and left, and that's it.' She hesitated, and then added, 'He left his backpack.'

I admit I perked up a little at that. 'What was in it?' I asked.

'Traces of blood,' she said, as if she was admitting she had taken the last cookie. 'It matches Tammy Connor's.'

'Well then,' I said. It didn't seem right to say anything about the fact that she'd had somebody else do the blood work. 'That's a pretty good clue.'

'Yeah,' she said. 'It's him. It has to be him. So he did Tammy, took the head in his backpack and did Manny Borque.'

'It does look like that,' I said. 'That's a shame – I was just getting used to the idea that I was guilty.'

'It makes no fucking sense,' Deborah complained. 'The kid's a good student, on the swimming team, good family – all of that.'

'He was such a nice guy,' I said. 'I can't believe he did all those horrible things.'

'All right,' Deborah said. 'I know it, goddamn it. Total cliché. But what the hell – the guy kills his own girlfriend, sure. Maybe even her roommate, because she saw it. But why everybody else? And all that crap with burning them, and the bulls' heads, what is it, Mollusk?'

'Moloch,' I said. 'Mollusk is a clam.'

'Whatever,' she said. 'But it makes no sense, Dex. I mean . . .' She looked away, and for a moment I thought she was going to apologize after all. But I was wrong. 'If it does make sense,' she said, 'it's *your* kind of sense. The kind of thing you know about.' She looked back at me, but she still seemed to be embarrassed. 'That's, you know – I mean, is it, um – did it come back? Your, uh . . .'

'No,' I said. 'It didn't come back.'

'Well,' she said, 'shit.'

'Did you put out a BOLO on Kurt Wagner?' I asked.

'I know how to do my job, Dex,' she said. 'If he's in the Miami-Dade area, we'll get him, and FDLE has it, too. If he's in Florida, somebody'll find him.'

'And if he's not in Florida?'

She looked hard at me, and I saw the beginnings of the way Harry had looked before he got sick, after so many years as a cop: tired, and getting used to the idea of routine defeat. 'Then he'll probably get away with it,' she said. 'And I'll have to arrest you to save my job.'

'Well, then,' I said, trying hard for cheerfulness in the face of overwhelming grim grayness, 'let's hope he drives a very recognizable car.'

She snorted. 'It's a red Geo, one of those mini-Jeep things.'

I closed my eyes. It was a very odd sensation, but I felt all the blood in my body suddenly relocating to my feet. 'Did you say red?' I heard myself ask in a remarkably calm voice.

There was no answer, and I opened my eyes. Deborah was staring at me with a look of suspicion so strong I could almost touch it.

'What the hell was that,' she demanded. 'One of your voices?'

'A red Geo followed me home the other night,' I said. 'And then somebody tried to break into my house.'

'Goddamn it,' she snarled at me, 'when the fuck were you going to tell me all this?'

'Just as soon as you decided you were speaking to me again,' I said.

Deborah turned a very gratifying shade of crimson and looked down at her shoes. 'I was busy,' she said, not very convincingly.

'So was Kurt Wagner,' I said.

'All right, Jesus,' she said, and I knew that was all the apology I would ever get. 'Yeah, it's red. But shit,' she said, still looking down, 'I think that old man was right. The bad guys are winning.'

I didn't like seeing my sister this depressed. I felt that some cheery remark was called for, something that would lift the gloom and bring a song back to her heart, but alas, I came up empty. 'Well,' I said at last, 'if the bad guys really are winning, at least there's plenty of work for you.'

She looked up at last, but not with anything resembling a smile. 'Yeah,' she said. 'Some guy in Kendall shot his wife and two kids last night. I get to go work on that.' She stood up, straightening slowly into something that at least resembled her normal posture. 'Hooray for our side,' she said, and walked out of my office.

From the very beginning it was an ideal partnership. The new things had self-awareness, and that made manipulating them much easier – and much more rewarding for IT. They killed one another much more readily, too, and IT did not have to wait long at all for a new host – nor to try again to reproduce. IT eagerly drove IT's host to a killing, and IT waited, longing to feel the strange and wonderful swelling.

But when the feeling came, it simply stirred slowly, tickled IT with a tendril of sensation, and then vanished without blossoming and producing offspring.

IT was puzzled. Why didn't reproduction work this time? There had to be a reason, and IT was orderly and efficient in IT's search for the answer. Over many years, as the new things changed and grew, IT experimented. And gradually IT found the conditions that made reproduction work. It took quite a few kills before IT was satisfied that IT had found the answer, but each time IT duplicated the final formula, a new awareness came into being and fled into the world in pain and terror, and IT was satisfied.

The thing worked best when the hosts were off-balance a bit, either from the drinks they had begun to brew or from some kind of trance state. The victim had to know what was coming, and if there was an audience of some kind, their emotions fed into the experience and made it even more powerful.

Then there was fire – fire was a very good way to kill the victims. It seemed to release their essence all at once in a great shrieking jolt of spectacular energy.

And finally, the whole thing worked better with the young ones. The emotions all around were so much stronger, especially in the parents. It was wonderful beyond anything else IT could imagine.

Fire, trance, young victims. A simple formula.

IT began to push the new hosts to create a way to establish these conditions permanently. And the hosts were surprisingly willing to go along with IT.

31

When I was very young I once saw a variety act on TV. A man put a bunch of plates on the end of a series of supple rods, and kept them up in the air by whipping the rods around to spin the plates. And if he slowed down or turned his back, even for a moment, one of the plates would wobble and then crash to the ground, followed by all the others in series.

That's a terrific metaphor for life, isn't it? We're all trying to keep our plates spinning in the air, and once you get them up there you can't take your eyes off them and you have to keep chugging along without rest. Except that in life, somebody keeps adding more plates, hiding the rods, and changing the law of gravity when you're not looking. And so every time you think you have all your plates spinning nicely, suddenly you hear a hideous clattering crash behind you and a whole row of plates you didn't even know you had begins to hit the ground.

Here I had stupidly assumed that the tragic death of Manny Borque had given me one less plate to worry about, since I could now proceed to cater the wedding as it should be done, with $65 worth of cold cuts and a cooler full of soda. I could concentrate on the very real and important problem of putting me back together again. And so thinking all was quiet on the home front, I turned my back for just a moment and was rewarded with a spectacular crash behind me.

The metaphorical plate in question shattered when I came into Rita's house after work. It was so quiet that I assumed no one was home, but a quick glance inside showed something far more disturbing. Cody and Astor sat motionless on the couch, and Rita was standing behind them with a look on her face that could easily turn fresh milk into yogurt.

'Dexter,' she said, and the tromp of doom was in her voice, 'we need to talk.'

'Of course,' I said, and as I reeled from her expression, even the mere thought of a lighthearted response shriveled into dust and blew away in the icy air.

'These children,' Rita said. Apparently that was the entire thought, because she just glared and said no more.

But of course, I knew which children she meant, so I nodded encouragingly. 'Yes,' I said.

'Ooh,' she said.

Well, if it was taking Rita this long to form a complete sentence, it was easy to see why the house had been so quiet when I walked in. Clearly the lost art of conversation was going to need a little boost from Diplomatic Dexter if we were ever going to get more than seven words out in time for dinner. So I plunged straight in with my well-known courage. 'Rita,' I said, 'is there some kind of problem?'

'Ooh,' she said again, which was not encouraging.

Well really, there's only so much you can do with monosyllables, even if you are a gifted conversationalist like me. Since there was clearly no help coming from Rita, I looked at Cody and Astor, who had not moved since I came in. 'All right,' I said. 'Can you two tell me what's wrong with your mother?'

They exchanged one of their famous looks, and then turned back to me. 'We didn't mean to,' Astor said. 'It was an accident.'

It wasn't much, but at least it was a complete sentence. 'I'm very glad to hear it,' I said. '*What* was an accident?'

'We got caught,' Cody said, and Astor poked him with an elbow.

'We didn't *mean to*,' she repeated with emphasis, and Cody turned to look at her before he remembered what they had agreed on; she glared at him and he blinked once before slowly nodding his head at me.

'Accident,' he said.

It was nice to see that the party line was firmly in place behind a united front, but I was still no closer to knowing what we were talking about, and we had been talking about it, more or less, for several minutes – time being a large factor, since the dinner hour was approaching and Dexter does require regular feeding.

'That's all they'll say about it,' Rita said. 'And it is nowhere near enough. I don't see *how* you could possibly tie up the Villegas' cat by accident.'

'It didn't die,' Astor said in the tiniest voice I had ever heard her use.

'And what were the hedge clippers for?' Rita demanded.

'We didn't use them,' Astor said.

'But you were going to, weren't you?' Rita said.

Two small heads swiveled to face me, and a moment later, Rita's did, too.

I am sure it was completely unintentional, but a picture was beginning to emerge of what had happened, and it was not a peaceful still life. Clearly the youngsters had been attempting an independent study without me. And even worse, I could tell that somehow it had become my problem; the children expected me to bail them out, and Rita was clearly prepared to lock and load and open fire on me. Of course it was unfair; all I had done so far was come home from work. But as I have noticed on more than one occasion, life itself is unfair, and there is no complaint department, so we might as well accept things the way they happen, clean up the mess, and move on.

Which is what I attempted to do, however futile I suspected it would be. 'I'm sure there's a very good explanation,' I said, and Astor brightened immediately and began to nod vigorously.

'It was an *accident*,' she insisted happily.

'Nobody ties up a cat, tapes it to a workbench, and stands over it with hedge clippers by *accident*!' Rita said.

To be honest, things were getting a little complicated. On the one hand, I was very pleased to get such a clear picture at last of what the problem was. But on the other hand, we seemed to have strayed into an area that could be somewhat awkward to explain, and I could not help feeling that Rita might be a little bit better off if she remained ignorant of these matters.

I thought I had been clear with Astor and Cody that they were not to fly solo until I had explained their wings to them. But they had obviously chosen not to understand and, even though they were suffering some very gratifying consequences for their actions, it was still up to me to get them out of it. Unless they could be made to understand that they absolutely must not repeat this – and must not stray from the Harry Path as I put their feet upon it – I was happy to let them twist in the wind indefinitely.

'Do you know that what you did is wrong?' I asked them. They nodded in unison.

'Do you know *why* it is wrong?' I said.

Astor looked very uncertain, glanced at Cody, and then blurted out, 'Because we got caught!'

'There now, you see?' said Rita, and a hysterical edge was creeping into her voice.

'Astor,' I said, looking at her very carefully and not really winking, 'this is not the time to be funny.'

'I'm glad somebody thinks this is funny,' Rita said. 'But I don't happen to think so.'

'Rita,' I said, with all the soothing calm I could muster, and then, using the smooth cunning I had developed in my years as an apparently human adult, I added, 'I think this might be one of those times that Reverend Gilles was talking about, where I need to mentor.'

'Dexter, these two have just – I don't have any idea – and you—!' she said, and even though she was close to tears, I was happy to see that at least her old speech patterns were returning. Just as happily, a scene from an old movie popped into my head in the nick of time, and I knew exactly what a real human being was supposed to do.

I walked over to Rita and, with my very best serious face, I put a hand on her shoulder.

'Rita,' I said, and I was very proud of how grave and manly my voice sounded, 'you are too close to this, and you're letting your emotions cloud your judgment. These two need some firm perspective, and I can give it to them. After all,' I said as the line came to me, and I was pleased to see that I hadn't lost a step, 'I have to be their father now.'

I should have guessed that this would be the remark that pushed Rita off the dock and into the lake of tears; and it was, because immediately after I said it, her lips began to tremble, her face lost all its anger, and a rivulet began to stream down each cheek.

'All right,' she sobbed, 'please, I – just talk to them.' She snuffled loudly and hurried from the room.

I let Rita have her dramatic exit and gave it a moment to sink in before I walked back around to the front of the couch and stared down at my two miscreants. 'Well,' I said. 'What happened to We understand, We promise, We'll wait?'

'You're taking too long,' said Astor. 'We haven't done anything except the once, and besides, you're not always right and we think we shouldn't have to wait anymore.'

'I'm ready,' Cody said.

'Really,' I said. 'Then I guess your mother is the greatest detective in the world, because you're ready and she caught you anyway.'

'Dex-terrrr,' Astor whined.

'No, Astor, you quit talking and just listen to me for a minute.' I stared at her with my most serious face, and for a moment I thought she was going to say something else but then a miracle took place right there in our living room. Astor changed her mind and closed her mouth.

'All right,' I said. 'I have said from the very beginning that you have to do it my way. You don't have to believe I'm always right,' and Astor made a sound, but didn't say anything. 'But you have to do what I say. Or I will not help you, and you will end up in jail. There is no other way. Okay?'

It is quite possible that they didn't know what to do with this new tone of voice and new role. I was no longer Playtime Dexter, but something very different, Dexter of Dark Discipline, which they had never seen before. They looked at each other uncertainly so I pushed a little more.

'You got caught,' I said. 'What happens when you get caught?'

'Time out?' Cody said uncertainly.

'Uh-huh,' I said. 'And if you're thirty years old?'

For possibly the first time in her life, Astor had no answer, and Cody had already used up his two-word quota for the time being. They looked at each other, and then they looked at their feet.

'My sister, Sergeant Deborah, and I spend all day catching people who do this kind of stuff,' I said. 'And when we catch them, they go to prison.' I smiled at Astor. 'Time out for grown-ups. But a lot worse. You sit in a little room the size of your bathroom, locked in, all day and all night. You pee in a hole in the floor. You eat moldy garbage, and there are rats and lots of cockroaches.'

'We know what prison is, Dexter,' she said.

'Really? Then why are you in such a hurry to get there?' I said. 'And do you know what Old Sparky is?'

Astor looked at her feet again; Cody hadn't looked up yet.

'Old Sparky is the electric chair. If they catch you, they strap you into Old Sparky, put some wires on your head, and fry you up like bacon. Does that sound like fun?'

They shook their heads, no.

'So the very first lesson is not to get caught,' I said. 'Remember the piranhas?' They nodded. 'They look ferocious, so people know they're dangerous.'

'But Dexter, we don't look ferocious,' Astor said.

'No, you don't,' I said. 'And you don't want to. We are supposed to be people, not piranhas. But the idea is the same, to look like something you are not. Because when something bad happens, that's who everyone will look for first – the ferocious people. You need to look like sweet, lovable, normal children.'

'Can I wear makeup?' Astor asked.

'When you're older,' I said.

'You say that about *everything*!' she said.

'And I mean it about everything,' I said. 'You got caught this time because you went off on your own and didn't know what you were doing. You didn't know what you were doing because you didn't listen to me.'

I decided the torture had gone on long enough and I sat down on the couch in between them. 'No more doing anything without me, okay? And when you promise this time, you better mean it.'

They both looked slowly up at me and then nodded. 'We promise,' Astor said softly, and Cody, even softer, echoed, 'Promise.'

'Well then,' I said. I took their hands and we shook solemnly.

'Good,' I said. 'Now let's go apologize to your mom.' They both jumped up, radiating relief that the hideous ordeal was over, and I followed them out of the room, closer to feeling self-satisfied than I could remember feeling before.

Maybe there was something to this whole fatherhood thing after all.

32

Sun Tzu, a very smart man, in spite of the fact that he has been dead for so long, wrote a book called *The Art of War*, and one of the many clever observations he made in the book was that every time something awful happens, there's a way to turn it to your advantage, if you just look at things properly. This is not New Age California Pollyanna thinking, insisting that if life gives you lemons you can always make Key Lime pie. It is, rather, very practical advice that comes in handy a lot more than you might think.

At the moment, for instance, my problem was how to continue training Cody and Astor in the Harry Way now that they had been busted by their mother. And in looking for a solution I remembered good old Sun Tzu and tried to imagine what he might have done. Of course, he had been a general, so he probably would have attacked the left flank with cavalry or something, but surely the principles were the same.

So as I led Cody and Astor to their weeping mother I was beating the bushes in the dark forest of Dexter's brain for some small partridge of an idea that the old Chinese general might approve of. And just as the three of us trickled to a halt in front of sniffling Rita, the idea popped out, and I grabbed it.

'Rita,' I said quietly, 'I think I can stop this before it gets out of hand.'

'You heard what – This is already out of hand,' she said, and she paused for a large snuffle.

'I have an idea,' I said. 'I want you to bring them down to me at work tomorrow, right after school.'

'But that isn't – I mean, didn't it all start because—'

'Did you ever see a TV show called *Scared Straight*?' I said.

She stared at me for a moment, snuffled again, and looked at the two kids.

And that is why, at three thirty the next afternoon, Cody and Astor were taking turns peering into a microscope in the forensics lab. 'That's a *hair*?' Astor demanded.

'That's right,' I said.

'It looks *gross*!'

'Most of the human body is gross, especially if you look at it under a microscope,' I told her. 'Look at the one next to it.'

There was a studious pause, broken only once when Cody yanked on her arm, and she pushed him away and said, 'Stop it, Cody.'

'What do you notice?' I asked.

'They don't look the same,' she said.

'They're not,' I said. 'The first one is yours. The other one is mine.'

She continued to look for a moment, then straightened up from the eyepiece. 'You can tell,' she said. 'They're different.'

'It gets better,' I told her. 'Cody, give me your shoe.'

Cody very obligingly sat on the floor and pried off his left sneaker. I took it from him and held out a hand. 'Come with me,' I said. I helped him to his feet and he followed me, hopping one-footed to the closest countertop. I lifted him onto a stool and held up the shoe so he could see the bottom. 'Your shoe,' I said. 'Clean or dirty?'

He peered at it carefully. 'Clean,' he said.

'So you would think,' I said. 'Watch this.' I took a small wire brush to the tread of his shoe, carefully scraping out the nearly invisible gunk from between the ridges of the tread into a petri dish. I lifted a small sample of it onto a glass slide and took it back over to the microscope. Astor immediately crowded in to look, but Cody hopped over quickly. 'My turn,' he said. 'My shoe.' She looked at me and I nodded.

'It's his shoe,' I said. 'You can see right after.' She apparently accepted the justice of that, as she stepped back and let Cody climb onto the stool. I looked into the eyepiece to focus it, and saw that the slide was everything I could hope for. 'Aha,' I said, and stepped back. 'Tell me what you see, young Jedi.'

Cody frowned into the microscope for several minutes, until Astor's jiggling dance of impatience became so distracting that we both looked at her. 'That's long enough,' she said. 'It's my turn.'

'In a minute,' I said, and I turned back to Cody. 'Tell me what you saw.'

He shook his head. 'Junk,' he said.

'Okay,' I said. 'Now I'll tell you.' I looked into the eyepiece again and said, 'First off, animal hair, probably feline.'

'That means cat,' Astor said.

'Then there's some soil with a high nitrogen content – probably potting soil, like you'd use for houseplants.' I spoke to him without looking up. 'Where did you take the cat? The garage? Where your mom works on her plants?'

'Yes,' he said.

'Uh-huh. I thought so.' I looked back into the microscope. 'Oh – look there. That's a synthetic fiber, from somebody's carpet. It's blue.' I looked at Cody and raised an eyebrow. 'What color is the carpet in your room, Cody?'

His eyes were wide-open round as he said, 'Blue.'

'Yup. If I wanted to get fancy I'd compare this to a piece I took from your room. Then you would be cooked. I could prove that it was you with the cat.'

I looked back into the eyepiece again. 'My goodness, somebody had pizza recently – oh, and there's a small chunk of popcorn, too. Remember the movie last week?'

'Dexter, I wanna see,' Astor whined. 'It's my turn.'

'All right,' I said, and I set her on a stool next to Cody's so she could peer into the microscope.

'I don't see popcorn,' she said immediately.

'That round, brownish thing up in the corner,' I said. She was quiet for a minute, and then looked up at me.

'You can't really tell all that,' she said. 'Not just looking in the microscope.'

I am happy to admit that I was showing off, but after all, that's what this whole episode was about, so I was prepared. I grabbed a three-ring notebook I had prepared and laid it open on the counter. 'I can, too,' I said. 'And a whole lot more. Look.' I turned to a page that had photos of several different animal hairs, carefully selected to show the greatest variety. 'Here's the cat hair,' I said. 'Completely different from goat, see?' I flipped the page. 'And carpet fibers. Nothing like these from a shirt and this one from a washcloth.'

The two of them crowded together and stared at the book, flipping through the ten or so pages I had put together to show them that, yes indeed, I really can tell all that. It was carefully arranged to make forensics look just a tiny bit more all-seeing and all-powerful than the Wizard of Oz, of course. And to be fair, we really can do most of what I showed them. It never actually seems to do much good in catching any bad guys, but why should I tell them that and spoil a magical afternoon?

'Look back in the microscope,' I told them after a few minutes. 'See what else you can find.' They did so, very eagerly, and seemed quite happy at it for a while.

When they finally looked up at me I gave them a cheerful smile and said, 'All this from a clean shoe.' I closed the book and watched the two of them think about this. 'And that's just using the microscope,' I said, nodding around the room at the many gleaming machines. 'Think what we can figure out if we use all the fancy stuff.'

'Yeah, but we could go barefoot,' Astor said.

I nodded as if what she had said made sense. 'Yes, you could,' I said. 'And then I could do something like this – give me your hand.'

Astor eyed me for a few seconds as if she was afraid I would cut her arm off, but then she held it out slowly. I held it and, using a fingernail clipper from my pocket, I scraped under her fingernails. 'Wait until you see what you have here,' I said.

'But I washed my hands,' Astor said.

'Doesn't matter,' I told her. I put the small specks of stuff onto another glass slide and fixed it to the microscope. 'Now then,' I said.

CLUMP.

It really is a bit melodramatic to say that we all froze, but there it is – we did. They both looked up at me and I looked back at them and we all forgot to breathe.

CLUMP.

The sound was getting closer and it was very hard to remember that we were in police headquarters and perfectly safe.

'Dexter,' Astor said in a slightly quavery voice.

'We are in police headquarters,' I said. 'We're perfectly safe.'

CLUMP.

It stopped, very close. The hair went up on the back of my neck and I turned toward the door as it swung slowly open.

Sergeant Doakes. He stood there in the doorway, glaring, which seemed to have become his permanent expression. 'You,' he said, and the sound was nearly as unsettling as his appearance as it rolled out of his tongueless mouth.

'Why yes, it is me,' I said. 'Good of you to remember.'

He clumped one more step into the room and Astor scrambled off her stool and scurried to the windows, as far away from the door as she could get. Doakes paused and looked at her. Then his eyes swung back to Cody, who slid off his stool and stood there unblinking, facing Doakes.

Doakes stared at Cody, Cody stared back, and Doakes made what I can only call a Darth Vader intake of breath. Then he swung his head back to me and clumped one rapid step closer, nearly losing his balance. 'You,' he said again, hissing it this time. 'Kigs!'

'Kigs?' I said, and I really was puzzled and not trying to provoke him. I mean, if he insisted on stomping around and frightening children, the least he could do is carry a notepad and pencil to communicate with.

Apparently that thoughtful gesture was beyond him, though. Instead he gave another Darth Vader breath and slowly pointed his steel claw at Cody. 'Kigs,' he said again, his lips drawn back in a snarl.

'He means me,' Cody said. I turned to him, surprised to hear him speak with Doakes right there, like a nightmare come to life. But of course, Cody didn't have nightmares. He simply looked at Doakes.

'What about you, Cody?' I asked.

'He saw my shadow,' Cody said.

Sergeant Doakes took another wobbly step toward me. His right claw snapped, as if it had decided on its own to attack me. 'You. Goo. Gik.'

It was becoming apparent that he had something on his mind, but it was even clearer that he ought to stick with the silent glaring, since it was nearly impossible to understand the gooey syllables that came from his damaged mouth.

'Wuk. You. Goo,' he hissed, and it was such a clear condemnation of all that was Dexter, I at last understood that he was accusing me of something.

'What do you mean?' I said. 'I didn't do anything.'

'Goy,' he said, pointing again at Cody.

'Why, yes,' I said. 'Methodist, actually.' I admit that I deliberately misunderstood him: he was saying 'boy' and it came out 'goy' because he had no tongue, but really, one can only take so much. It should have been painfully clear to Doakes that his attempts at vocal communication were having very limited success, and yet he insisted on trying. Didn't the man have any sense of decorum at all?

Happily for all of us, we were interrupted by a clatter in the hallway and Deborah rushed into the room. 'Dexter,' she said. She paused as she took in the wild tableau of Doakes with claw upraised against me, Astor cringing against the window, and Cody lifting a scalpel off the bench to use against Doakes. 'What the hell,' Deborah said. 'Doakes?'

He very slowly let his arm drop, but he did not take his eyes off me.

'I've been looking for you, Dexter. Where were you?'

I was grateful enough for her timely entry that I did not point out how foolish her question was. 'Why, I was right here, educating the children,' I said. 'Where were you?'

'On my way to the Dinner Key,' she said. 'They found Kurt Wagner's body.'

33

Deborah hurled us through traffic at Evel Knievel-over-the-canyon speeds. I tried to think of a polite way to point out that we were going to see a dead body that would probably not escape, so could she please slow down, but I could not come up with any phrase that would not cause her to take her hands off the wheel and put them around my neck.

Cody and Astor were too young to realize that they were in mortal danger, and they seemed to be enjoying themselves thoroughly in the backseat, even getting into the spirit of things by happily returning the greetings of the other motorists by raising their own middle fingers in unison each time we cut off somebody.

There was a three-car pileup on U.S. 1 at LeJeune which slowed traffic for a few moments and we were forced to cut our pace to a crawl. Since I no longer had to spend all my breath suppressing screams of terror, I tried to find out from Deborah exactly what we were racing to see.

'How was he killed?' I asked her.

'Just like the others,' she said. 'Burned. And there's no head on the body.'

'You're sure this is Kurt Wagner?' I asked her.

'Can I prove it? Not yet,' she said. 'Am I sure? Shit yes.'

'Why?'

'They found his car nearby,' she said.

I was quite sure that normally I would understand exactly why somebody seemed to have a fetish for the heads, and know where to find them and why. But of course, now that I was all alone on the inside there was no more normal.

'This doesn't make any sense, you know,' I said.

Deborah snarled and hammered the heel of her hand on the steering wheel. 'Tell me about it,' she said.

'Kurt must have done the other victims,' I said.

'So who killed him? His scoutmaster?' she said, leaning on the horn and pulling around the traffic snarl into the oncoming lane. She swerved toward a bus, stomped on the gas, and wove through traffic for fifty yards until we were past the pileup. I concentrated on remembering to breathe and reflecting that we were all certain to die someday anyway, so in the big picture what did it really matter if Deborah killed us? It was not terribly comforting, but it did keep me from screaming and diving out the car window until Deborah pulled back into the correct lane on the far side of U.S. 1.

'That was fun,' said Astor. 'Can we do that again?'

Cody nodded enthusiastically.

'And we could put on the siren next time,' Astor said. 'How come you don't use the siren, Sergeant Debbie?'

'Don't call me Debbie,' Deborah snapped. 'I just don't like the siren.'

'Why not?' Astor insisted.

Deborah blew out a huge breath and glanced at me out of the corner of her eye. 'It's a fair question,' I said.

'It makes too much noise,' Deborah said. 'Now let me drive, okay?'

'All right,' Astor said, but she didn't sound convinced.

We drove in silence all the way to Grand Avenue, and I tried to think about it by myself – clearly enough to come up with anything that might help. I didn't, but I did think of one thing worth mentioning.

'What if Kurt's murder is just a coincidence?' I said.

'Even you can't really believe that,' she said.

'But if he was on the run,' I said, 'maybe he tried to get a fake ID from the wrong people, or get smuggled out of the country. There are plenty of bad guys he could run into under the circumstances.'

It didn't really sound likely, even to me, but Deborah thought about it for a few seconds anyway, chewing on her lower lip and absentmindedly blasting the horn as she pulled around a courtesy van from one of the hotels.

'No,' she said at last. 'He was cooked, Dexter. Like the first two. No way they could copy that.'

Once again I was aware of a small stirring in the bleak emptiness inside, the area once inhabited by the Dark Passenger. I closed my eyes and tried to find some shred of my once-constant companion, but there was nothing. I opened my eyes in time to see Deborah accelerate around a bright red Ferrari.

'People read the newspapers,' I said. 'There are always copycat killings.'

She thought some more, and then shook her head. 'No,' she said at last. 'I don't believe in coincidence. Not with something like this. Cooked and headless both, and it's a coincidence? No way.'

Hope always dies hard, but even so I had to admit that she was probably right. Beheading and burning were not really standard procedures for the normal, blue-collar killer, and most people would be far more likely simply to clonk you on the head, tie an anchor to your feet, and fling you into the bay.

So in all likelihood, we were on our way to see the body of somebody we were sure was a killer, and he had been killed the same way as his own victims. If I had been my cheerful old self, I would certainly have enjoyed the delicious irony, but in my present condition it seemed like just another annoying affront to an orderly existence.

But Deborah gave me very little time to reflect and become grumpy; she whipped through the traffic in the center of Coconut Grove and pulled into the parking area beside Bayfront Park, where the familiar circus was already under way. Three police cruisers were pulled up, and Camilla Figg was dusting for fingerprints on a battered red Geo parked at one of the meters – presumably Kurt Wagner's car.

I got out and looked around, and even without an inner voice whispering clues, I noticed right away that there was something wrong with this picture. 'Where's the body?' I asked Deborah.

She was already walking toward the gate of the yacht club. 'Out on the island,' she said.

I blinked and got out of the car. For no reason I could name, the thought of the body on the island raised the hair on the back of my neck, but as I looked out over the water for the answer, all I got was the afternoon breeze that blew across the pines on the barrier islands of Dinner Key and straight through the emptiness inside me.

Deborah jogged me with her elbow. 'Come on,' she said.

I looked in the backseat at Cody and Astor, who had just now mastered the intricacies of the seat-belt release and were trickling out of the car. 'Stay here,' I said to them. 'I'll be back in a little while.'

'Where are you going?' Astor said.

'I have to go out to that island,' I said.

'Is there a dead person there?' she asked me.

'Yes,' I said.

She glanced at Cody, then back at me. 'We want to go,' she said.

'No, absolutely not,' I said. 'I got in enough trouble the last time. If I let you see another dead body your mother would turn me into one, too.'

Cody thought that was very funny and he made a small noise and shook his head.

I heard a shout and looked through the gate into the marina. Deborah was already at the dock, about to step into the police boat tied up there. She waved an arm at me and yelled, 'Dexter!'

Astor stomped her foot to get my attention, and I looked back at her. 'You have to stay here,' I said, 'and I have to go now.'

'But Dexter, we want to ride on the boat,' she said.

'Well, you can't,' I said. 'But if you behave I'll take you on my boat this weekend.'

'To see a dead person?' Astor said.

'No,' I said. 'We're not going to see any more dead bodies for a while.'

'But you promised!' she said.

'Dexter!' Deborah yelled again. I waved at her, which did not seem to be the response she was looking for, because she beckoned furiously at me.

'Astor, I have to go,' I said. 'Stay here. We'll talk about this later.'

'It's always later,' she muttered.

On the way through the gate I paused and spoke to the uniformed cop there, a large heavy man with black hair and a very low forehead. 'Could you keep one eye on my kids there?' I asked him.

He stared at me. 'What am I, day-care patrol?'

'Just for a few minutes,' I said. 'They're very well behaved.'

'Lookit, sport,' he said, but before he could finish his sentence there was a rustle of movement and Deborah was beside us.

'God*damn* it, Dexter!' she said. 'Get your ass on the boat!'

'I'm sorry,' I said. 'I have to find somebody to watch the kids.'

Deborah ground her teeth together. Then she glanced at the big cop and read his name tag. 'Suchinsky,' she said. 'Watch the fucking kids.'

'Aw, come on, Sarge,' he said. 'Jesus Christ.'

'Stick with the kids, goddamn it,' she said. 'You might learn something. Dexter – get on the goddamn boat, now!'

I turned meekly and hurried for the goddamn boat. Deborah strode past me and was already seated when I jumped on, and the cop driving the boat headed for one of the smaller islands, weaving between the anchored sailboats.

There are several small islands on the outside of Dinner Key Marina that provide protection from wind and wave, one of the things that makes it such a good anchorage. Of course, it's only good under ordinary circumstances, as the islands themselves proved. They were littered with broken boats and other maritime junk deposited by the many recent hurricanes, and every now and then a squatter would set up housekeeping, building a shack from shattered boat parts.

The island we headed for was one of the smaller ones. Half of a forty-foot sports fisherman lay on the beach at a crazy angle, and the pine trees inland of the beach were hung with chunks of Styrofoam, tattered cloth, and wispy shreds of plastic sheeting and garbage bags. Other than that, it was just the way the Native Americans had left it, a peaceful little chunk of land covered with Australian pines, condoms, and beer cans.

Except, of course, for Kurt Wagner's body, which had most likely been left by someone other than Native Americans. It was lying in the center of the island in a small clearing, and like the others, it had been arranged in a formal pose, with the arms folded across the chest and the legs pressed together. The body was headless and unclothed, charred from being burned, very much like the others – except that this time there had been a small addition. Around the neck was a leather string holding a pewter medallion about the size of an egg. I leaned closer to look; it was a bull's head.

Once again I felt a strange twinge in the emptiness, as if some part of me were recognizing that this was significant, but didn't know why or how to express it – not alone, not without the Passenger.

Vince Masuoka was squatting next to the body examining a cigarette butt and Deborah knelt down beside him. I circled them one time, looking at it from all angles: Still Life with Cops. I was hoping, I suppose, that I would find a small but significant clue. Perhaps the killer's driver's license, or a signed confession. But there was nothing of the kind, nothing but sand, pockmarked from countless feet and the wind.

I went down on one knee beside Deborah. 'You looked for the tattoo, right?' I asked her.

'First thing,' Vince said. He extended a rubber-gloved hand and lifted the body slightly. There it was, half covered with sand but still visible, only the upper edge of it cut off and left, presumably, with the missing head.

'It's him,' Deborah said. 'The tattoo, his car is at the marina – it's him, Dexter. And I wish I knew what the hell that tattoo meant.'

'It's Aramaic,' I said.

'How the fuck would you know that?' Deborah said.

'My research,' I said, and I squatted down next to the body. 'Look.' I picked a small pine twig out of the sand and pointed with it. Part of the first letter was missing, cut off along with the head, but the rest was plainly visible and matched my language lesson. 'There's the *M*, what's left of it. And the *L*, and the *K*.'

'What the hell does that mean?' Deborah demanded.

'Moloch,' I said, feeling a small irrational chill just saying the word here in the bright sunshine. I tried to shake it off, but a feeling of uneasiness stayed behind. 'Aramaic has no vowels. So *MLK* spells Moloch.'

'Or milk,' Deborah said.

'Really, Debs, if you think our killer would tattoo *milk* on his neck, you need a nap.'

'But if Wagner is Moloch, who killed him?'

'Wagner kills the others,' I said, trying very hard to sound thoughtful and confident at the same time, a difficult task. 'And then, um . . .'

'Yeah,' she said. 'I already figured out "um."'

'And you're watching Wilkins.'

'We're watching Wilkins, for Christ's sake.'

I looked at the body again, but there was nothing else on it to tell me more than I knew, which was almost nothing. I could not stop my brain from going in a circle; if Wagner had been Moloch, and now Wagner was dead, and killed by Moloch . . .

I stood up. For a moment I felt dizzy, as if bright lights were crashing in on me, and in the distance I heard that awful music beginning to swell up into the afternoon and for just that moment I could not doubt that somewhere nearby the god was calling me – the real god himself and not some psychotic prankster.

I shook my head to silence it and nearly fell over. I felt a hand grabbing my

arm to steady me, but whether it was Debs, Vince, or Moloch himself, I could-
n't tell. From far away a voice was calling my name, but it was singing it, the
cadence rising up to the far-too-familiar rhythm of that music. I closed my
eyes and felt heat on my face and the music got louder. Something shook me
and I opened my eyes.

The music stopped. The heat was just the Miami sun, with the wind whipping in the clouds of an afternoon squall. Deborah held both my elbows and
shook me, saying my name over and over patiently.

'Dexter,' she said. 'Hey Dex, come on. Dexter. Dexter.'

'Here I am,' I said, although I was not entirely sure of that.

'You okay, Dex?' she said.

'I think I stood up too fast,' I said.

She looked dubious. 'Uh-huh,' she said.

'Really, Debs, I'm fine now,' I said. 'I mean, I think so.'

'You think so,' she said.

'Yes. I mean, I just stood up too fast.'

She looked at me a moment longer, then let go and stepped back. 'Okay,'
she said. 'Then if you can make it to the boat, let's get back.'

It may be that I was still dizzy, but there seemed to be no sense in her
words, almost as if they were just made-up syllables. 'Get back?' I said.

'Dexter,' she said. 'We got six bodies, and our only suspect is on the ground
here with no head.'

'Right,' I said, and I heard a faint drumbeat under my voice. 'So where are
we going?'

Deborah balled up her fists and clenched her teeth. She looked down at the
body, and for a moment I thought she was actually going to spit. 'What about
the guy you chased into the canal?' she said at last.

'Starzak? No, he said . . .' I stopped myself from finishing, but not quite
soon enough, because Deborah pounced.

'He said? When did you talk to him, goddamn it?'

To be fair to me, I really was still a little bit dizzy, and I had not thought
before I spoke, and now I was in a somewhat awkward spot. I could not very
well tell my sister that I had spoken to him just the other night when I had
taped him to his workbench and tried to cut him up into small neat pieces.
But the blood must have been flowing back into my brain, because I very
quickly said, 'I mean, he seemed,' I said. 'He seemed to be just a . . . I don't
know,' I said. 'I think it was personal, like I cut him off in traffic.'

Deborah looked at me angrily for a moment, but then she seemed to accept
what I had said, and she turned away and kicked at the sand. 'Well, we got
nothing else,' she said. 'It won't hurt to check him out.'

It didn't seem like a really good idea to tell her that I already had checked
him out quite thoroughly, far beyond the boundaries of normal police routine, so I just nodded in agreement.

34

There was not a great deal more worth seeing on the little island. Vince and the other forensic nerds would spot anything else worth the trouble, and our presence would only hamper them. Deborah was impatient and wanted to rush back to the mainland to intimidate suspects. So we walked to the beach and boarded the police launch for the short trip back across the harbor to the dock. I felt a little better when I climbed onto the dock and walked back to the parking lot.

I didn't see Cody and Astor, so I went over to Officer Low Forehead. 'The kids are in the car,' he told me before I could speak. 'They wanted to play cops and robbers with me, and I didn't sign up for day care.'

Apparently he was convinced that his line about day care was so sidesplittingly funny that it was worth repeating, so rather than risk having him say it again, I simply nodded, thanked him, and went over to Deborah's car. Cody and Astor were not visible until I was practically on top of the car, and for a moment I wondered which car they were in. But then I saw them, crouching down in the backseat, looking at me with very wide eyes. I tried to open the door, but it was locked. 'Can I come in?' I called through the glass.

Cody fumbled with the lock, and then swung the door open.

'What's up?' I asked them.

'We saw the scary guy,' Astor said.

At first I had no idea what she meant by that, and so I really couldn't say why I felt the sweat start rolling down my back. 'What do you mean, the scary guy?' I said. 'You mean that policeman over there?'

'Dex-terrr,' Astor said. 'Not dumb, *scary*. Like when we saw the heads.'

'The *same* scary guy?'

They exchanged another look, and Cody shrugged. 'Kind of,' Astor said.

'He saw my shadow,' Cody said in his soft, husky voice.

It was good to hear the boy open up like this, and even better, now I knew why the sweat was running down my back. He had said something about his shadow before, and I had ignored it. Now it was time to listen. I climbed into the backseat with them.

'How do you know he saw your shadow, Cody?'

'He said so,' Astor said. 'And Cody could see *his*.'

Cody nodded, without taking his eyes off my face, looking at me with his usual guarded expression that showed nothing. And yet I could tell that he trusted me to take care of whatever this was. I wished I could share his optimism.

'When you say your shadow,' I asked him carefully, 'do you mean the one on the ground that the sun makes?'

Cody shook his head.

'You have another shadow besides that,' I said.

Cody looked at me like I had asked him if was wearing pants, but he nodded. 'Inside,' he said. 'Like you used to have.'

I sat back against the seat and pretended to breathe. 'Inside shadow.' It was a perfect description – elegant, economical, and accurate. And to add that I used to have one gave it a poignancy which I found quite moving.

Of course, being moved really serves no useful purpose, and I usually manage to avoid it. In this case, I mentally shook myself and wondered what had happened to the proud towers of Castle Dexter, once so lofty and festooned with silk banners of pure reason. I remembered very well that I used to be smart, and yet here I was ignoring something important, ignoring it for far too long. Because the question was not what was Cody talking about. The real puzzle was why I had failed to understand him before.

Cody had seen another predator and recognized him when the dark thing inside him heard the roar of a fellow monster, just as I had known others when my Passenger was at home. And this other had recognized Cody for what he was in exactly the same way. But why that should frighten Cody and Astor into hiding in the car—

'Did the man say anything to you?' I asked them.

'He gave me this,' Cody said. He held out a buff-colored business card and I took it from him.

On the card was a stylized picture of a bull's head, exactly like the one I had just seen around the neck of Kurt's body out on the island. And underneath it was a perfect copy of Kurt's tattoo: MLK.

The front door of the car opened and Deborah hurled herself behind the wheel. 'Let's go,' she said. 'Get in your seat.' She slammed the key into the ignition and had the car started before I could even inhale to speak.

'Wait a minute,' I said after I managed to find a little air to work with.

'I don't *have* a goddamned minute,' she said. 'Come on.'

'He was here, Debs,' I said.

'For Christ's sake, Dex, who *was* here?'

'I don't know,' I admitted.

'Then how the fuck do you know he was here?'

I leaned forward and handed her the card. 'He left this,' I said.

Deborah took the card, glanced at it, and then dropped it on the seat as if it was made out of cobra venom. 'Shit,' she said. She turned off the car's engine. 'Where did he leave it?'

'With Cody,' I said.

She swiveled her head around and looked at the three of us, one after the other. 'Why would he leave it with a kid?' she asked.

'Because—' Astor said, and I put a hand on her mouth.

'Don't interrupt, Astor,' I said, before she could say anything about seeing shadows.

She took a breath, but then she thought better of it and just sat there, unhappy at being muzzled but going along with it for the time being. We sat there for a moment, the four of us, one big unhappy extended family.

'Why not stick it on the windshield, or send it in the mail?' Deborah said. 'For that matter, why the hell give us the damn thing at all? Why even have it printed, for Christ's sake?'

'He gave it to Cody to intimidate us,' I said. 'He's saying, "See? I can get to you where you're vulnerable."'

'Showing off,' Deborah said.

'Yes,' I said. 'I think so.'

'Well goddamn it, that's the first thing he's done that's made any sense at all.' She slapped the heels of her hands on the steering wheel. 'He wants to play catch-me-if-you-can like all the other psychos, then by God I can play that game, too. And I'll catch the son of a bitch.' She looked back at me. 'Put that card in an evidence bag,' she said, 'and try to get a description from the kids.' She opened the car door, vaulted out, and went over to talk to the big cop, Suchinsky.

'Well,' I said to Cody and Astor, 'can you remember what this man looked like?'

'Yes,' said Astor. 'Are we really going to play with him like your sister said?'

'She didn't mean "play" like you play kick the can,' I said. 'It's more like he's daring us to try to catch him.'

'Then how is that different from kick the can?' she said.

'Nobody gets killed playing kick the can,' I told her. 'What did this man look like?'

She shrugged. 'He was old.'

'You mean, really old? White hair and wrinkles?'

'No, you know. Old like you,' she said.

'Ah, you mean *old*,' I said, feeling the icy hand of mortality brush its fingers across my forehead and leave feebleness and shaky hands in its wake. It was not a promising start toward getting a real description, but after all, she was ten years old and all grown-ups are equally uninteresting. It was clear that Deborah had made the smart move by choosing to speak to Officer Dim instead. This was hopeless. Still, I had to try.

A sudden inspiration hit me – or at any rate, considering my current lack of brain power, something that would have to stand in for inspiration. It would at least make sense if the scary guy had been Starzak, coming back after me. 'Anything else about him you remember? Did he have an accent when he spoke?'

She shook her head. 'You mean like French or something? No, he just talked regular. Who's Kurt?'

It would be an exaggeration to say that my little heart went flip-flop at her words, but I certainly felt some kind of internal quiver. 'Kurt is the dead guy I just looked at. Why do you want to know?'

'The man said,' Astor said. 'He said someday Cody would be a much better helper than Kurt.'

A sudden, very cold chill rolled through Dexter's interior climate. 'Really?' I said. 'What a nice man.'

'He wasn't nice at all, Dexter, we told you. He was scary.'

'But what did he look like, Astor?' I said without any real hope. 'How can we find him if we don't know what he looks like?'

'You don't have to catch him, Dexter,' she said, with the same mildly irritated tone of voice. 'He said you'll find him when the time is right.'

The world stopped for a moment, just long enough for me to feel drops of ice water shoot out of all my pores as if they were spring-loaded. 'What exactly did he say?' I asked her when things started up again.

'He said to tell you you'll find him when the time is right,' she said. 'I just said.'

'How did he say it?' I said. '"Tell Daddy?" "Tell that man?" What?'

She sighed again. 'Tell *Dexter*,' she said, slowly so I would understand. 'That's you. He said, "Tell Dexter he'll find me when the time is right."'

I suppose I should have been even more scared. But strangely enough, I wasn't. Instead, I felt better. Now I knew for sure – someone really was stalking me. Whether a god or a mortal, it didn't matter anymore, and he would come get me when the time was right, whatever that meant.

Unless I got him first.

It was a silly thought, straight out of a high-school locker room. I had so far shown absolutely no ability to stay even half a step ahead of whoever this was, let alone find him. I'd done nothing but watch as he stalked me, scared me, chased me, and drove me into a state of dark dithering unlike anything I had ever experienced before.

He knew who, what, and where I was. I didn't even know what he looked like. 'Please, Astor, this is important,' I said. 'Was he real tall? Did he have a beard? Was he Cuban? Black?'

She shrugged. 'Just, you know,' she said, 'a white man. He had glasses. Just a regular man. You know.'

I didn't know, but I was saved from admitting it when Deborah yanked open the driver's door and slid back into the car. 'Jesus Christ,' she said.

'How can a man be that dumb and still tie his own shoes?'

'Does that mean Officer Suchinsky didn't have a lot to say?' I asked her.

'He had plenty to say,' Deborah said. 'But it was all brain-dead bullshit. He thought the guy might have been driving a green car, and that's about it.'

'Blue,' Cody said, and we all looked at him. 'It was blue.'

'Are you sure?' I asked him, and he nodded.

'So do I believe a little kid?' Deborah asked. 'Or a cop with fifteen years on the force and nothing in his head but shit?'

'You shouldn't keep saying those bad words,' Astor said. 'That's five and a half dollars you owe me. And anyway, Cody's right, it was a blue car. I saw it, too, and it was blue.'

I looked at Astor, but I could feel the pressure of Deborah's stare on me and I turned back to her.

'Well?' she said.

'Well,' I said. 'Without the bad words, these are two very sharp kids, and Officer Suchinsky will never be invited to join Mensa.'

'So I'm supposed to believe them,' she said.

'I do.'

Deborah chewed on that for a moment, literally moving her mouth around as if she was grinding some very tough food. 'Okay,' she said at last. 'So now I know he's driving a blue car, just like one out of every three people in Miami. Tell me how that helps me?'

'Wilkins drives a blue car,' I said.

'Wilkins is under surveillance, goddamn it,' she said.

'Call them.'

She looked at me, chewed on her lip, and then picked up her radio and stepped out of the car. She talked for a moment, and I heard her voice rising. Then she said another of her very bad words, and Astor looked at me and shook her head. And then Deborah slammed herself back into the car.

'Son of a bitch,' she said.

'They lost him?'

'No, he's right there, at his house,' she said. 'He just pulled in and went in the house.'

'Where did he go?'

'They don't know,' she said. 'They lost him on the shift change.'

'What?'

'DeMarco was coming in as Balfour was punching out,' she said. 'He slipped away while they were changing. They swear he wasn't gone more than ten minutes.'

'His house is a five-minute drive from here.'

'I know that,' she said bitterly. 'So what do we do?'

'Keep them watching Wilkins,' I said. 'And in the meantime, you go talk to Starzak.'

'You're coming with me, right?' she said.

'No,' I said, thinking that I certainly didn't want to see Starzak, and that for once I had a perfect excuse in place. 'I have to get the kids home.'

She gave me a sour look. 'And what if it isn't Starzak?' she said.

I shook my head. 'I don't know,' I said.

'Yeah,' she said. 'I don't know either.' She started the engine. 'Get in your seat.'

35

It was well past five o'clock by the time we got back to headquarters and so, in spite of some very sour looks from Deborah, I loaded Cody and Astor into my own humble vehicle and headed for home. They remained subdued for most of the ride, apparently still a little bit shaken by their encounter with the scary guy. But they were resilient children, which was amply demonstrated by the fact that they could still talk at all, considering what their biological father had done to them. So when we were only about ten minutes from the house Astor began to return to normal.

'I wish you would drive like Sergeant Debbie,' she said.

'I would rather live a little longer,' I told her.

'Why don't you have a siren?' she demanded. 'Didn't you want one?'

'You don't get a siren in forensics,' I said. 'And no, I never wanted one. I would rather keep a low profile.'

In the rearview mirror I could see her frown. 'What does that mean?' she asked.

'It means I don't want to draw attention to myself,' I said. 'I don't want people to notice me. That's something you two have to learn about,' I added.

'Everybody else wants to be noticed,' she said. 'It's like all they ever do, is do stuff so everybody will look at them.'

'You two are different,' I said. 'You will always be different, and you will never be like everybody else.' She didn't say anything for a long time and I glanced at her in the mirror. She was looking at her feet. 'That's not necessarily a bad thing,' I said. 'What's another word for normal?'

'I don't know,' she said dully.

'Ordinary,' I said. 'Do you really want to be ordinary?'

'No,' she said, and she didn't sound quite so unhappy. 'But then if we're not ordinary, people will notice us.'

'That's why you have to learn to keep a low profile,' I said, secretly pleased at the way the conversation had worked around to prove my point. 'You have to pretend to be *really* normal.'

'So we shouldn't ever let anybody know we're different,' she said. 'Not anybody.'

'That's right,' I said.

JEFF LINDSAY

She looked at her brother, and they had another of those long silent conversations. I enjoyed the quiet, just driving through the evening congestion and feeling sorry for myself.

After a few minutes Astor spoke up again. 'That means we shouldn't tell Mom what we did today,' she said.

'You can tell her about the microscope,' I said.

'But not the other stuff?' Astor said. 'The scary guy and riding with Sergeant Debbie?'

'That's right,' I said.

'But we're never supposed to tell a lie,' she said. 'Especially to our own mother.'

'That's why you don't tell her anything,' I said. 'She doesn't need to know things that will make her worry too much.'

'But she loves us,' Astor said. 'She wants us to be happy.'

'Yes,' I said. 'But she has to think you are happy in a way she can understand. Otherwise *she* can't be happy.'

There was another long silence before Astor finally said, just before we turned onto their street, 'Does the scary guy have a mother?'

'Almost certainly,' I said.

Rita must have been waiting right inside the front door, because as we pulled up and parked the door swung open and she came out to meet us. 'Well, hello,' she said cheerfully. 'And what did you two learn today?'

'We saw dirt,' Cody said. 'From my shoe.'

Rita blinked. 'Really,' she said.

'And there was a piece of popcorn, too,' Astor said. 'And we looked in the microphone and we could tell where we had been.'

'Microscope,' Cody said.

'Whatever,' Astor shrugged. 'But you could tell whose hair it was, too. And if it was a goat or a rug.'

'Wow,' Rita said, looking somewhat overwhelmed and uncertain, 'I guess you had quite a time then.'

'Yes,' Cody said.

'Well then,' Rita said. 'Why don't you two get started on homework, and I'll get you a snack.'

'Okay,' Astor said, and she and Cody scurried up the walk and into the house. Rita watched them until they went inside, and then she turned to me and held onto my elbow as we strolled after them.

'So it went well?' she asked me. 'I mean, with the – they seemed very, um . . .'

'They are,' I said. 'I think they're beginning to understand that there are consequences for fooling around like that.'

'You didn't show them anything too grim, did you?' she said.

'Not at all. Not even any blood.'

'Good,' she said, and she leaned her head on my shoulder, which I suppose is part of the price you have to pay when you are going to marry someone. Perhaps it was simply a public way to mark her territory, in which case I guess I should be very happy that she chose not to do so with the traditional animal method. Anyway, displaying affection through physical contact is not something I really understand, and I felt a bit awkward, but I put an arm around her, since I knew that was the correct human response, and we followed the kids into the house.

I'm quite sure it isn't right to call it a dream. But in the night the sound came into my poor battered head once again, the music and chanting and the clash of metal I had heard before, and there was the feeling of heat on my face and a swell of savage joy rising from the special place inside that had been empty for so long now. I woke up standing by the front door with my hand on the doorknob, covered with sweat, content, fulfilled, and not at all uneasy as I should have been.

I knew the term 'sleepwalking,' of course. But I also knew from my freshman psychology class that the reasons someone sleepwalks are usually not related to hearing music. And I also knew in the deepest level of my being that I should be anxious, worried, crawling with distress at the things that had been happening in my unconscious brain. They did not belong there, it was not possible that they could be there – and yet, there they were. And I was glad to have them. That was the most frightening thing of all.

The music was not welcome in the Dexter Auditorium. I did not want it. I wanted it to go away. But it came, and it played, and it made me supernaturally happy against my will and then dumped me by the front door, apparently trying to get me outside and—

And what? It was a jolt of monster-under-the-bed thought straight from the lizard brain, but . . .

Was it a random impulse, uncharted movement by my unconscious mind, that got me out of bed and down the hall to the door? Or was something trying to get me to open the door and go outside? He had told the kids I would find him when the time was right – was this the right time?

Did someone want Dexter alone and unconscious in the night?

It was a wonderful thought, and I was terribly proud to have it, because it meant that I had clearly suffered brain damage and could no longer be held responsible. Once again I was blazing new trails in the territory of stupid. It was impossible, idiotic, stress-induced hysteria. No one on earth could possibly have so much time to throw away; Dexter was not important enough to anyone but Dexter. And to prove it, I turned on the floodlight over the front porch and opened the door.

Across the street and about fifty feet to the west a car started up and drove away.

I closed the door and double-locked it.

And now it was my turn once more to sit up at the kitchen table, sipping coffee and pondering life's great mystery.

The clock said 3:32 when I sat down, and 6:00 when Rita finally came into the room.

'Dexter,' she said with an expression of soporific surprise on her face.

'In the flesh,' I said, and it was exceedingly difficult for me to maintain my artificially cheerful façade.

She frowned. 'What's wrong?'

'Nothing at all,' I said. 'I just couldn't sleep.'

Rita bent her head and shuffled over to the coffee-maker and poured herself a cup. Then she sat across the table from me and took a sip. 'Dexter,' she said, 'it's perfectly normal to have reservations.'

'Of course,' I said, with absolutely no idea what she meant, 'otherwise you don't get a table.'

She shook her head slightly with a tired smile. 'You know what I mean,' she said, which was not true. 'About the wedding.'

A small bleary light went on in the back of my head, and I very nearly said Aha. Of course the wedding. Human females were obsessive on the subject of weddings, even it if wasn't their own. When it was, in fact, their own, the idea of it took over every moment of waking and sleeping thought. Rita was seeing everything that happened through a pair of wedding-colored glasses. If I could not sleep, that was because of bad dreams brought on by our upcoming wedding.

I, on the other hand, was not similarly afflicted. I had a great deal of important stuff to worry about, and the wedding was something that was on automatic pilot. At some point I would show up, it would happen, and that would be that. Clearly this was not a viewpoint I could invite Rita to share, no matter how sensible it seemed to me. No, I had to come up with a plausible reason for my sleeplessness, and in addition I needed to reassure her of my enthusiasm for the wonderful looming event.

I looked around the room for a clue, and finally saw something in the two lunch boxes stacked beside the sink. A great place to start: I reached deep into the dregs of my soggy brain and pulled out the only thing I could find there that was less than half wet. 'What if I'm not good enough for Cody and Astor?' I said. 'How can I be their father when I'm really not? What if I just can't do it?'

'Oh, Dexter,' she said. 'You're a wonderful father. They absolutely love you.'

'But,' I said, struggling for both authenticity and the next line, 'but they're little now. When they get older. When they want to know about their *real* father—'

'They know all they'll ever need to know about that sonofabitch,' Rita snapped. It surprised me: I had never heard her use rough language before.

Possibly she never had, either, because she began to blush. 'You are their real father,' she said. 'You are the man they look up to, listen to, and love. You are exactly the father they need.'

I suppose that was at least partly true, since I was the only one who could teach them the Harry Way and other things they needed to know, though I suspected this was not exactly what Rita had in mind. But it didn't seem politic to bring that up, so I simply said, 'I really want to be good at this. I can't fail, even for a minute.'

'Oh, Dex,' she said, 'people fail all the time.' That was very true. I had noticed many times before that failure seemed to be one of the identifying characteristics of the species. 'But we keep trying, and it comes out all right in the end. Really. You're going to be great at this, you'll see.'

'Do you really think so?' I said, only mildly ashamed of the disgraceful way I was hamming it up.

'I *know* so,' she said, with her patented Rita smile. She reached across the table and clutched at my hand. 'I won't let you fail,' she said. 'You're mine now.'

It was a bold claim, flinging the Emancipation Proclamation aside like that and saying she owned me. Still, it seemed to close off an awkward moment comfortably, so I let it slide. 'All right,' I said. 'Let's have breakfast.'

She cocked her head to one side and looked at me for a moment, and I was aware that I must have hit a false note, but she just blinked a few times before she said, 'All right,' and got up and began to cook breakfast.

The other had come to the door in the night, and then slammed it in fear – there was no mistaking that part. He had felt fear. He heard the call and came, and he was afraid. And so the Watcher had no doubt about it.

It was time.

Now.

36

I was bone weary, confused, and, worst of all, still frightened. Every light-hearted blast of the horn had me leaping against the seat belt and searching for a weapon to defend myself, and every time an innocent car pulled up to within inches of my bumper I found myself glaring into the mirror, waiting for an unusually hostile movement or a burst of the hateful dream music flung at my head.

Something was after me. I still didn't know why or what, beyond a vague connection to an ancient god, but I knew it was after me, and even if it could not catch me right away, it was wearing me down to the point where surrender would seem like a relief.

What a frail thing a human being is – and without the Passenger, that is all I was, a poor imitation of a human being. Weak, soft, slow and stupid, unsee-ing, unhearing and unaware, helpless, hopeless, and harried. Yes, I was almost ready to lie down and let it run over me, whatever it was. Give in, let the music wash over me and take me away into the joyful fire and the blank bliss of death. There would be no struggle, no negotiation, nothing but an end to all that is Dexter. And after a few more nights like the one just past, that would be fine with me.

Even at work there was no relief. Deborah was lurking in wait, and pounced after I had barely stepped out of the elevator.

'Starzak is missing,' she said. 'Couple of days of mail in the box, news-papers in the drive – He's gone.'

'But that's good news, Debs,' I said. 'If he ran, doesn't that prove he's guilty?'

'It doesn't prove shit,' she said. 'The same thing happened to Kurt Wagner, and he showed up dead. How do I know that won't happen to Starzak?'

'We can put out a BOLO,' I said. 'We might get to him first.'

Deborah kicked the wall. 'Goddamn it, we haven't gotten to anything first, or even on time. Help me out here, Dex,' she said. 'This thing is driving me nuts.'

I could have said that it was doing far more than that to me, but it didn't seem charitable. 'I'll try,' I said instead, and Deborah slouched away down the hall.

I was not even into my cubicle when Vince Masuoka met me with a massive fake frown. 'Where are the doughnuts?' he demanded accusingly.

'What doughnuts?' I said.

'It was your turn,' he said. 'You were supposed to bring doughnuts today.'

'I had a rough night,' I said.

'So now we're all going to have a rough morning?' he demanded. 'Where's the justice in that?'

'I don't do justice, Vince,' I said. 'Just blood spatter.'

'Hmmph,' he said. 'Apparently you don't do doughnuts, either.' And he stalked away with a nearly convincing imitation of righteous indignation, leaving me to reflect that I could not remember another occasion when Vince had gotten the best of me in any kind of verbal interchange. One more sign that the train had left the station. Could this really be the end of the line for poor Decaying Dexter?

The rest of the workday was long and awful, as we have always heard that workdays are supposed to be. This had never been the case for Dexter; I have always kept busy and artificially cheerful in my job, and never watched the clock or complained. Perhaps I had enjoyed work because I was conscious of the fact that it was part of the game, a piece of the Great Joke of Dexter putting one over and passing for human. But a really good joke needs at least one other in on it, and since I was alone now, bereft of my inner audience, the punch line seemed to elude me.

I plodded manfully through the morning, visited a corpse downtown, and then came back for a pointless round of lab work. I finished out the day by ordering some supplies and finishing a report. As I was tidying up my desk to go home, my telephone rang.

'I need your help,' my sister said brusquely.

'Of course you do,' I said. 'Very good of you to admit it.'

'I'm on duty until midnight,' she said, ignoring my witty and piquant sally, 'and Kyle can't get the shutters up by himself.'

So often in this life I find myself halfway through a conversation and realizing I don't know what I'm talking about. Very unsettling, although if everybody else would realize the same thing, particularly those in Washington, it would be a much better world.

'Why does Kyle need to get the shutters up at all?' I asked.

Deborah snorted. 'Jesus Christ, Dexter, what do you do all day? We've got a hurricane coming in.'

I might well have said that whatever else I do all day, I don't have the leisure to sit around and listen to the Weather Channel. Instead, I just said, 'A hurricane, really? How exciting. When did this happen?'

'Try to get there around six. Kyle will be waiting,' she said.

'All right,' I said. But she had already hung up.

Since I speak fluent Deborah, I suppose I should have accepted her telephone call as a kind of formal apology for her recent pointless hostility. Quite possibly she had come to accept the Dark Passenger, especially since it was gone. This should have made me happy. But considering the day I had been having, it was just one more splinter under the fingernail for poor Down-trodden Dexter. On top of that, it seemed like sheer effrontery for a hurricane to pick this moment for its pointless harassment. Was there no end to the pain and suffering I would be forced to endure?

Ah well, to exist is to wallow in misery. I headed out the door for my date with Deborah's paramour.

Before I started my car, however, I placed a call to Rita, who would be very nearly home now by my calculations.

'Dexter,' she answered breathlessly, 'I can't remember how much bottled water we have and the lines at Publix are all the way out into the parking lot.'

'Well then we'll just have to drink beer,' I said.

'I think we're okay on the canned food, except that beef stew has been there for two years,' she said, apparently unaware that anyone else might have said something. So I let her rattle on, hoping she would slow down eventually. 'I checked the flashlights two weeks ago,' she said. 'Remember, when the power went out for forty minutes? And the extra batteries are in the refrigerator, on the bottom shelf at the back. I have Cody and Astor with me now, there's no after-school program tomorrow, but somebody at school told them about Hurricane Andrew and I think Astor is a little frightened, so maybe when you get home you could talk to them? And explain that it's like a big thunder-storm and we'll be all right, there's just going to be a lot of wind and noise and the lights will go out for a little while. But if you see a store on the way home that isn't too crowded be sure to stop and get some bottled water, as much as you can get. And some ice, I think the cooler is still on the shelf above the washing machine, we can fill it with ice and put in the perishables. Oh – what about your boat? Will it be all right where it is, or do you need to do something with it? I think we can get the things out of the yard before dark, I'm sure we'll be fine, and it probably won't hit here anyway.'

'All right,' I said. 'I'll be a little late getting home.'

'All right. Oh – look at that, the Winn-Dixie store doesn't look too bad. I guess we'll try to get in, there's a parking spot. Bye!'

I would never have thought it possible, but Rita had apparently learned to get by without breathing. Or perhaps she only had to come up for air every hour or so, like a whale. Still, it was an inspiring performance, and after wit-nessing it, I felt far better prepared to put up shutters with my sister's one-handed boyfriend. I started the car and slid out into traffic.

If rush-hour traffic is utter mayhem, then rush-hour traffic with a hurri-cane coming is end-of-the-world, we're-all-going-to-die-but-you-go-first insanity. People were driving as if they positively had to kill everyone else who might come between them and getting their plywood and batteries. It was not a terribly long drive to Deborah's little house in Coral Gables, but when

I finally pulled into her driveway I felt as if I had survived an Apache manhood ordeal.

As I climbed out of the car, the front door of the house swung open and
Chutsky came out. 'Hey, buddy,' he called. He gave me a cheerful wave with
the steel hook where his left hand used to be and came down the walkway to
meet me. 'I really appreciate the help. This goddamned hook makes it kind of
tough to put the wing nuts on.'

'And even harder to pick your nose,' I said, just a little irritated by his cheerful suffering.

But instead of taking offense, he laughed. 'Yeah. And a whole lot harder to
wipe my ass. Come on. I got all the stuff out in back.'

I followed him around to the back of the house, where Deborah had a
small overgrown patio. But to my great surprise, it was no longer overgrown.
The trees that had hung over the area were trimmed back, and the weeds
growing up between the flagstones were all gone. There were three neatly
pruned rosebushes and a bank of ornamental flowers of some kind, and a
neatly polished barbecue grill stood in one corner.

I looked at Chutsky and raised an eyebrow.

'Yeah, I know,' he said. 'It's maybe a little bit gay, right?' He shrugged. 'I get
real bored sitting around here healing, and anyway I like to keep things neat-
ened up a little more than your sister.'

'It looks very nice,' I said.

'Uh-huh,' he said, as if I really had accused him of being gay. 'Well, let's get
this done.' He nodded toward a stack of corrugated steel leaning against the
side of the house – Deborah's hurricane shutters. The Morgans were second-
generation Floridians, and Harry had raised us to use good shutters. Save a little money on the shutters, spend a lot more replacing the house when they
failed.

The downside to the high quality of Deborah's shutters, though, was that
they were very heavy and had sharp edges. Thick gloves were necessary – or
in Chutsky's case, one glove. I'm not sure he appreciated the cash he was saving on gloves, though. He seemed to work a little harder than he had to, in
order to let me know that he was not really handicapped and didn't actually
need my help.

At any rate, it was only about forty minutes before we had all the shutters
in their tracks and locked on. Chutsky took a last look at the ones that covered the French doors of the patio and, apparently satisfied with our outstanding craftsmanship, he raised his left arm to wipe the sweat from his
brow, catching himself at the very last moment before he rammed the hook
through his cheek. He laughed a little bitterly, staring at the hook.

'I'm still not used to this thing,' he said, shaking his head. 'I wake up in the
night and the missing knuckle itches.'

It was difficult to think of anything clever or even socially acceptable to say to that. I had never read anywhere what to say to someone speaking of having feeling in his amputated hand. Chutsky seemed to feel the awkwardness, because he gave me a small dry snort of non-humorous amusement.

'Hey, well,' he said, 'there's still a couple of kicks left in the old mule.' It seemed to me an unfortunate choice of words, since he was also missing his left foot, and any kicking at all seemed out of the question. Still, I was pleased to see him coming out of his depression, so it seemed like a good thing to agree with him.

'No one ever doubted it,' I said. 'I'm sure you're going to be fine.'

'Uh-huh, thanks,' he said, not very convincingly. 'Anyway, it's not you I have to convince. It's a couple of old desk jockeys inside the Beltway. They've offered me a desk job, but . . .' He shrugged.

'Come on now,' I said. 'You can't really want to go back to the cloak-and-dagger work, can you?'

'It's what I'm good at,' he said. 'For a while there, I was the very best.'

'Maybe you just miss the adrenaline,' I said.

'Maybe,' he said. 'How about a beer?'

'Thank you,' I said, 'but I have orders from on high to get bottled water and ice before it's all gone.'

'Right,' he said. 'Everybody's terrified they might have to drink a mojito without ice.'

'It's one of the great dangers of a hurricane,' I said.

'Thanks for the help,' he said.

If anything, traffic was even worse as I headed for home. Some of the people were hurrying away with their precious sheets of plywood tied to their car roofs as if they had just robbed a bank. They were angry from the tension of standing in line for an hour wondering if someone would cut in front of them and whether there would be anything left when it was their turn.

The rest of the people on the road were on their way to take their places in these same lines and hated everyone who had gotten there first and maybe bought the last C battery in Florida.

Altogether, it was a delightful mixture of hostility, rage, and paranoia, and it should have cheered me up immensely. But any hope of good cheer vanished when I found myself humming something, a familiar tune that I couldn't quite place, and couldn't stop humming. And when I finally did place it, all the joy of the festive evening was shattered.

It was the music from my sleep.

The music that had played in my head with the feeling of heat and the smell of something burning. It was plain and repetitive and not a terribly catchy bit of music, but here I was humming it to myself on South Dixie Highway, humming and feeling comfort from the repeating notes as if it was a lullaby my mother used to sing.

And I still didn't know what it meant.

I am sure that whatever was happening in my subconscious was caused by something simple, logical, and easy to understand. On the other hand, I just couldn't think of a simple, logical, and easy-to-understand reason for hearing music and feeling heat on my face in my sleep.

My cell phone started to buzz, and since traffic was crawling along anyway, I answered it.

'Dexter,' Rita said, but I barely recognized her voice. She sounded small, lost, and completely defeated. 'It's Cody and Astor,' she said. 'They're gone.'

Things were really working out quite well. The new hosts were wonderfully cooperative. They began to gather, and with a little bit of persuasion, they easily came to follow IT's suggestions about behavior. And they built great stone buildings to hold IT's offspring, dreamed up elaborate ceremonies with music to put them in a trance state, and they became so enthusiastically helpful that for a while there were just too many of them to keep up with. If things went well for the hosts, they killed a few of their number out of gratitude. If things went badly, they killed in the hope that IT would make things better. And all IT had to do was let it happen.

And with this new leisure, IT began to consider the result of IT's reproductions. For the first time, when the swelling and bursting came, IT reached out to the newborn, calming it down, easing its fear, and sharing consciousness. And the newborn responded with gratifying eagerness, quickly and happily learning all that IT had to teach and gladly joining in. And then there were four of them, then eight, sixty-four – and suddenly it was too much. With that many, there was simply not enough to go around. Even the new hosts began to balk at the number of victims they needed.

IT was practical, if nothing else. IT quickly realized the problem, and solved it – by killing almost all of the others IT had spawned. A few escaped, out into the world, in search of new hosts. IT kept just a few with IT, and things were under control at last.

Sometime later, the ones who fled began to strike back. They set up their rival temples and rituals and sent their armies at IT, and there were so many. The upheaval was enormous and lasted a very long time. But because IT was the oldest and most experienced, IT eventually vanquished all the others, except for a few who went into hiding.

The others hid in scattered hosts, keeping a low profile, and many survived. But IT had learned over the millennia that it was important to wait. IT had all the time there was, and IT could afford to be patient, slowly hunt out and kill the ones who fled, and then slowly, carefully, build back up the grand and wonderful worship of ITself.

IT kept IT's worship alive; hidden, but alive.

And IT waited for the others.

37

As I know very well, the world is not a nice place. There are numberless awful things that can happen, especially to children: they can be taken by a stranger or a family friend or a divorced dad; they can wander away and vanish, fall in a sinkhole, drown in a neighbor's pool – and with a hurricane coming there were even more possibilities. The list is limited only by their imaginations, and Cody and Astor were quite well supplied with imagination.

But when Rita told me they were gone, I did not even consider sinkholes or traffic accidents or motorcycle gangs. I knew what had happened to Cody and Astor, knew it with a cold, hard certainty that was more clear and positive than anything the Passenger had ever whispered to me. One thought burst in my head, and I never questioned it.

In the half a second it took to register Rita's words my brain flooded with small pictures: the cars following me, the night visitors knocking on the doors and windows, the scary guy leaving his calling card with the kids, and, most convincingly, the searing statement uttered by Professor Keller: 'Moloch liked human sacrifice. Especially children.'

I did not know why Moloch wanted my children in particular, but I knew without the slightest doubt that he, she, or it had them. And I knew that this was not a good thing for Cody and Astor.

I lost no time getting home, swerving through the traffic like the Miami native I am, and in just a few minutes I was out of the car. Rita stood in the rain at the end of the driveway, looking like a small, desolate mouse.

'Dexter,' Rita said, with a world of emptiness in her voice. 'Please, oh God, Dexter, find them.'

'Lock the house,' I said, 'and come with me.'

She looked at me for a moment as if I had said to leave the kids and go bowling. 'Now,' I said. 'I know where they are, but we need help.'

Rita turned and ran to the house and I pulled out my cell phone and dialed.

'What?' Deborah snapped.

'I need your help,' I said.

There was a short silence and then a hard bark of not-amused laughter. 'Jesus Christ,' she said. 'There's a hurricane coming in, the bad guys are lined up five deep all over town waiting for the power to go out, and you need my help.'

'Cody and Astor are gone,' I said. 'Moloch has them.'

'Dexter,' she said.

'I have to find them fast, and I need your help.'

'Get over here,' she said.

As I put my phone away Rita came splattering down the sidewalk through the puddles that were already forming. 'I locked up,' she said. 'But Dexter, what if they come back and we're gone?'

'They won't come back,' I said. 'Not unless we bring them back.' Apparently that was not the reassuring remark she was hoping for. She stuffed a fist into her mouth and looked like she was trying very hard not to scream. 'Get in the car, Rita,' I said. I opened the door for her and she looked at me over her half-digested knuckles. 'Come on,' I said, and she finally climbed in. I got behind the wheel, started up, and nosed the car out of the driveway.

'You said,' Rita stammered, and I was relieved to notice that she had removed the fist from her mouth, 'you said you know where they are.'

'That's right,' I said, turning onto U.S. 1 without looking and accelerating through the thinning traffic.

'Where are they?' she asked.

'I know who has them,' I said. 'Deborah will help us find out where they went.'

'Oh God, Dexter,' Rita said, and she began to weep silently. Even if I wasn't driving I wouldn't know what to do or say about that, so I simply concentrated on getting us to headquarters alive.

A telephone rang in a very comfortable room. It did not give out an undignified chirping, or a salsa tune, or even a fragment of Beethoven, as modern cell phones do. Instead, it purred with a simple old-fashioned sound, the way telephones are supposed to ring.

And this conservative sound went well with the room, which was elegant in a very reassuring way. It contained a leather couch and two matching chairs, all worn just enough to give the feeling of a favorite pair of shoes. The telephone sat on a dark mahogany end table on the far side of the room, next to a bar made of matching wood.

Altogether the room had the relaxed and timeless feel of a very old and well-established gentlemen's club, except for one detail: the wall space between the bar and the couch was taken up by a large wooden case with a glass front, looking something like a cross between a trophy case and a shelf for rare books. But instead of flat shelves, the case was fitted with hundreds of felt-lined niches. Just over half of them cradled a skull-sized ceramic of a bull's head.

An old man entered the room, without haste, but also without the careful hesitance of frail old age. There was a confidence in his walk that is usually found only in much younger men. His hair was white and full and his face was smooth, as if it had been polished by the desert wind. He walked to the telephone like he was quite sure that whoever was calling would not hang up until he answered, and apparently he was right, since it was still ringing when he lifted the receiver.

'Yes,' he said, and his voice, too, was much younger and stronger than it should have been. As he listened he picked up a knife that lay on the table beside the telephone. It was of ancient bronze. The pommel was curved into a bull's head, the eyes set with two large rubies, and the blade was traced with gold letters that looked very much like *MLK*. Like the old man, the knife was much older than it looked, and far stronger. He idly ran a thumb along the blade as he listened, and a line of blood rose up on his thumb. It didn't seem to affect him. He put the knife down.

'Good,' he said. 'Bring them here.' He listened again for a moment, idly licking the blood from his thumb. 'No,' he said, running his tongue along his lower lip. 'The others are already gathering. The storm won't affect Moloch, or his people. In three thousand years, we've seen far worse, and we're still here.'

He listened again for a moment before interrupting with just a trace of impatience. 'No,' he said. 'No delays. Have the Watcher bring him to me. It's time.'

The old man hung up the telephone and stood for a moment. Then he picked up the knife again, and an expression grew on his smooth old face.

It was almost a smile.

The wind and the rain were gusting fiercely but only occasionally, and most of Miami was already off the roads and filling out insurance claim forms for the damage they planned to have, so the traffic was not bad. One very intense blast of wind nearly pushed us off the expressway, but other than that it was a quick trip.

Deborah was waiting for us at the front desk. 'Come to my office,' she said, 'and tell me what you know.' We followed her to the elevator and went up.

'Office' was a bit of an exaggeration for the place where Deborah worked. It was a cubicle in a room with several others just like it. Crammed into the space was a desk and chair and two folding chairs for guests, and we settled in. 'All right,' she said. 'What happened?'

'They . . . I sent them out into the yard,' Rita said. 'To get all their toys and things. For the hurricane.'

Deborah nodded. 'And then?' she prompted.

'I went in to put away the hurricane supplies,' she said. 'And when I came out they were gone. I didn't – it was only a couple of minutes, and they . . .' Rita put her face in her hands and sobbed.

'Did you see anyone approach them?' Deborah asked. 'Any strange cars in the neighborhood? Anything at all?'

Rita shook her head. 'No, nothing, they were just gone.'

Deborah looked at me. 'What the hell, Dexter,' she said. 'That's it? The whole story? How do you know they're not playing Nintendo next door?'

'Come on, Deborah,' I said. 'If you're too tired to work, tell us now. Otherwise, stop the crap. You know as well as I do—'

'I don't know anything like it, and neither do you,' she snapped.

'Then you haven't been paying attention,' I said, and I found that my tone was sharpening to match hers, which was a bit of a surprise. Emotion? Me? 'That business card he left with Cody tells us everything we need to know.'

'Except where, why, and who,' she snarled. 'And I'm still waiting to hear some hints about that.'

Even though I was perfectly prepared to snarl right back at her, there was really nothing to snarl. She was right. Just because Cody and Astor were missing, that didn't mean we suddenly had new information that would lead us to our killer. It only meant that the stakes were considerably higher, and that we were out of time.

'What about Wilkins?' I demanded.

She waved a hand. 'They're watching him,' she said.

'Like last time?'

'Please,' Rita interrupted, with a rough edge of hysteria creeping into her voice, 'what are you talking about? Isn't there some way to just – I mean, anything . . . ?' Her voice trailed off into a new round of sobs, and Deborah looked from her to me. 'Please,' Rita wailed.

As her voice rose it echoed into me and seemed to drop one final piece of pain into the empty dizziness inside me that blended in with the faraway music.

I stood up.

I felt myself sway slightly and heard Deborah say my name, and then the music was there, soft but insistent, as if it had always been there, just waiting for a moment when I could hear it without distraction, and as I turned my focus on the thrum of the drums it called me, called as I knew it had been calling all along, but more urgently now, rising closer to the ultimate ecstasy and telling me to come, follow, go this way, come to the music.

And I remember being very glad about that, that the time was here at last, and even though I could hear Deborah and Rita speaking to me it didn't seem that anything they had to say could be terribly important, not when the music was calling and the promise of perfect happiness was here at last. So I smiled at them and I think I even said, 'Excuse me,' and I walked out of the room, not caring about their puzzled faces. I went out of the building, and to the far side of the parking lot where the music was coming from.

A car was waiting for me there, which made me even happier, and I hurried over to it, moving my feet to the beautiful flow of the music, and when I got there the back door of the car swung open and then I don't remember anything at all.

38

I had never been so happy.

The joy came at me like a comet, blazing huge and ponderous through a dark sky and whirling toward me at inconceivable speed, swirling in to consume me and carry me away into a boundless universe of rapture and all-knowing unity, love, and understanding – bliss without end, in me and of me and all around me forever.

And it whirled me across the trackless night sky in a warm, blinding blanket of jubilant love and rocked me in a cradle of endless joy, joy, joy. As I spun higher and faster and even more replete with every possible happiness, a great slamming sound rolled across me and I opened my eyes in a small dark room with no windows and a very hard concrete floor and walls and no idea of where it was or how I got there. A single small light burned above the door, and I was lying on the floor in the dim glow it cast.

The happiness was gone, all of it, and nothing welled up to replace it other than a sense that wherever I might be, nobody had in mind restoring either my joy or my freedom. And although there were no bulls' heads anywhere in the room, ceramic or otherwise, and there were no old Aramaic magazines stacked on the floor, it was not hard to add it all up. I had followed the music, felt ecstasy, and lost conscious control. And that meant that the odds were very good that Moloch had me, whether he was real or mythical.

Still, better not to take things for granted. Perhaps I had sleepwalked my way into a storage room somewhere, and getting out was simply a matter of turning the knob on the door. I got to my feet with a little difficulty – I felt groggy and a bit wobbly, and I guessed that whatever had brought me here, some kind of drug had been part of the process. I stood for a moment and concentrated on getting the room to hold still, and after a few deep breaths I succeeded. I took one step to the side and touched a wall: very solid concrete blocks. The door felt almost as thick and was solidly locked; it didn't even rattle when I punched my shoulder against it. I walked one time around the small room – really, it was no more than a large closet. There was a drain in the center of the room, and that was the only feature or furnishing that I could see. This did not seem particularly encouraging, since it meant that either I was supposed to use the drain for personal tasks or else I was not expected to be here long enough to need a toilet. If that was the case, I had trouble believing that an early exit would be a good thing for me.

Not that there was anything I could do about it, whatever plans were being made for me. I had read *The Count of Monte Cristo* and *The Prisoner of Zenda*, and I knew that if I could get hold of something like a spoon or a belt buckle it would be easy enough to dig my way out in the next fifteen years or so. But they had thoughtlessly failed to provide me with a spoon, whoever they were, and my belt buckle had apparently been appropriated, too. This told me a great deal about them, at least. They were very careful, which probably meant experienced, and they lacked even the most basic sense of modesty, since they were clearly not concerned in the least that my pants might fall down without a belt. However, I still had no idea who they might be or what they might want with me.

None of this was good news.

And none of it offered any clue at all as to what I could do about it, except sit on the cold concrete floor and wait.

So I did.

Reflection is supposed to be good for the soul. Throughout history, people have tried to find peace and quiet, time all to themselves with no distractions, just so they can reflect. And here I was with exactly that – peace and quiet with no distractions, but I nevertheless found it very difficult to lean back in my comfy cement room and let the reflections come and do good for my soul.

To begin with, I wasn't sure I had a soul. If I did, what was it thinking to allow me to do such terrible things for so many years? Did the Dark Passenger take the place of the hypothetical soul that humans were supposed to have? And now that I was without it, would a real one grow and make me human after all?

I realized that I was reflecting anyway, but somehow that failed to create any real sense of fulfillment. I could reflect until my teeth fell out and it was not going to explain where my Passenger had gone – or where Cody and Astor were. It was also not going to get me out of this little room.

I got up again and circled the room, slower this time, looking for any small weakness. There was an air-conditioning vent in one corner – a perfect way to escape, if only I had been the size of a ferret. There was an electric outlet on the wall beside the door. That was it.

I paused at the door and felt it. It was very heavy and thick, and offered me not the tiniest bit of hope that I could break it, pick the lock, or otherwise open it without the assistance of either explosives or a road grader. I looked around the room again, but didn't see either one lying in a corner.

Trapped. Locked in, captured, sequestered, in durance vile – even synonyms didn't make me feel any better. I leaned my cheek against the door. What was the point in hoping, really? Hoping for what? Release back into the world where I no longer had any purpose? Wasn't it better for all concerned that Dexter Defeated simply vanish into oblivion?

Through the thickness of the door I heard something, some high-pitched noise approaching outside. And as the sound got closer I recognized it: a man's voice, arguing with another, higher, insistent voice that was very familiar.

Astor.

'Stupid!' she said, as they came even with my door. 'I don't have to . . .' And then they were gone.

'Astor!' I shouted as loud as I could, even though I knew she would never hear me. And just to prove that stupidity is ubiquitous and consistent, I slammed on the door with both hands and yelled it again. 'Astor!'

There was no response at all, of course, except for a faint stinging sensation on the palms of my hands. Since I could not think of anything else to do, I slid down to the floor, leaned against the door, and waited to die.

I don't know how long I sat there with my back against the door. I admit that sitting slumped against the door was not terribly heroic. I know I should have jumped to my feet, pulled out my secret decoder ring, and chewed through the wall with my secret radioactive powers. But I was drained. To hear Astor's defiant small voice on the other side of the door had hammered in what felt like the last nail. There was no more Dark Knight. There was nothing left of me but the envelope, and it was coming unglued.

So I sat, slumped, sagged against the door, and nothing happened. I was in the middle of planning how to hang myself from the light switch on the wall when I felt a kind of scuffling on the other side of the door. Then someone pushed on it.

Of course I was in the way and so naturally enough it hurt, a severe pinch right in the very back end of my human dignity. I was slow to react, and they pushed again. It hurt again. And blossoming up from the pain, shooting out of the emptiness like the first flower of spring, came something truly wonderful.

I got mad.

Not merely irritated, narked by someone's thoughtless use of my backside as a doorstop. I got truly angry, enraged, furious at the lack of any consideration for *me*, the assumption that I was a negligible commodity, a thing to be locked in a room and shoved around by anyone with an arm and a short temper. Never mind that only moments ago I had held the same low opinion of me. That didn't matter at all – I was mad, in the classic sense of being half crazed, and without thinking anything other than that, I shoved back against the door as hard as I could.

There was a little bit of resistance, and then the latch clicked shut. I stood up, thinking, *There!* – without really knowing what that meant. And as I glared at the door it began to open again, and once more I heaved against it, forcing it closed. It was wonderfully fulfilling, and I felt better than I had in quite some time, but as some of the pure blind anger leached out of me it occurred to me that as relaxing as door thumping was, it was slightly point-less, after all, and sooner or later it would have to end in my defeat, since I had no weapons or tools of any kind, and whoever it was on the other side of the door was theoretically unlimited in what they could bring to the task.

As I thought this, the door banged partially open again, stopping when it hit my foot, and as I banged back automatically I had an idea. It was stupid, pure James Bond escapism, but it just might possibly work, and I had absolutely nothing to lose. With me, to think is to explode into furious action, and so even as I thumped the door shut with my shoulder, I stepped to the side of the doorframe and waited.

Sure enough, only a moment later the door thumped open, this time with no resistance from me, and as it swung wide to slam against the wall an off-balance man in some kind of uniform stumbled in after it. I grabbed at his arm and managed to get a shoulder instead, but it was enough, and with all my strength I pivoted and shoved him headfirst into the wall. There was a gratifying thump, as if I had dropped a large melon off the kitchen table, and he bounced off the wall and fell face-first onto the concrete floor.

And lo, there was Dexter reborn and triumphant, standing proudly on both feet, with the body of his enemy stretched supine at his feet, and an open door leading to freedom, redemption, and then perhaps a light supper.

I searched the guard quickly, removing a ring of keys, a large pocketknife, and an automatic pistol that he would probably not need anytime soon, and then I stepped cautiously into the hall, closing the door behind me. Some-where out here, Cody and Astor waited, and I would find them. What I would do then I didn't know, but it didn't matter. I would find them.

39

The building was about the size of a large Miami Beach house. I prowled cautiously through a long hallway that ended at a door similar to the one I had just played bull-in-the-ring with. I tiptoed up and put my ear against it. I didn't hear anything at all, but the door was so thick that this meant almost nothing.

I put my hand on the knob and turned it very slowly. It wasn't locked, and I pushed the door open.

I peeked carefully around the edge of the door and saw nothing that ought to cause alarm other than some furniture that looked like real leather – I made a mental note to report it to PETA. It was quite an elegant room, and as I opened the door farther I saw a very nice mahogany bar in the far corner.

But much more interesting was the trophy case beside the bar. It stretched along the wall for twenty feet, and behind the glass, just visible, I could see row after row of what seemed to be assorted ceramic bulls' heads. Each piece shone under its own mini-spotlight. I did not count, but there had to be more than a hundred of them. And before I could move into the room I heard a voice, as cold and dry as it could be and still be human.

'Trophies,' and I jumped, turning the gun toward the sound. 'A memorial wall dedicated to the god. Each represents a soul we have sent to him.' An old man sat there, simply looking at me, but seeing him was almost a physical blow. 'We create a new one for each sacrifice,' he said. 'Come in, Dexter.'

The old man didn't seem very menacing. In fact, he was nearly invisible, sitting back as he was in one of the large leather chairs. He got up slowly, with an old man's care, and turned a face on me that was as cold and smooth as river rock.

'We have been waiting for you,' he said, although as far as I could tell he was alone in the room, except for the furniture. 'Come in.'

I really don't know if it was what he said, or the way he said it – or something else entirely. In any case, when he looked directly at me I suddenly felt like there was not enough air in the room. All the mad dash of my escape seemed to bleed out of me and puddle around my ankles, and a great clattering emptiness tore through me, as though there was nothing in the world but pointless pain, and he was its master.

'You've caused us a great deal of trouble,' he said quietly.

'That's some consolation,' I said. It was very hard to say, and sounded feeble even to me, but at least it made the old man look a little bit annoyed. He took a step toward me, and I found myself trying to shrink away. 'By the way,' I said, hoping to appear nonchalant about the fact that I felt like I was melting, 'who are us?'

He cocked his head to one side. 'I think you know,' he said. 'You've certainly been looking at us long enough.' He took another step forward and my knees wobbled slightly. 'But for the sake of a pleasant conversation,' he said, 'we are the followers of Moloch. The heirs of King Solomon. For three thousand years, we have kept the god's worship alive and guarded his traditions, and his power.'

'You keep saying "we,"' I said.

He nodded, and the movement hurt me. 'There are others here,' he said. 'But the we is, as I am sure you are aware, Moloch. He exists inside me.'

'So *you* killed those girls? And followed me around?' I said, and I admit I was surprised to think of this elderly man doing all that.

He actually smiled, but it was humorless and didn't make me feel any better. 'I did not go in person, no. It was the Watchers.'

'So – you mean, it can leave you?'

'Of course,' he said. 'Moloch can move between us as he wishes. He's not one person, and he's not in one person. He's a god. He goes out of me and into some of the others for special errands. To watch.'

'Well, it's wonderful to have a hobby,' I said. I wasn't really sure where our conversation was going, or if my precious life was about to skid to a halt, so I asked the first question that sprung to mind. 'Then why did you leave the bodies at the university?'

'We wanted to find you, naturally.' The old man's words froze me to the spot.

'You had come to our attention, Dexter,' he continued, 'but we had to be sure. We needed to observe you to see if you would recognize our ritual or respond to our Watcher. And, of course, it was convenient to lead the police to concentrate on Halpern,' he said.

I didn't know where to begin. 'He's not one of you?' I said.

'Oh, no,' the old man said pleasantly. 'As soon as he's released from police custody he'll be over there, with the others.' He nodded toward the trophy case, filled with ceramic bulls' heads.

'Then he really didn't kill the girls.'

'Yes, he did,' he said. 'While he was being persuaded from the inside by one of the Children of Moloch.' He cocked his head to one side. 'I'm sure you of all people can understand that, can't you?'

I could, of course. But it didn't answer any of the main questions. 'Can we please go back to where you said I had "come to your attention"?' I asked politely, thinking of all the hard work I put into keeping a low profile.

The man looked at me as though I had an exceptionally thick head. 'You killed Alexander Macauley,' he said.

Now the tumblers fell into the weakened steel lock that was Dexter's brain. 'Zander was one of you?'

He shook his head slightly. 'A minor helper. He supplied material for our rites.'

'He brought you the winos, and you killed them,' I said.

He shrugged. 'We practice sacrifice, Dexter, not killing. In any case, when you took Zander, we followed you and discovered what you are.'

'What am I?' I blurted, finding it slightly exhilarating to think that I stood face-to-face with someone who could answer the question I had pondered for most of my slash-happy life. But then my mouth went dry, and as I awaited his answer a sensation bloomed inside me that felt an awful lot like real fear.

The old man's glare turned sharp. 'You're an aberration,' he said. 'Something that shouldn't exist.'

I will admit that there have been times when I would agree with that thought, but right now was not one of them. 'I don't want to seem rude,' I said, 'but I like existing.'

'That is no longer your choice,' he said. 'You have something inside you that represents a threat to us. We plan to get rid of it, and you.'

'Actually,' I said, sure he was talking about my Dark Passenger, 'that thing is not there anymore.'

'I know that,' he said, a little irritably, 'but it originally came to you because of great traumatic suffering. It is attuned to you. But it is also a bastard child of Moloch, and that attunes you to us.' He waved a finger at me. 'That's how you were able to hear the music. Through the connection made by your Watcher. And when we cause you sufficient agony in a very short time, it will come back to you, like a moth to a flame.'

I really didn't like the sound of that, and I could see that our conversation was sliding rapidly out of my control, but just in time I remembered that I did, after all, have a gun. I pointed it at the old man and drew myself up to my full quivering height.

'I want my children,' I said.

He didn't seem terribly concerned about the pistol aimed at his navel, which to me seemed like pushing the envelope of self-confidence. He even had a large wicked-looking knife on one hip, but he made no move to touch it.

'The children are no longer your concern,' he said. 'They belong to Moloch now. Moloch likes the taste of children.'

'Where are they?' I said.

He waved his hand dismissively. 'They're right here on Toro Key, but you're too late to stop the ritual.'

Toro Key was far from the mainland and completely private. But in spite of the fact that it's generally a great pleasure to learn where you are, this time it raised a number of very sticky questions – like, where were Cody and Astor, and how would I prevent life as I knew it from ending momentarily?

'If you don't mind,' I said, and I wiggled the pistol, just so he would get the point, 'I think I'll collect them and go home.'

He didn't move. He just looked at me, and from his eyes I could very nearly see enormous black wings beating out and into the room, and before I could squeeze the trigger, breathe, or blink, the drums began to swell, insisting on the beat that was embedded in me already, and the horns rose with the rhythm, leading the chorus of voices up and into happiness, and I stopped dead in my tracks.

My vision seemed normal, and my other senses were unimpaired, but I could not hear anything but the music, and I could not do anything except what the music told me to do. And it told me that just outside this room true happiness was waiting. It told me to come and scoop it up, fill my hands and heart with bliss everlasting, joy to the end of all things, and I saw myself turning toward the door, my feet leading me to my happy destiny.

The door swung open as I approached it, and Professor Wilkins came in. He was carrying a gun, too, and he barely glanced at me. Instead, he nodded at the old man and said, 'We're ready.' I could barely hear him through the wild flush of feeling and sound welling up, and I moved eagerly toward the door.

Somewhere deep beneath all this was the tiny shrill voice of Dexter, screaming that things were not as they should be and demanding a change in direction. But it was such a small voice, and the music was so large, bigger than everything else in this endlessly wonderful world, and there was never any real question about what I was going to do.

I stepped toward the door in rhythm to the ubiquitous music, dimly aware that the old man was moving with me, but not really interested in that fact or any other. I still had the gun in my hand – they didn't bother to take it from me, and it didn't occur to me to use it. Nothing mattered but following the music.

The old man stepped around me and opened the door, and the wind blew hot in my face as I stepped out and saw the god, the thing itself, the source of the music, the source of everything, the great and wonderful bull-horned fountain of ecstasy there ahead of me. It towered above everything else, its great bronze head twenty-five feet high, its powerful arms held out to me, a wonderful hot glow burning in its open belly. My heart swelled and I moved toward it, not really seeing the handful of people standing there watching, even though one of those people was Astor. Her eyes got big when she saw me, and her mouth moved, but I could not hear what she said.

And tiny Dexter deep inside me screamed louder, but only just loud enough to be heard, and not even close to loud enough to be obeyed. I walked on toward the god, seeing the glow from the fire inside it, watching the flames in its belly flicker and jump with the wind that whipped around us. And when I was as close as I could get, standing right beside the open furnace of its belly, I stopped and waited. I did not know what I was waiting for, but I knew that it was coming and it would take me away to wonderful forever, so I waited.

Starzak came into view, and he was holding Cody by the hand, dragging him along to stand near us, and Astor was struggling to get away from the guard beside her. It didn't matter, though, because the god was there and its arms were moving down now, outspread and reaching to embrace me and clasp me in its warm, beautiful grip. I quivered with the joy of it, no longer hearing the shrill, pointless voice of protest from Dexter, hearing nothing at all but the voice of the god calling from the music.

The wind whipped the fire into life, and Astor thumped against me, bumping me into the side of the statue and the great heat coming from the god's belly. I straightened up with only a moment of annoyance and once more watched the miracle of the god's arms coming down, the guard moving Astor forward to share the bronze embrace, and then there was the smell of something burning and a blaze of pain along my legs and I looked down to see that my pants were on fire.

The pain of the fire on my legs jolted through me with the shriek of a hundred thousand outraged neurons, and the cobwebs were instantly cleared away. Suddenly the music was just noise from a loudspeaker, and this was Cody and Astor here beside me in very great danger. It was as if a hole had opened up in a dam and Dexter came pouring back in through it. I turned to the guard and yanked him away from Astor. He gave me a look of blank surprise and pitched over, grabbing my arm as he fell and pulling me down onto the ground with him. But at least he fell away from Astor, and the ground jarred the knife out of his hand. It bounced along to me and I picked it up and holstered it snugly in the guard's solar plexus.

Then the pain in my legs went up a notch and I quickly concentrated on extinguishing my smoldering pants, rolling and slapping at them until they were no longer burning. And while it was a very good thing not to be on fire anymore, it was also several seconds of time that allowed Starzak and Wilkins to come charging toward me. I grabbed the pistol from the ground and lurched to my feet to face them.

A long time ago, Harry had taught me to shoot. I could almost hear his voice now as I moved into my firing stance, breathed out, and calmly squeezed the trigger. Aim for the center and shoot twice. Starzak goes down. Move your aim to Wilkins, repeat. And then there were bodies on the ground, and a terrible scramble of the remaining onlookers running for safety, and I was standing beside the god, alone in a place that was suddenly very quiet except for the wind. I turned to see why.

The old man had grabbed Astor and was holding her by the neck, with a grip much more powerful than seemed possible with his frail body. He pushed her close to the open furnace. 'Drop the gun,' he said, 'or she burns.'

I saw no reason to doubt that he would do as he said, and I saw no sign of any way to stop him, either. Everyone living had scattered, except for us.

'If I drop the gun,' I said, and I hoped I sounded reasonable, 'how do I know you won't put her in the fire anyway?'

He snarled at me, and it still caused a twinge of agony. 'I'm not a murderer,' he said. 'It has to be done right or it's just killing.'

'I'm not sure I can see a difference,' I said.

'You wouldn't. You're an aberration,' he said.

'How do I know you won't kill us all anyway?' I said.

'You're the one I need to feed to the fire,' he said. 'Drop the gun and you can save this girl.'

'Not terribly convincing,' I said, stalling for time, hoping for that time to bring something.

'I don't need to be,' he said. 'This isn't a stalemate – there are other people on this island, and they'll be back out here soon. You can't shoot them all. And the god is still here. But since you obviously need convincing, how about if I slice your girl a few times and let the blood flow persuade you?' He reached down to his hip, found nothing, and frowned. 'My knife,' he said, and then his expression of puzzlement blossomed into one of great astonishment. He gaped at me without saying a thing, simply holding his mouth wide open as if he was about to sing an aria.

And then he dropped to his knees, frowned, and pitched forward onto his face, revealing a knife blade protruding from his back – and also revealing Cody, standing behind him, smiling slightly as he watched the old man fall, and then looking up at me.

'Told you I was ready,' he said.

40

The hurricane turned north at the last minute and ended up hitting us with nothing but a lot of rain and a little wind. The worst of the storm passed far to the north of Toro Key, and Cody, Astor, and I spent the remainder of the night locked in the elegant room with the couch in front of one door and a large overstuffed chair in front of the other. I called Deborah on the phone I found in the room, and then made a small bed out of cushions behind the bar, thinking that the thick mahogany would provide additional protection if it was needed.

It wasn't. I sat with my borrowed pistol all night, watching the doors, and watching the kids sleep. And since nobody disturbed us, that was really not enough to keep a full-grown brain alive, so I thought, too.

I thought about what I would say to Cody when he woke up. When he put the knife into the old man he had changed everything. No matter what he thought, he was not ready merely because of what he had done. He had actually made things harder for himself. The road was going to be a long tough one for him, and I didn't know if I was good enough to keep his feet on it. I was not Harry, could never be anything like Harry. Harry had run on love, and I had a completely different operating system.

And what was that now? What was Dexter without Darkness?

How could I hope to live at all, let alone teach the children how to live, with a gaping gray vacuum inside me? The old man had said the Passenger would come back if I was in enough pain. Did I have to physically torture myself to call it home? How could I do that? I had just stood in burning pants watching Astor nearly thrown into a fire, and that hadn't been enough to bring back the Passenger.

I still didn't have any answers when Deborah arrived at dawn with the SWAT team and Chutsky. They found no one left on the island, and no clues as to where they might have gone. The bodies of the old man, Wilkins, and Starzak were tagged and bagged, and we all clambered onto the big Coast Guard helicopter to ride back to the mainland. Cody and Astor were thrilled of course, although they did an excellent job of pretending not to be impressed. And after all the hugs and weeping showered on them by Rita, and the general happy air of a job well done among the rest of them, life went on.

*

Just that: Life went on. Nothing new happened, nothing within me was resolved, and no new direction revealed itself. It was simply a resumption of an aggressively plain ordinary existence that did more to grind me down further than all the physical pain in the world could have done. Perhaps the old man had been right – perhaps I had been an aberration. But I was not even that any longer.

I felt deflated. Not merely empty but *finished* somehow, as if whatever I came into the world to do was done now, and the hollow shell of me was left behind to live on the memories.

I still craved an answer to the personal absence that plagued me, and I had not received it. It now seemed likely that I never would. In my numbness I could never feel a pain deep enough to bring home the Dark Passenger. We were all safe and the bad guys were dead or gone, but somehow that didn't seem to be about me. If that sounds selfish, I can only say that I have never pretended to be anything else but completely self-centered – at least not unless someone was watching. Now, of course, I would have to learn to truly live the part, and the notion filled me with a distant, weary loathing that I couldn't shake off.

The feeling stayed with me over the next few days, and finally faded into the background just enough that I began to accept it as my new permanent lot. Dexter Downtrodden. I would learn to walk stooped over, and dress all in gray, and children everywhere would play mean little tricks on me because I was so sad and dreary. And finally, at some pathetic old age, I would simply fall over unnoticed and let the wind blow my dust into the street.

Life went on. Days blended into weeks. Vince Masuoka went into a furious frenzy of activity, finding a new, more reasonable caterer, fitting me for my tuxedo, and, eventually, when the wedding day itself came, getting me to the overgrown church in Coconut Grove on time.

So I stood there at the altar, listening to the organ music and waiting with my new numb patience for Rita to sashay down the aisle and into permanent bondage with me. It was a very pretty scene, if only I had been able to appreciate it. The church was full of nicely dressed people – I never knew Rita had so many friends! Perhaps now I should try to collect some, too, to stand beside me in my new gray, pointless life. The altar was overflowing with flowers, and Vince stood at my side, sweating nervously and spasmodically wiping his hands on his pants legs every few seconds.

Then there was a louder blare from the organ, and everyone in the church stood up and faced backward. And here they came: Astor in the lead, in her beautiful white dress, her hair done in sausage curls and an enormous basket of flowers in her hands. Next came Cody in his tiny tuxedo, his hair plastered to his head, holding the small velvet cushion with the rings on it.

Last of all came Rita. As I saw her and the children, I seemed to see the whole drab agony of my new life parading toward me, a life of PTA meetings and bicycles, mortgages and Neighborhood Watch meetings, and Boy Scouts, Girl Scouts, soccer and new shoes and braces. It was an entire lifeless, colorless secondhand existence, and the torment of it was blindingly sharp, almost more than I could bear. It washed over me with exquisite agony, a torture worse than anything I had ever felt, a pain so bitter that I closed my eyes—

And then I felt a strange stirring inside, a kind of surging fulfillment, a feeling that things were just the way they should be, now and evermore, world without end; that what was brought together here must never be rent asunder.

And marveling at this sensation of rightness, I opened my eyes and turned to look at Cody and Astor as they climbed the steps to stand beside me. Astor looked so radiantly happy, an expression beyond any I had ever seen from her, and it filled me with a sense of comfort and rightness. And Cody, so dignified with his small careful steps, very solemn in his quiet way. I saw that his lips were moving in some secret message for me, and I gave him a questioning glance. His lips moved again and I bent just a little to hear him.

'Your shadow,' he said. 'It's back.'

I straightened slowly and closed my eyes for the merest moment. Just long enough to hear the hushed sibilance of a welcome-home chuckle.

The Passenger had returned.

I opened my eyes, back again to the world as it should be. No matter that I stood surrounded by flowers and light and music and happiness, nor that Rita was now climbing the steps intent on clamping herself to me forevermore. The world was whole once again, just as it should be. A place where the moon sung hymns and the darkness below it murmured perfect harmony broken only by the counterpoint of sharp steel and the joy of the hunt.

No more gray. Life had returned to a place of bright blades and dark shadows, a place where Dexter hid behind the daylight so that he could leap out of the night and be what he was meant to be: Dexter the Avenger, Dark Driver for the thing once more inside.

And I felt a very real smile spread across my face as Rita stepped up to stand beside me, a smile that stayed with me through all the pretty words and hand-holding, because once more, forever and always, I could say it again.

I do. And yes, I will, I really will.

And soon.

EPILOGUE

Far above the aimless scurrying of the city IT watched, and IT waited. There was plenty to see, as always, and IT was in no hurry. IT had done this many times before, and would do so again, endlessly and forever. That was what IT was for. Right now there were so many different choices to consider, and no reason to do anything but consider them until the right one was clear. And then IT would start again, gather the faithful, give them their bright miracle, and IT would feel once more the wonder and joy and swelling rightness of their pain.

All that would come again. It was just a matter of waiting for the right moment.

And IT had all the time in the world.